obsessed

Other novels by Ted Dekker:

House (with Frank Peretti)
Saint
Showdown
Black
Red
White
Three
Blink
The Martyr's Song
Heaven's Wager
When Heaven Weeps
Thunder of Heaven

With Bill Bright:

Blessed Child
A Man Called Blessed

obsessed

TED DEKKER

THOMAS NELSON
Since 1798

NASHVILLE DALLAS MEXICO CITY RIO DE JANEIRO BEIJING

Published in Nashville, Tennessee, by Thomas Nelson. Thomas Nelson is a trademark of Thomas Nelson, Inc.

Thomas Nelson, Inc. books may be purchased in bulk for educational, business, fund-raising, or sales promotional use. For information, please e-mail SpecialMarkets@ThomasNelson.com.

Library of Congress Cataloging-in-Publication Data

Dekker, Ted, 1962–
    Obsessed / Ted Dekker.
    ISBN 10: 0-8499-4373-6 (hard cover)
    ISBN 13: 978-0-8499-4373-7 (hard cover)
    ISBN 10: 1-59554-031-8 (international)
    ISBN 13: 978-1-59554-031-7 (international)
    ISBN 10: 1-59554-078-4 (trade paper)
    ISBN 13: 978-1-59554-078-2 (trade paper)
    ISBN 10: 1-59554-311-2 (mmpb)
    ISBN 13: 978-1-59554-311-0 (mmpb)
    I. Title.
    PS3554.E43O27 2005
    813'.6—dc22

2004015647

Printed in the United States of America

07 08 09 10 11 QW 7 6 5 4 3

This one's for The Circle.

1

ROTH BRAUN SLOWLY TWISTED THE DOORKNOB and gave the door a slight shove. A familiar medicinal odor stung his nostrils. Outside, the sun warmed a midsummer day, but here in the dungeon below the house, the old man lived in perpetual twilight.

Roth imagined a Jew stepping into a delicing shower and let himself relish the horror he might feel in that moment of realizing that more than lice were meant to die in this chamber.

Roth was in a very good mood.

The smothering quiet was broken by the sound of the old prune's tarred, seventy-eight-year-old lungs rasping for relief. Gerhard's wheezing annoyed Roth, ruining his otherwise perfect mood.

The only living soul he despised more than the Jew who'd stolen his power was Gerhard, who had allowed the Jew to steal his power.

He glanced at Klaus, the gangly male nurse who had tended his father for three years. The white-smocked man hovered over Gerhard in the corner of the room, refusing to meet Roth's eyes. Gerhard Braun

3

sat in a dark-red leather recliner, blue eyes glaring over the nasal cannula protruding from each nostril.

"Good morning, Father," Roth said. He closed the door quietly and stepped into the room, pushing aside a curtain of tinkling glass beads that separated it from the entryway. "You wanted to see me?"

His father looked at a servant, who busied himself over the table in the adjacent dining room.

"Leave us."

By the trembling in his voice, either Gerhard really was dying, or something was upsetting him, which invariably sowed its own sort of death. How many men alive today had been responsible for as many deaths as his father? They could be counted on two hands.

Even so, Roth hated him.

The servant dipped his head and exited through a side door. The steel door closed and the nurse flinched. Glass in a cabinet behind the table rattled despite the room's solid-concrete walls. The nineteenth-century Russian crystal—one of dozens of similar collections pilfered during the war—had once belonged to the czar. The Nazis' defeat should have sent Gerhard to the gallows; instead, the war had left his father with obscene wealth. The paintings alone had netted him a significant fortune, and these he owned legally. He'd shipped them to Zurich, where a hotly contested law made them his after remaining unclaimed for five years. Compliments of the Swiss Federation of Art Dealers.

Until the day I suck the energy from your bones, I will love you for showing me the way.

Until the day I suck the energy from your bones, I will despise you for what you did.

Gerhard held up a newspaper. "Have you read this?"

Roth walked across the circular rope rug that covered the black cement slab and stopped five feet from Gerhard. A hawk nose curved over his father's thin, trembling lips. Wispy strands of gray hair backlit by a yellow lamp hovered over his scalp. Skeletal, blue-veined fingers clutched what appeared to be a *Los Angeles Times*. A stack of news-papers—the *New York Times*, *Chicago Tribune*, London's *Daily Telegraph*, and a dozen others—sat a half-meter thick on the small end table to his left. Gerhard routinely spent six hours each day reading.

Gerhard flung the paper with a flick of his wrist, never removing his eyes from Roth. It landed on the floor with a *smack*.

"Read it."

The male nurse pretended to fiddle with the oxygen tank. Roth stood still. This attitude of Gerhard's was no longer simply ruining his mood, but destroying it altogether.

"I said, 'Read it'!"

Roth calmly bent and picked up the paper. The *Los Angeles Times* was folded around an article in the Life section, "Fortune Goes to Museum." Roth scanned the text. A wealthy woman, a Jew named Rachel Spritzer, sixty-two years of age, had died three days ago in Los Angeles. She'd been survived by no one and had donated her entire estate to the Los Angeles Museum of the Holocaust.

"So another Jew's dead." Roth lowered the paper. "Your legacy lives on."

His father clutched the arms of his chair. "Read the rest." His chest sounded like a whistle.

If Roth wasn't a master of his own impulses, he might have done something stupid, such as kill the man. Instead, he set the paper on the windowsill and turned away. "You've read it, Father. Tell me what it says. I have a ten o'clock engagement."

"Cancel it."

Roth walked to the bar. Control. "Just tell me what has you so concerned."

"The Stones of David have me concerned."

Roth blinked. He poured a splash of cognac into a snifter.

"I'm finished chasing your ghosts." He swirled the brandy slowly before sipping it. "If the Stones still exist, we would have found them long ago."

Gerhard managed to stand, trembling from head to foot, red as a rooster around the neck.

"They *have* been found. And you know what that means." He launched into a coughing fit.

Roth's pulse quickened a hair and then eased. If the man wasn't dying, he was losing his mind. Surely the Stones hadn't been found after all this time.

Gerhard staggered three steps to the windowsill, pushing his startled nurse out of the way, and grabbed the newspaper. He leaned on the wall with one hand and held the paper up in the other. He threw the paper toward Roth. It fluttered noisily and landed on the black slab.

"Read it!" Gerhard's eyes drilled him. So then maybe there was something to this.

Roth picked up the paper, found the article, and slowly read down the column. What if Gerhard was right? What if the relics did exist after all? They would be priceless. But the Stones' monetary value didn't interest Gerhard—he already had enough wealth to waste in his final years.

Gerhard's obsession was for the journal that had gone missing with the Stones.

And Roth's obsession was for the power that had gone missing with the Jew who'd taken the journal.

He had spent nearly thirty years tracking down innumerable leads, searching in vain. There was no telling how much wealth had been stripped from the Jews when Hitler had gathered them up and sent them to the camps. Much of the fortune had been confiscated by the gestapo and recovered after the war, but a number of particularly valuable items—priceless relics that belonged in museums or in vaults—had disappeared. Some of those treasures could be found in this very house. But any well-heeled collector knew that the most valuable collection had vanished for good in 1945.

The Stones of David.

One stunning item in Spritzer's collection is an extremely old golden medallion, better known as one of the five Stones of David. According to legend, the medallions are the actual stones selected by David to kill the giant Goliath. The smooth stones were subsequently gilded and stamped with the Star of David. The collection was last verified in 1307, when they were held by the Knights Templars. The collection was rumored to be held by a wealthy Jewish collector before World War II but went missing before the claim could be verified.

Alone, each medallion may be worth over $10,000,000. But the collection in its entirety is valued at roughly $100,000,000. The relic will be displayed in a museum yet to be disclosed with the following cryptic caption at Rachel Spritzer's request: "The Stones are like the lost orphans. They will eventually find each other."

Sweat cooled Roth's palms. He set the paper on the bar, set an unsteady finger in its margin, and scanned to the end.

Rachel Spritzer lived alone in an apartment complex she owned on La Brea Avenue and died a widow. The complex will be sold by the estate, along with much of Spritzer's noncollectible property.

Rudy and Rachel Spritzer immigrated to the United States sixteen years ago, five years before Rudy was killed in an automobile accident. (See B4.)

For a moment Roth's vision clouded. His mouth went dry.

"Now I have your attention?" Gerhard demanded.

Roth read the article again, searching for any phrase that might undermine the possibility that this Jew could be anyone other than whom Gerhard was suggesting.

"She was sixty-two," Gerhard said. "The right age."

Roth's mind flashed back to those war years when he was only twelve. Even if the connections were only circumstantial, he could hardly ignore them.

"I *knew* the Jew survived," Gerhard said.

"She donated only one Stone. There were five."

"If one Stone exists, then the journal exists. Someone has that journal!"

"She's dead."

"You will make her speak from the grave." Gerhard swayed on his feet, right fist trembling. His eyes looked black in the basement's shadows. "She knew. She knew about the journal."

"She's dead!" Roth snapped. He took a deep breath, irritated with himself for losing control. The fact was, Gerhard's history with the Stones gave him knowledge that no one else could possibly have.

"You know well enough that the journal implicates the entire line of elders. It lists each of our names and the names of the women we killed. It must be found!"

Mention of the women triggered a coppery taste in the back of Roth's mouth. The last time he'd seen the journal, it contained 243 names. Roth would one day surpass that number, he had vowed it.

But even a thousand or ten thousand would not compensate for the one that had escaped Gerhard.

"That woman would toy with me even in her

death," the old man said. "In her house, in her belongings—somewhere, the old bat left a trail. You will go to Los Angeles." The nurse, Klaus, moved to assist Gerhard back to his seat, but the old man shook him off. Klaus retreated.

Gerhard was right. The Stones could lead to the journal. The journal could lead to the Jew. The Jew would lead to power, a supernatural power that his father had never attained. But Roth would.

The prospect of finding the Jew after so many years felt delightfully obscene.

Roth realized that his fingers were trembling.

"The United States," Roth said absently. "We don't have the same liberties there."

"That's never stopped you before."

The notion swarmed Roth like bees from a disturbed hive. Hope. More than hope—a desperate urgency to possess. Pounding heart, dry mouth. He was no fool. He would neither fight the emotion nor show it. After lingering so long on the edges of his mind, the desire to possess this one lost hope swallowed him. This is what Roth lived for, the purest form of power found in the very emotion that at this very moment raged through his body.

In his mind's eye he was already flying to America. He would have to move quickly, set the trap immediately. There was no telling how long they would keep the old Jew's collectibles in Los Angeles.

Roth stared into his father's blue eyes for a few long seconds, torn between the man's mad obsession with the past and his own with the future. What

Roth did for tomorrow, Gerhard did because of yesterday. Who was the better man?

He remembered the first dead Jew he'd seen in the camps twenty-eight years ago. He'd been eating fresh eggs and sausage prepared by one of the Polish servants from the village for breakfast. It was the most delicious breakfast he'd ever tasted. Perhaps leaving his mother in Germany to spend the summer with his father up in Poland would be a good thing after all. He was twelve at the time.

"Papa?"

"What?" his father asked, walking toward the window overlooking the concentration camp.

"Why do Polish eggs taste better than German eggs?"

His father pulled back the curtain, and Roth saw a woman hanging from the main gate. Gerhard answered him, but Roth didn't hear the response. The year was 1942, and hers was the first of many dead bodies Roth would see in Poland. But there was something about the first.

Roth let the memory linger, then returned his mind to the Stones. His father's eyes glistened with tears; his face wrinkled.

"The Jew took my soul. *She* took my soul! I beg you, my son." Roth felt a terrible pity for him. A single tear broke free and ran down Gerhard's right cheek.

"If the Jew is alive, she will be drawn by the Stone," Roth said.

"Forget the Jew. I must have the journal. You see that, don't you? More than anything, I must have it." He held out a spindly arm laced with bulging veins.

"Swear it to me. Swear you'll bring me what is mine."

Roth looked at the large swastika on the gray wall, sickened by Gerhard's weakness. He would make it right, because the Stones meant far more to him than they could possibly mean to his father.

"Come here," Roth said to the nurse.

Klaus glanced at Gerhard then stepped out from the shadows.

Roth backed up and stepped off the rug. There was the right way and the wrong way to do this, and the purest in mind knew the difference.

"Farther, to the middle of the rug," he said.

Klaus took another step so that he stood near the center of the rug.

"I would like to repay you for your care of my father," Roth said. "Few men could put up with a whining old man the way you do. Is there anything you would like?"

No response. Of course not.

"Anything at all?"

The nurse lowered his head. "No sir."

Roth pulled out his gun and shot Klaus through the top of his head while he was still bent over. The slug likely ended up in his throat.

The man dropped in a pile.

Roth looked at his father. "You should have sent him out."

"You're working against your own kind," Gerhard said. "He was pure."

"Then I did him a favor by sending him to his grave pure."

2

Los Angeles
July 18, 1973
Wednesday Morning

STEPHEN FRIEDMAN MARCHED ALONG THE south edge of the vacant Santa Monica parking lot, mind whirling. This was a primo deal, baby. Definitely, absolutely, one of the most primo deals he had come across in the seven years he'd played the real-estate market.

His partner on occasion, Dan Stiller, followed closely at Stephen's heels, black portfolio under his arm.

Stephen leaped over a chain and kept an energetic pace along the uneven asphalt. Tufts of stubborn brown grass grew among the cracks. The crumbling brick wall across the lot had been decorated by hundreds of white droppings. Seagulls. Someone had scrawled some word art on the wall: BIG DADDY ROCKS. To any ordinary pedestrian, the parking lot would have looked desolate, and perhaps worthless.

To Stephen, this piece of ground looked like a slice of potential paradise.

He smiled at Dan, who'd walked around the chain. Prevailing Santa Ana winds slapped at the wide lapels of Dan's plaid polyester blazer and whipped his hair back. The effect accentuated his sloping forehead and turned his bulbous nose into something that might have fit a Boeing 747. But behind that nose, Dan's brain was proportionally as large. They made a good team for the odd investment—two young Jews, both immigrants, carving out a new life in this magnificent land of opportunity. Where Dan's conservatism held them in check, Stephen's enthusiasm drove them on.

"It's a natural," Stephen said.

"Like the condo in Pasadena was a natural?" Dan referred to the complex Stephen had insisted they convert to a neighborhood amusement park. But the notes came due before construction could begin.

"I got us out of that, didn't I?" Stephen said.

"Involving a crook like Joel Sparks isn't exactly my idea of getting us out."

"The mob rap is totally hearsay. He's a businessman; he has money. He bailed us out."

"We lost a hundred thousand dollars."

"You've never lost a hundred thousand before? You win some, you lose some." Stephen turned to the vacant lot. "Besides, this one's a winner, guar-an-teed." He took a long whiff of the air. "I can practically smell it. You smell that, Dan? That's money you smell."

"Actually, that's exhaust I smell. And it's the carbon monoxide in the exhaust, the stuff you *can't* smell, that worries me."

"It may just be me, but I get the distinct impression you have some doubts. You don't trust my nose?"

Dan wiped his brow. "I don't doubt your ability

to choose them, Stephen. But, yes, I'm struggling with this particular idea."

Stephen had made and lost a million dollars a dozen times already—and they both knew as much. The very same impulsive passion that pushed him to seize opportunity also landed him in trouble from time to time. He made a million dollars easier than most. He also lost it easier than most.

Never mind. The fact that he now understood this about himself tipped the scales in his favor. He was up at the moment—eight hundred thousand up. Not bad for a thirty-one-year-old immigrant from Russia. Dan, for all his cautiousness, was only liquid to the tune of half that much. Which was why he needed Stephen. The only real issue separating them was what to do with the property.

Stephen tapped his temple. "You have to imagine it, Daniel. Open your mind!" He scanned the property and spoke with animated gestures. "Americans love entertainment. Cotton candy, ice cream, a roller coaster." He pointed to the deteriorated brick wall. "Right over there you see gull droppings; I see balloons. This lot is most definitely a coastal amusement park begging to be built."

Three teenagers passing by on the sidewalk turned to look at Stephen as his voice grew louder.

"I'm not saying that it couldn't happen, but a museum is more reasonable, if not to you, then to the city planners. Stephen, think. We have to submit our intentions with the down payment by next Wednesday. There are two other parties bidding. If the city rejects our plan, we lose the deal.

All I'm suggesting is that we go with a more conservative plan."

"And I say the people here are secretly crying out for a roller coaster. They're praying every night for us to put thoughts of museums and office buildings out of our minds, because they want clowns and the sound of laughing children to invade their neighborhood."

Dan stared at him.

Stephen saw an opportunity and seized it. He stepped toward the teenagers and motioned to a boy with long blond hair and a pooka-shell necklace. "Excuse me, Sir Hamlet, there. Could I get your opinion on something?"

The blond boy glanced at a younger rail-thin girl with large freckles and an embroidered blouse, and a skinny boy who towered over both of them.

Stephen fished out a ten-dollar bill. "I'll give you ten bucks for five minutes of your time."

"Ten bucks?"

"Ten bucks."

"For what?"

"Just to act something out for me and my business partner here."

Dan objected. "Come on, Stephen."

"Act what out?" the blond kid asked.

"We're investors, and we're trying to decide if this parking lot should be an amusement park or a museum." Stephen pointed to the freckled girl. "I want you to stand over there"—he pointed, then gestured toward the other two—"and you two over there and there."

"Ten bucks for each of us?" the boy asked in a small voice.

Stephen saw that they were sloppily dressed. Not *cool* sloppily, but poor sloppily. The girl's sandals were tied together with string, and the tall skinny kid's bell-bottoms were ankle-high. For a moment he just stared at them, struck by an odd sense of empathy that he couldn't place. The city was full of kids like this—why these three suddenly pulled at his heart, he didn't know.

No, he did know. At this moment they were him. They were decent, wide-eyed kids mesmerized by the possibility of making a quick ten dollars.

"What's your name?" Stephen asked the blond boy.

"Mike." If the boy were a smart aleck, Stephen might have changed his mind. But no snot-nosed kid would have answered the question so innocently. Several others on the sidewalk had stopped and were watching.

"I'll tell you what, Mike. I'll give you each *twenty* dollars if you help me out here. That's a lot of money for five minutes, but my friend and I are going to make a bundle on this piece of property, so I think it's fair. What do you say?"

"You mean it? Twenty dollars?" the small girl asked, eyes wide.

"I mean it."

One last glance at each other, and they scrambled over the chain to their posts.

"What do we do?"

"I want you to pretend you're an amusement

park." He pointed to each in succession. "You're a
Ferris wheel, you're a merry-go-round, and you're a
roller coaster. Just stick your arms up like this"—he
threw his hands up over his head—"or like this"—
he waved them out at his sides—"and when I tell
you to, pretend you're machines."

"You better not be pulling our legs about the
twenty dollars," the blond boy said.

"Scout's honor," Stephen said.

The kids adjusted their arms.

"Perfect!" Stephen faced Dan. "Okay, Dan, now
you stand over here—"

"I'm not doing this, Stephen."

"You have to! I need you to do this. You need to
stand over there like a statue. How else are we going
to compare?"

"No way."

Stephen took his arm, turned him from the kids,
and whispered, "Be a good sport, Dan. For their sakes.
Look, you need my five hundred grand, right? Just
go along with me here."

Dan looked at the three kids and then walked to
one side.

"Act like a statue, Dan," Stephen said.

"I am like a statue."

"Stick an arm up or something, so you look more
like a statue."

Dan hesitated and then raised an arm and went
stiff, like a German soldier saluting.

The gawking crowd on the sidewalk now
included a dozen kids and several adults. Stephen
faced them.

"Ladies and gentlemen, we're conducting a quick survey here. We have to decide whether we want to build an amusement park or a museum here. You guys are the judges."

He spun and faced the three kids like a conductor cuing up his orchestra. "Ready?"

The freckled girl chuckled. "You're pretty crazy, mister."

"You'd better believe I am. Ready?"

"Ready."

"Okay, make like an amusement park." He waved his arms.

The tall skinny kid was the roller coaster. He stuck his arms out like a cross, which wasn't Stephen's idea of how to show a coaster, but at least the boy was playing along. The girl turned in a slow circle like a merry-go-round, and the blond boy made a circle with his arms. Ferris wheel. They grinned wide.

"Sound! Sound!" Stephen called.

"Sound is an extra five bucks," the blond boy said.

"Make it ten," Stephen said. Shoot, he'd probably give them forty if they wanted it. "Give me some sound!"

"*Vroom, vroom. Whir.*" Wasn't much, but it earned some laughs from the gathering crowd. "*Honk honk*," snorted the girl.

"Excuse me," Stephen said. "What's *honk honk*? If I'm paying ten bucks for a noise, I need to know what it is."

"It's the line of cars waiting to get in," the girl said.

Stephen smiled wide, delighted. "There you go,

then. Cars waiting to get in to the amusement park!"
He faced the crowd. "All in favor of the amusement
park, raise your hands."

Two dozen hands went up amid chuckles.

"All those in favor of a museum"—Stephen
pointed to Dan—"raise your hands."

A middle-aged couple walking by raised their
hands and grinned.

"There you go. Case settled. Thank you for your
cooperation. You're dismissed." Some loitered, some
moved on.

The kids ran up to him and Stephen handed each
thirty dollars.

"That's it?" Mike asked. "We're done?"

"You're done. Don't blow it all at once."

They hurried off, looking back over their shoulders.

Dan shook his head. "Okay, Mr. Hot Shot. So
you have a bit of charm with the locals. I can assure
you that the bank, which holds the papers on this
lot, doesn't care about your antics. And I guarantee
the city will look more favorably on a museum than
on a playground. Especially a museum that already
has its backers. You know the Jewish Public Affairs
Committee has talked about bringing the Holocaust
museum under its umbrella and then relocating it.
Why not here? If they follow through, we'll do well.
That was the whole idea."

"Just because we're Jewish doesn't mean everything we do has to promote the Jewish cause,"
Stephen said. "This is nothing but business."

"Of course. But you *are* a Jew. A secular Jew without much sentimentality for our history, maybe, but

still a Jew. You can't ignore that. You're irrevocably tied to the war."

Stephen's morning paled. Dan's problem was that he knew too much.

"No, Dan, nothing is irrevocable. Especially not memories of the war. This is the United States of America, not Poland. Just because my great-great-great-great-grandmother dug potatoes in Poland or wherever doesn't mean I have to build a monument to her here."

Stephen had left both Russia and his past at age twenty to find a new life, and for the most part he'd succeeded. Anything that threatened to take him back, even if only in his mind, offended him.

"You're being unfair," Daniel said quietly. "You owe your life to your mother. And you know very well that she probably gave her life in one of the camps. How can you turn your back on that?"

"Because I don't *know* that she died in a camp," Stephen snapped. "I don't even know who she was. Why do you bring this up? I'll give you money for your museum. Just don't pretend we're crusaders here. I spent twenty years trying to find my mother and finally came here to give up that search. I don't have the stamina for that kind of thing."

"Seek and you will find—"

Stephen flung an arm into the air, his irritation flaring to anger. "Don't patronize me. For all I know, my mother and father *were* killed in some gas chamber. Whoever brought me into this world obviously suffered enough—is it incumbent on me to suffer too? As far as I'm concerned, it never happened. I don't have a mother. I'm not even Jewish anymore."

He paused, surprised by the emotion shortening his breath.

"And if there's a God in heaven who cares that I should seek, then I challenge him to create something . . ." He pinched his thumb and forefinger together. "Even a small morsel of some goodness worth seeking. Anything but the death that turns up everywhere I look."

Dan blinked at his outburst. "I'm sorry—"

"Then leave it. Give me some breathing room. Build your museum, but don't exploit my conscience."

Dan held up both hands.

For a few seconds that stretched into twenty, they stood in the vacant lot, making a good show of studying it. How they had managed to go from amusement parks to prison camps was beyond Stephen. Why, he wasn't entirely sure, but the subject never failed to resurrect ugly feelings he couldn't deal with.

Actually, he could deal with them. By burying them. Burying them deep and letting them lie dead in an unmarked grave. Certainly not by building a monument to them.

"You know, you may be right," Dan said. "An amusement park could transform this neighborhood."

"Forget it," Stephen said. "You already have backing for the museum. It's the safer plan. Though not as much fun, you have to admit."

"No, not as much fun. Your call."

"Couldn't we build a museum as part of an amusement park?"

Dan chuckled. "Now, there's an idea. I have three hundred thousand. We need eight by Tuesday. Can I count on you for the five?"

"Yes. And forget the amusement park for the time being. I'll run some comps and get the money to you by Tuesday."

"Okay." They shook hands.

"Sorry, huh?" Stephen said. "I can get carried away sometimes."

"Don't be ridiculous. I shouldn't have brought it up." He nodded at Stephen's blue Chevy Vega. "Go buy yourself a new car; it'll help you feel better."

"What, you don't like my car?"

"It's a bucket of bolts."

"It's my friend. Maybe the only one I have. Other than you and Chaim, of course. And I just installed an eight-track." He snapped his fingers to a few bars from James Taylor's "You've Got a Friend."

They stared at each other. For some strange reason a great sadness crept into Stephen's chest. He suddenly felt very lonely. He was standing in the middle of a parking lot in Santa Monica, surrounded by pedestrians and cars, contemplating a deal that could make him hundreds of thousands of dollars, and he felt oddly abandoned.

Like an outcast. Or like a child who couldn't find his mother. Both.

Stephen swallowed. *Bury it.* He grinned and slapped Dan on the back. "Man, you have got to stop being so serious. I'll see you later."

Dan smiled back. "Okay."

3

ROTH BRAUN STOOD ATOP THE GUTTED
building across the street from Rachel Spritzer's
apartment. The warm California breeze swept over
his face, through his hair, around his arms. He
hated America, but he loved the purity of nature,
and despite the smell of exhaust, the wind held
some of the power that came with that purity. Even
those who thought they understood the psychic
energy in nature rarely really understood its true
unspoiled power.

It was the energy of a million nuclear detonations.

It was the force of a billion dying babies crying
out at once.

It was the substance of creation—raw, staggering.
A plea to reverse the chaos suffered at the hands of
ruined humanity.

Purity. This was the true meaning behind the
Nazi swastika.

Roth unbuttoned the top three buttons on his
black silk shirt and let the breeze reach inside. The
others were waiting in the car with the agent who
would show them Rachel Spritzer's building. Roth
had insisted they wait while he scouted out the
neighborhood. The Realtor had objected, and Roth
wanted to crush his windpipe, but his practiced and

generous self-control had allowed him simply to repeat the demand and thereby receive a nod.

The Realtor undoubtedly assumed that Roth was walking around the buildings to get a feel for the value of the adjacent land. Instead, he had climbed the stairs of this abandoned building opposite the Spritzer place and now stood unseen above them all.

Like a god.

Still, they were waiting; otherwise he might have performed a ritual to the spirit of the air, right here on the black tarred roof.

He'd slept less than four hours since shooting the male nurse in Gerhard's flat, but he felt as though he could go another week without closing his eyes. This time, the success of his mission was within reach.

Roth put his hands on his hips and walked to his right, keeping his eyes on Rachel Spritzer's apartment.

"Who are you, Rachel Spritzer?" He spoke low. "What secrets do you hold? Hmm? Who will come to find you? Who, who, who? I know who."

He did not doubt that this rather plain-looking four-story apartment complex held the secret to more power than most of the neighbors who'd lived like rats around it for the last thirty years could imagine. He knew this because he had disciplined his mind to connect with the psychic energy that said it was so.

The Stones had surfaced through the death of yet another Jew. Fitting. There was Gerhard's fortune to be found, yes. But more. Much more.

Roth lifted his eyes and scanned the city stretching into the haze. He breathed deeply and closed his eyes. In his younger days, before he'd perfected his exquisite self-control, he might have succumbed at a time like this to the compulsion to kill. The discovery of Rachel's Stone called for a celebration, no doubt about that. But he would wait until the sun was down. What he had in mind here could not be compromised by weak-minded indulgences.

What he had in mind here would make an indiscriminate killing laughable. He would discriminate with utmost care.

Roth exhaled completely, allowed a shiver of eagerness to work its way through his body, and turned to the roof access.

Let the game begin.

4

TWO OR THREE TIMES A WEEK, STEPHEN CAME home for lunch. Today was one of those days, and Chaim Leveler was glad. The boy was clearly troubled by an altercation he'd had with Dan Stiller.

Evidently, Stephen had said a few things he now regretted. For all his ambition, the lad was actually quite sensitive. He tried to cover up the deep wounds of a hapless past, but no spin could change what had happened. Stephen would always be a war child: subject of all worlds, master of none. Lost in the folds of history without a true mother, a true father, or a true home.

Stephen sat at the chrome-rimmed dining room table, spreading mayonnaise on his bread. "You should spend less time figuring out how to make money and more time thinking about love," Chaim said, laying a hand on Stephen's shoulder as he walked to his green vinyl chair. "Look at you. You are smart, good-looking. Although you could use a haircut, never mind what is culturally accepted. Either way, what woman can resist a dimpled smile? You're thirty-one. You should have three children already."

"Yes, of course. Sylvia."

"Now that you mention it . . ." Chaim had always

thought Stephen and his bright young niece, as he insisted on calling her, would make a handsome pair.

"Please, Rabbi, I don't need a matchmaker."

Chaim wasn't technically a rabbi, at least not in the eyes of the synagogue. No Messianic Jew could truly be a rabbi. But the retired fire marshal had never been able to suppress his spiritual fervor. Not that he ever tried. He smiled at Stephen's term of endearment and rounded the table, stroking a full beard. The smell of fresh mint tea and salmon sandwiches whetted his appetite more than he cared to admit. Age had snuck up on him like a wolf on a rabbit; he had to stay fit enough to flee the snapping fangs. He touched his belly.

Chaim had left Russia immediately after the Second World War. Two years in the Sobibor prison camp had exhausted his interest in Europe. His brother, Benadine Leveler, had survived the war fighting with a Polish resistance group. Afterward, Benadine had stayed in Russia and opened the orphanage where Stephen was deposited as a child. At times, Chaim felt guilty for coming to this land of plenty, but how could he feel bad with Stephen at his table? The lad may never have come to America if Chaim hadn't blazed the trail.

The call from his brother, informing him that Stephen was coming to America, had been one of Chaim's brightest moments. It had been a pleasure to help Stephen, no longer a child, find his feet. As it turned out, Stephen hardly needed help. He'd completed his studies with honors and entered the lucrative world of real estate at the age of twenty-four. Still, Chaim felt he could take some credit for that.

The boy had elected to live in Chaim's two-bedroom home all these years despite the alternatives his considerable earnings provided. Even in the best years, Stephen never ran out and bought a new Mercedes or otherwise advertised his wealth. America had a difficult time understanding Stephen. He didn't run through women, didn't drive fast cars, didn't spend half his earnings on parties and clothing. But not because he was too frugal or conservative.

Stephen could walk into a Las Vegas casino and drop a thousand dollars in a game of craps inside of ten minutes. He was as impetuous and bold as they came.

Stephen didn't flaunt his success for the simple reason that the trappings of American life didn't appeal to him. At least not the kind of trappings a few million dollars could buy. When Stephen dreamed, he dreamed of owning jets and buying islands. Of obscuring the past and buying himself a new future. He was a tie-dye dreamer; he dreamed big, audacious, colorful dreams that held certain appeal, even if they were absurd fantasies to most.

"What you need, dear Stephen, is some love in your life," Chaim said again.

"You don't give up, do you?"

"Why should I? Pass me the mayonnaise, will you?"

Stephen passed the jar.

"It wasn't so long ago that I was in love, you know," Chaim said. "Sofia. A beautiful Jewish girl in St. Rothsburg. When she entered my life, the rocks began to smell like chocolates. Nothing became everything overnight."

Stephen shook his head. "Enough."

Chaim acquiesced. They made small talk and ate their fish sandwiches. Delicious.

Stephen finally wiped his mouth and stood. "Speaking of love, didn't you invite Sylvia to supper tonight?"

"Dear me, I had forgotten!" Chaim stood and hurried to the sink. "And I'm cooking, yes?"

"We could order—"

"Nonsense! She loves my cooking. Did I promise her anything in particular?"

"Veal parmesan, wasn't it? Or was it fondue?"

"You're not sure?"

"I had more on my mind at the time than the menu." Stephen lifted his chin, stepped onto the kitchen floor, and began dancing with an imaginary partner. His lips twisted into that whimsical, dimpled smile. "Love, dear Rabbi. Remember? Love is in the air, and I am caught in its draft."

"Nonsense. I don't think you would know love if it smacked you upside the ear. Seriously, Stephen. Was it veal?"

Stephen spun around once. "Love, Rabbi. The food of life itself. Cook us love for dinner."

"Be serious, boy! I've forgotten what I told her!"

"It won't matter what we eat. Feed us stones, and we'll think they're chocolates, Rabbi. You do remember love, don't you?"

"Ha! I was born for love." Chaim impulsively stepped around the counter, grabbed the taller man's upheld hand, and swung into his dance. "Although I doubt I make a suitable partner."

Stephen didn't miss a beat. He spun Chaim around and feigned a swoon. "Abandon yourself, Rabbi. Tonight, I will feed on love."

Chaim dropped Stephen's hand, suddenly embarrassed. "Oy, what has become of us? What am I going to do about dinner?"

Stephen spun into the living room and abruptly dropped his arms. He walked to the stereo and punched the power button. "Veal sounds wonderful. I'm certain it was veal. In fact, I was sure all along. I just wanted to see your moves."

"My moves! Please!"

The telephone rang shrilly and Chaim picked it up.

THE RABBI was right, Stephen thought. He really could use a little romance in his life. He spun the radio dial. Stopped on the alto voice of Carly Simon. Stephen returned the mayonnaise to the refrigerator while Chaim spoke into the phone. Of course, it meant finding the right woman to romance or, more to the point, finding a woman who wanted to be romanced by him. He'd had one major love fresh off the boat as a freshman in college. *"You gave away the things you loved, and one of them was me,"* Carly drawled. A girl named Betsy who had been utterly infatuated with him for two weeks before moving on to some other prey. The experience had left him less than confident. *"You're so vain, you're so vain."*

"Are you sure?" Chaim's tone caught Stephen's attention. "How is it possible?"

"What?" Stephen asked, closing the fridge.

Chaim responded by turning his back.

Something had happened. Stephen walked to the table to clear off the remaining dishes. Perhaps it was Marjorie Stillwater, the old lady from Chaim's church. She'd died? Or was this Joel Sparks, insisting that Stephen owed him money? What if something had happened to Sylvia?

The suggestions trotted through his mind, but none paused. It was probably nothing.

"Thank you, Gerik." The rabbi set down the phone.

"Well? What was that about?"

Chaim still didn't turn.

Alarm spread through Stephen. This wasn't like Chaim. Not at all.

"What's going on? For heaven's sake, tell me."

When the rabbi turned, the blood had faded from his already pale face—he looked like a ghost. He reached for the newspaper, flipped through the sections, stared at a page for a moment, then showed it to Stephen. "Did you hear about this?"

The page was open to the story about Rachel Spritzer's death. They had all heard of the reclusive woman, of course, at least of her reputation. Stephen glanced at the paper and shifted his eyes back to Chaim.

"I heard of it, yes. She lived alone in an old, vacant apartment complex off La Brea. The property is worth roughly five hundred thousand dollars, demolition costs factored. Why? You know something I don't?"

"She had in her possession one of the Stones of David, which she donated to the museum."

Stephen looked up. "No, I hadn't heard that." Surprising. Even stunning. But this information wouldn't have turned Chaim white. "You're serious? The Stones of David?" He reached for the paper. It came out of Chaim's limp hand.

Stephen glanced down the article, settled on the part about the relic, and read. His interest in the Stones of David had been started by his foster father. He glanced up, saw that Chaim was staring at him, and returned his eyes to the paper.

"I knew about the listing," he said. "But I didn't know about the Stone. This is proof, then. They do exist." Stephen quoted from the article: "'The Stones are like the lost orphans. They will eventually find each other.'"

The rabbi was still quiet. Stephen closed the paper and dropped it on the table. "What gives?"

"She was an emigrant from Hungary," Chaim finally said. "A very wealthy emigrant who had in her possession one of the Stones of David. Not too many wealthy Jews survived the war."

"I can read that much for myself."

"She used to visit Gerik down at his antique shop. She left a note with him to be opened in the event of her death." Chaim stopped. "Evidently, she'd been sick for some time."

"And?"

"Do you mind . . . would you mind showing me your scar, Stephen?"

Odd request. He had a scar below his collarbone—a crude half circle with three points inside it, like a half-moon some creature had taken a bite out of. He'd searched for the meaning of the mark. Chaim had asked Gerik about it once, and the old man drew a blank. It was a mark from the war; they guessed that much, but no more.

Stephen pulled down his collar, revealing the scar. Chaim stared and seemed to shrivel.

Stephen released the shirt. "What? Tell me—what!"

"Stephen, Rachel Spritzer's note says that she branded her son—who was born in a Nazi labor camp—with the image of half a Stone of David."

The words made no sense to Stephen. Rachel Spritzer marked her infant son. Half a Stone of David. Surely this wasn't connected to him.

Tears filled the rabbi's eyes. "She had been searching for her son since the war, but she had to be very secretive."

"You're not saying . . ."

Stephen felt the air slowly vacate his lungs. Heat washed down his neck and back.

"I'm saying that I think you've found your mother, Stephen. I think that Rachel Spritzer was your mother."

The room shifted out of focus. Stephen reached out to steady himself on a chair.

He couldn't breathe.

5

Poland
April 24, 1944
Early Morning

MARTHA PRESSED HER EYE AGAINST THE THIN crack between the two boxcar planks for the thousandth time in four days. Outside, dawn colored Poland's horizon gray. Where in Poland, she didn't know. Why to Poland, she didn't know. But she was certain if they didn't stop soon, some of the women in this car never would know.

How long could a human live in a cramped box without food or water?

There was this gray sky above them, and there was this constant *clank, clank, clank* of railroad tracks below them, and there were vacant stares inside, and there was enough heartache to have wrung the tears from every one of them days ago, and that was the sum of the matter. Nothing to say, nothing to do, not much even to feel anymore.

Except for the baby. She had to feel for the sake of the baby inside her.

Martha clenched her jaw, turned back to the dark car, and slid to her seat. She hadn't urinated for two days, but the dull pain was manageable for the time being. There were three waste buckets on the far side, all full after the first day. Having nothing to eat or drink did have its advantages, however small.

The freight car held roughly seventy women, made up of two groups: a motley crew of fifty who'd accompanied her from the prison in Budapest, and another twenty who'd joined them much later, well inside Poland. Late on her second night in the car, the train had pulled into a large plant with huge smoking stacks. Martha had stared through the cracks at hundreds, maybe thousands of men, women, and children. They wore gaunt faces and walked slowly in long lines to the big brick buildings near the train's caboose. Music floated over the compound—Bach. Something felt horribly wrong with the scene, but she couldn't put her finger on it.

Soldiers swapped out the buckets, hustled the new prisoners on board, slammed the gate shut, and locked it tight. The boxcar began rolling again about an hour later.

Ruth had been in the second group, which was mostly comprised of Jews from Slovakia. The petite young woman had eyed Martha for a full day before edging past the others to her side. She'd taken Martha's arm at the elbow and stood in silence.

Martha smiled as best she could and placed her hand on Ruth's. They remained like that for several hours. No need for talk. Human touch was all the young woman seemed to want, and Martha found it indescribably comforting. *Everything will be all right because I can feel you, and you are all right. See, it's not so bad—your arm is warm.*

Ruth had finally stretched up on her toes and whispered into Martha's ear. "Are you from Hungary?"

Martha nodded. "Yes."

"I am Ruth Kryszka," she said in decent Hungarian. "They took my husband a week ago from a farm where we were hiding in Slovakia. I think they may have killed him." Her voice trembled slightly, but she seemed brave.

Martha drew her closer and felt compelled to kiss her on top of her head.

"Who are you?" Ruth asked.

The question was Martha's first normal exchange in four weeks, and it made her want to cry.

"I am Martha," she whispered. "Martha Spieller." She wasn't entirely sure why they were whispering. Perhaps because they clung to their own histories as the last bastion of meaning in a world gone mad. Sharing it was like sharing the deepest secret.

"I am from Budapest," Martha said.

"I studied in Budapest once," Ruth said. "It's a beautiful city. They are killing Jews in Hungary?"

Killing Jews? She said it as if she spoke of eating bread.

"Some. Not so much in Budapest, but my father was well-off. The gestapo came with the gendarmes three or four weeks ago. They confiscated our house and my father's collections. I was taken to the prison outside of Budapest, and now I'm here."

"Are you married?"

Martha had cried herself to sleep for two straight weeks in prison, remembering the brutality of that day. They'd been eating lunch—imported Swiss cheese and strawberries with a wonderful white wine—listening to Father talk confidently about the return of better days, when the pounding came on the door. Not just a knock, but smashing fists and shouts. For a moment they'd all frozen, even Father. Then he'd dabbed his lips, pushed back his chair, and assured them it would be all right. Yes, of course, he'd set things up with Kallay's high-ranking officials. No harm would come to his family.

But they all knew that one day harm would come. Most able-bodied Jewish men already had been sent to labor camps. All Jewish property had been legally confiscated.

Martha closed her eyes, doubting whether she could share this particular secret of hers. "My husband and father were killed in our home," she said with an ease that surprised her. "They took my mother and younger sister, but I haven't seen them."

It was enough for a few hours. After a period of rocking quietly with the clanking train, Martha rested her cheek on the shorter woman's head and quietly cried for the first time since boarding.

They whispered above the sound of the tracks several times over the next day, exchanging precious secrets that were really not secrets at all. They were both Jews. They had both lost their husbands and their homes. They were both young—Ruth twenty-five and Martha thirty-two—and above all, they were both on the same train, rolling and grunting and whistling its way steadily closer to some unknown destination.

Now, the dawn outside marked Martha's fourth

morning aboard the cattle car, and still the train rumbled north, always north. Ruth sat next to Martha, knees bunched up to her chin, brown eyes bright, a fighter who'd accepted whatever comfort Martha could offer.

Ruth faced her and whispered, "Do you think we will both be in the same place?"

"I don't know where we're going."

"To a labor camp."

"A labor camp? You know this?"

"I think so." Ruth hesitated. "Do you know what they are doing? The Germans?"

"In the war?"

"No, to us. To the Jews."

Martha had heard rumors, hundreds. "They are killing some and forcing the rest to work."

"They are exterminating us," Ruth said. "It's why Paul and I went into hiding. The station where I was put on the train—I think that was a camp called Auschwitz, where they kill us like cattle. There are other death camps, but not this far north, I don't think."

Martha stared into the darkness. Surely Ruth was exaggerating. "They can't just kill like that."

"But they do. I heard it from someone who escaped from a camp called Sobibor. They kill with gas and then burn the bodies."

A chill swept over Martha. Gas?

She felt Ruth's eyes on her. "You're pregnant?"

"What?"

"You're pregnant, aren't you?"

Martha sat up, terrified that her secret was

known. Was it so obvious? A cotton shirt and a loose wool sweater hid her belly well. This was her first child, and even without the loose shirt she wasn't showing much.

"I am also," Ruth whispered.

"You . . . you're pregnant?"

"I don't think we should let them know."

Martha was at a loss for words. If Ruth could see that she was pregnant in this dim light, surely others would see it as well. She'd refused to consider what the Germans might do to her when they learned of it, but she couldn't escape the certainty that they would eventually discover her child.

"How did you know?" she finally asked.

"Don't worry, it's not so obvious. I see these things."

"And they won't?"

"If they do, they'll know that I'm pregnant too," Ruth said. There was a comforting sweetness in her voice. She had a heart of gold, this one.

"How many months are you?" Martha asked.

"Six."

"Six? I am almost six!"

"Five then? You hardly show! It's your first? It must be your first."

Martha wondered if any of the others could hear their excited whispers. She lowered her voice.

"Yes, my first. And yours?"

"Yes."

For a minute, the secret lives they carried within them overshadowed any sense of pending doom. Martha could feel Ruth glowing beside her.

"What will you name it?" Ruth asked.

"I . . ." Now the desperation of their plight surfaced again. Martha looked away. "I don't know."

Ruth placed her palm on Martha's belly. "He feels like a David to me," she said.

"And if it's a girl?"

Ruth hesitated. "Esther. David or Esther."

———

THE TRAIN'S whistle pierced the silence. The cadence of the wheels immediately slowed. Martha tensed, then stood and peered through the thin crack.

"What is it?" Ruth asked over her shoulder. "We're stopping?"

"I don't know."

"Do you see buildings?"

"Yes. Yes, there are buildings!"

Murmurs swept through the boxcar. A woman to their left demanded that someone tell them what was going on. It occurred to Martha that the question was directed at her. She had the best eye-level view out of this box.

"I think we're stopping," she said. "There are buildings and a fence."

"A fence?"

Voices bubbled up in the car. A loud hissing confirmed her suspicions. The train was stopping.

Martha's palms were wet already. Good news might greet them here. A drink of water. Some soup and bread—stale, soggy, moldy; it wouldn't matter. There would be a toilet. Even a hole in the ground would be a welcome sight.

Ruth laced her fingers with Martha's and squeezed tight. "This is it! This has to be it."

"I think so."

The air felt electric.

Only Martha and another woman, who poked her head past Martha's knees, could see clearly. The train passed guards who held back dogs straining against their leashes. Soldiers lined a road beside the tracks, rifles slung, some staring casually, others smoking. A tall fence topped with rolls of barbed wire ran along the perimeter of a compound, which housed dozens of long rectangular buildings.

Martha glanced over her shoulder. The women who could stand had done so. They'd grown quiet again, eyes wide in the dim light, staring at her or at the cattle gate. Their door to freedom.

Ruth leaned into Martha's ear and whispered. "The strong are allowed to work. Stand tall and suck your belly in."

Martha put her arm around the woman and drew her tight. "Thank you, Ruth." She kissed her head again.

She wasn't sure why she was thanking young Ruth.

"Promise you won't leave me," Ruth said.

"I won't."

The car jerked to a standstill.

They heard the dogs then, a chorus of barks that seemed to have started on command. The lock rattled. Martha's heart hammered at twice its normal rate.

The gate swung open, and light flooded the car. Martha strained for a view.

The first thing to catch her attention was a

German officer standing thirty feet away beside a line of trucks. He wore a freshly pressed SS uniform with a bright red-and-black armband, arms folded behind his back, legs spread in bulging slacks, shiny black holster at his side. But more riveting than these were his eyes. Even at this distance, she saw them clearly. They were blue. And they were dead.

The next thing Martha saw was the sign above the gate.

TORUŃ

"Out. Step off the train and line up by the trucks." A guard pointed at a caravan of seven or eight flatbed transport trucks behind him.

For a moment, none of the women moved.

"No need to be afraid. Hurry!"

They surged out of the train as quickly as aching joints would allow. Ruth released Martha's arm, and they walked down the ramp into the crisp morning air side by side. All the way down the train, women emerged from the freight cars, which were fewer now than Martha remembered from when she had boarded in Hungary. Maybe ten cars remained.

"Make a line. Make a line!" The guards hustled the women into a long line, several deep. They weren't beating or shooting, simply bringing order to a situation that required it. This was not the way soldiers intent on extermination behaved.

Martha hurried for the line, Ruth by her side. The morning air felt fresh; she could smell something, maybe baking bread. They might even have hot showers. It had been a month since her last hot shower.

Or perhaps they would be gassed.

"Follow the guards into the camp. We have food and blankets. Follow the guards into the camp."

They hurried as best they could past the gate and into the camp called Toruń. Martha gazed at the sprawling compound and tried to remain calm. The other women weren't hysterical. Ruth wasn't crying or showing fear. She had to be strong. Martha straightened her back against the terror.

The yard was a slab of brown mud beaten into submission by thousands of feet. Not a blade of green grew between the buildings. Four guard towers rose above the fence, each manned with three guards. Overlooking the entire yard, a red house stood on a rise to the right. A large German flag rolled lazily on a pole from the highest gable.

"Form a line, form a line!"

"I think we might be in for some trouble," Ruth said, staring at the large brick buildings to the left.

"Silence! Single file!"

The women extended their line until they stood shoulder to shoulder at the center of the yard. A dozen women dressed in frayed shirts and slacks, women who apparently lived here, walked past the new group in single file, watching. Several others dressed in gray uniforms worked with the new arrivals, jostling them into order, issuing commands even though they looked to be prisoners too.

Martha saw an SS officer from the corner of her eye; she turned. Ruth glanced over, saw the man, and stood still. It was the officer Martha had first seen, the one with dead eyes.

The officer strode toward the group from the left, a long overcoat now draped over his shoulders, a stick gripped in both hands. He walked to the middle of the yard and faced them.

"You have arrived at Toruń, subcamp of Stutthof, in Poland. My name is Gerhard Braun, and I am god." He spoke in Hungarian, and his eyes remained flat. They settled on Ruth and lingered there as he spoke.

"I have selected each one of you. For that you should feel fortunate. Your train came through Auschwitz, yes? In Auschwitz, you would never receive such personal service.

"Now, I imagine that most of you would love a bowl of hot soup and the opportunity to relieve your bladder. Am I right?"

None of them responded.

"Answer me when I speak!" The officer's face flushed.

"Yes," Ruth said loudly. Martha hesitated, unnerved by her friend's bold response, then mumbled the same with the others.

He paced, calming himself. "I was sent to this stink hole only because I speak Hungarian fluently, and I will tell you that this place easily can put me in a bad mood. In fact, most of the time I am in a bad mood. There's no need to exasperate me. At this very moment, my twelve-year-old son is watching us from the window of my house. He's visiting from Germany. His name is Roth. I would like all of you to wave at him."

Martha glanced at Ruth and then up at the red house a hundred meters away. First a few, then all of the women waved at the window, though they could see no one behind the glass.

"Good. Now, I have a decision to make," Braun said. "I can send you to the barracks where you'll be assigned duties and then fed. Or I can send you to the building to your left." Without turning, he let his stick flop in the direction of a large brick building. "This building is where we give you a shower. Has anyone heard of the showers?"

Martha felt her muscles stiffen, but she dared not speak.

"No? The showers at Auschwitz are ten times as large as ours. They say you should never hold your breath while taking a shower." He paced, lifted his face to the sky, and then faced them.

Martha's stomach twisted. Surely he didn't mean to kill them. Birds were chirping in a huge poplar by the gate; the morning sun was bright on the horizon; they'd done nothing wrong. Besides, he surely wouldn't toy with them in this manner if he intended to kill them. She let out a slow breath.

None of the women had spoken.

"Take your clothes off and leave them on the ground with your belongings. Now!"

"Suck your belly in!" Ruth whispered.

Martha quickly pulled off her shirt and then her slacks, holding her belly as tight as possible. In less than thirty seconds, they were naked.

Braun stretched his arm toward the showers. "Move!"

They turned and filed through the mud like a flock of white geese. Two female guards hurried them on each side. The dead-eyed commandant watched them go.

Martha refused to let her mind assess the situation. Thoughts of warm showers and hot soup had fled. Perhaps being treated as cattle on a cattle car had been better.

They marched into the brick building, past a line of square wooden toilets, and into a large cement room with a dozen shower heads protruding from one wall. Martha felt a wedge of panic rise in her chest. She had to be strong!

She bumped into Ruth, who had stopped in front of her.

"Keep moving!" one of the guards yelled. "Move!"

Ruth spun, eyes wide. "It's a shower!" She ran to one of the shower heads that dribbled a steady stream of clear liquid, cupped her hand to catch some, sniffed it, and whirled about.

"Water! It's water, Martha!"

The showers suddenly began to spit and spray. Ruth grabbed handfuls of water and splashed her face and mouth. Martha stood rooted to the concrete as the women rushed to the flowing water, crying out with delight. How many of them had suspected something other than water, she didn't know, but she felt their rapture.

To her right, two expressionless female guards watched.

"Martha!" Ruth called.

Martha ran into the cool streams. Life flooded her skin and reached into her soul. She lifted her hands and shrieked with exuberance. She couldn't remember feeling so alive.

There was a God in heaven, and he was kissing them with this water.

Or was he?

6

STEPHEN AND CHAIM APPROACHED RACHEL Spritzer's abandoned apartment building from the north. Ordinarily, Stephen drove with the ease of someone who'd found a thousand addresses in Los Angeles—one hand on the wheel, the other on the listing; one eye on the map, the other on street signs. Today, the nervous twitches of a new driver ran through his bones. Both hands on the wheel, both eyes glued to the windshield.

They'd stopped by Gerik's antique shop to retrieve the note, an unexpectedly innocuous note written on white paper with thin blue lines. The words still bounced around Stephen's head.

> *I have searched all of Europe for my son. An orphan after the war, perhaps. His name is David, and his father died during the war. I placed half of David's Stone on his right shoulder, under his collarbone.*

49

That was what the note had said just above a sketch identical to Stephen's scar.

And, *They must not know that he is my son. I would fear for his life if they were ever to find out.*

And, *I had hoped he would come because of the Stones, but I could not make it widely known. This note is my only remaining hope. Tell no one unless it is he. May God forgive me.*

That was it.

So who was Rachel Spritzer?

How had she come into possession of a Stone of David?

For that matter, who was *he*? Stephen's foster father had named him, upon collecting him from an orphanage in Poland. But his name was really David. It simply had to be.

Gerik had been little help. He had been as surprised as anyone that Rachel had harbored such a treasure all these years. Rachel had given Gerik the note six months earlier when her health began to fail. But he hadn't opened it until after her death, as instructed. If Chaim hadn't made a comment about the scar on Stephen's chest, Gerik never would have connected the note to Stephen.

Whatever had prevented Rachel Spritzer from revealing her connection to a lost child had held power over her until the day she died.

Stephen had received the note with a trembling hand and paced for fifteen minutes, asking unrelenting questions. But there were no answers. Not from Gerik, who knew Rachel better than most, he said. Rachel was a private woman.

Three blocks off La Brea, the traffic thinned considerably. Amazing how neighborhoods changed from one street to the next. Here stands a million-dollar home with elegant palms and a mermaid fountain in its front lawn. There, a mere slingshot's distance off, stands a home surrounded by lumps of clay.

"It could be coincidence," Stephen said.

"Yes, it could," Chaim responded. "I can't see it though. Can you? The mark on your chest matches the sketch in her note."

"Still. Could there be any proof?"

"They've already buried her. I don't know."

"What about the will? Maybe she mentioned something in the will?"

"Gerik said no."

Stephen nibbled on a fingernail and tried to think clearly. All these years his mother lived not twenty miles away? He wasn't sure whether it was preposterous or tragic. Why hadn't she found him? Why hadn't he found *her*?

This couldn't be his mother. Not this rich woman

who'd died and made the local news. The woman
may have abandoned him in Poland, then gone on
to live a life of luxury while he scraped to build a life
from scratch. The woman quite possibly had given
birth to him, but she could not be his mother.

"It should be up ahead on the left," Chaim said.

Stephen fought a sudden urge to turn back, afraid
of what he might find. Or what he might not find.

You are my Stone of David, his foster father,
Benadine, used to say, kissing him on the forehead.
He asked Benadine what it meant. His foster father
had smiled. "You are a survivor, Stephen. No Goliath
can touch you." That was enough to make any boy
of six walk around with a puffed chest for the day.

You are my Stone of David.

But he'd never been Rachel Spritzer's Stone of
David.

A tall, gray structure loomed ahead. He glanced at
the listing and scanned the building again. Four stories
high. Cracked and discolored stucco siding. Chipped
red-tile roof. Mexican tiles displaying the building
numbers embedded in the stucco under an exposed
light bulb. A Caldwell Realty sign in the lawn.

"This is it," Chaim said. "I have the distinct feeling that your denial has been compromised. Perhaps
this is all for the best."

"I'm not in denial," Stephen said. "I'm living
beyond the past."

Chaim didn't respond.

Stephen pulled to the curb and peered up at the
structure. Dying vines spilled from flower boxes
below dirty windows. A lone palm tree listed

slightly, its dead, bushy fronds in desperate need of a trim. Concrete steps led to a single brown entrance door. A patchy brown lawn surrounded the corner lot, separating it from the nearest structure—a dilapidated apartment building with boarded windows across the street. The buildings looked to have been built at the same time, although Rachel's building was in far better condition than its twin.

They climbed out of the car, Stephen clutching the newspaper with its old black-and-white photograph of Rachel Spritzer and her husband, Rudy, shortly before his death. Three yards to his right sat a dog, stubby tail madly twitching, tongue hanging limply out of its jaw. It was a cocker spaniel, not fully grown, perhaps a year old or so.

"Are you okay?" Chaim asked.

Stephen gazed up at the four-story building. "Yes."

"Arrff!"

"Easy, boy."

The dog offered a brief whine, bounded toward him, stretched up on its hind legs, and tried to lick his hand with a large wet tongue.

Stephen glanced around, saw no sign of the dog's owner, and tentatively petted the spaniel behind its ears, welcoming the distraction.

Stephen straightened and flipped his hand "Go home. *Shoo*."

The dog sat on its haunches, tilted its head, and stared at him with big brown eyes.

"Go on now. *Shoo!*"

The dog turned away and bounded a few feet before turning back and sitting again. Good enough.

"Maybe it would be best to come back later, after you've had more time to digest this news," Chaim said.

"No." Stephen let out a long breath. "I don't know why I'm so nervous. It's just a house."

Chaim said nothing, but Stephen was sure he was thinking *denial.*

They walked to the entry. Chips in the stucco and small cracks in the door's brown paint showed the building's age. A lock box hung on the door handle. According to the article, Rachel Spritzer had spent the last month of her life in a hospice facility, where she'd made preparations to settle her estate. The complex had been on the market for a week. Stephen entered his code, removed a corroded brass key, and opened the front door.

Chaim poked his head in, then studied Stephen. "I think I'll wait in the car."

"There's no need for that."

"Yes, I think there is. You should be alone."

Stephen nodded. "Okay. I won't be long."

"Take your time." He descended the steps. "Please, take your time."

The dog suddenly barked and bounded up the steps and into the building.

The dog had no business inside, but the moment Stephen stepped in, a sense of wonder swept away any thought of issuing the canine out. The entire entry level had been converted into a parking garage similar to those found under office buildings. Three rows of bare steel posts stood in the place of load-bearing walls. Judging by two large cobwebs, the garage door hadn't been opened in at least a month. He noticed a single elevator to his right, next to a door that read, "Stairs."

This was his mother's house?

The dog had stopped ten feet in and once again stared at Stephen, head tilted.

Stephen shut the door behind him. "You can't be in here," he said. But again, he welcomed the dog's presence. Despite Chaim's insistence, Stephen wasn't sure he wanted to be alone.

The dog bounded for the elevator, sat by the door, and stared eagerly at the call buttons. Seemed to know the building. What was the chance that this was Rachel's dog? Surely she would have made arrangements for it, as she had for the rest of her estate.

Stephen walked toward the elevator, breaking the silence with the *clack* of his shoes on hard concrete. With a whole lot of remodeling, the apartment building could be restored. Then again, if the rusted pipes overhead were any indication, the entire infrastructure would need an overhaul. Cheaper to start over.

See, it didn't feel like his mother's house to him. He was a Realtor examining a building, not a son coming home. Maybe because he wasn't really her son.

A twinge of guilt pricked his mind. He should feel more like a son.

"You stay here," he told the dog. But the moment he cracked the door to the stairwell, the cocker spaniel bolted for it, squeezed between Stephen's legs, and disappeared down a flight of steps.

"Hey!" His voiced echoed through the stairwell. He considered following the dog into the darkness below. "I'm going up." He was talking to this dog as if it could understand. "You hear me? I'm going up. Don't you dare poop down there."

Stephen headed up the concrete steps. He would deal with the dog before leaving. Letting it wander around the basement for a few minutes wouldn't hurt anyone.

The second floor still housed three apartments, but they looked as if they'd been abandoned for a decade, maybe two. Green carpet, fifties all the way.

Third floor, same as the second. Musty, dark, and vacant. She had lived in the building only a month ago, but where? Caldwell may have removed her belongings, but the first three floors had been vacant for a long time.

Stephen walked up the last few steps, saw the heavy oak door that led into the fourth floor, and stopped. This was it. His hammering heart was driven as much by nerves as by the climb.

The dog sat by the door. Must have run up while he was on the third floor. Maybe this really was Rachel's dog. Did that make it his dog? It really was a beautiful dog, and by the look in its eyes, quite intelligent. No, this wasn't his dog. Rachel had left everything to someone else. To a museum.

"You poop down there?"

The dog barked and Stephen jumped. "Hush."

This was ridiculous. He should just go in there, see what this Rachel Spritzer had left, and then be on his way.

He gathered himself, transferred the newspaper to his left hand, pushed the door open, and stepped into the fourth floor. A smell that reminded him of cherry blossoms tinged with licorice filled his nostrils. The odor of . . . Russia. His foster grandmother's apartment in Moscow. If he was right, he would find some mothballs hanging around somewhere as well.

The dog ran around him and headed straight for the back of the apartment. Stephen peered through the dim light. He was breathing through his nostrils. Loudly. He opened his mouth. Better.

The entire level had been converted into a single apartment. Plush carpet, textured gold wallpaper, lavender drapes—Turkish, if he was right.

A light switch to his right brought a large crystal chandelier to life in the entryway. He walked farther in, taken by the contrast between the floors below and this one. Judging by a scattering of empty picture hangers leaning against the walls, someone had selectively removed some of the paintings. Undoubtedly, the museum had picked through her belongings and taken what they considered truly valuable. There certainly weren't any Stones of David lying around.

You are my Stone of David.

Stephen stood in place for a full minute, gazing about the room, trying to decide what it meant to him. Was there some deep, mysterious connection between the apartment and his life? He tried to imagine Rachel Spritzer living here. He lifted the paper and stared at the picture of Rachel and Rudy Spritzer. The black-and-white photograph was slightly out of focus. Dark hair pulled up in a bun. A kind face. Thin. Before coming to the United States, and during his first year here, he had searched for any record of his true parents. Nothing. Not a scrap of information in the hundreds of war records he'd pored over.

He folded the paper, took a deep breath, and walked into the room. He would look around, sure. It would be good to know who had given him birth. But to pretend there was any meaningful relationship between this woman and him was nothing more than misguided sentimentality. He'd shut this door once and had found a certain amount of peace in doing so. He couldn't afford to open that door now. This was about closure, not a new beginning.

Stephen walked slowly through the sprawling five-bedroom apartment, feeling distant from it all.

Some of her clothes still hung in the master-bedroom closet, clearly the source of the mothballs he'd smelled. A king-size canopy bed sat draped in lace. The kitchen boasted the latest appliances. A cookie jar with a rose inlaid in gold leaf still held sugar biscuits. Although the museum evidently had no interest in the furniture, most of the pieces in the living room were antiques, probably from Europe, and would fetch some money with the right dealer. The dinner table was hand carved from cherry.

History seemed to leak from every knickknack and every doily. But Stephen didn't want to engage that history right now. The trappings of unmistakable taste were everywhere. No photographs though. She hadn't even left him a photograph.

Stephen stopped in the middle of the room, struggling against a terrible urge to cry. He couldn't, of course. He was a grown man. He didn't even know if she really was his mother. And even if she was his mother . . .

A wellspring of sorrow rose through his chest. He struggled to hold back tears and failed.

He stood straight, sniffed hard. It was enough. He'd come, he'd seen, and he'd cried. He couldn't afford any more.

Stephen walked to the dining room table, slapped down the paper, and cracked his knuckles. All right, then. There you have it. Finished. Chaim was waiting. He headed for the door.

The dog.

"Hey, do—" His voice cracked and he cleared it. "Hey, puppy?" He headed back to the master bedroom. "Hello? Puppy?"

A brown nose poked out from under the bed skirt. No eyes, just the nose. "Come on, Spud, time to go."

In response, the spaniel eased its head out, still flat to the carpet, eyes rolled back for a view of Stephen. The dog was certainly no stranger to this apartment. If it wasn't Rachel's, it had to be one she'd befriended.

"Come on." Stephen turned and walked into the living room, hoping the dog would follow. It bounded past him, pulled up by the elevator, and barked.

"You want to ride the elevator? Is that the way you normally go?" He punched the call button. "Sure, why not?" He was feeling better already.

He punched the call button, stepped in behind a happy cocker spaniel, and pressed the lowest button before realizing it had a B on it. Basement. The number on the button above was worn off, and when he pushed it, no light illuminated. The car rumbled slowly for the basement. Stairs would have taken half the time.

Stephen rested his head against the wood paneling. What would he tell Chaim? He would be reasonable. He had found some closure. Maybe they could come back later and walk through the apartment together. Maybe they should take a closer look at her will—she may have left something for him in the fine print. Something that had meaning.

He tried again to imagine the Jewish woman who had carefully packed her precious treasures and crossed the seas in search of a new life. Rachel Spritzer. She'd survived Hitler's reign of terror. He'd spent the last ten years pushing it from his mind.

The car reached the bottom, and its door slid open. He hit the close button, but the dog leaped through the gaping doors.

"No, Spud, not here! Hey!" Stephen stepped from the elevator, hit the switch to his right, and let his eyes adjust.

The dog stood by a door across the empty room, swapping expectant looks between the door and Stephen.

"You know this place, don't you? Is this where you slept?"

Curious, Stephen quickly poked his head into three other doorways. Two led to empty storage rooms, the other to an old coal room. He cracked the door Spud had fixated on—utilities. The dog hurried toward a plump, black cast-iron boiler that sat against the far wall, then found an old blanket in the corner. Spud had obviously slept here on more than one occasion.

Stephen scanned the room. The building had been constructed in the forties or fifties, before electricity dominated the water-heating industry. Black water pipes ran out of the boiler and disappeared into the ceiling. A newer electric water heater stood in the corner. Several fifty-five-gallon drums lined the wall next to the black boiler. The room smelled a bit like kerosene. Or was that charcoal he smelled?

He walked to the drums and tapped them. Two gonged loudly, empty. The third thudded, and the liquid caught in its rim vibrated. It smelled stagnant. A drop splashed on the drum, and Stephen glanced up. The culprit appeared to be a slowly leaking pipe.

He grunted and was about to turn when the dog caught his eyes. Spud was sniffing at a round plate set in the concrete floor behind the boiler. Something like a manhole cover, only smaller, maybe eighteen inches in diameter.

"You find something?" He crossed the room and leaned over the dog for a better view. Spud was pawing the edges of the cover now. Careful not to rub against the boiler, Stephen squeezed behind, bent down beside the dog, and examined the dirt-encrusted surface. A pattern had been stamped into the steel, but he couldn't make sense of it. The cover probably gave entry to a sewer system or a large drain. Of course, you never knew with these old buildings.

He straightened, dug for his keys, and scraped at the dirt. No luck. A screwdriver or crowbar would probably do the trick, but he didn't make a habit of lugging around either in his back pocket. Interesting though. The dog was certainly taken by it.

It occurred to him that he was squatting over a sewer grate behind a potbellied boiler with a dog. The day's revelations had messed with this mind. He grunted and stood. Black dust covered his right hand, and he wiped it as best he could against the cement wall.

He found a certain quality about the utility room appealing. The fact that it had survived all these years, maybe. Its utter silence, perhaps. Peace and bliss at the bottom of a hole. Or was it isolation and death? Abandonment. Misery loves company.

"That's it, Spud."

The dog looked up wistfully; returned a longing gaze to the circle.

"If only my life were as simple as yours. Let's go."

Amazingly, Spud obeyed.

They opted for the stairs this time. The ancient elevator deserved a wrecking ball through its gut. It was amazing that the thing still worked. Stephen pushed his way into the garage and stopped.

The rolltop door was open. A black Cadillac with tinted glass gleamed under the lights—a rental from California Limousine Service, according to the insignia on its doors.

"Stephen Friedman, what on earth are you doing in a dump like this?"

Stephen turned to face Mike Ryder, a Realtor he'd bid against on a piece of property in Hollywood last year. The dog ran past Mike and through the garage door.

"Hey, Mike. Never know where you'll find the deals. You showing the place?"

"Second time today. To the same party. That mutt follow you in?"

"It slipped in before I could stop it," Stephen said. No sign of Chaim. "Know who he belongs to?"

"I think he's a she," Mike said. "Used to belong to the owner, but I guess she found another home. Been meaning to call the pound."

"Who's the lucky prospector?" Stephen asked, glancing around.

"German investor. Working on an offer."

Stephen arched an eyebrow. "Just like that? How much?"

"Asking price. He's on the top floor now with two business associates. Forget this place, Stephen—no short-term money in this one."

The thought of someone buying the building struck Stephen as profane. He may not have a legal right to the place, but if Chaim was right and he was Rachel's son, his own history was tied to this building.

Stephen nodded and looked at the limousine again. Odd for a foreign investor to snap up a property like this so quickly.

"Your listing, right? Can you give me a day on this?"

"You really interested?" Mike wore a crooked grin. He shrugged and headed for the elevator. "Nothing's going to happen in a day anyway. You got it. But don't tell me I didn't warn you. You may have a nose for a deal here or there, but trust me, this ain't one of them."

"Appreciate it."

Stephen left the building feeling dazed and

confused, and clueless as to why. It was just a building from the past. Like the Holocaust, he should just leave it for history.

The thought made him sick.

7

Los Angeles
July 18, 1973
Wednesday Evening

THE RICH AROMA OF VEAL GREETED STEPHEN
when he stepped into the house at five thirty.
He'd dropped Chaim off after their visit to the
apartment and gone for a long drive before making
some inquiries at the courthouse and the museum
that had acquired Rachel's estate. In the end, he'd
learned nothing new. The afternoon had been a
complete waste of his time. He had to get beyond
this crazy assault on his emotions.

But Chaim and Sylvia would want to talk about
it. Maybe it would be for the best.

He stood by the door and gathered his resolve; the
last thing he wanted to do was spoil the evening with
his problems. The fact was, he really didn't have any
problems. Nothing had changed, really. Only history. So he'd been born to a woman named Rachel
Spritzer. Maybe. So what?

He walked toward the sound of voices in the
kitchen.

"The carrots and onions do the trick, I'm telling
you," Chaim was saying.

65

"Smells delicious." Sylvia's soft voice. "You really didn't have to go to so much trouble for—"

"Nonsense. Besides, Stephen insisted."

She chuckled. "I hate to break it to you, dear Rabbi, but Stephen is only a friend. And I think the feeling is mutual."

Stephen pulled up short.

"Are you accusing me of meddling?" Chaim objected. "How does an old man like me propose to meddle in the lives of two young pups?"

A pot boiled gently on the stove.

"Two lovely, beautiful young pups, I might add." Chaim said. "A lonely man and a lonely woman, searching for love, practically ordained for each other."

"Please! I don't know where you get the idea that I might be interested in Stephen. As a friend, sure. But trust me, he's not my type."

"Oh? And what is your type? You're both Jewish."

"There's more to a relationship than religion."

"You don't find him physically attractive? And he's ambitious, smart, strong willed—you could never go wrong with a man like him."

"Don't get me wrong, I like him, I really do. I just can't imagine him as any more than a brother."

There was a pause. Long enough for Stephen to realize that he'd started to sweat.

"I think you're wrong about him," Chaim said.

"Please, what's wrong with a brother?"

Stephen backed up a few paces then walked forward, hoping they could hear him. He rounded the corner, saw Sylvia kiss Chaim on the forehead.

Brown hair fell to her shoulders. She had a small nose, dwarfed next to the rabbi's. Chaim was no beast, but Stephen couldn't help but think that Sylvia was indeed the beauty kissing the beast.

"And you're like a father to me," Sylvia said.

"What is that incredible smell?" Stephen asked, stepping into their view.

Chaim and Sylvia both started.

He winked at them. "Is this the talk of love that I smell? Or is it veal parmesan?"

"Hello, Stephen." Sylvia exchanged a quick glance with Chaim. "It seems that God has informed the rabbi that you and I should fall madly in love and raise a dozen children in marital bliss."

"Oy, I said no such thing!"

Stephen stepped to Sylvia and kissed her on the cheek. "Thank you for coming."

"My pleasure."

Stephen withdrew a box from under his arm and handed it to Sylvia. "In case the rocks still taste like dirt."

"Chocolates." Chaim arched an eyebrow.

"Rocks?" Sylvia asked.

"Chaim was telling me this morning how even the rocks taste like chocolates when you fall madly in love. From his own vast experience, of course."

Sylvia took the box. "Thank you. These look wonderful."

Chaim eyed him. "Are you okay?"

"Fine? Why wouldn't I be? Today I found my mother. Her name was Rachel Spritzer. She was a very wealthy woman. A few days ago she died and left me nothing." He shrugged. "So what has changed? Nothing."

"She was your mother," Sylvia said.

"Was she? And what is a mother?"

They both looked at him.

"How is the district attorney today?" Stephen said. "Keeping our streets safe from thugs?" He made no secret of his skepticism when it came to her boss, Ralph Ferguson, the bald, potbellied DA who'd come to Los Angeles from the East Coast seven months earlier. Sylvia still hadn't committed to liking or not liking the man, even after going on four months as one of his attorneys fresh out of law school.

"That would be the police chief's department," she said. "We only lock them up."

"Lock 'em up . . . take 'em off the street . . . same thing. People don't give you enough credit. That whole department would fall apart without you."

She laughed. "Last I checked, I was still chained to the research desk, but thanks for the vote of confidence."

They avoided the subject of Rachel Spritzer for the next twenty minutes. They were all thinking about it, Stephen knew. It was in their eyes and on the tips of their tongues. But they were giving him the space he demanded.

The veal smelled wonderful, but Stephen hardly tasted a bite. They made small talk about the church Chaim attended, about Sylvia's research, about the deal Stephen was working with Dan Stiller.

"I visited the Holocaust museum," Stephen finally said after a stretch of silence.

Chaim set down his fork. "You did?"

"Yes. And the will makes no provision for any other party."

"You told them who you were?" Sylvia asked.

"I told them I was Stephen Friedman."

"But they knew you're related?"

"Of course not. How am I supposed to prove that? 'Hi, my name is David Spritzer, son of Rachel Spritzer; hand over the goods'?"

"There has to be a way."

"I don't even know if I *am* her son."

"You must be," Chaim said. "How could she ever know about the scar? No, there is no doubt."

"Legally there could be," Stephen said.

"Hire an attorney," Sylvia said.

"I don't *want* to hire an attorney. I want closure. And I think I have it now. She was my mother; I can probably accept that. End of story."

"It can't be the end of the story," Chaim said. "She alluded to some danger. Sylvia, can't you talk to the police about this?"

"Please, no," Stephen objected. "Really, whatever was in her past is in the past. Finished. I just want to get on with my life."

Stephen pushed a piece of meat into his mouth. "I'm not the only one she abandoned. Her dog's on the street as well." He immediately regretted the remark.

Chaim raised his eyebrows. "That was her dog?"

"I think it might live in the basement."

"The building has a basement?" ·

"Not so uncommon for a building that size. Nothing but an old boiler and utilities down there."

"How old is the place?"

"Built in 1947. The boiler isn't in use, of course. Maybe she stashed all her gold in the sewer." He couldn't seem to stop this flood of spiteful comments.

Sylvia looked up from the meat she was cutting. "What sewer?"

"There was a manhole in the boiler room. I assume it leads to an old drainage sewer of some kind."

Chaim glanced at Sylvia and then back. "A manhole? How big?"

Stephen set down his empty fork and indicated with his hands. "About so." It was absurd to think that Rachel Spritzer would put anything in a sewer. Besides, the cover hadn't been touched in years.

"Since when do they put entrances to public sewers in private buildings?" Chaim asked. "In Russia maybe, but not here."

"They don't," Stephen said. "But if the sewer predated the building, it's possible. I've seen it. These days, they would simply collapse the sewer and reroute it, but not in the forties."

"Could be submerged utility valves," Sylvia said.

The rabbi began to eat again. "Could be a bomb shelter."

"It could be a secret entrance to Fort Knox," Stephen said. "Please. It was in the utility room."

"How big did you say?" Chaim asked.

"Eighteen inches?"

"I would think that was a floor safe," Chaim said.

"No, it was a manhole cover of some kind," Stephen insisted.

"How do you know this?"

"Well, I don't."

"There you go, then. A floor safe."

"Makes sense to me." Sylvia winked. "You walked away from a fortune without knowing it."

"The cover was caked with an inch of grime," Stephen said. "No keyhole either."

"Still, I like the idea of a safe. A woman who owned one of the Stones of David would like the idea too."

Stephen rolled his eyes. "Don't be ridiculous. Nobody has touched it for years—does that sound like a safe to you? I can't believe we're even talking this way."

Chaim nodded. "You're right. It was a drain." He sliced into a potato. "I'm very sorry about all of this, Stephen. Maybe Sylvia is right. You should hire an attorney."

"I don't need an attorney. I have Sylvia. Honestly, I don't have a case, do I?"

"No telling without digging deeper," Sylvia said.

"But from what you know."

"No, probably not. But you never know until you dig deeper."

The image of that manhole cover, or whatever hid behind the potbellied boiler, fixed itself in Stephen's mind.

"I don't think I could handle digging deeper. I'll just . . . things will be fine. I'm working on a very good deal with Dan; I have a wonderful home. Wonderful friends." He attempted his best smile. "This will all pass, and things will be fine. You'll see."

SYLVIA LEFT at nine, and Stephen retired to his room at ten.

He climbed under the sheets and turned off the lamp, but he could not sleep. What if Chaim was right about the safe? Absurd. Eighteen inches—about right for a safe. A big safe, anyway. Too small for a manhole, really. Floor safes weren't that uncommon, although a safe behind a boiler was odd. Maybe he should return with a few tools and clean off the lid. Settle the matter. A safe would have a lock of some kind.

He tossed and turned. The hour hand on the white-faced alarm clock by his bed crept past midnight.

Say, for the sake of argument, that there was a safe behind the boiler. And say that there was more to Rachel's estate than what her will revealed. Wasn't it possible she would have left it in a safe? Maybe for her real son to find? He considered the note.

I had hoped he would come . . .

Even if the circle behind the boiler did belong to a safe, there might be no way to open it. Short of owning the building, breaking into the compartment was out of the question. Had she hidden a key in the basement? Or in her apartment?

Stephen crawled out of bed at one, went to the bathroom and returned, careful not to slough off what little grogginess had set in after three hours in the dark. *Sleep. Please, let me sleep.* He plopped into bed and shut his eyes.

What would she hide in a safe anyway?

The Stones of David.

No, she'd donated the one Stone in her possession

to the museum. If she would have had two or three or all five, she would have donated the entire collection.

She'd had a month to settle her estate before dying—surely she would have itemized her estate. Rachel hardly seemed the kind who would lock up a treasure in a floor safe and then forget to list it among her assets. Especially something so valuable as the Stones of David.

Unless she wanted her son to find them without tipping off whomever she was afraid of. There was a thought. A silly, stupid thought. But a thought that kept him awake.

———

ROTH BRAUN sat in the black sedan and peered into the night. It was now well past midnight, and the long journey from Germany had worn him thin. If not for his anticipation of the satisfaction that lay ahead, he would have collapsed long ago.

But Roth wasn't fueled by regular flesh and blood and muscle and sinew. He drew his power from the blackest part of night.

He picked up the penlight with his gloved hand and snapped it on. A round circle of light lit the book that lay on his lap.

A telephone directory of greater Los Angeles. A monstrous thing that he would have preferred to leave back at the hotel. But he needed options in the event that the Jew he'd selected was unavailable or hard to reach.

There was always the possibility that he might

select the wrong woman. Name alone couldn't confirm heritage. For all he knew an American Indian married a Jewish man and now bore the name Goldberg. But that didn't really matter. The selection of a Jew as opposed to an Indian or a German wasn't critical, though certainly more rewarding.

It did have to be a woman. His father had selected women. A woman had been his father's undoing. Yes, it had to be a woman.

His penlight illuminated the first name he'd chosen. Hannah Goldberg. Sounded like a Jew. Certainly a woman. Hopefully living alone.

According to the phone book, she lived across the street from where he was parked now. The number on her mailbox read 123423. Such a big number for an address. The Americans were far too many.

By night's end they would be at least one fewer.

Roth snapped the light off and set the book on the passenger seat. His fingers were trembling, but he knew he could subdue this visible anticipation with a single squeeze. He had this power. For the moment he would indulge the slight physical response.

Roth picked up a red scarf, ran the silk under his nostrils, inhaled slowly, then tucked the long scarf into his pocket.

He opened the car door, stood in the night, glanced up and down the vacant street, pushed the door closed. He rounded the hood and headed across the street. A single porch light lit the entryway. Otherwise the house was dark.

It was going to be a good night.

8

Los Angeles
July 19, 1973
Thursday Morning

BLINDING RAYS STREAMED THROUGH THE windows when Stephen pulled himself from sleep the next morning. He swung his legs to the floor. Nine o'clock. When had he fallen asleep?

He hurried to the shower. First stop, Rachel Spritzer's apartment. He considered running the comps he'd promised Daniel first but decided that could wait. He had to get this other business out of his blood.

He'd go, find nothing, and be done with his mother's apartment. End of story.

He couldn't remember ever feeling so knotted up. The obscure hope that had kept him awake last night now demanded that he get into the apartment complex and down to the safe.

What if?

No, Stephen, not what if. Impossible, crazy, stupid.

But what if?

From his clock radio, Diana Ross was belting out "Ain't No Mountain High Enough."

THE REALTOR'S sign was missing from Rachel Spritzer's yard when Stephen pulled up an hour later. Huh. Even if the Germans had made an acceptable offer, the sign usually remained until closing.

A single brown car Stephen recognized as Mike Ryder's waited along the curb. No pedestrians. And no cocker spaniel. Probably off licking someone else's hand.

Stephen got out of the Vega, grabbed a hefty screwdriver and a hammer from the floor behind the driver's seat, shoved the first in his slacks' front pocket, and slid the hammer into the inside pocket of his blazer. The folds of his pants easily concealed the screwdriver; the hammer wanted to lean out. He tried to flip the hammer around so the head would sit in his pocket. No luck. He would have to hold it in place with his left forearm.

He patted his left breast pocket and headed toward the front door. If he was lucky, he would miss Mike. A quick trip down to the basement, and he would be gone. He was a Realtor with legal access—he wasn't exactly breaking and entering. Still, sweat glistened on his brow. Hot day.

Stephen stopped at the door. No lock box. No sign; no lock box. For a brief moment, he actually panicked. How could . . .

The door swung open and Mike stood in the frame. "Stephen!" He clearly hadn't expected any-one. "Whoa, too strange. I was just going to call you." He stepped out and shut the door behind him, then donned a pair of mirrored aviator shades. "Sorry, man. It's off the market."

"What do you mean, 'off'? Pulled?"

"Sold."

"Sold?"

"Closes tomorrow morning. Impossible, I know, but true. What can I say? Sometimes they go your way; sometimes they don't." A slight smile curved his mouth.

"How can it close tomorrow?" Stephen asked, seeking a new angle. He still wanted in, to satisfy his curiosity if nothing else. "Paperwork takes longer than that."

"Not necessarily. Clean title, cash deal."

"The German?"

"Roth Braun. Asking price. Paid for the furnishings too. Signed the papers yesterday."

"He's here?"

"Not at the moment, but I'm sure he will be. Sounds like he intends to live out of the top floor for a few days while he finishes his business here in the States." Mike locked the door and walked down the steps.

"Any chance you could let me in?" Stephen asked.

"In? Why? It's sold."

"Not technically. It'll be sold tomorrow morning. If they make closing. Either way, I think I left my wallet somewhere inside."

"As far as I'm concerned, it is closed," Mike said. "They put half down in earnest money. Two hundred fifty thousand smackaroos, my friend. That sound anything but done to you? I'm not sure I'd want to be caught inside the property when Braun shows up. Considering the size of the deposit, we're giving him access. I'm surprised he's not here already."

Stephen almost walked away then—he really had nothing to gain at this point.

Except maybe an inheritance that was rightfully his. Except maybe four more Stones of David.

"I'll be sure to hurry. Just let me in. I'll lock up. I'm a Realtor, for heaven's sake. This is what I do. Five minutes max. For my wallet." The hammer felt heavy in his jacket, and he turned slightly away.

"If he shows up—"

"My *wallet*, Mike! He won't."

Mike looked around and shrugged his shoulders. He pulled out a key, jogged up the stairs, and unlocked the door. "Locks from the inside. Make it quick. Trust me, you don't want to run into Braun. The dude gives me the creeps."

"If it becomes an issue, I'll tell him I entered the building while you were still inside. You left without knowing I'd come in, and I left shortly after."

"Yeah. Okay. You have a hammer in your pocket?"

Stephen froze briefly. Recovered. "Oh, yeah. I forgot it was still there." He pulled it out, thinking it was impossible to forget such a bulky object. "Pounded in a sign just a bit ago."

Mike stared at him for a moment. "You always keep hammers in your jacket pockets?"

"Gosh, no. I don't know what I was thinking. I was in a hurry." He pushed his way past the door. "You sticking around?"

"Not a chance. You're on your own. Don't forget the door."

Mike left wearing a puzzled expression. Stephen closed the door and let out a sigh. Not exactly the smoothest of cover-ups. A few white lies. He *was* going to pound a stake, if he could call the screwdriver a stake. Hadn't exactly done it yet, but he wouldn't call it a bold-faced lie. Never mind, this was his mother's house. Or had been.

He took the stairs to the basement, flipped the light switch, and gazed around. A single caged incandescent bulb cast a yellow hue over the four doors, all closed. Had the German been down here yet? He crossed to the boiler room, stepped in, and lit the room with another switch.

Three fifty-five-gallon drums, large water heater, potbellied boiler. Nothing had changed. The smudge marks where he'd wiped his hand yesterday stood out on the wall behind the boiler. A small hiss from the water heater broke the stillness.

Stephen pulled out the screwdriver and walked to the boiler. The circle in the concrete hadn't been disturbed. He moved one of the empty drums to gain working space. Settling to one knee, he chipped at the dirt that encrusted the lid. It broke off in small, crusty chunks. At this rate, cleaning the lid would take ten minutes at least.

He paused to listen. Silence. What was he doing? This was nuts. An image ran through his mind— him spilling out of the building, smeared with dirt and sweat. *Hello, Mr. Braun. The boiler works just*

*fine, just fine. No need for a plumber. Yeah, that's what
I am, a plumber.*

He attacked the lid with determination, needing
to be done with this madness. The screwdriver kept
catching on the pattern's small edges. Could be anything. He cleared the edges and saw that the lid was
indeed just that, a steel lid set into the concrete.

Questions racked his mind as he worked. Why
would anyone put a safe here? Assuming it was a
safe, which it probably wasn't. But then why would
anyone put a sewer entrance here? Unless it wasn't a
sewer entrance or a drain or anything of the sort.
Unless it was really a safe . . .

He shook his head and used his fingertips to
brush the surface clear. The relief appeared to be a
single insignia stamped into the metal. Still no keyhole, which meant it probably wasn't a safe. Not a
chance this thing was a—

And then, suddenly, there was a keyhole.

A dime-sized slab of dirt flipped off the lid, revealing a round cylinder and the telltale zigzag of a key slot.

Stephen knelt over the lid and blinked. He ran
his eyes around the edges and then refocused on the
keyhole. His heart pounded. It had to be a safe!

He stuck the screwdriver into the slot and tried to
turn it but gave up immediately. There had to be a key.

So, it was an old floor safe, hidden here behind an
ancient boiler. Didn't mean it held anything but air.
On the other hand, what if? What if there really was
something hidden in there? For him. Rachel's son.

Stephen stood and hurriedly looked around for a
key. The wall, the boiler, the furnace. Nothing. He

paused to listen. Nothing. How long had he been here? Ten minutes at least.

He took a deep breath and sighed. Now what? He stepped up to the safe. The overhead light bulb glared on it. He'd actually managed to clear most of the grit from the surface. Small dirt chunks now ringed the safe. Anyone setting foot in the room would see it immediately. *Here I am; open me and find hidden riches.*

The least he could do before leaving was sweep away the dirt and make some attempt at hiding his hack job. He was about to look for a broom when the steel edges of the lid's pattern suddenly tripped a wire of recognition in his brain. Something familiar. Letters?

Stephen fell to his knees, snatched up the screwdriver, and attacked the dirt with renewed vigor.

The dirt came up in stubborn flakes but slowly revealed letters and then words. He tossed the screwdriver in favor of his fingernails. He clawed at the surface, brushed the dirt off again, and jumped up.

The Stones are like the lost orphans. They will eventually find each other.

Stephen's heart rose into his throat. A high-pitched ring sounded on the edge of his consciousness. *The Stones.* At his feet was a hidden safe that made specific reference to the Stones of David. He was a Stone of David. He was David. This meant what?

His breathing sounded loud in the chamber. *You're jumping to conclusions, Stephen. This is where she once kept the single Stone she owned. You're letting your imagination run wild down here.*

A faint *hum* ran through the walls. Stephen spun. The garage door! It had to be the German. And unless he was blind, he would have noticed the blue Vega parked out front.

Sweat covered Stephen's face. He instinctively wiped it away and then swore when his hand came away smeared black. He dived for the safe. Landed on his knees hard enough to send pain up his spine.

Using his arms as two brooms, he swept all the loose dirt back over the lid. Never mind the huge smudges that dirtied his blazer; he had to hide what he'd done here. The building might belong to some German named Braun, but as far as he was concerned, this safe belonged to him.

Footsteps sounded faintly above. He jumped to his feet, grabbed one of the empty drums, and drag-rolled it along the wall as quietly as possible, which was far too noisily.

If they barged in on him, what would he say? The plumber thing wouldn't have a prayer. Maybe he was from the city inspector's office, checking on compliance issues. A requirement for closing on the property. Cross the t's and dot the i's and all that rot. Unfortunately, he'd gotten a tad involved, thus the painted face and smudged arms.

Stephen grunted and maneuvered the drum directly over the floor safe. He stepped back. Looked natural enough, except that now a ring showed on the concrete from where he'd taken the drum. He brushed at it with his feet and managed to at least confuse the issue.

He ran from the room. Doubled back, grabbed his hammer and screwdriver, checked the room one last time, and headed back out. He hung out at the bottom of the stairwell for several minutes, begging a God he didn't really believe in to make the people upstairs disappear.

They ascended in the elevator. *Thank God, thank God.* Good enough, then.

Stephen crept up the stairs on his toes, poked his head into the garage, saw no one, took a deep breath, and headed for the front door. He made it all the way without taking a breath. Unfortunately, he was forced to breathe before he got out. His gasp echoed through the garage. Perfect stealth.

Stephen ran for his car. If the German was to look out the window at the moment, he would see a dirtied man making a break for the blue Vega. Let him draw his own conclusions. At least Stephen was in disguise of sorts.

"Arf!"

He pulled up ten yards from his car. The dog sat by his door, stubby tail wagging furiously.

"Shoo! Shoo!"

Spud did not shoo. Stephen leaned over him and unlocked the door. He expected the dog to bolt then. Instead, Spud licked his hand.

The dog had bad timing. At any minute someone would begin yelling out the door for Stephen to get back in there and explain what in tarnation he'd been doing in the basement.

"Okay, okay, go easy on me. I'm not a salt lick or whatever it is you guys—I mean gals . . ."

The dog jumped into the car, hopped into the passenger's seat, and looked away.

"Out." He didn't want to yell or make a scene. "Get out, dog!" he whispered harshly.

Spud refused to acknowledge him.

"Get out!" he whispered again.

No luck.

Stephen slid in, closed his door, and leaned across to open the passenger door so he could shove the mutt out the other way. Now Spud turned huge, eager eyes on him. The dog licked his hand as Stephen reached for the lock.

Maybe he should take the dog. Stephen straightened and gripped the steering wheel. Mike planned to call the pound, which meant the cocker spaniel might find a new home. Or an early grave.

Now was not the time to weigh his options.

Spud barked.

"Okay, but just for a day. That's it." He fired up the car and pulled into the street.

The dog looked forward, apparently pleased.

"And if you poop in the car, you're out for good. You got that?"

She whined and lay down on the seat. If Stephen didn't know better, he would think Spud here could actually read his intentions.

Which were what?

To find out what was in that safe. Rachel's safe. Mother's safe.

A tremble in his fingers refused to settle. He studied them. He didn't think he was prone to shaking.

He fought a sudden desire to wheel the car around, slip back into the apartment, and have at the safe. But he rejected the idea immediately. His eagerness might have landed him a case of the shakes, but he hadn't lost his mind to this thing. Right?

9

B E THANKFUL," GOLDA SAID IN A SOFT, HUSKY voice. She must have heard Martha's hushed cry. Only one day had passed, and Martha doubted she could survive another.

Moonlight cast gray shadows on the wall opposite the small window. A hundred women crowded Block D, the barracks reserved for Jews. Most of them slept, exhausted from a long day's work at the soap plant. Martha couldn't remember ever feeling quite so hopeless, lying here on the planks they called beds. At least in Budapest, she was in a familiar city. Here, she was abandoned and so far from home. Golda was right, she should be thankful, but she couldn't bring her emotions in line with her reason.

"You're alive," the barracks leader said. "Full trains leave Stutthof for Auschwitz all the time. And you came on a train *from* Auschwitz. There will be no crying in my barracks."

Martha could not answer. An apology seemed unwarranted, and any defense would be insensitive to the hardship they all faced.

85

On the bunk opposite Martha's, Ruth rolled over, rose to her elbows, and faced Golda. "Your body's alive, but maybe they've killed your heart. Who ever heard of such a rule, no crying?"

"In another week, you'll be begging for a dead heart," Golda snapped under her breath. "When the war is over, you may cry all you like. In here, you will keep your driveling to yourself. You aren't the only one trying to survive this madness."

Ruth didn't retreat, but she didn't respond either. Martha could see the whites of her eyes glancing from Golda's bunk to hers. Maybe she was tempted, as was Martha, to tell the hard woman that pregnant women couldn't afford to shut down their hearts, for fear it would shut down the child's heart within them.

Toruń was a labor camp for about five thousand women, mostly Polish dissidents and political prisoners from the Baltic region, but quite a few Jews lately as well. The food, a daily helping of a liquid they had the nerve to call soup and one slice of a white cardboard substance they called bread, was not enough to keep both mother and child alive. Martha had spent her first day at the plant, thinking the problem through until her head throbbed. As long as a woman could work, she was spared death, but between disease and malnutrition, life expectancy was only a few months at best. Between disease, malnutrition, and a growing baby, she couldn't expect to live more than half as long.

Unless she and Ruth found a way to eat more, neither would likely bear their babies.

Ruth's eyes returned to Golda. "Don't think that

because we're new here, we don't know the meaning of suffering in silence," she said. "But if you can't protect your passions in this life, then stepping into the next might be better, don't you think?" Ruth, the brave one. "What good is surviving if you survive with a dead heart?"

Golda hefted herself to one elbow and studied Ruth. "What, you're a rabbi? There *is* no passion in this place! It was the first thing the Nazis stole from us."

"Not from me. The desire to live and thrive is a drive granted by God. Fine, we will learn not to cry, but you waste your time trying to kill our passions."

The leader squared off with Ruth in silence.

"She's right," a voice said quietly from above Martha. Rachel, another Jew from Hungary who'd been here for a month already, leaned over the bunk. "It's the most sensible thing I've heard since coming here. If we can't have hope, then why live at all?"

"Animals don't feel hope," Golda said.

When no immediate response came, Golda lay back down, satisfied she'd made her point. "We should be thankful for one thing only, and that is that we are alive," she said. "Braun might be the devil in white skin, but if you play by his rules, you may actually live awhile. Talking of hope and passion will only get you killed."

"Some things are worth dying for," Ruth said.

"Not your passions. Trust me, you can't afford to be passionate."

"I can't afford not to be passionate," Ruth said, soft and sweet, like an angel. "I'm pregnant."

Martha felt her pulse surge in the sudden vacuum created by Ruth's statement.

Golda sat up, swung her feet from the bunk, and stared at Ruth.

Rachel slid to the floor. She sat on Ruth's bed. "You're with child?" she whispered.

"Yes."

"I have a child. A three-year-old boy. They took him away in another holding camp."

Martha could hold her tongue no longer. "I'm pregnant too," she said.

They turned to her as one.

"Six months," Martha said. Her voice held a slight tremor.

"*Both* pregnant?" Rachel asked.

"Yes," Ruth and Martha said together.

"Do you know what this means?" Golda demanded.

"It means that we both carry joy and passion in our bellies," Ruth said.

"Don't be a fool! You'll likely be dead by tomorrow evening!"

"Don't be so harsh, Golda!" Rachel said. "You can't know that."

"I'm required to report this immediately. You have no idea what this means to the barracks."

"You have no right—"

"If they are discovered without my reporting it, five of us will be shot for hiding it!"

Martha felt a welcome resolve sweep through her. She could only hide so much without sacrificing her sanity. "Then tell him," she said. "I can't hide forever. Report me—"

"Report both of us," Ruth said. "We're not afraid, are we, Martha?"

Martha considered the question. "I'm scared to death."

Ruth stared back, white. "So am I."

Rachel and Golda did not move and offered no words of comfort. Were they so insensitive? Martha could understand Golda's dilemma, but the woman's silence sent a chill through her bones.

"What has the commandant done to others who are with child?" she finally asked.

"He sends some away." Golda's voice sounded tempered, perhaps by Ruth and Martha's display of strength. "He's allowed only one to have her child. This one finds some twisted pleasure in exercising power over life. Letting one live extends hope. He uses your hope as a weapon, to make the suffering worse for everyone."

Martha took a deep breath, fighting to hold on to courage. "Even if he does allow us to live, we don't have enough food to keep the babies alive."

"We will depend on God's will," Ruth said.

"God's will?" Golda said. "God's lost his will. I'm not sure God hasn't lost *himself* in this war."

"No, Golda," Ruth said. "Don't mistake man's weakness for God's."

She humphed. "Braun will want to see you." She sighed impatiently. "Whatever you do, don't slouch or look stupid. Don't anger him. And don't try to seduce him. If he tries to seduce you, resist, but not too much. It's a dangerous game. He's not permitted to touch a Jew, but that doesn't mean he won't."

The thought nauseated Martha. "I . . . I couldn't."

"Think of the little bundle of passion in your belly, and you can do anything." Golda faced Ruth. "There's your sentiment for you." She swung her legs back onto the bunk and lay still.

"I would pay any price to keep my child," Rachel said. She paused and looked at her hands. "I marked my son before they took him away." Her lips began to quiver with emotion, and she lifted her fingers to cover them. She stifled a cry and whispered. "I burned him. What else could I do? He's too young to remember his name. How will he know I am his mother? I had to mark him so maybe one day I could tell him that mark means he's my son. I could write letters and search for him that way. I wanted to tattoo him, like they do with all of us, but I didn't have the ink, and they were going to send me away the next day."

Martha wondered what could drive a woman to burn a mark on her baby. There must have been a better way. She could never imagine doing anything so painful to her own child. But to question this tormented woman who'd lost her boy felt scurrilous.

Rachel glanced up, anxious, as if realizing how shocking her confession must seem. "It's not so different from giving a baby a shot, is it? You poke a needle into the child so that he won't become ill. He screams today, but you've saved his life. It's all I did."

"Yes," Ruth said, rubbing Rachel's back. "It's exactly what you did, Rachel. And it's what I would do too. These are not normal times. We must cling to each other—to our children, our families—no matter what the cost. It's all we have left. This is our hope."

Martha lay back, empty of the courage she'd felt less than a minute earlier. If only she weren't pregnant. What had she and Paul thought, even considering bringing a child into this cruel war? It had been her idea. She'd practically begged him, and now look at her! What a fool she had been, thinking that a baby would make her feel alive again.

Martha stared at the pitted bunk boards above her, blinded by bitterness. She hated herself; she hated the war; she hated Golda; she hated the baby.

The baby? Tears sprang to her eyes. Dear God, what was she thinking? No! She could never hate the life that grew within her body. *Never!*

10

THE NEXT DAY CREPT BY, TORMENTED BY THE burden of the unknown. Golda had made the report to one of the guards before the eight o'clock work bell. Ruth and Martha were assigned to the fat vats, a hot, grueling place that would have sweated the women dead in a single day if not for the extra rations of water.

The bell signaling the end of the workday customarily rang at six. At five, when one of the guards signaled for her and Ruth to follow him, Martha rose from her stool with terrible anxiousness.

The guard marched them to the red house on the hill.

The air felt cool, promised rain. Birds chirped, full of life, a far cry from the deathlike hissing of the fat vats. Martha glanced over her shoulder at the camp below. From this vantage point, it looked crisp and clean, except for the huge mud hole in the center yard. It could easily be a Hungarian factory or a large college for boys.

A prisoner tended a flower bed that lined the walkway to the porch. Her eyes caught Martha's for the briefest of moments and then turned away. Did she know something? No, how could she? Except perhaps that few prisoners who entered the house fared well.

Martha swallowed and climbed the steps, legs weak and shaking.

Be strong. Don't slouch. He likes pretty women.

Both she and Ruth were pretty. Maybe that would give them favor. A petite doll from Slovakia and a tall brunette from Hungary. The thought sickened her.

Ruth took her hand and squeezed. She could feel a slight tremble in the fingers of the younger woman, who was brave not because she didn't feel fear, but because she faced it with surprising strength. Little Ruth needed her, didn't she? It was why she'd found Martha on the train. It was why she had taken Martha's hand now.

Martha squeezed back. "Be brave," she whispered. "He will never send away two such beautiful women. We are in God's hands, remember?" She didn't know which hope would prove true, that they'd find themselves in God's hands or that the commandant would find something in them to favor. Maybe both, maybe neither.

The guard opened the door and pushed them in. A young boy standing behind a chair, perhaps Braun's twelve-year-old son, stared at them for a moment and then ran down the hall.

The door shut behind them. They faced a spacious living room, handsomely decorated with crystal and paintings and golden velvet drapes, not unlike her father's country home outside Budapest.

Leather couches surrounded a large, turquoise Oriental rug, well-worn but tightly woven. A long dining table was set with silver goblets and tall red candles.

Without warning, Braun stepped into the room from the kitchen. He'd been waiting there, staring at them with his dead, blue eyes.

It occurred to Martha that her hand was still in Ruth's. She tried to pull it free, but Ruth clung too tightly. The commandant wore his uniform slacks and knee-high black leather boots, but above his waist, only a white undershirt. His eyebrows arched.

His eyes drifted over them. "The two pretty ones." He walked to a cabinet and withdrew a bottle of red wine. "Would you like to join me in a drink?"

Martha heard the question, but she felt as though she were trying to breathe through syrup. Her heart sounded too loud in her ears. Her hand was still in Ruth's tight grip. They should decline, right?

"That would be nice," Ruth said evenly, finally releasing Martha's hand. "Thank you."

"Wonderful. It's not exactly German wine, but it is quite fine." Braun pulled out the cork and sniffed the bottle. "When in Poland, do as the Polish." He grinned, poured three shallow glasses, and stepped forward with two.

Ruth and Martha each took a glass.

"Thank you."

"Thank you." Martha thought her voice sounded like a mouse, and she determined to be stronger.

Braun retrieved his own glass. "So I understand that these two feisty Jews are pregnant. Honestly, I never would have guessed. You're both so"—he turned—"*fresh* looking."

Ruth lowered her eyes. "Thank you, sir."

Thank you? Was Ruth going too far?

Braun regarded Ruth with a pleasantly surprised look. Maybe her friend was onto something. What if the commandant chose to let her live, but sent Martha away?

"You're too flattering," Martha said, lowering her eyes as Ruth had done.

"Hmm. Yes, I suppose I can be. But you should know that I detest the fat guts of pregnant women. Especially bloated Jewess guts. If I know that the pure Aryan race is to be extended by a birth, I can stomach the sight. Otherwise I find myself wanting to vomit."

Martha stared into her glass. For a moment, he had seemed almost human. Now, she resisted a sudden urge to throw his wine at him and scratch out his eyes. Not even Ruth had a quick answer.

Braun was watching them carefully. "Which is why, whenever I oversaw the execution of Jews before being sent here, I personally shot the pregnant women. Himmler insists that no more than two bullets be used for each Jew. When I shoot a pregnant whore, I can take out two Jews with one bullet. How does that strike you?"

"It strikes me as inhuman," Martha said evenly.

Ruth glanced at her, then back at the SS officer. "It strikes me as diabolical. Only a coward would even find such a thing admirable."

Braun's grin seemed to stick in one place. They'd surely committed themselves to death.

He suddenly grinned wide and set down the glass. "Fortunately for you, neither of you has a pig gut. Lift your shirts, please."

Martha hesitated only a fraction of a second before lifting her shirt to reveal her belly. Ruth did the same.

"Amazing. You can hardly see it. They tell me six months."

"Yes."

"I like children, of course. I love children, actually. Even, dare I say it, the odd Jewish child. Young, impressionable minds waiting to be formed. Innocence. Innocence can be intoxicating. That's why we sometimes kill a hundred Jews at once, you know. So that when we kill only twenty, we are practicing a kind of innocence."

"I can see the logic," Ruth said. "But wouldn't killing *no* Jews lend itself to an even purer innocence?"

Braun stared at her, as if considering the argument for the first time. "But then we are confronted with another evil," he said.

"Allowing Jews to live?"

"Precisely." He held her gaze. "Sometimes the death of one satisfies the wrath of a just God. Isn't that why God demanded blood sacrifice from the Jews?"

"The death of a lamb," Ruth said. "Not a human. A long time ago."

"The last sacrifice of the Jews wasn't a lamb. It was a man. Jesus Christ. You don't remember?"

"You use the indiscretion of a few men to justify a slaughter?"

He stared at her and then abruptly diverted his

gaze. "You will both live. You will be given double rations and allowed to give birth, should you survive so long. In exchange for this, I ask only that you visit me on occasion. You don't need to be afraid; I won't touch you, although I do find you both very beautiful. I would just like your company from time to time."

Ruth dipped her head without removing her eyes from his. "Thank you, sir. You can be very kind."

"Well, I suppose we all have it in us." He walked to the wall and plucked a red scarf from a hook and handed it to Ruth. "I would like you to do me a favor. Take this scarf into your barracks and place it on the bed five down from your own. The woman will know what it means."

Ruth took the scarf. "Just place it on the bed?"

"Yes. Just drape it over the bed. Will you?"

"Of course."

Braun smiled. "Good. Good, then. You may leave."

Ruth folded the scarf and tucked it under her waistband.

Martha wasn't sure how to feel about their good fortune.

The barracks were still empty when they arrived. Together they ran to the window and watched the guard walk away. Ruth was clearly more elated than Martha. She lit up like a Christmas bulb and threw her arms around her friend.

"See what Golda says to that!" Ruth said. "You see what passion can do?"

"It's not over, Ruth. It's a beginning, but—oh, you're right! Thank you!" She kissed Ruth on the cheek. "Thank you, thank you, thank you."

Ruth pulled out the scarf and walked to the bunk five down from hers—Rebecca's, if Martha remembered right—and unfolded it over the corner of the bed.

"Come, let me show you something," Martha said. She led Ruth to her bunk and slid onto the bed, where she'd scratched ninety small marks into the wall. "This is how we will know when the baby is due. Each day, I will cross one off."

"I can hardly believe he's agreed."

A morsel of doubt tempted Martha. Golda had insisted that the commandant only lifted hope to crush it. She pushed the thought aside.

"The end of July."

The door suddenly creaked open. Women began filing in, worn to the bone. Ruth and Martha exchanged a glance and then bounded out of the bed.

"Where's Golda?"

Golda was the eighth person to step through the door. The first seven had stopped and were staring. They knew? Golda had frozen in the doorway. They knew already? They *all* knew?

But Golda wasn't staring at her, was she? Not at all. Her eyes were fixed past Martha's shoulder, down the aisle. They were all staring down the aisle.

She turned with Ruth, but there was nothing to see. Only the red scarf.

Martha faced Golda. "What?" The woman's face had drained of blood. "What is it?"

"The scarf," Golda said matter-of-factly. "It's on Rebecca's bed."

"The commandant told me to put it there," Ruth said. "Is—what does it mean?"

Golda walked past them, picked up the scarf, stared at it for a second, and then set it back on the bed. Two dozen women now crowded the aisle by the door, all eyes fixed on the red scarf. A few lowered their heads and walked off.

"What is it?" Ruth cried.

"It's Braun's game," Golda said softly. "Every few days, he orders a guard to place the scarf on a bed. The selected woman is required to visit the commandant at six thirty for dinner."

"For dinner? Oh, my dear, poor Rebecca. I had no idea! I didn't—"

"The woman does not return. The next morning she is found dead, hanging by her neck from the front gate." Martha felt the blood drain from her face.

Ruth lunged for the scarf, but Golda stopped her short. "You can't do anything! Stop it!"

A loud gasp silenced the group. There in the doorway stood Rebecca, eyes fixed wide on the red scarf. She slowly lifted a trembling hand to her mouth. Her face went white like paste. Nobody moved.

Then three women converged on her. They placed their arms around her neck and began stroking her hair in a kind of silent ritual that struck terror in Martha's heart. No one made a sound.

Except Rebecca. Rebecca suddenly sagged and began to whimper.

———

"YOU'RE TWELVE—grow up! This isn't a world made from fairy tales. It's a world where lions eat sheep and powerful men eat inferior animals like Jews."

Roth watched his father, terrified and in awe at the same time. He lowered his eyes to his knees, bared between his shorts and knee socks. No matter what Father said, thinking of other boys his age as animals was still a little strange, although he wouldn't dare admit such a thing.

This was his third visit to the camp, and each time the sights became easier to accept, but he doubted very much that young boys were meant to see the things he saw. His friends back in Berlin walked around all proud in their uniforms, but they hadn't seen what he'd seen.

"Come here," his father said in a softer tone, stepping toward the window. He stretched out his arm and beckoned with his fingers. "Come on, I want to show you something."

Roth approached and looked out at the work camp below them. It was brown everywhere. Mud and dirty buildings and women plodding around in brown clothes. Some of them wore white scarves on their heads.

Father placed a calloused hand on Roth's shoulder. "What do you see?"

Roth thought about it. "Jews?"

"Yes, that's what most would say. Jews. But when I look I see more than Jews. What I see separates me from most men."

Roth looked up. There was something almost

magical about the way his father looked at him with those mesmerizing blue eyes.

"What do you see?" Roth asked.

Father lifted his eyes. "What I see isn't for children."

Roth felt a stab of disappointment. The feeling quickly changed to humiliation.

"But I'm not a child," he said. "How can I grow up if you don't let me see things that other children don't see?"

His father considered this.

"Once you cross the threshold, there's no turning back. Are you sure you're ready for that?"

He wasn't sure. Not at all. But he nodded anyway. "Yes."

Father stepped back and arched one eyebrow. His eyes dropped to Roth's feet then up his body. Roth stood tall, uncomfortably aware that he was quite short for such a bold statement.

But judging by the look on his father's face, Gerhard was proud of his answer. He'd stood there like a man and said yes.

The commandant stepped forward and smoothed Roth's blond hair. "You come from good stock, boy." He paced in front of the window, one hand stroking his chin. "Do you remember what I told you about the swastika?" he asked.

"Yes."

"Tell me."

"That it is an old symbol that has been changed."

"The Sanskrit word, *svastika*, means good fortune. It's a spiral spinning with the sun. Only those who have a clear understanding of the occult know that a chaotic force can be evoked by reversing the symbol. This is behind the design of our swastika."

His father stopped and turned to him. "This war, all that the Third Reich is doing"—he stretched his hand out to the camp below—"in camps like these, is about power. It's about reversing the effect of a terrible degeneration that has ruined civilization over thousands of years. This is the führer's primary objective. Do you understand?"

His father had tensed and his hand shook a little. It made Roth nervous.

"Do you understand?"

"Yes, Father."

Father stared at the camp. "When I look at that mud hole down there, I don't see Jews. I see degenerated humanity. I see a wrong that needs to be righted. And I see the perfect solution. In ridding the world of them, yes, but not in the same way I did at Auschwitz. They are killing enough Jews each day to satisfy our objective. Marching them into the chambers like zombies, ignorant of their fate." The man's lips twisted in disgust. "Here . . . here our task is far nobler. Here we are finding a way to power the new world."

Roth followed his stare. How Father saw a way to power the world with the sad-looking Jews below was beyond him, so he said nothing.

"They are like batteries," his father said.

"Batteries?"

"Psychic fuel cells. If you know how to take that power, it becomes yours and makes you strong. Like taking the power out of one battery and putting it in your own."

His father had closed his eyes. His lips trembled. Roth quickly lowered his eyes, afraid to be caught looking.

"Do you know what hope and fear have in common?"

Was he meant to answer? Roth wondered briefly if his father was speaking to him, or to himself.

"They both hold great power. But that power is dependent on both fear and hope together. Think about it. Without the fear of something terrible, you cannot have the hope that it won't happen, you see? Without having hope for something wonderful, you can't have any fear of losing it. They work together, the two most powerful forces we possess."

Father turned from the window, walked to the bar, and poured a drink into a glass. "I play a game of high stakes here, Roth. I play for the kind of power that few men will ever have. Not the power of deciding who will live and who will die—that's child's play. But the power of taking another human being's power. The power to harvest their souls."

He paused, eyes glimmering, as if this was a great revelation that should impress Roth. And indeed it did. His heart was beating very fast.

"I lift their hopes to the heavens"—he lifted his hand high in the air, then swung it down hard—"then dash them. *Why?* you may want to know. I'll tell you why. The anguish they feel in that moment weakens their will. Their resolve turns to putty. Their anguish becomes my power."

Then his father said one more thing that would
never leave Roth.

"This is how the Prince of Darkness has always
gained his power—through the suffering of his victims. That's how he took the life of the Christian
God, Jesus Christ. Raised him up and dashed him to
the ground. And he was a Jew too."

Father chuckled, took a drink, then set the glass
down with a satisfied sigh.

"There are many of us, Roth, not just me. Our
work is meticulously recorded, and one day I will
show you what we have done. The deaths of our
enemies—these Jews—is a happy bonus. But it is
the power that feeds us. Does this excite you?"

Only then did Roth realize that he was squeezing
his hand into a fist. He relaxed, but he found that he
couldn't speak.

Father smiled reassuringly. "Not to worry. It was
all quite strange to me as well. I still remember the
first ritual I witnessed. It scared me to death. But the
power, Roth . . . the power was intoxicating!"

He laughed and Roth joined, glad for the relief.

"Would you like to join me tonight?" his father
suddenly asked.

"Join you?"

"Well, not join me. You can watch me through
the slit in the door. I've picked a woman. At this
moment she's down there in the camp, plumbing
the deepest wells of her soul, dredging up horror.
Tonight I will ravage her soul. Don't worry, it won't
be gory or brutal. I have no need for theatrics. A
little blood is all."

Roth said the only thing that came to mind. "Okay."

Father beamed his pride, a look irreversibly seared into Roth's mind. "That's my boy!"

11

STEPHEN RETURNED HOME TO FIND THE RABBI gone. Yes, of course; Chaim always spent Thursday afternoons down at the mission, serving soup and spreading good cheer. But this was good. Stephen couldn't tell anyone about the safe, not even Chaim.

Two things had changed during his last visit to Rachel's apartment. The first had to do with secrecy. Some things in life had to remain private. Matters of love. Matters that were deeply sacred. If Rachel was his mother, and if she had gone to the grave with some deep, dark secret, then he should pursue that secret with reverence.

The second change had to do with objective. The scales of his desire had tipped from a simple need to discover to a surprising need to possess. If Rachel, being his mother, had searched for him as the note to Gerik claimed; and if taking out a full-page advertisement in search of her son placed him—David—in terrible danger; and if, failing to find him, she'd secretly hidden something for him, then it was his right to possess this last remaining link to his mother.

The Stones are like the lost orphans. He was an orphan. The other orphans would be the other four Stones of David. Either way, he had the mark; the safe had the mark, or at least the words. The safe should be his.

Stephen left Spud on the front porch. He brought the dog a bowl of water and some lunch meat, which Spud gulped down without chewing. "Stay here." Stephen pointed a finger. "Don't move."

He hurried into the bathroom and stopped in front of the mirror. He'd forgotten about the black dust. He looked like a native warrior trapped in a business suit. It was a wonder Spud hadn't barked at him all the way home. Now that he thought about it, several drivers had peered at him quizzically on the trip home. *What's wrong, never seen a treasure hunter before? Just returning from a coal mine where I've found a stash of diamonds.*

He stripped off his shirt and paused to trace the small scar near his left breastbone. Whatever he'd speculated about it before, he now knew the truth.

Stephen showered, dressed, and drove straight to the library with Spud in the passenger seat. "You have to stay in the car, you know. No way I can take a dog into the library."

He parked in the shade of a jacaranda and cracked the window. "I'll be back."

His first challenge was to research without tipping his hand. He couldn't very well run around conducting interviews about his mother without bringing attention to the possibility that she had hidden the other four Stones in her apartment.

A series of searches through the periodicals turned up nothing on Rachel Spritzer. As Gerik had said, she'd lived privately. She had been hiding her secret.

Who were you, Mother?

Stephen turned to the Stones of David. He flipped through library cards, found dozens of titles that contained information on the Stones, and pulled five of them. Settling in a quiet corner, he began to read.

None of them told him any more than he already knew. He'd done a research project on the Stones for a history class nearly a decade ago. But now he read the coverage in each book with renewed interest.

Although the biblical record made no mention of what happened to the five stones David chose to slay Goliath, historians' first note of their existence cropped up in 700 BC, when they were taken to Babylon along with other treasures from the kingdom of Judah.

They next appeared in AD 400 in Alexandria. Christian folklore claimed the Stones represented the seed of David, the purest surviving symbol of Israel, which was Christ. According to Genesis, God put enmity between the serpent's seed and the woman's seed, and the woman's seed would crush the head of the serpent. David had crushed the head of Goliath with a stone, and the Messiah had come to deliver the final deathblow.

Nevertheless, most Christians weren't even aware of the relics. They'd been lost again in AD 700, and for a thousand years their very existence was in dispute. Here the record became somewhat fragmented. Various rumors surfaced and then faded, until the

Knights Templars claimed to hold them for almost two hundred years before the order's sudden demise in 1307, when the French king Philip IV drove them into obscurity. *You are my little Stone of David.* Why would his foster father use that particular phrase of endearment for Stephen?

Most experts valued the collection at between $75 and $150 million. The idea caused the slight tremble to return to Stephen's fingers.

Rachel had donated a Stone of David to the Los Angeles Museum of the Holocaust. He returned to the library's newspaper section. Virtually every major newspaper in the country had picked up the story, and several already debated the existence of such a relic. Others doubted the authenticity of Rachel's Stone. But to think that a World War II survivor such as Rachel would lie about the Stone seemed somehow profane. It *had* to be genuine.

As for the Spritzers, they had immigrated to the United States sixteen years ago from Hungary. They spent their time working with orphanages around the world. Low-profile. Wealthy. That was all he could determine.

Stephen checked out three of the volumes and headed home, nerves taut. He'd learned nothing new.

The rabbi still wasn't back. Stephen led the dog into his room and ordered her to stay in the corner. Spud jumped onto his bed, eyed him as if asking permission, and, when Stephen made no objection, curled up by the pillow.

Stephen looked at the books. Who was he trying to fool? There was only one way to do this. He had to get back into the building, find a key, and open the safe. He was just delaying the inevitable, subconsciously trying to work up the courage.

But he couldn't just waltz up to the front door and demand they let him look for a key. The moment the owner sniffed anything remotely like a safe, he'd slap the crazy Realtor with a restraining order and take the treasure for himself.

"Stephen?"

Stephen whirled. Chaim stood in the doorway.

"Sorry, didn't mean to startle you." The rabbi looked at him questioningly. "You okay today?"

"Why wouldn't I be? Sure. Why, what's up?"

"That's what I was just asking you. Isn't that the dog from the apartment?"

"I'm just watching over her for a day or so."

"So you went back?"

Stephen shrugged. "Just to collect the dog. I'm okay, Rabbi. Really."

The rabbi shifted his gaze to his left and Stephen followed it. The books lay on his desk, one cracked open to a chapter titled "Stones of David: Fact or Fiction?"

"Maybe you should take a few days off," Chaim said. "Your mother has died. You missed the funeral, but you should grieve in your own way."

"Grieve what? I didn't know my mother."

"Then grieve the fact that you didn't know her."

"I've spent my whole life grieving that fact already."

"I think you may be in a bit of denial."

"That's what you keep saying." Maybe he should confide in Chaim. Only Chaim. Caution argued against it, but since when had he let caution guide his path?

"I want to tell you something, Rabbi. But I want you to swear to secrecy. Can you do that?"

"Have I ever broken your confidence?"

"No, you haven't, but this you have to swear to. No matter what, you have to agree not to breathe a word. Do I have your word?"

The rabbi smiled. "Do I have to prick my finger?"

"I'm not kidding." Stephen leaned back against the desk. "I just need your confidence on this."

They held stares. "Then you have it."

"You swear?" Stephen asked.

"Swear by neither heaven nor—"

"Just swear it."

"I swear, then."

"You won't tell a soul?"

"Stephen, I won't tell a soul that you went back to Rachel Spritzer's apartment and discovered a floor safe in the basement." Chaim arched an eyebrow.

"You know?"

"Simple deduction. And a few filthy clothes." Chaim glanced at the coal-blackened blazer on the floor.

Stephen let his enthusiasm rise to the surface. He ran both hands through his hair. "Okay, you were right; it's a safe."

"Doesn't surprise me. I know Jews. Especially Jews from the era. I'm going to eat. Would you like something?" The rabbi turned and walked toward the kitchen.

Stephen hurried after him, incredulous at the

man's ambivalence. "It's a floor safe, Rabbi! My mother's floor safe!" The dog jumped from the bed and pattered along behind him.

"I don't mean to be insensitive, Stephen. But I don't think you should do anything without proper legal representation. Rachel Spritzer went to great lengths to hide the Stone she donated to the museum."

"The Stone should be mine! I could contest the will."

"If you could prove you were her son, perhaps. But why was your mother so careful to hide it? There are those who would stop at nothing for something so valuable. Rachel was frightened. You have to be careful."

Chaim's wariness made Stephen pause. Telling him had been a mistake. Though the rabbi did have a point.

"Involving attorneys could take months. It's hopeless. How could I ever prove that I'm her son?"

"That would be for the courts." Chaim sighed. "Although you're probably right in the long run. She's donated everything to the museum."

"But not"—Stephen's mind spun—"not necessarily what is in the safe. Not if the safe wasn't listed among her assets. I can find that out. But trust me, if it was listed, the museum would have made the claim already. They obviously haven't."

"Perhaps because it's empty." Chaim pulled out the leftover veal and set it in the oven. "I know these may be hard days for you, but you must be careful."

Stephen decided then not to tell the rabbi about the inscription on the safe. If anything, he would have to divert attention away from the safe now.

"There might be another way," Chaim said.

"Another way to what?"

"To take possession of whatever is left in Rachel's apartment. Who's handling the estate?"

"The building's sold," Stephen said.

"Already? We were just there yesterday."

"A German investor."

Chaim studied Stephen with an amused expression. "Then buy the place from this German investor."

The suggestion hit Stephen like a bucket of ice water. Yes. He could offer the investor a quick turn-around profit. Once the building was in his name, he could open the safe.

He turned away, worried that the rabbi might note his eagerness. He had to downplay the whole thing.

"Maybe. Aw, you're probably right. I should just forget it. What do I have to gain? I've seen what's there, right?"

"I'm not suggesting that you forget it," Chaim said. "She was your mother. You need space and time to deal with that. And your true inheritance should be yours. But you must walk very carefully."

"You're right." Stephen clapped his hands and squinted at the oven. "Veal sounds great."

"That's my boy. Now. The reception at the Board of Realtors is formal?"

Stephen looked at him, not understanding.

"The reception you invited Sylvia and me to?" Chaim said. "Tomorrow night? It's a formal affair, right?"

That reception. It was this weekend? "Formal, yes, I think so."

They ate veal together.

Ten came before they retired. "Good night, Stephen. Sleep well."

"Good night. I will."

But he didn't. He hardly slept a wink. The dog, on the other hand, slept like a baby nestled against his shoulder.

12

Los Angeles
July 20, 1973
Friday Morning

THE SLEEPING MIND WORKS IN STRANGE WAYS when hung up somewhere between out-like-a-light and bright-eyed, Stephen had always believed. In this no-man's-land, the challenges of the next day's plans walk about like relentless trumpeters. IRS agents and bill collectors loiter. A few hastily spoken words of a friend echo and transform themselves into vile threats.

On this night, Stephen's no-man's-land was populated by his mother, a faceless German crook, Chaim Leveler, and a hole in the ground filled with black air. He himself was mysteriously absent. The rabbi spent most of the night walking around inside the safe, waving his arms like a leprechaun, insisting that danger lay ahead. Rachel Spritzer spent most of the time holding her one golden Stone up to the light, asking it to lead David home. The German stood guard at the boiler room, his rocket launcher aimed at the elevator. And the hole . . .

The hole was just an empty hole, apart from the munchkin rabbi.

Stephen awoke late, at eight. He stumbled out of bed, pulled on a pair of olive-green slacks and a white shirt. No time to shower. A shave was in order, but a bit of scruff wouldn't hurt. He had plans for this day.

The dog! Where was Spud? He ran out to the living room. The cocker spaniel sat by the front door, waiting patiently. "There you are." The rabbi must have heard her whine and let her out. What was Stephen going to feed her? "Come on, let's take a ride."

Stephen hopped into the Vega after Spud and fired the engine before realizing he'd forgotten to brush his teeth. "Wait here, dog. I have to brush my teeth." Spud eyed him smugly. "*You* should try it sometime." The dog turned away.

Stephen left the car purring, ran into the house, gave his teeth a quick scrub, and returned. The prospect of the deal he was set to propose ran through his veins as hot as any he could remember. Purchasing a building that held a secret treasure trove in the basement was nothing less than the stuff of fantasies. And yet that was precisely what he was about to do.

The German had purchased Rachel Spritzer's apartment building for four hundred ninety thousand dollars. With a little work, the building could easily go for six or seven hundred thousand. Maybe more. The bank might just finance the deal without a down payment, based on his portfolio. This would accomplish two things. One, he would still have the money he had promised to Dan. And two, he would have unfettered access to that safe.

Assuming the German would sell.

The whole plan was perhaps a tad impulsive, but really it involved little more than shifting a few funds around.

And if the German didn't want to sell?

He would. He just would.

He pulled up to the curb in front of the apartment. It seemed as familiar to him as his own home now, even though this was only his third visit.

"Okay, dog, here's the deal. I can either leave you here or let you out, but if you get out, no running around getting into trouble."

Spud whined and glanced through the windshield. These were her stomping grounds. She would probably just run off, which could be a good thing. For all Stephen knew, someone else had taken the dog in and was waiting for her to return.

"Come on, let's have a look."

He got out and walked up to the door. Spud trotted proudly alongside. Stephen pressed the intercom buzzer. Butterflies took flight in his belly.

He pushed the call button. "Hello? Anyone home?"

Nothing.

The doorknob twisted freely in his hand. The building was open? He hadn't locked the door behind him yesterday—maybe they hadn't noticed. They used the garage door for access.

Stephen glanced up the street before stepping into the garage with Spud. It was empty. He scanned the room. Like a tomb. Hallowed. His pulse quickened. Where would Rachel hide a key to the safe?

"Let's go," he whispered. They walked toward the elevator in tandem, the son and the dog. Stephen's shoes clacked loud on the concrete and he rose to his tiptoes. Next time, he would wear sneakers.

He winced when the elevator started its grinding ascent. The four-story climb took twice the time a climb up the stairs would take. When the doors finally clanged open, empty space greeted him. Silence rang in his ears.

"Hello?" A faint echo from the elevator. He poked his head into the flat. "Hello?"

Unless he was hiding to pounce on him, the German was gone. The closing, perhaps.

Spud stepped cautiously past the door, ears perked, mouth closed, testing the air with her nostrils.

"What is it?" Stephen whispered. The dog relaxed and trotted for the bedroom as she had yesterday.

The scent of licorice filled Stephen's nose. "Hello?" Empty. If the new owner was at the closing, then the transaction hadn't been completed, had it? The building was still technically for sale. As a Realtor, he had the right to inspect the place. Find a key, maybe. Open the safe.

He walked slowly into the living room, taken once again by the unspoken history here. He'd left the first time determined to leave this history behind him, but now, inexplicably, he felt the irresistible urge to seek it out. To embrace it. To hear his mother speak to him from beyond the grave.

He ran his fingers over a white doily and then gently picked it up. His mother had purchased this doily, perhaps in a small shop somewhere in Budapest. He set it down.

And there, that painting of a young girl smelling

a rose. Why had it attracted Rachel? Had it been a careful purchase, or one made simply to fill a hole? The former, probably. Rachel struck him as a careful person.

He walked on the carpet in a daze. He looked for a brass or silver key in all the places people normally hid keys—kitchen cupboards, jars of potpourri, dresser drawers, bookcases—but really he was looking past it all to find his mother. Did she hum while she worked in the kitchen? What kind of food did she cook? Did her sweet breads and rich stews fill the apartment with their aroma? He inhaled deeply and tried to smell her over the scents of licorice and cherries.

The walls creaked. He jerked up. Wind? Or just the frame expanding with the warming sun? He returned to his search.

Rachel had left signs of a careful life everywhere. Silver bells and crystal butterflies lined a bookcase, perfectly positioned in small groupings. Intricately designed rugs, woven in rich reds and blues, lay precisely where he would have placed them. A painting of a yellow daisy growing out of a bleak, rocky landscape hung above the couch.

If the new owners had spent the night here, there was no sign of it. Why?

Stephen had finished a full round of the apartment and was tiptoeing through the master bedroom when he noticed an odd strip of molding behind the window drapes. He stepped around the bed, drew the curtain back. A door? Here, to the left of the window, was a door. He turned the handle and eased the door open.

A sunroom. Stephen walked in.

White curtains were drawn on three windows. A single rocking chair sat beside a doily-covered oak lamp table. Dozens of framed photographs lined the wall, mostly black-and-white. Hundreds. They were pictures of the war. Of concentration camps. Of people, some in prison clothes, others in street clothes.

It was a sanctuary. Rachel's special room.

History charged the air, electric enough to lift the hair on his arms when he moved.

A photograph to his right showed a mass grave filled with hundreds of emaciated bodies, tangled as they had fallen. The fuzzy image showed a woman, two children, and two men standing in their underwear with their backs to the pit, hugging themselves. One of the children was looking back into the grave. The caption above read, *Jews await execution in Belzec.*

Stephen's vision blurred. He tried to move his foot, but he stood rooted to the carpet. He'd seen similar pictures before but refused to engage them. He'd come to America to start over, not to wallow in this horrible chapter of history. But here . . .

Here in Rachel's shrine, this chapter of his mother's history—of his history—grabbed him by both arms, yanked him in, and would not let go. She was here, one of the faces in these pictures. He might be here.

His eyes moved to a picture of a young girl, maybe ten, mouth open and toothless. Round, innocent eyes. Legs and arms crossed, preserving her modesty. Hardly more than a skeleton. She was bald and she was naked.

The picture said she was Greta's daughter, Susan.

Medical labs. He'd heard that the Nazis had conducted experiments on children, but he'd never seen them, not like this. What had they done to this child?

Stephen lifted both hands to his cheeks, as if that would somehow quell the nausea in his gut. These were Jews. His people. How could any sane human do this to another living person? He wanted to run from the room, but his legs refused to move. Part of him hated Rachel Spritzer for leaving this grotesque monument.

But no, it was also lovely, a lovely thing. It was a monument to love. By showing this picture of the toothless girl, Rachel was speaking to her through time. *I will not forget you, Susan. You are not ugly to me. You are beautiful, and I will cherish you forever.*

And Mother would surely say the same to him. I love you, David. I will cherish you forever. Tears filled his eyes. To think that he'd turned his back on the memories of his mother's own suffering . . .

He searched the walls for a picture that resembled the picture from the newspaper. He wanted to cry out, *Mommy, Mommy.* And the fact that he wanted to cry out brought a fresh flood of tears to his eyes.

Stephen's eyes stopped on an eight-by-ten frame that sat beside the lamp on the oak table. The black-and-white photo captured a woman with long black hair. Rachel? He stumbled forward on numb legs and lifted the photograph.

The woman seemed to stare through him. Round, melancholic eyes. Innocent lips. She was beautiful.

He turned the photo over and saw that there was no backing. He read the black cursive.

*My dearest Esther, I found this picture in
Slovakia after the war. It is your mother,
Ruth, one year before your birth.*

*Not an hour passes without my begging God
that you and David will find each other. I will
never forget. You are the true Stones of David.*

Stephen's heart bolted. *You are the true Stones of
David?* He flipped the picture over. The woman's
name was Ruth. Her daughter was Esther. Esther was
also a Stone of David? But the daughter of Ruth, not
Rachel Spritzer.

Esther and David were meant to find each other.

Stephen sank into the rocker and stared at Ruth's
picture. For a moment he imagined that Ruth was
actually Esther. Was Esther alive? A secret bound
them all together. Ruth and Rachel and Esther and
David. He stared into the eyes of the young Ruth,
and he knew with unequivocal certainty that his life
had just been irrevocably changed.

His own destiny stared him in the face. Nothing
would ever matter as much as understanding what
secrets lay behind these eyes. He vowed it silently.

The air felt thick. He wiped his eyes and drew
long breaths.

*The Stones are like the lost orphans. They will even-
tually find each other.*

The safe.

A hum ran through the floorboards. Elevator?

Hands shaking, he pried the photograph out of
the frame with his fingernails, slipped it into his

shirt, shoved the empty frame under the end table, and hurried out of the room.

The key. He hadn't searched the room for a key.

Spud scrambled from under Rachel's bed, went rigid for a moment, and then raced from the room.

Stephen ran after the dog. "Spud! Get back here."

But the dog already stood on guard by the door. She uttered a low growl. "Down, girl!"

———

THE ELEVATOR doors slid open. Stephen leaned nonchalantly against the wall and took a settling breath. Two men dressed in dark suits stepped out and stopped at the sight of the dog.

"Well, it's about time," Stephen said. "Don't mind Spud. She doesn't bite."

They looked up at him, unfazed.

He unfolded his arms and straightened. "Hope you don't mind—the door was open, and I was look-ing for the owner." He reached out a hand. "Name's Stephen Friedman. I'm a Realtor. Sit, Spud."

The man ignored his hand.

Spud growled and bared her teeth. "No, Spud. Relax, girl."

Amazingly, Spud quieted and backed up.

"You're trespassing." Heavy German accent.

Stephen lowered his arm. "I'm sorry, maybe you don't understand. I'm here with an offer. I have a client who is willing to pay a substantially higher price than what you paid for this building. I realize it's a bit unusual, but—"

"We really have no interest in selling," the man said with an amused smirk. "You said the door was open?"

"Yes. I was looking for a Roth Braun."

"I can assure you Mr. Braun has no interest in selling. I apologize for the inconvenience, but you really should leave now. He will be here soon."

"Then I'll wait for him," Stephen said.

"You're not listening. Please leave. Now."

"I'm offering—"

"I don't care if you're offering twice what was paid; we're not interested."

Stephen stared at them, taken off guard by their dismissal. "You hear that, Spud? They aren't interested in the million dollars I was going to offer them." He had no intention of offering a million dollars, of course. But saying it might make them think twice. "May I ask what Mr. Braun's interest in the building is?"

"Actually, no; that would be completely inappropriate," the dark-haired man said. His friend looked on without expression. He was white enough to be an albino. Blond hair and eyebrows. Pale blue eyes that forced Stephen's stare away. They obviously weren't impressed.

"Is he going to tear it down?" Stephen asked.

The dark-haired man glanced at the blond, then back to Stephen, apparently amused. "Are all Americans as dense as you?"

Perhaps the man was more incensed than amused.

"I will now give you precisely thirty seconds to vacate the property, or I will personally show you the door," the German said.

Stephen lifted both hands in a sign of surrender. "Easy. I'm just a businessman interested in business. It's a simple matter of money. How could any sane man refuse to double his investment in a day? It makes me wonder what you're doing here. In America."

"That is none of your concern. Now, please"— the man bowed his head in an unsuccessful attempt at graciousness—"leave."

He wore thick gold rings on several fingers, one with an onyx carved in the shape of a lion. A heavy gold chain hung on his neck. And under his jacket? Stephen would be surprised if the man didn't wear a gun.

"Okay. I'm leaving." He turned to the stairs, paused, and turned back. "Does the owner have any interest in Rachel Spritzer?"

The man stepped forward, grabbed Stephen above his elbow, drew him roughly toward the stairs, and shoved him down the first two steps. "Now you're trying my patience. Get out!"

Pain flared up Stephen's arm. "Ouch! I'm going."

Spud barked and dodged a swift kick. She ran deftly past them and into the stairwell.

"I know you're going. And I'm going with you."

Stephen twisted his arm away and hurried down, stunned by their treatment of him. When had he ever been physically removed from a building by a bodyguard? *Ouch?* Had he actually said "ouch"?

"This is crazy. You're actually physically throwing me out of the building?"

"I'm protecting the interests of my employer. You, on the other hand, are breaking the law."

Braun's bodyguard pushed him across the garage floor, ignoring Spud, who'd found her courage again and was hopping to their left, barking furiously. The man pulled the front door open, swung his foot at Spud, who bolted out in a hasty retreat, and shoved Stephen through.

"The door was open—"

"Forgive the confusion. You won't find it open again." The door slammed in his face.

"Uh! You . . . *idiot*!" Stephen turned to find an elderly lady on the sidewalk watching him.

He forced a grin and shrugged. "Brothers."

She smiled knowingly and went on her way.

Stephen hurried for his car, trailed by an indignant dog. They climbed in and sat side by side, staring out the front window. He hadn't actually talked to Braun, but somehow he doubted the treatment would have been any different.

"What do you think, Spud? Maybe we overdid it a bit?"

He pulled out Ruth's picture and stared into her eyes for a long minute.

"Well, I don't think we did," he said. "I'm going to find a way in, Spud. One way or another, I'm going to find out what's in that basement."

The dog whimpered.

A black limousine drove by, took a left at the stop sign and rounded the apartment. Braun. Stephen slipped the picture between the seats and gripped the wheel with both hands.

Several thoughts flashed through his mind. His deal with Dan Stiller. The reception tonight.

Chaim and Sylvia, whom he'd invited to the reception tonight.

All were distant distractions from the driving urge to get to the bottom of Rachel Spritzer's apartment complex. Literally.

Stephen decided then that he would cancel the rest of his plans for the day and apply his energy to one end and one end only: getting at that safe.

He started the engine and angled for La Brea.

"A REALTOR named . . ." Claude turned to Lars.

"Stephen Friedman," Lars said.

"Stephen Friedman. Don't worry, he won't be back."

"He was inside?"

"Yes. Up here, in fact. He claimed to have a client willing to pay a million dollars for the property."

"How did he get in? I said no one enters. Is that too complicated for you?" Roth wanted to hit one of them. Not because the man had come in, but because Claude and Lars had broken his trust. He immediately set the impulse aside.

"He said the front door was open," Claude said. "I can promise you, he won't be back."

On second thought, reprisal of some kind was in order. And the appearance of the Realtor confirmed that the game was in full swing.

Could it be the Jew?

He had to play the game perfectly now. One slip and all would be lost.

"If anyone else enters, kill them. We have too much riding on this to risk exposure."

"Killing a Realtor will draw attention," Lars said.

"Not the Realtor. Kill anyone else. The Realtor, bring to me."

Roth turned away and walked to the living room. He withdrew a white handkerchief and dabbed at the sweat that had gathered on his forehead. He couldn't remember ever feeling so terrified over the prospect of failure.

The Stones were here. They called out to him. But also, more than mere fortune. With calculating, deliberate moves, he would finish what Gerhard had started in Toruń.

"We have to move quickly. Start in the kitchen. I want every drawer emptied of every spoon and fork." He faced Claude and Lars, who waited with folded arms. "Every word she wrote, no matter how insignificant it seems, comes to me." He looked around at the remaining artwork and sniffed at the air. "They're here, I can smell them. Can you smell them?"

They exchanged glances. Fools, pawns, oblivious to the game. "I can smell Jew," Claude said, the corner of his mouth lifting slightly.

Roth ignored the bourgeois response and glanced out the window. He'd expected more activity around the building. The wench had possessed one of the Stones of David, for heaven's sake. He'd half-expected the museum to be out here with a wrecking ball, searching for the others. Their assumption that someone who'd gladly donated her entire estate would not cunningly hide a greater fortune betrayed them for the fools they were. They'd picked through the apartment and removed a number of valuables but conducted no thorough search. Like most men, they were psychically impaired.

All the better for him.

He stripped off the black silk jacket. His shirt was also silk. Black silk. He loved the way it felt on his skin, smooth and slick. He draped the jacket over a chair. They would blockade the entry door, bring in only food and what tools they needed, and live on the third floor while they worked.

"Take off your jackets," he said.

Claude and Lars stripped down to white undershirts.

"Place your guns on the table where we can get to them. Just as a precaution."

They did so.

"What about the sunroom?" Lars asked. The man's gray eyes had always fascinated Roth. You could look in his eyes and guess that he was ruthless, but at other times those eyes seemed as innocent as a child's.

"I will work in the sunroom," Roth said. Rachel Spritzer's own private museum had been a delightful surprise. The pictures excited Roth, gave him the unexpected thrill of reliving his formative years.

He turned and headed for the master bedroom.

13

EVEN WITH DOUBLE RATIONS OF THE BROTH and bread, Martha didn't know how her baby would survive another two months. She and Ruth had both lost weight in their arms and legs—everywhere but in their bellies, which had grown slowly to show the life curled up within.

Prisoners came and went, most bearing long expressions of desperation and hopelessness. News of the outside world filtered in with the new arrivals, but separating the rumors from the truth was nearly impossible.

Warplanes flew high above, presumably on bombing runs to the south. Rumors of the Russians advancing with their allies, advancing to crush the Germans, rippled through the camp but provided little hope. Here in Toruń, such possibilities could not rise above the resignation of five thousand women plodding on dry mud, clinging to a life few were sure they wanted anymore.

They said the Germans were gathering all the Hungarian Jews in the camp at Kistarcsa, outside Budapest, but Martha could hardly remember what her homeland looked like, much less cry over what was happening in the bleak landscape of her distant memory. The exceptions were her sister, Katcha, and Antonette, her mother. She pressed every prisoner from the south for news of the two women, but no one had any. How could they? Trainloads of Jews shuttled here and there, and they were supposed to remember a face or a name among them all?

Martha stood outside the barracks and stared at the gray sky. Heavy clouds stretched from horizon to horizon, dark like the mud under her feet. To her right, the gate to Toruń, where she'd seen eighteen women hanged with bags over their heads over the past month, stood exposed to the gathering storm. To her left, the commandant's house rose like a monument painted red with the blood of his victims.

Rebecca was the first she'd seen hanging from the gate, but always, every two days, or three at most, the camp awoke to another body, swinging like a sack of rocks. It wasn't enough for Braun to kill the women. He insisted on this inconceivable torture before the slaughter, of dining them and God only knew what else. The wails of some victims cut through the camp at midnight. But the cries would always end abruptly, cut off by the sudden snap of the noose.

Martha heard movement behind her. She turned to see Ruth walking toward her from the barracks, smiling. No other woman in the compound could smile as much as the young mother-to-be from Slovakia. Unfortunately, her optimism was lost on most of the others. At times even Martha felt a hint of contempt, perhaps a bit of jealousy as well. Ruth's talk of passion and joy sometimes struck Martha as offensive in this place of death.

Ruth slipped her arm around Martha's and pulled her close. "It's getting warmer," she said. "Summer will be here soon."

On the other hand, Ruth exhibited an unrelenting need for companionship. Since their meeting on the train, she had been more like a sister to Martha than a friend. When they stood side by side like this, as they often did before the evening roll call, Martha felt more alive, and more hopeful, than at any other time during the day.

"It's going to rain again," Martha said.

"Hmm. Look at the flowers out there," Ruth said, gazing at the field.

"They've painted the guard towers," Martha said. "Why would they paint the guard towers?"

"Perhaps they want to brighten the guards' mood."

Her optimism was incorrigible. Martha nearly laughed, but the gray skies held her back.

"Little David's been kicking me silly today," Ruth said. She put her hand on Martha's belly. "Yours?"

"Quiet. I think he has the days and nights mixed up. I could hardly sleep last night. Anyway, how do you know yours is a David?"

"Then she's an Esther, and yours is a David. Or they are both Esthers."

"Or both Davids."

"But it would be better if one is a David and one is an Esther."

"Why?"

Ruth smiled wide. "So they can fall in love and be married, of course. Wouldn't that be something?"

Martha had to chuckle. "You're impossible. Women are being hung from the gate, and your mind is skipping through the daisies, planning weddings."

Ruth's smile faded. She reached up and swept a strand of hair from Martha's cheek. "If you have a daughter, she will be very beautiful, like you. She'll run through fields of daisies and marry my beautiful David."

"Aren't you forgetting something?"

"That dead babies can't grow up to be married men and women?"

"Yes."

Ruth looked out at the field, shifting to one of her rare, somber moods. "You're right. That's the problem with this world. But do David and Esther know that? They're warm and snug in our bellies, jumping for joy, oblivious to the trains and the camps. We should take a lesson from them."

"We're not oblivious to the stink of death, though."

"No. But we aren't oblivious to the joy that awaits us either."

"Joy? You mean the possibility of a noose around our necks? Or a train ride back to Auschwitz?"

"No, I mean what awaits us when we are born into the next life."

Martha sighed. "Yes, of course, how silly of me. The next life. After we've been killed."

"Or after we have lived long and full lives. Death is the one thing that happens to every person. So what if our passing is a little strenuous? What awaits will be no less delightful."

Ruth had never spoken so frankly about death, and Martha wasn't sure she liked it much.

A guard approached them from the commandant's hill. Ruth looked his way, silenced for a moment. Braun had asked both of them to his house only once since that first meeting—a ridiculous social affair during which they sat on his couch and talked nonsense. Ruth had been called up on three other occasions, by herself.

"He likes you," Martha said, still watching the guard.

"I'm not sure I can go again." Emotion crowded Ruth's voice.

"You have to. But please tell me you won't let him touch you."

"There's a letter opener on his desk. I would stab him in the heart before I let him touch me."

"Maybe you should do it anyway."

"I've been tempted."

Ruth turned to Martha. "I would like to ask you something. If anything were to happen to me after my child is born, will you take him as your own?"

"Of course. I would think of nothing else."

"And if anything happens to you, I will care for your child." Ruth's eyes searched hers, concerned, which alarmed Martha.

"What is it, Ruth? Do you know something?"

"No. No, of course not. I swear it, Martha. I will care for your child as if it were my own."

Martha nodded. "And I will take care of yours."

"At all costs. Forever. Swear it."

"At all costs, forever. I swear it."

"As do I," Ruth said.

The guard stopped twenty feet away. "You. The short one. The commandant wants to see you."

Ruth squeezed Martha's hand. "Thank you."

"Be strong," Martha whispered.

The admonition was more for herself than her friend.

14

Los Angeles
July 20, 1973
Friday Evening

CHAIM LEVELER SCANNED THE RECEPTION HALL again, but Stephen was nowhere to be seen. He hadn't seen or heard from the boy since they'd retired last evening. The Realtors' semiannual reception had started an hour ago, and still no sign. This wasn't entirely unlike Stephen, but given the circumstances of the last two days, Chaim worried.

Three hundred voices of realty professionals and their significant others filled the room with a steady murmur. Guests dressed in black jackets and trendy maxis surrounded a few dozen tables, each decorated with miniature homes—whether edible or not, the rabbi wasn't sure. The crab cakes and truffles certainly were edible, and quite good too.

"Hello, Rabbi."

He turned to see Sylvia, dressed in a long black gown and smiling softly. "My, you look stunning, dear." He took her hand and kissed it. "Have you seen Stephen?"

"No. He's not here yet?"

"Not that I've seen. He's distracted. I think this

discovery of his mother is getting to him." He'd given his word not to breathe a word about the safe, not even to Sylvia. "Not that I blame him."

"He's not doing anything stupid, is he?"

Chaim looked at her, surprised. She'd touched on his fear exactly, but to say it so plainly seemed insensitive. "No, no. Why would you say that?"

"Stephen is unpredictable and impulsive. I wouldn't put anything past him. You talk to Gerik again?"

"Yes," Chaim said.

"And he's worried about Stephen's safety?"

"You know Gerik. Sure he's concerned, but he also sees this as a private matter. And he thinks Stephen should follow his heart to whatever resolution awaits him."

"Well, if any danger does exist, Stephen is the type to find it."

"Listen to us. It's probably nothing." Chaim smiled. "We're seeing ghosts. Stephen is a grown man, not a child. Maybe Gerik is right—let him follow his heart."

Sylvia sighed. "Probably right. I'm a bit uptight. All this talk about a serial killer has the office in knots."

"Serial killer? What are you talking about?"

"You should turn on the television more often, Rabbi. Two women killed in two nights, each found with their wrists slit."

"That's reason to assume it was a serial killer?" Chaim asked. "It's a big city—"

"Both women were Jewish. Both were left in identical states. A red scarf was draped over the face of both women. These are deliberate killings."

"My, my." The rabbi shook his head slowly.

"The mayor isn't too thrilled that the information was leaked to the press. Last thing we need is panic among Jewish women."

"Does it concern you?" he asked.

"What? That I'm Jewish?" She scanned the floor. "Honestly, I hadn't thought about it."

"Well, I'm sure a good party is just what you need to get your mind off work."

Chaim patted her hand and took a step before stopping short. She followed his gaze. Stephen angled toward them from the main entrance. He wore a white shirt without a jacket. No tie. His dark, thinning hair had been hastily slicked back.

Sylvia watched him approach. "Distracted, you said?"

Stephen zigzagged his way around curious stares, mounted the steps into the hall, and hurried to them, winded. A light sheen of sweat coated his unshaved face.

He cracked a boyish grin. "Hey. Boy. Sorry I'm late. I've been tied up doing some"—he paused and shifted his eyes—"research."

Chaim stared.

"I feel a bit underdressed," Stephen said. "It was either that or miss the whole thing." He looked around. "Whole gang's here."

"Daniel Stiller is looking for you," Chaim said. "Something about the Santa Monica property. Where have you been?"

"Stiller . . ." Stephen stared off in a daze.

"You okay?" Sylvia asked.

"Right. Fine. I just lost track of time. Do I look okay? I tried to freshen up a bit in the restroom."

"A jacket wouldn't hurt," Sylvia said. "But hey, who's looking? Nothing wrong with the . . . earthy look."

"You think someone has a jacket I could borrow?" He attempted to smooth his rumpled shirt.

"I doubt it," Chaim said. They stood in silence for a moment. He'd never seen the lad so frazzled. It was hardly his business, but Chaim felt compelled to ask the question again. "So, where were you?"

Stephen looked from him to Sylvia and then back. He glanced around, bright-eyed now. He took them both by their arms and eased them around so their backs were to the main hall.

"Did Chaim tell you, Sylvia?"

"Tell me what?"

"About the safe. That's good, Rabbi. I knew you were a man of your word. Promise me you won't tell a soul, Sylvia." He glanced over his shoulder. Evidently, the coast was still clear.

"How can I promise you what—"

"Just promise me."

"Fine. I promise," Sylvia said.

"It *is* a safe. And she has a room in her house filled with pictures of the camps. She had to be a camp survivor. I found a note on a picture—there's a girl she referred to as a Stone of David. Her name's Esther. I think she may still be alive. My foster father used to call me his Stone of David."

He looked at them as if expecting this information dump to fill their minds with amazement. Chaim heard it all, but he'd been so distracted by Stephen's near-rabid performance that he'd missed the point. He caught Sylvia's eye. She took Stephen by the arm.

"Stephen, I don't have a clue what you just said, but I think you need some rest. Maybe we should go."

"What do you mean, you don't have a clue? Aren't you listening?" Another quick look over his shoulder. He whispered harshly. "It's a *safe!* And I swear the people who bought the building know something's there. Don't you see? I'm an orphan from the war. *The orphans will find each other.* She wants me to find the safe. For all we know, it just might have the other four Stones."

He stopped midgesture, looked from Sylvia to Chaim, and lowered his arms. "You don't see it, do you?"

Chaim finally found his voice. "We see that you are quite taken with this thing, my boy. But this is neither the time nor the place to show the world your interest."

"You're right. You're right. I don't know what came over me. Sorry."

"Don't be," Sylvia said.

He closed his eyes. "I must look like a fool."

"Don't be silly. A crazed maniac, maybe, but not a fool." She smiled.

Stephen grinned. "Okay. Sorry. Not another word about it tonight. I swear."

"Honestly, you have to be careful," Chaim said.

"Not to worry, Rabbi." He patted Chaim on the shoulder. "How's the food?"

"The crab cakes are among the best I've tasted."

"You've both had a chance to meet some new people?"

"Not yet," Sylvia said. "But I'm sure there are plenty of Realtors who'll willingly serve an attorney her drink. Would you mind?"

"Not at all," Stephen said.

But Stephen didn't move to get Sylvia her drink.

"Listen." Stephen stroked his chin and glanced around furtively. "I'm not sure this was a good idea. I shouldn't have come in the first place, and the thought of having to mingle is giving me the shivers."

"Please, Stephen, we didn't mean to suggest that—"

"No, Rabbi." He held up his hands. "I really, really think I need to go. I'm not dressed right." He winked and put a hand on Chaim's shoulder. "Do me a favor, will you? If you run into Dan Stiller again, tell him I'll get in touch with him in the morning."

"Actually, I was thinking of leaving myself. It—"

"No. Absolutely not. I forbid it! You will stay and enjoy yourself. I have a few errands to run, and then I'll be home."

"Errands? It's nine o'clock."

Stephen grinned deliberately. "Exactly. Need to buy some shampoo and a razor. Thank you for coming, Sylvia. I would love to stay and chat, but the shower is bellowing my name. Stay and have some fun."

"Don't worry about me. I'm just getting started."

He cocked his finger at her like a gun. "That's the spirit. Show the rabbi how an attorney parties, will you?" He began to back away. "Good night."

He turned and hurried toward a side door, leaving Chaim and Sylvia staring after him with raised brows.

—⁓—

STEPHEN RAN out of the building, more relieved than he could remember feeling in a long time. He hadn't been roped into a conversation with a single one of his peers—luck was definitely on his side. It was going to be a good night. Even the dog seemed eager, perched on the edge of the passenger's seat.

"Don't worry, Rabbi," Stephen muttered. "If you knew what I know . . ."

Which was? That he had indeed done some research, if stalking Rachel Spritzer's apartment building from every conceivable angle and setting every last cell in his brain to the task of getting at that safe could be classified as research. As a result, he'd stumbled upon information only a fool could ignore: the contents of the safe did not belong to the museum.

At least that's the way he read the provision buried in the will.

He'd left the apartment and visited Caldwell Realty, where he'd persuaded a secretary named Sally to let him take a peek at the documents. No harm— they would soon be part of the public record in a transaction like this anyway. He found the portions of Rachel Spritzer's will that dealt with the apartment. According to the document, in addition to the building itself, Rachel Spritzer had donated to the museum all of her earthly possessions "currently located in the fourth-floor apartment of #5 Thirty-second Street . . . including but not limited to . . ." The document contained an inventory of her most valuable possessions.

The contents of the safe weren't in the fourth-floor apartment. They were in the basement. And they weren't technically part of the building. The safe itself was, but not the contents.

True, the specific mention of her residence may have simply been intended to address her living quarters in general, but as far as Stephen was concerned, that was open to debate. Which could mean there *was* something in that safe Rachel Spritzer didn't want the museum to possess. He was no attorney, but considering everything else, the implications read like absolute fact to Stephen.

He'd also taken the time to flesh out the man who'd bought the building on such short notice. Roth Braun. A German investor with no ties to the United States that he could find. Not one. He had a name in Germany, owned a bunch of businesses that read like Mafia cover-ups to Stephen, especially in light of his earlier exchange with Braun's henchmen. Still, the man looked clean on paper. Maybe he really had purchased the building as a legitimate investment.

Not a chance. Braun knew something. Specifically, something about Rachel Spritzer. It struck Stephen that the man could be the very danger his mother alluded to in her note. All the more reason to get into that safe.

Stephen had spent three hours thinking through a dozen ways to get into the building. He watched as a woman, apparently someone from the city, approached the front door, spoke briefly to the dark-haired German, had him sign something, and then left. An inspector, maybe, getting a waiver.

His challenge was to get in without them knowing he was in. No matter how he broke down the problem, this meant the front door was out of the question. A dozen times he told himself that he was charting dangerous waters. And a dozen times the photograph of Ruth reached into his soul, demanding he liberate the Stones of David. The authorities were out, absolutely out. He had no claim against the Germans. Retaining an attorney was even more impossible. If Braun learned about the safe, he and the treasure would be long gone before any court could even hear a case.

Stephen's only option was to move alone, and quickly. He felt sick—or was it giddy?—with the impossibilities of the situation.

And then one thought healed his sickness.

A plan.

An improbable, highly creative plan that no one would suspect of anyone but a fool. Improbable enough to actually work.

He returned to the apartment building, drove around it three times, each time gathering his resolve, and finally settled on his course. A visit to the hardware store ate up the remaining daylight and the first hour of darkness. But the time proved invaluable. He refined options and details by careful calculation until the plan was perfect.

Skipping out of the reception without talking to Dan Stiller may not have been wise, but they still had ample time to submit their proposal to the city. Next Wednesday was still a long ways off. He had to get this small matter of history and destiny and several hundred million dollars off his chest before he could really concentrate on the Santa Monica property anyway.

Chaim and Sylvia no doubt believed him a tad whacked-out, but he'd covered well enough. They couldn't possibly understand the true significance of the safe.

Stephen glanced at his watch. A little over two hours before midnight. Perfect.

15

Los Angeles
July 20, 1973
Friday Night

SURPRISINGLY, LA BREA AVENUE SEEMED TO have more traffic near midnight than midday. Stephen parked the Vega on a side street two blocks south of his mother's apartment. He pulled a backpack from the backseat, checked to see that no one was watching, and hefted the bag over his shoulders. *Natural. Look natural.* Just an ordinary Joe taking a midnight stroll with a pack strapped to his back.

"You stay put, Spud. I'll be back before you know it."

The dog jumped out before Stephen could shut the door. "Spud!" But the dog ran up the street and disappeared. This was getting to be a bad habit.

Stephen locked the car and turned north, searching for the dog on his way. Surely she would come back. He felt oddly lost without the dog's carefree presence.

The sidewalk was deserted except for a woman walking directly toward him, half a block up. Where had she come from? *Avoid eye contact. Natural.* They passed each other without incident. Had she seen his car?

He cut east at the next street and then turned left into an alley that approached the rear of the abandoned complex across the street from Rachel's building. Darkness swallowed him. He hurried his pace. So far, so good, but still no sign of Spud. Maybe just as well for the time being.

Stephen stopped at the end of the alley and poked his head around the corner. The windows of what he'd decided to call "Building B" were patched up with plywood. Graffiti covered the back wall. How many pimps and drug pushers frequented these shadows each night? He hoped not to encounter any. Beyond Building B, across the street, stood Rachel's apartment. If he could get into Building B, he might be able to find a window with a view of her apartment. He glanced at his watch—11:30. Half an hour to burn. He looked down the empty alley and then stepped lightly toward the back door.

Something clattered noisily on the asphalt and he jumped. His foot had hit a bottle. Enough of this. He ran for the building, pulled up beside a rear service entrance, and twisted the knob. To his surprise, it opened. He slipped in, shut the door, and heaved a sigh of relief.

His breathing sounded like billows in the hollow chamber. The lines of walls slowly grew out of the darkness. A long hall and stairs. Couldn't use the light yet.

He mounted the stairs and felt his way up one flight, then two, then three. Fourth floor. He pushed on the door exiting the stairwell and stepped cautiously through it.

Moonlight shone through a single window on the opposite wall. The rooms had been gutted—sections of framing lay in tangled heaps in every direction. But the floor seemed sound enough. He picked his way across the room to the window.

There it was, illuminated by a bright moon—Rachel's apartment. Stephen's pulse surged. The lights in her fourth-floor suite were still on. The lights of her master bedroom. The sunroom.

He instinctively pulled back from the window. Rachel's curtains were drawn. Made sense—the men who'd thrown him out didn't seem the kind to walk around in their underwear with the drapes wide open.

Stephen slid the backpack off and settled to one knee. They were up there all right, picking through her belongings. How dare they? But on the bright side, if they were preoccupied with the fourth floor, they wouldn't be in the basement.

If.

Thank God he'd taken the picture of Ruth from the sunroom. He straightened, struck by a terrible thought. The picture! Where had he put it?

He remembered immediately and relaxed. He'd left it on his desk. For a brief moment, he considered retracing his steps, racing home, retrieving the photo, and returning. What if the rabbi entered his room and found it? He could trust Chaim. After all, it was only a picture.

Stephen studied his mother's building. The real trick was to get in and out without dropping any clues. Leaving a trail to the boiler room would only proclaim that it possessed something noteworthy. In the unlikely event that he failed tonight, he couldn't afford to tip his hand. He was smarter than that.

Eleven thirty-five. His fingers trembled with anticipation. There was nothing magical about midnight. It had just seemed a good time. The neighborhood was already quiet; maybe he should just go now.

No. He had to follow the plan, and the plan was midnight.

Was it illegal, this plan of his? Maybe. Maybe not.

On second thought, absolutely. But at times, principle should supersede the law, and this was one of those times.

The sum of the matter was this: if Rachel had intended the museum to have the contents of the safe, she would have specified as much in her will. The fact that she hadn't meant its contents were for someone else. Someone like him. That's why she'd inscribed the safe with words that would have meaning only to an orphan branded with a Stone of David.

An element of danger trailed Rachel, a secret that put her son's life at risk. She had hoped that her son would recognize the caption in the paper—"the Stones are like the lost orphans"—and figure out the rest. As he was doing.

As Chaim would say: *If you want to have what others do not have, you must be willing to do what others are unwilling to do.* If ever there was a time to prove such an axiom, it was tonight.

One hundred million dollars—more money than he'd ever dreamed about. The idea made his mind hurt. He could walk down Sepulveda slipping hundred-dollar bills to the down-and-out and watch their eyes light up. He could buy an island with a yacht parked in the slip down by the shore.

On the other hand, his passion for this safe was as much about principle, about his mother and her secret, and about a little girl named Esther who'd been lost to Ruth. Put together—the safe, the Stones, Rachel, Esther—the sum was too much to ignore. As a Stone of David, he had an obligation. A calling.

It occurred to him that his liberation of this treasure was, in some convoluted way, not terribly unlike the liberation of a concentration camp by the Allied soldiers. He was redeeming what belonged to the Jews. Restoring their inheritance. His inheritance. This would be his part in the war. Stephen's mind reeled with a dozen thoughts, some completely reasonable, others admittedly less.

Desperate times; desperate measures.

Watch. Eleven forty. Time was crawling.

Something thumped softly across the room. Stephen started, nearly choking on his heart. He pressed himself against the wall and gazed into the shadows.

A dog bounded silently over the rubble, grinning wide, tongue flopping. Spud! She jumped up and stretched to lick his face. "Where'd you go? Okay, enough. Enough!" Stephen hugged the dog. "Boy, am I glad to see you."

No, he wasn't. What was he going to do with her now?

"She likes you," a woman's voice said.

Stephen bolted up, knocking the dog to the ground. "What?"

"I said, she likes you." A petite woman in her twenties stepped out of the shadows. She wore torn bell-bottom jeans with a light-colored blouse and beads. Hundreds of beads: on her wrists, on her neck, in her braided hair.

"What are you doing up here?" she asked.

"I was . . . I was just looking around."

"Is that right?"

What was he supposed to say? Nothing came to mind.

"The last time I saw anyone wearing those kind of duds up here was three months ago when they put this building up for sale. But nobody's buying. You know why? Because it belongs to us."

"Oh."

She stared at him, uncertain, then a smile slowly formed on her lips. "Well, the dog likes you, so maybe I do too. You can call me Melissa."

"Okay." She was a hippie type. Stephen had only one thing on his mind now. Get past this and pretend she'd never seen him. This wasn't in the plan. "Groovy," he said.

"Groovy." Melissa walked around him, wearing a whimsical smile, smelling like jasmine tea. "Groovy. Well, Mr. Groovy, you are in the wrong building. This building belongs to the Brotherhood of Bohemia. What's in the backpack?"

"Nothing."

"Mr. Groovy, whose bulging backpack has nothing in it, and who doesn't like to talk. That about cover it?"

He just nodded, then glanced out the window over his shoulder. Street still empty. Almost midnight.

Melissa suddenly started to chuckle, and Stephen smiled with her.

"What's so funny?"

"You."

Her laughter grew until it echoed around the room. He stepped forward and tried to wave her down. "Could you hold it down? The whole place will hear you!" Across the street, the curtains were still drawn.

"There's no one in the building right now but us, baby." She controlled her laughter. "I think you just might do. You could play the city slicker who wants to be groovy but doesn't have a clue."

He had no idea what she meant.

"Okay, you can stay for a bit. But I've gotta cruise—city's just coming alive for us bohemians. Wanna join us?"

"No thanks. I've got some stuff to do."

She looked out the window. "They moved in a few days ago. Friends of yours?"

"Who?"

"The people you're looking at. You know, Rachel's place."

"You . . . you knew Rachel?"

"Not really. She was friendly, and she asked me to take care of Brandy here." Melissa bent and rubbed the dog's back. "But that's about it. You knew her?"

"No."

Melissa nuzzled the dog playfully, cooing. She jumped up. "Gotta go. Come on, girl." She hurried off. Spud—no, Brandy, the dog's name was Brandy—gave Stephen a long, indecisive gaze, then bounded after the girl.

It took ten minutes for Stephen to recover from the intrusion. He wasn't sure how he felt about Melissa's attachment to the dog. A constant companion like little Brandy, although something he never would have sought, appealed to him. But there Brandy went, bounding after the girl.

Stephen surveyed the street one more time. Not a soul had walked by in ten minutes. Time for Mr. Groovy to boogie.

16

STEPHEN MADE HIS WAY DOWN THE STAIRS, stopping on every floor to listen. Apart from his own pounding heart, he heard nothing. Melissa and Brandy were gone.

Every Special Forces movie he'd ever watched barked the same mantra: *Get in quick, and get out.* Made sense. In his case: Get in quick, secure the fortune, and get out. Without leaving a calling card, of course. Or, better yet, leave a calling card with the wrong address.

Stephen huddled at the base of the gutted building for a full minute, trying to overcome an acute case of hesitation. Once he went to work there would be no backing out, no explanation that any cop would buy.

A hundred million dollars.

Esther.

He headed toward the apartment. *Natural. Look natural.* But when his foot hit the lawn, he couldn't resist hunching over and scurrying for the apartment's dark shadows, natural or not. He squatted at the wall and looked back. Coast clear.

Keeping low, Stephen rounded the corner and walked to the metal garage door. As he saw things, the garage was the best way in, because it faced the side street rather than the main thoroughfare, and also because it was hidden from view. The most brilliant break-in artists always found the weak holes, however unexpected. Besides, the windows were high and covered with wrought iron—no easier to deal with than the garage door.

He fell to his knees, unzipped the backpack, and yanked out a roll of heavy, dark gray plastic. Gray, same color as the building's stucco. The plastic unfurled noisily with a whip of his wrists. He shoved his hand into the pack, pulled on a pair of gloves, withdrew a roll of duct tape, and quickly taped the plastic onto the garage door over his head, so that it covered him like a lean-to. Working under the crackling plastic, he was sure half the neighborhood could hear him. It was possible that from the street he looked like a gray ghost, flailing under the plastic sheeting in the moonlight. No, he'd made sure the plastic was thick, hopefully thick enough to block the light. Of course, the plastic was thick enough to prevent him from noticing whether a crowd had gathered to watch the specter.

The roll of tape slipped out of his sweaty fingers. He drew back the plastic and peered toward the street just to make sure. No one.

He fumbled for the roll and completed his disguise. Now he crouched under the plastic lean-to, taped above him and on both sides. The idea was to blend in, but he couldn't shake the suspicion that he was doing more poking out than blending in.

Cutting torch. He'd used one once, in Russia many years ago, a monster consisting of twin bottles

on a dolly. The largest part of the setup he'd purchased today was the torch itself, a foot-long silver
tube with a ninety-degree cutting tip. Green and red
hoses fed into two football-sized canisters in his
backpack. One oxygen, one acetylene. He fired up
the device in an alley after buying it—seemed simple enough despite the clerk's warning that it wasn't
a toy. No, of course not.

Stephen cracked the acetylene valve and lit the
cutting tip with a lighter. Yellow light filled his hideout. Safety glasses. He reached into the bag, came
out with a set of dark glasses, and tried to fix the
band around his head with one hand. No go. Sweat
snaked past his left eye. He raised his right hand to
nudge the goggles into place.

The plastic to his left sizzled. He jumped back and
inadvertently dropped the torch. Flame licked at his
legs and he cried out, kicking at the torch. The plastic to his right pulled free, exposing him to the world.

Stephen dived for the pack and twisted the canister's knob. The flame died. He sat on his knees,
shaking. He'd burned a hole in the plastic and
singed his leg hair.

It took him a minute to calm down, resecure the
plastic camouflage, and set up for a second, informed
attempt. Goggles on, nerves under control, flame
down. With dark goggles on, he found he couldn't
see to light the thing, and his nerves were anything
but under control. Bringing focus to bear, he finally
managed to light the torch, pull his glasses into place,
and set up for the burn.

He took a deep breath. This was insane.

The words of his foster father blazed through his mind. He'd spoken them a hundred times during Stephen's adolescence: *Try to see trouble as you would see a brick wall, Stephen. Then try not to run smack into it at every turn. Seriously, son, I worry for your life at times.*

He felt like a fifteen-year-old boy at the moment, running straight for a brick wall.

Then again, there was Chaim: *If you want to have what others do not have, you must be willing to do what others are not willing to do.*

Like run straight at the brick wall.

He cranked the oxygen, adjusted the flame until it was bright blue, and tested the pressure trigger. The miniature jet flared to life. Stephen leaned forward on his knees and committed an irrevocably criminal act.

He cut into the building. That was the *breaking* part of *breaking and entering.*

But he was smart about his breaking. Cutting too close to the plastic would melt the tape. He cut a foot in, slicing right through the thin sheet metal as if it were butter. With any luck, he didn't look like a glowing Christmas bulb from the street. He shielded the light with his body as much as possible.

If Braun was in the garage at the moment, watching red sparks spray over his floor, Stephen would be toast. And if the metal fell inward onto the concrete, it might wake the world. But if he could cut this hole without setting off any alarms, the plastic would hide the hole while he did his real business.

Halfway through the long arc, Stephen concluded that his idea wasn't so brilliant after all. No doubt he *did* look like a glowworm. No doubt the metal *would* fall in.

As it turned out, the sheet did fall inward, despite his attempt to pry it toward him with the torch's cutting tip. But the sound it made wasn't so much a *clang* as a *whap*.

Stephen yanked off his goggles and held his breath. A dome-shaped hole led into the dark garage. No Braun. Only the black limousine parked on the right-hand side.

He wrapped a rag around the hot torch, shoved it into his pack, and pulled the bundle into Rachel's garage behind him. The plastic settled into place, masking the ragged opening.

He let his eyes adjust to the deeper darkness. If they came down now, he would roll under the Cadillac. Or maybe he'd just dive back out the hole. Out the hole, he decided, definitely out the hole.

Now for the car. He had to make it look like some local hoodlum had seen the car and broken in to steal it. Sleight of hand. Get their attention on the garage so the real damage in the basement would go unnoticed.

He pulled out a screwdriver and approached the Cadillac's driver-side door. It was unlocked. And the key was on the front seat. His first real stroke of pure fortune.

He left the car door wide open for his return later, cut across to the garage, and eased through the door. The stairwell was an echo chamber. He tiptoed down into the basement.

A buzz grew louder in his mind. He'd made it into Rachel's basement. His plan was unfolding in brilliant fashion. Had his pulse eased even a beat or two since breaking and entering, it would have surged now, but his heart already was maxed out.

No windows down here. He hit the light, acquired the boiler room, turned the light off, and angled for the door. He found it with his forehead in ten strides. Good to remember that—ten strides.

He opened the door, closed it behind him, flipped on the light. New gas water heater, black potbellied boiler, empty fifty-five-gallon drum. And under the drum . . .

The safe.

Stephen stared, mesmerized. The room was black and gray and smelled musty from concrete and dust and water. But the bland colors were inviting and the musty smell intoxicating. He'd let his mind walk into this small room a hundred times over the last forty-eight hours, and to actually be here again . . . the feelings of comfort and accomplishment surprised him.

For several long seconds, Stephen stood immobilized with anticipation. His world was spinning in a new direction, and this room was its axis.

He crossed the floor and tugged at the drum. It scraped loudly against the concrete. Could they hear that? He had to get the torch out first. Get the torch out, pull the drum off, slice through the safe's metal lid, extract the treasure, flee.

He grabbed at his backpack and then abandoned it in favor of the drum again. He had to see the safe, just to be absolutely sure that it hadn't been opened by the idiots upstairs. The drum slid with another wake-the-dead scrape. Stephen tilted it on edge and froze.

Exactly as he remembered. Undisturbed beyond his own work. An irresistible sense of urgency swarmed him. He released the drum and yanked the backpack from his shoulder. The drum clanged to the concrete. The fact that he was now making enough noise to wake Braun from a coma occurred to him as a distant abstraction. The man was four stories above him anyway.

Stephen dragged the drum out of the way, pulled out his tools, donned the protective goggles, and lit the cutting torch with the confidence of an experienced journeyman. No problem. *Whoosh* goes the acetylene, *pop* goes the oxygen, and we're in business. He could cut through Fort Knox with a big enough one of these, right?

His unsteady fingers betrayed his frayed nerves.

He dropped to one knee and lowered the cutting tip to the lock. If he could cut out the bolt, hopefully the lid would lift out. The torch eased into the hard steel with a blast of oxygen. Not exactly like cutting through butter, but the metal melted away and fell inside.

He jerked back, struck by a horrifying thought. What if the glowing steel fragments melted the gold on the Stones of David? Too late. Surely Rachel had protected whatever she'd hidden in the safe.

Drawing the full molten circle around the lock took Stephen several minutes, time enough to heighten his fears that he was ruining the safe's contents. He finished the cut, turned the torch off, and pulled off the goggles. A ragged but complete gap ringed the two-inch lock.

He flipped the torch over and tapped the circle. It fell in and landed with a dull *thunk*. Stephen reached for the hole and jerked back from the heat before he made contact with the metal. He hooked the cutting tip into the hole and pulled up, but the lid refused to budge.

"Come on . . ."

Stephen jumped to his feet and jerked back as hard as he could. The lid suddenly released, sending him back two steps and then to his rear end. He stared at the safe, lid dislodged, half covering a hole in the concrete.

He'd done it.

He was afraid to look.

Slowly he rose, hardly aware of the dull pain in his tailbone. He bent over the hole but saw only darkness. He tested the metal for heat, felt it quite cool opposite the cut, and shoved the lid aside. A hole, eighteen inches wide and maybe two feet deep, opened up before his eyes.

And at the bottom of the safe, an object.

His movements seemed too slow. The buzzing settled in his ears. There was something in the safe. There was a shallow metal cookie box down there. And there was a picture taped to the top of the box. Several black burn holes spotted the picture.

Ruth's picture. Only it said "Esther" on it.

Stephen stared into her eyes. Esther was a Stone of David. But was there more? *See, there's a tin can under that picture, and in that tin can is something your mother left for you. A hundred million dollars' worth of something.* He could hardly breathe.

Far above Stephen's head, a voice yelled.

Stephen jerked his head up. They'd found his hole in the garage door!

He plunged his hand into the safe and grabbed the box, but immediately a warning bell clanged in his head. If the Germans were in the garage at this moment, there was a decent chance they would discover him—bad enough. But what would happen if they discovered him *with* the box under his arm or shoved into his pack?

For the first time that night, true-blue panic flooded Stephen's veins. He reacted without conscious thought, like a finely tuned machine masterfully created for a single purpose.

To hide the treasure.

He dropped the box back into the hole, shoved the lid over the top, kicked at it until it clanked into place, and then spun the drum back over the whole mess.

The car. He had to make them think someone had broken in for the car. If they found him down here, they would want to know why a man had broken into the building with a cutting torch and made straight for the boiler room.

It was all he could do to ignore the whispers in his head that demanded he take the box now. There was a fortune in that box, for heaven's sake!

Not a chance. Not that dumb.

He donned the backpack, grabbed the cutting torch, and scanned the floor. To his eye, it looked undisturbed. At this juncture, he was more concerned with the safe's well-being than his own. If they found the safe—end of story. If they found him, he still had a chance.

Stephen turned off the light, slipped out of the room, then poked his head back in and hit the switch one last time just to be sure he'd left no clue. Reason should have him fleeing for safety already, he realized. But he was beyond reason. He slapped off the light and closed the door.

Now what? Instinct vacated him. Footsteps sounded on the concrete over his head. He had to get out of the basement. Anywhere but down here with the safe.

Stephen ran for the stairwell and took the steps two at a time. The hum of the elevator told him they were using it rather than the stairs. Maybe he could wait them out here. He pressed up against the wall behind the door into the garage.

No. He had to get closer to the car—away from the stairs.

He stepped up to the door and cracked it. Two large forms dressed in T-shirts stood by the large hole in the garage door, backs to him. How far could he get in his tennis shoes before they heard him? The front door had been chained—no exit there. Apart from the Cadillac, thirty yards away, the garage offered no cover.

The sound of his heart, pounding like a tom-tom, might give him away before his footsteps did. He took a careful breath, squeezed into the garage, and eased the door closed.

He moved quietly on the edges of his soft-soled shoes, rolling from heel to toe. A shadow in the night, gliding toward the car. He couldn't bring himself to look up, as if doing so might alert them. He had to reach the car. Every step was one closer to freedom.

This was idiotic! He was out in the open! At any moment they would glance back and see the thief strolling across their garage, armed to the teeth with his cutting torch. He almost turned to retreat.

Then again, they hadn't seen him yet. If they'd seen him, they'd be yelling—

"Hey!"

Stephen jerked up. "Hey!" he yelled back.

The two bouncers he'd met earlier stared at him. Maybe if he distracted them with some clever move, like torching one of the car's tires, he could buy himself enough time to sprint between them and dive through his hole to freedom.

The smaller of the two, if "small" could be used in reference to either man, walked toward him. In a moment of lucidity, it struck Stephen that this man was no ordinary thug. No insults, no demands to know what he was doing in their garage, no cautious approach or gun. The man pulled out a cigarette and lit it as he walked. He stopped by the car and leaned on the hood. His friend walked up casually beside him. Neither spoke.

"You're leaning on my car," Stephen said.

The larger man, the blond, spoke quietly into a radio. German.

"Get *off* my car. If you don't get off the car, I'm going to call the police," Stephen said. "I don't know who you think you rented it from, but this limousine belongs to me. My employer. She's my wife."

That was stupid. "I only came to take what does not belong to you."

They appeared not to have heard him. A voice crackled on the radio.

"I have to talk to your boss. I know this may look a bit out of the ordinary, but it's imperative that I talk to Roth Braun."

They just stared at him. The man with the radio spoke into it again.

They were probably discussing how to dispose of his body. "Do you recognize me?" Stephen demanded. "I'm the guy who was here this morning, claiming to be a Realtor. Well, I must confess, I'm not a Realtor. But what I am will definitely interest Roth Braun."

The quiet blond stepped forward and indicated the elevator across the room. "Please step into the elevator."

Stephen hesitated. This was unquestionably one of those life-or-death junctures.

The man on the hood tossed his cigarette and stood up. "Move."

Stephen turned and walked toward the elevator.

17

ROTH BRAUN SAT AT RACHEL SPRITZER'S DINNER table dressed in a black silk shirt. A heavy gold chain hung around his neck. Stephen stood before the man, unable to hold his eyes. The blond German had blue eyes too, but his were soft, distracted. Braun's were cold, still. Like death.

Stephen's backpack sat on the floor, contents dumped out and thoroughly examined. Piles of kitchenware were stacked neatly on the dinette. The knickknacks so carefully arranged by Rachel Spritzer had been taken from the walls and shelves along with the paintings. They were conducting a methodic search of the apartment.

"What's your name?" Braun asked.

"Parks," Stephen said, and cleared a croak from his voice. "Jerry Parks."

Braun looked at the blond man. "You said his name was Friedman?"

"That's what he told us this morning."

Back to Stephen, eyes bland. "Well?"

"Do you mind if I have a drink?" Stephen asked. "Surely the old woman left some scotch around here."

"You burn a hole in the side of my building and ask me for a drink?" A slight grin curved Braun's wet lips. "Sure, why not? Lars?"

The blond went to the cupboard and returned with a bottle and a glass. He poured Stephen a finger of amber liquid and then stepped back.

"Scotch," Braun said.

Stephen never touched the stuff, and he barely managed to throw it back without gagging. He set the glass on the table, mind scrambling. One look at Braun, and he knew this man wouldn't hesitate to do him bodily harm. But he hadn't betrayed the boiler room, had he? The safe was . . . safe.

He glanced at his knapsack. "I know this looks a bit strange to you." Insane was more like it. Stephen forced a tentative smile. "I mean, it's not every day someone lies about his identity, offers a million dollars for a gutted building, gets thrown out, and then returns at midnight to burn a hole in the garage door, right?"

Braun's right eyebrow arched.

"Well, it makes perfect sense when you know what I know." Stephen walked to his right and stared around at the bare walls. He was about to make a very big gamble. "Trust me, it does."

"Trust doesn't come naturally to me," Braun said.

Stephen had abandoned his theft story during his climb, somewhere around the third floor. Depending on who Braun really was, he would either turn him over to the police or worse.

"For starters, I'm not a Realtor and I'm certainly not a thief," he said. "Do I honestly strike you as being desperate enough to risk my life for a Cadillac? I'm interested in the building, not the car."

"And what about a run-down building interests you?"

"You'll have to ask my employer. Maybe the same thing that interests you."

Braun looked amused. Stephen cleared his throat and pushed ahead. "I mean, you have to admit, burning a hole in a garage door might be strange, but refusing an offer of one million dollars for this heap is just as strange, don't you think?"

The German studied him for a moment. "Claude."

The dark-haired man walked forward. His hand flashed out and struck Stephen on the cheek with enough force to drop an ox. Stephen fell to his seat.

"You broke into my building, Mr. Parks," Braun said. "I believe it would be within the law to shoot you."

Stephen struggled to his feet. "Then I've succeeded, haven't I?" The night's emotion suddenly surged in him. "Stop being so dense." *Too much, Stephen, way too much.*

Braun took the insult without any visible reaction, which for some reason unnerved Stephen more than if he'd whipped out a gun. Stephen felt as if he might fall if he didn't sit. He put a hand on a chair to steady himself. "My employer will pay you two hundred thousand dollars for a three-day lease of the building."

His mind worked furiously. He had to get their attention completely off the basement. If he rented the top floor, he could find a way to the basement unnoticed. "Actually, two hundred thousand for a three-day lease of the top two floors."

Braun smiled softly. "You burned a hole in my garage door to tell me this? Why don't you call my Realtor?"

Stephen hesitated. "Your Realtor doesn't do property management. His work on this deal is done."

"I'm not interested."

"That's . . . that's ridiculous! Two days, then."

"Ridiculous? I would say that offering two hundred thousand for two days is ridiculous."

If Braun took him up on the offer, he might actually pay. The Stones of David were in that cookie tin down in the safe—they had to be. He could take them and be on his way. Actually, he needed only fifteen minutes, but he had to consider what impression he would leave if the offer failed. He had to persuade them there was something on the upper floor that would require a two-day search.

"I think he wants to search this flat," Stephen said. "Something of sentimental value—your guess is as good as mine. Maybe the pictures. Humor him."

"Pictures?"

"The ones in the sunroom. I saw them the last time I was here."

"Out of the question."

"There's another hundred thousand in it for me. I'll give you half of my take. That's two hundred and fifty—"

"No." Braun stood, almost as tall as the man he called Lars, but broader in the shoulders. "Take our guest down to the basement and show him our hospitality," he said, turning.

Stephen stepped back. The basement? They were going to hurt him. "If I'm not back by two, my employer will call the police," he said. He meant to sound matter-of-fact, but his pitch sounded more scared-to-death.

"I doubt it," Braun said, turning back.

"He said you might say that. He also said you were even less likely to want the police involved. You touch me again, and I swear I'll have the police crawling through this building like bees in a hive. My employer assures me his motivations were purely sentimental. Somehow, I doubt yours are."

For several long moments they faced off. A thin smile finally curved Braun's mouth.

"Claude, Lars, please excuse us."

The two men left and descended the stairs.

"Jerry Parks?" The man walked up to him. There was enough power in his arms to snap Stephen's neck with a single twist. He was breathing heavily, deliberately, and Stephen got the impression that he was enjoying himself.

Braun walked around him. Circled him slowly, arms clasped behind his back. He stopped behind Stephen, lingered for a few seconds, then stepped easily to Stephen's left.

The man seemed delighted and doing his best to hide it. *Whoever he was, Roth Braun was a man possessed by evil,* Stephen thought.

"There's nothing to be found here except some old photographs of Jews who deserved to die," he eventually said.

A strange brew of emotions bubbled in Stephen's chest. The picture of the toothless young girl in Rachel Spritzer's sunroom filled his mind.

He looked back at Braun. "You won't know that until you've taken a wrecking ball to these walls," he said, then added, "Up here."

"You're dancing on your own grave." Roth spoke

in a low, gravelly voice. "I can smell it on you. Fear. Sorrow. Desperation. Hope. The most powerful forces known to man. You stink of them all."

Stephen barely managed the fear that gripped his mind. Roth's heart was as black as his shirt.

"If you ever set foot on my lawn again, I will track you down in your home and burn you along with it. Tell your employer to search for pictures of dead Jews somewhere else. These are mine."

Braun turned and walked toward the master bedroom. "Claude will see you out."

The tremble that overtook Stephen's limbs should have been triggered by relief. Braun was setting him free. But the shaking was full of dread. Fear, sorrow, desperation, hope. As Braun had said.

Susan. Toothless Susan. She might just as easily have been Ruth's daughter, Esther. For all he knew, Esther had ended up in the same medical lab, and this beast Braun took some kind of demented pleasure in it all.

Stephen scooped up his backpack and hurried to the door. He wanted out nearly as much as he wanted that safe in the basement. He met Claude in the stairwell and the man escorted him to the hole he'd burned in the garage door.

The moment the plastic fell into place behind him, Stephen began to run.

He couldn't go home. What if they followed him? Could he dare risk exposing Chaim to these people?

Stephen ran east, away from the neighborhood, but the moment he was out of Claude's sight, he doubled back through the alley toward Building B, yanked open the same back door he'd used earlier, and climbed the stairs to the fourth floor. He sat down by the window that overlooked Rachel's apartment. The sunroom was right there, across the street, nearly at eye level. He lowered his head between his knees and began to cry.

Understanding didn't seem important. Emotion shouted down reason. Anguish, horror, anger. In a strange way, he felt that he had to right what had been wronged for little Susan, the victim of his mother's oppressors. He had to become what the Jews couldn't become in their cages. For Susan's sake, his mother's sake, Esther's sake, he had to take back what was theirs.

He had to possess that tin box left for him in the safe.

My little Stone of David.

If he'd been eager to get to the treasure before, he was now desperate for it. His urgency made no sense; his desire had become a compulsion. How he'd gone from reasonable Realtor to manic desperado in the space of three days, he had no clue.

He stood, paced, bit his fingernail, and stared at that building across the street.

Stephen had once heard that over half of the homeless suffered from some sort of mental delusion. Many were once-successful people who'd vacated reason for a small spot in one abandoned building that overlooked another.

He finally slumped in the corner and rested his head against the wall. The last thing Stephen remembered thinking was that he was losing his mind.

18

Toruń
July 21, 1944
Just before Dawn

SHE HEARD MOANING AND WHISPERS AND THE sound of pattering feet, but these were common fragments in many of Martha's dreams. But when whispers hissed into her left ear and hands began to jerk her body, she knew this was no dream.

"Martha! Ruth's giving birth; wake up! Hurry, hurry, wake up!"

She bolted up in the darkness, rolled out of bed, and began to run before her feet hit the floor. "Ruth?"

Three steps along, she realized she was running the wrong way. She spun.

Ruth lay in her bed, knees bent, moaning softly. Half a dozen women were huddled around her.

"Water!" Golda stood up and barked the order. "Bring a bucket from the showers!"

Martha slid up close to Rachel and knelt by Ruth's head.

"Give Ruth room," Golda bossed. "Stand back, some of you. Let her breathe, for heaven's sake. Who's getting water?"

"I am," someone said. The door banged behind the voice as someone ran to the showers for water.

"And blankets. Someone else, hurry."

"Martha!" Ruth suddenly buckled with a spasm. "The pain . . . Martha!"

Martha grabbed Ruth's hand. "It's okay, dear. I'm right here. Breathe. Breathe."

Ruth rolled her eyes and looked at Martha. The early morning moon shone through the windows and gently reflected the sweat glistening on her face.

"Martha." She smiled. "Martha."

"Shh, shh. Save your strength." She turned to Golda. "We need more light."

Normally, light was prohibited. Golda hesitated, then said, "Get some candles, Rachel." Rachel ran for three small candles they saved for special occasions. This indeed qualified. Golda shooed the women away from the bunk. "Stand back. You'd think none of you had ever seen a woman give birth before. And keep yourselves quiet, or the guards will hear."

"Let the guards hear," Martha said. "What do they expect, a nice calm Sabbath affair?"

"No, but they may want to take her to the clinic. Believe me, we don't want her to give birth in the clinic."

Martha hadn't considered the possibility that the camp doctor would not share the commandant's feelings about Ruth giving birth. He could easily kill the child and claim it was dead at birth!

"Okay, then we have to keep quiet," she said.

"We are quiet," Rachel objected. "But she's in pain; you can't just muzzle—"

"Shut up, all of you!" Ruth gasped.

They stared at her, silenced. The scene was both terrifying and wonderful at the same moment, Martha thought. She herself would soon be in this position, lying on her back begging God for mercy.

The women went to work like a flock of hens intent on the coop's only chick. Rachel lit the candles. Golda slid blankets under Ruth. Martha rubbed Ruth's back and spoke softly in her ear. They set the bucket of water at the foot of the bed.

Some of the others spoke in hushed tones or watched from a distance. But even the most jaded women could not completely ignore the bustle about Ruth's bunk.

A baby was being born. New life was coming into the world.

Here, perhaps more than any other place on earth, the wonder of it felt monumental. Martha knew that some of the women despised her and Ruth because the commandant had favored them. Or because they intended to bring their babies into this horrible war. Some even murmured that an abortion, however crude, would be better than a delivery.

For three months, Ruth had talked to them about joy and passion, scolding them for their long faces as she rubbed her belly. She'd upset more than one woman along the way, but she'd lightened the hearts of many others. There was not one woman in the barracks who didn't have some stake in this baby.

The women piled up on the nearby bunks and peered at the scene as if it were a theatrical play unfolding before their eyes. An hour later, well after Ruth's water had saturated the blankets, Martha ran through the barracks for dry ones. She saw that only one woman remained in her bunk at the far end of the barracks—Latvina, a twenty-year-old from Russia who'd been beaten the day before for spilling a bucket of mud in the brick factory.

"Is she having the baby?" Latvina asked.

Martha spun back. "Yes!"

"It's . . . alive?"

The simple question frightened her. "I think so. Lie down and get your rest; we'll bring the baby to you later." Then she ran for the blankets, suddenly panicked for not being at Ruth's side. Why hadn't she let someone else get the blankets?

"Blankets!" She held them over her head.

"Let her through!" Golda barked. "Let Martha through!"

The women parted like the Red Sea, and Martha edged through the narrow aisle, brushing half of them with her own pregnant belly. She gave Rachel the blankets and knelt beside the bed.

Tears ran down Ruth's face, and Martha grabbed her elbow in alarm. "Ruth? Ruth, what's happening?"

Ruth opened her eyes and smiled through her tears. "I'm having a baby, Martha." She gripped her belly with both hands and cried it out, an impossible blending of pain and gratitude. "I . . . am having . . . a baby!"

"A baby." Martha put her hand on top of Ruth's and smiled with relief. "Yes, you are having a baby." She faced the others, flooded with joy. "She is having a baby," she cried through a sudden burst of laughter.

Several dozen women stared at her, some smiling wide, others lost in their own thoughts.

Ruth's body began to quiver, and Martha turned back. Her friend's mouth was open in silent agony. And then it wasn't silent at all. She began to scream, long and loud. Loud enough for the whole camp to hear.

The final push lasted only thirty seconds, with Golda and Rachel easing the new life into the world, and Ruth wringing Martha's hands until they were white.

It happened almost unexpectedly. First there was only Ruth, screaming on the bed. And then there was Ruth and a baby, cradled in Rachel's arms, covered in fluid.

The room fell silent under the gaze of a hundred women stretching for a clear view of the birth. Then one question cut through the silence, braved by someone too far away to see. Latvina.

"Is it alive?"

As if in answer, the baby's cry sliced through the room.

Pandemonium swept the barracks, dozens of voices piled on top of each other.

"It's a girl!" Rachel announced, working quickly. She wiped away most of the fluid and handed the child to Martha, who carefully laid her in her mother's waiting arms.

Ruth was crying again, this time with loving eyes on the new life in her arms. She held the baby tenderly and began to shake with sobs.

Martha wept with her, unable to speak. Behind

them, the women had quieted to sniffles and soft sobs. The barracks was held captive to the emotion bound up in the miracle of this new life. For a few minutes, no one spoke.

"Do you have a name?" Rachel asked.

Ruth caught her breath, wiped her eyes, and drew a finger down the tiny girl's cheek. "Her name will be Esther. She—"

The name passed through the room on the lips of the women, covering Ruth's next words.

"Hush!" Golda ordered. "Please, have some respect."

The women grew quiet.

"What is it, Ruth?" Golda asked.

"Let every woman here look at my child and see that there is hope. She is a star in the sky, pointing the way." She started to cry again, but stopped herself. "What price can you place on this treasure? Esther is the hope of our people. The seed of Israel."

A young woman pushed her way through the others. Latvina.

"May I hold her?"

Golda held out her hand. "This is no time—"

"No, it's okay," Ruth said.

Latvina stepped forward and gingerly lifted the child. She smiled, kissed little Esther on the forehead, and began to sing a soft lullaby in Russian. This young woman who perhaps wondered if she would ever complete her womanhood by bearing a child held tiny Esther as if she were the mother herself.

Then another woman, Margaret, wanted to hold her, and Ruth again overturned Golda's objection.

Margaret held the child delicately. She'd lost her two-year-old daughter at Auschwitz before being shipped here to work. A surreal calm settled on the barracks in the dim glow of first light. The candles flickered silently as the six or seven women closest to Ruth took turns holding the baby. Hushed tones of awe and wonder rippled through the onlookers. Quiet tears of hope and love.

Martha silently questioned the wisdom of exposing the child to so many so soon, but one look at Ruth's beaming face, and she knew it was the right thing. Allowing these women to hold this moving, breathing hope was life-giving. Its own kind of birth.

The baby came to Golda, who hesitated at first but then reluctantly took the child. The woman stared into Esther's tiny, wrinkled face. Her own face slowly knotted, and a tear made its way down her right cheek. "Hope," she whispered, and kissed the baby on the head. "Ruth's hope."

"Our hope," Ruth said.

Golda stepped forward and passed Esther into Martha's arms. "Israel's hope."

19

STEPHEN AWOKE TO A HOT SHAFT OF SUNLIGHT on his right cheek. A warm, musty-smelling towel licked his cheek. For a moment, nothing else registered except this most peculiar sensation and the ache in his neck.

The dog. It had to be the dog.

He pushed himself to his elbow and stared into the mug of Brandy, who stood over him grinning wide and wagging her tail. Behind the dog stood Melissa, now clad in a halter top and gauchos. Beside her were two men, both dressed in corduroys and army jackets. Hippies.

"Welcome to the world of the living, Mr. Groovy," Melissa said.

The man on her left reminded Stephen of Shaggy from the *Scooby Doo* cartoon, only with longer hair. The other was squatty with a touch of Asian in his face. All three looked at him as if he were a specimen to be studied, but he doubted this motley crew would threaten a flea.

"Stephen," he said. "My name's Stephen."

"Excuse me. Stephen. I thought I told you this building belongs to us."

Stephen looked around. He was lying on what had once apparently been carpet, worn thin and so packed with dirt that it now resembled concrete. Portions of an old wall clung to steel supporting posts, but someone had taken an ax or a chain saw to most of the rest. He could see straight through the building to an empty elevator shaft thirty yards away. A pile of twenty or thirty old tires leaned against one wall. The room smelled like mud.

He stood unsteadily, trying to remember why he hadn't gone home. Then he remembered. He turned to the window, ignoring the pain in his neck. The morning sunlight bathed Rachel's building across the street. The night's events crowded his mind.

"Hey, dude. Did you hear the lady? We're not offering a lease on this spot, dig?"

He turned back and faced Shaggy. "I was just resting."

"You running?"

"No."

"He's interested in Rachel Spritzer's building," Melissa said.

The gangly man looked out the window. "That so?" He walked up and peered across the street. "Why's that?"

"I'm a Realtor," Stephen said.

"That so? And why would a Realtor sleep in a dump like this, watching a building that's already sold?"

"Why would an intelligent man like yourself take leave of his senses and claim to own a building like this?" Stephen asked.

The man's eyebrow arched. He grinned. "What makes you think I'm intelligent?"

Stephen hesitated. "Your choice of jacket?"

Melissa chuckled.

The gangly man winked. "We got us a Realtor with spunk, dudes." He stuck out his hand. "Name's Sweeney."

Stephen shook the hand. "Nice to know you, Sweeney."

"You've met Melissa, and that's Brian. And for the record, intelligence can be overrated. I should know. I not only attended UCLA, I graduated with honors. Believe it or not, under this skin I'm really an architect, although I haven't actually worked as one in the fake world. Melissa's old man runs a law firm downtown, and Brian's just hanging with us for the day."

He walked back to his friends, crossed his arms, and turned around. "So what are you really doing here?"

Stephen wasn't sure he knew. He'd broken into the apartment last night and come out empty-handed. But he *had* come out. And he knew some things now. He was sure that Braun knew about the Stones of David. Nothing else explained his intense and unreasonable interest in the building. He was also quite sure that Braun *didn't* know about the safe.

And he was sure the safe wasn't empty.

"I'm not sure," he said.

They held stares.

"Why are you here?" Stephen asked. "You throw it all away?"

"No, my man. I'm finding what I couldn't find in

the books. Life, love, and the pursuit of happiness. The second bohemian revolution."

"Sounds interesting." Brandy was sniffing through a pile of wood ten feet away. Stephen suddenly felt tightness in his chest, and he wasn't sure why. He looked back out the window.

"It has its downsides," Sweeney said, "but in the end, we're all just children chasing after the rainbow."

"Maybe that's why I'm here, then," Stephen said. "Chasing the rainbow."

"Looks like some idiot tried to break into Rachel's building last night. Cut a hole in the garage. You know anything about that?"

Stephen blinked. "You're kidding. Cut a hole?"

"That's what it looks like. Cutting torch or something."

"How stupid is that?"

"Definitely not the intelligent way to approach life's problems. Some druggies will try anything for a fix."

"Idiots," Stephen said.

"What do you say, kids? Should we let Mr. Groovy hang?"

Melissa winked at Stephen. "Sure. Why not?"

Brian just shrugged.

Sweeney spread his hands. "There you go. You can hang. But don't tell anyone about this place—it's quiet and far enough out of the main drag to stay that way. We on?"

"Sure."

"Gotta split."

Stephen watched them go. Brandy eyed him cockeyed for a few seconds. "Hey, Brandy," he whispered.

The dog trotted over to him and licked his hand eagerly.

Melissa whistled. "Come on, puppy. Let's leave him in peace."

"No—"

The dog galloped for the hippies, stopped at the stairs for one last look, and then disappeared.

Stephen stared at the stairwell until the sound of their footsteps faded. The door slammed far below. Gone. He was alone in the world—even the dog had left him again.

He sighed and faced the window once more. The image of the tin box with Ruth's picture, which he was now thinking of as Esther's picture, loomed in his mind. Like mother, like daughter. The woman he'd been destined for.

He stared at the sunroom across the street, trans-fixed by the drawn curtains, wondering what Roth Braun was doing in secret over there.

Who are you, Esther?

The perplexing obsession that had taken him out of his game yesterday taunted him again. Now, in ret-rospect, it felt rather childish. He really had to get back to being normal. The thought of trying to explain why he'd spent the night in an abandoned building made him cringe.

But with each passing second, Rachel Spritzer's apartment continued to draw him, like a wraith beckoning a man to his appointed death; like a siren seducing a fool to his destruction.

Only it wasn't a wraith or a siren; it was a tin box with a picture of Esther. Stephen sat heavily against the wall.

That and the Stones of David, which, incidentally, were worth millions.

He closed his eyes and swallowed. Maybe he had gone over the edge last night, but he couldn't just dismiss his connection to the Stones of David.

His mind drifted. If he was right, no one knew how valuable that safe really was. He was faced with the kind of opportunity that presented itself to one lucky soul maybe once every century. Like stumbling onto a lottery ticket worth ten million dollars. Only this was far more significant. How far to the Spritzer building? Thirty yards. Then straight down about another thirty yards in the corner of the boiler room.

He should've grabbed the tin box last night. Stephen gritted his teeth. No, they would have found it on him. But he could have at least opened the box and stuffed its contents in his pockets, right? No, too risky.

With any luck, he'd stalled Braun with the bit about the upper floors. How long before the creep made his way into the basement? Then again, even if he did search the basement, there was no guarantee he would find the safe. If Stephen was lucky, he had a couple of days. Maybe three.

Stephen stood slowly, determined to fight off waves of gloom. He looked around, dazed. The thought of going home to the rabbi made him queasy.

A thought struck him. The picture of Ruth was still on his desk at Chaim's house. He really should have brought it with him, really should get it and keep it with him. Besides the note from his mother, it was his only tangible link to his past. And perhaps to his future.

He would go home, get that picture, and then decide on a reasonable course of action.

Stephen turned and headed for the stairs. Maybe he could show the picture to Gerik. The old Jew knew everything about everybody from the war. But could he trust Gerik with more than the antique dealer already knew? Not a chance. He couldn't trust anyone. Even if he could, he didn't want to. This was solely his business. Besides, you trust one person with your once-in-a-lifetime, and it becomes someone else's once-in-a-lifetime.

On the other hand, what if the antique dealer actually knew Ruth? Or Esther? Unlikely, but possible. Stephen stepped up his pace to a jog.

The Vega sat where he'd parked it. If anyone saw the haggard man climbing in, they might guess he was stealing it. Stephen eased the car into traffic. At least he hadn't forgotten how to drive. How to comb his hair, perhaps, and how to sleep in his own bed, but out here on the streets he was incognito. On a mission. To do nothing more than retrieve a photograph from his own desk, true enough, but at least he was making progress again.

The Beatles insisted he let it be, let it be. Stephen ejected the tape from his eight-track and threw it on the floor of the passenger seat. Whispered words of wisdom, please. They had no idea.

His next bit of progress was to get into his bedroom unseen. Facing Chaim's scrutiny at this juncture was as unappealing as chewing quinine tablets.

The plan was simple. He was getting pretty good at sneaking into buildings. If Chaim wasn't home, he would just walk in the front door, clean up a bit, take the picture, and leave—five minutes max. If the rabbi *was* home, then Stephen would climb in through his bedroom window, which he was quite sure he'd left open. The trick would be to get in without the neighbors seeing his butt hanging out the window.

He parked the car a block from the house. Chaim's old Peugeot was in the drive.

Stephen sat in silence for a good minute before stealthily climbing out of the car. He ducked into the backyard and crept as naturally as possible along the wall toward his window. He reconsidered the plan—walking in and explaining himself to the rabbi would be so much simpler. On the other hand, the thought of baring his soul really was unnerving. What was he going to say? *Oh, good morning, Rabbi. Yes, well, I look like a vagabond because I've decided to become one. To kick things off in the right spirit, I torched a hole in the German's garage door last night and then spent the night in the dump across the street.*

He reached the window, glanced around, and pushed it up. He'd forgotten about the screen, but a hard punch put his hand right through it. A few more, and the mesh sat in tatters. Another quick look, a kind of pull-up dive, and Stephen spilled into his room, no worse off than a bruised hip bone, compliments of the windowsill.

He had to move quickly. The unframed photograph sat on his desk next to several phone messages left in Chaim's handwriting. He couldn't read Ruth's piercing eyes, a mysterious blend of resilience and tenderness. She was perhaps the most beautiful woman he'd ever seen.

He shoved the photo into his shirt and immediately withdrew it. His sweat would ruin it. Besides, he was going to take a shower. He tiptoed for the bathroom. No. Running water might alert the rabbi. Maybe he should skip the shower. He really didn't have time anyway.

Stephen stood before the mirror, photograph in hand, and looked at himself. His hair stood on end, and his face was coated with dust. He quickly patted his hair and reached for the faucet, but stopped before twisting the knob. The house had noisy pipes that were known to even groan on occasion.

He really should just walk out into the living room and tell Chaim he was home. He'd gone out with some friends last night, partied until dawn, and come home for a shower. Fun, fun, fun. And the hole in the screen? Well, a bird must have crashed through.

Stephen grunted. This was ridiculous. He had to get out.

Using some water from the tank behind the toilet, he managed to clean his face. He took a stab at fixing his hair and brushed his teeth without using water. Three minutes in the bathroom, and he suddenly felt sure the rabbi would walk in on him at any moment. He wrapped his treasured picture in a towel, stuffed it under his shirt, and climbed back out the window.

───

"I DON'T know what he's up to," Lars said, "but his name *is* Stephen Friedman, and he *is* a Realtor. He lives up north with an old Jew."

"Another Jew," Roth said.

"Both father and mother dead. Has connections with the DA through a friend. A Jewish girl named Sylvia Potok."

"Married?"

"Stephen, no. The woman, I don't know."

Roth suddenly wanted off the subject. It wasn't an issue that Lars or the others should concern themselves with.

"He should be easy enough to deal with if he becomes a problem," Lars said.

Three more men had arrived from Germany this morning to join the deconstruction project. They were carefully removing the plaster from the walls in the kitchen and would work their way through the entire floor. The task would take them a couple of days, coincidentally the term of the Realtor's suggested lease. If either the journal or the other four Stones were in this house, they would find it.

But Roth had already found what he had come for. Stephen Friedman.

The boy had come home. Exactly as Rachel Spritzer had wanted. The game. The game was on.

Roth had spent the first part of the night in the sunroom, desperate to coax secrets from the pictures. So much pain. But like hope and fear, pain and pleasure yielded the most power when they could be found together.

Afterward he satisfied himself by selecting another Jewish woman, this one from Pasadena. Toruń had come to Los Angeles. And soon, if the powers of the air were smiling on him, he would take Los Angeles back to Toruń.

"We move on the grave site tonight and the museum tomorrow night," he said. "How much will the grave cost us?"

"Half a million U.S. dollars to exhume the body, leave us alone with it for an hour, and return the grave to normal by morning. The guards at the museum, on the other hand, can't be bought."

He had expected this. "We only want to look at the contents. Surely we can find someone there who will accept a million dollars for a few hours alone with some old trinkets. We don't want to see the Stone, just her belongings." He paused. "Offer two million if you have to. If all else fails, we'll go in with gas."

Lars didn't respond.

"I want access to every last item from her estate, every scrap of paper, every photograph, and I want it within the next forty-eight hours. Frankly, I don't care what it costs."

"Understood."

"And the next time Gerhard calls, tell him I'm occupied. I will not speak to him again."

"Of course."

Roth was an unusually patient man, but he'd never been in a position quite like this, with such high stakes and on foreign soil. He stood and slowly paced.

In under a week, he would finish what his father should have finished thirty years ago.

The fact that his plans were proceeding exactly as he'd envisioned was almost too much to bear. His success made him feel warm. He wanted to look at the pictures again.

20

FROM THE STREET, GERIK'S ANTIQUE SHOP looked like nothing other than one more flea-infested hole that might sell used clothes, half of which had been soiled and never properly cleaned. But step past the bell that clanged upon entry, and even an amateur would know this shop was unique.

The store ran long and narrow, crowded by hundreds of antiques that sat and hung and leaned and balanced in every conceivable space. The walls could be plastered with mud or coated in gold and no one would know, because there was no wall to see. Instead, there were Queen Anne chairs and ornate mirrors and huge brass plates and myriad paintings. A large cherry four-poster bed purportedly once owned by Thomas Jefferson himself hung from the ceiling.

Stephen stood at the door and peered into the shadows for a glimpse of Gerik Dlugosz, "Gary" to all who frequented his store. A middle-aged woman with a splotchy red face and a blue silk blouse glanced up at him from some silver vases. She was looking at the towel wrapped under his arm, he just knew it. *What*

191

*does that man have under his arm, pray tell? It looks
valuable. It looks secretive. I wonder if he'll show it to me.*

Stephen hurried up the left aisle, past long glass
cases stuffed with coins and copper figurines and
sprawling collections of silverware. If it was old and
valuable, it belonged here. The floor creaked with
each step. You'd think that with all the money Gerik
made, he could invest in a new place.

"Stephen?"

Stephen instinctively gripped his wrapped picture
and jerked at the sound of Gerik's voice.

The thin man walked toward him with an out-
stretched hand. A scraggly gray beard hung off his
chin. "So good to see you again." He put an inviting
hand on Stephen's shoulder and steered him to the
side. "And how are you holding up?"

"Fine. Good."

"Excellent. Excellent." The proprietor stopped by
a case and ran curious eyes over Stephen. "You've
been to Rachel's apartment, then?"

"Yes."

"And?"

"Nothing much. The museum had already been
through."

"Yes, of course. I am very sorry, Stephen. I wish I
could help you. You've contacted an attorney?"

"No."

"No. I don't blame you. You should follow your
own heart until things become clear."

They stood in silence.

"Maybe I could help you in some other way,"
Gerik said.

"No, nothing." Stephen was feeling hot under the neck. It had been a mistake to come. "I just came by for a visit."

"Is that so?" Gerik smiled softly. "I don't believe you. But I'm willing to pretend. So then, let's visit."

A mistake. Definitely a mistake. The shop had four or five other customers at the moment, and Stephen was sure they were all at least curious about him, if not downright fixated on him. His hair was a mess, his clothes wrinkled and dirty, his face haggard, and he clung to a bundle under his arm as if it were his last worldly possession. He relaxed and leaned on the counter, determined to appear somewhat normal.

"Business good?" he asked.

"Always."

Stephen looked at an old pocket watch in the case. A handwritten tag hanging off it read 3000. Nothing else. Surely that couldn't be the price. Twin horse heads graced either side of the silver piece. He dared a glance at one of the other customers and saw that the man wasn't staring at him after all. But if he knew what Stephen knew, his eyes would be popping out of his skull. *Fess up, boy, where are the other four Stones? You have no right to them. They are for a serious collector with millions to spend.*

"Three thousand," Stephen said. "What does that mean?" Question sounded dumb, but he had to say something before making a retreat.

"It means that someone will give me three thousand dollars for a watch I paid five hundred dollars for," Gerik said.

Stephen looked up, surprised. "Three thousand dollars? It's worth that much?"

"It's worth what someone will pay for it. What's the value of a diamond? Whatever someone is willing to pay for a pretty stone that makes him feel important."

"And someone will want that old watch enough to pay three thousand dollars? Amazing."

"They aren't buying an old watch, my boy. They're buying an idea. The value of an idea is determined by how appealing the idea is to someone. If you want something desperately, you will pay desperately. Isn't that true?"

"Yes. Yes, I suppose so."

"I sell ideas. Actually, if you think about it, everything is really no more than idea. The past is nothing more than a memory, which is one kind of idea. The future is still a hope, another kind of idea. The present is fleeting and becomes a memory before you can put your hands on it. All ideas. I sell ideas."

"That's a bit cynical, isn't it? Am I just an idea?"

"No. But what I think of you is." Gerik grinned. "And, of course, there's the greatest of ideas," he said with a twinkle in his eyes. "Love. You could even say that I sell love. Obsession. A good thing."

Stephen chuckled nervously and looked at the three-thousand-dollar watch. "Sure—love. I would say that's stretching things a bit."

"Is it? Last week, I sold a brass masquerade mask with red feathers to a woman from Hollywood. It is said the mask was worn by a wealthy French nobleman known for his extravagant parties. She'd been seeking that mask for seven years, and I was fortunate enough to track it down for her. I honestly think she might have parted with her husband for it. She loved it as much as she loved anything. Another collector offered me ten thousand dollars for the mask. She paid me twenty-five. What was it worth? Twenty-five."

"Most people associate love with other people," Stephen said.

"And I associate it with any object of desire. People who buy from me are in love with what they purchase. Many are obsessed. I'm not sure some wouldn't risk their lives for a particular obsession. Which isn't all that crazy—some ideas are actually worth dying for." Gerik winked. "I think Rachel was such a person."

Stephen looked at him, taken off guard. He couldn't think of a response.

"Life is hardly worth living without an obsession. God himself is obsessed."

Stephen stared on dumbly. What was this man talking about?

"With his creation. With humans. With the love of humans. You think he created with nonchalance? Let's throw some mud against the sky and see if any of it sticks? Not a chance. We are created for love, for obsession. So we do indeed obsess, though usually not over the right idea." He hesitated and eyed Stephen's shirt again.

"I had a rough night." The words about this obsession business echoed through Stephen's head. "Is that . . . Judaism?"

"What? That we are created to obsess? Sure, why not? What do you have there?"

Stephen shifted nervously. "This? Nothing. Really. Just some stuff I picked up. Some, you know, personal effects that I picked up from my place and wrapped here. In this towel. For safekeeping. You know." *You babbling fool!* He looked around again. "This is a beautiful place, Gerik. A wonderful . . . little place. You should be proud of what you've done here in this . . . place."

"Thank you." The man was eyeing him without a break now. "Would you like to clean up in the back?"

"Me? Why would I want to clean up? I'm fine. I just picked up some things, and I wanted to stop by and see, you know, all this things." *This things?* "I'm fine, really."

"Fine."

"Good."

Stephen felt terribly exposed. As if he were in one of those dream sequences in which he walked out onto a stage, only to realize that he was naked. He was chewing on his fingernail without remembering exactly when he'd lifted his finger to do so.

"Okay, so I'm not completely good," Stephen finally said. The antiques dealer arched an eyebrow. "Do you mind if I have a word with you?"

"Not at all," Gerik said.

Stephen glanced around. "Not here."

Gerik hesitated, then turned and walked deeper into the store, where the furniture hung lower and the shadows were darker. He stopped and turned around.

"This is private?" Stephen asked.

"We might as well be in a vault," the old man assured him.

"Our voices might carry."

"No one can hear us."

"No, but voices can travel."

"I've practically lived in this room for twenty years, and I can assure you—"

"Please, Gerik."

Stephen looked back at the man browsing thirty feet away and saw that they'd attracted his attention.

"I'm sorry, where are my manners? Please, I'm not thinking clearly. Follow me."

They walked past the last of the stacked furniture way in the back and stepped into an office cluttered with books and papers. Gerik closed the door, picked up a pipe, and lit it. A blue cloud billowed over his head. Stephen held the wrapped photograph against his chest now.

"You found something at the apartment," Gerik said.

Stephen didn't respond.

"May I see it?"

"This?"

"You did want to show me, didn't you?"

"I guess so, yes." He began to unwrap the picture, suddenly unsure if he wanted to show it. "I . . . came across this." The picture of Ruth stared up at him, mesmerizing.

He hadn't noticed it before, but her hair was swept back so that it exposed her left ear. That would be her right ear if the photo had reversed her image. A nice ear. A stunning ear actually, one that looked as if it had been painted on with a skilled—

"And?"

Stephen looked up and blinked.

"I . . . I found this photograph and thought maybe you could take a look at it."

Gerik held out his hand. The towel fell to the floor. Stephen gave him the picture. "Her name's Esther."

Gerik puffed on the pipe and studied the image. He turned the picture over. "It says her name is Ruth."

"Right. I mean Ruth."

"Taken before or during the war." He read the note on the back. "Stone of David," he said, and glanced up at Stephen. "Taken before the war. Esther would be your age, if she survived."

"Exactly," Stephen said. "That's exactly my point!"

"It is?"

Was it?

"You found this in her apartment?"

Stephen cleared his throat. "It was with some other pictures of . . . of victims. Maybe I shouldn't have taken it, but I just . . . it was quite moving."

"Of course you should have taken it. She would have wanted you to have it. Most of the world wants to forget the Holocaust, you know."

Gerik knew nothing about the safe; he was speaking from his heart only. He set his pipe down and examined the edges of the photograph with a trained eye.

"Did Rachel tell you anything else? About Ruth."

"No, nothing," Gerik said. "She asked about the Stones, of course. Do you know what one Stone of David is worth?"

"Millions."

"Like I said earlier, it's worth what someone will pay for it, which means twenty million as of this morning."

"Someone offered twenty million to the museum?"

"A group of Jewish moguls who insist the relic belongs in Israel. I'm not sure I disagree. But Christians also lay claim to the Stones, as you may know. The seed of Adam to strike Lucifer on the head, in the line of David. Christ. I know of collectors in Rome who would pay well over one hundred million for the collection. Perhaps even two hundred."

Stephen felt his heart thump a little harder. "Hmm." He was chewing his fingernail again.

Gerik handed the picture back and Stephen took it carefully.

"Thank you."

"I doubt they'll be found in our lifetime," Gerik said.

"No? Why not?"

"Because they were part of some Nazi's war spoils. No one knows which officer took them, but it's rumored that they were pillaged from a wealthy Polish collector's home in Warsaw. If the Nazi survived the war-crimes trials, he won't be eager to show off his loot, I can promise you that."

"Maybe Rachel had all five."

"Unlikely."

Stephen went rigid. Did Gerik know something definitive, or was he just guessing?

"Think so?"

"Why give one Stone and not five?"

"Exactly! That's exactly what—no, that makes sense."

"I really should get back to the store. Half of my inventory could be gone by now." Gerik walked toward the door, and Stephen followed him.

"You're right to treasure the picture, Stephen," the old man said, turning back. "Wherever she is now, little Esther is worth more than all the Stones of David together. Now, there would be an obsession worth dying for, don't you think?"

Stephen felt his face blush, and he shifted his gaze. "I don't know. It's just a picture."

"No. It's an idea. A memory. Perhaps a hope, but not simply a picture. I'm sorry I can't help you find her."

"That's not—"

"Of course it is. If I'm not mistaken, you're quite taken by her, which is understandable. I'm a Jew. I was there. She deserves your obsession, dead or alive. Your obsession gives her life value." Gerik smiled politely and left.

Stephen didn't remember actually leaving the antique shop. He drifted rather than walked. The old man was right about some things and wrong about some things. Right about Esther deserving someone's obsession, wrong about the Stones not being found.

Unless they weren't in the tin box.

He wasn't willing to dwell on that possibility.

He drove to Rachel's apartment. Still there. Still alone on the lot, towering in the midday sun while the busy beavers scurried through the upper floor, chewing, chewing, chewing. He drove around it once, then twice, doubling back three blocks away so as not to be too obvious. Too many passes of a blue Chevy Vega, and someone might raise an eyebrow. Or a gun.

Shades were pulled. The hole in the garage door had been sealed with boards. They wouldn't leave the bottom floor unguarded this time, not a chance.

That's right. This time. He had no choice but to go again.

They probably had men or dogs or machine guns rigged to go off upon unauthorized entry. This time it would take more than a torch and a lighter to get in.

Fifteen minutes. Fifteen minutes alone in the basement, and he would be finished.

He finally parked the Vega on a side street and crept back up the stairs to his hiding spot on the fourth floor of Building B. He had to think this through. There was a way. There had to be a way.

He leaned against the wall beside the window and slid to his seat. There was always a way. This one hid in the dark corners of his mind and refused to step into the light, but Stephen knew he could eventually coax it out. With enough patience, with enough focus, the right plan would present itself.

He unfolded Ruth's picture and gazed into her eyes. "Speak to me, Esther. Tell me."

21

SYLVIA SAT AT HER DESK STUDYING THE PHOTO-graphs in the file. Forty in all, taken from every conceivable angle. They were duplicates from homicide, a precaution that the DA insisted on.

"I want a parallel file compiled now, and I want you to build that file with every last bit of evidence that you can scrounge from every detective on this case. Baby-sit them if you have to, but I need that file to be up-to-the-minute."

It was Sylvia's first high-profile case. No telling how long before they apprehended the killer, or when it would eventually go to trial, assuming he lived that long. But if and when the time came to prosecute, the DA would be ready. Sylvia would make sure of it.

Three nights; three victims; same MO.

She stared at the bodies. Blood pooled around each. Enough to conclude that whoever had killed the women had wanted them to bleed out.

Why?

The last victim had struggled more than the first

two, according to the preliminary investigative reports. Bruises on the wrists.

The sight sickened her. She'd become an attorney to protect the rights of victims, not analyze their brutal deaths.

Jewish women across the city were double-bolting their doors or moving in with relatives. The fact that the case had gone public was a good thing, despite the fear it caused. Better fear than death.

And what about you, Sylvia? She glanced at the office door. The rest of the staff had already gone home. How easy would it be for a killer to break into the DA's office?

But really. What were the chances that she would be singled out? Besides, all three had been killed in their homes.

Still, the quiet was disconcerting.

The phone rang shrilly and she jumped. She snatched up the receiver.

"Hello?"

"I'm worried, Sylvia." It was Chaim. "Very worried. This isn't like Stephen. Something's wrong."

She reoriented her attention from the killer to Stephen.

"Sylvia?"

"I'm thinking, Rabbi." She sighed. "He's probably out on a hot date. What did you expect with all of your love talk?"

"A hot date is the farthest thing from his mind. I would have thought at least he'd call."

"Maybe he did and the line was busy. Maybe he

has something he wants to surprise you with. Maybe he's at that Santa Monica property."

"He tore out his own window screen, for heaven's sake!"

That silenced her for a moment. "Like I said, he can be irrational at times."

"Impulsive, not irrational," he said.

He had a point.

"Really, Sylvia, I'm worried, and this conversation isn't helping me."

"Look, I'm sure he's fine. He may be reeling from this news about his mother, and God knows he can do some crazy things when he puts his mind to it, but he's not an idiot."

"This from the same woman who insisted that if anyone could find danger, Stephen could?"

"Well, maybe I was wrong."

"And maybe you weren't."

"He's smart, Rabbi. Like you said, he really is. Let him follow his heart."

"Now you sound like Gerik."

"Would you like me to come over? I could bring some Chinese."

"Would you? Yes, I would like that."

STEPHEN HAD reviewed the situation a hundred times. Maybe a thousand, counting all the subconscious assessments. The long of it was that he was in a vicious circle of dilemmas; the short of it was that the dilemmas ended at an impasse. He just couldn't see a way out.

Still he paced in front of the window and rehashed his problem.

His head hurt, and he wasn't sure he was thinking so effectively anymore. Nevertheless, he was thinking: he was thinking that Gerik was much smarter than he'd imagined. His words of wisdom had set Stephen free.

He was thinking he had wasted the day pacing and driving and avoiding the house.

He was thinking he was avoiding the house because he didn't want to answer to Chaim.

He was thinking involving Chaim could be dangerous for the rabbi.

He was thinking Roth Braun knew the Stones were in Rachel's house and would kill for them.

He was thinking he would either go home tonight or get a motel room. He might be a tad whacked-out, but he wasn't loony enough to sleep here again.

He was thinking he really should go to the police.

Then again, he knew a few things too: he knew he couldn't go to the police because he, not Braun, was the one committing crimes here.

He knew the Stones of David were in the basement over there.

He knew the Stones in the basement were his.

He knew there had to be a way into that basement to take the Stones that were his.

Stephen peered out the window. A city worker walked up to Rachel's building. His heart skipped a beat, but then he saw that she was only reading the meter on the back wall. Maybe he could take her place and demand to read the meters in the basement. Were there any meters in the basement? He couldn't remember. Of course, they would see his face and end it right there. He had no reason to doubt their threats.

He resumed his pacing.

He also knew that nothing he knew was really for certain, except the fact that he couldn't go to the police.

There had to be a way into the building.

He did know how *not* to get into the building. Not with a cutting torch.

Not with a truck through the garage door.

Not on a hang glider to the rooftop.

Not via a helicopter pounding above their heads.

Not through the front door.

Not in a huge wooden horse, or in a cake, or in a massive scrumptious pizza delivered for the Wolfmeister.

Not through the front door. Said that already.

Not on a rocket . . .

Stephen stopped. Not through the front door. Why was that again? Why not?

His heart bolted. Could it work? He jumped to the window again. The meter reader was down the street now, climbing into a black Datsun. Why not?

He resumed pacing, frantically now. It was bold. It was daring. It was the kind of thing no one could possibly expect.

It was lunacy!

Which made it perfect.

He glanced at his watch. Almost seven. Almost dark. That was even better.

But where would he get an outfit at this hour? His mind revved into overdrive. It was Saturday night.

He knew something else. He knew that every Saturday night, Marjorie Stillwater played bingo.

———————

THE CHURCH Chaim attended was a small inter-denominational affair, a study in cultural diversity. Black, white, Korean, Jewish—you name it—a hodgepodge of seekers who'd found their answer in Christianity. The old church building had a steeple on the outside and exactly thirty pews on the inside. Two hundred or so managed to squeeze into the sanctuary every Sunday.

They were a friendly lot, a little too friendly for Stephen's tastes. Hugs and kisses and smiles, smiles, smiles. They seemed genuine enough, but to an outsider like Stephen, who didn't want to care about God, much less Christianity, their sincerity came across as a pressing invitation to join them. Fine for the meek and mild, not so fine for the headstrong.

Stephen had attended services on three separate occasions, and each time he'd left feeling both welcomed and repelled by the oddity of it all. The fact that he suspected some truth in Chaim's assertions that Jesus of Nazareth was more than a man only complicated the matter.

He'd always seen religion as a function of some folks' need for meaning and a moral compass. Whatever it was, it was not an object of personal faith. Father had led him and his foster brothers through the seven feasts, spring and fall, with an emphasis on Passover, and Stephen had dutifully followed the course expected of all non-Orthodox Jewish boys until he'd come to the United States.

He'd found in Chaim a different kind of religion altogether. His was born less out of tradition than simple faith. The rabbi still was attracted to much of Judaism, but he also believed the Messiah had already come. He'd put his faith in Jesus of Nazareth, and he talked regularly about falling madly in love with him. Christianity: faith, love, and lots of wet kisses on the cheek from old ladies who wore wigs.

Actually, *one old lady* would be more truthful, and *one* wet kiss even more so. He'd met Marjorie Stillwater within a few minutes of entering the church the first time, and he'd spent at least half the service watching her. Her big, flowing, blond wig had slipped to one side, and no one but him seemed to notice or care.

One of the pastor's teachings suddenly returned to Stephen. He'd heard it on his second—or was it his third?—visit. The pastor recounted a story Jesus had apparently told, about a man who was walking in someone else's field one day, found a treasure, and basically went ballistic.

That was the way the pastor had put it. Ballistic. In the parable, the man hadn't told the landowner about the treasure on his land. No, he was far too focused on the treasure to do any such decent thing. Instead, he'd hidden it again, snuck out and sold all that he owned, approached the owner, and bought the field without telling the man about the treasure. A tad deceptive, to be sure. Surprising that Jesus would tell such a story. All things considered, one might think he was trying to say that man's passion for God needs to look more like desperation than reason.

Stephen nibbled on a fingernail and made a connection. His own ordeal with his mother's building wasn't so different from the man's ordeal with the field, was it? Stephen might not be after the kingdom of God, but then neither was the man in the story. They really weren't so different, he and this man. Neither was a Christian, both were after a treasure, and both were singularly focused on the task.

The thought gave him some courage.

Stephen had been to Marjorie's tiny house six blocks from the Santa Monica Pier only once, but he'd seen enough to know precisely what he had to do now.

He slowed the Vega to a crawl in front of the house. Light glowed through the living-room curtains, but he couldn't tell if she was home. He had to either get her out of the house or verify that she already was. Pay phone.

He found a phone three blocks over, searched the directory for her number, and made the call. The plan was simple enough—if she answered, he would call Marjorie to the church for an emergency. *Come quick, Miss Stillwater! Don't have time to explain, just get down here as fast as you can. It's life or death.* Click. That would send her scrambling.

But ten rings later, she hadn't answered, which meant she was probably at bingo, exactly as he'd suspected. Perfect. Bingo ended . . . when? Probably not before eight o'clock. That gave him almost an hour. Very perfect.

Stephen drove to within a block of Marjorie's house and approached her front porch on foot. He was getting in the habit of parking his car a block away from all his destinations these days, a noteworthy but not necessarily incriminating fact. He walked straight, without daring to look left or right. Nothing that would make him look suspicious to neighbors. Just nephew Stephen coming for a visit.

The trusting old woman had locked her keys inside and used a spare from under the third flowerpot when Stephen had visited. The flowerless pot sat where he remembered it, full of dirt that had spilled to the wood porch more than a few times, judging by the stains. Stephen bent, withdrew the key, unlocked her door, and returned the key.

And if she was still here?

He stepped in. "Marjorie?"

Her bedroom door stood open to a dark interior. Stephen closed the front door. "Marjorie?"

The tiny house rang of silence. She was gone. Which meant she would be back sooner or later. With his luck, probably sooner. Stephen hurried into the bedroom, found the sliding doors that presumably led into her closet, and slid the door open.

Two dozen dresses hung organized by color—reds and blues and purples. He had absolutely no business being here, staring at Marjorie Stillwater's dresses. They smelled like talcum powder.

Stephen ran his hand lightly down the row of hangers, parting each dress for a better view. This was how women shopped at Sears. For hours, inexhaustibly running their hands down the rows and around the carousels, imagining what, only God could really know. He'd gone shopping once with Sylvia and was exhausted after the first rack.

A business suit of some kind would be best, but Marjorie just wasn't a business-suit kind of person. He wasn't sure he cared for her selection of colors. Lots of purples. Dresses might be too . . . feminine. A pantsuit would be better. At least it had pants and a jacket thing. Question was, did Marjorie own any pantsuits? He continued down the row and stopped three outfits from the end at a lime-green polyester pantsuit, freshly pressed. Maybe she'd bought the outfit in a moment of youthful extravagance and not yet worked up the courage to actually wear it.

He wrestled the suit jacket from its hanger and held it up to his shoulders. Marjorie wasn't thin, and he wasn't large—should work. The idea was preposterous, but that was exactly the point. No one would suspect this woman could possibly be Stephen Friedman. Dressing as a man in disguise would be nearly impossible without the help of someone who knew what he was doing. Arriving as a woman, on the other hand . . .

Still, he wasn't thrilled with the prospect of donning Marjorie's lime-green pantsuit. He walked to her dresser and started rummaging through the drawers for the rest of his outfit. What else? Nylons—definitely nylons. Couldn't walk in with hairy ankles. Maybe socks would work. Depended on the shoes.

He bounded over to the closet again, dropped to his knees, and scanned her shoes. High heels, mostly. They'd never fit. Working women did wear men's shoes on occasion, didn't they? Shoes that looked like men's? He stared down at the tassels on his own black leather shoes and tried to imagine them with Marjorie's lime-green pants.

He really had no choice but to split the difference—he'd go for the nylons and wear his own shoes. It wasn't unbelievable that a woman in his occupation might wear comfortable shoes on the job.

Stephen hauled his bundle into the bathroom and plopped it down on the floor. Flared lime-green polyester pants, matching suit jacket, lavender shirt with paisleys, white pantyhose or nylons (he wasn't sure what this particular variety was called), white gloves, and the crowning element of this disguise—the reason Marjorie had been a brilliant selection—a blond wig.

He dropped his pants and pulled on one leg of the nylons. Tight, but they were supposed to be tight. The hair on his legs was still visible, but the pants would take care of that. He stood and hopped into the second leg.

This particular method of donning nylons proved to be less brilliant than he'd imagined. He had his leg halfway in before it occurred to him that things were going wrong. He started to fall forward, hopped once, tried to free his leg, and succeeded only in catapulting himself headlong toward the wall.

After betraying him so boldly, his masculine prowess came to his aid. He performed a duck/roll/flip and hit the wall with his back instead of his head. The whole house shook with the impact. A shelf full of knick-knacks slipped off the wall and crashed over his head before he could get his arms up to protect himself.

Stephen lay on the floor, one leg still half-caught

in the nylons, and took quick stock of the situation. Silence. No one banging on the door, demanding to know who was in there trying to get into a pair of pantyhose.

A broken plate lay in pieces a foot from his head—not unheard of with all the earthquakes that rolled through these parts. All in all, he'd averted any real setback.

Stephen rolled to his back and tugged on the second leg of the nylons. He felt as if he was being strangled from the ankles up. Why women quietly suffered in these contraptions, he couldn't imagine.

The rest of the outfit slid on with ease—lime-green pants, lavender paisley shirt, lime-green jacket. His own shoes. No need for a bra, not with the jacket. See, that was smart too; judging by his battle with the pantyhose, he might very well hang himself trying to don a bra. Stephen slipped his shoes back on and stood in front of a full-length mirror behind the door.

Lime green was clearly not his color, but the lavender blouse actually brought a glow to his face. He tugged at the jacket sleeves and managed to extend them another inch, enough to cover what hair the gloves would miss.

The weakest link in the disguise was clearly the length of the pants, which flared wide and hung short, six inches above his ankles. Three-quarter-length pants—he was sure he'd seen a model or two wearing an outfit something like this. They might even pass for gauchos. His black shoes looked a bit out of fashion—maybe he would leave them in the car.

Now for the second reason Marjorie Stillwater was a brilliant solution—makeup. Even if he had bought a new outfit at Woolworth's, he needed makeup and the dressing room to apply it.

He walked into the bedroom and glanced at the dresser clock. Seven thirty. Plenty of time.

He fished in her shower, found a razor, and shaved his face as clean as the dull blade would allow. Patted his skin dry with a towel. Face powder, lots of face powder. A touch of reddish stuff he found in her third drawer that he thought might be rouge or perhaps blush. He examined himself in the mirror.

More. More makeup.

Five minutes later, he pulled on the blond wig and stood back for a view. His image was actually quite frightening, with all the hair and the red lipstick. He looked like a stick of celery with blond leaves. But apart from the heavy eyebrows, there wasn't a hint of man on him. The heavy eyebrows and the square jaw. And the shoes.

On the other hand, he imagined he might look quite sexy to someone who didn't know. He would kick off his shoes before entering and walk light on his feet. In the dim light, he would easily pass for a city inspector. He cleared his throat and tried out a fitting voice.

"Hello?" Too low. Sounded nothing like a lime-green celery stick.

He tried again, leaning on his falsetto. "Hello. My name is Wanda."

A door slammed. She was home early!

For one eternal second, Stephen froze. The bathroom drawers were open, his clothes were in a pile behind him, the fallen shelf and its broken plate lay scattered to his left. He tore himself from terror's grip and flew about the room, scrambling to hide his tracks. The broken plate went in the laundry hamper; the fallen shelf went under the sink with a little brass elephant that had plunged with it; the lipstick went back in the third drawer down. Or was it the second?

No time. He scooped up his clothes and ran for the bedroom, slapping off the lights as he passed. He evaluated the bedroom window. Short of burning holes in garage doors, diving out windows was one of the best ways to enter and leave other people's buildings unawares.

Unless they were covered with wrought iron.

So Stephen did what any man in his situation would do: he dropped to his hands beside the bed and rolled under the mattress in one smooth motion. Immediately, two problems presented themselves. One, his feet were sticking out of the bottom. This he remedied with an instinctive jerk/curl. His left knee slammed into the box spring, bumping the whole bed a few inches into the air. He reacted to the sharp pain up his leg by dropping his knee. The box spring *thumped* softly back to the frame.

The second problem he saw while the bed was momentarily elevated: he'd dropped his clothes upon rolling under the bed. They sat in a mound just beyond the bed skirt. He snatched them into darkness not a moment too soon.

The lights popped on. "Hello?"

Stephen held his breath in the stillness, but his heart was echoing down here.

Apparently satisfied, Marjorie hummed a few notes and walked into the bathroom. He couldn't see her, which meant she couldn't see him. He should slip out now.

Stephen began to execute his turn, but Marjorie walked back into the bedroom, still humming. At least she hadn't discovered the evidence in the hamper. Or, for that matter, the shelf missing from her wall.

She tossed something on the bed and headed back for the bathroom. Stephen waited a few seconds and resumed his turn toward the foot of the bed, where he would roll/spring/run stealthily from the bedroom.

But Marjorie, who'd graduated from humming to opera, came back before he could get even halfway around. She sat heavily on the edge of the bed, opera voice now gaining volume.

Stephen knew that beds with poor frames and cheap springs bowed under weight, but he had an awful premonition that *bow* would be far too gracious a term to describe—

Marjorie catapulted herself into the air and slammed into the bed with a shrill, high-pitched vibrato. The mattress pounded into his chest, and he grunted. Her virtuoso halted abruptly. After a few moments of silence, she humphed, shifted her weight for comfort, and turned off the light.

Turned off the light? It was what—seven thirty? Who went to bed at seven thirty? This was not good. A celery stick with blond leaves pinned in the darkness under the body of a woman who went to bed before the sun did.

Stephen considered his predicament. Not even

Gerik with all his talk of obsession would approve of this.

Did I say go stark-raving mad? he would ask the jury. *No, I said we were created to obsess. Not to don women's clothing and crawl under strangers' beds.*

Stephen waited ten minutes before a soft snore put him at ease. He put both palms flat on the springs and carefully pushed up. Like a bench press. How much? Felt like two hundred if it was an ounce. Dead, heavy, sagging weight that—

Marjorie rolled over, and Stephen slid three inches to his right, masked by the motion. That was it! Move when she moved.

He waited a minute and then pushed up again. She lay like a log, so he pushed harder. She shifted, and he slid another inch or two. It was working. Five pushes later, he was free.

Stephen tucked his own clothes under one arm and crawled from the room on his remaining limbs like a thieving monkey.

The moment he stepped on the porch, he regretted his decision to park the car a block down. There were streetlights out here! He would be strutting his stuff down the sidewalk, exposed for the whole neighborhood to see. On the other hand, it would be an opportunity to practice. He needed a crash course on walking confidently, like a woman. This was nothing less than an unexpected gift.

Stephen headed out to the sidewalk. He tried several gaits and decided the short-step one, with cocked arms and a limp wrist, did the trick as well as any.

A whistle cut through the air. He jumped. A man

leaned against the streetlight across the road, staring at him. Her. Stephen hurried for the Vega.

By the time he slid behind the wheel, Stephen was feeling quite buoyant. He was on a roll. His plan was going to work; he had a feeling about this. The dashboard clock read a quarter of eight—a bit late for a city inspector, but time wasn't something he had to play with.

22

HE MADE TWO STOPS ON HIS WAY TO THE apartment and arrived at eight thirty, later than expected, but he had the angle covered.

Stephen grabbed a black leather doctor's bag, took a deep breath, adjusted his wig in the rearview mirror, and stepped out. From here on out, it was purely professional. Confident. Purposeful. He turned and strutted up the sidewalk, up the steps to the porch, and pushed the doorbell.

He cleared his throat and tested the voice he'd used for the duration of the ride. Sounded thoroughly male, but with a good half hour's practice he managed to capture a decidedly female quality.

He quickly reached into the bag, withdrew a round plastic lemon, and squirted a shot of juice into his mouth. He'd bought the lemon juice with his other supplies, thinking it might help his voice.

Chains rattled. Startled, he tossed the lemon over the rail and did his best to ignore the waves of heat washing over his skull. From now on, he was a her. Remember that. Her, her, her.

The door parted a crack; the one called Claude stood in the gap. "Yes?"

"Alicia Ferguson with the city," Stephen said in his practiced falsetto. "I'm here for the pest inspection."

Claude's eyes swept down his body. Her body. They stopped at her shoes. Stephen glanced down. He'd forgotten to take them off. They looked absurd, sticking out all black and gangly.

"Feet kill me on this job," Stephen said. "I can't afford to care about fashion."

"It's night," Claude said. "I was told nothing about an inspection. We can't accept any visitors at this hour."

"I'm afraid you don't have a choice; 5031CBB isn't something we debate. I'll need to come in and run a few tests, and then I'll be out of your hair."

Five minutes alone in the basement was all he needed.

"We were told nothing of this."

"Doesn't surprise me," Stephen said. "I spend half the day explaining myself to owners, which is one reason I'm so late today." He pulled a sheaf of paperwork from the bag. "Had a guy on Thirty-fourth who made me call the authorities in. Set me back two hours." He flipped open the pages. "Here it is, city ordinance 5031CBB. *The city shall at its election inspect any building suspected for pest contamination within seven days of the sale of such property.* It goes on, but that's the gist of it. Ten, fifteen minutes is all I should need."

Claude eyed the paperwork suspiciously and pulled a walkie-talkie off his hip. He spoke to someone in German. A dog barked in the garage. Two dogs.

Claude lowered his radio. "I'm sorry. You can't enter at this time. Come back on Monday."

"I don't think you're hearing me, sir. I will inspect the building now. If you refuse me, I will be back with the police and several colleagues."

"It's after eight o'clock. Why are you working so late?"

"I thought I told you why. I had another stubborn foreigner who forced me to call in the police. I don't have a choice on this; they give me ten properties, I have to finish ten properties. Any less and it affects my bonus, and I'm not about to let you cost me any money." Claude just stared and Stephen wondered if he'd heard. He spread his hands, careful to appear as delicate as possible. "Fine. I'll be back in a few minutes with the LAPD."

He turned to go. Claude spoke quickly into the radio. A static-filled response came back.

"Where do you need to run your tests?" Claude demanded.

"Five basic pest groups," Stephen said. "I'll have to take a look."

Another quick exchange on the radio.

Claude pushed the door open. "Please be quick. We will be leaving soon."

"Is that so? Don't wait on my account. Go ahead and leave—I'll be happy to lock up."

"Just hurry your tests. Please."

Stephen stepped in and looked around the huge garage. Two large dobermans growled at him from a spot halfway across the room, where they'd been tethered to a metal pole.

To the right, the stairs.

"Okay, why don't you leave me to run a few tests," he said. "Say, fifteen minutes?"

"I would rather watch."

"Well, I would rather be home in bed, off these

poor feet. I'll tell you what, Claude, why don't you sit down here and let me do what they pay me—"

"How do you know my name?"

Stephen blinked. "You are Claude, aren't you? Associate to a Mr. Roth Braun, I think the paperwork said."

Claude hesitated. "Yes."

"Well, Claude, if you don't mind, I'd rather do what I do without you breathing over my shoulders. Now, where are there pipes in this rats' nest?"

"Everywhere—"

"Does this thing have a basement?"

"Yes."

"Then I suppose I'll start there. How do I get down?"

Claude motioned at the staircase.

Stephen gripped his bag and walked without further hesitation. Any luck, and Claude would stay put. No further hints necessary.

He reached the door and stepped into the stairwell. No Claude. A tremble coursed through him. He was going to make it! Just stay here, big boy. He ran down to the first landing. Just stay—

The door pushed open; Claude stood above him. Stephen felt his heart drop to his heels. If he'd had a gun, he might have pulled it and winged the guy then.

"Don't you have something better to do?"

Claude descended the stairs without responding.

"Fine," Stephen said, turning back up the stairs. He wasn't about to lead the man anywhere near the safe. He'd have to regroup above.

He mounted the steps and walked up briskly, mind racing. This wasn't the plan. "If you're going to insist on badgering me, I'll come back tomorrow with more help. This is absolutely ridiculous. I have to say, I've never . . ."

Cool air flooded the crown of his head. His hair suddenly felt liberated.

Stephen jerked around and saw that a few loose hairs from the wig had caught on a splintered wooden beam above. It swung by the strands, six inches from his matted hair.

For a moment they stood in silence, struck by the sight of the blond furry ball swinging in space above Stephen's dark head of hair. Their eyes met.

Stephen threw the bag at Claude, hurled himself up the stairs, and slammed past him while he clutched the bag. The German yelled, stumbled, and came after him. Had Stephen elected to wear the heels, he would be dead now. But he had a head start, and he was dressed in pants. He flew across the garage, a streak of green.

The front door was still open. Stephen crashed through it and fled toward his Vega.

Claude stopped on the porch and yelled something in German, but Stephen could hardly make out the words, much less the meaning.

He threw the car into drive before his door was properly closed and squealed for La Brea. It took him two blocks to fully realize what had just happened.

He'd survived. This was good.

He'd failed. This was bad.

23

ROTH BRAUN DESCENDED THE STEPS ONE AT A time, feeling destiny and purpose course through his veins like liquid gold. The man had played his cards as expected.

With this latest charade, the Jew had given away more than he had intended: he was after the basement. From the beginning he had been interested in the basement.

It was why he drew attention to the top floor. It was why he'd broken into the garage and then emerged out of thin air from below. It was why he had tried to descend the stairs then reverse course when Claude insisted on following.

The Jew's heart was in the basement.

He stepped into the garage and stared at the dogs. Their eyes shone yellow in the dim light, but they didn't move. They sensed something in him. They perceived his power, like a high-pitched sound inaudible to the human ear.

He *tsked* and was rewarded with their soft whines.

Roth opened the door to the stairwell and walked down, not bothering to turn on the lights.

In the basement he elected to flip the light switch. His breath sounded hollow and welcoming in the concrete chamber. The Jew had been here—

he could feel the emotions in the air. Excitement. Fear. Hope.

The scent of the room reminded him of the basement in his father's house at Toruń. Mildew and dirt. Not so different from a grave.

This was an unexpected little treat, wasn't it? Here in America, so far from home, yet home after all.

Roth Braun felt compelled to sing. He shut the door behind him, stared at the gray room with its sealed steel doors and sang the German war anthem. His voice echoed with vibrato and he pumped his fist and sang louder, the whole song, just as he had as a child.

Gratified, he twisted his head, stretched his neck, and walked toward the door directly opposite him.

It was his third time in the boiler room. The other rooms were made of concrete and had no furnishings, so if anything had been hidden in the basement, it would likely be in the utility room. The previous two visits had been cursory, but this time he would look for evidence of the Jew.

The potbellied stove looked undisturbed. No sign of anything that . . .

Roth caught himself. The drum behind it had been moved. He could sense it as much as see it, although a thin line of dust a centimeter from the base confirmed the same.

Roth stepped forward and pulled the drum aside. A steel lid sat in the floor. It had been scraped clean.

A floor safe.

Rage overcame him. The Jew had beat him to it. In this delicate game, Roth had been outmaneuvered. By a Jew.

Just as his father had been.

The feelings that had warmed him while singing the anthem were gone. He tightened his fists and closed his eyes. Control.

Not all was lost, of course. The Jew hadn't been down here on his last unbelievable visit as a city employee. Claude had assured him of that much. Whatever Stephen had found earlier was still here, or he wouldn't have risked so much to come back for it.

Roth bent down, pulled the steel lid to one side and stared into the hole. He withdrew the tin box and stared at the picture of a woman whom he immediately recognized.

Seeing her here, on this box in America, offended him. The fact that they'd managed to smuggle even a picture of her out was an insult to his father. To him.

Roth demonstrated considerable restraint in not tearing the picture from the lid. Instead he pried the cover off with a controlled hand. Inside, a piece of cloth wrapped around Rachel's treasure.

But was it his father's treasure?

He set the tin box down and carefully unwrapped the cloth.

Heat gathered at the top of his skull and rushed down his head, making him momentarily dizzy.

The journal.

No Stones, but that didn't really surprise him. A relic as valuable as the Stones of David would never present itself so easily.

The journal was treasure enough for now. It was true then. She had smuggled the journal out with the Stones. The journal that could incriminate not only

Gerhard, but dozens of others. She'd hid it all these years knowing that if Gerhard were executed for crimes, her hope of finding her son would be dashed.

She was a smart one.

Roth lifted the old leather cover and gazed at the contents. Every woman that Gerhard had ever killed was listed, by date of execution. Details of the ritual and a small smudge of their blood by each name.

With the journal was a letter. The letter told the rest of the story. Rachel's story.

Roth sank to his knees and began to weep with gratitude. There was so much hope here. So much fear and desperation and longing. So much power. His resolve to finish what he'd started when he'd bought this building crashed through him like a waterfall.

Gerhard wanted the journal because it threatened his very life. But Roth knew that the journal would call to Stephen. Roth hadn't come to Los Angeles for the Stones, no. Nor the journal.

Roth had come for Stephen.

He spent an hour with the treasure, soaking in its meaning, plotting his next move. This was good. This was very good. It confirmed everything he'd guessed. He was perhaps the most fortunate man alive at this moment. But fortune had little to do with his success. He was here because he had earned his good fate and been patient in the working for it.

Thirty long years.

He set the journal back into the cookie tin as he'd found it, replaced the box in the safe, pulled the lid over the hole, and slid the drum back into place.

Stephen must find the treasure, and he must find

it on his own, in a way that elevated his hope to the highest heavens.

He stood to his feet. A celebration was in order.

Roth walked from the basement, determined to find not one, but two women this night.

24

THE BIRTH OF LITTLE ESTHER HAD FILLED
Martha's barracks with a surreal hope that lingered
against all odds. The rumors of mass gassings at
Auschwitz came so regularly now that none of the
women doubted them any longer. Hungary had been
all but emptied of its Jews, they said, and most of
them had vanished into the camp at Auschwitz. Only
the strongest were occasionally spared and sometimes
sent north, to Stutthof. Martha could hardly bear to
think of what had happened to her mother and sister.
Part of her insisted that she couldn't afford to think
about them—she had to think about one thing only:
giving birth to the child within her. Any day now,
maybe even tonight. A few days at the most.

Her heart hammered every time she thought
about going into labor. Imagine, not one baby in the
barracks, but two! Esther and David. Or if she had
a baby girl, Esther and Esther. Two stars of hope.

Ruth and Martha hurried from the factory and
walked quickly to the barracks, where Rachel had
been given charge of the baby today. The comman-

dant had allowed Ruth to stay with Esther for ten days before issuing the order that she return to work.

"She's going to be famished," Ruth said breathlessly. "It's been eight hours since I fed her. He's a beast!"

"Of course he is," Martha said. "But he's been good to you. And Esther is alive." She looked up at a group of women passing the other way. "Half the women in this camp grumble about how you're favored."

"Not in our barracks."

"No, not those who know you, but they all see you walking up to his house every day with Esther. It drives them mad. They think he likes you."

"Then they should try to spend some time with him! He insists I go; what am I supposed to do, slap him in the face? I have Esther to think about now. He hasn't touched me. Do they know that?"

"I've told them. Keep your voice down."

Streams of women crisscrossed the camp, making their way back to their barracks or the bathrooms before the roll call. Here in Toruń, roughly five thousand women, over half of them Jews, clung to the hope that they might be spared, yet they all knew a single order could change everything. The Russians were advancing from the east. If they could just hang on a little longer, surely the nightmare would end. Little Esther had been spared and allowed a new life outside her mother's womb—perhaps they, too, would be spared.

Martha imagined an army advancing over the fields to the east, coming to liberate them. What a day that would be. She and Ruth holding their tiny babies bundled in blankets, being whisked away to begin a new life. They rounded the showers and angled for the barracks where Rachel waited with baby Esther. Fifty yards. Ruth quickened her pace.

"This waiting is making me crazy," Martha said.

Ruth faced Martha, eyes bright. "Oh, Martha, you will be so excited. It's a miracle. You can feel the new life coming from you, and nothing else in the world matters."

Martha laughed. "Except for the pain."

"No, the pain tries to distract you, but the baby is stronger than the pain, Martha! A baby! You're giving birth to a baby, and the whole world stops for that." Ruth touched Martha's belly. "Can't you feel it?"

"Yes. Honestly, I'm terrified."

Ruth took her hand and squeezed it. "I was too. I was so scared that I couldn't breathe right. You were telling me to breathe, and while part of me was thrilled with what was happening, the other part was terrified." She smiled wide, as if her confession had been a secret.

But Martha knew her friend too well. Ruth, the courageous one who spoke the truth with chin held high, needed comfort and assurance as much as any woman in the camp. She was like a little girl in some ways—wise and confident, as long as Martha was by her side to hold her hand.

Ruth began to skip.

"Stop it, Ruth. Do you want to rub salt in their wounds?"

"They could use a touch of salt now and then. The red scarf hasn't touched one of their beds since Esther was born. Don't they see that? They should be grateful

for my skipping and all my trips up the hill. Little
Esther and I stand between them and that monster.
He does like her, you know. It horrifies me to think
about it, but that pig is actually fond of my baby."

She hurried the last twenty meters, threw open the
door, and ran in with Martha on her heels. "Rachel?"

Ruth pulled up three paces in, and Martha nearly
ran her over. Down the aisle between the bunks
Rachel faced them, holding the baby in her arms,
tears streaming down her cheeks.

"What's wrong?" Ruth ran for her baby. "What
did they do?" she demanded.

Something had happened to Esther? Martha felt
her heart bolt. She ran after Ruth, who carefully
took the bundle from Rachel.

"Is she okay? Please, tell me she's okay."

Rachel's lips were quivering. She still said nothing. Ruth peeled the blanket from her baby's face.
The child cried. So she was alive!

"Shh, shh. It's okay now. Mommy's here." Ruth
cradled the child and rocked her gently. "What is it,
Rachel? She's hungry?"

Rachel didn't respond. Why should she? It was a
rhetorical question. Several others entered the barracks behind them.

Ruth pulled her shirt up and let the baby suckle.
The child quieted and began to eat noisily. "You see,
Rachel? She's fine. What is it?"

Someone gasped behind them. "The scarf!"

Martha looked past Rachel and saw the scarf immediately. The bright red material was draped on a
lower bed, six or seven bunks down the aisle.

The first thing Martha thought was that Ruth had been wrong about the commandant.

The second thing was the realization that the red cloth lay terribly close to her own bed.

On her bed.

She blinked, unable to process the meaning. This silk scarf angled across the corner of her bed. This splash of red against the drab gray blanket. There was a mistake, of course. That bunk was her bunk. She was about to give birth to her baby. The commandant had promised it.

The barracks filled with more women. Questions—What is it? What's going on? Why is everyone standing here?—then silence.

Martha stared, still stunned.

Ruth's baby suckled quietly beside her.

"Ruth?" Martha faced her, suddenly very worried. "What . . . ?"

"I'm sorry," Rachel said, weeping. "The guard, he came in and asked me which was Martha's bed. I didn't know; I swear, I didn't know. He put the scarf there and then left." She fell to her knees and gripped Martha's dress. "I'm so sorry, Martha. I'm so sorry."

"Stop it!" Ruth snapped. "Stop your blubbering, Rachel."

Golda pushed through the gathered women. "What's going on?" Then she saw the red scarf and her lips formed a grim line.

All of this ran through Martha's mind: Rachel's weeping, Ruth's anger, Golda's silence. They all meant the same thing.

She would be hanged tonight, before her child was born.

Her legs started to give way, and she reached out to break her fall, but Rachel and Golda both held her up. She wanted to scream, but she was suddenly hyperventilating. The others were silent, and she hated them for it. A breathy moan escaped her lips.

They would come for her at six thirty, in ten minutes. But the baby! No, he couldn't do this! It was inhuman! Why had he placed this cloth on her bed? Didn't he love little David as he loved little Esther?

"Ruth." She touched her belly. "Ruth!" Her voice sounded distant, inhuman. She could see her friend still staring at the scarf, baby cradled in her arms.

"Hold Esther, Rachel," she heard Ruth say.

"Where are you going?"

"To the commandant."

"No!" Golda objected. "You can't just go—"

"He's going to kill her!"

"And if you go, he may kill you as well."

"It's my life!" Ruth yelled.

"Stop it!" Martha cried. Her limbs trembled, but she couldn't bear these women screaming at each other. She sat heavily on the nearest bunk. "Please, don't argue. Ruth, you know you can't go up there. You have to think of Esther."

Ruth stared at her, face flushed. She looked at the scarf then back at Martha. Slowly, she relaxed.

"I know this is a horrible thing," Golda said, "but he's killed dozens of women this way already."

"She's pregnant!" Ruth snapped. "He gave his word!"

"We have to accept it."

Martha knew she was right, but the truth did nothing to temper a sudden urge to claw the woman's eyes from her face. How many pregnant women had the commandant hanged from his gallows? How many within a day of their child's birth?

"No," Ruth said. "We don't have to accept it."

She walked up the aisle, took the scarf in her hands. "He told me once that the woman presented to him wearing the red scarf was the Jews' sacrificial lamb. She would die for the whole camp, to appease his wrath."

What she did next could not have been anticipated by any of them. She walked to her own bed, lay the red cloth across the corner, and smoothed it.

"Now the scarf is on my bed. I will go."

What was she saying? A sliver of hope sliced through Martha's heart. Ruth would make an argument for Martha's life? What if the commandant would listen? There was some hope in that, wasn't there?

"What do you mean, you will go?" Golda asked.

Ruth looked at Martha and then at her own baby. Tears misted her eyes, and she raised her hand to her lips.

Then Martha understood. "No! No, Ruth!"

Her friend wasn't listening. Ruth returned to Rachel, took her child lovingly. Kissed the baby on her forehead and then on her lips, tears dripping on the infant's cheek. She sniffed softly and then swallowed back her tears.

"I love you, dear Esther. I love you so much."

Martha was horrified by this display. She staggered to her feet. "Ruth—"

Ruth put a finger on her lips. "Shh. Listen to me, Martha."

"What are you doing? You can't take the scarf!"

"Listen to me! This is the only—"

"No!" Martha sobbed. She couldn't hear this. The panic she'd felt only a moment ago felt small next to the notion that Ruth would follow through with her plan.

"No, you can't—"

"Listen to me!" Ruth shouted. "They'll be coming soon."

Martha blinked.

"I'm sorry, I don't mean to shout." Tears slipped from Ruth's eyes again. "This is the only way to save both of our babies, Martha."

"He will never allow it."

"Your child will die with you," Ruth cried. "How can we allow that? Your child has as much right to live as I do. Should both of you die so that I can live?"

"Yes! I was chosen, not you."

"And now I choose."

"You don't even know if he will accept your choice."

"He will. I know him. He will, and he will let you live and have your baby." She kissed her infant again, several times, all about the face. "Promise me, Martha. Raise her as your own."

She handed the child to Martha, who took her, fingers numb. "Ruth . . ."

The women stared at the scene, dumbstruck. Not even Golda found the courage to object. Martha didn't know what to say. She didn't want this to be happening any more than she wanted to die herself. She should stop Ruth. Push the baby back into her arms and run up the hill to demand that Braun hang her.

She could do none of these.

For an endless minute, Ruth and Martha stared into each other's eyes. Then Ruth's show of bravery slowly began to fold. Her lips began to curve downward and quiver. Her breathing came quicker and sounded forced. She was trying to be courageous, but she couldn't stand against this terrible onslaught of fear and sorrow on her own.

This was Ruth, the young woman with more courage than the whole camp put together. But this was Ruth, the girl who'd edged her way through the train to find Martha's comfort in a time of loneliness.

Martha gave the baby to Rachel and wrapped her arms around Ruth's shoulders. The younger woman hugged Martha's pregnant belly, buried her face in her neck, and began to sob.

The pain in Martha's heart threatened to tear a hole through her chest. She wanted to die. She had to say something, anything that would stop Ruth from what she was going to do.

Golda's cheeks glistened with tears, and she made no attempt to wipe them away.

"Please, Ruth. Please . . ."

The door banged open. "Get back! What is going on?"

Martha began to panic. "Please, Ruth."

The women parted, and there stood the guard, the same young blond who'd come on several occasions to lead away women. She was accustomed to some emotion, but this scene made her hesitate.

"Whose bed is that?" she demanded, pointing her stick at the red scarf.

"If you have a boy, tell him to marry my Esther," Ruth whispered. She faced the guard and wiped her tears. "That's my bed."

She retrieved the scarf and glided down the hall, past Martha's clinging hands, past her baby with one last kiss and one last sob, and past the guard, out the door.

Martha slumped to the bed, curled into a ball, and began to cry uncontrollably.

25

THINK, THINK, THINK. HE'D PRACTICALLY thought himself to death these last five days.

Stephen had returned to the hiding place in Building B two nights before, stripped off the green pantsuit, donned his old dirty slacks, paced, and made an important decision.

He would not go home tonight.

He would rent a motel room.

And so he had. An old, flea-infested room seven blocks down on La Brea. Sunday, he'd made another important decision.

He would not rent a motel room that night.

He would sleep here overlooking Rachel's apartment on the off chance that the German entourage would vacate the building for a spell. Monday, he would go home. After he found a way into that basement. But Monday had come, and he had neither found a way into the basement nor gone home.

He'd lost his mind to this thing, and he no longer cared.

Braun had made a threat, and Stephen had dared

to defy him. For the first time, he feared for Chaim's life. He couldn't go home. As long as he stayed out of reach, Braun couldn't hurt him or endanger Chaim.

Besides, Stephen didn't want to go home.

On the other hand, he had to at least let Chaim know that all was well, even if it wasn't. He'd made a phone call from a booth on La Brea. The conversation lasted less than a minute.

Where are you? Are you okay? What are you doing?

I'm in a . . . motel. I'm okay. I'm taking a few days to think things through. Are you okay?

Of course I'm okay. When will you be home?

Soon. Don't worry. Please don't worry.

But he knew from Chaim's tone that the rabbi was worried, so he added the warning. *Be careful, Rabbi. Promise you'll be careful.*

Stephen looked around the ten-by-ten living space he'd pulled together while thinking. He'd scavenged wood and some tires from the piles around the room and built up a semblance of walls to cordon off his area. Two walls, each stabilized by nothing more than its own weight, leaned against trusses and angled from the floor to the building's outer wall. A few tires added stability. It was a lean-to of sorts.

Some might think he'd flipped his lid. Sylvia, for example. The rabbi even. But it wasn't madness that drove him. He was no more mad than the rest of God's children, chasing after their rainbows.

See, Stephen, even that sounded a bit mad. Your reasons for not being mad are mad.

In a bohemian kind of way, what he was doing made perfect sense. He was pursuing an idea that really mattered. The safe was his pot at the end of the rainbow. Until some dramatic breakthrough would put his hands on that safe, he would carefully block out any part of the world that took his attention off the goal. Did that sound like madness? Of course not. The greatest achievements in history were accomplished by men willing to do what others were not willing to do.

The antique dealer, Gerik, had said that man was created to obsess. The rabbi had said that the only thing worse than not getting what you desperately want is not desperately wanting anything at all. Well then?

Stephen straightened from his work over the left wall. What was that diatribe the rabbi had once delivered at the breakfast table?

You can have nothing to die for until you first have something to live for. The Holocaust did that for Jews. It revealed the incomparable value of another idea. Life. Love! Love, Stephen. We should be daily ravaged by love. The Nazis hated us. If from this we do not learn to love, we dishonor the lives of six million Jews.

"That's right, Rabbi," he muttered. "So then I will desperately want and I will love. This is my labor of love."

He nudged a two-by-four into place—an extra brace required because the wall swayed every time he touched it—and stood back.

"Lovely," he mumbled.

Another preposterous idea had been brewing over the last twenty-four hours, and with each passing hour its preposterousness faded. The notion that Joel Sparks could be his salvation seemed counterintuitive, given the man's less-than-honorable character. But Stephen was in pursuit of love, not necessarily reason.

Stephen reached into his backpack, carefully pulled out the eight-by-ten photograph of Ruth, and looked into her eyes. In his mind's eye, this woman was Esther. As Gerik had said, the daughter of this woman would today be about the age of her mother in the picture. She would look like her mother, perhaps.

This was Esther. This was the woman he was meant to find. She was an orphan, a true Stone of David, and her picture was in the safe, on top of the tin box that Stephen would soon have.

He had stared at Esther's picture for hours in these last three days.

He was meant for her.

Honestly, he thought he might be falling in love with the woman in this picture. Her daughter, Esther. Chaim would call it infatuation, but Stephen knew the difference.

"You have ruined me," he whispered lovingly, and he kissed the picture lightly.

He stood and looked around. The two haphazardly erected walls bordered the window that overlooked Rachel's apartment. A piece of plywood layered with some insulation made a bed in the left corner. Three cans of beans and two cans of corn stood in a neat pile in the right corner. A crate with a candle, some matches, a spoon, a can opener, and a comb he hadn't yet used sat dead center.

He'd slept on his bed here last night, if *slept* could be broadly defined. *Moaned* and *rolled about* and *stared* at the sagging ceiling might be more accurate word choices. He tried to walk the beach yesterday, figuring a bit of sun and a change of scenery might do him some good. The walk lasted fifteen minutes. He'd fled the crowds in a near panic, desperate to be alone to think things through, as if he hadn't done enough of that.

Think, think, think. The thinking was driving him loopy.

On the bright side, the short exposure to the real world had stimulated his appetite. The idea of going to a restaurant unnerved him, so he made one stop at a grocery store, gathered a handful of necessities, endured the checkout line, and retreated to safety here.

Stephen approached the wall to the left of the window, dropped to his knees, and carefully taped the corners of the photograph to the drywall with duct tape. He stepped back, sat cross-legged, rested his elbows on his knees, and stared at the picture.

Was there another woman in the world as beautiful? Was it even physically possible for the world to produce not one, but two women as stunning as the woman who gazed at him from this black-and-white photograph? The sweep of her hair; the subtle curve of her jaw; soft, steady eyes. He could swear the photo had been touched up with a skilled brush. No nose could be that perfect, no lips so symmetrical. But he knew that no artist had retouched this photo. This was Ruth, who was Esther, who was perfect.

Stephen closed his eyes and swallowed. Time was running out. He had to make contact with Joel Sparks. Illegal, insane, impossible.

But he had to do this. For Ruth's sake. For his mother's sake.

He opened his eyes and stared at the picture. For Esther's sake.

Stephen grunted and rose quickly to his feet.

———

GREAT WESTERN Bank was bustling with a late-morning crowd when Stephen walked through its doors just before noon. To say he felt conspicuous sporting two days' growth of stubble and a rumpled shirt was only half-true. The crowd, not his appearance, was to blame for his anxiety.

The white Converse tennis shoes he'd bought to replace his impractical wing tips stood out like fluorescent bulbs. Maybe he should have dirtied them a bit. Still, he was doing nothing illegal. He really had no reason to be nervous.

Wait. What if Sweeney and gang returned to the fourth floor and stole his picture of Ruth? Some vagabond could ransack his shrine and disappear without a trace. He should have brought the picture with him. Too late.

Stephen made a halfhearted attempt to smooth his shirt and walked straight for the closest banker's desk. A middle-aged woman with a ball of blond hair, meticulously shaped by curlers, looked up. A gold nameplate on her desk read "Nancy Smith." Her eyes scanned him from head to toe.

"May I help you?" she asked, her politeness all but forced.

Stephen slid into a chair, glanced around, and leaned forward. "I would like to make a withdrawal," he said.

"You need to go to one of the tellers for a withdrawal—"

"No, I need to withdraw a lot of money."

Her face slowly turned white. "I . . . we don't keep money in our desks."

"Of course not. But you have it in the vault. I need a hundred thousand. Surely you keep that much on hand."

Her eyes shifted with a look of panic. What was her problem? He knew that banks didn't like to shell out large sums of cash without prior arrangements, but her reaction was uncalled for. It wasn't like he was holding her up.

"I'm . . ." She swallowed. "Please . . ."

Understanding came in a flash. "You think I'm trying to rob you?"

Her look was answer enough.

He found it within him to laugh kindly. "Don't be ridiculous," he said. "I have money in this bank, and I need to withdraw some of it."

"You do?"

"Yes." Her eyes dropped to his shirt, and he pulled the tails to straighten the wrinkles. "I'm sorry, I . . . I got mugged in the alley, and the . . . people got my shirt dirty." He felt his face flush, and he grinned. "Druggies. They'll do anything for a fix these days."

She just looked at him.

"I need a hundred thousand dollars," he said.

"Wait here, please."

She stood and walked toward the manager's office. Stephen hunched down and watched her speak to a balding bank manager. Both looked out at him, and he looked away until he sensed someone approach.

"My name is Bruce Spencer; I'm the bank manager. Can I help you?"

"Do you have cash in your vault?"

The manager grinned. "We're a bank—we always have money."

"Then you can help me. I have an account with your bank—just over eight hundred thousand. I need a hundred thousand in twenties. Can you do that?"

The man's left eye twitched. "That's a lot of money."

True enough. Any normal investor would have put it to work in more aggressive ways than what a bank could offer. But Stephen's rearing on foreign soil had given him this incongruous conservative streak when it came to saving money.

"Which is why I have it in your vault rather than stuffed under my mattress." He pulled out the check he'd prepared and handed it to the man. "If you don't mind, Mr. Spencer, I'm in a bit of a hurry."

Spencer glanced at the check. "Are you in some kind of trouble?"

"Do I look like I'm in some kind of trouble?"

"Frankly, yes."

"There you go, then. I'm in a spot of trouble, and I need some money. Isn't that what money's for?"

"That's a lot of money," Spencer repeated.

"I think we've already established that." He had no reason to treat the manager with condescension, but he was growing impatient.

The manager handed the check to Nancy. "Please verify the funds and get Mr. Friedman his money." Then to Stephen, "This will take a few minutes, I'm sure you understand. Most large withdrawals are arranged in advance."

"I'll wait. No problem. But please don't take all day. I am in a hurry."

Stephen walked out twenty minutes later, sweat leaking down his back, big bag of cash under his right arm. So far so good.

26

JOEL SPARKS WAS A DEVELOPER IN PASADENA known for his low-income housing developments. But a closely held rumor suggested that Sparks had more than casual Mafia ties. The possibility had nearly paralyzed Dan Stiller two years earlier, when Stephen had proposed Joel bail them out of their deal gone bad. After all, the Mafia bit was only a rumor, Stephen had insisted. But judging by the way the man carried himself, Stephen thought the rumor might have some credence.

He drove north, nibbling on a nail, knowing that he was about to plunge into very deep waters.

Then again, there was no guarantee the man was even available on this particular Monday afternoon.

Sparks's large white mansion stood against a hill in north Pasadena, surrounded by palms and a sweeping red-brick driveway. Stephen leaned out his window and punched the call button at the main gate.

"Yes?"

"Uh . . . yes, Stephen Friedman here to see Joel Sparks."

The intercom remained silent. He pushed the button again.

"Hello?"

"You have an appointment?"

Not good.

"Uh . . . well, yes. Better, I have business he won't be able to refuse."

The wait was longer this time, but just as Stephen was again reaching for the call button, the gates began to swing inward.

Okay, baby. Calm and collected. He drove up to the house, parked the Vega, and walked up the steps to the front door. The cash would stay in his trunk for now. One step at a time.

A bodyguard who passed himself off as a butler led Stephen over marble floors to a spacious office. Details registered in his mind but didn't stay—the paintings on the walls, the crystal chandelier, the floor-to-ceiling cases of leatherbound books. Then his attention was consumed by the large man at the sliding glass doors, back to Stephen, phone plastered to his ear.

"Of course, don't I always?"

The butler-bodyguard closed a door behind Stephen, and Joel Sparks turned. His deep-set eyes tried to hide behind pronounced cheekbones. He smiled, but to Stephen it looked more like a grimace. He had nasty written all over him. Amazing he wasn't locked up yet.

Or was Stephen just imagining things?

"Good. I'll call as soon as I hear." He set down the phone. "Well, well. If it isn't the man who sold me that overpriced piece of junk on Wilson." He stepped forward and offered his hand. "How's business these days?"

"Good." Stephen took the hand. "Yeah, good."

"Really? You're driving a Vega and you're dressed like a schmuck. Can't be that good. Have a seat."

Stephen sat on a black leather couch. "Yeah, I know. I didn't have time to change."

"What can I do for you?"

Right to business. Just like any deal. Stephen crossed his legs, then set his foot back down.

"I need a favor."

"You owe me a favor. What makes you think I'm in the mood to give you even more credit?"

"This one will make up for both."

Sparks leaned against his desk. "I'm listening."

"Let's say you left something important in a building, but when you went back to get it, the owners wouldn't let you in."

"And?"

"How would you go about getting it?"

Sparks's plastic smile softened. "I'm not sure I understand. I deal in real estate, not the law. I think you have the wrong party. Come back with a building to sell me at half price, and we'll do business." He reached for a call button on his desk.

"It's worth a lot to me," Stephen said, "this thing that I left behind. Family heirloom that dates back to the war."

Sparks withdrew his hand and studied Stephen for a few long seconds. "Just out of curiosity, how much is it worth to you . . . this heirloom? I may know a good lawyer."

"I'm not sure. A lot of cash."

"How much cash?"

"You tell me."

"Tell you what? You're the one with the heirloom, not me. Lawyers don't come cheap these days."

"Twenty?"

"Twenty thousand."

"Twenty thousand cash."

"Tell you what, I'll mention this to a lawyer I know, and maybe he'll give you a call."

"I need to retrieve the heirloom tonight."

Sparks sighed. "Then I'm afraid I can't help you. Try the yellow pages."

"How about fifty?"

"Exactly what kind of heirloom are we talking about here? You walk into my office looking like you fell off a cliff, offer me fifty thousand dollars in cash to break into a building, and I have to wonder if you're on the wrong side of the law. I don't mess with the law."

"Of course not. I'm just trying to get something that belongs to me without having to go through a lengthy process. I may not look like it now, but I've done quite well for myself these last few years. Some things are more important than money. I'll pay you fifty thousand in cash to distract the owners long enough for me to take what's mine. Totally copacetic. No harm, no foul."

"Paying for something like this could be illegal."

"Why? I'm not stealing anything."

"You have fifty thousand cash?"

"In the car."

Sparks took a deep breath. "Well, God knows I could always use fifty thousand cash, but this is just not something I do."

"It so happens that these guys have guns. They're in an abandoned apartment complex—five of them now, I think. German Mafia types. Considering the circumstances, how about seventy-five thousand?"

"I'm not sure you realize what you're asking."

"I pay you, and I'm the one incriminated in any crime, right? But this isn't even a crime per se. I've got seventy-five thousand dollars in a bag that says you know someone who can help me out."

"What's the heirloom?"

"Some photographs."

Sparks stood and walked toward the sliding glass door that led out to a pool. He stood, hands on hips, doing what mafioso types do best, making a judgment call. Stephen could practically hear his thoughts. *Do I trust this punk with my true identity? Do I let him into the inner circle of the unlawful? Do I tell him that I look like a bat because I am one, feeding at night on the weak and the lonely, like this poor sap?*

Then Stephen thought to himself, *I'm already in your circle, mafioso. I've lost my mind and I'm chasing after a rainbow, and I've gone too far to turn back now. Take your best shot, baby.*

"If you double back on me, I will destroy you." Sparks turned around, lips drawn tight. His transformation from aboveboard businessman to underworld criminal was complete. "Do you understand me?"

"Absolutely."

"Something goes wrong—someone gets hurt and

you even sneeze—I guarantee, you'll spend your life regretting it."

The sincerity of Sparks's tone sent a chill down Stephen's back. He could hardly have hoped for more. If the man who stood before him now couldn't distract the Germans for a few minutes while Stephen retrieved his treasure, it couldn't be done.

He smiled. "Nothing will go wrong."

"Bring me a hundred thousand and we'll talk."

"A hundred?"

"Not a penny less."

Stephen stood. "Okay. I have it in the car."

TWO DAYS and nothing but one short, cryptic phone call from Stephen. Chaim had taken nineteen messages for Stephen, eight from a desperate Dan Stiller. The rest were from a variety of sources, mostly related to real estate.

The rabbi stood and walked into the kitchen. He decided against a glass of orange juice, breathed a prayer, and headed for the phone.

His initial alarm slowly had been replaced by curiosity. Stephen was no doubt disturbed by the discovery of his mother and her death, but if Chaim was right, this recent strange behavior wasn't connected to remorse. Stephen was after what he believed was his. He was maybe even after the Stones of David, and, apparently, he believed he could get them.

Gerik answered on the third ring.

"Hello, Chaim! So pleased you called."

"Hello, Gerik. Have you heard from Stephen lately?"

"Not since last Friday. He's missing?"

"You saw him Friday?"

Gerik relayed his encounter with Stephen and the photograph without the slightest hint of concern.

"This doesn't worry you?" Chaim asked.

"What? That a young Jew has discovered something worth throwing his life into? Not in the least."

"The something is a *picture*—"

"Hardly, Chaim. That something is a girl named Esther who may or may not have survived the death camps. His passion is for Esther and everything she represents. Grace in the face of horrible suffering. Love. Let him run. Let him redeem her. Let him obsess. God knows, we could use a few hundred thousand more like him."

"Yes, of course, let him obsess. Have you ever considered the dangers of obsession? Just because you love someone doesn't mean you have the right to break the law in their name."

"I don't think Stephen is planning on breaking the law, do you?"

"I truly can't say. But I'm worried. He has a tendency for this, Gerik. He's done it before."

"He's gone after his mother's inheritance before?"

"No. But there's more here. He's a war child, an abandoned orphan, an immigrant without a true home. He compensates for his loneliness with some of his antics. But at times like this, I fear he retreats into isolation, searching for meaning. For belonging. Family. He becomes the lost child again, and he doesn't follow reason."

"Maybe becoming a child again isn't so bad," Gerik said. "He needs time to work through this, Chaim. Let him search for his identity. Let him feel his need to belong to someone. We all might consider the same with God."

Chaim took a deep breath and nodded. "I think he may be after more than his identity. There are the Stones of David."

"If he is so fortunate to have stumbled on information leading to the other Stones, he should go after them. Especially if they are his rightful inheritance."

Chaim didn't necessarily disagree. "Rachel's note mentioned danger. I'm thinking of calling the police."

"The police would put an end to whatever hope Stephen has for finding what he's searching for. Surely you know that."

"The police could save his life."

"How many times have you told me your Christ taught that man should abandon this kingdom for the next?"

"These are Stones, not the kingdom of God. The passionate dedication that Christ requires of his followers can destroy a man if misdirected."

"But this isn't really about the Stones," Gerik said. "It's about love. Isn't the kingdom of God about love?"

"Yes."

"There you go, then."

"I'm still worried."

"Then you don't trust him," Gerik said.

"Exactly. I don't trust him. Passion has a way of making people do stupid things. Especially people like Stephen."

There was kindness in Gerik's laughter. "Yes, passion is dangerous, but it's also a requirement for good living."

"This isn't God he's pursuing, Gerik."

The antique dealer turned somber. "Then help him, Chaim. Be with him to keep him from falling over himself. But don't kill his passion."

Chaim let the man's suggestion settle in. "Maybe."

"Perhaps we should all be so obsessive of love."

Chaim didn't answer.

27

STEPHEN MET FIVE OF SPARKS'S THUGS IN THE alley at nine and led the black-clad men to the fourth floor of Building B as agreed. The leader, Bert, was a burly man with a pitted face who looked as though he'd grown up on a diet of thumbtacks.

The other four were no more congenial. Three had each survived a tour in Vietnam. This pleased Stephen more than he would ever admit. They were his salvation, and he welcomed them with a giddiness he didn't know he was capable of.

"What's this?" Bert asked, motioning to Stephen's makeshift hiding place.

"This place? I don't know. Looks like a . . . hangout. I found it here."

"Someone lives here. What if they come back?"

"No one lives here," Stephen said. "It's been abandoned."

"Doesn't look abandoned to me. Picture on the wall, food cans in the corner. No way." Bert eyed Stephen. "You do this?"

"You take me for an idiot? Why would I do this?

Forget it. Doesn't matter anyway. You do your thing, and I watch from here like we planned. If someone comes, it's my problem, not yours."

"I don't like it," one of the others said. "You should wait somewhere else."

"Fine. I'll find another window." He had no intention of doing any such thing. The fact that these thugs were tromping all through his place was annoying enough without them ordering him around in his own home. Who did they think they were?

"Let's get going," he said.

Bert lifted his binoculars and peered across the street. "Top floor's lit, the rest are dark. Looks simple enough. You're sure there's only two dogs?"

"Does it make a difference? You're using a stun grenade—that should knock them all out."

"Everything matters. Joey, you think you could get the gas canister through one of those windows from here?"

Joey eyed the top floor. "Should be easy enough. But a ground-level shot will be just as easy. That puts me in position when we go in."

Bert nodded and lowered the glasses. "Okay, everyone follows the plan. We gas the top floor, knock out the dogs in the garage, and hold the stairwell and the elevator for seven minutes from the all-clear. That means you"—he jabbed a finger at Stephen—"have exactly seven minutes from the time we signal three short flashes to get your butt across the street, into the basement, collect these . . . heirlooms of yours, and get out. Two long flashes, and we abort. Clear? You see two, and we're out of here, no questions, no refunds."

"What if I fall or get delayed somehow? I know we agreed on seven minutes, but—"

"Seven means seven. What you do in those seven minutes is up to you. Any longer and we'll have cops swarming the place, especially if whoever's in there starts firing off unsilenced rounds."

They'd been over this several times already. Their entry would be relatively painless, but there was no telling what the Germans would do if they got off the fourth floor before the gas knocked them out. If one of the neighbors called in gunshots, it would take the nearest precinct seven minutes to show, less if a squad car happened to be nearby—a risk they would have to accept. If a cop did show before the seven minutes were up, they would blow a hole in the back of the garage and vanish into the night. Stephen would be on his own.

That was the plan, and Stephen thought it was stupendous. The way he figured it, three minutes would be all he really needed to drop into the basement, move the barrel, scoop up the tin box, and do his own vanishing act.

"Let's do this," Bert said. He caught Stephen's attention, brought two fingers to his eyes, and then pointed them at the building. "Don't take your eyes off the target."

"Not a chance."

"Seven minutes."

"Seven minutes."

They pounded down the stairs, and Stephen took up his position at the window. He lifted the binoculars and strained to see shapes beyond the drawn curtains. Nothing. If someone pulled back a curtain and saw a man staring at them through binoculars from across the street . . .

He lowered the glasses and edged to his left. A dark shadow crossed the street to the right—that would be Joey with the grenade launcher. Stephen's pulse pounded. He scanned the neighborhood for pedestrians. All clear.

Could this actually work? What if the gas canister from Joey's launcher bounced off the window? No, these guys knew what they were doing. They were in the zone, man. They would crash the party and put Braun out of business.

The other four men broke for the side of the building and slid into the shadows below one of the ground-floor windows. He could hardly believe this was happening. Should've done this three days ago.

The curtains suddenly parted at one of the fourth-floor windows. Stephen jerked back. They'd been spotted!

No, not necessarily. Maybe the Germans had only heard something. Stephen sneaked another peek. A man stood at the window, studying the street. Come on, Joey! Light them up! Do it, do it now!

But Joey was out of sight, and the south side of the building remained dark. The man in the window didn't seem satisfied. Stephen dismissed a sudden temptation to stick his head out the window and direct their attack.

A dull *thump* sounded, followed by a crashing window. Joey had fired. And hit.

The curtain dropped shut. Stephen leaped to the center of the window and strained for a view of the attack. Another crash, this one from ground level. A definite *whump!* Maybe more than definite. Maybe thundering. The stun grenade. The cops were probably already on their way.

Stephen watched five men hoist themselves into the window and disappear. Still no sign of anything from the top floor. Maybe they were all unconscious. Or racing down the stairwell bearing arms.

"Come on," he growled. "Come on!"

"What's up, Groovy?"

Stephen spun. Sweeney and Melissa!

"Lotsa commotion out there tonight," Sweeney said. "You in on it?"

"What are you doing here?" Stephen demanded.

"I asked first."

Stephen whirled back to the window. What had he missed? He had to watch for the flashes! Nothing seemed to be happening.

The bohemians had walked up beside him and peered out. "You looking at anything in particular or just gazing at that missed opportunity over there?" Sweeney asked.

Stephen turned sideways, keeping the building in his peripheral. He could feel sweat snake past his right temple.

"I need some privacy right now."

Melissa looked at his flimsy walls. "You want us to knock before entering, is that it? Come on, dude, let's knock." She led Sweeney out of Stephen's square with a straight face and lifted her fist to knock. "Oops, no door, Groovy. I would knock on the wall, but it might fall if I do."

This could not be happening.

ROTH BRAUN was seated on what was left of Rachel
Spritzer's leather sofa when the canister crashed
through the dining-room window, rolled to a stop
under the table, and hissed white gas.

A sliver of fear immobilized him momentarily
before his training took over, returning to him his
full power of control.

The Jew had returned. This was good.

He bolted from the couch. "Gas!"

The effects were surprisingly quick—three men
seated at the table were on their knees already, gasping for air. Roth was far enough away to escape its
initial effects. Surely it wasn't lethal. Or had he misjudged the man?

A dull *thump* shook the floors below them.

Lars ran from the master bedroom, stared at the
scene with wide eyes, and stepped aside just in time
to avoid Roth's rush.

"A blanket!" Roth said. "Hurry!"

They'd shredded the bed to its springs. Lars
grabbed a blanket from the floor and threw it at
Roth, who quickly stuffed it into the crack at the
bottom of the door.

"It'll seep around the door," Lars said.

"Give me an ax." Braun shoved the closet doors
leaning against the wall to the floor. "The stairwell's
behind this wall."

Axes were one thing they weren't short on, and
they'd already taken the plaster off the bedroom side
of the wall. They wouldn't find anything by tearing

down the walls—the treasure was in the basement. But Stephen had to believe that he was in a race against time to retrieve the treasure. So Roth would keep up the charade. He would play the game until Stephen found his own way in. There was no point in crushing the Jew's hopes until they had been elevated to a point of fanaticism.

Roth caught the ax with his left hand and broke a two-by-four with his first swing.

"They will be coming up the stairs." He cursed himself for leaving the masks on the third floor and swung again. The ax shattered two timbers this time.

Roth grinned and swung again. This time, the entire wall sagged. Nothing was so satisfying as the game. They were coming to the finish line, neck and neck.

"Come on, Jew!" Roth bellowed, swinging again. "Come on!"

Another three quick chops, and a three-foot portion splintered off and fell out.

Roth dropped the ax, shoved his head into the stairwell, saw a clear path, and crawled out. He dropped to the third-floor landing, followed by Lars. The attackers were still below, waiting for the gas to complete its work. He slammed through the door and ran for a cache of supplies in the first bedroom.

"The ventilation system. Flood the building with tear gas."

Lars tore through a large black duffle bag, yanked out two gas masks, and tossed one to Roth. Gas masks secure, they each grabbed three small canisters. Lars snatched up a rifle.

"Gas first," Roth snapped. He shoved a crowbar at Lars. "Use the return vents." He ran into the hall, turned the thermostat to manual vent, dropped the canisters, and crammed his crowbar under a large return vent above his head. The grill popped off in two attempts. He could hear Lars doing the same in the adjacent hall.

Roth popped the tabs on all three canisters and dropped them into the vent. Perhaps the men below already had gas masks in place, but with any luck they would wait to don the gear until they secured the stairwell. Masks limited field of vision.

It would take no more than a minute for the gas to work its way through the building. Without another word, they collected their weapons and reentered the stairwell.

Roth motioned Lars to cover. The blond German swung his rifle over the rail. "Clear."

So, they were still in the garage? Or was this the work of a lone fool, firing off a canister of gas with the intent to crawl up after half an hour to collect his treasure?

"No killing," he ordered. "Not now."

He descended the stairs to the second-floor landing and covered for Lars. They took up positions on the first landing, weapons trained on the door to the garage. If anyone cracked that door, Roth would put a bullet in his gut.

THE FIRST *clunk* came while Melissa's hand was still raised, and for a moment Stephen thought she'd stomped her foot to imitate a knocking sound. The noise came again, distant.

All three of them looked out the window together. The sound was hardly more than a knock, but there it came again. Stephen froze. Someone was taking a hammer or an ax to one of the walls in Rachel Spritzer's apartment.

"What's that?" Sweeney asked.

They'd entered his hiding place without knocking again.

"I . . . I don't know." Stephen was desperate. He turned and held up both hands to ward them off. "Please! I have to do something here."

"What's up, man? Something's going down and—"

"Just leave!" Stephen shouted.

They flinched.

He flung his arm toward the door. "Can't you take a hint? Leave!"

"Now you've gone and hurt my feelings, man," Sweeney said. "What gives you the right? And after we extended our hospitality to you?"

"Is that what you call this? Hospitality? You're hurting my feelings by being here. I'm telling you, I have something real important to do, and you can't be here!"

"Then maybe you should apologize," Melissa said, crossing her arms.

Stephen stared at her, mouth open. The whole scene felt surreal. He glanced back at the building. No flashes, right? He would have seen the light from the corner of his eye. Nothing but black on the garage level. What was keeping Bert? They should have given the all-clear by now. He swung back.

"I'm sorry!" He was frantic, and he knew that they knew he was frantic. "Believe me, I'm so sorry."

"For kicking us out of your little shrine here."

"Yes! For kicking you out of—"

"What was that?" Sweeney asked.

Stephen turned back to the window. "What?"

"I thought I just saw some flashes."

"You did? How many?"

"I don't know. Two, I think. Maybe it was three."

"Well, was it two or three?" Stephen demanded.

"I don't know. Lighten up."

Stephen turned on Sweeney. "It was either two or three, it couldn't be both! And they were either long flashes or short flashes. Two long flashes or three short ones. Tell me!" he yelled.

Sweeney stared back, shocked.

"Sorry. I'm sorry for that. Look, I just need to know exactly what you saw. You have no idea how important it is to me."

"That your signal?" Melissa asked. "That's why you're looking over there. You're waiting for a signal from someone inside. You've been holding out on us."

"You're right, I have. And I'm sorry, okay. Just tell me what—"

"I think it was three short," Sweeney said. "But I saw only two."

"Then why is it three?"

"Because the two flashes I saw were short. You said three short or two long right? These were short, so there must have been three. I just saw the last two."

He had seven minutes! He'd already wasted at least one. Stephen bolted for the stairs.

"Hey, someone's climbing out the window down there," Sweeney said.

Stephen slid to a stop. "What?"

"No, two! Check that, make it three . . . five! Five people dressed in black just dived out that window down there."

Stephen ran for the window. Sure enough, Bert and gang were out of the building, along the wall, bent over.

Two long flashes blazed from one of their flashlights.

"What?"

"Are they okay?" Melissa asked.

"What happened?" Stephen asked, disbelieving. "What are they doing?"

The men ran to the east, crouched low. They rounded a building and were gone. Stephen faced the apartment, still not comprehending exactly what had just happened. There had been three short flashes followed by two long flashes. The team had entered, secured, and then been beaten back by Braun somehow.

But how?

It didn't matter how. The fact was, they were gone.

The desperation came quickly, pummeling him like a breaking wave.

He spun from the window, suddenly panicked. He should go anyway! He should run over there, dive through the window, zip into the basement, and grab the tin box! For all he knew, Sparks could have told his men to shut it down before he got in.

But Braun had managed to beat back five trained soldiers. He was either a lot smarter or a lot stronger than Stephen previously assumed.

He slowly lowered himself to the crate. The world faded. Five days of pent-up frustration flooded his chest. It was time to give up. It was time to go home and explain everything to the rabbi. To crawl out of this hole and rediscover the land of the living. Tears blurred his eyes, and he fought to contain himself.

"You okay, man?" Sweeney asked.

No, man, I'm dying here. Can't you see that? Of course I'm okay. I'm a successful Realtor with eight hundred thousand dollars in the bank. Make that seven.

Melissa put her hand on his shoulder. "It's okay, honey. We all have bad days."

He lowered his head and tried to shake off the emotion. The attempt failed miserably. Silence swallowed them for a few minutes.

"Man, you have it bad, don't you?"

Stephen cocked his head to see Sweeney sitting cross-legged in the corner of his hiding place.

"I have what bad?"

"The desires. You've got a case of the desires, and you have it bad. Maybe that's good."

Stephen didn't bother with a response.

"That's what I'm looking for, you know. It's why I left the world behind and took on the bohemian ideals. I don't know what about Rachel Spritzer's place has you like this, but you've given yourself to it. Know what happens when you abandon yourself to something like that?"

"No, tell me."

"It either ruins you or makes you. Drugs, for example. There's something that you give yourself to, and it ruins you. But give yourself to love, and it makes you."

"Whatever."

Sweeney stood. "Come on, Melissa, let's leave Groovy to figure things out. He's got me all inspired again."

"Take care, Stephen," she said. They looked at him from his doorway that wasn't, and he knew that somewhere in his breaking down he'd earned their respect. Somehow, the realization comforted him. His new family was embracing him.

They left, and Stephen curled up on his bed.

"TEAR IT apart!" Roth thundered. "Every wall, every post, every carpet, the whole building, from top to bottom, starting with the third floor. We begin now!"

"It's midnight," Balzer said.

Roth glared at the man.

"We're still recovering," Balzer said.

The gas had rendered them unconscious for an hour before its effects faded. From what they could tell, four or five men had orchestrated the attack and been driven out by the tear gas. One of them had dropped a magazine of 627 rounds in their quick exit, most likely from an M-16. A stun grenade had killed one dog and knocked the other out.

The attackers had used a grenade launcher for the gas canister. Whoever they were, they didn't lack resources.

Roth was pleased with the Jew's efforts. It was critical that he find his own way in. Then, and only then, could Roth make his next move. If Stephen suspected at any point that he was being played for a fool, he would be compromised. He might even quit.

And what if the Jew actually outwitted him as his mother had outwitted Gerhard?

Roth would have to take that risk.

Suddenly angered, he lifted his pistol and shot Balzer through the head.

"Balzer was ill," Roth said. "We don't have time for illness. Is anyone else ill?"

No one challenged him.

"Good. I want this building stripped to the basement in two days."

He faced Lars. "What was the name of the woman at the district attorney's office?"

"Which woman?"

"The friend of the Realtor."

Lars hesitated. "I don't . . . maybe Sylvia. Yes. Sylvia Potok."

"I need her address," Roth said.

28

Ruth's first moment of redemption came when she stepped through the door to Braun's house on the hill.

She'd been here at least a dozen times, and always she was greeted with a coy smirk, a look that said, *Aren't you fortunate to be in my presence?* Tonight, the commandant stood by his dinner table, dressed in full dashing uniform, and his look went from coy to shocked in the space of two seconds. Ruth took a tiny measure of comfort in his surprise.

The guard shut the door behind her, and she faced Braun with as much courage as she could muster. Bitterness and fury had marched her up the hill, but now, looking at him blinking in his silly uniform, she felt more ill than angry.

"What are you doing here?" he demanded. His eyes shifted to the red scarf hanging from her arm. "I didn't send for you."

"You sent for a woman who is pregnant. Of course you would. Why waste a rope on one when you can hang two with the same rope?"

He stared at her, unmoving. "You think this is a joke?"

"Is it?"

Behind him, the table was set with two place settings of Dutch china, crystal glasses, white serviettes rolled in silver rings, and a single red rose.

Braun walked around the table, fingers dragging lightly on the silk tablecloth. "I sent for Martha, not you. There has been a mistake. I'll send a guard—"

"I took the scarf." She said it with her usual confidence, as if her visit was just another contest of wills. But she knew this one was different.

"You don't have the right." His face darkened. "I sent for Martha."

"You insist on your sacrificial lambs. What kind of sacrifice does an unwilling victim make? I'm here willingly. Or don't you have the courage to match mine?" She walked toward the table and met his eyes. "We'll see who has more courage tonight, a small Jewish girl with a gun to her head, or a big, strapping Nazi thug."

Ruth stepped past the commandant, lifted the lid on the white porcelain dish. Steam rose, scented of chicken and celery with a touch of ginger. She paused, gripped by the incredible sensations that ran through her mind with this single, delightful odor. She hadn't smelled real food in many months, but this . . . this tantalizing scent seemed to spread right through her. And another scent—fresh bread from the kitchen. Fresh, hot, sweet. The back of her tongue tightened and immediately flooded her mouth with saliva. The rose that stood eighteen inches from her eyes was fragrant too. And it seemed redder than the roses she remembered in Slovakia. Such beauty blossoming from a stalk of thorns. The commandant said something, but she didn't hear it.

What was coming over her? All her own words of new birth and hope and passion were now, at this very moment, being tested. In a way, she was coming alive, wasn't she?

But what if it all was just talk? What if there was no true virtue or meaning in this madness of hers?

She swallowed and looked up at the commandant. "Shall we eat? It smells . . . delightful."

He glared at her, but his shock seemed to have lost its edge. "I could have you both shot for this."

"You could have had us both shot months ago. But you're tired of shooting Jews; you told me that yourself. The challenge is gone, remember? So now I give you a new challenge. Accept a sacrifice in the place of another. You may be the only one in the entire war to have done so."

"You're worthless to me like this!"

She wasn't sure what he could mean by that.

"How can you abandon your own child?" he demanded.

"How can you kill Martha's child?"

"She is a Jew!" he shouted.

"So am I!"

To Braun, the war was a game in which he played god. Anything that elevated his status moved him closer to winning. Anything that diminished that status compromised his power. The fact that the Russians were advancing three hundred miles to the east hardly mattered. His game was here, in Toruń, and in Toruń he was winning.

Ruth pulled out the chair she assumed was hers and sat.

"You really believe that I will hang you and let the others live?" Braun demanded. "That's your understanding of how I work?"

She immediately lost her appetite. It was his use of the word "others." He meant Esther and Martha and Martha's child, and she knew that he was fully capable of hanging her and then marching straight over to the barracks to murder Martha and the children. Esther would be most difficult for him, because he regarded himself as Esther's benefactor. She was his proof that he was still human, merciful.

"I expect you to honor the rules of the game," Ruth said. "You may be a murderer, but you still have honor, don't you?" It was a bold-faced lie, but she knew he believed it.

The commandant pulled out his chair, sat, crossed his legs, and studied her carefully. "You never cease to amaze me," he said. "Honestly, I don't understand you. Are you positive that you're Jewish?"

"Yes." Fear began to work its fingers into her mind. He was going along with this. She knew he would, but she expected more of a fight. Maybe a quick gunshot to her head in a fit of anger. The thought of being hanged by a rope—

"Okay, then. Have it your way. But I'll have to kill your daughter. We can't have a baby here without its mother. Maybe I'll send it to Auschwitz in a potato sack."

Ruth was suddenly moving without a clear understanding of what she was doing. She jumped to her
feet. The hot porcelain dish with the ginger chicken
was in her hands, and then she was hurling it against
the back wall. It smashed into the wood with a horrendous crash.

"No!" She knew this wasn't the way to deal with
him. For a moment, she'd taken control of the game,
but now he'd trumped her. "Don't you dare touch
her! Ever!"

He chuckled. Ruth stood, fists shaking at her
sides. Her noble sacrifice felt foolish now. She had to
control herself. For Esther's sake.

"You have the spirit of twenty men," Braun said.
"But you should know by now that you can't tell me
what I can or can't do. If I decide to kill your baby, I
will. And if I decide she goes to Auschwitz in a potato
sack, she goes. Your pathetic sacrifice means nothing."

Ruth sat hard. She took a deep breath and set her
hands, palms down, on the table. "I'm sorry. You
struck a raw nerve," she said, and then she swallowed to rid her voice of its tremor.

He was smiling, but she noticed that his upper lip
was beaded with sweat. "Understandable," he said.

"Thank you."

*Think, Ruth. Say what you came to tell him now,
before he ends this game.*

"But you shouldn't kill my daughter or Martha. In
fact, you should honor them. It follows the cleverness
of your method here. You extend hope and then dash
it. The problem with butchers like Himmler is that
they don't extend any hope. They simply take life, and

take life, and take life, until the whole mess becomes meaningless. You've said that yourself."

His smile softened. "And?"

"If after my sacrifice you kill Martha or Esther, you will crush the hope of the others completely. They'll know you no longer play by the rules. The scarf will come, and they won't care. You'll become nothing more than yet one more cog in this killing machine."

He regarded her with a long stare. The truth of her words struck her, and she hesitated, but she would say anything now to keep Esther and Martha alive.

"But if you honor them, you will flood the barracks with hope. The next time your scarf settles on one of their beds, they will be crushed. Killing the body is much easier than crushing the spirit."

"All of this at the expense of your own life?" he said.

Her stomach turned. "Yes."

"You really do love them, don't you?"

"Yes."

"I can't guarantee that they will live."

"Then you aren't as powerful as you think you are."

Braun pushed back from the table, stood, gave her a long look, and walked to the window that overlooked the compound. Abandoned to silence once again, she considered what it would feel like to be hanged by the neck. Would the world go black immediately, or would she choke to death? Would her legs jerk?

Dear God, she was abandoning her baby! Her face flushed hot and she suddenly stood. How could she do such a thing to the beautiful, innocent life she'd given birth to only ten days earlier?

No, but there was Martha and Martha's child. If Martha were standing here right now, two lives would be lost for certain. This was the only chance Martha's child had.

Braun turned from the window, face fixed in a frown. "Have it your way, then." He walked to the phone.

"Then make me a promise," Ruth said.

"You've ruined my plans for the evening," he said. "I'm not interested in giving the others hope. I had my heart set on taking Martha's. You're right about the power of hope. Desperation. Desire. I live for it. But you've disturbed me."

"Promise me that you will let them live," she said.

He picked up the field phone and spoke in a soft voice. "Now. Yes, now." He set the phone back in its cradle.

"Promise me." The tears sprang from her eyes before she knew that she was going to cry. The room swam, and she didn't know what to do. Braun watched her, then walked to a dresser and opened a drawer.

Ruth looked away and closed her eyes. She had run out of smart arguments. The guards were coming up the hill. She'd committed herself to death, and she didn't know what to do.

Except cry. She thought that crying now would be okay, because she'd already been strong enough. What did it matter if she died with tears in her eyes? No one would see except for a few guards, who had probably placed bets on how long she would jerk about on the end of the rope. Either way, she would be dead within the hour.

She let the tears stream, but she didn't make a peep. No, that was too much in front of this monster. And she wouldn't beg anymore, no matter how much she wanted to. Braun would not respond well to a begging woman.

"Look at me."

Braun stood three feet from her. In one hand he held a sharp, thin knife. In the other he held a crystal wine glass. He looked like a demon.

"I will do as you request on one condition."

A wedge of hope. She felt suffocated.

"Anything," she said. A sob. "Anything, I swear, anything."

"I will let them live, Ruth. But I need some of your blood. I want you to give me some of your blood. Willingly."

"My blood?"

"Just a small cut on your wrist."

His request made no sense.

"I need it to verify your child's bloodline."

Ruth was beyond caring about his reasoning. She believed him. And with her belief came a flood of hope unlike any she'd felt in a very long time.

She stood, trembling from head to foot. He was blurry from her tears, but she held out her arm, wrist up. "Cut me," she said. "Just save my baby. I beg you to save my baby."

He took her hand gently. Rubbed her palm with his finger, fascinated by her skin. It was the first time he had touched her. "I will. I swear I will let your baby live. And I will let you live as well."

Electricity shot through her veins. Could he mean it?

She felt the cold edge of the blade on her wrist.

"I swear you will survive this war."

He jerked the knife. The blade stung. She gasped. The cut was deeper than she had expected.

Braun twisted her wrist and watched the blood dribble into the glass beneath. His eyes were wild and his lips were parted.

Ruth felt a pang of fear.

He dropped her arm and lifted the glass to his nose. Sniffed it like a delicate flower. For a moment she thought he was going to taste it.

Braun looked at her as if suddenly realizing that she was still in the room. They exchanged stares. Then he smiled.

"There is one force in this universe that rules them all," he said. "It is the power behind war and love and life and death. It is hope. Desire. It is passion. It is what enables a mother to give her life for a child. It is what sends man on his search for God. It is what set Lucifer on his ambitious course. It is heaven and it is hell. The desires and affections of man are in the crosshairs."

She was too shocked to move.

"Like Lucifer, I have entered the fray, my dear."

A knock sounded on the door.

He lifted the glass and swirled the blood like a red wine. Then Gerhard Braun lifted the glass to his lips, tilted it back, and drank it to the last drop. When he lowered his arm, his eyes were closed, his breathing ragged, his lips red.

The blood drained from Ruth's head. "You made a promise . . ."

The door opened.

"Which I have no intention of keeping," Braun said. He set the glass on the table. "Hang her. Now."

Boots clumped.

Ruth's throat had frozen shut with horror. They pulled a black bag over her head and quickly bound her arms behind her back. She gave in to their handling completely.

They pushed her forward, down the stairs she'd climbed so many times. Maybe he would let Esther live. Maybe hanging her would be enough for him.

Father, give my baby hope!

She blinked in the pitch darkness and tried to push the picture of the front gate from her mind. The musty cloth pressed into her nostrils. Did they force this same cloth over all of their victims' heads? She imagined the other women who'd taken this walk, how they must have felt all alone in complete darkness, certain only that their lives were about to end. Did they cry? Was it dried tears that she smelled?

Her breathing quickened.

"Step up!"

She stepped up—a chair or a crate. She could feel the rope as they worked it over her head. The adrenaline came in waves, hot to her skin, slicing through her nerves like a million tiny razor blades, each one urging her to run, run away. But there was nowhere to run.

"Dear God in heaven, I beg you to save the children."

Whoever was working on the rope paused for moment, and then cinched it tight.

"Don't let my death be in vain. Save the children."

Her voice rose in pitch and in volume. "Give them love and hope."

---———---

MARTHA AWOKE before dawn, disorientated in the dark. A baby lay against her belly.

Ruth's baby.

Ruth!

Dread swept through her chest and she moaned. She could look now if she wanted to. She could climb out of bed, sneak over to the window and have a clear view of the gate to Toruń.

But she couldn't.

She lay still for ten minutes before the need to know compelled her to throw off the covers and hurry for the window. She would have to be strong now; the babies depended on her alone. Part of being strong was facing the truth. Knowing. She had to know.

She edged her head into the window slowly.

Then she knew.

The body hung in silence a hundred yards away. There was a black hood over Ruth's head. Her arms and legs hung limply. So innocent and still there across the yard.

Martha clenched her jaw and swallowed the knot in her throat. No more crying. She now had one objective only. Keep the babies alive. Nothing else mattered. Her life mattered only because the children needed her to survive. The war's end mattered only because such an end would set the children free.

The price that had been paid for the child in her
womb demanded her unfailing devotion.

Martha stared at Ruth's body and vowed to live so
that Ruth's death would not be in vain.

29

STEPHEN DREAMED OF LEECHES CRAWLING through his toes and woke to find the dog licking his bare feet. Brandy matched his stare, whined, and crept up the bed to nuzzle his neck before lying down beside him.

It was the most touching moment in Stephen's recent memory. The dog had returned. He was loved. The world had not ended, despite his conclusion of several hours past.

He drifted back into an exhausted sleep—three days without a decent nap had worn him onionskin thin. He'd gone up to the giant, he'd fought with all of his strength, and he'd been sent home packing. Goliath had not fallen.

Someone shook him. Goliath was mocking him, egging him on for a fifth round.

"Stephen."

Goliath knew his name.

"Wake up, dude."

Stephen jerked up. "What?" Brandy lay across the

room on Melissa's lap. Sweeney sat cross-legged beside his bed.

"What's up?"

"Sorry to wake you from such a blissful sleep, but I have something I think we should talk about."

Stephen sat up, groggy. "What's up?"

"I just told you what's up."

"I mean, what do you want to talk about? What time is it?"

"It's time to face the dragon, baby." Sweeney grinned.

What was this guy talking about? This was the problem with bohemians—they were too idealistic to be useful. Poetry was fine, but you couldn't wear it, eat it, or sleep in it.

He wanted to reach out and slap the man for waking him.

"How much is it worth to you to get into that building?" Sweeney asked.

"What do you mean?"

"I mean, how much would you pay?"

Stephen sat up, suddenly awake. "Could you get in?"

"Maybe. Depends. But let's say I did have a way in. I mean, an absolutely guaranteed way in. What would it be worth to you?"

"Just tell me if you have a way in!"

"You think I'd wake you up from such serenity to toss around esoteric hypotheticals?"

"I doubt it's beyond you."

"See, there you go, hurting my feelings again. Just go with me, baby. Give me a figure."

"Okay. A thousand dollars."

Sweeney looked long and hard. "That's it? This whole thing is only worth a thousand dollars to you?"

"You have a thousand dollars now?" Stephen asked.

"I don't want a thousand dollars now."

"So why are you asking?"

Sweeney waved a hand. "Forget it, man. I don't know how to get into the building anyway."

"What do you mean, you don't have a way in? You just sat there and told me you did!"

"What does it matter—it's hardly worth a thing to you, right? A thousand bucks—please, man."

"Okay, ten thousand," Stephen said.

"I have a way in, you know. I really do." Sweeney grinned. "But I was under the impression that this thing really meant a lot to you. I'm hearing numbers like a thousand and ten thousand, and I'm thinking that I was wrong."

Sweeney wasn't bluffing, was he? He actually might have a way in. Stephen scrambled to his knees. "You get me in there, and I'll pay you whatever you want."

Sweeney looked over at Melissa, who was watching quietly. "Hear that, babe? Now we're getting somewhere. But that's not the way it works, Groovy. I need to know what it's worth to *you*. It's not what I want that matters here. It's how much you want whatever's over there that matters. How much will you pay?"

"Twenty thousand."

Sweeney just stared at him.

"Fifty thousand—if you get me in."

"Not enough."

"For crying out loud, then! How much *is* enough?"

"Your desire's bigger than that, Groovy. I've seen it in your eyes. You would sell your soul for whatever's in that building."

Stephen settled to his haunches and looked at the smiling bohemian. A bright moon hung in the window. The traffic from La Brea hummed faintly, even though the sun wasn't up.

"You're asking me what I'll pay you, not what it's worth," he said.

"They're synonymous. You'll pay whatever it's worth. It's worth what you'll pay for it. What price are you willing to pay for this obsession of yours? That's what I want to know."

Stephen looked up at Ruth's picture. The moon cast a soft hue over her face.

"That's an unfair question."

"So few are really willing to put their money where their mouths are, isn't that the truth? That's what sets the greatest apart. Gandhi. Jesus. They gave their lives. All I'm asking for is money."

Stephen wasn't sure if he wanted to hit the man or cry on his shoulder. He had promised Dan Stiller five hundred thousand. He'd spent a hundred on Sparks. He had two hundred to spare.

"A hundred thousand," he said.

"Not enough. Guaranteed access to the building."

"Two hundred."

Sweeney hesitated. "That's it? You would walk away from here if it cost you more?"

"No! I didn't say that!"

"Then stop messing around!" Sweeney yelled.

His fury startled Stephen. Tears welled in his eyes.

"Put your gut into it, man!"

"Five hundred!" Stephen cried. Dan would have to forgive him.

"Stop it, Sweeney!" Melissa said. "That's enough. You're torturing him!"

"This is exactly what he needs. It's what we all need." He reached out and rubbed Stephen on the shoulder. "You did well, my man. You did well."

The man stood up and walked to the window. "How will you pay me?"

Stephen cleared his throat. "You're serious?"

"As a heart attack."

"How do you want it?"

"Cash?"

"The bank doesn't like to give me cash, but I think I can arrange it."

"Just curious—how much money do you have in the bank?"

"Seven hundred thousand."

"See, that leaves you with two hundred thousand. Minus expenses."

"Expenses?"

"We'll need some equipment. Shouldn't cost more than a few thousand. I want twenty thousand in cash, and the rest in a cashier's check made out to the charity of your choice."

"What?" Stephen rose slowly to his feet.

Sweeney shrugged. "I don't really have use for money. Twenty thousand will keep me for a couple of years, high on the hog."

"Then why—" He looked at Melissa; she was smiling.

"You're paying every dime, my friend. If this is worth five hundred thousand, then someone's gonna pay five hundred thousand, and that someone is you. Let's just say I'm legitimizing your desire. Either you'll pay, or you won't. And there's one more thing. You pay even if you don't find what you're looking for. I get you in, that's all."

"But you have to guarantee me access."

"If I can't get you in, I'll tear up the check."

An image of the floor safe with the tin box sitting inside filled Stephen's mind. "Okay, when do we go? How's this work? Can you show me now?"

"First things first. I need the money."

"No, I don't think you get it. We can't wait! I'll get your money, I swear, but the people over there are after the same thing I am. They're tearing down the walls as we speak. For all I know, they might already have it! We have to move."

"This isn't an overnight thing," Sweeney said, eyebrow cocked.

"How long?"

"Two days. Maybe longer. Depends."

"Two days? Come on!"

"Two days. At least."

Stephen paced. "Then we have to start now. I'll get you a check as soon as the bank opens. I'll bump the amount to forty thousand if you'll show me now."

Sweeney looked at Melissa. "Okay. You can keep the extra dough, but you renege, and I go to the police and expose what you're doing down here."

"I'm not going to renege," Stephen said firmly.

Sweeney's eyes twinkled like an excited child's. "You wanna see?"

"Yes! Yes, I want to see!"

"Come on."

———~~~———

THEY HURRIED down the three flights of stairs to the ground floor in near darkness. "Wait here," Sweeney instructed. He returned thirty seconds later holding a makeshift torch. "We'll need light down there," he said.

"Down? I have a flashlight in my bag upstairs," Stephen said.

"Too small." He struck a match and set rags ablaze. Flames licked at the cloth and filled the stairwell with dancing light. "Besides, this is much more exciting, don't you think? Come on!"

He flew down the basement stairs, leading a ribbon of oily smoke. "This building was planned in tandem with the other one," Sweeney said, pushing into the basement. "Same basic layout, same foundation, same utilities. If you ask me, they're both trash, but they haven't caved in yet; I guess that's all some people want."

Stephen recalled that Sweeney studied architecture at UCLA. Stephen's blood pressure surged. They'd entered a basement almost identical to Rachel's. He stopped, fixed on one of the doors directly opposite the stairs.

That was the boiler room. The rest of the basement suddenly faded. Sweeney was saying something, but it sounded distant. They were actually in the basement! This was his mother's basement, and that was the boiler room, and in there was the safe!

Stephen tore for the room, slammed into the door, gripped the knob and yanked it open. Dark.

"Hurry!"

"Stephen—"

"Bring the light!" He motioned frantically and stepped in.

Flame light spread into the room from behind. "What is it?" Melissa asked.

Stephen blinked. No drums. The Germans—

"You see something?" Sweeney asked.

"I . . ." The door was missing from the boiler room. The water heater had been ripped out. "Is this the same?" No, of course it wasn't. What was he thinking? This was the boiler room in Building B. A mixture of relief and disappointment washed over him. "Boy. For a moment there I thought this was Rachel's."

He faced Sweeney and Melissa. Brandy trotted into the room, tested the air with a raised nose. All three looked at Stephen.

"It's in the boiler room?" Sweeney asked. "What you want is in the boiler room across the street?"

No use denying what he'd made painfully obvious. "Yeah. I'm sorry, I just kinda flipped out."

"Boy, are you going to love me," Sweeney said with a big smile.

"Why?"

"I said I could get you into the building. What I didn't tell you was that I could get you into the basement."

"You mean just the basement?"

"You'll see. Come on." He turned, walked out, and stopped in the middle of the basement as if undecided where to lead them next.

"By the way, just out of curiosity"—Sweeney faced him—"I know this thing of yours is a closely guarded secret, but so is what I'm about to show you. So first, what exactly are you after over there?"

A compulsion to tell them surprised Stephen. "A box," he said. Surely, anyone who wanted to donate four hundred eighty thousand dollars to a charity wasn't the kind who would steal to feed their greed.

"And what's in the box? Just curious. Are we talking the Ring here? My precious?"

Stephen stared at Sweeney and then at Melissa. He liked them. He liked these two people very much—at this moment, maybe more than he had ever liked anybody his entire life. That was strange, considering the fact that he hardly knew them. The sentiment choked him up a little and he just stared at them, swimming in this fondness.

"You okay?" Melissa asked.

He nodded. "You guys are pretty neat, you know."

She walked over and rubbed his back. "We think you're neat too. That's why we want to help you. We weren't going to ask for money—that was Sweeney's idea." She flashed Sweeney a glare. "He insisted it would make the whole experience more rewarding for you."

"And it will," Sweeney said. "You're feeling it already, aren't you, Groovy? The more you pay for the diamond, the more you love it. I can feel a whole lot of love in this room right now. You understand what I'm saying?"

Stephen nodded. He wanted to hug them both. "To be honest, I don't know for certain what's in the box," he said. "But I'm sure it came from Nazi Germany, and I know it belongs to a girl named Esther, the daughter of the woman in the picture upstairs. If she's alive."

"Oh, how sweet," Melissa said, rubbing his back again. "You're doing this for love."

"What's in it could be worth a hundred million dollars," Stephen said, but saying it to these two, the detail seemed insignificant. Silly.

Still, the added detail earned him a moment of silence.

"Even so," Melissa said, "you're doing this for love. I can see it in your eyes." She walked over to Sweeney. "All this talk is making my knees weak, baby."

He took her under one arm and kissed her on the lips. "Love, baby. It's all about love."

They looked over at Stephen, smiling like two jack-o'-lanterns. He let out a short sob-laugh, the kind that mothers cry at weddings, the kind of sound he'd once sworn only a woman could make.

"Ready, Groovy? We don't have all night. I'd hate to get caught down there with a burned-out torch."

"I was born ready."

Sweeney winked and walked for a door. They were in a dingy basement in the middle of the night, headed wherever "down there" was, talking gushy and conquering the world. Sweeney was going to march him into the basement, right to the safe.

They entered a room blackened by coal.

Sweeney had said that it would take two days, but that was because he'd wanted the money up front. Without that caveat to hold them up, they would probably have the box by daybreak.

"What's this?" Stephen asked, looking around.

"This is it, man."

Black lumps lay scattered on the floor or stacked in small piles. "The coal room."

Sweeney walked to one end and kicked at the floor. "No. just watch."

Stephen hurried over. "What?"

"Hold this, honey." Sweeney handed the torch to Melissa, dropped to one knee, and yanked on a steel lid. The metal slab slid free with a loud grate and a clang. A two-foot black hole gaped in the floor.

"I give you a drain," Sweeney said proudly, hand extended in majestic presentation.

"A drain?" Stephen looked up. "Where does this lead?"

"Follow me."

Sweeney plopped to his seat, swung his legs into the hole, mounted what Stephen could now see were iron rungs, and climbed down. "You might want to roll up your pants," he called. "It's a bit wet down here." The announcement was followed by a splash.

Stephen stood in dumbfounded stillness. The dog barked, and he flinched.

"It's okay, puppy," Melissa said, rubbing the dog's head. She turned to Stephen and gave the light to him. "Hand this to me when I get set."

Stephen handed her the torch when she was

halfway in and stared down at the glowing hole. There was definitely water in there.

"Come on, dude! We don't have all night."

He thought about rolling up his pants, but neither of them had, so he crawled in after them. Brandy stuck her head into the drain and whined, but she made no attempt to take the plunge.

"Hold on, girl; we'll be back."

Stephen lowered himself gingerly into the sewer drain and turned to face Sweeney and Melissa. The concrete tunnel ran past them into darkness—round, about six feet in diameter. Brown slime covered the walls. He looked down at his feet, but they weren't visible in the murky water. Or whatever it was.

"Don't worry, the city has upgraded," Sweeney said. "This drain isn't in use. They moved the street twenty years ago when they rezoned the neighborhood to accommodate the hordes of people who wanted to live by the sea in bliss. Part of the drain was rerouted, but this section was just cut off. This manhole is the only service entrance. Code. You can't have a drain that's inaccessible, even if it's out of use. A piece of bureaucratic brilliance hard at work."

"How do you know all this? This is the only entrance?"

"I designed two buildings to replace these two as part of an assignment for a design class. So you see, this building has sentimental value to me. I'm not here by accident. I chose it."

"But there's only one manhole?"

"It's all that's left of the old sewer system. Come on, let me show you."

Sweeney turned and plowed up the drain, bent slightly to keep the slime out of his hair. Stephen slogged after them. His mind was still suspended between the romance of their moment up on dry ground and the less-appealing sogginess here. There had to be another service entrance that led up into Rachel Spritzer's apartment.

"Ladies and gentlemen, we have arrived." Sweeney spun around and spread his arms.

"Where?" Stephen looked up. Nothing but slime. "What is it?"

"Another drain," Sweeney said, shoving the torch to his left. A round hole no more than eight inches in diameter exited the side of the sewer.

Stephen looked at the hole, glanced back at a smiling Sweeney, and stared at the hole again, hoping this was not Sweeney's answer. His mind fell free of any romantic threads that had kept it in suspension.

"What's this? It's a hole," he said.

"Well said. A hole that leads into the basement of Rachel Spritzer's apartment."

"But it's tiny. I don't see—"

"It's tiny now." Sweeney had not lost his smile. "When we're done with it, it'll be big."

"How?"

Sweeney lifted up his forefinger. "One word, my bohemian understudy. Jackhammer. Or is that two words?"

"Jackhammer."

"Hammer by Jack. Exactly."

"You're telling me that I just shelled out five

hundred thousand dollars for you to point out a tiny hole that you expect me to take a jackhammer to?"

Sweeney's smile faded. He lowered his finger. "It's more than a tiny hole. It's the sewer. It's a way into the basement! It's love and passion and the pot at the end of your rainbow."

"It's crazy!" Stephen's voice echoed down the tunnel.

"What did you expect, Groovy? A rocket ride? I said two days."

"No, I didn't expect a rocket ride, although for five hundred thousand maybe I should have. You think we're dealing with idiots up there? You saw how they sent those soldiers packing. The sound of a jackhammer pounding away down here will echo up every drain in the building. Every sink, every toilet, every shower, booming like machine guns. And even if they are deaf, the whole building could fall in on us!"

Sweeney stared at him in silence, smile gone.

"I told you he might not dig it," Melissa said. "No pun intended."

"This can work, man," Sweeney said. "Where's your suck-it-up, I-gotta-have-it-at-any-cost desperation? I *know* these buildings. There's only seven feet of earth and some concrete between us and where that drain takes a turn for the boiler room. That turn is buried in twelve inches of foundation directly below the coal room. I'll admit, there are a few challenges—like the sound thing—but five hundred thousand dollars says that won't stop us."

Stephen ran a hand through his hair and slopped through the muck in a half circle. Maybe he had expected a rocket ride and maybe he was overreacting to the disappointment. He wanted the safe, and he wanted it tonight.

"How do we deal with the sound?"

"Baffles."

"Brilliant. Baffles," he said cynically. "Why don't we tie some earplugs to a rock and throw it through one of their windows? Who wouldn't turn down a free set of earplugs?"

Melissa giggled. Sweeney looked hurt.

"Sorry," Stephen said. "I . . . I just wasn't expecting this." He stared at the hole. Seven feet. He'd never operated a jackhammer, but surely it could cut its way through seven feet in a day, depending on how much concrete they ran into. Maybe they could baffle the drain. Maybe with all their own hammering, the Germans wouldn't hear. And if they did, they might have trouble identifying the source. Or they could be distracted.

The idea began to take root. Imagine breaking in through the bottom of the safe itself. Like breaking into Fort Knox and taking a hundred million dollars' worth of bullion, only this would be legal. At least the taking part would be legal. The breaking-in part could be a problem.

Stephen grunted.

"I'm telling you, Groovy. This is a lot smarter than going in dressed as a woman."

"You know about that?"

Sweeney winked. "You looked marvelous, although I'll admit it was a bit dark and we were a ways down the street. We saw your exit. The Vega gave you away."

"You know my car?"

"Melissa figured that one out."

"Man. You think anyone else saw me?"

"If they did, they couldn't have put it all together. Your secret's safe with us."

Stephen stared at the hole. This idea might actually be the smartest thing he'd tried yet, though that didn't necessarily put it in the brilliant category. He leaned over and peered into the hole. Couldn't see the end.

"Seven feet. Man, wouldn't that be something if we pulled it off. Come up under them like that. Ha!"

"I said I could get you into the building, and I can. That much we definitely will pull off. Whether or not they will be standing over the hole with guns is another issue altogether."

It could work. Stephen stroked the stubble on his chin. It really could. In fact, in its own way, it *was* brilliant. Braun would *never* expect it.

"Okay," Stephen said, turning from the small drain. Nervous anticipation swept through his nerves. "How do we get power down here?"

"Groovy," Sweeney said.

30

Los Angeles
July 24, 1973
Tuesday Afternoon

ELECTRIC JACKHAMMERS DON'T FALL OUT OF the sky upon request. This is what Stephen learned Tuesday morning.

Nor do cashier's checks for four hundred eighty thousand dollars, but the fact that Stephen had the bank make it out to the Los Angeles Museum of the Holocaust seemed to earn him some respect. "I'm having a stellar year," he told them. "I need the tax break this donation will give me." Donating such a large sum to the same museum his mother had selected seemed fitting.

He walked out at nine thirty with thirty thousand in cash—twenty for Sweeney, ten for operating expenses—and the cashier's check, to be sent posthaste to the museum.

The jackhammer, on the other hand, proved more difficult. They weren't available at the local five-and-dime, and the only rental company that had an electric one ready to go was all the way out in Riverside. By the time Stephen finally made it to the shop, rented the beast, and returned home, noon bells were ringing.

Half a day and they hadn't even started. Meanwhile, Braun was tearing through the walls next door.

Stephen parked in the alley behind the abandoned building and climbed out. Sweeney approached and threw open the back door.

"You get it?"

"Got it. The manager assured me it would cut through concrete like butter. You get the extension cords?"

"Ready to go, man. Lights blazing, just waiting on you."

Stephen popped the trunk, and they gazed upon the mammoth rig together. Bold black letters that had once read "Sledge Master" were worn thin in some spots and off in others. Streaks of crusted tar ran down one side. The bit looked as though it had eaten one too many nails.

"He said the gas one would be better 'cause it's heavier," Stephen said.

"He doesn't know that we're digging up, not down—carburetor wouldn't work at that angle. Besides, without ventilation, the exhaust would kill us."

"You sure we have enough power?"

"I blew a fuse not three minutes ago testing it. Sparky's live. Let me give you a hand with this."

They hauled the tool out of the trunk, each on one end. "You have any idea how this works?" Sweeney asked, squinting in the noon sun.

"No. Don't you?"

"Seems awful heavy. I can't imagine what the gas one must weigh."

"But you do know how these work, right?"

"What I do know is that we're standing still, and my arms are about to drop off. It vibrates, right?" He chuckled. "Just pulling your leg, man. I could operate this monster in my sleep."

"This isn't funny, Sweeney!" Stephen felt a trickle of desperation leak into his mind. What if it didn't work? He stumbled backward for the door and stepped through. "Just how many times have you worked one of these?"

"Awake or in my sleep?"

Stephen stopped. "You're kidding, right?"

"Relax, dude. How hard can it be? We plug it in and chop away."

The desperation swept in like a wave. "If this doesn't work, I swear I'm going to strangle you."

"Watch the steps."

They struggled down the stairs, into the basement, and into the coal room. Both were sweating steadily by the time they set down the jackhammer.

Melissa scrambled up the ladder and stuck out her head. "You get it? Wow, that thing's huge!"

"Get the rope, honey."

She came back up with a coil of rope, which they tied around the handle. "I'll guide it from below," she said.

"Not a chance. This thing drops, and it'll crush you like a ripe tomato," Sweeney said.

"And we're supposed to dig up with it?" Stephen asked.

"Have faith."

They were doomed.

They managed to lower the jackhammer into the

hole and lug it up the tunnel, which Sweeney had strung with several lights while he was gone. Stephen felt his frustration grow with each step. "I swear, Sweeney. There's no way this is going to work. Maybe I should let you do this while I try something else."

"Something else like what?"

"I don't know, but we're running out of time."

"Did I ever tell you I graduated from UCLA with honors?"

"Meaning what?"

"Meaning I'm not an idiot."

They came to the hole, and Stephen looked up at a contraption that hung from the sewer's ceiling.

"What's that?"

"That's my genius at work." They propped the jackhammer against the wall.

Stephen examined Sweeney's creation. The rig was pieced together with ropes, pulleys, and springs, all anchored into the concrete above by three large screws. It looked like a huge spider dangling from a web.

"I'm not a mechanical engineer, but I did take several engineering classes," Sweeney said. "The way I figure it, those three anchor bolts I've secured into the concrete will hold a hundred pounds without a problem. Maybe twice that. But we'll have a lot of vibration, and the last thing we need is for the whole thing to come crashing down with one of us under it."

"Ripe tomato."

"Exactly. The beast will hang on two ropes that pass through these pulleys and then attach to this spring, which will absorb most of the vibration. Presto. In my sleep."

A grin crept across Stephen's face.

"And you doubted me," Sweeney said.

"Okay. Never again. Let's try it."

"First, we try the jackhammer."

The extension cord was strung from the ceiling with the lights. Melissa plugged the jackhammer in and eyed them. "Who goes first?"

"I will," Stephen said, stepping forward. His confidence was making a comeback. He dragged the machine upright and examined the two levers, one right, one left. Seemed simple enough. A single knob switched the power on. This done, he stood the jackhammer at an angle in the water, braced himself, and pulled the right-hand lever.

Nothing.

Panicked, he grabbed the left-hand lever.

An awful scream filled the tunnel, and the jackhammer started to jump. The power was fierce, like a bull desperate to buck its rider. Stephen hung on for dear life. The beast bounced away from him, jerking madly down the slippery floor.

Sweeney was yelling something, but the noise swallowed his words. Didn't matter, Stephen knew what he should do. He should let go. But if he let go, the whole machine might fall down, land in the water, and fry its circuits.

It was quick thinking, not panic, that made Stephen hang on to the jackhammer gone berserk. He slipped and splashed in a scramble to keep up with the apparatus, which continued to race away from him.

It died suddenly, and he nearly overran it. Shrieking laughter echoed down the tunnel from behind. He spun and saw that the cord had come unplugged.

"Quiet!" he yelled.

Melissa lifted a hand over her mouth. "I'm sorry, it's just . . . my goodness."

"They'll hear us!" Stephen yelled.

Of course, that was ridiculous. They were about to pound a hole up their noses with a machine that screamed like a banshee. A little laughter was nothing.

Stephen suddenly began to cackle. Melissa removed her hand and laughed out loud. Sweeney howled. For a solid minute, they were incapacitated with relentless laughter in the bowels of the earth.

"It works," Stephen finally said.

This sent Melissa off again, so much so that Stephen and Sweeney both eventually suggested she'd laughed enough. What would they do if she had a hernia down here? Call an ambulance?

It took them another twenty minutes to hoist the jackhammer into place and fill the pipe with as much insulation as they could stuff up it. The baffling wouldn't stop noise from traveling through the ground, but at least it wouldn't pound through the pipes.

They still had one major test. The hammer was designed to operate with gravity doing the hard labor, like a sledgehammer. Pound at a rock hard enough and long enough, and it would break down. But with the weight now suspended from the ceiling, and only Stephen's or Sweeney's strength to bear on the hammer, would the device exert enough force to break up the concrete?

"Ready?"

"Go for it," Sweeney said.

Stephen braced his lower body against the wall behind him, leaned into the jackhammer, and pulled the lever. The tunnel filled with that awful scream and the machine pounded furiously. Stephen had to clench his jaw to keep his teeth from clacking.

"Come on, baby!" he grunted.

First a chip. Then a tiny chunk. Then a very small slab dislodged and splashed into the water. Stephen let up on the lever. His ears rang. All three stared at the damage. It wasn't much, but it was something.

"Yeehaa!" Sweeney bellowed. "Am I a genius, or am I a genius?"

"I need earplugs," Stephen said.

Sweeney grabbed some insulation, tore off a piece, and stuffed it into his ears. Thirty seconds later, they all had pink fuzzballs sticking from their ears. Stephen pulled on the gloves Sweeney had purchased with the rest of the supplies, and set himself up again.

"Ready?"

"I am," Stephen said and pulled the lever.

The progress was slow, and he had to swap out with Sweeney every ten minutes to realign his jarred bones, but slowly the jackhammer chipped away a two-foot circle of concrete around the small drainpipe. Melissa periodically went up to the fourth floor to see if the Germans were peering out the windows or putting their ears to the sidewalk, seeking the source of any noise they heard. The afternoon passed without any sign of them.

The first foot took ten minutes—nothing but gravel packing.

The next foot took three hours.

Stephen let off the lever and squatted, exhausted. His sopped shirt clung to his chest. He pulled off the goggles and painter's mask Sweeney had insisted they wear, and looked up at the hole. Maybe fourteen inches. They'd cut through the sewer wall and were into some rock.

"We're not going to make it," he said.

Sweeney looked into the hole. "Sure we are."

"You're the genius; do the math. You said seven feet."

"If I remember right. Could have been nine."

"Seven times three is twenty-one hours of straight digging. I don't think I can last that long. And I doubt the hammer will either. I think it's already slowing down."

"Not a chance. We'll have to start letting it cool down every now and then, but—"

"And there's another problem. You said the last foot would be solid concrete. Even if we get that far, the last bit will be three hours of straight banging on the foundation. The whole building will echo like a gong."

"Not necessarily."

"Necessarily."

"You're way too moody, man. Have I let you down yet? I told you I could get you in, and I intend to."

The likely outcome of his situation suddenly struck Stephen. He was in a drainpipe under an apartment complex, digging his way into the basement to break into a safe. San Quentin was full of people who'd executed far better plans.

"Okay, here's the truth," Sweeney said. "The digging will get much easier as soon as we hit the gravel base. These buildings are set on footers that run deep, but here in the center it's all gravel, designed to give with the earthquakes. Digging through the gravel will be quiet, but you're right about the noise when we hit the concrete. We'll have to set up a distraction."

"A distraction."

"You're repeating me. Once we break through, you nab the box and we immediately fill the hole with quick-setting concrete. No one ever knows we were even in there."

Stephen was surprised by Sweeney's forethought. He stood up. "You can do that with quick-set? How long will it take to dry?"

"Couple hours. Won't matter, we'll scatter coal over it—unless someone sweeps the room within a couple of hours, we're home free." He grinned. "See?"

"They have dogs in the garage."

"I'm not sure the dogs survived your friends."

"Okay." Stephen paced. His body quivered, and he doubted it had anything to do with the jackhammer. "This could really work."

"Of course. That's why we're doing it. Why don't you catch a couple hours of sleep? We may be in there by noon tomorrow, and we're definitely going to need you awake."

"Noon, huh?" He could hardly stand the wait. "Why can't we press through tonight? If the gravel is that easy, we could be in by morning!"

"Maybe, but we can't start beating on their floor in

the middle of the night when the whole world's asleep. They'll hear us for sure. We need a distraction."

"You could blast music from the sidewalk. You know, just a couple of hippies playing their music too loud."

"I don't have a stereo."

"I'll buy you one."

"Not loud enough."

"You want louder?"

"You want a ring of guys with guns standing over the hole when we come out?"

Stephen paced again. This one small problem could be a spoiler. Maybe he could call Sparks and ask his boys to create a distraction. Not a chance.

Another idea dropped into his mind, a gift from the God who favored the oppressed. He stopped and turned slowly to Sweeney.

"I've got it."

31

THE BOY WAS CLOSE. STEPHEN WAS VERY CLOSE.
This might be Roth's last night of hunting.
Tonight he would plan a special surprise for Stephen.
He'd decided that the friend named Sylvia would be
his next victim. She wasn't exactly a blood relative of
Stephen's, but she was a Jew and she was a woman.

He'd considered killing the old man and spent two
hours watching Chaim Leveler's house earlier that
evening. But breaking protocol could adversely affect
the cosmic order of power, so he rejected the idea.

Few people understood that the powers of the air
were carefully balanced and even the slightest
change could upset this perfection. Rituals had to be
performed with precision. If you decided to harvest
the souls of Jews, but then switched to Russians, for
example, you might lose all of the benefit derived
from taking Jews.

This was Gerhard's downfall. He'd broken the
rules of his own ritual by allowing Martha and the
children to live after selecting them with the scarf.

As a result he'd lost all of his power. A single

decision made in a moment of weakness had robbed him of power. Now the only way to restore that power was to kill those who should have been killed in the first place. Gerhard would be vindicated. His power restored.

Then Roth could take that power and kill him.

Roth's present indulgences, on the other hand, weren't a matter of precision. He was simply adding to his pleasure. He was showing the powers of the air that he was the kind of vessel that deserved the might they would pour into him when it was all over, in a matter of days now.

Then again, he could use the woman Sylvia as a pawn against the Stephen. Yes, yes, he could do that. Roth smiled, pleased with himself for thinking so broadly about the challenges that lay before him.

He parked the car in the alley behind her apartment complex. He'd killed eight women since coming to Los Angeles. Eight in six nights. He would decide when he saw her whether she would be the ninth. A part of him was tempted to delay killing so that when he took Stephen, his thirst for blood would be ripe.

Another interesting thought.

Roth pulled out another red silk scarf and pressed it to his nose as he always did. Inhaled. He draped it over his neck and tucked it into his shirt. If anyone saw him strolling the alley with a red scarf, they might connect him immediately to the other killings, and the thought excited him.

He wouldn't be caught, naturally. He might have to change his plans for the night, but they would never catch him.

Roth pulled his black gloves on and stepped into the dark alley.

———

SYLVIA HAD spent the evening as she had spent the last three evenings—returning to her apartment late from work, eating a meat-loaf TV dinner and talking to Chaim about Stephen and the Red Scarf Killer, as they were calling him, before retiring at about eleven.

Chaim had left five messages and then called her from a hotel. He was nearly frantic about something Stephen had told him about danger. And he'd seen a black car parked down his street, so he'd packed up and moved into a hotel room for the night.

Sylvia's first response was one of alarm. The rabbi was overreacting. Stephen was a grown adult, not a child.

If anyone had something to be concerned about, it was Sylvia, she said. The killer was still selecting only single Jewish women. He'd upped his nightly quotient to two.

"Then you must come, Sylvia! Spend the night here with me."

"In the Howard Johnson's?"

"In another room, of course. I insist."

"Please, Rabbi. You're taking all of this too far. What is the likelihood that I would be selected by a serial killer in a city this size? He's never broken into an apartment. I have neighbors on all sides here. And I lock my doors with dead bolts."

"Then come for my benefit. Maybe I am overreacting, but that doesn't change the fact that I'm frightened."

She'd spoken to him for nearly half an hour, and when she finally hung up she wondered if her refusal to go was insensitive. She peered out of her window, but saw nothing but an empty alley and the glow of distant city lights.

The one-bedroom apartment was silent. Kitchen with breakfast bar to her right. Bedroom to her left. What if the killer had sneaked in before she'd returned home?

After a moment of contemplation, she satisfied the ghosts of concern by checking the lock, the closet, even the cupboards in the kitchen.

No killer. Of course not.

She brushed her teeth, washed off her makeup, slipped into a yellow-and-blue-flowered cotton night-gown, and rolled into bed. Bathroom light, on. Kitchen light, on.

Soon thoughts of an intruder were replaced by thoughts of Chaim, wringing his hands in the Howard Johnson's. She should have gone over, she thought. At least to reassure him.

Sleep came quickly.

The first foreign sound came even more quickly. A scratch from deep inside of Sylvia's dream.

She made nothing of it, though it did wake her momentarily. The glowing clock face by her bed read almost 2:00 a.m. She'd been asleep that long?

She rolled, and pulled in her second pillow. Sleep was one of the most wonderful sensations. Blissful sleep.

The sound again. A creak this time.

In the space of two heartbeats, Sylvia's world changed from sweet dreams of sleep to blood-stopping terror. Her eyes snapped open and she caught her breath.

She could hear nothing but silence.

Don't be ridiculous. You hear a single sound and you jump out of your skin. It's nothing. Nothing . . .

"Hello, Sylvia."

The words were whispered behind her, low, so low that she wasn't absolutely sure she'd heard them.

"If you make even a very small sound, I will bury this knife in your temple. Can you hear me?" Still whispering very low.

This time she could not mistake the words, try as she did. Someone was behind her. Someone who knew her name. Someone who had a knife.

Sylvia could not move. Her heart crashed violently. Repeatedly.

"Are you awake? You're awake. Your breathing's changed."

She could hear his heavy breathing now.

"Turn over. Let me see you."

She couldn't. *Dear God, help me!*

A cold blade touched her cheek. She clenched her eyes tight and suppressed a whimper.

"Now, now, no need to ruin things with your fear. I'm not going to kill you. Not necessarily. Unless you make noise; then I will kill you." He paused. "Roll over."

Slowly, as if rolling through thick tar, she turned. He stood tall over the bed. A black shirt, white face. Built like a bulldog with short cropped hair above grinning face.

There was a red scarf around his neck and a large silver knife in his gloved hand.

"Sit up," he said.

She sat up without thinking, because her mind was filled with other thoughts. She was going to die. She knew she was going to die because this was the same serial killer who'd killed eight single Jewish women in six nights.

She was a single Jewish woman and it was the seventh night. She was going to die.

The man stood looking at her for a long time, pleased with himself—or with what he was doing, or with her, she didn't know which—but pleased.

He sat down on a chair he'd brought in from the kitchen. He'd been here that long? Maybe he'd climbed the fire escape and broken the window. But why hadn't she heard him? Maybe the neighbors had heard him and called the police already.

"So, I understand that you are a female friend of Stephen's; is that so?"

Stephen? This man knew about Stephen?

"You may speak now," the killer said. "No yelling or loud noises, but you will answer my questions."

"Stephen?" she whispered.

"Stephen Friedman, yes? The Jew. You know him?" German accent.

"Yes."

"Good. What can you tell me about him?"

This killer, for whom the whole city was looking,

was interested in Stephen? Maybe the man wasn't going to kill her.

"Then should I just kill you? If you don't answer me, I'll have no choice."

"He's a friend. He's a Realtor."

"Yes, I know. But what drives him? Is he religious?"

"He's . . . he's Jewish."

"But is he a man of faith? You know the difference, don't you? Does he put his hope in powers beyond him, or is he just another self-motivated fool who can't see beyond the night?"

The room felt cold. *You have to be strong. Think of a way out. Keep him happy. Maybe if you keep him happy, he won't kill you.*

"He's not really a man of Jewish faith," she said.

"Then maybe Christian, like the old man he lives with? Does he realize that the power of life is in the blood? That's why the Christians drink the blood of Christ. The power is always in the blood. It's why I have to cut my victims. It's why I drink their blood. Do you know this?"

"No." She had to keep him talking. He was absorbed by this train of thought, so she had to let him follow it long enough for her to think of a way out of this madness.

"No, of course not. He isn't easily discouraged; that's good."

Stephen again.

"No."

How did this man know Stephen? A disgruntled client? A Jew-hater certainly. But why?

"Do you want to know why I'm doing it? Why I killed all of those Jews?"

She didn't, but she couldn't bring herself to say no.

"Because it makes me strong. Pure. What most Aryan purists won't tell you is that the Jews have more power than any other race—that's a spiritual matter we don't have time to go into. Hitler's solution was to eradicate them. Not a bad plan, but shortsighted. Better to take their power." He sat slightly hunched over. Unbreaking stare.

"Have you ever tasted another person's blood, Sylvia?"

"No."

"Its flavor changes with the donor's mood. Anguish, Sylvia. The greater the anguish, the sweeter the blood."

His talk made her sick. She'd recovered enough to speak in a reasonably normal voice.

"Why are you telling me all of this?"

"Because it excites me."

"Then you're a sick man," she said.

He chuckled. "You remind me of Ruth. She was a strong woman too. So strong, you Jews." He shuddered. "I'm tempted."

Tempted to kill her. Sylvia said nothing.

"I'm playing him like a mouse, Sylvia. He doesn't know, of course. He thinks that he's outwitting me. That's good; I need him to feel like he's outwitting me. It raises his hopes. But in the end I will finish what my father started."

For a long time he just looked at her. She knew she should be saying something, distracting him, stalling him. Instead she held very still and silently cried for him to leave.

She would alert the police. Stephen. Chaim. The serial killer was sitting in her room.

"What's your name?" she asked.

The killer suddenly stood. "Turn around."

She instinctively pulled her sheets tight.

"Face the wall. Now."

"You promised—"

"And if you don't do exactly as I say, I may change my promise."

She faced the wall away from him.

The sound of cloth flapped behind her. He'd pulled the scarf off of his neck and snapped it open. It whooshed over her head and then smothered her face.

She wanted to tear it free, but resisted the impulse.

His gloved hand pulled the cloth down into her mouth. He tied it tight behind her head. She could breathe through her nostrils, but her mouth was effectively gagged.

"Step off the bed."

She followed his order and stood shaking.

He jerked her arms back and bound them together with string. Then he ripped tape from a roll and strapped her wrists. Her hands felt as if they were in a plaster cast.

"Lie down on your back."

Again she did as he instructed. It took him a minute at most to tie her legs to the bedposts and her neck to the headboard. Another strap of tape went over her mouth.

He wasn't taking any chances of her escaping, but that was good, she kept telling herself. That meant he was going to let her live. She lay still and let him finish his work.

When he was done, he stood beside the bed and looked down at her. The moments stretched in a long vacuous silence. He grinned.

"Forgive me, but I've changed my mind," he said.

Then he reached down and flicked his knife across her left wrist. Pain flashed up her arm.

He'd cut her!

"Good-bye, Jew."

His fist came out of nowhere and crashed into her temple.

The room went dark.

32

EVEN FROM HER SMALL ROOM IN THE BASEMENT of the commandant's quarters, Martha could hear the faint thunder of the Russian artillery to the east. Braun had been beside himself for a week now, taken to muttering from time to time, scurrying from room to room and always to the room down the hall from her own, "the vault," as he called it, which he kept bolted and locked at all times.

Her door was closed now, but he'd stomped past not ten minutes ago, and she hadn't heard him return. He was in his vault. She sat on her bed, staring at the door, willing it to remain closed. Little Esther slept peacefully in a bundle of wool blankets behind her.

His demands had become more absurd as of late. Wash the floor, wash it again, scrub the walls, scrub them again. Scrub them again. He seemed intent on making her life as difficult as possible. She'd given birth four days after Ruth's hanging, and it was a boy after all. She named him David. The barracks had been flooded with hope, perhaps even more than after Esther's birth. See, the commandant wasn't completely evil. He had allowed Martha and Esther and now little David to live because of Ruth's sacrifice.

For five wonderful days, Martha had nursed and coddled the two babies, Esther and David, giving herself completely to the mandate before her. Save the children. At all costs, save the children.

Then a guard came and told her that she was to leave the barracks and be Braun's personal servant. She was to bring Esther. And David? No, not the boy. The boy would stay with Rachel. Bring only Esther.

She'd kissed her son and left in tears, clinging to Esther.

That night, not knowing what the commandant intended for her, Martha had served dinner to Braun and a woman, Emily, whom she recognized from one of the other barracks. Was he going to hang her in Emily's stead? What would happen to her precious David?

The commandant had dismissed Martha at the end of the meal, but she listened with her ear to the door. Emily had squealed with joy, then gasped in horror not two minutes later. What Braun could have said to cause such a reaction, Martha could hardly guess.

The woman's body hung from the gates the next morning. Then, with full view of the body out the picture window, Martha served Braun breakfast while he made his intentions for her utterly clear. She was alive only because of Ruth's sacrifice. She was to care for Esther, but under no circumstances would she be allowed to see her own child, David, even though David would also be allowed to live. He owed this to Ruth.

It was Braun's twisted method of punishment. Of extending hope while maintaining the power and will to withdraw it at any moment. *Please me here, and I will allow your son to live there.*

She'd served him for five months. Or was it six? And no, she was serving Esther, not the commandant. He beat her with his stick on occasion for not cleaning well enough or quickly enough or burning a batch of buns, but otherwise he never touched her.

His footsteps clumped back down the hall. Martha instinctively put her hand on the baby and slowed her breathing. How many nights had she imagined sneaking upstairs to Braun's bedroom and sticking a knife in his throat? If it weren't for the babies, she might have done it.

The door swung open and the commandant stood in the door frame, face drawn, collar unbuttoned and skewed. He stared at her like a man who wanted consolation. She turned her face away.

"We've received orders to evacuate the prisoners," he said.

She looked back and stood, stunned by the news.

"Those who are able to march will be gone in the hour. The weak and the sick will stay."

Why was he telling her this?

"I have been ordered to stay," he said. "You will stay as well."

Her heart hammered. "David?"

"Rachel will stay. So will your son."

If he'd said that David was going, she might have flown at him. The Russians could break through any week and liberate the camp—surely Braun knew his days as a god were numbered. By the haggard look on his face, he did know.

"Follow me," he said and turned for the stairs.

Martha checked Esther, saw that she was still sleeping, and hurried up the stairs after the commandant. He stood at the picture window overlooking the winter-locked camp. Long lines of prisoners filed through the windblown snow toward the front gate. The windchill had to be well below zero.

"How far are they going?" Martha asked.

Braun sighed. "Seventy kilometers. Let's put it this way: I am extending your life by making you stay."

The women weren't dressed for a one-kilometer march through the snow, much less seventy. They walked proudly, as if to their freedom, but half of them didn't even have coats or proper shoes. Martha doubted that this was Braun's idea, but it would have fitted his methods perfectly. Give them hope, make them think the day of their deliverance had finally arrived, then march them to their deaths.

The door to her old barracks suddenly opened, and out came a troop of women led by Golda. Golda! Martha stepped closer to the window and searched for Rachel's face. She would be the one holding a bundle, her little David. Others whom she recognized followed.

"It would have been easier to send them all to Auschwitz last month," Braun said bitterly. "I told them that. They are too concerned with covering their tracks. Now even Major Hoppe will be leaving. And who stays behind to cover their backsides?"

The last woman spilled from Martha's old barracks—no Rachel.

"It's inhuman," Martha spat. "For such a proud race, don't the Germans even know how to surrender with honor?" Her words surprised her. It was a bold accusation, something Ruth would say.

Braun only shrugged into his coat and opened the door to a blistering wind. The door slammed shut.

Where would they keep the ones who stayed behind? Maybe the commandant would allow her to see David. Maybe even to care for him!

Martha stared, enraged, at the lines of women marching steadily from the camp. But David was still alive. Esther was sleeping peacefully in the basement. They were her concern. For their sakes and for Ruth's, she couldn't allow herself to do anything stupid in her grief over these other women. Grief was useless anyway. Just because she had a warm bed and plenty of food while the rest marched to their deaths didn't mean she had the power to change any of it. She would put what little power she had into protecting the hope of David and Esther.

She turned from the window, ran down the stairs, and was about to enter her room when she noticed that the padlock to Braun's vault lay open.

Open? He never left the lock unlatched! She glanced into her room, saw that the baby hadn't moved, and stood frozen by indecision. Silence filled the house, empty except for her and Esther. Outside, five thousand women blindly marched to their deaths. What kind of courage would it take for her to step into this room and see what the commandant had hidden for so long?

In the distance, a large gun boomed like thunder.

Martha walked quickly to the door, unlatched the lock, and shoved the door open before she could stop herself. The room was dark. If Braun caught her, she would pay a dreadful price.

She found the light switch and eased it up. Twin incandescent bulbs popped to life, baring a sight that made no sense to her at first. She saw the paintings first—a dozen, maybe two—stacked against one wall. Degas, Cézanne, and Renoir—she recognized them from her father's art books. A fortune. Behind her, the house slept on.

She stepped in and glanced around. To her left stood a writing desk with neat stacks of passports, ledgers, a few books, a typewriter, and a quill pen.

The floor was littered with piles of artifacts. A suit of armor that looked very old, with a large shield and sword, the type she imagined a gladiator might wear. There were piles of china and more paintings and spears and several chests. Shelves lined two of the walls, and on the shelves, carefully sorted relics, gold and silver and bronze. An entire wall of Jewish artifacts.

Museum pieces. Spoils of war! Martha clamped her mouth shut and swallowed. Such wealth! Braun had been busy before his assignment to Toruń.

She stepped up to a shelf and lifted a gold candlestick. If she wasn't mistaken, this very piece came from a collection she'd seen in Hungary, although she couldn't remember which. How was that possible? Had he been in Hungary before coming here?

She caught sight of a small, very old mahogany box, perhaps thirty centimeters square, beside the candlestick. She found it familiar but couldn't say why. She set down the candlestick and lifted the lid. Five golden spheres lay embedded in purple velvet. They varied in size and shape, each a few centimeters in diameter, flat like river-washed stones. Each had a six-pointed star stamped on its surface.

Martha's heart nearly seized in her chest. She knew these! They were the Stones of David! Her father had known the collector, who had secured these very stones just before the war—he'd taken Martha to see them several years ago. Pure gold gilded to the five stones David had chosen to slay Goliath, they said. Over the course of history they'd gone missing for hundreds of years at a time.

She reached out and picked one of them up between her thumb and forefinger. This one Stone in her hand was worth many millions of forints, pounds, dollars—take your pick. The entire collection was worth more than her father's entire estate, he'd told her.

What if she were to slip it into her pocket? Not the entire collection, of course, just the one Stone. With all the relics in this room, Braun surely didn't inspect this box often. He might never notice.

She cupped her left hand around her right to steady it. On the other hand, these five Stones could be the most valuable artifacts in the entire collection. For all she knew, Braun inspected them every day.

She set the stone back in its velvet housing, stepped back, and gazed around, pulse throbbing. A treasure trove worth hundreds of millions. She lifted the lid to one of the trunks. Brilliant jewels. Ancient gold coins. How many museums had he raided for these? And how many of these had been confiscated from Jews? She stared at a diamond necklace with large rubies displayed in a glass case. It alone might be worth several million. And the coins?

Martha took a deep breath and let it out slowly. *What do you think you'll do? Pack all of this in a purse, grab the babies, climb over the fence, and hike to the Baltic Sea?*

She closed the box that held the Stones of David.

But one small Stone . . . What if she were to find a way to keep it in Jewish hands? The reward alone could take care of the children for a very long time.

David and Esther were the true Stones of David. Israel. The seed of Abraham. Ironic that one of the most valuable icons in Jewish history should now be in the hands of their enemy.

She was about to turn when she saw a leather book behind the box. She wasn't sure what made her pick it up and open it. It was a journal, and it contained the names of hundreds of women.

Slowly the meaning of this book came to her. What she held in her hands was a trophy of Gerhard Braun's serial killings. She wanted to throw up.

This was a record of his red-scarf game. Only it wasn't a game. It was a ritual, very different from the mass murders at other camps.

Martha replaced the journal, slipped from the vault, set the latch back exactly as she'd found it, and tiptoed to her room.

She decided then that, at the right time, she would take the journal.

And maybe one of the Stones.

33

Toruń
February 28, 1945
Night

THE WAR WAS COMING TO AN END. YOUNG Roth Braun knew that, even though the radio announcers insisted it wasn't. He knew it because he'd heard Father talking about it. The Russians were coming, Gerhard said.

Roth had been to Toruń six times since he'd first seen the woman hanging from the gate. If his mother had been more cooperative, he would have gone at least ten or twelve times, but she insisted that his spending time at a labor camp, away from her, was too risky. But with bombs falling on Berlin, her perspective changed.

Each visit had lasted a week. Once ten days, when the supply routes had been clogged by a bomb. Before each visit, he'd spend a month dreaming of what his days at the camp would be like. There were no other boys. No games, nothing to do really, except to watch the camp and dream about what Father did to the women.

There was nothing else in the world he wanted more than to serve the power, and thereby gain more power.

The Jew servant, Martha, lived in the basement with the baby, Esther, and Roth was on his third visit when he first began to think about killing the baby.

He grew more powerful every time Father let him drink the blood and chant the oaths late at night. Gerhard spoke until dawn about how many leaders in the Third Reich secretly followed Adolf Hitler in his fascination with the occult. But it was a privileged membership, a secret society, reserved for the superior even among Germans.

Roth decided on his third visit that he would be one of those superior people. He could hardly think of anything else. He was bursting at the seams to reveal his plans to his friends in Berlin, despite his promise not to tell.

He finally broke down one afternoon and told Hanz that he drank the blood of Jews when he visited the labor camp where his father was the commandant. Hanz had laughed and Roth had beaten his face with his fist. When his hand began to hurt, he grabbed a rock and pounded the boy until he stopped moving.

That night, after lying awake for two hours, still exhilarated from beating Hanz, he decided he would definitely kill Martha's baby. For one thing, she was just a Jew. For another thing, he was sure that there was more to Gerhard's ritual than drinking blood. His father was actually responsible for killing the women. That was a big part of it.

Every night until he returned to Toruń, Roth tossed and turned, dreaming of how he would sacrifice the baby and drink her blood. The fact that

Father had allowed the child to live in his house made no sense to him.

Father had told him how he'd selected Martha and her baby to be hanged, and how Ruth had taken her place. But in Roth's mind, Martha had been chosen to die. If she lived, she would be the only Jew chosen by Gerhard to actually survive.

The only Jew to outwit his father. To take back all the power that he'd harvested all these years. This one woman and her child could be the undoing of his father. And, by extension, of Roth.

He despised Martha. She was a Jew—even without the scarf, why would Father allow her to live? He had a weak spot for the baby, and Roth thought it was because Gerhard had had a weak spot for her mother—Ruth.

By killing the baby, Roth would gain power and save his father from his own weakness.

On his fourth visit, he plotted and watched and waited for the opportunity. If his father learned of his plans, he would probably forbid it, saying that he was too young. If he just did it, he was sure Gerhard would see the wisdom of it and praise him.

The closest he got to killing the baby on that visit was when he sneaked down the hall late one night and peeked into the Jew's room. But the servant was asleep with the baby in her arms—he would never be able to take it without waking her. He'd returned to Berlin determined to rethink his strategy.

Three weeks later he returned to Toruń. Three nights had passed and he couldn't wait any longer. He would either kill the baby tonight or be caught trying. Roth was agitated; Gerhard hadn't brought a woman up to the house for three nights.

At dinner, he asked his father why.

"Tomorrow night," Gerhard said. He'd nearly finished a whole bottle of wine. "You have to learn to pace yourself. Control, boy. Control."

Roth thought about that.

"If I wanted to show some of my power, would you let me?"

His father seemed confused by the question. "How?"

"Why can't I have a servant?"

"Well . . . you can, boy."

"Then I want Martha," he said.

"No, not Martha. She has a debt to pay to me."

"What better way to show her your power than making her obey your son?"

Gerhard laughed. "Well, then, since you asked, Martha can be your servant tomorrow."

"Tonight," Roth said.

"Tonight? What can she do for you tonight?"

"Cut some wood. It's cold, and I would like a fire."

Gerhard seemed amused. "So tonight it is, then! She's in the kitchen; call her out."

"Not now. Later, when she's already settled for the night. That will show who the boss is."

His father grinned. "I can see you will make a very good soldier."

Roth waited two hours. His father had drunk himself into a warm stupor in his bedroom, and the house was quiet. He told Father that he would have his fire now. Gerhard laughed and waved him on.

The stairs creaked as he descended into the basement where Martha had gone to bed for the night. He stopped in front of her room and lifted his fist. Should he knock?

The thrill of what he was about to do shook his body. He knew why, of course. He was feeling the power of true hope. The kind of desire that had made Lucifer denounce God. He had the power of Satan in him because he'd stolen the hope of Father's Jews with him. It really did work, just as Gerhard had said.

He knocked, because it seemed like the right thing to do.

The door opened a few seconds later, and Martha stared at him, dressed in a dirty night dress.

"I am cold, and I want a fire," he said. "Go outside and chop some firewood and build me a fire."

She stared at him, confused.

"You have to obey me. I am your master."

"You're just a boy. It's not very cold. It's already late."

"If you question me, then my father will take your baby away from you. I have his authority now."

She looked too shocked to react, and Roth felt the thrill of his power over her. Martha started to say something but thought better of it. She grabbed the tattered German coat Gerhard had given her, stepped into the hall, and pulled the door closed behind her.

Roth marched up the stairs ahead of her. He didn't want to give her any ideas. It was bad enough that his hands were shaking like leaves in anticipation already. He put them in his pockets, hoping she hadn't noticed. The pocketknife he'd sharpened felt cold against his fingers.

As soon as he heard the back door close, Roth tip-toed back down the stairs. He pushed the door to Martha's room open.

The baby lay on the bed, like a lump of laundry.

He could hear her breathing. He could hear himself breathing. The room was nearly dark. Quiet. Peaceful. In a way he couldn't explain, he felt sorry for the baby.

Standing there in the doorway, Roth was suddenly horrified. Could he really kill a baby? What kind of power did that require, really?

It didn't matter. He'd dreamed of this moment and told himself that he'd probably be scared. But it was the power of Lucifer in him that would over-power the weakness he felt.

Roth stepped toward the bed.

He couldn't hear the sound of wood chopping outside, probably because he was in the basement. But he had to hurry.

He stepped to the bed and pulled the wool cover down. The baby lay on her side, facing the wall, breathing steadily.

Roth pulled out the pocketknife and pried the blade out.

There was great power in this baby's life. Esther and others like her were the hope of the Jews. And as Gerhard said, the greatest power in the universe is hope. Without it, no one could become like God.

Killing the baby was Satan's hope.

Saving the baby was God's hope.

In the end, hope was the fuel that empowered both sides, and right now Lucifer was winning.

This was the war.

But standing over the child, Roth couldn't ignore the fact that his heart was hammering with more than hope. What if she cried out? What if he couldn't cut her skin with the blade? Or what if he became too frightened to actually do it?

Give me strength.

He immediately felt a surge of confidence. Father never should have let the child live in the first place. Gerhard should have killed Ruth and Martha and both of the children. Now Roth would finish the job, or at least this part of the job.

He lifted the baby's small wrist and turned it so that he could cut the veins. A terrible shaking overtook Roth's body. He suddenly felt like throwing up.

But he knew that this was only his weakness. It would pass.

He rested the blade against the baby's wrists and whispered another prayer.

Please give me strength to become like you.

"What are you doing?"

Roth whipped around at the sound of the servant's voice. Martha stood in the doorway, eyes white in the dim light. Roth's heart bolted into his throat.

"What are you doing?" Her voice was higher. Louder.

Roth couldn't move.

Martha saw the knife in his hand. She screamed and flew at him like a ghost. Her voice was so loud, so piercing, that Roth thought she might actually be a ghost.

He jumped to the side at the last moment. Her fist beat on his shoulder, but she turned her attention to the baby and scooped it up in her arms.

Cut them! Cut them both now, while her attention is on the baby!

Roth swung his knife at Martha's head. It stuck her arm, but he couldn't tell if he'd cut her. He had to go for her throat. Or the baby's . . .

"What is this?"

Father loomed in the doorway, scowling. He glanced from Roth, who stood with the knife, ready to strike again, and the Jew, who sheltered the baby.

"What is going on?"

"I'm killing the baby, Father."

Silence filled the room. The Jew began to sob softly.

"Get out of here!"

At first Roth thought that Father was yelling at Martha. Leave the baby for my son to kill and get out of here!

But then he saw that Gerhard was glaring at him. Why was he so angry? And in front of the Jew!

Gerhard stretched his arm toward the stairs behind him. "Get out of here!"

"Father—"

"Now!"

Roth felt himself blush.

"You can't let them live," he said. "If you do, they'll be the only ones who escape you. They have to die. Why can't I kill one?"

"Out!" his father screamed.

Roth stared at him, stunned by the anger. Surely his father understood that they had to die.

"I said *out,*" Gerhard snapped.

Roth hurried past his father and ran up the stairs. A pile of wood sat by the stove. Maybe it had already been cut. He walked to the window overlooking the camp and stared into the darkness.

He decided then that he hated his father.

If Martha and her child lived, he would hunt them down and kill them. He had to. They had been sentenced by the scarf.

34

Los Angeles
July 25, 1973
Wednesday Morning

CHAIM WASN'T SURE WHY THE BLACK CAR HAD
alarmed him so much. Perhaps because of those
three words spoken by Stephen two days ago: *Be
careful, Rabbi.*

What if there really was danger? What if someone
else was after what Stephen was after? And what if
he, Chaim Leveler, was about to be squeezed in the
middle?

And what if there was someone in that black car,
watching him? Or watching to see if Stephen came
home?

He'd called Sylvia at eight in the morning. No
answer. He'd called her office. She was likely running late and on her way to work.

It was time to put an end to this craziness. If he
couldn't find Stephen himself, he would go to the
police.

Chaim approached Rachel Spritzer's old apartment complex, whispering prayers for Stephen's
safety. Chaim had no indication that the lad was
anywhere near here, but his fixation on the place

made perfect sense. It was, after all, his mother's home. And Stephen had found a safe.

He drove from the north, toward the front of the building. A repair crew was working on the corner today. One man with a yellow hard hat wielded a gas-powered jackhammer in an area cordoned off with orange caution signs. What a racket that thing made.

He crept past the house—no sign of life. For all he knew, Stephen was actually in some trouble. Kidnapped, or worse. He couldn't ignore the possibility any longer.

The construction worker looked at him as he passed, smiled, and returned a wave. A bit odd to see that these days.

The building adjacent to Rachel Spritzer's was another abandoned apartment building. Was it remotely possible that Stephen was in there, watching him drive by at this very moment? He'd said that he was in a hotel, but Chaim wouldn't put this past him.

Chaim *humphed* and parked the car by the alley behind the building. He climbed out and headed for a back door on the off chance it was open. Even here, the jackhammer rattled his ears.

The door stood ajar. He stepped in and let his eyes adjust to the dim light.

"Stephen?"

No answer.

"Stephen!"

His voiced bounced around with the jack-hammer. A quick look upstairs wouldn't hurt—he'd come this far. He mounted the steps and made his

way up through the floors, calling out Stephen's
name at each stop.

Last floor. He poked up his head, saw that it was
stripped and vacant, and started back down. What
was that across the room there? A picture on the wall
next to the window. Someone had been here, maybe
not so long ago. The window overlooked Rachel's
apartment.

Curious, Chaim climbed up and walked across
the room. What he saw stopped him. The photograph was of Ruth, the picture Stephen left in his
room for a day before breaking in through his window. A bed lay in the corner, and next to it cans of
food—half opened, half still sealed. Beans, corn,
cranberry sauce. The area was cordoned off with
tires and sections of broken wall.

Chaim had found Stephen's . . . place.

"My, my," he muttered. "My, my, my, my. What
have you gone and done, my boy?"

What had come over his Stephen? The boy was
obsessed with this treasure.

He turned and called out loudly. "Stephen?"

Still no answer. Wherever Stephen was, it looked
as though he intended to return. Chaim walked into
the space and turned around in a slow circle, imagining what it would be like to sleep here for a few
days. Whatever had taken hold of Stephen, he'd lost
himself in this thing. And so quickly!

Chaim looked out the window at Rachel's apartment. Was it possible that the Stones of David really
were hidden in there?

"Hello?"

He jerked around. A young woman looked at him from the stairs.

"May I help you?"

"Yes, hello. Yes. Do you know Stephen?"

"Stephen?" She was a petite girl, pretty, with bright eyes and dark braided hair heavy with beads. "There's a lot of Stephens around."

He walked out of the square. "I'm looking for a Stephen who is tall. Thin. Dark hair. A Realtor." He pointed back at the shrine. "This is his place. I am his friend."

She glanced at the picture of Ruth. "Is that so? For all I know you're an old kook looking for a scam."

"Really?" He cocked his right eyebrow. "I strike you as an old kook. Funny, but I've never actually been called that before. I just want to talk to him. He lives with me, you see. If I can't find him, I will have to report him missing to the police. They'll want to search this building."

She stared at him evenly, expression now flat.

"Can you at least tell me if he's okay?"

"He's fine. What's your name?"

"Chaim Leveler. Stephen calls me Rabbi, even though I'm not."

"You only want to talk?"

She knew where he was! "Definitely. Just to know that he's safe."

"You swear not to tell anybody about this place?"

"Of course not."

"Swear it."

For the second time in a week, he broke his vow not to swear. "I swear it."

"Follow me. He isn't going to like this."

"THERE IT is again," Lars said. "The sound is different. Faster."

Except for Roth, they all stood with ears pressed against the bared apartment wall, listening intently to the sound of a strange thumping that didn't match the racket outside.

Lars straightened. "He's digging under us."

They'd heard the hum through most of the night, but it was morning before Lars suggested that it might not be traffic. Then the thumping in the street had broken the silence—a lone worker breaking up the sidewalk. After an hour, the worker had made no progress, and they knew that something was wrong.

Roth crossed to the window and peered down at the construction worker again. It did make sense— what better way to cover up a jackhammer underneath the building than to run a second jackhammer on the street.

If so, the Realtor's gall was unprecedented. Roth grinned. *Come to me, Stephen. I've been waiting so long. So very, very long.*

Roth descended the stairs. His men followed. He shoved the basement door open and stepped into the concrete room. A steady thumping echoed softly through the entire structure. He faced the east wall, then the west. It was impossible to pinpoint the source of the sound.

Lars ran his fingers along one wall, listening. "It could be from the street, but I don't think so. It's too loud. I think he's actually planning to break in through the floor."

"Idiot!" Claude said. "He'll come up to a rifle in his mouth."

"No," Roth said. "We can't be sure where he'll come up. Even if we could, he'll drop back down and be gone if he sees us. I want him, and I want him alive."

He walked to the doors lining the basement and opened them one by one. He could feel the vibration run through his feet—stronger on the east side away from the boiler room, if his imagination wasn't playing tricks on him.

The worker on the street was a cover-up. Unless the wrong person happened by, no one would know he wasn't who he seemed to be.

Who would have imagined this, tunneling of all things? Then again, if Roth was in his position, he might have done the same. There must be an old sewer or something below the foundation.

"It is critical that we allow him to enter," he said, turning back. "One man stays in the stairwell—Claude. The rest of you, finish upstairs. The moment he breaks through, key your radio three times. Watch him. Take no other action." Roth frowned and then grunted. "Let the mole dig."

35

"IN THERE?" CHAIM SHOUTED. A HORRENDOUS clamor rang from the hole in the ground.

"It's wet down there, Rabbi. You sure you want to do this?" the girl asked.

"Stephen's down in that hole? Is he a prisoner?"

She laughed. "I suppose that's a matter of perspective. Come on."

The dog that had come home with Stephen last week braved the noise to lick his hand. It whined and backed up several steps.

"It's okay, puppy," the girl said. "We're almost done."

The dog retreated out the door, tail between her legs.

The girl lowered herself into the hole and disappeared.

Chaim took a deep breath and swung his legs into the sewer. "My, my, my. What have you done?"

The tunnel glowed under a string of lights. Muddy water covered his leather shoes. Chaim covered his ears and waded toward the pounding.

At first all he saw was a rear end and legs protruding from a hole in the tunnel's wall. The person was operating a jackhammer or something inside the hole, up at an angle. A strange contraption dangled free from the ceiling.

The girl slapped the person's backside. The hammering stopped.

Chaim didn't recognize the man who pulled himself out of the hole. White dust covered a mask and glasses. He looked freshly buttered and rolled in flour. The man saw Chaim, rubbed the lenses, and then pushed them to his forehead.

"Rabbi?"

He heard the voice and knew immediately. "Stephen! I didn't recognize you. What on earth are you doing down here?"

Stephen looked at the girl.

"He said he was going to call the police if I didn't bring him down," she said.

Stephen looked back into the hole, stricken.

"You're tunneling up?" Chaim asked.

Stephen didn't answer.

"Isn't this city property you're tearing up?"

"We're going to fix it," Stephen said.

Looking at the boy now, Chaim knew that he could not hope to stop him. He wasn't even sure he should try. In fact, he probably *would* do more service to Stephen if he helped him, as Gerik had suggested.

"That's Rachel Spritzer's basement up there, isn't it?"

"Um . . . yes."

"The Stones of David? They really are inside?"

"Well . . . I think so."

"And the front door is no longer open to you?"

"No."

"My, my, my." Chaim shook his head. "I do love your spirit. Could you get arrested for doing this?"

"I . . . I don't think we will. The new owners don't

want anything to do with the police. They're after the Stones too."

"I see."

"How . . . how did you find me?"

"Detective work." Chaim tapped his head. "My powers of deduction. I think to myself, where would Stephen seek love and happiness, and I narrow it down to two possibilities. One, in Sylvia's arms, or two, the sewer under Rachel Spritzer's apartment. I checked with Sylvia, and her arms were empty, so I rushed here."

The girl chuckled. A crooked grin twisted Stephen's mouth.

"How can I help?" Chaim asked.

"You're serious?"

"This is about a girl named Esther, isn't it? Love. And about your inheritance. I'm not sure I can operate that monster, but anything else, you name it."

A thought seemed to flip a light switch behind Stephen's eyes. No longer concerned with any threat presented by Chaim's sudden appearance, he stuck his head in the hole and pulled out a large jackhammer. The handle thumped to the ground, and Melissa helped him lean it against the wall. He grabbed a flashlight and dived back into the hole, all but disappearing this time.

"My name's Melissa," the girl said, hand extended.

"Pleased to know you, Melissa. How deep is the hole?"

"Seven feet, about."

"How far to go?"

"I'm surprised he hasn't broken through yet."

Stephen slid out, ignoring the dirt that encrusted his stomach. "I'm eight inches through the floor. If Sweeney's right, that leaves four inches." His eyes darted around. "The drill. Hand me the drill."

Chaim stood back and watched them. Melissa unhooked a large red drill from the ceiling and handed it to Stephen. "How long is this bit?" the boy asked. "Six inches? That should work, right?" His frantic pace would impair his judgment.

He virtually threw himself back into the hole and wiggled up till only his muddy tennis shoes stuck out. His voice echoed back after a moment.

"What's he saying?" Melissa asked.

Chaim stuck his head in. "What?"

"Plug it in," Stephen said. "Power!"

"He says to plug it in," Chaim told Melissa.

"Oh. Suppose that would help." She switched the jackhammer's cord for the drill's and then swatted his shoe.

"What's he doing?" Chaim asked.

"Playing it safe. Despite the distraction, there's a possibility that whoever's in there has heard us. He's drilling a small hole to check it out before he breaks in."

Stephen's feet suddenly wiggled in farther. For a moment they remained still.

"I think he's in." Melissa looked into the hole. "Stephen?"

He suddenly scrambled backward, as if he'd met a brood of vipers. He piled out and stripped off his glasses.

"We've got a problem. They're in the basement!"

"They're inside? How do you know?" Melissa demanded.

Stephen took two splashing steps through the water and wheeled back. "Oh, man. Oh, man, this isn't good."

"How do you know?"

"I heard someone cough, that's how I know. And the light's on. You have to get Sweeney."

"You want him to stop?"

"We have to figure this out." He paced, desperate. Chaim felt his own pulse quicken. "Get him!" Stephen snapped.

Melissa ran down the tunnel and up the ladder.

Stephen flexed his jaw and slowly beat his head against the concrete wall. "They heard us. They're in the basement."

"There has to be something you can do," Chaim said.

"They probably have it already."

"Can I go in? The front door?"

Stephen ignored him. He dived back into the hole, pulled himself way in, lay still for a moment, and then slid back out.

"They're definitely in there."

"I'm sorry—"

"Please." Stephen held up a hand and closed his eyes. "Just let me think."

⁓

THEY STOOD in silence, feet planted in six inches of water. Sweeney, Stephen, Melissa, and the rabbi.

Stephen clenched his teeth, furious. He fought a terrible urge to run across the street and slam through the front door. Maybe the dogs were dead; maybe he could bluff his way in; maybe he could race down the stairs, grab the box, and lock himself in the coal room while Sweeney finished the digging. Another five minutes of hard hammering would surely crack open the hole.

"We have to get them out of the basement," Sweeney said.

"Smoke 'em out," Melissa said.

Stephen glared at her. "Well, sure, that's just brilliant. We could build a fire down here and let the smoke seep through the little hole I drilled."

"Lighten up."

He lowered his head and kneaded his skull.

"There's got to be a way," Sweeney insisted. "Why don't we burn down the building?" They looked at him. "Strike that."

"You need to get them out of that building, correct?" Chaim asked.

"Yes. At least out of the basement."

"For how long?"

"There's about four inches of concrete, but without any support behind, it's going to crack pretty quickly. Maybe fifteen minutes."

"Plus time to repair the damage?" Chaim pressed.

"Forget that—"

"No, hear him out," Sweeney said. "What's on your mind, old man?"

"Maybe nothing, but it might start you thinking. The city has very specific evacuation policies for fires.

If a fire breaks out in any building, they immediately evacuate not only that building, but any building next to it. It's the law. They have to verify safety before allowing the occupants back into their homes."

"So what are you saying?" Sweeney asked. "We start a fire?"

"No, we could never do that. But I know the fire department, and I know that if this building were to catch fire, the city would force the evacuation of all the buildings—"

"That's it!" Stephen said. "That's it! Right?" His eyes were like saucers.

Sweeney smiled. "Actually . . ."

Stephen broke for the manhole.

"Stephen? Where are you going?" the rabbi demanded.

"To start a fire," he yelled. "Come on!"

36

"GET THE GUNS," ROTH SAID. "EVERYTHING, IN the car. Now!" Claude ran for the stairs. Three fire engines had screeched to a halt in front of the building across the street. Thick black smoke boiled out of the windows on the upper floor. He could see no flames, only smoke.

The construction worker had run out to the street, heaved the jackhammer and the signs into the back of a car with the help of an older man, and then careened around the corner.

Still no sign of a breakthrough in the basement.

"He's burned himself out," Lars said. "The fool stumbled over a gas can or something—"

"Quiet," Roth snapped.

The game had escalated. It was more than he'd hoped for. The others had no clue what was happening, but they weren't meant to. This was between him and the Jew.

Naturally there was the possibility of failure, but that was part of the exhilaration—success was still a hope.

Lucifer's hope.

In reality, the possibility of failure was very small. Roth was far too powerful. He just had to bring that power to play in a reasoned, methodical way, as he had last night.

He would be out of the country before anyone figured out that he was connected to the killings. This thought made Roth feel warm.

The streets filled with running people. Firemen quickly strung a hose, yelling at the gathering crowd to stay back. How likely was it that something had caught fire and was forcing the Jew to shut down?

A fist pounded on the front door. "Fire Marshal. Open up!"

Roth took a deep breath and turned from the building. He glanced at the car. Claude slammed the trunk on the last of the equipment they'd retrieved from the third floor and nodded. Roth walked to the door and pulled it open.

A fireman stood in a yellow slicker. "I'm sorry, but you'll have to evacuate this building."

He looked past the fireman and gazed at the fire. "Is everything under control? What happened?"

"We need everyone out. Don't worry, it won't touch this building."

"Then we'll stay here." He began to close the door.

The man leaned forward, barring the door open. "I'm sorry, but you have to leave. City ordinance. No more than half an hour, with any luck. Let's go."

Roth motioned Claude out with a nod. "You won't be entering the building?"

"Just to clear it." The man waited while they filed out. "Anyone else inside?"

"No."

"Wait here." The man ran for the stairwell and disappeared.

"Spread out along the street," Roth ordered his men. "Keep your eyes open. No one enters without my knowing."

The fireman ran out, slammed the door, and stretched a piece of wide yellow tape over to seal it. "This one's clear. Stay back on the street. We'll let you know when it's safe. Unauthorized entry is a crime, understand?"

Roth ignored him and looked at the burning building. Three police cruisers had joined the party. Stephen was up to something.

Think, Roth. Outthink the Jew.

———

"GO, GO!" Sweeney yelled down the manhole. "They're out!"

Stephen turned to the rabbi. "Cut the lights!"

The string of lights went out. He scrambled into the hole, put his full weight into the jackhammer, and squeezed the lever. The machine shook furiously in his hands. Four inches. With any luck, the Germans wouldn't hear the sound now that they had evacuated. Not that it mattered. With a little more luck, the slab he was pounding on would break free along the circle of holes he'd drilled while they waited for the fire trucks to respond.

They were taking three calculated risks, any of which could sink them. The most obvious was the whole arson bit. They'd laid down slabs of old asbestos on the top two floors, piled the slabs with tires, and lit the stacks on fire. Unless the fire department responded slowly, the smoldering tires would be extinguished and the building cleared in short order, though hopefully not too short. The stunt might cost them a slap on the wrist, but they already had their story in place. Sweeney wanted to see how much smoke tires made. He'd taken precautions. If there was a law against burning tires, he was totally unaware of it.

The second risk was possibly being discovered by the fire marshal down in the manhole, operating a jackhammer. To this end, Sweeney had closed the door to the coal room and presumably pulled the mound of insulation over the cover as planned.

The third risk was beyond them entirely. Stephen wasn't positive how many men Braun actually had over there. What if he'd hidden one away in the coal room with a gun?

He would find out soon enough.

So close. So, so close after so much effort. Stephen redoubled his pressure on the jackhammer. "Come on, baby, break. Break!"

He'd drilled twenty holes—surely that had weakened the slab. Sweeney had assured him there was no rebar in the floor, said they would've run into it by now if there was. Man, if there was rebar, they were dead. He would kill—

The jackhammer suddenly surged forward. He released the trigger. Chunks of large concrete lay over the bit. Above, a gray circle of light.

The breakthrough was so sudden, so complete, that Stephen wasn't sure it had actually happened.

"Guys?"

Stephen jerked his head up, slammed it into the ceiling and ducked back down, hardly aware of the pain. He lowered himself back into the sewer. Pitch black.

"Guys?"

"Here," said Sweeney.

"We're in!"

"We're in?"

"We're in!"

Stephen tugged at the jackhammer and jumped out of the way as it hurtled out of the drain.

Splash.

"What was that?" Sweeney asked.

"The jackhammer."

Stephen clambered back up the hole, saw that the broken concrete would need to be removed for him to climb past, and dragged the two largest pieces back down the hole.

Splash, splash.

"What was that?"

"Concrete."

He crawled up again, scooting all the way on knees and elbows. Shoved more debris past him, down the hole. Someone grunted.

"Sorry."

The slab had broken free along the line of holes he'd drilled. "Perfect. Perfect, perfect." He reached up, gripped the floor's edge, and pulled his head out.

The basement.

The sweet, sweet, beautiful basement. Silent and bare past the open door. No guns, no Germans. He could hardly stand such a sight.

Something bumped his foot. "Go, go!" Sweeney
called up.

Stephen climbed out of the hole and stood. The
door into this room stood open; it had a dead bolt
on the inside, which was strange. Maybe it had been
a study or hideout once. The bulb out in the basement glared. The cement on the floor was shiny. He
ran to the door, poked his head out, and then
stepped into the main room. The door to the boiler
room was closed.

"Please, please," he breathed. What if they had
found it? He couldn't think like that. Not now.

"Take my hand," Sweeney whispered behind him.
Stephen glanced back to see Sweeney kneeling over the
hole, helping one of the others. He looked up at
Stephen. "Hurry, man! We have to do this and get out!"

Stephen walked to the boiler room, cracked the
door, peeked into the dark. His heart pumped like
that jackhammer, breaking up his confidence. What
if the tin was gone?

He hit the light switch, and the lone incandescent
bulb snapped to life. The boiler was open. He'd left
it closed. The drums looked as if they might have
been shifted.

Braun had been here!

Stephen leaped for the boiler, grabbed the empty
drum behind with both hands, and sent it crashing to
the side. There lay the top of the safe, covered in dirt.

Stephen let out a soft, involuntary cry. For a
moment, he felt ruined by relief. Then he dropped
to his knees, swept the dirt off, and yanked the lid.
Esther's face stared up at him, serene.

He shoved both hands into the safe, latched his fingers around the tin box, and pulled it out.

Surprisingly light. What would four gilded Stones wrapped in cloth weigh? Less than the tin box perhaps. Maybe more. Maybe much more.

He spun around and ran into the rabbi, who had come in unnoticed.

"It's here?"

Stephen clutched the box with white fingers. "Yes."

The rabbi looked from the box to Stephen.

"I have it," Stephen said.

"Yes. Yes, I see that." A slight smile formed on Chaim's face.

Stephen rushed past him into the main room, driven by the adrenaline in his blood, not the thoughts in his head. There were no thoughts in his head. He had the box, that was all. The box was in his hands.

"Are you going to open it?" Chaim asked.

He whirled around, caught off guard by the question. "Here? Not here!"

Sweeney and Melissa stood by the coal room, staring. "That's it?" Sweeney asked.

For a moment, they all stared at it. Why? What were they trying to prove with their gawking? Sweeney had already mixed the quick-setting concrete, which sat in a bucket behind him. They should be moving, not gawking.

Sweeney stuck out his hand. "As much as I would love to sit around and look at your five-hundred-thousand-dollar box, the clock is ticking. It's been a pleasure, Groovy. If I don't see you in prison, I'll try to look you up." He grinned. "The concrete's already half-set, so as soon as I wedge the wood in place, you pour. Got it?"

Stephen's legs were numb. He nodded.

"You sure you're all right?"

"'Course." He cleared his throat.

"And you might want to stash the contents of that box in your pockets. It's a bit obvious."

It was Stephen's idea that he should be the one to stay behind, fill the hole, and escape through the garage. After all, it was his treasure, and someone had to do it. The notion struck him as a bit ambitious now.

Melissa kissed him on the cheek. "See you around, Stephen."

"Okay," Sweeney said. "Come on, Rabbi."

"I'll stay with Stephen," Chaim said.

"You have to get out, you know? Two will be harder than one."

"And three will be harder than two escaping from the smoking building. I think I should stay with Stephen."

"Okay, Stephen?"

"Okay."

Sweeney winked, followed Melissa down the tunnel, and wedged a piece of plywood behind him, forming a floor of sorts for the quick mix. He knocked on it from below. "Okay, all set. Good luck."

Stephen kept looking down at the box in his hands. It was an old cookie box, roughly twelve by eight inches. Orange wafers ran around the sides. No tape to seal it. Ruth's picture looked up at him in a surreal silence. He shook it gently once—something thumped softly inside. A knot filled his throat.

Chaim watched Stephen, and then, without a word, dumped the concrete into the hole. He smoothed it as best he could with the bottom of the bucket, and then shoved loose coal over the mess.

Stephen would have helped, but he couldn't bring himself to put down the box. He watched in silence, contemplating Sweeney's advice that he leave the box behind. A box was just a box. He could take the picture off and take out the Stones and leave the box.

Chaim finished in less than a minute. It wouldn't support a man's weight for another half hour, but the coal masked the job well. If Sweeney was as successful at hiding the manhole on his end, their tunnel might never be discovered.

All Stephen and Chaim had to do now was get out.

SOMETHING WAS wrong. Roth had never been so sure of his instincts before. It was the fire—something was wrong about the fire. So much smoke and yet no flames.

He paced the sidewalk, eyes peeled for any sign of a fireman, a policeman, a city inspector, anyone who might look like the Jew or the construction worker. For that matter, he wouldn't have to look like the Jew—Friedman wasn't beyond dressing as a woman. Anyone who approached the building would be suspect.

Ten minutes after their evacuation, he learned

why there were no flames. Tires. They were saying that someone had set tires on fire.

The Jew had set the tires on fire knowing it would force an evacuation, resumed his digging, and was now in the building.

Roth ran toward the front doors.

He pulled up. What was he thinking? The authorities had eyes everywhere.

He hurried back to Lars. Panic spread through his limbs, enough to make him want to scream. "They may have tunneled through the floor under cover of the fire. Have Ulrich set fire to one of the cars down the street—I need their eyes away from me. Do you understand what I'm telling you?"

"Start a fire? How?"

"I don't care how!" he yelled, then quickly turned in the event he'd attracted attention. "I don't even care if he's caught. Tell him to stuff a rag into the gas tank and set it on fire. Just do it!" His head swam with emotions he had never experienced before. He might be having a breakdown right here on the street. Control. He had to regain control.

"Hurry!"

37

"RABBI!" STEPHEN WHISPERED.

Chaim turned from the door that led into the stairwell.

"Maybe I should take them out."

"We have to hurry!" the rabbi said.

"I know, but maybe Sweeney's right. I should hide them somewhere else so that if they take the box, I'll still have the Stones. I think we still have time; it's only been ten minutes—didn't you say we had at least twenty?"

The rabbi looked at the door, then back. "Where would you put them?"

"In my pockets. Or my shoes."

Chaim walked back. "Okay." He looked at the box. "Open it."

"Okay," Stephen said.

He couldn't move his fingers though. They hadn't moved in five minutes.

The rabbi's hand reached out and touched the photograph. "She's very beautiful. Please, Stephen."

"Okay."

He gingerly set the box on the ground, knelt down, wiped his palms on his pants, and pried his fingers under one end of the lid. It came loose with a soft popping sound. Stephen felt such a terrible desperation in that moment that he nearly slammed the lid closed. Desire, of course; yes, desire. But fear as well. Terror!

What if the Stones of David weren't in this box?

He slid the lid over and let it clatter to the floor. Inside was a red bundle. Silk. He scooped it out with trembling hand. Beautiful, soft silk that felt like cream in his hands.

He looked down, thinking there could be more at the bottom of the box. There was. A worn journal. He scooped it out, leafed through it quickly, and handed it to Chaim.

Carefully, he unraveled the silk scarf. It felt empty. Panic crept up his throat. He shook the scarf. A folded letter fell to the floor.

No Stones.

Stephen sank to his haunches, horrified. He could hardly breathe. A red scarf and a folded letter. There had to be more. The safe! The safe had a false bottom!

He leaped to his feet, tore into the boiler room, and plunged his hand into the safe. His knuckles crammed against a hard bottom. He struck at it furiously, but it sounded dull. No false bottom.

Stephen stared into the hole and began to breathe hard, as if he were locked in an overheated sauna, desperate to get out.

"Stephen?"

The truth was unbearable. A mountain on his shoulders, crushing with its dead weight. There was no treasure. The children were the Stones of David. Esther. Ruth's picture flashed through his mind.

"Stephen!"

Chaim was at the door. Stephen turned slowly,

senses dulled. The rabbi looked at him, face white. The letter shook in his right hand.

Stephen stood unsteadily. "What?"

"I . . . you should read this." The rabbi held it out.

"It's a letter," Stephen said. "To Esther?"

"Yes. To Esther and David. From Martha."

"Martha?"

"I think you should read it."

Stephen walked forward and took the letter. Written in cursive. The ink was old, and the creases in the paper were worn nearly through.

My dearest son, David, and Esther, for whom you were born:

I've searched the world and cannot find you. I can only pray that someday one of you will find this letter and know the truth.

I have married a good man, Rudy Spritzer, and I call myself Rachel now in honor of the woman who cared for you, David, in the camp. There I was known as Martha. I was able to give birth to you at the labor camp Toruń only because of the sacrifice of Ruth, who had given birth to Esther just weeks earlier. I was chosen by the red scarf to die, but Ruth took the scarf for herself.

The commandant wouldn't let me care for you, David, but I cared for Esther. He took you both before the camp was liberated. I searched for five years and then came to the United States when I learned that many orphans had immigrated. I discovered only that the commandant left my dear David in an orphanage near Ketrzyn and took Esther into Germany.

Please forgive me, but I couldn't let him know that I had taken the journal, or he would hunt me down. It contains enough information to send him to his grave. But you must understand, I could not allow them to prosecute the commandant. He alone may have knowledge of your whereabouts.

I couldn't seek you out publicly, for fear that they would come for you as well. You will know you belong to me and to Ruth because I have marked both of you with half of David's Stone. I tried to find you through the mark— I'm so sorry I could not.

I have prayed every day that God will draw you to me and to each other as he draws a man seeking the pearl of great price. May he fill you with the hope we entrusted in you. You must find each other. Then you will know the real treasure, which makes the Stones look like toys for children. I am sorry, so sorry, dearest children. You are the true Stones of David, and I pray every day that if I cannot find you, you will find each other in good health.

As for the Stones, their hiding place will go to the grave with Ruth and me. Find each other and find God.

Martha
Sept. 1958

"Esther," Stephen said quietly. Tears welled in his eyes, and he was forced to swallow. "Dear God, I have to find her."

He owed his life to a woman named Ruth, and by extension to her daughter. *Esther* was the treasure. Not some ancient Stones covered in gold, but a child of the war. A woman. Esther, for whom he was born.

He couldn't explain what happened next, except to think that a week of madness had finally broken him down to a pulp. Stephen dropped to his knees, covered his face, and yielded to sobs. They started with soft shakes and grew to rob his breath completely. He bobbed on his knees, wanting to shake the emotion that ravaged his body, but it only tightened its grip on his throat and chest.

The photographs from Martha's sunroom flashed across his mind. Girls and boys, wives and mothers and daughters, husbands and fathers and sons. They had died, and he had lived—because of one named Ruth. He owed his every breath to another Jew. And for twenty years, he'd betrayed the memory of their deaths by ignoring their pain.

Chaim tried to comfort him, tried to suggest they must leave, but Stephen sank to the ground, letter clenched in his fist. For a few unbearable moments, he imagined that the picture of the little bald girl from the medical clinic was him. He was there, in Poland. Every day, the Germans carried him down to a room that smelled like alcohol, and they injected different parts of his body with cancer cells. That's how he lost his hair and his teeth.

But he wasn't dead from cancer. He was alive because someone else had died to give him life. Ruth. Esther.

Chaim was shaking Stephen violently. "Someone's coming!"

Stephen scrambled for orientation. "The letter!"

A door slammed somewhere.

Stephen struggled to his feet. They had to get out! He quickly shoved the letter into the ash tray below the boiler.

"You're leaving it?"

"What if they find it on me? We'll come back for it. Hurry!" He ran out, scooped up the tin box with the journal and the scarf, and turned for the door.

"No. Not this time."

Braun stood at the entrance to the stairwell, pistol in his fist. He walked straight for Stephen. The German's gun hand flashed out, and Stephen felt sharp pain shoot through his skull. Something crashed to the concrete. A tin box.

He hit the floor hard and lost consciousness.

38

STEPHEN HAD NO IDEA HOW LONG HE'D BEEN unconscious. He lay in a heap on the basement floor, stripped to his undershirt and briefs. His head pounded, and he lay still for a few minutes, listening to several men talking in German. Slowly, the details of the letter again filled his mind. He had to find Esther.

Stephen straightened his leg. The talking ceased immediately. Thirty seconds later, Braun stood above him.

"Have a seat."

Hands hauled him up from behind. They set him in a chair.

"Where's the rabbi?" Stephen asked.

"The rabbi?" Braun chuckled. "He's no rabbi. Which is a disappointment to me." Braun wore an unbuttoned Nazi SS jacket, revealing a black silk shirt beneath. His slacks and shoes were the same he'd worn before. The red scarf was draped over his left shoulder. He strolled to Stephen's right, drawing on a cigarette.

"I would have killed his worthless soul already, but for the moment he's more useful to me alive. The old ones always go quickly, my father used to say."

Stephen felt a chill snake down his spine. The large blond they called Lars stood by the stairwell, staring without emotion. Claude stood in front of the boiler room.

"Do you like my jacket?" Braun asked. "It was my father's. I wear it sometimes, when I make deals with Jews."

He held up the tin's lid and stared at Ruth's picture. "I want you to tell me where you put the Stones, Mr. Friedman. We found the floor safe. I must say, your juvenile bluffs successfully diverted our attention from the basement. We tore the upper floors to pieces, and all the while you had the safe covered by a drum in the basement. How did you get in?"

"What do you mean?"

"I mean, an hour ago you weren't in, and now you are. How did you get in?"

They hadn't discovered the covered tunnel yet. "Through the garage door."

Roth slapped Stephen hard across the cheek. "I don't have time for lies, Jew."

Stephen caught his balance, put his hand to his tingling face. "We . . . we knew the fire would force your evacuation. In the confusion, we forced the garage door open and walked in. I was dressed like a fireman."

"Where are the clothes?"

"We tossed them outside."

Judging Roth Braun by his expression was impossible. He showed no emotion. "And the jackhammer?"

"We were digging a hole from a sewer that connects the buildings, but the motor burned up. The fire was a last resort." Stephen took a deep breath. "There are no Stones," he said. "Only the scarf."

"And the journal." Braun raised it in one hand

and took a drag on the cigarette with the other. "Do you know who this scarf belongs to?"

"Rachel Spritzer."

"You mean Martha. She was my father's personal servant at Toruń. She stole this scarf from my father. I know it well. It was very special to him." He lifted the picture of Ruth, caught Stephen's eye, and sniffed the photograph as if testing her perfume.

Stephen felt sick.

"This is Ruth," Braun said. "Amazing how Esther resembles her."

Stephen's hands were free; he could rush the man and take the picture. But it would only prove that he knew about Esther. He couldn't tip his hand. Braun didn't know about the letter yet.

"You do know Esther?" the German asked, gaze studied.

Stephen didn't respond.

"Ruth's daughter." Braun's lips twitched. "My father sent her into the Alps after the war, to a small village named Greifsman." His eyes twinkled. "She's very beautiful."

She *was* alive! "He . . . I don't understand . . ."

"Why is she alive? Let's just say that Esther is our bargaining chip, in the event we ever found Martha. But her value has now expired, hasn't it?"

Braun grinned. "And you're Martha's son, David. My father made the mistake of allowing you to live as well. He wanted Martha's missing son to haunt her till her death. A good instinct, but fundamentally flawed. After all, you were chosen by the scarf."

"I don't know what you're talking about,"

Stephen said. He had to distract Braun from this line of thinking. "I knew Rachel Spritzer from an antique shop I used to frequent," he lied. "She purchased some things there. She talked about her Stones of David, but I always thought she meant her children, until I saw that she had donated one to the museum. I looked around and stumbled onto the floor safe. You know the rest."

"Another one of your inventive stories? My father took the Stones of David as spoils from a collection in Hungary, and I'm sure he would like to have them back. But this"—he held up the journal—"interests us the most. If you've seen the contents I'm sure you know why."

It occurred to Stephen that Braun was incriminating himself—something he would never risk if he intended to let Stephen live. A moan seeped from under the door to the coal room.

Chaim.

"I think the Stones were in this box with the journal," Braun said. "I'm willing to wager the old man's life on it. We can begin now, one finger at a time, or you can tell me what you did with them and make this painless."

"There are no Stones! Do whatever you want, but there was only the scarf."

The letter would prove there were no Stones here, but did he dare tell him about the letter?

"Fine." Braun turned to Claude, who stood by the door to the coal room. "Start with a thumb."

Stephen bolted to his feet. "Stop!" He had to stall. "Okay, listen. The scarf must mean something.

She left it for a reason. It leads to the Stones. Ask yourself how."

Braun hesitated. "Nothing comes to mind."

"Think about it. She wanted me to find the scarf. Why?" Stephen felt toothless, standing up to this monster while wearing nothing but Fruit of the Loom briefs and a torn T-shirt, but he would bite at any hope. "Because you're right. I am David. The scarf saved my life. She drew me in to find the scarf."

"Cut off his thumb," Braun said to Claude, who turned to enter the room where Chaim moaned.

"Wait, there's a letter! It's in the boiler."

Braun held up his hand to Claude. He glanced through the door into the boiler room.

"Well?"

Claude ran in and emerged a moment later bearing the smudged letter.

Braun took the letter, eyed Stephen, and then read it quickly. His left eye twitched once as he neared the end. Stephen sagged into the chair. Braun would now assume the Stones were hidden somewhere else. *The Stones' hiding place will go to the grave with Ruth and me.*

ROTH WAS having a hard time controlling his exuberance. He was playing the boy like a fiddle. He'd convinced the Jew that he was after the Stones of David as well as the journal. And that Esther was still alive in Germany.

He turned his back to Stephen and reread the

letter. The old man called Stephen's name softly once, and Claude thumped the door. "Shut up!" An eerie silence filled the basement.

Roth planted his feet wide and rolled his neck.

"The Stones aren't here," Roth said softly.

He took several deep breaths. He was so taken by his own game that he almost missed the significance of the last line. He'd missed it when he'd first read the letter several days earlier. Now it jumped out at him.

"What could she have possibly . . ." He read the last line out loud. "As for the treasure, its hiding place will go to the grave with Ruth and me."

The implication was what? That Ruth, not only Martha, had known something about the Stones' hiding place.

He turned around and would have grinned wickedly if not for his practiced control.

"Strip him!"

The others hesitated, not expecting the sudden order.

Roth walked to the Jew. "I said *strip* him!" He grabbed the neck of Stephen's T-shirt and jerked it down. The cotton fabric ripped, leaving half of Stephen's chest exposed.

Lars and Ulrich grabbed Stephen and pulled him to his feet.

Roth stared at Stephen's chest. He extended his hand and touched the scar. Traced it.

"David," Roth said. "Isn't it ironic that after all these years, your very survival continues to play into our hands? You've led us to this letter, which says more than Martha meant—I can promise you that. I have to pay our beloved Esther a visit now, so I'm afraid we won't be seeing each other again, but I want you to remember my face. I assure you, I look like my father. Your mother went to her grave with his face stamped in her mind. Why should you go any differently?"

He dropped the letter and walked to the door. "Lars, Ulrich, come with me." He opened the door and turned back to Claude. "Kill the old man and dispose of his body. Keep this other stinking Jew alive until I call. If he tries to escape the basement, kill him. I trust you can manage that."

The instructions were for Stephen's benefit, naturally. The game wasn't over—not yet.

Claude dipped his head, indicating that he'd understood. If he didn't, he would pay with his own life.

THEY WERE going to kill Chaim?

"Cover the stairs," Claude said to Carl. Stephen jerked his head around—Claude was screwing a silencer onto his pistol.

Stephen responded instinctively rather than with any kind of coherent plan. He leaped to his feet, hurled the chair at Claude with a furious grunt, and rushed the man before the chair struck.

Claude absorbed most of the flying chair with his left forearm, but one of the legs struck him square in the forehead. Stephen slammed into the chair, shoving Claude hard against the wall. The German batted at him with a thick hand, struck him on the shoulder, and pushed him into the coal room door.

Stephen grabbed the handle, jerked the door open, and spun inside. He slammed the door, once on Claude's hand, and again after the man sensibly withdrew it. Stephen crammed his palm into the dead bolt he'd seen earlier. It banged home.

Stephen took a step back, trembling from head to foot. He couldn't see—the room was pitch black. Fists pounded on the door. Bitter curses.

"Hello?"

Chaim's voice. From his left. The pounding stopped, and it occurred to Stephen that a bullet could pop through the door as if it were paper.

He dived to his left.

Phwet! Stephen hit the rabbi and both crashed to the floor. *Phwet! Phwet!* Bullets punched round holes of light in the door.

"Uhhh!"

"Down!" Stephen snapped. "Stay down!"

He jerked his eyes back to the door. They seemed to be shooting randomly, hoping for a hit, but it wouldn't take much to blow off the latch. In ten seconds they would be through.

"The tunnel!" Stephen coughed. The quick-drying cement they'd used set up in thirty minutes, but how long before it solidified?

Stephen rolled to his feet and tore for the center of the room. Somehow the spitting bullets missed him as he kicked at the coal they'd scattered over the tunnel. A circle darkened by coal quickly took shape.

"Chaim—"

"Hurry!" The rabbi was beside him, already stomping.

The shooting stopped momentarily, then started again, just below the dead bolt.

"Jump!" Stephen shouted. "Hard!"

He slammed both feet down and was rewarded with a teeth-rattling jolt. It had hardened.

"Together. One, two, three!" He jumped again, but the rabbi's leap came after his. Two more holes popped in the door, up toward the latch.

"Together. Together! One, two, three."

They both leaped; they both slammed into the fresh concrete together; they both fell when the concrete caved.

"Out!" Stephen pushed the rabbi, who quickly crawled out.

Streams of light blazed through the holes in the door. Stephen shoved his hands into the tunnel, grabbed chunks of concrete and wood, and threw them out.

A shot blew away the door latch. But the dead bolt above still held. Someone kicked at the door and swore again.

The tunnel couldn't possibly be clear of all the material Sweeney had used to prop up the concrete, but Stephen had pulled out the large slabs and the plywood. They were out of time.

"Follow me."

He went in headfirst, like a tentative child taking his first daring ride down a slide. His hands struck two-by-fours, and smaller chunks of crumbling cement littered the hole. He shoved them down, ahead of him, praying they wouldn't jam.

Wiggling and squirming, he slid down, plowing

the refuse until it splashed into the sewer ahead. He
didn't try to slow his exit, but he did tuck and roll
the moment his head cleared the tunnel. The sudden cold of sewer water sent waves of relief through
him. He wanted to cheer.

The rabbi was spared the bath; he fell on top of
Stephen like a huge sack of potatoes. The impact
knocked the breath from Stephen's lungs, but the
fact was lost to the whine of bullets. Claude was
shooting down the hole.

"Hurry!" Chaim gasped.

They ran through the blackness. The shooting
stopped, and Stephen knew the German was coming down after them. He hoped Sweeney hadn't
heaped bricks on the manhole cover.

Stephen managed to find the ladder, scrambled
up first. He heaved on the grate, but it refused to
budge. Behind them, Claude swore. He was feeling
his way out of the tunnel they'd dug. Stephen
pushed again. Not a chance.

"Move it! Move it," the rabbi whispered.

"It's stuck! Shh, quiet!" But even the *shh* carried
down the sewer like air brakes.

A huge splash. Claude was in. Stephen swallowed. This was it, then. They were trapped. He
gathered all of his strength and crammed his back
against the lid above. Nothing.

Far away, a dog barked.

"Brandy?" Stephen's whisper echoed down the
tunnel. His question was answered by a sudden slosh-
ing and another big splash, followed by another curse.

Now the dog was barking furiously.

The manhole cover suddenly slid off. Stephen stared up into the round eyes of Sweeney. Brandy attacked his face with a wet tongue.

"No, Brandy. Hurry, get me out!" he cried.

Sweeney and Melissa grabbed his arms and yanked him out of the hole. Brandy stood back, head cocked.

"The rabbi, hurry!"

Up came Chaim.

The sewer filled with splashing and yells. Stephen shoved the cover back over the hole. "How was it braced?"

Sweeney got behind a large timber that he'd found and pushed it back over the cover.

"Good night, what happened?" Sweeney asked.

The cover bounced up.

"More! He's strong."

"There is no more," Sweeney said.

Stephen looked around quickly. The cover rose a full two inches off the hole—he could see the German's gun hand. Without thinking, Stephen jumped up on the timber. The lid clanged back into place.

"Find something." The lid rocked crazily. "Hurry!"

Instead, Sweeney jumped up with him. This time the cover slammed home with confidence. "That'll give him something to think about," Sweeney said. "You're lucky we came back to check out the damage."

"My car's on the street," Stephen said to Chaim. "Spare key's in the gas well. Take Melissa and wait for us."

Chaim needed no encouragement. They left with Brandy bouncing behind.

The timber below them shifted, and Sweeney crouched like a surfer. "That guy's a bull!"

"There's more than one," Stephen said. "We have to get out of here. Four guys with guns could be crossing the street already."

"What went wrong?"

"Long story."

"Did you get it?"

Stephen hesitated. "Sort of."

"You don't have any pants on," Sweeney said.

"I about had my tail shot off. No time for pants."

Sweeney stared at him dumbly.

"Make sure you don't kick the wood off the cover when we push off," Stephen said. "Ready? You go first; I'm right behind. Go!"

Sweeney jumped off and sprinted from the room. Stephen followed on his heels. Behind them, the cover scraped concrete. A single bullet chipped the wall before they made the stairwell. They cleared the building, tore up the alley, and ran straight for Stephen's car, a happening hippie in blue bell-bottoms and a scruffy Realtor in white underwear.

Not until Chaim pulled the car into traffic on La Brea did Stephen feel his pulse ease. But the madness wasn't over, was it? In so many ways, it was just beginning.

For the first time, he knew what was happening; now he just had to follow through. A whole new world had just been opened up to him. He was being drawn by the pearl of great price. The pearl was Esther, for whom he was born.

———~~~———

STEPHEN PACED in the living room, peering repeatedly out the windows on either side of the house. They'd let Sweeney and Melissa off ten blocks down La Brea and returned home the long route. An hour had passed since their narrow escape, but Stephen's nerves still felt taut like piano wires.

They'd called the police, who'd dispatched a cruiser to check out Rachel Spritzer's apartment.

"Rabbi—"

"I'm sorry I didn't help you sooner, Stephen. I was afraid you were pulling back into yourself. But I see that you've been reaching out more than withdrawing. You're finding your own identity."

Stephen nibbled at his index fingernail. "I don't think I can hang out here for the police."

"They'll want to take a statement. We were shot at and nearly killed!"

Stephen looked in his eyes. "She's alive, Chaim."

"Who is?"

"Esther."

"She's alive and in a German town called Greifsman." He swallowed. "He's going to kill her. I have to stop him. He said the red scarf had selected—"

"Red scarf?" the rabbi interrupted, paling.

"The red scarf. You saw it. The letter—"

"He's the one behind the killings!"

"That's what the letter said. His father was the commandant in the camp where my mother was held."

"No, now. The killings in Los Angeles."

"What killings?"

"You haven't heard? Of course you haven't!" Chaim quickly filled him in.

"There's no direct link," Stephen said. "Either way, he's gone now. I have to get to Germany, Rabbi."

Chaim looked at him blankly.

"Braun's going to kill her, did you hear me? I have to beat him there."

"And maybe that's what he wants."

"Then he would have taken me with him. Or killed me when he had the chance."

"This is very dangerous, Stephen." The rabbi hurried to the phone, dialed a number. "You can't just run off to Germany. Do you even have a passport?"

"Yes. Who are you calling?"

"Sylvia. She's working on the Red Scarf case."

Stephen stared out the window as Chaim spoke on the phone. The possibility that Roth Braun was a killer failed to upstage the revelations of Martha's letter.

"Thank you," Chaim said into the phone. He dialed a second number.

On the other hand, this serial-killer business was extremely important. It meant that Esther was about to die. At least that's how Stephen saw it.

He bumped his forehead with his fist. The emotion that had consumed him for the last few days now felt like a hot branding iron on the brain.

Chaim dropped the receiver in its cradle. "She's not at work. No answer at home."

"I'm going, Rabbi."

They stood in silence for a moment. "Why would Braun want to kill her now, assuming he's known all along where she lives? Does she know where the Stones are?"

"No. I don't know. The letter says that their hiding place would go to the grave with Martha and Ruth."

"And they're both dead."

"Right."

"So what does Braun know?"

"I don't know. But I know he's going after Esther."

"Well, this is terribly dangerous."

"No, this is my life!" Stephen was yelling now. He might burst into tears at any moment. "I have to do this. I can't explain why any more than I can explain why I tunneled into the apartment, but I have to go."

"The police—"

"I can't afford to be questioned by the police. If Roth Braun is the man they're looking for, then the danger for Los Angeles is gone. Let them try to find him, although I can guarantee you that he's already in the air. It'll take time to coordinate any action with the German police."

His words echoed in the small house.

"I have to go now."

"Then I'll go with you."

"No. Stay and fill the police in. Tell Sylvia. Do whatever you need, but please give me a chance to get out of the country."

"They'll want to know—"

"Then tell them. Just don't tell them where I've gone. I'm not the criminal here. They can't hold me, can they?"

"Vandalism."

Stephen knew Chaim had a point, and it infuriated him. He gathered himself.

"I have to go, Rabbi," he said quietly. "Please, hear me. I have to go."

Chaim sighed and finally nodded. "Okay. Find her, but please remember what I said, Stephen."

The phone rang. Chaim snatched it up. The police.

In a moment the rabbi set the phone back down and faced Stephen wearing a frown. "You were right—no sign of Braun; no evidence of a crime. Other than a hole in the basement. They want a statement from both of us."

"I'll give mine when I get back."

The rabbi seemed to accept this.

"Obsession is a dangerous business, Stephen. You can't lose sight of virtue or morality for the sake of passion. Just because your intentions are noble, you have no right to break the law. Certainly not to kill or to—"

"I'm not going to kill anyone. I'm going to rescue Esther. God has answered my mother's prayers."

39

THE COMMANDANT'S EYES WERE RED AND watery from lack of sleep. He leaned over the table and sipped at a spoon of the corn chowder Martha had prepared for supper at his request. The china was set on a white cloth, and the commandant was dressed in the uniform he reserved for social events—black, pressed, and starched. For nine months she'd waited on the commandant, while the war slowly ground to a halt throughout the world. Auschwitz had been liberated, Belsen liberated, even Buchenwald in Germany itself liberated. But here in Toruń, just a few miles from Stutthof, the Germans had dug in and were fighting a fierce battle over these last camps. Why? And how could Braun sit so calmly while even now Russian planes flew overhead, armed with bombs for Stutthof?

Martha had long ago lost her fear of Gerhard Braun. "It's over," she said.

"It will never be over," he answered, not bothering to look up. "You're alive today. Does that mean you'll be alive tomorrow?"

381

Martha looked away. His threats hardly even registered anymore. Several other facts, however, did register, like glaring lights in her eyes. The first was that David was still alive. She hadn't seen him for nine months, but she knew he survived in the barracks below. The second was that in a matter of days, whatever end awaited them all would come.

And the third was a growing hope—yes, hope—that she could actually affect that end. How many nights had she lain awake, her mind filled with fantasies of revenge, plotting to use Braun's treasures to her advantage? Her only living mission was to save the children; perhaps she could do so with the help of the spoils hidden in the vault.

The only question was how? Anytime now, Braun would evacuate the vault and be gone.

Paper covered the picture window now, obstructing the view of the camp below where her little David lived. Most of the Russian bombs had descended on the main camp at Stutthof, but Toruń had suffered several raids as well. Braun had sent most of the remaining prisoners north to the Baltic nearly two weeks ago to be evacuated by sea, he said. All but a hundred, mostly wounded or sick, were gone. Rachel was among those who remained. Rachel and David. Rachel and David and Martha and Esther, pawns in his game, kept only to make Braun feel powerful.

If only there was a way to speak sense into this pig! "You have no reason to keep us," Martha said. "And you have no reason to kill us. What will any of this prove?"

Braun set his spoon into the empty bowl, dabbed his lips with a serviette, and ran his tongue over his teeth. She wanted to cut off his red lips with a knife. A fantasy as foolish as taking his treasure.

"Don't be a fool," he said softly. "I have more reasons than you can possibly know to kill you." He stood and picked up his hat. "As it turns out, I also have several compelling reasons not to kill you. Killing you would end your misery, and I have no interest in ending your misery. Also, the Allies are evidently frowning on the indiscriminate killing of prisoners—I'll be gone when they come, but I wouldn't want to leave any evidence to fuel their fires."

Martha, confused, watched him walk to the door. It was the part about her misery that sounded wrong. How would her liberation lead to extended misery—except in the memories she would take with her? Such relatively insignificant misery was beneath Braun. He meant to do more.

"I will be leaving in the morning, but the guards at the perimeter will remain. Don't think you can walk out of here."

He reached the door, put on his hat, and turned the handle. "Oh, and I've decided to take the children with me."

Martha's mouth dropped open. "No! No, you can't!" She took three steps toward him and stopped. "You . . . you can't!"

"But I am. What's more, I can promise you that you'll never find them."

Martha ran to him, fell to her knees, and grabbed his hand before considering the consequences of such an action. "No, I beg you!" she cried. "I beg you; they are children! They mean nothing to you!"

He looked at her as a scientist might look at a lab experiment, pleased by such an unusual reaction from her.

"Please, let me keep my child," Martha whispered.

"You don't think that I'd seriously allow Ruth's ridiculous obsession with hope to actually find life outside this camp, do you? There is no hope for the Jews."

He jerked his hand free and stepped out into the darkness. "If you make any attempt to escape, I would be delighted to shoot all three of you. Except Esther. I've taken a liking to the little girl."

"As has your son," Martha said bitterly.

His head snapped up. He glared. The night Roth had tried to kill Esther had been the last time Martha had seen him.

She pushed him, knowing the danger of it. "He's stronger than you."

Gerhard spat. "He's a child who doesn't know that the war is over. Yesterday's indulgences are today's death sentences. If I didn't know you better, I might think you were asking to be killed."

"I have no reason to live without my David."

"Which is the point. You'll live with the horror of this camp your whole life. Roth doesn't understand that death is sometimes the easy way out."

Gerhard made a disgusted, dismissing motion with his right hand and shut the door with a *thump*.

Martha jumped to her feet and ran for the stairs, mindless. Her right foot was already down two steps before the first clear thought forced her attention. She had to get David! The commandant was leaving, and she had to get her baby before then. She spun around, ran for the door, but pulled up without opening it.

What was she thinking? Even if she could get David, she could never escape with two children under her arms. Even alone, she would be killed.

She threw both fists toward the floor, jerked to the window and screamed through gritted teeth, like an animal. For several long seconds she just stood there, tensed from head to foot, trembling with fury. The thought of losing Esther and David was like the thought of dying. Maybe worse. What did he have to gain from this? Nothing!

But she knew that her scream would do nothing for either David or Esther. She forced herself to take a deep breath. Maybe she could still prevent him from taking the children. Or maybe he didn't really mean to carry out this threat. He was playing with her, one last sick joke before running off with this loot of his.

She blinked. The Stones of David. The journal.

Martha walked to the kitchen and then back, working quickly through ideas. There *was* no way to save the children. Nothing would prevent Braun from taking them.

She stopped by the kitchen table and stared at the far wall without seeing, never so hopeless since seeing the red scarf on her bed nine months earlier. Whatever Braun planned to do with the children could not be good. He might kill them outside the camp, leaving her with lingering hope and uncertainty.

"No, Martha," she muttered, wiping her eyes. "You have to be strong. You have to be strong."

She returned to an idea she'd massaged for dozens of hours late in the nights. A thread, however thin, of hope for the children.

She ran down the stairs, suddenly consumed with accomplishing this one task before Braun returned. Esther slept in peace—her night started at five, something the commandant had insisted on. He wanted the child asleep before he sat down for a quiet evening meal. Martha had wanted to dump poison in his quiet evening meal when he'd first made the demand, but tonight she was grateful.

First, the vault.

How long would Braun be gone? It could be five minutes, or it could be several hours. She ran back upstairs to his bedroom, to a beautifully engraved, white jewelry box on his nightstand, under which she'd discovered the key to the vault three months earlier while cleaning. Tilting back the box, she snatched up the key and flew to the basement. Most of her plan would require stealth, in the late-night hours after Braun was asleep. This first part, however, she could not do without disturbing the peace.

The idea had first mushroomed in her mind as she contemplated how renowned the Stones of David were. Certainly they were far more important to the world than two Jewish children, even if in her mind David and Esther were the true Stones. If her children were ever to be lost, they would be forgotten forever with untold thousands following the war.

But the Stones would always stand as icons, sought by the whole world.

What if she could somehow link both children to the Stones of David? Draw them by association to each other and to her? Rachel's confession in the barracks over a year earlier had haunted Martha. What if she could mark Esther and David as Rachel had done? And what if later she could make it clear in private circles that she was looking for a girl named Esther and a boy named David, both bearing this mark?

She unlocked the door with unsteady hands and stepped into the cool, dark room. It looked just as it had the first time she'd come in. But the journal was gone.

Gone?

Martha hurried to the box and opened it. There, on top of the five stones, lay the leather journal.

She emerged from the vault three minutes later with two green ammunition containers the size of shoe boxes under her right arm. Sweat slicked her palms, but she didn't falter. Not once. She locked the door, slid the boxes under her bed, and returned the key to its place under the commandant's jewelry box.

Returning to the living room window, she peered past a tear in the paper. No sign of him yet. She had to put the mark on Esther before he returned, or her crying would cause a terrible scene. And she would cry. Poor baby, she would cry.

Martha hurried to her room and reached under her thin mattress for the twisted piece of metal. She'd formed the symbol a week ago, using one paper clip, cut and folded back on itself to show the brand she intended.

It would never work! She paused, reconsidering, trying to think of a better way.

There was no time.

The child slept on her back. Martha looked at her supple, innocent body and started to cry silently. She tied the crude brand to the end of a wooden ladle and then bared little Esther's chest. Should she wake her?

Dear God, this was madness! How could she burn a child? She nearly abandoned the plan then, but this was the only way she knew to extend the very hope Ruth had died for. The thought gave her the strength to slowly heat the metal over a candle flame until it was red hot.

She had to clear her eyes of tears twice so she could see. "I'm sorry, dear Esther," she whispered, and then she pressed the metal into the baby's flesh, hard.

Esther did cry. She screamed through Martha's fingers. But thankfully, before the child fully realized she was under assault, the damage was done.

Martha hugged the child tight and rocked her. "Shh, shh, I'm so sorry. I don't mean to hurt you. Shh, shh, you must be quiet."

She dabbed the deep burn with an ointment she'd confiscated from Braun's personal medicine cabinet and then placed a bandage over it. Esther might tear it off, but Martha knew the burn must be hidden from Braun, at least for as long as he had both children.

Surely he wouldn't keep both—it wasn't in his character. He would rid himself of David; why would he keep David? No reason to keep a Jewish boy. The only reason he'd allowed the boy to live was for the sake of his game. He would rid himself of her son within a day or two, maybe sooner.

Martha's thoughts brought her no comfort. Had she burned in vain the child she had promised to care for as her own? Fresh tears streamed down her cheeks, and she lay down with the child, soothing her slowly back to sleep. Exhausted by the pain and tears, Esther finally settled.

She would have to wait now, lying here in bed, cold with sweat. Wait. And doubt.

The door upstairs banged an hour later, and Martha bolted up. Boots clomped on the wood floor, then down the stairs. Many boots, maybe four pair or more. They walked by her door, straight to the vault.

Panicked, she slid from the bed, dropped to her knees, shoved the ammunition boxes all the way under her bed, and then pushed some dirty clothes after it, knowing this cover-up was hopeless. If the commandant discovered anything missing from the vault, he would tear through the entire house, starting with her room, until he found it.

This wasn't just a few coins she'd relieved him of. The journal could destroy him. Dear God, what was she thinking?

They walked by nineteen times, and each time Martha lost a kilo in sweat. And then they didn't return. The house grew quiet. A sudden, terrifying thought struck her: What if he meant to take the children tonight?

She jerked upright. He'd said in the morning, but

what if he meant *by* the morning? What if he'd left already to collect David, with the intention of returning for Esther?

Martha threw off the covers and tiptoed up the stairs in her bare feet. Water, if he asked. She was getting a glass of water.

She peeked down the hall and saw his bedroom door closed. A thin line of light ran along the base of the door. She retreated, her bare feet whispering across the concrete. He'd emptied the vault, presumably without noticing anything missing. What kind of good fortune had extended her this grace?

And to what end? She wouldn't be leaving here with the children, much less the treasure. It was nearly midnight, at least eleven. Her plan would be for nothing if she didn't get down to David. She *had* to get to her son. How could she possibly explain this to Rachel?

Martha slipped to her seat and sat in the dark hall, sunk by a terrible hopelessness. What would Ruth do in a situation like this? Ruth would pray. She would cry out to God for his favor and his hope. She would believe that God would preserve the Stones of David. She would believe that God would protect the children without being compelled to explain why he hadn't protected countless others in this horrifying war.

Martha whispered her prayers to God and then assured herself that he would indeed preserve the true Stones of David. Her tears slowly dried, and her resolve returned. She finally took a deep breath and set about to do what she must.

She pulled out the ammunition boxes, rolled

them in a blanket, and ascended the stairs. The light was out beneath the commandant's door. So then, what was she waiting for? Ruth had given her life for hope; it was time for Martha to risk hers.

She would need a shovel, and although she had an idea where she could get one, she wasn't sure. This part of the plan she might have to abandon. She had one of the Stones at any rate, stashed in her underclothes. If all else failed, she could call to the children after the war using this one Stone.

Martha took a deep breath and slipped out the back door.

40

Germany
July 27, 1973
Friday

STEPHEN STOOD BY THE VOLKSWAGEN BUS
She'd rented in Hamburg and stared down at the
small town of Greifsman. A bird chirped from a
grove of trees to his right; the sky was blue and the
air was cool. It felt surreal to be here, so far from
home, yet so close.

Several children played in the village square; a tall
bell tower marked the church around which two or
three hundred homes crowded. The village wasn't
unlike any small Russian town, a far cry from the
sprawling cities of America. For every minute of the
past forty-eight hours, he'd imagined this moment,
driving into Greifsman and running into Esther's
arms, two soul mates finally and miraculously
reunited. He'd stared at Ruth's picture for hours,
considering every conceivable eventuality.

But the three-dimensional reality dashed his fantasies. If she wasn't here, he was lost. If she was here
but refused to go with him, he was lost. If she was
here and agreed to go with him, and Braun was also
here, they were both lost. For all he knew, she was

already dead. Or alive and happily married with
twelve children. Even one child. Spoke no English.
A dozen other possibilities.

Stephen had contacted Chaim upon his arrival
in Germany. The rabbi had terrified him with new
details.

Sylvia was dead.

Dead?

Dead.

The news still seemed impossible.

Chaim had gone looking for her after giving the
police a statement on the fire. She never had shown
up at work.

He found her bound in her apartment on blood-
soaked sheets. Gagged with a red scarf. Lifeless.

Chaim blurted the news through tears, demanding that Stephen return immediately. This changed
everything. Stephen couldn't return, of course. Another woman's life was at stake.

Esther. Her face was burned into Stephen's head,
begging, dying for his help. His love.

They'd already made contact with the German
authorities, but Stephen was right—these things
took time.

Now, standing over the village called Greifsman,
Stephen was suddenly sure that the next hour would
turn out badly.

In a moment of overwhelming resolve, however,
he ran for the Volkswagen, climbed in, and fired up
the van. Lack of sleep had made him emotional. He
looked over at the picture of Ruth on the passenger's
seat. This was insane.

He muscled the gearshift forward, released the clutch, and jerked with the bus. The gravel road was steep, and he found himself wondering how they managed in the winter. Maybe there was another road, although the man at the rental agency had assured him this was the only way to Greifsman, if he absolutely insisted on visiting. No one visited Greifsman. It was nothing but a pile of rubble in the middle of nowhere.

Stephen accelerated and shifted into a higher gear. He would blaze into town; he would search; he would find; he would leave.

Honestly, he wasn't sure he actually wanted to find her. Yes, as odd as that sounded, he really wasn't too thrilled about the prospect of searching for someone who was likely married or dead. And he wasn't just telling himself that to keep his hopes from boiling over. Or was he? Either way, he couldn't race through the streets yelling her name, now, could he? The residents might come out of the houses with pitchforks.

No, it would be a calm, collected affair. A simple question here, a suggestion there. He would compare faces against Ruth's picture, show it to others. If he wore his collar up, Braun might not even know he was in town.

He glanced at the picture and took a settling breath. "God help me."

Everyone who saw him drive up the cobblestone street into Greifsman stared. They didn't run out and clap their hands and dance in the streets as if he were the liberating army; they simply stared at him, as if they'd seen this before. The return of the gunslinger. Maybe the car rental man back in the airport knew a few things.

Stephen parked the van by the square and looked around. A bread shop, a butcher, the distant sound of children singing. School. An old man with a wrinkled face sat on a bench ten yards ahead, watching him with casual interest.

Okay, Stephen. Calm, collected, methodical. You've come this far.

He took the photograph, exited the van, and walked straight to the old man.

"Excuse me."

The man cracked a toothless smile and nodded.

"Excuse me, you speak English?"

"Anglesh," the man said.

Apparently not. He held up the picture. "Du yu no vwherr I ken fined dis wooman? Estar?" What was he thinking? He cleared his throat and spoke in normal English. "Do you know where I can find this woman?"

"Nein." The man shook his head and wagged one hand.

"Thank you." He walked up the street where a group of children watched him, smiling.

He held up the picture. "Esther? Anyone know this girl?"

A girl of eight or nine giggled. The rest ran off, squealing with delight.

He walked on, feeling more self-conscious than he had upon exiting the van. Several women were crossing the street to his left. "Excuse me." They ignored him and continued. "Excuse me, does anyone speak English? I'm looking for Esther."

They whispered to each other and moved on without paying him more than a sideways glance. Stephen stopped on the sidewalk, suddenly worried. What if she really wasn't here? Braun might have purposefully thrown Stephen off. He swallowed and hurried toward the bread shop. A woman with a plaid dress covered by a white apron walked out holding a large bag, gave him a quick glance, and moved away quickly. Not a good prospect. He stepped into the shop.

He stumbled out thirty seconds later. Not one of the seven people inside seemed to speak English. Not one showed any recognition when he showed them the picture. She wasn't here! And the people were treating him like a piece of trash that had blown in on the wind.

The calm, collected approach wasn't working.

Stephen ran to the corner and thrust the picture above his head. "Hey!" he yelled. "English! Who speaks English?" His voice rang out over the street. There were several cars, a dozen bicycles, and at least forty people in his field of vision. The bustle paused with his cry. A hundred eyes turned his way.

He had their attention.

"Please, I'm looking for Esther! The girl in this photograph." He pointed at the photo. "Can anyone tell me where I can find her?"

The pause lasted two seconds, and then as one they resumed their bustle, as if he didn't exist here on the corner, bellowing like a fool.

"Hey!"

This time, they ignored him entirely. They were hiding something! Of course! Why would so many people ignore him? Germans were well-known for their friendliness, even more so in the country. If one of them had responded kindly, tried to explain—but no. The whole village was conspiring against him.

The obsession he'd lived with in Los Angeles drove him forward now. Stephen ran down the sidewalk, waving the picture in front of startled villagers. "See her? This is Ruth. Esther's mother. Tell me where she is. Tell me!"

A middle-aged woman scolded him in high-pitched outrage. The only word he caught with certainty was "idiot."

He honestly didn't care whether she thought he was an idiot. If she had any idea what he'd gone through to be here, she would be running around frantically with him.

He showed the picture to at least fifty people, ignoring their blatant denial, gaining steam as he progressed, as much out of anger as hopelessness now. The main street ran for about a hundred yards, and he hurried all the way to its end, begging, yelling, whispering, any and every approach that came to mind. "Show me some respect, for heaven's sake. Look at the picture!"

Except for the occasional vacant or sympathetic stare and several angry lectures, the villagers continued to ignore him. He was doomed. No, he refused to be doomed.

Stephen pulled up and faced the street, beyond himself. "You lying hoard of insensitive—" He jumped up and beat at the air. "Speak to me!"

"They wouldn't tell you if they did know," a voice

said behind him. Stephen whirled. A young man leaned against the wall, stroking a black goatee.

"You speak English," Stephen said.

"So do half the people in this town. The younger ones."

"Then why—"

"This town is controlled by the . . . what do you call it? Like German Mafia. Do you want these people to be killed? Only a fool would tell you anything, whether they know or not. And only a fool would run around town yelling at them and jumping in the air. You'll be dead by sunset."

Stephen stared at him.

The man turned away.

"No, wait." Stephen stepped up and grabbed his arm. "Do you know her?" he whispered.

The man stopped. "Let go of my arm."

Stephen did.

"Are you deaf? Do you want a sniper to pop my head like a pumpkin?"

"No."

"Then don't ask again." He walked off. "No, I don't know her," he said so Stephen could hear.

No? No? Stephen scanned the roofs of the buildings, half expecting to see the glimmer of a rifle. Snipers in this tiny village? It had to be a figure of speech.

He hurried for a side street, suddenly feeling like a fool. Okay, so maybe calm and collected would have been better after all. But now he had a problem of incalculable proportions. He had to believe Esther lived here, in this village. He really had no

alternative. If no one would tell him where to find
Esther, then he would have to find her himself.

Stephen stopped and looked back toward the
town square. How many people lived in this place?
One thousand? Three thousand? Couldn't be more
than three thousand. How long would it take to
search thirty streets? He would go door-to-door if he
had to. If Esther was here, he would recognize her;
he was sure of that.

On the other hand, some of them would surely
recognize him from his circus act on Main Street—
maybe even report him to the snipers. Half the town
had probably seen or heard of him by now. He had to
be more discreet. But he also had to hurry; if Braun
hadn't taken her already, he couldn't be far behind.

He considered retreating to the van, but one
glance at the picture and he discarded the thought.
He hid the photograph under his shirt, shoved his
hands into his pockets, and walked on. He bought a
floppy black hat from a street vendor, hoping it
might alter his appearance at least some.

He entered a lazy cobblestone street that ran in
front of the towering church. Half a dozen people sat
or stood outside as many shops. Someone laughed,
but he didn't turn to see if it was directed at him. He
glanced as nonchalantly as possible at each face. None
of them was Esther. None of them was even a woman.

Another thought struck him. Maybe Esther
would find *him*. If it was true that they were soul
mates, wouldn't she recognize something special in
him? Maybe he should be less concerned about
being recognized by the Mafia types and more

concerned with letting everyone in the village get a good look at him. He would leave the rest in God's hands, if indeed God was interested.

He glanced up at the church across the street. A woman stood at the side of the building, by the entrance to an alley, arms crossed. She was staring at him.

Stephen stopped. Was . . . was it her?

The same dark hair, the same finely curved cheekbones. Eyes that drilled him with a bright stare. She wore an equally bright blue dress.

He was holding his breath.

He glanced up the street—no one was watching him. Except her. She was still looking at him. His mouth was open, he knew that, but he wasn't thinking clearly enough to close it. Worse, he couldn't move his feet. He just stood there, forty yards away, ogling her as if she were an apparition who'd come to sweep him off to heaven.

This didn't seem to faze her. She continued staring. Or was she glaring?

Stephen regained his composure and headed across the street, straight for her. She let him come. He stopped ten feet from her. This was Esther, the perfect image of Ruth. The same hair, flowing gracefully past smooth cheeks. The same disarming eyes and the same small nose. She was petite, no more than a couple of inches over five feet.

"What are you staring at?" she asked.

"What?"

"You're staring at me as if you were looking at a ghost. Haven't you ever seen a woman before?"

"Of course." His voice cracked, but he didn't bother to correct it. She was reacting out of shock at finally seeing him. Hiding her own need for him with this charade.

"Then stop staring as if you haven't," she said.

He blinked. "You speak English."

"Obviously."

"Do you have twelve children?"

It was her turn to blink. "Do I look like I've had twelve children?"

"No! Sorry." His face flushed. "You're just so beautiful, I had to know . . ."

"If I've had twelve children?"

"Are you married?"

"No."

It was too much for Stephen. He rushed to her and threw his arms around her neck before she could move.

"My name is Stephen. David. I've looked everywhere for you!"

She was stiff like a mannequin. He was overwhelming her. *Get ahold of yourself, Stephen. She's a tender twig; you'll snap her in two. This is no way to introduce yourself.*

He started to pull back and was aided by a shove from her.

She stepped away, horrified and angry. "What on earth do you think you're doing?" she said, eyes darting up the street.

"I'm sorry. I don't know what came over me. You're . . . you're Esther, right?"

"I don't know what you're talking about."

This couldn't be! Was she terrified out here on the street? Of course!

"Maybe we should go to the alley," he said.

She reached out and slapped him. "What do you take me for?"

For the first time, he wondered if he'd made a terrible mistake.

"What do you mean, prancing around the village, making a fool of yourself?" she demanded.

Stephen stepped back. "You saw me?"

"Half the village saw you. If there's an Esther who lives here, I don't know her. Now leave, before you get yourself killed."

She glanced over his shoulder, gave him a parting glare, and walked away.

41

WHO THE MAN WAS, SHE HAD NO IDEA, BUT IF he continued with these antics, neither of them would live out the day. She feared as much for him as she did for herself. Perhaps more.

That's why she'd slapped him.

Yes, that's why. Hard enough to really hurt. Tears came to her eyes now as she walked briskly from him. How he knew, she couldn't guess. He'd called her beautiful. She couldn't remember the last time a man had told her she was beautiful. It wasn't permitted.

But this bold fool from America named Stephen David didn't know that. He had maybe seen her somewhere and really thought she was pretty. Now he was coming after her in full daylight. Is this how Americans courted their women?

And yet she found herself undeniably attracted to the tall man with haphazard dark hair. He'd told her she was beautiful. Did he really believe she was beautiful? Was *he* beautiful? He did not fit her preconceived notion of American men. And yet, he could be missing his ears and she might think him beautiful. He desired her.

"Stop it," she whispered harshly. "What do you take yourself for? A whore?" Fresh tears filled her eyes. She bit her bottom lip. Some realities in life couldn't be changed.

The first: no man could love her.

The second: she could love no man, because she certainly could never love the man who'd imprisoned her here.

The third: she was trapped. If she set one foot outside this pathetic village, Braun would kill the only person who meant anything to her.

She rounded the corner and glanced back. No sight of the American. She stopped for a moment, swallowed, and then hurried down the street. Her memories flitted to Hansen. She was eighteen, and he was a strong young man with bright blue eyes and a wide smile. Braun had killed that budding desire. Literally. She'd cried for two straight weeks. Her first and last true love. Braun's decree could not have been more clear. The men stayed away from her after that. And she from them.

Her earliest memories took her back to age six, when she first began to realize that she was different from the other children. She had no mother, no father, only uncles. And her uncles were mean men who cursed often.

When she was eight, the other children seemed to turn on her. She remembered the day on the playground clearly. Freddy had called her a whore in front of all the other children. She didn't even know what a whore was. No one had stood up to him.

She learned the truth of her life when she was twelve—why she had no memory of her parents and lived with mean uncles and aunts.

She caught the eye of Armond across the street, keeping his eternal watch over her. She squared her shoulders.

What would they all say if the American ran up to her again and pronounced his undying love? Was she lovable? Was she not a woman? The American seemed to think so.

She secretly wished that Stephen David would do just that. That he would chase her at a full sprint and fall to his knees and cry out his adoration for all the village to hear.

But that was a foolish fantasy. And a dangerous one.

"Please leave," she whispered. "Leave this town."

STEPHEN LOOKED around. Three men angled toward him, intentions clear. They were coming to the aid of a woman who'd been attacked by a foreigner.

He stepped into the alley, took several long steps until he was sure he was out of their sight, and ran. What had he just done?

The alley ended. He veered to his right and slowed to a walk. How could she not be Esther? What was the probability that a woman who so closely resembled Ruth just happened to live in the very village Braun had named?

On the other hand, Stephen wasn't a student of faces. In the past twenty-four hours, a hundred women who resembled Ruth had made his heart jump. He had seen her face in the clouds, in the rocks, even in the Volkswagen emblem on the van's steering wheel.

Stephen began to run again, terrified by the possibility that he had just let Esther go. He had to at least warn her about Braun. Where could she have gone?

The answer came quickly when she walked out onto the same street, fifty yards ahead. He instinctively threw himself into a doorway. Somehow, skipping up to her for another hug didn't strike him as the most effective way to gain her confidence.

He poked his head around the corner and looked both ways. The men had either given up their pursuit or had opted to follow her to safety. The girl who wasn't Esther was walking away, deeper into the village.

He stepped onto the sidewalk, lowered his head, and followed. The floppy black hat was a beacon now; he pulled it off and tossed it in a doorway. Ten paces later, he braved a glance. She wasn't walking as if she was concerned. Even if she wasn't Esther, she was one of the most beautiful women he'd ever laid eyes on. Of course, that was probably because he'd imagined she *was* Esther, and his mind had been ruined by . . .

She began to turn. He leaped to his right, behind a garbage bin, and dropped to a crouch. Someone chuckled, and he turned toward the sound. It had come from an older gentleman seated in a doorway. The man waved, and Stephen waved back, embarrassed.

He sneaked a peek. She was entering another alley, headed back toward the church! Stephen stood, immobilized by indecision. If he ran down the street she'd emerged from a moment ago, he might be able to intercept her.

He ran. If she was Esther, Braun hadn't arrived

yet. The thought propelled him into a sprint, legs pumping like a world-class runner. The old man's cackle chased him down the street and around the corner. He ignored a dozen alarmed villagers, took a sharp left at the next corner, and blasted for the alley from which he knew she would emerge.

He slid to a stop at the corner, took one deep breath, and jumped out. Another second and he might have landed on top of her. She jumped back and shrieked.

The leap had been a bit much, he immediately saw. A nonchalant, suave entrance would have accomplished the same thing with far more subtlety.

She held a hand to her chest. "What are you doing, you idiot! Get away from me!"

He held up a finger. "Shh!" Looking into her eyes again, he was sure she was Esther. He felt as though he'd searched for those eyes his entire life.

"Why are you attacking me?"

Her accusation shocked him. "I wouldn't dream of hurting you. How can you say that? I'm here to save you!"

"Throwing yourself at me and then stalking me in broad daylight is your idea of saving me? They'll kill you for sure now."

"Stop it!" he yelled. Footsteps pounded behind him. They'd heard her cry and were coming. Stephen pulled out the photograph and spoke quickly. "Help me, I'm begging you. This is Ruth, Esther's mother. She gave her life for me in the concentration camp at Toruń. There isn't time—Braun's on his way here now. For Esther."

The woman stared. Running feet entered the alley.

"Please," Stephen said quietly. "I swear I thought you were Esther, otherwise I wouldn't have done that. Please, I have to help her."

A rough male voice spoke in German behind Stephen.

The woman hesitated. "I'm okay," she told the man. The footsteps left.

"Thank you." He was still holding the photograph out to her.

Her eyes searched his for several moments and then lowered to the photograph.

"I wish I could help you," she said. "But I can't."

"You must!"

She stood defiant, but he thought her eyes were misty.

"I don't know who Esther is," she said, "but I do know they will kill you if you continue. Braun's well-known here. He doesn't value life."

"And he's on his way here now."

She stepped around him and hurried for the street. Stephen walked after her. "Please—"

"You must leave before you get both of us killed."

He ignored the glares of onlookers and hurried to catch her.

"I'm telling you the truth. My name is David. I go by Stephen. I was born in Toruń. My mother's name was Martha. Do you know any of this?"

She veered up the stairs to the church doors. Her jaw was firm, but he saw a tear escape her eye, and the realization nearly crushed him. What had Braun done to make her so terrified?

He followed her into an arching foyer with stained glass high above. "I just came from Los Angeles. Braun was there looking for the Stones of David. Doesn't any of this mean anything to you?"

She spun. "You have no idea!" Her eyes blazed, but she could not hold back another tear that ran down her face. She was Esther after all! She had to be.

"Look at it!" he said, shoving the picture forward. "This is your mother! She gave her life!"

Esther looked at the photo. But her eyes stayed on the image. Surely she saw her own features in it.

"You are Esther!" He turned the photograph over. "Read it!"

Her eyes dropped to the writing.

> My dearest Esther, I found this picture in Slovakia after the war. It is your mother, Ruth, one year before your birth.
>
> Not an hour passes without my begging God that you and David will find each other. I will never forget. You are the true Stones of David.

"No. It can't be."

Her lips quivered. Stephen resisted an impulse to take her into his arms again. *Dear Esther, I am so sorry. What have they done to you?*

She shook her head. "You have the wrong person." Stephen grabbed his collar and ripped his shirt open, exposing the scar on his chest, daring her to deny it.

She stared, unable to move her eyes. Her face softened, and the tears began to run unrestricted. She lifted a trembling hand over her heart and slowly, as if in a dream, pulled the neckline of her dress down just enough to reveal the skin below her collarbone. There, burned into her flesh, was an identical scar.

"Esther," he said.

Her eyes rose to meet his. "Yes."

He stepped forward and put his hand on her shoulder. Anything else seemed inappropriate. She slowly rested her forehead on his chest and began to cry.

42

A YEAR HAD PASSED SINCE ROTH LAST VISITED the village. His men usually did the honors. From the road, the town looked unchanged.

Gerhard had his journal, but the Stones of David were still missing. With the threat posed by the journal behind Gerhard, Roth had little trouble stirring up his father's passion for the Stones.

Gerhard hadn't been so delighted in thirty years. Roth was pleased. And he had a plan.

When he'd received the phone call nearly two hours ago saying the Jew had arrived, Roth had nearly wept for joy.

Stephen had come, as surely as Roth had known in his remarkable judgment he would. The Jew would chase this fantasy of his to hell and back if necessary. Why not? After all, Christ had.

Little did Stephen know.

The danger of playing the game so close to the wire was both thrilling and unnerving to Roth. What if the Jew outwitted him as Martha had outwitted his father? Or worse, what if the Jew had already left?

"Straight to her house, Lars."

"If she's not there?"

"Then we'll find her at the church," he said. "Just hurry."

The car surged forward, down the steep grade.

He lifted his father's old red scarf, pressed it against his nose, and inhaled deeply. It smelled like Ruth, he thought. Like Esther. He glanced over his shoulder. Esther was about to get a wake-up call.

"Faster."

"Any faster, and we'll be off the side," Lars shot back.

Roth took a deep breath. The thought of what lay ahead tested even him.

~~~

STEPHEN WATCHED Esther pace behind the last pew, content to study her fiery brown eyes and her blue dress, which flowed lazily with each turn.

Esther. This was Esther. This stunning creature who paced before him was really Esther. He could still hardly believe she was Ruth's daughter.

They'd burned forty minutes in the church, far more than he knew was reasonable considering their predicament. But he was asking her to leave the only home she knew on a moment's notice. Half an hour ago, he was jumping out at her from the alleys; now, he was asking her to head to the hills with him. Unlike her confession, this wasn't something he could force.

He'd walked among the pews and discreetly watched her weigh the choice before her. There wasn't a shred of doubt in Stephen's mind: he was born for this woman. And he would win her love or die trying. No other woman could compare, not even in the smallest way—he was sure of this, though he hardly knew her at all.

Yet he did know some things. She had the spirit of an eagle caged by evil. If ever there was a victim of cruelty, it was her; and yet she endured it with her chin level. Because of this alone, he was utterly in love with her. He would set her free.

And there was more. The flip of her wrist, the darting of her eyes, the smell of her skin, the sound of her voice. She had the skin of a dove. She was his soul mate, created for him. And he for her.

His pearl of great price, as Martha had put it.

His obsession had taken flesh, and he would embrace it. Protect it. Its name was Esther. Gerik was surely right—man was created to obsess.

Despite the danger that now faced them, he could barely keep his mind on the task at hand. Perhaps because the task always had been love. It made sense that he was now as concerned about love as he was about staying alive or finding the Stones of David. Of course, staying alive was a prerequisite to winning Esther's love.

He knew she couldn't possibly feel the same about him. After all, she hardly knew him. But he thought maybe she was warming to him. Her apprehension was understandable. Once they got out of this mess, he'd give her time and space to grow to love him. He'd romance her properly. Candlelight, roses, moonlight strolls on the beach—the lot. She wouldn't be able to resist . . .

He looked over and stopped. She was gone! His heart jumped into his throat.

"Esther?"

"Yes?"

Her voice drifted in from the foyer. He vaulted the pew and ran in. "Don't you ever do that again!"

"Do what?" She stood before a large mirror, looking at her scar. "I walked ten paces. Just because I leave the room doesn't mean I've fled."

"I crossed the ocean to find you."

"And if I would have known about you, I would have done the same," she said.

This was good, right?

"I've been lost my whole life," Stephen said. "Until now."

She didn't respond, but her eyes spoke clearly enough. She was as lonely as he, just as desperate. The only difference was that she hadn't dwelt on the matter for a week as he had.

She looked back at the mirror. Even watching her now, his knees felt weak. He felt completely unreasonable and soft. Really, his whole life had been moving inexorably toward this day.

"Please don't go anywhere without telling me," he said. "Braun's out there somewhere."

"Stephen."

"Yes?"

"Will you come here?"

He walked over, feeling awkward. "Have you decided whether you'll come with me?"

"Yes," she said matter-of-factly.

He stopped. "Yes?"

She looked over at him. "Yes."

"So you'll come with me?"

"I said yes."

"Then we should go now."

She eyed him, amused. "Will you come here for a moment?"

He stepped up next to her in front of the mirror.

"May I see your scar?" she asked.

He exposed the burn on the left side of his chest.

"Come over here, on this side."

His hand that held the shirt open was trembling. He released it. "Please, Esther. If we don't get out now, we may never get out."

"Please," she said softly.

A strange faintness drained Stephen. Her words were a lovely, sedating drug. Just a simple word, *please*, yet he felt he might crumple where he stood!

Stephen swallowed. "Okay."

She guided him to her right side, so they stood shoulder to shoulder, exposing their burns to the mirror. Hers was a full foot lower than his.

"Wait here." She brought a padded stool that sat beside the door. "Here, kneel on this."

He watched her. She did everything with an incredible grace. The way she picked up the stool; the way she carried it over as if it were made of feathers; the way she bent her legs to set it down; the way she said "kneel on this." No woman could move or speak so gracefully.

He knelt on the padded stool. Now they were at roughly the same height.

"It's hard to believe, isn't it?" she said. "Your mother did this to us so we could find each other."

Stephen focused on her scar. Here they were, kneeling in front of a mirror, Esther and David, the two children from the camps, shoulders bared, branded for each other. The sight was so perfect. Terrifying. He jerked his shirt back up to cover his chest.

"Please, Esther, we have to leave."

She covered her shoulder and turned away. Was something wrong?

"Esther?"

She walked to the window, peered out, and then turned back. "You have to understand something, Stephen." The fire flashed in her eyes again. "I can't leave here yet. Not as long as Braun is alive."

"What? We don't have time for that! We should be somewhere else. As far away from here as possible. Why can't we just leave? He has nothing to gain by coming after us."

"No. He won't permit me to leave." Her jaw was set.

"What can he possibly do?"

"More than you can know."

"What do you mean? We *have* to leave. Now!"

She closed her eyes and took a deep breath. "I'm a prisoner of Braun." Her eyes snapped open. "Believe me, he'll find us both, and when he does he'll kill us. I can't leave as long as he's alive."

"You have to. We have each other; we can run."

"Where can we go that he will not follow? No. I will not run."

Urgency swelled in Stephen's chest. "He'll kill you if you stay."

"That is why I have to kill him before he gets to me. Leave if you have to, but I can't. There are other reasons."

"I can't leave you!" He placed both palms against

his forehead and paced. "That's crazy. If you only knew what I've been through."

"I'm sure it's no more than what I've been through. Or my mother. Or your mother. This doesn't end as long as Braun is alive. The man is obsessed."

Her use of the term stopped Stephen. "And so am I."

"Then go find your obsession."

"I already have."

Her eyebrow arched.

"You," he said. "You're the obsession I've searched for my entire life."

"Really? We met only an hour ago. In an alley, if you recall." She looked deep into his eyes. "To what ends will you go to protect this obsession of yours? Will you kill the beast who threatens her, or will you hide so that he can live to stalk her another day? Believe me, Stephen, there's more here than you can know. I can't leave this place as long as Braun is alive."

He frowned, struck as much by her suggestion that he would do anything less than protect her as by the sudden realization that he had to do exactly that.

He had to kill Braun.

He swallowed. What was he thinking? He had to kill Braun? He had to *run*! With Esther.

"But . . . if we kill him, aren't we becoming like him?"

"No. We're doing what Ruth and Martha would have done if they had the chance."

"Okay. Okay, then maybe we should kill him."

Hearing his own words, Stephen felt dizzy. Would he actually kill a man? Should he?

"Just like that?" Esther asked.

"I won't let anybody hurt you. Never again."

She walked up to him, eyes searching. "Are you a dream, Stephen?"

"No."

She was putting on a brave face, but he could see the fear in her eyes. She didn't know if she could trust him. Yet he was giving her no choice. *Dear Esther, what have they done to you?*

She suddenly turned and hurried for the sanctuary.

"Follow me."

43

THE BELL TOWER ROSE HIGH ABOVE THE church, and by the looks of the aged bricks that lined the bell housing, it had been built long before the war. Stephen stood against one wall, staring at Esther, who scanned the street over an old hidden rifle she'd extracted from the back of the tower's only closet.

"No sign of him," she said.

Her voice rose just above a contralto, impossibly sweet. He knew what was happening. Now that the truth of her identity had settled fully in his mind, the fixation he'd had with the Stones of David had been transferred, heart and soul, to Esther. He felt like a puppy in her presence. He'd followed her up the stairs, lightheaded as much from the scent of her perfume as from the climb, and listened as she explained how she knew the rifle was there. Something about having smuggled it there years ago during a lapse in her captors' attentiveness, but he was more interested in her.

"Stephen?" Esther turned her head.

She'd caught him staring? He jerked his eyes from her, aware of his flushed skin. Could she read his thoughts? No, how could she know his mind by looking at him? He was overreacting, which explained the hot and cold waves that spread over his skull and down his neck.

"Are you okay?" she asked.

"Yes. Yes, of course I'm okay. What are you doing?"

"I'm waiting for Braun—what do you mean, what am I doing?"

"Of course. What I meant was, why? Or . . . what are you thinking?"

Stupid. Stupid question!

Esther turned back to her study of the street without betraying any problem with his question. "I'm thinking that the moment this pig shows himself, his life is going to end."

"Sure. Of course. Makes perfect sense."

Did it? He hadn't been able to think clearly enough to imagine actually killing a man. The whole plan—coming up here to pick Braun off— seemed surreal.

Was he thinking straight?

Another thought occurred to him. How could a preoccupation that impaired his reasoning be a good thing? If God had created man to obsess, had he also created him to trade reason for intuition? Or worse, sacrifice reason for emotion? The rabbi would never agree. Not even Gerik would agree.

Stephen watched her as she peered over the rifle. Her lips were parted slightly, but she was breathing through her nose. A wisp of dark hair rested on her cheek. Her right hand, tender and white, gripped the trigger. This was the image of God before him. He was staring at a piece of God, and he could hardly stand the wonder.

Chaim had often preached passion for God. In this moment, Stephen thought he understood what the rabbi meant. If man could be as obsessed with God as Stephen was with Esther—what a thought.

And if Chaim was right, if man's emotions were only a dim reflection of the Creator's emotions, wouldn't God also have feelings like Stephen had? Was God obsessed? Was he preoccupied with an extravagant love for man?

How reasonable was dancing naked in the streets, as King David had done? How collected was Noah in building his huge boat in the desert? Or the prophets, being fed by birds or crawling around like an animal for years? Whatever had motivated those great shapers of history had been sparked by a moment of the deepest conviction and passion—maybe not so different from his own.

The entire line of reasoning took no more than ten seconds, and Stephen felt his confidence surge as a result of it.

"Are you really going to shoot him?" he asked.

"Do you have a better idea?"

"It just seems so . . . illegal."

"How can you stand there and talk to me about laws? This man kills. His father killed your mother. He will kill you too. And me. What he's done to me is illegal. Foul!"

She straightened and walked three steps to the still bell, then back to the window, tucking a strand of hair behind her ear.

Foul?

Rage blackened Stephen's vision. "What . . ." *No, not now.* He took a deep breath. "You're right; I'm sorry," he said.

"What am I supposed to do? You can run; I can't. He'll hound me!" For a moment, Stephen thought she might cry.

"No, I was wrong," he cried. "Kill him! We'll kill him for sure!" He took two steps toward her, sick that he'd hurt her again. What was his problem?

Chaim's words were burning a hole in his soul, that was his problem. *This obsession business is danger-ous, Stephen. You can't break laws in the name of love.*

Esther's eyes darted about the room and briefly settled on his face. She looked like a child caught between terror and hopelessness.

"Esther . . ."

She spun to the window and froze.

"What?"

She leaped forward and crouched at the sill. "He's here!" she whispered.

Stephen sprang forward, saw the black car roll to a halt across the street. How Esther knew it was Braun, he didn't know, but neither did he doubt. One glance at her face, and he knew this man was a living demon to her. Her lips quivered with fury.

Esther brought the rifle to her shoulder and angled the barrel toward the car. She was breathing hard, and the gun wavered with each breath.

The car's rear door swung open. Braun stepped out.

Stephen bent behind Esther, beating back panic. How could he stand here like a mouse while she fought off the beast?

Esther began muttering under her breath. Bitterly.

Stephen stared at the unfolding scene, aghast. *Foul,* she had said. Roth had abused her.

He lunged for the gun; grabbed the barrel. "Wait! I'll do it!"

The gun boomed in the enclosed tower. Stephen jumped back, rifle in hand. Below them, Braun ducked and ran across the street toward the church's entrance.

"What are you doing?" cried Esther, jumping up.

"I should do the shooting," Stephen said.

"You made me miss!" She gaped at him, and he wanted to explain, but words seemed inadequate.

Esther clamped her mouth shut and ran past him. "Hurry, we're sitting ducks up here!" She disappeared through the tower door.

"Esther!"

From the corner of his eye, Stephen saw the driver's door fly open. Lars dived out.

"Hurry, Stephen!" She was calling him.

His lover was calling his name.

"Esther!"

He worked the bolt, pivoted the rifle out the window, lined the sights in the man's direction, and jerked the trigger.

Boom!

Lars staggered.

Stephen ejected the spent cartridge and shot at the large target again. This time, the man turned and hopped back toward the car. He'd hit him! He'd shot a man through his leg! Or maybe his hip.

Stephen whirled and raced for the stairs. "Esther!"

She was running straight for Braun! Stephen took the stairs three at a time, rifle flailing overhead. His foot missed one of the steps and bounced over the edges of three more before finding purchase on the fourth. The rifle sailed free as he grabbed at the air. It clanged down a flight and came to rest on the floor directly below him.

"Es—" He cut the yell short. Braun would hear him screaming! The thought sent him flying down the stairs for the gun. He had to get into the sanctuary and cut Braun down before the man found Esther, assuming she didn't find him first.

Stephen reached the rifle, grabbed metal, and came up in a run.

The blow came out of nowhere, a sledgehammer that crashed into his head and sent him reeling back to the floor.

Braun, he thought vaguely. *That was Braun.* But his vision had clouded over, and he couldn't make sense of his surroundings. The gun lay on the floor to his right. He was sitting down. Maybe he'd run into the wall.

No, he'd seen movement. He tried to stand, but his muscles weren't cooperating.

Hands grabbed his collar and jerked him to his feet. "Where is she?"

The stench of the man's breath buffeted his face. Stephen's world cleared. He was standing just inside the sanctuary, supported by Braun. The man's white knuckles gripped a fistful of shirt and pressed against Stephen's nose. He nearly opened his mouth and bit the man's fingers but quickly decided that angering Braun more would only make matters worse.

"Where is she?" Braun said.

She'd eluded him! Esther had eluded this monster and, fortunately, Stephen had no clue where she could be. Hopefully halfway up the hill headed for Hamburg.

A hand slapped his face. "Where?" Braun dragged him into the sanctuary.

"She's gone," Stephen said. "She ran away when I told her about Martha. I told her Alaska would—"

"Jews don't run. They wait obediently; don't you know your history?"

"You'll never find her."

Braun dropped him to the floor by the altar and stepped back. He held a pistol in his right hand, angled casually at the ground. But there was nothing casual about the man's grin. Sweat wet his flushed skin, and his nostrils pulled at the air.

He pulled out the red scarf Stephen had found in the safe and wiped his face as he glanced around the sanctuary, searching the dark corners by the confessional and the doorways.

"She's gone," Stephen said. If he could keep the man occupied long enough, Esther could make her escape. Surely she would know to run. Without a gun, she would never confront Braun, no matter how much she despised him.

"I know what happened to the Stones of David," Stephen said. "Esther doesn't, but I do."

The man cast a sideways glance at him. He wasn't buying it.

Stephen cleared his throat and tried again. "She doesn't know because they belonged to my mother, not hers. You think I would tell her? I've been searching for them my whole life—I'm not about to confide in someone I hardly know."

Braun turned to Stephen and watched him for a moment. Slowly his face settled with a cold determination. "You'll tell me where she is," he said.

"Aren't you listening to me?" Stephen demanded. "She's out of this! Me, I alone, have what you want."

"The city inspector has what I want?"

"You think I would lie with a gun to my head? I didn't even know she existed until you told me. I'm after the same thing you are."

Braun's left eye twitched. "I doubt it."

Stephen was pushing—maybe too much.

"I'm just saying that we need each other," Stephen said. "I have what you want, and you have what I want."

"What do I have that you want?"

"My life! Obviously. You're standing over me with a gun. You let me live, and I'll split it with you."

"The Stones of David. Split them. You are more stupid than I thought, inspector. You think I would share the Stones with a Jew?"

"If you kill me, you'll never find the other four Stones."

A grin nudged the big man's lips. "I do not live for the Stones." Braun glanced around the room again. He dropped one end of the scarf so that it hung from his fingers. "I love games. Shall we play a game?"

He walked forward and held the red silk out so that it hung above Stephen. "You've become useless to me. The only reason you're still alive is because there's a slight possibility that the girl is as stupid as her mother. We'll find out soon enough."

Braun dropped the scarf. It spilled over Stephen's

shoulder and hung down his chest. "My father selected your mother, Martha, to die. It seems fitting that I should select you. Unless your guardian angel sweeps in to take your place, I will put a bullet in your forehead. Ten seconds." His voice rang throughout the auditorium.

"Let me live, and you can have it all," Stephen said. "I'll show you exactly where the treasure is, and then you can kill me if you want."

"Seven!"

"She's gone! Kill me, and it's over. I have the information."

"Five."

Stephen knew that his prodding had probably sealed his death, but he couldn't just sit here and die. *Dear Esther, what have I done?*

"Three!" Braun raised his revolver.

"Okay, you win," Stephen said. Panic swarmed him. He was going to die. A bullet was about to punch a hole through his head. He sat up, furious. "I said you win! I'll tell you everything!"

"Stop!" Esther's shrill cry echoed through the chamber. Stephen turned toward the sound of her voice. She stood at the entrance to the stairwell, arms limp at her sides, feet together.

44

STEPHEN FELT HIS HEART SINK TO THE FLOOR of his stomach. "Leave," he demanded. "Get out! Run!"

Esther regarded him with a casual glance and then stared at Braun. "There's an exit behind me," she said. "If you kill him, I will run, and you should know that I have a way out of this village that no one knows about. You'll never know what I know; I can promise you that."

"I don't need anything you know," Roth said. "And I don't think hiding will be so easy."

"Then let him go, and I'll cooperate." Her voice held a tremor.

"Esther, please," Stephen pleaded.

Esther ignored him. "Let him go."

Braun could hardly hide his excitement. "Like mother, like daughter. Take the scarf, and I won't kill—"

"I know how your disgusting game is played. How do I know you'll keep your word?"

"Did my father kill Martha when Ruth took the scarf?"

Esther shifted her gaze back to Stephen.

"Please, Esther, don't do this," he said. "He'll kill me either way."

"Maybe. Maybe not. But either way, I'm finished." She looked at Braun. "You hear that, you pig? I know that my life is worth something to you. If you kill him, I'll run, and you'll have to shoot me. I don't know what you have planned, but if I had no value to you, you'd have killed me long ago."

Braun tilted his gun up to the ceiling. "You have my word. He'll go free."

"I don't trust your word," Esther said. "Throw me the scarf."

"Come and take it."

"Do I strike you as a fool? You need me alive, so throw me the scarf."

Braun eyed her, clearly caught off guard by her audacity. But she was right. Braun wanted her alive. *Why?*

Braun snatched up the scarf and flung it at Esther. She caught the material, looked at it for a moment, and then casually draped it around her neck.

"Stand up, Stephen," she said calmly.

He scrambled to his feet.

"You'll find another exit through those doors behind you," Esther told him. "Walk out."

"No."

"Then my own life will be in vain," she said.

"He'll kill you," Stephen cried. "I couldn't live with myself."

"He'll kill me anyway," Esther said.

"If you run now, you can still make it. He probably won't kill me. I'm an American citizen, and the district attorney in Los Angeles knows I'm here with Roth Braun."

It hadn't occurred to him until he said it, but this did present a potential problem for Braun. Assuming the man cared.

Braun chuckled. Evidently not.

"Why are you arguing with me?" Esther asked, eyes now moist with tears.

"I'm not arguing—I'm trying to help you!"

"Why would you risk your life for me?"

"You're . . . you're Esther," he said.

"I am. I'm Esther, and no one has ever loved me."

Stephen took a step in her direction before remembering that Braun was in the room. "That's not true. *I* love you. I love you more than anything I can imagine."

"You don't even *know* me." Tears began to slip down her cheeks.

"I was *made* for you," Stephen said.

"Enough," Braun said.

Stephen ignored the man. Esther was offering to give her life for him, not because she loved him so dearly, but because she saw her own life as worthless. The few minutes of tenderness he'd shown her were more valuable in her mind than her life.

Dear Esther. My dear Esther! You are willing to throw your life away for a moment's love.

"Don't you see, Esther? Our hearts have been beating together for thirty years. The truth is, I don't think Martha hid the other four Stones of David. *We're* the Stones of David. I . . . I don't think I can live without you. Please, just run."

"I can't just—"

Boom! Stephen jumped. Braun had fired into the air.

Braun waved the gun at Esther. "Come here, please."

"Not until Stephen leaves," she said.

"You think you can outwit me at my own game?"

"Shoot me," she challenged.

The quiver in his fingers told the truth. Their ploy had stalled him. He couldn't kill Esther, not yet.

Braun twisted his head toward the door. "Lars!"

Lars?

It occurred to Stephen that Braun could easily stop Esther. A simple shot to her leg, and she would be powerless. He was either lost to this fact, or he was playing another game altogether.

If Stephen didn't move now, they could both be dead in a matter of seconds.

"Wait." He could hardly stomach the thought of leaving her here with Braun, but he had no choice. "She's right."

Stephen took a step back. "Okay, I'll leave. I'll leave."

———

THE GAME had been played out like chess match: for every move a countermove, for every victory a defeat, for every hope a helping of despair. Roth could not have hoped for more.

He was quite sure that he could be completely satisfied standing here for hours listening to their desperate ploys. But little did they know. It was just getting good. Really good.

He could toy with them both as if they were

made of clay. And compared to him, they were. Next to him, most humans were merely dirt that had been fashioned into walking objects.

Stephen backed toward the door. "I'm leaving. And since I'm an American citizen and people know I'm here, shooting me would be a mistake. I'll go."

Braun swung his gun in line with Stephen and waved at Esther. "I want you here, beside me, before he leaves."

She walked toward him slowly. "I'm coming. Now let him go."

Stephen took another step back, hands up. "Easy. I'm going. I'll be going." His back hit the door, and he felt for the knob.

Braun turned the pistol back on Esther. Stephen pulled the door open, stepped quickly through, and slammed it shut.

45

Stephen heard a slap that sounded like one of those tiny firecrackers, followed immediately by Esther's muted cry. The world tipped crazily. He had to go back in. He gripped the doorknob but stopped short. Braun was yelling at her in German.

Time was running out. Stephen turned, bounded for the outer door, and threw it open. A back alley; empty. He had to find his way back to the bell tower.

Hold on, Esther!

Stephen gritted his teeth and tore down the alley toward the door below the bell tower. Tugged on it.

Locked! Dear God, it was locked!

He sprinted around the corner, but he was running farther from her, not to her rescue. What if he couldn't find another way in? Inside, Braun was brutalizing Esther, and her only hope for survival was running in the wrong direction.

The species of panic that swallowed him in that moment was a rare kind, debilitating in dreams and deadly in waking life. His legs felt numb, and he wasn't running nearly as quickly as his heart suggested he was.

He ran straight for the street, barely aware of three women who gawked at him from across the lane. Rough brick tore at his fingers when he grabbed the building's corner for the turn.

The steps leading to the front entrance loomed, gray and empty. No other doors. The steps, the foyer, and then the sanctuary. And in the sanctuary, Esther.

From the corner of his eye, he saw Lars, limping, pulling something from the back of the car.

Stephen took the steps at a full run. A faint cry of pain drifted from the church. He was out of time.

He slammed through the heavy church doors. He crossed the foyer in three long strides and headed up the center aisle at a full sprint.

Braun knelt on the floor, directly ahead, bent over Esther.

A terrifying, throaty scream echoed off the arching walls, and Stephen realized it was his own. He rushed forward, blindly, pushed by the power of his own rage. Braun stared at him, frozen by the sudden intrusion.

Still Stephen ran. Still he screamed.

He was halfway up the line of pews before a thought redirected him, an image of that rifle he'd dropped at the base of the tower stairs.

He veered to his right, vaulted a pew, landed his foot on the seat of a second, and hurdled the pew tops toward the bell tower.

A gunshot boomed, but he didn't duck or stop. His momentum permitted neither.

Another gunshot. Stained glass shattered high above and rained down.

Stephen skipped over the entire bank of pews before his left foot finally betrayed him and came up short on the last bench. He threw himself forward in a dive, banged his shin hard, toppled over the pew, and landed on his side with a tremendous grunt.

Wood splintered above his head—Braun's shots tore at pews that momentarily shielded Stephen. He couldn't breathe. The bell-tower door was open, two yards away.

He clambered for it on his hands and knees.

Click! Click!

The gun-hammer fell on an empty chamber. Braun was out of bullets?

Stephen was still out of breath. He shoved himself to his feet and lunged through the door. The old rifle lay where it had fallen.

He snatched it up.

Chambered a round, desperate for breath.

Whirled back.

Lurched for the doorway, feeling faint.

His reason was making a comeback, and for once it sang in harmony with his passion. Kill Braun. He had to kill Braun.

Still no breath.

Stephen staggered into the doorway, gun extended, trigger halfway through its pull, sights lined for Braun.

But Braun didn't fill the sights. Esther did.

Stephen blinked. Braun had pulled Esther to her feet and stood behind her. A large, shiny blade pressed against her throat.

"Drop it," the German said. "Drop it, or I cut her and drink her blood here before it's time."

Stephen's lungs finally inhaled a pocket of usable air.

"Lower the weapon."

Stephen held the gun as steadily as he could, which amounted to wavering in favor of jerking. He had no chance of picking off Braun's head like they did in the movies. Esther's shoulder was exposed, baring the scar. Her eyes stared at him, glazed with indifference. She'd resigned herself to die.

"Let her go," Stephen said, still gasping.

"Drop the gun, and I'll release her."

Stephen groped for a way out, but came up empty-handed.

"I can't put the gun down, and you know it," Stephen said. "But I can promise you that if you draw blood, I'll take my chances and shoot."

"Then you'll kill her," Braun said.

"You'll kill her anyway."

The front doors crashed open. A woman's muffled cry.

Stephen froze.

A sick grin distorted Braun's mouth.

Lars staggered into the back of the sanctuary. Shoved a woman down the aisle. Her hands were bound. Lars held a gun to her back.

It took Stephen a few seconds to realize who he was looking at, not because she looked any differently than he might have guessed, not because the gray tape over her mouth hid her facial features, but because he simply couldn't understand what he was seeing.

Esther. Only older.

Ruth.

But this couldn't be Ruth.

Ruth was dead.

"Hello, Ruth," Braun said.

46

MARTHA STEPPED INTO THE YARD BEHIND THE commandant's red house and let her eyes adjust to the darkness. Ordinarily, the lights would be blazing from tall posts throughout the camp, but not since the Russians had begun their air raids. Not even the front gate was lighted. It was so dark tonight that Martha had to choose her way carefully. If the perimeter fence wasn't flowing with high-voltage electricity, she might have been able to find a way out with the children under the cover of this darkness.

She made it as far as the tool shed at the edge of the yard before a sound stopped her dead in her tracks.

A cough.

From the shed? Did Braun keep prisoners in the shed? She wouldn't put anything past Braun, but why? Most of the barracks below were empty.

There it was again. The cough.

It didn't matter; she had to keep her mind focused. She had to hurry, or she could endanger the children's lives. The fate of one or two prisoners locked in a concrete cell was no longer her concern. Maybe on the way back she would—

"God forgive me. God forgive me." The voice came now, a soft, mumbling voice that stopped Martha in her tracks. Didn't she know that voice?

She heard it again, coming from a small, barred window to her left. "God forgive me."

Martha held her breath and stepped up to the bars. "Hello?"

Nothing.

"Is anyone in there?" she whispered.

"Martha?"

"Ruth?" A knot tried to choke her off. "Is that you, Ruth?"

Hands grasped the bars. A face pushed up between them. Ruth's face.

"Ruth! Is it you? How . . . ? I thought he—"

"Martha! Thank God, Martha. You're alive!" Ruth frantically searched her face. "The children! Are the children—"

"Yes! Yes—oh, yes. I can't believe it's you! I was so certain that . . . I saw your body!"

"It wasn't me. I don't know who."

"But you're alive!" Martha kissed her fingers, then her forehead. "Oh, I have so much to tell you. So much! Esther is the most beautiful child. He won't let me see David."

"They're here? Can I see them?"

Martha glanced back toward the house. "They're here, but the commandant . . . I can't bring her out. She'll wake up. We are being liberated tomorrow, Ruth!"

"You're sure?"

"Yes! Yes, I'm sure of it." She had to leave; she knew she did. If Gerhard found them . . .

"Listen to me, Ruth. There is so much I will tell you. Tomorrow. If we get separated, then you should know that I've marked Esther, and I am going to mark David. Each with half a circle with a star of David in it. The Stone of David. You know it?"

"Yes."

She stepped back and lifted up the boxes. "I have them. And I am going to hide them. If for some reason we get separated from each other, or from the children, remember this."

Martha told her how she planned to hide the treasure.

"What good will that do? His gold is filthy!"

"Do I care? It's for the children, Ruth."

"They will have each other."

"He's . . ." Should she tell Ruth? She had to. "He's taking the children with him, Ruth."

"No!"

"Yes. I'm so sorry. Don't worry, God will protect them. You said so yourself. As long as he thinks I have stolen his treasure, he won't hurt them. Do you see? He'll keep them alive until he finds it. It's the only solution I have. We must have leverage. I have to go." She kissed Ruth on the forehead and nose.

"Thank you, Ruth. You saved my life. I love you more than I would my own sister. Tomorrow we will talk, okay?"

"Pray that God will draw the children with his hope. Like desperate children seeking the pearl of great price."

"I will, Ruth. I will pray it every day."

"God be with you."

"God be with you."

She hated leaving, but she walked with a new urgency. Ruth had survived! Think of it. A great weight was gone from her shoulders.

It took her half an hour to pick her way through the camp toward the barracks she thought would be David's. The door was unlocked. She slipped in and shut the door quietly. "Rachel?"

Silence.

Louder now. "Rachel?"

"Yes?"

Martha ran past empty bunks toward the sound. "Rachel. It's Martha."

"Martha?"

The woman lay on a lower bunk, one of only a few people in the beds as far as Martha could see. She set her bundle on the bed and threw her arms around the woman, noting Rachel's frailty through the cloth immediately. She was nothing but bones!

"Thank God you're alive."

"Martha?"

"Yes, it's Martha, dear. You have my baby? David. Where is David?"

Rachel shifted to reveal a small lump in the blankets behind her. "This is David," she said very quietly, almost as if it were a question. The woman's mind was slipping.

Martha stared at the form, afraid to ask anything more. She leaned in and eased back the blanket. There lay a small boy, white chest rising and falling slowly. Dark hair covered his head. Her David.

She lifted her fingers to her mouth to hold back

an urge to cry. But this scene was too much for her. She sank to her knees, folded her hands in gratitude to God, and began to shake with soft sobs.

Her son was more beautiful than she had ever imagined in thousands of hours of imagining. He lay with all of his arms and legs and a nose and such tender lips and eyes with long lashes. And he was breathing.

Martha knew she had to hurry, but she hadn't counted on such brutal emotion. The thought that she was about to lose her precious child again, this very night, consumed her.

She couldn't wake him.

Did she dare hold him? If he awoke, she would never have the strength to mark him. If she didn't mark him, she might never see him again. She might never see him again anyway. Shouldn't she just hold him now—her baby in her arms, his soft cheek against hers, his breathing in her ear?

She reached a trembling hand for his body. Touched him lightly on his head, pushed his hair back. He took a deep breath and turned his head toward her, still deep in sleep.

"This is David," Rachel said quietly.

Martha nodded but couldn't speak. There was no possible way for her to take him away from the commandant. Marking her beautiful baby boy might be the only way to find him again.

Martha closed her eyes and gripped her hands to fists. *Strong, Martha. You have to be strong.*

With Rachel and two other gaunt women in nearby bunks now staring on, Martha heated the brand until it glowed. She'd reversed it on the ladle to make it a companion to Esther's mark.

She could barely see to press the hot brand into David's flesh for all her tears. To make matters worse, Rachel began to hit her feebly as soon as the metal made contact. As with Esther, it took a moment for David to wake, but when he did, a scream was already in his throat.

For the first time in nine months, Martha pulled her baby boy to her neck and held him tight. His cries tore at her heart like knives, and she did her best to comfort him. He didn't know who she was, didn't recognize the scent of skin or the tone of her voice. Slowly, he calmed.

"It's my mark, Rachel," she said as she put the salve on David's burn. "Do you understand? My mark. So that later I will be able to find him."

Rachel stared at her with hollow eyes, but Martha thought she might understand, might remember what she had done once for her own son. One of the women looked out the dark window to their left. Martha followed her gaze and froze. A light! A guard was coming!

Now, so late? It couldn't be possible!

She spun to Rachel. "Where's his shirt?"

Rachel blinked.

"His shirt—we must cover this! Hurry!"

The woman picked up a small cotton shirt from the end of the bed, and Martha snatched it from her hands. If the guards caught her in here, all would be lost.

The light approached steadily, swinging at the end

of the guard's arm. Had Braun discovered her missing? She began to panic. There was no time. No time!

She handed her child to Rachel. "Lie down! Pretend you're sleeping. Don't let them see!"

She scooped up the ammo boxes, ran to the back around the last bunk, and climbed through a window just as the front door opened. If they would have turned on a light, they might have caught her with one leg still hooked in the window, but with the raids, they couldn't chance the brilliance.

Then Martha fled as fast as she dared in the darkness, pulse hammering in her skull, certain that all was lost.

47

Germany
July 27, 1973
Friday

MOTHER?" ESTHER'S EYES WIDENED.
"Esther?"

Esther stepped forward, but Braun grabbed her collar and yanked her back.

"Drop the gun," Lars said, shoving his pistol into Ruth's back.

Ruth's face wrinkled in empathy. She looked at Stephen. Then at Esther. Her eyes flooded with tears. Ruth began to cry.

"I thought . . ." Stephen didn't know what to say.

"Yes, you thought she was dead," Braun said. "She is. She's been dead for thirty years."

"Mama?" Esther gazed at her mother. There was something between them, Stephen thought. Something they knew that he did not.

The rifle wavered in his hands. "She . . . she's been alive all these years?"

"Naturally," Braun said. "My father's foolishness in allowing any of you to live has created several problems, but it would take too long to explain how the powers of the air work."

He ran a fat tongue over his upper lip. "When he found the journal and the Stones missing, Gerhard was . . . let us say, disturbed. Martha had outwitted him, and Gerhard was forced to keep Ruth alive. In the event we found Martha, she would reveal the location of the Stones if we hung Ruth's life over her head. So we kept Ruth alive, in my father's house."

He paused as if to let comprehension of Ruth's plight sink in.

"And, of course, what better way to keep Ruth in humble service than to let her know that her daughter was also alive, and would remain so only if Ruth stayed faithful? We told Esther the same about her mother. They've never met, as you can see, but they've lived in respect of each other's life."

Braun's smile faded. "You see what happens when you don't follow the rules? My father should have killed Martha when he selected her with the scarf. Instead she stole his power and handed him thirty years of misery. Today I intend to take that power back." He shivered.

"I'm sorry, Mother," Esther said. "I'm so sorry."

"Don't be. God has answered our prayers."

An awkward moment of silence passed.

"Please lower the gun," Braun said.

Stephen's head buzzed. Slowly his rifle came down, as if it had a will of its own.

"Rifle on the floor," Braun said.

"Forgive me, Mama," Esther said.

"Rifle on the floor!"

Stephen set down the rifle and stepped back.

"Don't be sorry," Ruth said. "Never. Every minute of my life has been worth this one."

Braun clasped his hands behind his back and spoke in a low voice. "Go on. Go to your mother." A chill descended over Stephen. Braun's eyes held wickedness.

Esther walked down the aisle, then hurried the last few paces and embraced Ruth. She kissed her graying hair and her cheeks, then turned to Braun.

"Untie her! What kind of animal leads a weak woman around by a rope?"

Braun's eyebrow arched. "The master of that woman. Back!"

Esther hesitated then walked back.

"David. You are such a lovely boy." Ruth looked between them.

It occurred to Stephen that Braun was reloading his pistol. He exchanged a short glance with Esther.

"And Martha?" Ruth asked. "How is my Martha?"

"She . . . she's dead," Stephen said. "She died in America two weeks ago. She died happy, and she led us to you."

"Did she?" Braun snapped the clip home in his pistol. "Let's give Martha credit, but not too much, shall we?"

Meaning what?

"This moment is . . . invigorating, it really is," Braun said. "But I'm afraid we have to shift our attention back to the Stones." He looked at Ruth. "I trust you don't need any more convincing."

Ruth didn't seem to have heard the man. She was captivated by Esther and Stephen.

Braun pressed his gun into Esther's hip. "Or do you?"

Ruth's face settled, and her jaw firmed. Her eyes met Braun's.

"You had us fooled all these years. Bravo. You convinced us that you couldn't possibly have known what Martha did with the Stones. Martha wasn't even aware that you'd survived your little hanging." He pulled the hammer back on his revolver. "But now I know the truth. You know where Martha hid the Stones. Don't you, dear Ruth? Martha's letter has spoken from beyond the grave."

No one moved. Stephen's mind tripped back to the letter. He could see the last sentence in his mind's eye now: *As for the Stones, their hiding place will go to the grave with Ruth and me.*

"As you can see, your daughter is as healthy as an ox. You have five seconds to begin speaking."

One glance at Ruth, and Stephen knew she had the information Braun wanted.

"If you kill her, I won't tell you," Ruth said.

"I will do much worse than kill her."

Braun lifted his pistol to Esther's head. The gun jumped in his hand. Esther jerked and cried out. Blood oozed from a crease in her skin where the bullet had grazed her neck.

Roth wiped the blood from her cheek and then sucked it off his finger. "That was a warning. I imagine she can take ten carefully placed bullets without dying."

Ruth stared at the man for a few seconds. There may have been a day when she would have called his bluff. But today she looked like a woman who'd been beaten down one too many times.

"They are buried at Toruń," Ruth said without batting an eye.

––––⁓––––

THE SOUND of the words sent a tremor through Roth. The Stones were buried in Toruń. His focused intellect had assumed as much for years. Gerhard had even swept the camp with electronic gear once without success.

Still, Roth knew. He had always known. His whole plan practically depended on Toruń. Which is why hearing that name brought such relief.

Toruń.

Toruń, Roth's spiritual birthing place. Where his father had shown him how to harvest souls.

Toruń, where his father had lost all of his power through one asinine decision.

Toruń, where Roth would finally become a god.

He could barely speak for all of his pleasure. "Where?"

Ruth hesitated. "Under the gates. But I will only show you when you have let her go as agreed."

It was too much! Under the gates! The confession was nothing less than an announcement from Lucifer himself. *Lead them like lambs to the slaughter, and I will deliver myself unto you.*

Roth wanted to shout out his joy, but he held it back in a final act of control. He would have to spread some joy throughout Hamburg to celebrate, but only when he'd finished what his cowardly father had failed to complete himself.

———

A FIRE had entered Roth Braun's eyes, Stephen thought. His eyes danced; an obscene grin tugged at his lips. Sweat dampened his face.

He walked to Stephen. "I want you to listen carefully, Jew, if you want to live. I'm sure the police in Los Angeles will have a problem with your disappearance, so go set their minds at ease. If you ever look for us, I'll kill them both. One word to the wrong people, and Esther will pay with her life. Carry that with you to your grave."

The man's arm flashed out. His pistol crashed against Stephen's skull, like bricks hurled from a catapult. He felt himself fall.

Hit the pew. Heard a sob.

Esther's.

Then nothing.

48

ESTHER DRIFTED BETWEEN REALITIES, VAGUELY aware that something was wrong. Something had happened—something furious and explosive—followed by the smell of a strong medicine, but that was surely a dream.

They were in a dark car, she and Ruth in the back, men's voices in the front. She thought they might have driven through a city some time ago, collected an old man with tubes in his nose, but he was surely a dream. The kind of nightmare the mind fabricated in deep, deep sleep.

In reality, she was driving with Stephen. Stephen and her mother, Ruth. They were going to Poland to deal with Braun, or they were running from him. She wasn't sure which. Mostly, they were just going. Together. In his car. She and Stephen in the front seat, Ruth in the back. Stephen obsessing after her from behind the wheel, she pondering him from the passenger's seat, her mother smiling with approval.

They were passing through the border into Poland, going after the Stones of David.

Stephen smiled and she smiled back, dreamy and hazy.

When the border guard waved them through,

Stephen revved up the van and took off with enough acceleration to produce a tiny squeal.

"Slow down," Esther objected. "You're driving as if we've just robbed a bank."

Stephen slowed and glanced in the rearview mirror. "Sorry. We're okay." He grinned. "Peachy."

"Peachy?" It was the American colloquialism he'd used during their long discussion in the church while waiting for Braun.

"Peachy."

"Peachy?" Ruth said. "I love peaches."

Esther chuckled. Her mother was here, safe and together with her for the first time in her memory. She couldn't stop looking at her, this woman who'd given birth to her and then given her life.

Then there was Stephen. Everything about Stephen struck her as a bit funny. Not funny as in comical, but funny as in nice. This man—who'd jumped out of the alley at her, who'd ruined her first good shot at Braun, and then who'd come screaming back into the church for her—made her feel funny. A nice kind of funny.

Esther turned and felt something that smelled like leather press against her face. Was she sitting up front with Stephen, or had she climbed in the back with Ruth?

Up front with Stephen, of course.

She'd never felt this way about a man before. Here was a man who claimed to be obsessed with her, a savior who'd come blazing out of the past to rescue her from her eternal prison. David, who had been born because of her mother's sacrifice and who now seemed willing to give his life for hers in repayment. No, not in repayment. In love.

With each passing minute, the realization that Stephen really did love her grew, until she began to wonder whether she herself was smitten with this obsession of his. For him. How ridiculous! Was his disease contagious?

How could any sane woman find herself so hopelessly attracted to any man in such a short time? This couldn't be love. It must be her irrational response to the first sign of real kindness shown her by any man in years. She'd been smothered by Braun's thick hand since birth, a bird caught in a cage, a tiger whipped into submission, a butterfly snagged in a web. And now she was suddenly free because of these two people. Her mother and her . . .

Her what? That was the question, wasn't it? Here was the kind of man she had longed for all these years. Here was her knight in shining armor. Here was the one who really did think she was beautiful. How could she possibly resist such a love? She couldn't. And Ruth, her mother, didn't want her to resist either. It was meant to be, and they all knew it. A fairy tale come true. She felt like laughing.

She sat with her hands folded in her lap, smiling, bouncing quietly along, wanting to see if he might be looking at her. She couldn't very well just turn and stare at him, now, could she? When they talked, she would have ample opportunity to look directly at him.

"I can't believe I actually found you," he would say.

Esther would face him. He would make a show of looking at the cattle in the field they were passing.

But she could tell that his mind was lost on her. Why else would he swallow like that, or lick his dry lips and then bite them? His hair curled around his ear, dark strands moved by a hidden breeze. He was such a gentle man, beautiful to look at and fascinating to think about. She could still see him running over the pew tops, screaming. What kind of man would do that for her?

"Right?" he asked, glancing at her.

He'd caught her staring? But she had the right to look at him because he said something and wanted a response. Still, she'd looked at him too long. Her face flushed. She'd betrayed herself. But she didn't look away.

He'd asked a question. What was the question?

"What?" she asked.

For an eternal moment, they stared deep into each other's eyes. "I was just thinking of how incredible it was that I actually found you," he said.

"Yes." She cleared her throat and looked at the cows he'd pretended to be interested in. "Incredible. Like finding a mouse in a haystack."

"A needle," he said.

Another of his colloquialisms.

"How silly. Whoever heard of losing a needle in a haystack? We say mouse. Have you ever tried to catch a mouse in a haystack?"

"No." He chuckled.

Another good opportunity to look at him. She did so, laughing with him. "What's so funny?"

"You."

"I'm funny?"

"No. You're . . . cute."

She blushed again. "Mice are cute; needles are not."

Why was she disagreeing with him? She should be throwing herself at him and thanking him from the bottom of her heart.

"Touché," he said.

"Yes, touché," Ruth said. They both looked at her and smiled.

"Talk, talk," Ruth said, waving her arms in encouragement. "I've waited my whole life for this moment; please don't spoil it for me. Talk about love."

Tears blurred Esther's vision. She reached a hand back and squeezed her mother's. "I'm so happy. Thank you." She looked at Stephen and touched his arm with her other hand. "Thank you both. Thank you for finding me. I feel . . ." She paused, suddenly unsure of what to tell them. She couldn't say she was falling madly in love with Stephen. That would sound stupid. She couldn't say she was so glad Mother was free. That sounded too plain.

David's right brow went up, urging her to continue.

". . . found," she finally said.

Esther rubbed Ruth's hand and smiled through tears. David frowned and nodded. "Hmm. Found. Like the treasure in the field. Wow, that's perfect."

It was? *Wow.* The American expression was new, and she liked it.

"If I'm right, he's already on his way," an uncomfortably familiar voice said.

Esther moaned and rolled. Funny how it felt as if she was lying down somewhere. And where was Stephen?

Maybe she was dreaming.

A FIERCE odor stung his nostrils. The sound of running feet. Stephen pulled himself from darkness. Slowly, he remembered what had happened. What was happening.

Braun had knocked him out and dumped him in the alley. He'd then taken Esther and Ruth and was on his way to Toruń.

This simple thought was filled with complex details. Details like Braun, the beast, and Esther, the beauty, and Ruth, his savior, and Toruń, the place where the beast played his game with the red scarf and killed the beauties.

Details like the fact that someone had waked him.

He pushed himself off the cobblestones in an attempt to stand. But his muscles weren't ready to execute the maneuver, and he fell flat on his face.

Roth Braun had let him go. Why?

Stephen moaned, rolled, and desperately willed his body's cooperation. Slowly, his arms and legs responded. Then he was tripping down the alley, one hand dragging on the wall, the other flailing for balance.

The panic hadn't abated. Nor could it. Surges of hot and cold swept over his body like storm-driven waves. They had taken Esther. They were taking Esther to Toruń. They were going to kill Esther at Toruń.

Stephen staggered down the alley and began to cry uncontrollably. His sobs echoed off the walls. When he broke into the street, people were staring at him.

"You should be ashamed of yourselves!" he cried.

The statement sounded absurd. Stephen began to run. There was no way to even begin telling them what they had just done. A princess had lived among them, and they had just killed her. Every last one of them should pay for their sin!

His vision was blurry. He overran himself and slammed into the Volkswagen van. He quickly recovered, tore the door open, and slid in.

How much time had passed? What if they weren't going to Toruń?

Pain hollowed his chest, a pain worse than long swords running him through. Nothing could be worse than this. Nothing!

Never had he wanted anything as terribly as he wanted to save Esther. His desire for the safe in Los Angeles paled by comparison.

And he knew that this was precisely what Roth expected. Stephen's reaction was the object of this mad game Roth was playing. He was lifting and dashing hopes as his father had with the women of Toruń.

He knew it, and he was powerless to stop it.

Stephen yelled at the windshield and slammed both hands against the steering wheel, once, twice. He fired the van up and screeched through a U-turn. A man on a bicycle dived for cover.

"Get out of my way!" He was briefly tempted to drive straight over the spinning wheels.

He roared from the village, redlining the VW's small motor before remembering to shift. When he did, he went right through the gears, blasting down the road.

The incline out of the village slowed the van, and he cursed his decision to rent the van over a Porsche.

Somewhere ahead on this very road, another car carried Esther, his dear, precious Esther, bound and taped and being led to her slaughter.

And what if he was wrong? What if Braun was still back in the village, beating the truth out of her?

Stephen shoved the brake pedal to the floor, sending the van into a precarious skid. A few hours had passed, judging by the light. Braun *had* to be on his way to Toruń. Either way, Stephen didn't have time to run through the village searching, while in all likelihood Esther was on the way to Poland.

He gritted his teeth and slammed the accelerator home.

The first fifty kilometers flew by. He didn't encounter any more than three vehicles. But then he pulled onto the autobahn headed east, and cars abounded. He felt lost in a sea of thugs, even though he knew these weren't the thugs. A hundred cars faded in his rearview mirror before it occurred to him that getting pulled over at this speed might actually put him in jail. Then again, he was on an autobahn, wasn't he? The square blue signs said 130 for cars and motorcycles and 80 for trucks.

He pushed the van to 140 km/h.

A hundred scenarios played through his mind. Images of Ruth. Of Esther speaking her mind and putting Braun in his place. Or being gagged and drugged. Or dead.

God, please. I beg you. Whoever you are, whatever your purpose, I beg you, bring Esther back to me.

He still had to cross the border into Poland. Thank God he had a Russian passport and the twenty thousand dollars he'd brought with him. He only prayed it was enough to buy his way across without the right visa. He still had to reach Toruń; he still had to avoid the police while shredding whatever speed limit lay in his way.

Esther still had to be alive.

Ruth still had to be alive.

And even if they were, what then?

49

ESTHER AND STEPHEN AND RUTH HAD A DOZEN exchanges, all dreamy, all vivid, all beautiful. And all while they were driving straight for this snake pit once known as Toruń.

What they would find there, she really had no clue, and she really didn't want to discuss the matter. There seemed to be an unspoken agreement between the three of them not to discuss the place, which was strange, considering they were headed straight for it. Stephen's preoccupation with her provided enough of a distraction.

Why were they going after the Stones of David? After all, she and David were the true Stones.

The car slowed, and Esther suddenly realized she was leaning against the door. And to her right, Ruth was also slumped over, sleeping. They apparently had fallen asleep while talking to Stephen.

She sat up and looked outside. Night. It was quiet, dark except for the bright moon. They were driving past a large, abandoned camp that looked like it had been turned into a museum. The sign over the gate . . .

STUTTHOF

Her heart bolted. Tall trees with sparse foliage surrounded the huge complex like shamed sentinels, bared for the whole world to see. Barbed fencing still surrounded the compound, and inside, dozens of identical barracks had fallen into various stages of disrepair.

A motorcycle headed the opposite way rushed past with a whine. How could anyone live near this place? But then, she'd lived in a place like this since her birth, hadn't she?

". . . after all these years. How can we Germans stand by and let them pretend this is a monument to the Jews?" The man spit in disgust. "It's a monument to the greatest time in history. The Third Reich."

For the first time in many hours, Esther began to realize that not all was as she'd imagined. She wasn't in the front seat. Stephen wasn't sitting next to her. She wasn't even in his car!

"She's awake," someone said. The old man she'd imagined in her dreams.

Adrenaline began to clear Esther's mind. She jerked her arms and found that they were bound behind her back. She cried out, only to discover that her mouth had been taped. And next to her, Ruth lay bound and gagged as well. She was still sedated.

The full reality of her predicament settled on her mind like a massive boulder, crushing any attempt to rise above it. Braun had struck Stephen in the church, maybe leaving him dead, and then left the village with her and Ruth drugged and bound. They'd stopped somewhere and collected the old man, who sat in the passenger seat now, breathing through an oxygen tube. The father. The one who'd hanged the women. With the son behind the wheel and the father in the passenger seat, they'd rolled through Poland, and had just passed Stutthof.

They were going to Toruń.

Esther leaned back, swung her feet up, and kicked at the heads on the other side of the seat. Her right foot struck the old man. She kicked at Roth, but the car swerved and she missed him. She struck out again, screaming through the tape, shutting out their curses.

The son reached up and wrenched her foot. Pain shot up her leg, and she arched her back.

"The next time I will break it," he said, and she had no doubt that he would. The father was silent.

She yelled at Roth through the tape, "What are you doing? Let me out!" But he couldn't understand her, and even if he could, the demand wouldn't generate a response. She knew the answer anyway.

They were taking her to Toruń because that's where the treasure was. Because that's where the hangings were.

The old man slowly twisted around and stared at her, and for a moment she thought he was part animal. Deep lines like canyons ran across his white face. His eyes looked black in the dim light, abysmal holes. She returned his gaze, terrified.

Gerhard turned back without speaking.

Silence settled around her once again. She was in a black car with leather seats, wet with her own sweat, sitting next to Ruth, who was still mercifully separated from consciousness. The drug had affected her older, frail body more severely. Her mother was a fighter to the end, though. Ruth had bought them some time, knowing that the moment she revealed the location of the treasure, their usefulness would end.

Esther forced her mind to dig deep, as deep as it could through the lingering effects of the drug. But she couldn't fathom a way out.

The car crested a small hill, and both men looked to the right. Two hundred yards off the road stood two old wooden posts with a crossbar, and beyond that the ruins of buildings jutted from tall grass. A second hill rose to the right of the dilapidated compound, and on that hill was a very old building that was shedding its red paint and looked to be hardly standing.

A pale moon hovered in the graying dusk sky.

Toruń.

Esther's heart hammered. The gates still stood! She had heard that most camps had been leveled.

They turned onto a gravel drive and drove across the field toward the looming gate.

Roth stopped twenty meters from the gate and turned off the engine.

Silence smothered them.

The engine ticked softly.

Esther stared past the entrance. She could see them now, as ghosts, a thousand starving women, dressed in gray clothing, standing in formation, waiting orders from a ruthless commandant.

"Parts still stand," Gerhard said. He slipped out of his nasal cannula and looked at the gate in wonder. "This is better than I could have hoped for." He faced Roth. "You knew?"

Roth didn't respond. He opened his door and stepped out.

A new sound filled Esther's ears. A field of crickets sawing at their own legs, like an orchestra greeting the new prisoners.

Roth's feet crunched on the gravel as he stepped forward, then stopped by the hood. For a moment he just gazed at the camp, then he lifted his chin, put both hands on his hips and breathed deep.

Gerhard stepped out and walked up to the gate. He touched the wood and brushed his hands together.

The crickets seemed to scream now. All of them.

Finally Roth retreated to the back of the car and pulled something from the trunk. He met Gerhard in front of the gate and they approached the entrance to Toruń together, father limping along slowly on thin legs, son holding a shovel and a large coil of rope.

The shovel was to dig. The rope . . .

Esther leaned back and shifted her gaze. She would not think about the rope. Ruth slept on, nostrils pulling audibly at the air.

When Esther looked back up, they were looking up at the crossbar. Even from here she could see the white mark worn on the wood. A rope mark from hundreds of hangings. Roth threw one end of the rope over the wood, lined it up with the groove, and then stood back.

This was their plumb line, Esther thought with sudden hope. The falling rope marked a spot directly beneath the worn mark. They were going to dig under the spot where they'd hanged their women so many years ago.

But couldn't they as easily estimate the center without a rope?

ROTH BRAUN could feel the power. What he now felt was new. How many souls had he stolen since the war? Too many to count.

These would be different.

These were the ones who'd stolen part of his soul first, a feat far more damaging to him in spiritual terms than any occurrence since.

As he saw it, the only way to undo his father's grievous sin was to return Gerhard's full power to him by beating these Jews in their own game, using as much cunning as Martha had.

Now he would outwit them, not by retrieving the Stones of David—although that was no small accomplishment—but by returning these Jews to the very fate they should have suffered in the first place.

By hanging them and then bleeding their souls.

Roth was in a very good mood.

He glanced at the road that led to the camp. Still no sign of pursuit.

"I know why you insist on the ritual," Gerhard said, "but please remember that the Stones are as important."

Roth's mood dimmed. But he was a patient man who could handle the weakness of others when required.

He couldn't bring himself to speak to the old man. Dealing with him would be the least of his pleasures, certainly not something to dwell on. Tragic how this man who'd introduced him to the great war of life—the struggle between God and Lucifer over the passions of man—now served the lesser master of greed and self-preservation.

But this would not stop Roth.

He turned away from his father and went to get the younger one.

———

THE SON walked back toward the car. Opened the door. "Get out."

Esther pushed herself away from the door and cocked her legs to protect herself.

"Is that necessary?" he said impatiently. His eyes were dark, emotionless.

He grabbed her foot and pulled roughly. She tried to kick—tried to strike him, even though she knew she would only provoke him—but she could not stop her slide. She landed on her back with a dull *thump*.

"Get up, or I'll drag you. And if you kick at me again, I'll put a bullet in your leg."

Esther rolled over, drew her knees under her belly, and struggled to her feet, her arms still tied behind her back. He prodded her and she walked for the gallows, numb.

Gerhard watched her. "Are you frightened now, little flower?"

Esther felt a lump fill her throat. Mama? She wanted to cry out, but her mouth was still strapped with tape.

Roth Braun took Esther's arm and shoved her to the ground. He quickly wound tape around her legs. Silent. Breathing steadily.

The old man stared at her, fascinated. His hands trembled by his sides, and his eyes glimmered with delight.

Roth fashioned a loop with a heavy knot on one end of the rope.

Esther began to panic again. But before she could even whimper, Roth had pulled her to her feet, spun her so she was facing the road, and shoved the noose over her head. He cinched it tight and tied the rope to the fence so that some pressure, but not too much, pulled on Esther's neck.

Braun walked to the car and shook Ruth awake. It took a minute before he finally helped her out of the backseat. Her mother stood unsteadily, gazing dumbly at the camp. Slowly, her eyes focused.

Braun had more rope in hands, from where, Esther hadn't seen.

Roth pulled the tape from her mouth. "No screaming," he said. "You'll have your chance to speak, but not now. Walk."

He directed Ruth to one side, threw the rope over the crossbar and set a twin loop over Ruth's head.

He threw a third length over the bar on Esther's right.

Ruth looked at Esther. A tear on Ruth's cheek glistened in the moonlight, but she showed no other sign of weakness or sorrow. Her mother's strength gave Esther some courage.

"Are we ready?" Gerhard asked his son.

Roth glanced past the car toward the road and hesitated. He was waiting?

He finally put one hand on the rope and faced Ruth. "If you don't tell us where it is, or if you direct us to the wrong location, your daughter will suffer painfully. If you cooperate, you will both live. Do you believe me?"

No answer.

Roth nodded at his father, who approached Ruth.

"Where did Martha hide the Stones?" Gerhard asked.

Ruth stared at him, emotionless. The moment she told them where the treasure was, they would both die, Esther thought, peering down.

"You're thinking that we will kill you anyway," Roth said. "Then what leverage would I have against Stephen? He would tell the world what he knows and I would have a problem. Your choice is a simple one: Either you tell us where the Stones are and live, or Esther dies first, then you."

He pulled on the rope, lifting Esther to her tiptoes.

"One pace south of the center," Ruth said softly. The words horrified Esther. So quickly! Ruth was too weak to resist.

Roth stared at Ruth for a long time as if caught off guard by her response. He had the look of a disappointed man.

He released the rope so that if Esther continued to stand on her toes, the noose wouldn't cut into her skin.

Roth removed his coat, placed it carefully on the fence, took up the shovel, and buried its blade deep into the earth roughly one pace to Esther's left.

She looked at her mother. Ruth gazed at her, eyes tearful. If Esther could speak past the tape, she would tell her mother that she was okay. That her sacrifice hadn't been in vain. That she loved Ruth more than she loved life itself.

Roth swung his shovel. *Chunk, scrape, chunk.* Metal on dirt. But it wasn't as loud as the sound of her own breathing. Or her heart.

It was louder than the crickets, but barely.

Don't panic, Esther. They won't kill you. He's right, they need you alive to keep Stephen from speaking. They've kept you alive all these years. What's a few more?

But she didn't believe it. She'd never felt such lingering horror.

Maybe someone would come over the hill and discover them. The car and the men were visible from the road. Seeing a man digging a hole at the base of this gate would surely draw the attention of anyone driving by. It had to! But whoever would come out to this dreadful place at night?

The old man stood stooped, dressed in wool pants that rose halfway up his belly and a gray sweater that looked as old as the war. Behind him on the hill stood the house from where he'd kept watch over his women.

Esther glanced at Roth steadily digging. There was only one outcome to this madness. Not three or two, but one.

Gerhard was walking around the hole now, like a vulture, waiting. If she could jump and kick him . . .

The shovel struck something solid. Gerhard stepped forward and stared into the hole. He dropped to his knees, thrust his arms below the dirt, and yanked on something that came loose reluctantly.

A container. Small, like a shoe box, maybe an ammunition holder, though she could barely see it.

They'd found Martha's treasure.

She closed her eyes. She heard a small whimper. From her own throat. Panic edged into her mind.

"Shh, shh, shh," Ruth whispered. "I will hold you in my arms forever, my dear Esther."

"Mama . . ."

"Be strong, Esther."

But Ruth was crying as well.

50

IN ROTH'S MIND, FINDING THE STONES WAS merely a bonus. not a small one, but still only a bonus.

Roth's skin buzzed with anticipation now. They'd set the table up ten meters from the gate, directly in front of Esther. It was a small folding table, not the lavish spread Gerhard had used in the war. But they had a white tablecloth and three crystal goblets. One tall bar stool.

And a silver knife.

The ammunition box sat on the ground behind them. Esther teetered on her toes, struggling to keep the rope from choking her. Ruth stood next to her. Gerhard stood by Roth's side before the table.

They were all here except Stephen.

The only thing that dampened Roth's spirits was Gerhard's obvious eagerness to hurry the ritual. The Stones were his prize.

Or were they? He hadn't actually opened the box yet.

Gerhard fidgeted and looked at him. "He may not come."

Roth watched the road. Still no sign.

"What are you waiting for?" Ruth demanded. "You have what you came for, and you're too cowardly to keep your word, so finish it. We've defeated you already."

He would have to be careful with Ruth. She was still capable of lowering the heights to which he anticipated ascending today.

"I have no intention of killing you, Ruth," he said. "Your daughter, perhaps, but not you."

"I don't believe you."

Esther's body was shaking with fatigue.

The road was still empty. Roth's eagerness to move forward forced him into a decision. Although patience was a strength, it had to be balanced against ambition and passion.

On balance it was time to move forward.

Roth picked up the bar stool. He stepped around the table.

"Think about it, Ruth," he said, but he was looking at Esther's frantic eyes now. He'd tried to do this once when she was a sleeping baby. It was immeasurably more satisfying now that she was fully aware.

"As stated, I need Esther alive to keep Stephen under control. And I need you to keep her in line. We really are one big happy family, just as we've always been."

"If you'd wanted to bleed us for your sickening ritual, you could have done that years ago," she said.

"Yes, but not with the same results. Bleeding is pointless unless the subject is in a particular state. I don't expect you to understand."

Esther stared at him with wide eyes.

He set the stool against her legs, ripped the tape off of her mouth, and walked toward the fence where the rope was tied off.

"I'm going to pull . . ." He untied the rope and applied some pressure, forcing her to stretch higher. "I advise you to climb the stool as I pull so that I don't break your neck."

Roth pulled. She stabbed at the stool with her legs and drew it under her. Clambered on the first rungs.

Roth snugged the rope. Watching her filled him with pride. His power was superior to hers. It always had been, but until now he'd never had the true opportunity to express it.

He pulled harder. "That's it. Up. Up, up."

She winced when the rope tightened on her neck, but she managed to get her knees on the round wood seat.

"Up, up."

He helped her by pulling her up, like drawing a caught fish out of the water. One leg under. The stool tipped, nearly spilled. That would have been disappointing. But she was a capable woman. She stood on the stool, trembling like a leaf, coughing and gasping. But standing.

Roth fed out a couple feet of slack and tied the rope off.

He walked to the table, picked up the knife and one of the glasses, then faced Esther, whose wrists were still taped together behind her back. Ruth had said nothing. He would have to watch her.

"I'm just going to cut you, Esther. If you look at your mother's palms, you'll see a scar. She's been cut before. Now it's your turn. The only reason I put you on the stool was to control you. If you try to kick me while I'm bleeding you, the stool will probably tip over and you'll drop."

She was trying so hard to be brave. But her face was white and stretched paper thin. She was balanced on that razor edge that divided hope and fear.

He stepped up to her hanging arms and held the glass under her fingertips. He set the blade against her white wrist, just below the gray tape, and pushed lightly.

She whimpered.

"You're in good company. Another Jew was bled by his enemy. Few think of Jesus Christ as a Jew, but he was. It's why we hate him."

Sweat ran down Roth's lip. His own hand began to shake.

Then Roth couldn't hold himself back any longer. He pressed the sharp silver blade down and slid it toward him.

Esther groaned. Her knees began to buckle, then found strength again.

A thin trail of blood seeped out of the cut, over her palm, down her forefinger, into the glass.

"You are a devil," Ruth said.

"I am," he said.

Roth was temporarily frozen by the moment. Lost in his own glory.

A tear slipped down his cheek.

He held the cup out to his father, who took it, mesmerized. Subservient.

"Drink it, Father."

"Not you?"

"She undermined you, not me."

"All of it?"

"All of it."

Gerhard tilted the glass back and swallowed the small pool of blood.

Roth trembled with anticipation. He turned to Ruth.

"It's your turn, my dear. Just a little blood."

"You are very sick," Ruth said.

"The power of life is in the blood," he said.

51

STUTTHOF.

Stephen roared by the old camp as the sun slipped closer to the horizon, choking on his own heart. The steering wheel was slippery from his sweat, but that didn't matter—there were no turns in this road. Stutthof was on this road, and Toruń was on this road. Sickness and death, that's all. Sickness and death and lots of buried Jews.

He would do anything to prevent Ruth's and Esther's names from being added to the long list.

Maybe he'd passed them on the autobahn. After an hour at 140, he'd pushed the van to its limit and held it there all the way to Poland. The border crossing had slowed him half an hour, but his money had bought a crossing. He could only hope that the border had slowed them as well.

Assuming they had even come this way.

He was driving blind, praying incessantly, hoping that he hadn't misjudged Braun's intent.

If he reached Toruń before them, he would dig a hole and pretend he'd found the treasure only to hide it again. If . . .

The camp suddenly rose into view like a monster from the sea. A black car was parked in front of the gate. Two people standing.

A body hung from the crossbeam. A second next to it, lower.

Stephen's heart seized. He barely glanced at the shoulder before yanking the van off the road, directing it through a shallow ditch and straight for the camp, two hundred meters off.

The van pounded over clumps of grass, threatening to wrest the wheel from his grasp, but Stephen hardly noticed. His eyes were locked on those bodies, and his mind was screaming bloody murder.

Esther's legs were partially obscured by the black car from this angle. He could no longer see Braun. He was bouncing over the field and whimpering and seeing nothing but red. Red and the black forms, hands tied, neck crooked, dangling on the end of the rope.

A sliver of reason sliced into his consciousness. Other than the knife in his right sock, he had no weapon. But the van was a weapon. They would begin shooting at the onrushing van at any moment—he had to bob and weave and he had to actually hit Braun.

One hundred yards. No shots.

Stephen swung the wheel to the right, sent the van into a fishtail. He began to weave through the grass.

———

AT FIRST, Esther thought the blur on the horizon was a bird, diving into the field for prey. Gerhard Braun was drinking their blood, and there was a bird diving from the road.

A car sliding into the field.

Stephen!

Esther couldn't hear the van streaking for them; her ears were filled with rushing blood and her heart was knocking. The old man might be half-deaf, and Roth too distracted, but sooner or later, they would hear. She had to distract them!

But she was still in shock. Her mind was hardly working, much less her mouth.

The van fishtailed crazily, only a hundred yards off now. She could already hear the racing engine as it bounced.

Behind her, Roth began to chuckle.

"The boy does not disappoint," he said.

———

STEPHEN SAW that the rope around Esther's neck was loose when he was still fifty meters out.

She was alive.

The sudden relief vanished immediately. She was on a stool. If she fell, she would die.

Three choices. He could try to angle directly for Roth Braun. He could ram the car and hope that it ran Braun over. Or he could crash into the gate, hoping to bring the whole thing down, including Esther.

Angling for Braun was a problem because he still couldn't see the man at thirty yards out. Ramming the car could be a problem because the black vehicle looked pretty solid—he might accomplish nothing except his own dismemberment. And rather than saving her, crashing into the gate might turn out to be a deathblow to Esther.

He slammed the brakes and brought the van to a skidding halt three feet from the large Mercedes. Esther stared, white-faced.

Stephen began to scream.

At the top of his lungs, as he threw the door open, as he vaulted the Mercedes' hood. He was nothing more than an enraged savage pushed to his limits by this brutal attack on Esther. His woman. His life.

The rage became awareness in the space of two steps. He pulled up abruptly.

Roth stood beside Esther, gripping one of the stool's legs, ready to yank it out. A gun in the other hand, hanging loosely by his side. Face amused.

"Nice of you to join us," Roth said.

"Stephen?" Esther's voice was breathy. High-pitched.

Ruth stood strung to Esther's left. Only then did he see the third rope, hanging on Esther's right. This was for him?

An old man stood by a small table behind Esther. This was Gerhard, Ruth and Martha's tormentor. There were three glasses on the table. One was stained dark; one held a small puddle of black wine; one was empty.

Then he saw the blood dripping from Esther's bound hands. And Ruth's hands. Their wrists had been cut and still bled.

Their predicament settled into his mind. He heaved and vomited on the hood of Braun's car.

Roth smiled softly. "That's right, the situation is quite hopeless, isn't it? For you, that is. For me . . . I'm pleased to have played you so well."

Stephen's head was reeling. It struck him that Roth would now kill all three of them.

"Played me?"

"Surely you don't think you're here without my approval? I'm after more than the Stones of David. The fact is, I've played you like a fiddle from the moment you showed up at Martha's apartment in Los Angeles, as I knew you would. Assuming you were still alive."

"You were there for the Stones," Stephen said.

"I was there for you. I knew the minute I read the news story in the *Los Angeles Times* that Martha suspected you were alive and was calling out to you. She was, and now here you are. Consider yourself called."

Stephen laughed bitterly.

"I'm here because Martha was one step ahead of your father," Stephen said. "I'm here because I've stayed one step ahead of you." His voice held no conviction.

"Have you? I drew you, Jew boy. I let you find the scarf. Build your hope to the point of a mad obsession."

Roth Braun spoke the words as if tasting each with immense satisfaction. Stephen had underestimated the power of this man.

"How do you think you escaped unharmed from the basement? Why did I let you walk out of the church in Greifsman and have my men wake you in the alley? I had to make you believe it was all your own doing—this fuels courage—but you've done nothing without my allowing it."

Roth glared at him smugly.

"And why am I now telling you this, knowing

that the game isn't yet finished? Because I know how it will crush you. I intend to return all of you to the death you should have met thirty years ago. I intend to bleed and hang all three of you."

He swayed slightly on his feet.

"Desperation, do you feel it working on your mind?"

The words bounced around Stephen's skull like a Ping-Pong ball.

"Turn around."

52

EVERYTHING WOULD PROCEED EXACTLY AS Roth had planned now.

All three faced him, Esther on the stool, Ruth and Stephen on either side, necks tight in their nooses, hands bound and bleeding behind them.

Gerhard tipped back the chalice containing Stephen's blood and drained it. The evening air was cool, silent except for the cricket's song, screeching through the fields. Tears stained the faces of all three Jews.

Roth trembled.

His father set the glass on the table, eyes closed, face tilted to the dim sky. *Can you feel it, Father? I have restored your power to you.*

Gerhard said nothing. His frail frame looked white in the moonlight. For a moment Roth couldn't help thinking that he was one of the starving Jews that had filled the camps, a ghost of his former self.

But inside, where it mattered, Gerhard had now recaptured the full power once lost to him by his own stupidity.

Roth walked toward the car slowly, a master committed to the grandest of all ceremonies.

He withdrew a rope from the car and brought it back. Without looking at his father, he slung the noose over the cross bar. It slapped the wood noisily, then swung into place, eight feet from the ground.

Gerhard's eyes grew wide. With wonder though, not fear. He still did not understand.

"How do you feel, Father?"

Gerhard glanced at the rope. "A fourth rope?"

"For Martha," Roth said. "All four have to hang, even if Martha's hanging is only symbolic. How do you feel?"

Red stained the man's lips. He looked dazed. Drunk on the blood.

"You were right," he said. "Forgive me for ever doubting you. I feel alive."

Roth stepped to his side, withdrew the pistol from his belt, and slammed it into Gerhard's temple.

His father slumped, unconscious.

The Jews seemed too shocked to express their surprise. Good.

Roth hefted his father up under the arms, dragged him to the rope, and dropped him on the ground. Working calmly, he strapped Gerhard's wrists with tape as he had the Jews. Then he pulled the noose down, slipped it over his father's head, and drew it tight.

~~~

STEPHEN COULD not comprehend the events playing out before his eyes. The ache in his wrist where Roth had cut him faded when Gerhard collapsed in a heap.

The rope was cutting off the circulation in his neck, but he found that if he stood on his tiptoes, the blood flowed freely. This, too, was now only a distraction.

To his right, Esther's knees were shaking on the stool.

To his left, Gerhard Braun lay bound and noosed.

Roth was going to hang them all, including his own father.

"I have decided to let each of you witness a hanging before I hang you," Roth said. "I want you to see the horror on a man's face when he realizes that he has not found freedom and glory. He has to die so that I can take his power."

Roth's face shone with sweat, not from exertion. His eyes fixed on his father.

"I would have to say that it's worked out better this way. You've all spent your lives searching. Whether you knew it or not, seeking, seeking. And tonight you've found your treasure. But it isn't the treasure you were hoping for, is it? Not what Martha had in mind at all. Your hope for love and all that nonsense is now smothered by horror. Emptiness. Death. Hope, on the other hand, will belong to me."

An image of Chaim and Sylvia flashed through Stephen's mind. A week ago he'd been busy trying to convince Dan what a good investment the property in Santa Monica would make. He'd forsaken all that was once dear for the woman who now teetered on a stool beside him.

What had happened to him? He'd lost his mind. Or had he? No, he'd found his heart.

Esther, I am so sorry.

"If you can see his eyes, watch them carefully," Roth said. "You can see the horror in the eyes."

He looked at Stephen for a moment, and then

frowned as if disappointed that, in his current state, Stephen wouldn't be watching Gerhard's eyes, at least not carefully.

Roth suddenly stepped forward, grabbed the end of Gerhard's rope that hung free, and began to haul his father off the ground, headfirst.

The father came to his knees.

Gerhard coughed once, sputtered, and threw his hands around his neck. He clawed at the rope, disoriented. Finally he got his feet under himself and staggered to his feet.

"What . . . ," he screeched. He began to cough before he could finish the sentence.

Roth tied his end of the rope around the post, walked to Gerhard, who was now hacking and wheezing in agony, and spread gray tape over the old man's lips. The father's eyes bulged wide and he strained to breathe through flaring nostrils.

Roth uttered a short cry of delight and jumped back to the post. He grabbed the rope with both hands and yanked Gerhard off the ground.

His father began to kick.

"You should have let me kill her, Father," Roth said. "Now look what you've gone and done."

Roth tied the rope off again. Gerhard's struggles eased. His wheezing was choked off. Only the crickets screeched.

Roth bounded behind his father, slipped a silver knife from his belt, and lined it up along the man's wrists.

Another kick from Gerhard.

"Be still!"

Roth cut him. Then jumped back, delighted. He ran to the table, scooped up one of the glass chalices and hurried back to his father. He worked frantically now, driven to drain his father's power and satisfy his obsession.

Gerhard went limp.

Roth lifted the glass and drank.

And then the air went silent again. Even the crickets had momentarily stalled their wails.

All the while Ruth had kept her eyes fixed dead ahead. Esther had followed her mother's cue and stood tall, despite the trembling in her legs.

And Roth . . . Roth stood panting behind them.

Stephen wasn't sure why, but the entire scene suddenly struck him as nothing more than child's play, which was odd because his quest for power certainly wasn't child's play. Still, in context, it now seemed hardly more than silly.

Foolish ambition in the face of far greater power.

What could possibly drive a man to such insane depths? What made one man crave another man's blood?

Obsession. A craving to have what he could not have. Power. Like Lucifer himself defying God in hopes of elevating himself. This moment was nothing less than the collision of two obsessions, theirs and Roth's. God's obsession with man. Lucifer's obsession with himself. Humankind's obsession with God on one hand, or themselves on the other hand.

Stephen turned his head to Esther and Ruth. He smiled. "I love you, Esther. God has given you to me as my obsession, and I love you."

"And I love you, David," Esther said bravely.

"Take courage," Ruth whispered. "God is our deliverer."

<hr />

THE JEWS were talking, but Roth couldn't make out what they were saying. His head throbbed with an expansive pride that elevated him to a state of heavenly perfection.

It was finished. He had restored his father's power and now taken his soul. Even the Stones of David were now his. The Jews were cowering. He would hang them next. Then he would cut down the bodies and bury them behind the forest.

"Roth!"

The sound of his name cut through his heavy head.

"Roth. Oh, Roth, you do have a problem."

It was the Jew. Stephen. What was he saying?

Roth turned around and stared at them blankly.

"You're drunk on your father's blood, so you may not realize it yet, but you have a very significant problem," Stephen said boldly. Too boldly. "Your plan to harvest souls in anguish has failed."

Roth's mind started to clear. The Jew was trying to sabotage this glorious evening?

"You have not killed our hope. You can't."

<hr />

THE MOMENT he saw Roth's bewildered expression, Stephen knew he'd struck a chord of fear in the man.

This simple yet genuine display of courage undermined him in a way that no physical power could.

Stephen laughed, loudly, deliberately. "Ha! You've lost the upper hand, man. Our simple love overpowers you with a single word. Hang us! Hang us and see that it gains you nothing!"

He felt giddy. Perhaps it was the result of the emotional strain he'd suffered for a week now. Perhaps there was some truth in his claim—surely some of that. But mostly Stephen yelled the words because they really did fill him with a sense of power.

He laughed again, louder this time. "You've taken nothing from us!"

———

ROTH STARED at him. This was a farce.

Stephen was smiling because he'd gone mad with fear.

Then the Jew looked up at Esther, but continued to address Roth. "You thought you brought me for a death, but instead I have found love." Stephen faced him and set his jaw. "I love Esther!" he cried, eyes bright with passion. "I love her. I love her deeply, and I can die easily, happily, knowing that I have found my love."

He kept laughing. A genuine laugh.

Roth was too shaken to move.

"And I have found love," Esther said. "God has given me love instead of fear."

Roth slammed his fist on the table. "Stop it!"

Ruth was smiling.

This couldn't be! He couldn't hang them while they were in this frame of mind. It would undermine his whole plan. Anguish! He had to return them to a state of anguish!

"I am about to hang you fools by the neck until you are dead!" He thrust a finger toward Gerhard. "Look at my father. Look at his white, dead face!"

They did not look.

The mother, Ruth, stared at him between the eyes. "You have another problem," she said. "The box that you believe holds the Stones of David is empty."

What was she saying?

"Don't be a fool," he said.

"Check it."

"You're lying."

"Check it," Stephen said. "Then hang us if you want. You've lost whatever you came here to gain anyway. We have no regrets, no fear. Only love at finding each other."

Roth didn't want to check the box. He knew that even considering their lies was a sign of weakness. But the thought of owning the Stones had set its claws deeper into his mind than he had guessed.

He walked to the box as slowly as possible.

THE MOMENT Roth turned, Stephen lifted his right heel and grabbed at his ankle with his bound hands.

He managed to grab his slacks and support his leg with one hand while he groped for the knife in his sock with his other hand. His fingers closed around the handle. Pulled it free.

He lowered his leg. If he dropped the knife now, there would be no retrieving it. He had to saw through the tape that bound his wrists before Roth returned his attention to them.

And if he did, then what?

Yes, then what?

He pointed the knife up and dug at the tape. Missed. Stuck his wrist instead. He ignored the pain and sliced upwards again.

Roth dropped to his knees by the box. He clawed at the lid.

Come on, Stephen.

The lid flew open. Roth stared into the box.

Thrust his hand inside. Pulled out bundled cloth. Stephen recognized it as one of the old shirts issued to prisoners in the camp. Martha had wrapped the Stones in a shirt.

Stephen felt something cutting, but he couldn't tell how much progress he was making. *Come on, Stephen, cut!*

Roth stood slowly to his feet, kneading the cloth, feeling for the Stones.

He turned to Ruth, eyes frenzied. Or delighted?

He let one end of the shirt fall. The cloth unraveled. Empty.

Ruth was right; the box was empty.

Their tormentor began to moan. He faced them all, eyes darting, arms spread like a gunslinger. A white ghost in the moonlight, living on rage now.

"Where are they?"

Ruth said nothing.

Stephen prayed the German wouldn't see his shaking as he sawed at the tape. But he had no choice. He had to cut himself free now.

"Where are they?" Roth screamed. "Tell me, you filthy Jew!"

Ruth stared at him defiantly. "Now it is you who are in anguish. You've lost all of your power."

Roth rushed forward with surprising speed. He rounded the table, headed straight for Ruth. But he didn't go to Ruth.

He veered toward Esther at the last moment, grabbed the stool with both hands, and yanked it out, just as Stephen felt the tape give way behind his back.

Esther fell a foot before reaching the end of the rope. She bounced and swung three feet off the ground.

He'd hanged her!

——◦◦◦——

WHEN ESTHER saw Roth veer toward her, she knew the worst was about to happen. She instinctively took a huge gulp of air, tensed her muscles, and clenched her eyes.

Then she was airborne. She hit the bottom and bounced. Pain flashed down her spine. She swung like a piñata.

It took a moment for her to realize that she was alive. Not only was she alive, but her neck, though stretched, wasn't broken. And she could breathe. Barely.

She opened her eyes. She was dangling from the

rope above the ground, but fully conscious and fully alive. Was this what it felt like to be hanged? Others' necks were broken by the snap, but hers wasn't. How long would she swing here before dying?

Stephen was swinging too! Had he been hanged as well?

She moved her legs but immediately felt pain stab at her neck. At any minute her neck could break. She wondered if it might be easier to just relax and let the noose take her life quickly. A buzzing began in her ears.

Her vision began to cloud.

———

ROTH LIFTED the stool and smashed it on the ground. It splintered into a heap of sticks.

Stephen wrenched his wrists free from the tape and grabbed the rope above his head for support. He threw his weight forward, lifted both legs as high as he could, and struck out with as much force as he could gather.

Roth spun, stunned by the sudden movement.

Stephen's heel caught him square in the temple. Any smaller of a man and he might have broken his skull. The impact sent a sharp shaft of pain clear up to his hip.

Roth staggered back several steps, fell heavily to his seat, then fell on his side, unconscious.

———

STEPHEN WAS only halfway out of his noose when Roth moved.

Already?

Stephen ripped the noose from his head and dropped to his feet, facing the German, who was now pushing himself up.

Behind Stephen, Esther hung on the end of the rope.

Roth stood, blinking. His eyes darted to the left, and Stephen followed them to a black lump on the earth, behind the table.

His pistol.

Esther began to rasp.

You have time to save her. Not much, but enough.

Stephen spun and grabbed Esther before realizing his mistake. He couldn't turn his back! The snake could easily have a second gun and put a bullet into both of their heads.

He whirled back, Esther in his arms.

Roth was withdrawing a small, snub-nosed revolver from his pocket. The man was still dazed, which slowed him down.

Stephen let Esther go, tore for Roth, and swung his hand, open palmed, for the man's face. The night crackled with a loud snap, like a firecracker.

Stephen's hand flashed with pain.

He formed a fist and drove it into Roth's nose. *Crack!* Roth grunted and fell back to his seat.

"Stephen!" Ruth was crying out for him. "Esther . . . you have to get Esther."

Esther's rasping had intensified. He grabbed the fallen gun, smashed its butt into Roth's head, and hurled the weapon into the grass as Roth slumped to the ground.

He should have kept the gun, he thought. No time now. He had to get to Esther.

"Stephen!" Ruth cried.

He leaped for Esther and grabbed her legs and shoved her up to ease the pressure on her neck.

"Are you okay?"

She coughed and gasped.

"Are you okay?" he demanded.

"Down!"

Stephen glanced around, suddenly struck with the slight problem of getting her down. Ruth stared at them helplessly. He wasn't quite sure what to do. So he asked her again, "Are you okay?"

"I'm hanged!" she barely croaked.

"Are . . . are you hurt somewhere?"

"Everywhere!"

"But not bad?" Surely not a broken neck!

"Bad!" she said.

"Is your neck broken?" he cried in alarm.

She looked down at him and held his gaze. She let out a breath and her face wrinkled, but it was relief, not pain in her eyes.

Stephen's vision blurred with gratitude. "Thank God."

"Stephen?"

"Yes?"

"Free my hands."

"How?"

"Stephen!"

He twisted at Ruth's cry and saw that Braun was struggling to lift his head. Ten yards from him lay the pistol that had fallen free during the confusion.

This was not good. He couldn't let go of Esther. Couldn't get to Braun. Couldn't reach to untie the tape around Esther's wrists. He saw it all, and he knew in a single, dreadful moment what he must do.

Roth slowly pushed himself to his knees.

"Esther, please—"

"Yes!"

"Hold on!" He eased her down, felt the rope take up her weight, felt nauseated. He took two long steps, snatched his fallen knife from the ground, and hurried back. If he thought she could withstand the pressure, he would have gone after Roth before returning to support her.

But the risk of her neck breaking was too high.

He grabbed her legs and shoved her back up. She gasped.

Braun got one leg under himself. Started to rise. Settled back down and tried again.

"Hurry!"

"I'm hurrying!" He held her up with one arm and searched for the tape with a shaking hand. He pressed the blade against it, afraid he might cut her skin.

Braun faltered, then staggered toward the gun.

Esther wheezed a cry.

Stephen sawed, wincing. The tape came apart.

She struggled above him, gripped the noose under her chin, and wrestled with the rope. "Go!"

He ran for Braun like a place-kicker running for a kickoff. His foot landed in the man's rear.

Braun grunted and sprawled to his face.

Stephen flew over him and scooped up the handgun. "Ha!" He spun around, knelt by the killer, and hit him on the head with the butt of the gun.

"Ha!"

This was the third major blow to the man's head. Surely it would keep him out.

In his peripheral vision he saw that Esther was falling.

She'd freed her neck and dropped cleanly to the ground, where she tried to hold her balance and then sank to her seat. She tried to stand, but fell back.

Stephen scrambled to his feet. "Are you okay?"

Esther touched her neck. The bleeding from her wrist had stopped.

Stephen jumped over Braun's prone body and rushed to them. He grabbed the knife and attacked Ruth's bonds. Freed her from the noose.

Dropped the knife.

Faced Esther. They were free.

Stephen sat and took Esther in his arms. She clung to him and began to cry softly.

"It's okay. It's okay, you're safe now."

He wanted to wash away her tears and squeeze her forever. Instead, he took her face in both hands and kissed her.

"I love you."

She couldn't respond for her tears. She didn't need to.

Stephen held her tight, her face planted in his neck as she wept. His eyes swept the camp behind her.

Roth Braun lay still.

This is where we were born. This is where our mothers' lives were once stolen.

He'd never felt so full of life as he did at this moment.

Epilogue

THE AMMUNITION BOX WAS EMPTY FOR GOOD reason, Ruth told them. Martha had buried two boxes in the event that the treasure's location was forced from them. She would confess taking one Stone and burying an empty canister. When they dug it up and confirmed her story, they would assume someone else had stolen the other four Stones at the end of the war.

But Ruth knew the location of both boxes. Now the second ammunition box sat on the ground—green, dirty, and latched shut. Martha had buried it five paces from the other, directly under the same beam.

They knelt before it in silence.

They'd wrapped their wrists in cloth and then strapped them tight with gray tape. Stephen had gagged and bound Roth like a hog, lowered Gerhard to the ground, and dragged them both around the fence, where the authorities would find them once the call was made. He'd then dug in the spot Ruth had indicated as her best guess.

She'd been right. What thirty years of mystery had covered, five minutes of digging had uncovered.

Ruth unceremoniously reached out, flipped the latch, and pulled open the lid.

On one hand, Stephen wasn't sure he wanted to see what was inside. Considering all the impossible directions the road had taken them these last two weeks, nothing would surprise him. The box might contain the Stones of David. It might just as easily contain a letter. He wasn't sure which he preferred any longer. He had Esther. Didn't he? They had Ruth. Martha's plan had succeeded. In the end they had beaten the diabolical plan to steal their hope, their love, their very lives.

On the other hand, he was desperate to see what was inside this box.

"It's . . . it's full," Ruth said.

"Full?" Stephen leaned forward.

Gold coins.

His heart pounded.

"Coins?" Esther reached her hand in and pulled out one of the coins.

"It's . . . it's Roman," Stephen said. He was staring at a single coin worth at least a hundred thousand dollars.

He pulled the canister closer and tipped it to one side. Gold clattered from the tin box, the unmistakable sound of priceless metals. The treasure rushed out all at once, gold coins, emeralds, rubies, diamonds, others he couldn't immediately name. There had to be a hundred!

Stephen dropped the box and gawked in silence. There on top of the pile rested a round lump of gold. Imprinted with a six-pointed star. And another . . . three more similar . . .

The Stones of David.

Esther touched one, then lifted it up. "The Stones of David?"

"Yes," he whispered. He cleared his throat and said it again. "Yes."

Her eyes were round and bright, like the diamonds. "Is this worth very much?"

They both looked back at Ruth. She gazed at them, smiling. She didn't know. She didn't care. Her eyes were on her treasure.

"A . . ." Stephen cleared his throat. "A hundred . . ." He didn't know how much. "Yes."

She set the Stone back on the top of the mound. "Wow," she said.

"Ha."

They looked at each other. A mischievous smile slowly lifted her cheeks. Stephen felt like hollering, like yelling, like screaming for joy. Not simply for the treasure on the ground, but for the treasure before him. For all of it. For the reward that had been bought and paid for by his mother. By Ruth. By Esther. And now by him.

This was their inheritance.

"You are my Stone of David," Esther said.

"You are my Stone of David."

"I was born for you," she said.

"I was born for you."

She leaned forward slowly, then kissed him on the lips.

Beside them, Ruth began to cry.

THE KINGDOM OF HEAVEN IS LIKE A TREASURE hidden in a field. A certain man learned that the treasure existed and he developed a terrible obsession to possess it. He wasted all of his wealth and secretely sold everything he had to purchase the field so that he could own the treasure.

Again, the kingdom of heaven is like a pearl of great price. When a man found it, he sold all that he had and purchased the pearl.

Unless you, too, obsess after God's kingdom, like this man did over his treasure, you will not find it.

Knock and keep on knocking. Seek and keep on seeking. When they send you away again and again, come back and seek still again. Then you will find the treasure you seek.

Parables of Jesus
Paraphrased and expanded
Found in the book of Saint Matthew

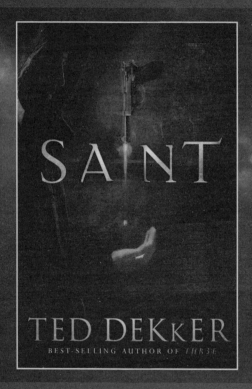

FROM THE MIND OF TED DEKKER

SAINT

TED DEKKER

BEST-SELLING AUTHOR OF *THR3E*

THOMAS NELSON
Since 1798

An Excerpt from
SAINT

I SEE DARKNESS. I'm laying spread eagle on my back, ankles and wrists tied tightly to the bedposts so that I can't pull them free.

A woman is crying beside me. I've been kidnapped . . .

My name is Carl.

But there's more that I know about myself, fragments that don't quite make sense. Pieces of a puzzle forced into place. I know that I'm a quarter inch shy of six feet tall and that my physical conditioning has been stretched to its limits. I have a son whom I love more than my own life and a wife named . . . named Kelly, of course, Kelly. How could I hesitate on that one? I'm unconscious or asleep, yes, but how could I ever misplace my wife's name?

I was born in New York and joined the army when I was eighteen. Special Forces at age twenty, Ranger at twenty-one, now twenty-five. My father left home when I was eight and I took care of three younger sisters—Eve, Ashley, Pearl—and my mother, Betty Strople, who was always very proud of me for being such a strong boy. When I was fourteen, I hit Brad Stenko over the head with a two-by-four and called the police when he slapped my mother. I remember his name because his proposal to marry my mother terrified me. I remember things like that. Events and facts cemented into place by pain.

My wife's name is Kelly. See I know that, I really do. And my son's name is Matthew. Matt. Matt and Kelly, right?

I'm a prisoner. A woman is crying beside me.

Carl snapped his eyes wide, stared into the white light above him, and immediately closed his eyes again.

Opening his eyes had been a mistake that could have alerted anyone watching to his awakening. He scrambled for orientation. In that brief moment, eyes wide to the ceiling, his peripheral vision had seen the plain room in which he was held captive. Smudged white walls. A single fluorescent fixture above, a dirty mattress under him.

And the crying woman, strapped down beside him.

Otherwise the room appeared empty. If there

was any immediate danger, he hadn't see it. Then it
was safe to open his eyes.

Carl opened his eyes again, quickly confirmed
his estimation of the room, then glanced down at
a thick red nylon string bound around each ankle
and tied to two metal bedposts. Beside him, the
woman was strapped down in similar manner.

He was dressed in black dungarees pushed up to
his knees by whomever had tied them down. No
shoes. The woman's left leg had been pulled over
his and was strapped to the same post that held his
right leg. Her legs had been cut and bruised and the
string was tied tightly enough around her ankles to
leave marks. She wore a pleated navy blue skirt,
torn at the hem, and a white blouse that looked like
it had been dragged through a field with her.

This was Kelly. He knew that, and he knew that
he cared for Kelly deeply, but he was suddenly
unsure why. He blinked, searching his memory for
details but his memory remained fractured.
Perhaps his captors had used drugs.

The woman whose name was Kelly faced the
ceiling, eyes closed. Her tears left streaks down
dirty cheeks and into short blonde hair. Small
nose, high cheek bones, a bloody nose, and several
scratches on her forehead.

I'm strapped to a bed next to a woman named Kelly who's been brutalized. My name is Carl and I should feel panic, but I feel nothing.

The woman suddenly caught her breath, jerked her head to face him, and stared into his soul with wide blue eyes.

In the space of one breath Carl's world changed. Like a boiling heat wave vented from a sauna, emotion swept over him. A terrible wave of empathy laced with a thread of bitterness he couldn't understand. What he did know was that he cared for the woman behind these blue eyes very much.

And then, as quickly as the feeling had come, it fell away.

"Carl . . ." Her face twisted with anguish. Fresh tears flooded her eyes and ran down her left cheek.

"Kelly?"

She began to speak in a frantic whisper. "We have to get out of here! They're going to kill us." Her eyes darted toward the door. "We have to do something before he comes back. He's going to kill . . ." Her voice choked on emotion.

Carl's mind refused to clear. He knew who she was, who he was, why he cared for her, but he couldn't readily access that knowledge. Worse, he didn't seem capable of actually feeling, not for more than a few seconds.

"Who . . . Who are you?"

She blinked, as if she wasn't sure she'd heard him right. "What did they do to you?"

He didn't know. They'd hurt him, he knew that, but he didn't know who *he* was much less who they were.

She spoke urgently through her tears. "I'm your wife! We were on the cruise, at port in Istanbul when they took us. Three days ago. They . . . I think they took Matthew. Don't tell me you can't remember!"

Details that he now remembered rehearsing in his mind before waking flooded him. He was with the army, Special Forces. His training was extensive and dark. They'd been taken by force from a market in Istanbul. Matthew was their son. Kelly was his wife.

Panicked, Carl jerked hard against the restraints. He was rewarded with a squealing metal bed frame, no more.

Another mistake, he thought. Whoever had the resources to kidnap them undoubtedly had the skill to use the right restraints. He was reacting impulsively rather than with calculation. Carl closed his eyes and calmed himself. *Focus, you have to focus.*

"They brought you in here unconscious half an hour ago and gave you a shot," she said hurriedly. "I think . . . I'm pretty sure they want you to kill someone." Her fingers touched the palm of his hand above their heads. Clasped his wrist. "I'm afraid, Carl. I'm so afraid." Crying again.

"Please, Kelly. Slow down."

"Slow down? I've been tied to this bed for three days! I thought you were dead! They took our son and you want me to slow down?"

The room faded and then came back into view. They stared at each other for a few silent seconds. There was something strange about her eyes. He was remembering scant details of their kidnapping, even fewer details of their life together, but her eyes were a window into a world that felt familiar and right.

They had Matthew. Rage began to swell, but he cut it off and was surprised to feel it leave as quickly as it had come. His training was kicking in. He'd been trained not to feel. So then his not feeling was a good thing.

"I need you to tell me what you know."

"I've told you. We were on a cruise—"

"No, everything. Who we are, how we were taken. What's happened since we arrived. Everything."

"What did they do to you?" she asked again.

"I'm okay. I just can't remember—"

"You're bleeding." Her eyes stared at the base of his head. "Your hair . . ."

He felt no pain, no wetness from blood on his neck or in his hair. He lifted his head and twisted it for a look at the mattress under his hair. A fist-sized red blotch stained the cover.

The pain came then, a deep throbbing ache from the base of his skull. He set his head back down and stared at the ceiling. With only a little effort he disconnected himself from the pain.

"Tell me what you remember."

She blinked, still breathing deliberately. "You had a month off from your post in Kuwait and we decided to take a cruise to celebrate our seventh anniversary. Matthew was buying some sugared ginger when a man grabbed him and went into an alley between the tents. You went after him. I saw someone hit you from behind with a metal pipe. Then a rag with some kind of chemical was pushed over my face and I passed out. Today's the first time I've seen you." She closed her eyes. "They tortured me, Carl."

i

"This excellent book offers patients and physicians an exciting theoretical framework that exposes the procedures they unconsciously use in making the critical medical decisions and suggests how these procedures might be improved."

—LESTER GRINSPOON, M.D.,
author of *Marijuana Reconsidered,*
Professor of Psychiatry,
Harvard Medical School

"Anyone—whether patient or doctor—who has ever been uncertain in a doctor's office needs to read this book—and that, of course, should include áll of us."

—A. STONE FREEDBERG, M.D.,
Emeritus Professor of Medicine,
Harvard Medical School

"One cannot help but view this book and its thesis as a watershed in contemporary medical thinking. With its rich and diverse set of referenced ideas, ranging from Niels Bohr to Lester Thurow to Norman Cousins, it provides a compelling argument for a new way of viewing medical reality. Family medicine could do well to take note of the ideas presented by these authors and to lead in incorporating them into the framework of medical care."

— *The Journal of Family Practice*

"A skillful, subtle exploration of the assumptions which guide contemporary thinking in medicine, this offers in place of the outmoded mechanistic model a far more workable probabilistic framework."

— *Kirkus*

"A thought-provoking book: recommended."

— *Library Journal*

MEDICAL CHOICES, MEDICAL CHANCES

How Patients, Families, and Physicians Can Cope with Uncertainty

with a New Preface by Hilary Putnam

HAROLD J. BURSZTAJN, M.D.   RICHARD I. FEINBLOOM, M.D.
ROBERT M. HAMM, PH.D.   ARCHIE BRODSKY

Routledge
New York   *London*

Published in 1990 by
Routledge
an imprint of
Routledge, Chapman & Hall, Inc.
29 West 35 Street
New York, NY 10001

Published in Great Britain by
Routledge
11 New Fetter Lane
London EC4P 4EE

Published in 1981 by Delacorte Press

Cover: Henri Matisse, *Icare* from the volume *Jazz*, 1947. Francis H. Burr Fund. © President and Fellows of Harvard College 1985.
The use of the Matisse on the cover was suggested to us by Harold J. Bursztajn. The publisher wishes to thank Stephanie Zelman for submitting a cover design for the book.
Photographs by Michael Lutch, courtesy of Beth Israel Hospital, Boston, Massachusetts. Permission to publish elsewhere may be granted by Beth Israel Public Relations.
Photograph accompanying Chapter 8 courtesy of A. Stone Freedberg, M.D.
Photograph accompanying Chapter 13 courtesy of Diana, Don, and baby Maxwell Jillie.

Library of Congress Cataloging-in-Publication Data

Medical choices, medical chances : how patients, families, and physicians can cope with uncertainty / Harold Bursztajn ... [et al.].
   p. cm.
  Reprint, with new preface. Originally published: New York, N.Y. : Delacorte Press/Seymour Lawrence, c1981.
  Includes bibliographical references.
  ISBN 0-415-90292-4 (pbk.)
  1. Medicine—Philosophy. 2. Medical logic. 3. Medicine—Decision making. 4. Probabilities. 5. Uncertainty. 6. Physician and patient. I. Bursztajn, Harold.
  [DNLM: 1. Decision Making. 2. Philosophy, Medical. 3. Physician -Patient Relations. W 61 M489]
R723.M36 1990
610—dc20
DNLM/DLC
for Library of Congress   89-70211
                    CIP

British Library Cataloguing in Publication Data
Medical choices, medical chances.
  1. Medicine. Decision making
  I. Bursztajn, Harold
  610

ISBN 0-415-90292-4

To
A. Stone Freedberg
a model of wisdom in clinical practice
and
Stanley Sagov
a model family physician

CONTENTS

viii   CONTENTS

PREFACE

In *Medical Choices, Medical Chances,* the four authors bring
together different kinds of knowledge and experience—three
of the authors represent different sorts of medicine, including
psychoanalysis and experimental psychology, and one is a social
critic—to discuss a problem that is potentially important to
every one of us: that is the role that a certain image of "objective
science" plays in determining doctors' decisions. This is a problem with practical consequences, but it also connects with one
of the greatest and most characteristic issues in European
thought since the age of Kant.

To see what that issue is, imagine that someone gets you to
understand a person or a work of art or your own life in a
different way. The one who does this—call him your mentor—
will be unable to tell anyone how he changed your sensibility
except by constructing a narrative. On the other hand, if a firm
builds a piece of laboratory equipment for you, the engineers
who designed the equipment and the engineers who designed
the machinery that made the equipment will be able to tell you
how they achieved their goals using the precise languages of
the physical sciences and engineering. The difference between
these two ways of understanding events—the difference between controlling objects and relating to subjects, between

"objectivizing reason" and human (or humane) understanding, if you like—has exercised thinkers in every generation in the last two hundred years.

The authors of the present volume believe that the medical professions are in the grip of a particular picture of what it is to be "scientific." According to this picture—and the picture is one that every one of us has absorbed, whether we have any formal scientific education or not—science is characterized by being reductionistic: to be scientific we must get down to the molecules or the atoms or the elementary particles, to the level of basic physics or basic chemistry. In addition, according to this picture, science is characterized by the conclusive character of the knowledge it affords. As applied to medicine, what the picture leads to is the idea that if causes are unclear, then more tests must always be performed. But even if laboratory "samples" are objects on which tests can be endlessly performed without worrying about the effect on the sample (one can, after all, always get another sample), human beings are not like that. This point is driven home by the case (described in detail in this book) of a 21-month-old child who was literally tested to death in a Boston hospital. No case could bring home more dramatically the conflict between the objectivizing attitude and the empathetic attitude, between objectivizing reason and narrative understanding.

The authors suggest that, in retrospect, it seems likely that what the child really needed was to be treated with a mixture of antibiotics, love, and distraction. But the child had ear infections, refused to eat, and so forth, and the causes were unclear. The child was being examined in one of the great research hospitals for which Boston is famous, and that, paradoxically, was the trouble. For a vicious cycle developed: test results were obscure; so further tests were ordered to remove the unclarity, and this happened over and over again. As the tests went on and on, the child stopped eating again. The doctors responded by installing a hyperalimentation line, thinking that all the child needed to survive was proper nutrition. But the line "carried only calories, not love," and at this point the child had become weak from the combined effects of infection, malnutrition, and testing—so much so that he had to have blood transfusions to make up for the "iatrogenic blood loss" from all of this. Two days before a scheduled biopsy of the thalamus gland the child died.

One thing that was lacking in this approach, besides the neglect of the child's emotional needs, was any notion of probability, the authors point out. "The questions that needed to be asked about each diagnostic or therapeutic procedure were 'How likely is this to do good? How likely is it to do harm?' Also, there was no assessment of values. 'What, in this situation, is good? Whose good are we working for? What is best for the patient? What does the patient want?'"

Following a certain image of science, the physicians acted as if they were investigating a process in a laboratory sample (hence they did not treat their own actions as subject to questions of moral responsibility). Indeed, they conducted a number of tests which, if they had revealed anything, would have showed conditions for which there was no presently known cure. "What then was the purpose of testing?" ask the authors. "Was it to treat K. more effectively or to give the clinicians the reassurance of certain knowledge?"

The authors are concerned to free doctors from this stereotype of science so that they can be more humane and also so that they can be more aware of the need for probabilistic as opposed to deterministic models for decision-making. The doctor, they argue, should not see himself on the model of an astronomer who can predict the position of the constellations millions of years in the future using astronomical data and physical laws. Instead, he should see himself as engaged in *gambling*—but gambling with moral responsibility, because he has the welfare of a fellow human being in his hands, and without pretending to himself that there is some knowledge that can be obtained without a gamble which will always point to an "objectively correct" decision.

In thinking about these issues, I recalled a book by three well-known cognitive psychologists, a book that studied the fallacies people commit when they reason probabilistically.[1] As one part

[1]*Judgement under Uncertainty: Heuristics and Biases,* edited by Daniel Kahneman, Paul Slovic and Amos Tversky, Cambridge University Press, 1982.

of their study, these psychologists studied one way in which doctors decide to order a risky operation. It is true that they were not concerned with the normative issues that are at the center of the present book; their purpose was to construct a model of actual decision-making, rather than to prescribe. But their study is nonetheless instructive in the present context.

The psychologists in question (Amos Tversky, Daniel Kahneman and Paul Slovic) found that their subjects regularly "ignore base rates." Here is an example: suppose that when the drivers from one taxicab company ("the blue cabs") have a minor accident they stop and report it ninety percent of the time while the drivers from a second company ("the green cabs") only stop and report it ten percent of the time. A detective wants to know whether Mr. Jones took a blue cab or a green cab (Mr. Jones is color blind, and did not notice the name of the cab company). Mr. Jones did notice that the driver had a minor accident and did not stop to report it to his company. On this data, most people would feel justified in concluding that the probability is .9 that the cab in question was a green cab. This tendency is not affected by being told that there are ten times as many blue cabs as green cabs.

The fallacy in this reasoning is easy to demonstrate. If the number of blue cabs is 1000 and the number of green cabs is 100, and each cab has one minor accident a month, then in one month there will be 100 blue cabs that fail to report an accident and 90 green cabs that fail to report an accident. So the probability that a cab which has failed to report a minor accident is green is 90 / 190, which is less than .5, and not .9. The "base rate" (the prior probability that a cab is blue or green) has to be known to estimate the probability, and not just the chances that a cab of each of the two kinds will stop and report an accident.

To come now to the medical example, if a test for cancer of a particular type is correct nine times out of ten, doctors (in Kahneman, Slovic, and Tversky's sample) generally relied on the test, and ordered very risky operations if the result was positive, without regard to the frequency of that type of cancer in the population. Yet if the base rate is very low, the majority of all positives will be "false positives." More patients will die than if the test were not used at all.

On the one hand, these results reinforce one of the morals of the present work: the need for a better understanding of decision-making under uncertainty. But there is also a danger here—one to which the authors of the present work are extremely sensitive. This is the danger of the easy thought that there is nothing wrong with scientism; it is just that our scientism has to be a *probabilistic* scientism. What is wrong with scientism is not that it neglects probabilities but that it neglects simple humanity; and an overemphasis on the ins and outs of probability can be as dehumanizing as the ideal of certainty and "objectivity" that led to the disaster in the case of K. In the area of nuclear strategy, thinkers at places like the Rand Corporation have sometimes argued that "scenarios" on which the survival of the entire human race may depend can be studied mathematically, and "rational" policies can be invented for the case of "nuclear emergencies" by employing game theory, probability theory, and so on. George Kennan has referred to these theorists as "nuclear metaphysicians" because of the way in which they forget that they are employing idealized models which are as far from reality as Plato's realm of Forms. It is true that a modicum of knowledge of probability theory and cost benefit analysis would be a good thing for doctors to learn: certainly everyone who makes repeated decisions involving serious consequences should know what the base rate fallacy is, and doctors need to know that small costs can add up. Many of the tests that K. had to undergo involved a cost to K. (in physical or emotional terms) that doubtless seemed small in comparison with the possible payoff of the test, but the cumulative sum of the costs was enormous. But thinking in terms of mathematical models can be totally unrealistic, whether the models be probabilistic or deterministic. K. may have been small and unable to communicate very well, but K. had, nevertheless, a subjective point of view: a point of view that saw endless "procedures" as a kind of torture. The subjective point of view of an individual is not something we can describe in the language of probabilistic models. It is for this reason that the present authors stress the importance of empathetic understanding and the importance of moral responsibility as well as probabilistic thinking. In no area have we benefited more from scientific discoveries than in the realm of medicine. That is why it is so important that antiscientism not be allowed to turn the clock back and that scientism not be allowed to corrupt medical progress. There is no mathematical rule that will enable us to calculate a "weighted average" of "objective" knowledge and understanding of human beings in all their subjectivity. But if there is no mathematic formula, there is still the simple principle that we all know, *be decent to one another*.

Since one of the authors of this work is a psychoanalyst, and psychoanalytic considerations make an occasional appearance in this work, I would like to take this opportunity to say a word about the much-discussed question of the "validity" of psychoanalysis. This will not be a mere opportunistic digression on my part, for, if I am not mistaken, the same deep cultural conflict between the claims of objectivizing reason and the claims of human understanding is behind much of the debate over psychoanalysis.

I don't mean that the debate is a simple reflex of ideological debates; indeed, it cuts across the major ideological lines. Thus the most famous positivist philosopher of the century (Rudolf Carnap) regarded psychoanalysis as a science, albeit an immature one. Marxists tended to regard psychoanalysis as "bourgeois," but the French communist theoretician Althusser was influenced by the "French Freud" (Lacan). In universities, medical schools frequently teach psychoanalysis as a specialization within psychiatry, while departments of psychology often exclude it from their teaching.

In trying to reach a sane view of this messy controversy, it is well to keep in mind that each one of the various psychological and social studies—psychology, sociology, economics, linguistics—as well as philosophy—have advanced the claim to be "sciences." Putnam's Law, if I may call it that, is that every thirty years or so a new theory—Hume's Association of Ideas, or Kant's Transcendental Philosophy, or Marx's Theory of Capitalist Development, ... or Noam Chomsky's Theory of Government and Binding in Linguistics—always claims to represent a "Copernican Revolution" in this or that subject. I don't mean to suggest that these theories are nonsense, but

they are not sciences. My purpose in saying this is not to
debunk new ideas in psychology and social "science," but to
say that we would be in a better position to determine what
is and is not a real insight contained in any one of them if we
stopped discussing them in such grandiose terms.

Thus, even though Freud was in the grip of a picture of
science which led him to present his work as a grand theory
(one which he hoped would eventually link up with neurology),
I would argue that the lasting value of psychoanalysis is that
it teaches us a new kind of observation. Of course, there are
critics who will not concede even that: critics who would claim
that all there is to psychoanalysis is "suggestion." But these
critics forget that "suggestion" is itself a phenomenon which
involves the *unconscious*. The fact is that we cannot go back
to viewing neurotic behavior as random and senseless.

Description of neurotic behavior in fine detail is not new; for
example, the fourth-century philosopher Theophrastus
described the behavior of the "rumormonger" and other
neurotics with great brilliance in *The Characters*. But what
Theophrastus missed—what his paradigm did not permit him
to see—is the rumormonger's *motivation*. The craving for
attention that immediately strikes us is not apparent to
Theophrastus, although the compulsiveness of the behavior is.
Any modern reader will be struck by Theophrastus' failure to
attribute any motive at all; for him, the neurotic is just someone
whose behavior manifests senseless irrationality. Yet few
people today would miss the craving for attention here; and
when we see it in the rumormonger, we are led to see it in
ourselves.

What I am saying is that Freud discovered that neurosis is
not senseless. And just as we cannot inhabit a pre-Marxian
world or a pre-Kantian world, we cannot inhabit a pre-Freudian
world.

I referred to the worry that Freudian therapy is "suggestion."
A complementary worry is that post-Freudian observation is
"projection." (Note that, like "suggestion," "projection" is an
unconscious process; even when we criticize Freud, our criticism reflects his influence.) There is not and cannot be a

general answer to this worry. But we enjoy works of art, even
though there too is the worry that we are falling for a fashion
(in the case of contemporary art) or being subservient to what
authorities have drummed into our heads (in the case of works
which belong to the canon). The problem of compensating for
the effect of fashion is one that Samuel Johnson and other
eighteenth-century critics indeed worried about, and as Johnson
pointed out, there is no set of fixed rules for discriminating good
art from bad; instead Johnson suggested reading and looking at
works from other times and other cultures in order to widen
one's sensibility. In the same way, an observer who is both
sensitive and widely experienced may be a better interpreter of
the motives and attitudes of other people, even though there
is no formal procedure for such interpretation. As Wittgenstein
writes, almost at the very end of his masterpiece, *Philosophical
Investigations*:

> Correcter prognoses will generally issue from the judgements
> of those with better understanding of people.
> Can one learn to understand people? Yes, some can. Not,
> however, by taking a course in it but through *'experience'*.—Can
> someone else be a man's teacher in this? Certainly. From time
> to time he gives him the right _hint_. —This is what 'learning'
> and 'teaching' are like here. —What one acquires here is not a
> technique; one learns correct judgements. There are also rules,
> but they do not form a system, and only experienced people can
> apply them right. Unlike calculating-rules.
> What is most difficult here is to put this indefiniteness, cor-
> rectly and unfalsified, into words.[2]

Once again we are up against the issue that I mentioned at
the beginning of this introduction, the issue raised by the fact
that in some cases we have only narrative understanding, and
not the kind of understanding possessed by the physicist or
the engineer. Indeed, this was an issue for Freud himself: in
commenting on the case of Elizabeth von R., he writes: "I have
not always been a psychotherapist. Like other neuropatholo-
gists, I was trained to employ local diagnoses and electro-
prognosis, and it still strikes me myself as strange that the case
histories I write should read like short stories and that, as one

---

[2]*Philosophical Investigations;* Basil Blackwell, Oxford, 1958; p. 227. I have
corrected the translation.

might say, they lack the serious stamp of science. I must console myself with the reflection that the nature of the subject is evidently responsible for this, rather than any preference of my own."[3]

Of course the student of the thought and life of Freud has to take into account Freud's desire to give his work "the serious stamp of science," a desire which sometimes led him to give psychoanalysis a highly dogmatic form; but Freud's own attitudes—attitudes which are understandable given his training and his period—need not prevent us from looking at what he gave us in a very different way. As I said, my own view is that what Freud gave us that is of lasting value is not a set of scientific laws, but a new form of observation. The tension in Freud himself—the tension between the two great cultural poles of scientific theory and narrative—is revealed by the way in which Freud writes case histories that "read like short stories," in his own phrase, and then proceeds to generalize, often in a dogmatic way. I believe that the "short stories" are valuable to the extent that they suggest to us ways of constructing our own "short stories," about ourselves and about other people, and to the extent that those "short stories" enable us to better understand ourselves and other people; the dogmatic generalizations represent the operation of Putnam's Law, the force that drives theorists to claim that they have discovered the "Laws of Motion" of this or that, or effected a "Copernican Revolution" in this or that.

Even if psychoanalytic understanding (and, more generally, narrative understanding) of ourselves and others is valuable (and, indeed, indispensable), it has been suggested by a number of writers that understanding may not be "curative." In other words, awareness of one's unconscious motives may not do anything to relieve one's "neurotic symptoms." Psychoanalysis may be of use as what I called a "new kind of observation" without being "valid" as a method of treatment. Attempts to study the issue "empirically" have produced a number of studies. The issue was first raised by insurance companies a

---

[3]Cf. *The Standard Edition of the Psychological Works of Sigmund Freud, Volume II (1893–1895), Studies in Hysteria by Josef Brewer and Sigmund Freud*, ed. James Strachey, London: The Hogarth Press, 1955, p. 160.

half a century ago, who wanted evidence before they paid out medical benefits to employees for what was then a novel form of treatment. (Today it is the National Institutes of Health that have the same worry.) Not surprisingly, the only criterion of "recovery" used in these early studies was the patient's being back on the job. More recent studies use additional criteria, including self-evaluation by the patient and evaluation by others. There have also been studies which looked at the correlation between "recovery" and various approaches and/or traits of the therapist, including the use of psychoanalytic or non-psychoanalytic methods, directive or non-directive approach, manifestation or non-manifestation of affect (by the therapist) in the therapeutic session, and so forth. The studies seem to show that while there are substantial differences in success rate from therapist to therapist, these do not correlate with the therapist's theoretical approach. The picture is confused, however, because some studies claimed to show a higher rate of success of behavior modification therapies, while later studies claimed to show a high rate of recidivism for the same therapies. (Of course, both findings could be right, given the criteria of "recovery" employed.) Moreover, the studies suggest that there *is* a correlation between the personal traits of the therapist—especially the ability of the therapist to show warmth and empathy, the ability to "confront" the patient if need be—and the therapist's success rate.

While such empirical findings are not unimportant, there is an ethical dimension to notions like "treatment" and "cure" which it is easy to overlook. An "objective" criterion of recovery can be as dangerous as a battery of "objective tests." A friend of mine once told me that the behaviorist therapy he received in college "made me a more efficient neurotic." What this friend believes is that the refusal to even discuss childhood events and feelings—or even his present feelings, insofar as they did not directly relate to the "symptoms" being treated—left him with as little understanding of himself as he had before the therapy. But what is it to "understand oneself"?

The maxim "know thyself" is as old as Socrates, and so is the belief that knowing oneself (or understanding oneself) does have consequences for what one does and how one lives; consequences that are to be prized. Of course this belief cannot be "objectively validated"; for the activity referred to is one that lies in the sphere of what I call narrative understanding, as opposed to the sphere of technological control. If this seems too quick, reflect on the activities that each one of us undertakes and must undertake that cannot be "objectively validated"; we choose friends, we reflect on our lives, we find mentors and role ✓ models, and self-understanding is often an important part of our aim when we do this. And it is true that in all of these cases we run the risk of being deceived or exploited; but it does not follow that we are *always* deceived or exploited. We need objective scientific knowledge, but we also need what used to be called "wisdom"; and the present book helps to fill that need.

HILARY PUTNAM
WALTER BEVERLY PEARSON PROFESSOR OF
MATHEMATICAL LOGIC AT
HARVARD UNIVERSITY
1990

ACKNOWLEDGMENTS

We wish to acknowledge some of the people who have contributed to this book and to our lives and works. They range from patients to philosophers, doctors to typists—and of course, loved ones and friends. They are: Joel Alpert, M.D., William Bayer, M.D., William Berenberg, M.D., Judith Ann Bevis, Sissela Bok, Lilly Bursztajn, Sherry Bursztajn, Buzzy Chanowitz, Sey Chassler, André Churchwell, M.D., Max Day, M.D., John Drimmer, Robert Ebert, M.D., Werner Erhard, Peter Farquhar, Betty Forman, Thomas Gates, M.D., Donna Gertler, David Gordon, M.D., Robert Haggerty, M.D., Michael Harris, Reid Hastie, Leston Havens, M.D., Harvey Jackins, Charles Janeway, M.D., Frances Judkins, Arthur Krieger, M.D., Robert Lawrence, M.D., Duncan Luce, James Lyons, M.D., Peter McFarren, Melissa Mahaney, Matthew Movsesian, M.D., Alexander Nadas, M.D., Thomas Nagel, Norman Paul, M.D., Eric Proctor, Hilary Putnam, Howard Raiffa, Julius Richmond, M.D., Klaus Riegel, Kim Ruth, Paul Schrecker, Miles Shore, M.D., Harold Solomon, M.D., John Stoeckle, M.D., Michael Sukale, Joanne Sullivan, and Daniel Tosteson, M.D. We also thank the staffs of the Family Practice Group of Cambridge, Massachusetts, and the Ambulatory Screening Clinic at Massachusetts General Hospital.

We are deeply grateful to the many patients and families who have worked with us in developing our ideas in practice. The experiences we have shared with them form the basis of the accounts in this book. In the course of preparing these case studies a number of families have given freely of their time to review experiences that were sometimes painful in order that others might benefit. In so doing they have made this their book as well as ours. The same is true of Merloyd Lawrence, a gifted editor whose critical readings have helped to clarify and at times inspire our ideas. This book would not have been possible without her support. Nor would it have been possible without the warmth and wisdom of the families in which our education began.

Since the initial publication of *Medical Choices, Medical Chances,* the authors have enjoyed the benefit of learning from its readers. Although we cannot list all of them individually, it would be a profound sin of omission not to name three: Erika W. Feinbloom, Patricia M.L. Illingworth, Ph.D., and Ingrid Young. Finally, we thank Maureen MacGrogan for inspiring us to bring this book to light a second time in its new home with Routledge.

H.B.
R.I.F.
R.M.H.
A.B.

INTRODUCTION

When we deal with questions of health and illness, as patients or concerned family members, as doctors or other health professionals, each of us has some notion of what is true and what is good. We are all guided by some implicit philosophy of science. That philosophy, whatever it may be, has a lot to do with how we feel about the pain, fear, and risks associated with illness, how we think about the decisions that are to be made, and what actions we take on our own behalf or that of someone else who is ill.

Of course, most of us don't think in terms of an *explicit* philosophy of science when we are confronted with illness. But we do have some idea of what we know, how we know it, and how sure we are about it. That is our implicit philosophy of science. Even if we don't think of ourselves as scientists, we do think of medicine as a science. We have some idea of what science is and of what constitutes good science and bad science. One question we need to ask ourselves is whether our ideas about science correspond to what scientists today understand science to be. Another is whether these ideas can help us make the best possible decisions about illness and health.

When a number of writers, dissatisfied with medicine as it is generally practiced by physicians, address these questions, they argue that medicine should not be thought of as a science at all (Carlson, 1976; cf. Cousins, 1979). Science cannot be an adequate basis for medicine, they claim, because medicine deals with human life and human feelings. The logic behind this critique is as follows: Science is "exact"; human beings cannot be understood exactly; therefore human beings cannot be understood by means of science.

But science is not what these critics of medicine seem to think it is. By their definition not only medicine but all of the biological and social sciences (at least in the twentieth century) fail to qualify. Although the sciences that deal with living beings cannot claim one hundred percent predictability, it still is useful to characterize particular ways of understanding living beings as scientific.

What the critics really seem to be saying, then, is that medicine cannot be a science because it is not like physics. But physics, too, has changed during this century from a *science of certainty* to a *science of probability.* Most of us have at least heard of the Heisenberg Uncertainty Principle. We are aware that the physics of Einstein and his successors is not the physics we learned in high school, where cause-and-effect relationships could be known with precision and predicted with certainty through the use of Newton's laws. But we haven't thought systematically about what it means to "know" in the age of quantum physics, because we haven't tried to apply the new science to everyday thought, feeling, and action. We still think we can "know" in the old, mechanistic way.

Physicists have realized that the new way of thinking has revolutionary implications. Indeed it represents what T. S. Kuhn (in *The Structure of Scientific Revolutions,* 1962) calls a "paradigm shift"—i.e., a change in the fundamental assumptions and procedures of science. As long as scientists work within a familiar, agreed-upon paradigm, the philosophy that guides their work can be left implicit. During the period of a paradigm shift, however, this implicit philosophy becomes a matter of explicit discussion. After a period of questioning, debate, theorizing, and experimentation, it is replaced by a new philosophy which, once articulated, agreed upon, and learned, can itself become implicit as the new paradigm that guides scientific investigation.

Paradigm shifts tend to occur when an existing paradigm isn't working— when scientists can no longer use it to solve the problems they set out to solve. Such a crisis of confidence exists today in the science of medicine. Amid malpractice suits, the holistic medicine and "patient's rights" movements, and a growing concern over the cost of medical care, we need to make explicit the assumptions that guide our thinking in medicine. In making these assumptions explicit, we have the opportunity to change them. In this book we will show that medical questions can continue to be approached scientifically if the science of medicine partakes of the standards of twentieth-century physics. It took two hundred years for medicine to incorporate the insights of classical physics, the physics of Newton. More than fifty years after the "quantum revolution" in modern physics, medicine has yet to incorporate its standards.

It may be natural to think that medicine always was and always will be what it is today, but in fact, what we know as "modern medicine" is less than a century old. In the latter part of the nineteenth century the French physiologist Claude Bernard introduced principles adapted from classical physics into experimental medicine, thereby revolutionizing all of medical practice, experimental and clinical. With medicine now in search of a new science we can once again turn to physics as a model. We will refer to the Newtonian paradigm of science as the Mechanistic Paradigm, and to the paradigm that guides the work of modern physicists as the Probabilistic Paradigm. The new science of the Probabilistic Paradigm is one that accepts a degree of uncertainty as an inherent part of reality. It questions whether causation can be specified with certainty, whether there is such a thing as a conclusive experiment, and whether subjective knowledge can be entirely separated from objective knowledge.

Under the Probabilistic Paradigm, a set of probable causes in constantly changing configurations replaces the concept of a definite cause or causes for a given effect. Experimentation, rather than linking cause and effect in a relationship of certainty, becomes a way of exploring what probabilities may obtain. Instead of an "objective" reality that exists independently of the observer, there is a many-sided reality that includes the effect of the way one observes on what one observes. Instead of a strict distinction between facts that are "value-neutral" and values that have no basis in fact, there is a recognition of the subjective component of factual knowledge and the objective, rationally discussable aspect of values and feelings.

All of these distinctions have vast implications for medical practice. Of particular significance for medicine is the fact that the Probabilistic Paradigm recognizes values and feelings to be an inescapable concern of science. A paradigm of science is a paradigm of thought and action. The Probabilistic Paradigm, as distinct from the Mechanistic, incorporates the realization that thought and action take place in the context of feeling. Under the new paradigm the scope of thought and action in medicine is enlarged to take into account the feelings that affect people's health and well-being.

We are all, to some degree or other, afraid of uncertainty. Because our conception of rationality is grounded in the Mechanistic Paradigm, which has no place for uncertainty, we find it difficult to be rational about uncertainty. Instead, when faced with uncertainty, we become anxious—most of all when our lives are on the line. When we are sick or are in the presence of illness (as family members or medical personnel), pain and fear make it hard to be as rational as we would like to be. We are tempted to retreat into a false sense of certainty, which affects our capacity to make decisions. For when uncertainty is too painful to face directly, we block it out. But we cannot make wise decisions when we deny ourselves the benefits of conscious awareness of uncertainty.

Not only patients and their families are prey to anxiety. While a patient may have reason to fear imminent death, a doctor may dread the intimations of mortality that come when the limits of knowledge and power are revealed. Just as a patient may seek to evade the unknown future consequences of an illness by simply failing to acknowledge them, so a doctor may do anything to avoid being exposed as uncertain or in error—in his or her own eyes, in the eyes of colleagues, in the eyes of patients and families who have been taught to expect "scientific" accuracy from medicine, and perhaps even before a court of law. A woman who fails to perform regular breast self-examinations and a doctor who relies on laboratory readings in place of clinical judgment may both be fleeing from the responsibility of making choices in an uncertain world.

One way to avoid the anxiety that accompanies uncertainty is to bury one's head in the sand. Another way is to seek assurance from technology. While much is said about overtreatment in critical commentaries on contemporary medicine, the damaging influence of the Mechanistic Paradigm can also be felt in overdiagnosis. In practically any teaching hospital conscientious interns and residents daily bring to bear every available piece of diagnostic machinery on difficult cases in an effort "not to take any chances" and "to find out for sure." Trained to seek certainty, they may not realize that they *are* taking chances, not only with time and money, but with the health of patients who are already in a weakened condition. Putting needles or tubes into a person's body and drawing blood (or whatever) drains the patient's strength and increases the risk of infection —often in a search for esoteric conditions that are unlikely to be found and would be untreatable if diagnosed. Mechanistic medical science all too frequently loses sight of the goal (treatment) in the exaltation of the means (increasingly refined diagnosis). The aim of medicine traditionally has been, and should still remain, that of making people who are ill feel better, not that of making doctors feel better about the state of their knowledge.

We are thus in agreement with those who criticize physicians for often being too hasty in turning to technological intervention instead of observing the natural course of illness, being emotionally supportive, and providing treatment in the context of a patient's life. But we come to this conclusion from a different perspective. Rather than question the value of reason as a tool for solving medical problems, we would suggest that reason is often abandoned in "establishment" medical practice. Technical procedures, valuable as they are when there is a rational basis for using them, are invoked mindlessly and automatically, as rituals to reassure anxious physicians. Precise laboratory measurement is accepted as a substitute for a complex, elusive reality that may be understood only with patience and sensitivity. Indeed, future anthropologists may look at our medical rituals the way we look at, say, the savage ritual of offering sacrifices to bring rain. We take the healing rain that eventually comes as conclusive evidence that we have finally chosen the right sacrifice.

The Probabilistic Paradigm offers both patients and doctors a way to make peace with uncertainty without paying the high costs involved in denying uncertainty altogether. Once it is understood that science accepts uncertainty, it should be easier for people to accept uncertainty. By using the new science of probability, people can support each other in uncertain situations by sharing the risks and helping each other cope with them consciously and rationally. The acknowledgment of uncertainty removes a large barrier to trust (whether between family members or between doctor and patient), since people can trust one another more readily when the unreasonable expectation of certainty is removed. At the same time, the realization that uncertainty is inescapably a part of reality motivates people to work at creating the trusting relationships and mutual support necessary in a world where no one can have a sure or final answer. Thus, along with its other benefits, the new science of medicine offers patients and doctors the opportunity to deal with each other as *allies* instead of *adversaries*, which is too often the case today.

An understanding of probabilities also enables patients and doctors to exert all possible influence over the outcome of an illness and to gain the satisfaction and the sense of control that comes from doing so. Although shielding ourselves from uncertainty may reduce anxiety in the short run, it does not help us achieve better outcomes in the long run. By giving up the dream of total certainty and sharing the uncertainty that does exist, we can realistically make decisions that in effect reduce uncertainty. We can better predict how things will turn out, do something about making them turn out for the better, and (when that is not possible) live with disappointment. It is only when we face the fact that we are taking chances that we can begin to make choices.

*   *   *

Medicine provides a natural focus for bringing the perspectives of twentieth-century science into our lives. Some of our most powerful fantasies about ourselves are nurtured and expressed (or left unexpressed) in our relationship to medicine: the fantasy of omniscience and omnipotence, as embodied in the doctor who commands the wondrous apparatus of modern science; the fantasy of ignorance and weakness, as embodied in the uncertain, dependent patient. Medicine is where our very existence may be at stake in the choices we make. It is one of the places where we learn early in life about certainty and uncertainty, trust and mistrust. If in the past medicine has contributed to teaching us mechanistic habits of thought, feeling, and action, perhaps we can now change medicine so that it can teach those who come after us different habits, habits that are more useful and more humane.

The new approach to medicine we propose here contains some ingredients that in themselves may seem familiar. The language of probability is already used a great deal in medicine. For example, doctors may obtain informed consent from patients by specifying the odds for success of various treatment outcomes. In addition, many recent developments in medical practice, emanating from the public as well as the profession, are aimed at breaking down both the intellectual rigidity of mechanistic medical science and the authoritarian doctor-patient relationship that coexists with it. They include self-care, holistic medicine, family medicine, patient's rights, patient advocacy, and patient education. Supporters of these changes may find much in these pages that strikes a sympathetic chord.

From a scientific perspective, however, the current efforts to humanize medical practice (admirable as they are) are a probabilistic icing on a mechanistic cake. When an outmoded paradigm breaks down, scientists naturally try to patch it up before giving up on it completely. This is what is happening in medicine today. While the patchwork repairs now being attempted may be moves in the right direction, they are not likely to have much effect in the absence of a systematic change in our habits of thought, feeling, and action. Until we learn to think about medical decision-making in a new way, the old way of thinking will continue to shape the questions we ask and the ways in which we answer them.

This is why we propose to use the Probabilistic Paradigm, originally developed in physics, in the applied science of medicine. We wish to explore this theme in a useful and not unnecessarily forbidding manner, since we believe that philosophy has meaning only insofar as it is consciously applied in everyday life—in this case by patients, doctors, and all who are concerned with medicine. We have therefore written this book as an episodic tale of how a doctor and his patients attempt to learn and practice the new paradigm. As our fictional Dr. S. makes a pilgrim's progress that loosely reflects the experiences (including the mistakes) of the two of us who are physicians, his thinking and personal reactions reflect those of all four authors. In keeping with the Probabilistic Paradigm, S. is committed to helping patients and their families to make their own choices and work out their own medical destinies. At the same time, as a physician he sees himself as having knowledge and skill to contribute and comfort and caring to offer.

At the beginning of our story, S., as a hospital intern, witnesses a case of overdiagnosing and under-caring—a case that haunts him throughout his practice—that dramatizes the devastating impact mechanistic thinking can have, even in the hands of well-meaning people. It is then that S. begins to articulate the principles of the Probabilistic Paradigm. The remainder of Part I ("A New Science of Medicine") lays out these principles and shows how they depart from those of the Mechanistic Paradigm—first in scientific theory and research (with emphasis on physics), then in medical practice, and finally in everyday life. For after S. and his patients realize the advantages of the new paradigm, they must come to terms with the fact that life in our society—in the family, on the job, in the consumer marketplace, and in the doctor's office—continues to reinforce the use of the old paradigm that has shaped our society in the first place. The bulk of our social institutions, including our profit-oriented economic system, have not been set up to encourage independent critical thinking. It will be far from easy for patients and doctors to think probabilistically in their medical encounters when they are accustomed to thinking mechanistically in other areas of their lives.

In Part II ("Chance and Choice") S. seeks to translate the Probabilistic Paradigm into tools for decision-making that he and his patients together can use. First he tries the formal procedure called decision analysis, which has recently been introduced into medicine after having been developed in business and public policy planning. Although he finds it useful to learn decision analysis as a way of teaching himself what to keep in mind when making decisions probabilistically, he and his patients conclude that guiding their actions with decision analysis creates as many problems as it resolves. Even with decision analysis, they are still faced with large questions of judgment at every step of the way.

Realizing that they cannot avoid making judgments, they turn to a more practical, informal approach, one that treats every decision (in medicine and in life) as a gamble and attempts to distinguish between good and bad gambles according to the contexts in which they occur. The word *gambling* here does not have its usual connotations: a trivial recreation, a highly profitable business activity, or a form of compulsive, self-destructive behavior. Instead, the gambling we speak of here is guided by the principles of scientific experimentation under the Probabilistic Paradigm. On the one hand, it requires critical judgment, i.e., the capacity to doubt. On the other, it requires trust, i.e., the capacity to believe. Actually people gamble all the time, in everything they do. Because they don't always like to admit it, they gamble unconsciously. By gambling consciously together, S. and the families with whom he works are able to gamble in a way that is both reasonable and effective.

To do so, however, they have to learn to trust one another, and that is not always easy in a world that is full of mistrust. In Part III ("Relationships") S. and his patients confront the fact that decision-making takes place in the context of relationships among people (in the family, in the workplace, between doctor and patient, and so forth) and the feelings those relationships engender. When there is little trust in a family (as, for example, in the case that begins Part III), the family members are not likely to have the emotional security needed to gamble consciously. By working to achieve greater trust and mutual concern, S. and his patients become better able to gamble together. Conversely, through the experience of gambling together, they develop trust and concern. In this process of discovery and growth S. learns from his patients just as they learn from him.

Although S. is portrayed as a family doctor, a doctor who works not only with individual patients, but with families, one does not need to be or to have a family doctor in order to make decisions as S. and his patients do; any doctor or patient can do so. On the other hand, probabilistic thinking lends itself particularly well to situations in which a doctor, patient, and family work together.

Part IV ("Family Decisions") shows how families can make medical decisions in keeping with the Probabilistic Paradigm when an atmosphere of trust and caring is present. Here, with guidance and support from S., families create their own ways of coping with illness, death, and birth, even as they go through the range of emotions attendant upon these events. The cases in this section, which include a birth and a death in the home, center around the decision to use the home or the hospital as a site for care. They show how families can exercise varying degrees of control in different settings. They also show that it is much easier for patients to exercise critical thinking under conditions of uncertainty when there is a family to support them in facing uncertainty.

From the doctor's point of view we see how S. shares his understanding of the new paradigm with patients and their families. By working with families he can observe and point out the complex contexts of causation that affect the course of an illness, showing that each individual cause has effects that vary with time and cannot be precisely specified. He and his patients soon realize that the family itself can simultaneously be both a factor contributing to illness and a source of recuperative strength.

Like physicists who unintentionally influence the movement of electrons merely by turning on a light to observe them, the

Chas.

patient, family, and doctor cannot be detached observers. They
are all involved observers affecting and being affected by the
observed situation in countless ways that no laboratory test can
measure. With regard to the doctor's observations, every form
of diagnosis, from a kindly gaze to a complex X-ray procedure,
has an impact, great or small, on what it is designed to reveal.
By the same token, the patient's and family's understanding of
symptoms can have a significant impact on the course of illness.

A doctor who maintains contact with families, rather than
just individuals, can also more easily understand the many
different ways in which people think, feel, and act, and the
importance of values in medical decision-making. Does a
lonely, disabled, elderly man want to prolong his life at the cost
of having a painful, risky, and perhaps further disabling operation? Does a woman about to give birth want to go through an
uncomplicated labor under anesthesia and pain medication or
with coaching from her family? Does a single mother with
severe high blood pressure want to try to live out a normal life
span by taking pills that make her too drowsy to earn a living
and care for her young children? Do a father and mother want
to authorize surgery to save the life of a three-day-old baby with
a heart condition who may also have Down's syndrome ("mongolism")? These are questions of value, and in the new science
of medicine values are considered along with probabilities in
reaching decisions. In this new science any doctor, regardless
of specialty, needs to be a bit of a family doctor as well; and any
patient, however isolated, needs to be in contact with the source
of his or her values, i.e., the family, even if it is accessible only
through memory.

Finally, as indicated in Part V ("Contexts"), even the most
fully aware and committed doctors and patients will be practicing the new science in a world that is not yet hospitable to
probabilistic thinking or to the spirit of trust and cooperation
in which probabilistic thinking can most readily take place.
Inevitably there will be obstacles, both in the immediate contexts of practice, where the setting (be it home or hospital)
influences medical choices, and in the larger contexts—economic, legal, political—where further barriers of misunder-

standing are raised. If one patient, doctor, or family learns to make decisions under conditions of uncertainty by thinking critically, it will not change the character of the social relations that limit everyone's freedom to make decisions, but it will mean more freedom and control for that one patient, doctor, or family. If we can all begin to think critically and to work together, then perhaps basic change will be possible.

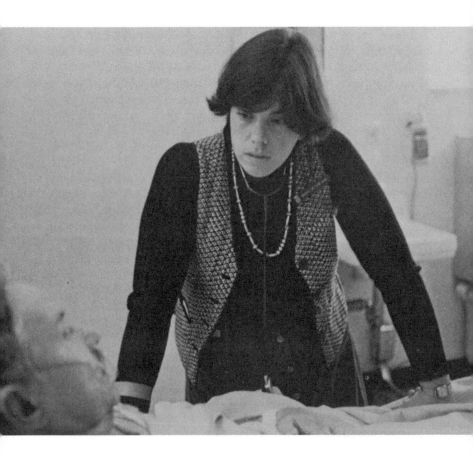

PART I

A NEW SCIENCE OF MEDICINE

1

A CASE OF UNCERTAINTY

In a large city with several renowned medical schools there is a leading teaching hospital which enjoys a well-deserved reputation (as hospitals go) for being efficient and humane at the same time. The pediatric facility of this hospital benefits from close association with the practitioners of adult medicine in an enlightened medical community. Yet its staff almost always has time to give a child a smile.

Not long ago the hospital admitted a twenty-one-month-old boy. It is difficult even now to write about him, using his full name. It is easier just to call him K.

What was wrong with him? Nearly everything. In addition to the ear infection that brought him to the hospital in the first place, he was emaciated, pale, and withdrawn. Though obviously starving, he refused to eat. What was *right* with him? It was hard to tell. He could not communicate verbally, and his capacity to experience and express love was not very well developed.

While K. was in the hospital, he came under the care of two groups of physicians who took very different approaches to diagnosis and treatment. His case enables us, therefore, to com-

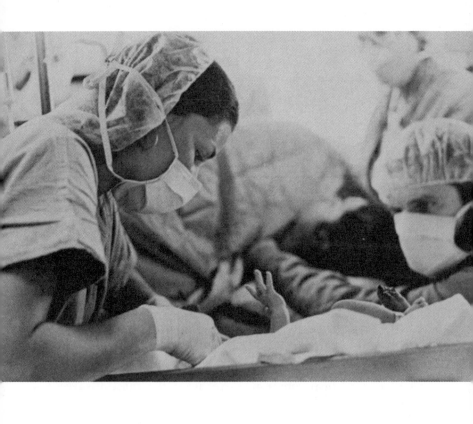

pare two ways of thinking and two strategies for making choices.

K. lived in a working-class neighborhood far from the hospital-medical school complex. He was the only child of a young mother who claimed that the anesthesia used during childbirth had left her in a daze for two weeks. As a result, she said, when she was finally able to start taking care of the child, he refused to accept food from her. Under these circumstances her husband took charge of the boy's feeding.

When K. was seven months old, his father lost his job as a warehouse loader and subsequently moved out of the house, leaving K. in his mother's care. The mother, who was often out "partying," sometimes missed feeding him altogether. When she did feed him, it was on an inadequate diet consisting of jar baby food, skim milk, and potato chips. When he refused these feedings, as he usually did, she would force the food down his throat with a spoon and hold his mouth closed until he swallowed. More often than not he would spit the food up again.

At the time his father left home, K. was at the fiftieth percentile (i.e., average) in height and weight for boys his age. Within a few months he began to decline. In a classic picture of malnutrition he first stopped gaining weight, then stopped growing. By the time he came to the hospital, he was about thirty inches tall and weighed less than eighteen pounds. Fewer than three percent of all boys his age are shorter and lighter than this.

Meanwhile he kept getting middle ear infections (otitis media). According to his records he had twenty-six such episodes before coming to the hospital. These recurrent infections were, in fact, what brought him to the hospital. The neighborhood doctor who had been seeing him felt, quite properly, that he needed more specialized attention. But this physician, who did not himself have privileges at the hospital and was not well acquainted with its staff, did not make the referral in the spirit of a family doctor actively supervising his patient's care. He did not refer K. to a particular individual at the hospital; nor did he write a referral letter detailing his condition. Instead he simply told K.'s mother that the pediatric ward of this hospital was *the* place for a sick child. In the jargon of the trade this is called *dumping.* The doctor had had enough of this frustrating case.

K. was seen in the infectious-disease clinic. There was no effective provision at the hospital for a general evaluation of the child's health before the specialty consultation. The clinic staff found no apparent reason for the recurrent ear infections, and K. was sent home, with an appointment for a follow-up visit three months later. No one noticed that he was starving.

A few months later, when he showed up again, someone did notice. K. was then admitted to the hospital for failure to thrive, feeding problems, developmental delay, and recurrent otitis media. First seen by house officers (interns and residents) on the infectious-disease rotation, he was referred to Dr. S., a new intern on the acute-care ward. Having just come through four weeks of drawing blood, starting IV's, and other intensive-care procedures on this difficult rotation, Dr. S. felt confident enough to take charge of a case in the manner of the family doctor he aspired to be. And K. was a peculiarly appropriate patient for him to have. On the telephone the house officer referring K. had said of him, "He looks like one of those concentration camp survivors you see in films." And indeed he did, with his sunken eyes, his long eyelashes, his wasted arms and legs, and his distended stomach and protruding ribs. From the beginning, the resemblance made Dr. S., who had had relatives die in Auschwitz, take a special interest in K.

Under Dr. S.'s supervision the admission lab workup was kept to a minimum. Aside from minor metabolic abnormalities, all the test results were normal except for an elevated red blood cell sedimentation rate (indicating chronic infections and inflammations), a low white blood cell count (in particular, a low count of one kind of white blood cell that is crucial in fighting infections), and a slightly abnormal liver function (consistent with malnutrition). The tests, in other words, confirmed what the initial physical exam had already revealed.

At this point what were the options? Any doctor might have been uncertain. Dr. S. knew that he was, as were the other physicians with whom he consulted. But he was able to reach three conclusions:

First, whatever else was wrong with the child, he was

severely malnourished. He was also suffering from an immune deficiency, i.e., an inability to fight off infections. But the lab tests had failed to establish primary (genetic or constitutional) immune deficiency, as opposed to secondary (environmentally caused) immune deficiency. Malnutrition itself is a major environmental cause of immune deficiency. The tests had, moreover, ruled out most of the clearly treatable conditions that could contribute to immune deficiency. Thus it was unlikely that K.'s lack of resistance to infection could be specifically diagnosed or directly treated. But one *could* treat his malnutrition, and perhaps in so doing build up his immune defenses as well.

Second, K. would starve to death if he wasn't fed.

Third, K. was very brittle. While performing the initial lab workup, Dr. S. felt very uncomfortable having to draw blood from this emaciated child. Noticing even then that K. refused to eat after being poked with needles, Dr. S. resolved to limit any further invasive testing to the necessary minimum. "God knows," he thought, "he's had enough invasive things done to him with a spoon, let alone needles." He realized that he was thinking of the child, at least sometimes, as a survivor of a kind of concentration camp. He might have dismissed these feelings as mere "projections," but he did not.

Dr. S.'s treatment plan evolved from these perceptions. He decided to forgo the more powerful diagnostic tests, since these had not proved very powerful anyway, and since they were likely to harm the child (by weakening him physically, by increasing his resistance to food, and by alienating him further from those caring for him). Dr. S.'s aim was to treat what could be treated, and to diagnose by continuing to observe how well the child thrived under treatment. Here was a child whose response to food—and to people—took the form of an extreme reaction to real and expected abuse. The first priority was to build up his strength by seeing that he was fed in a loving atmosphere. Since it was likely that K.'s malnutrition was exacerbating, if not causing, his immune deficiency, the extent of this effect could be assessed by seeing whether he became more resistant to infection once he was better nourished. If he did not, invasive testing would be resumed, since in that case more precise information would clearly be required. But by then K. would also be stronger and better able to withstand the testing.

To help set up K.'s feeding program, Dr. S. brought in the hospital's one-man volunteer "feeding team," a genial man who inspired trust in children by speaking to them patiently until they were ready to eat. This "specialist" noticed that even though K. would not eat, he liked to suck on empty bottles. So he and Dr. S. set up a positive-reinforcement schedule for K. When he ate, they let him suck on a bottle. When he spat up food, they did not give him this reward, but they also did not punish him. They just let it pass. Previously the only emotion K. had been able to elicit from his mother was the anger she displayed when he spat up food. Now he was getting love when he ate. To make sure he would get it consistently, Dr. S. put one nurse in charge of K. Together they recognized that this was an emergency, and that love was needed on an emergency basis.

Meanwhile K. continued to run fevers. Instead of always trying to specify the nature and cause of these infections by testing, which involved restraining the child for up to fifteen minutes while fishing for a still-functioning vein in his neck, Dr. S. made educated guesses and treated the infections empirically. That is, he tried a particular antibiotic, which worked, and kept using it as long as it continued to work. As long as K.'s infections could be brought under control in this way and he continued to thrive, the infections would not interfere with his overall therapy. Therefore Dr. S. felt no need to investigate them more closely. He was more interested in watching K. eat and begin to gain weight. One test was taken during this period —a liver function, which was now normal.

K. progressed for about ten days. Then he developed a fever while Dr. S. was off duty. Dr. S. had left instructions that if this happened, K. was not to be given a septic workup (which includes a blood culture and a spinal tap) to determine the source of infection, but was to be treated empirically as before. When he came back on the floor, Dr. S. found that K. had had a complete septic workup, with "a tube in every orifice, and a needle wherever there wasn't an orifice." Two medications dripped into K.'s arm through an intravenous needle. The house officer in charge explained to Dr. S., "If we hadn't done this and he had gotten worse, it would have been my head!"

The septic workup revealed nothing—which was exactly how much K. ate for the next three days. After his trust was regained, he resumed eating and again gained weight.

In his effort to play the role of a family doctor for K., Dr. S. went beyond his duties on the hospital floor. By now the parents were back together (as often happens when a child becomes seriously ill), and Dr. S. tried to get to know them. He succeeded in establishing a relationship with the father, but found that he could only maintain contact with the mother by referring her to a psychiatric social worker. He could not help but notice the lack of emotion she showed on her occasional visits to her child in the hospital.

Dr. S.'s superiors in the hospital did not encourage him in these efforts. And on the acute-care ward the prevailing attitude toward his spending time with K. in order to feed and communicate with him was a patronizing one. "That's nice," thought his colleagues. "Dr. S. is playing with this feeding therapy. Now let's get back to what's important." What was important to them was diagnosing K.'s infections. Like K.'s original physician, the hospital staff was more concerned with his ear infections than with his diet.

As Dr. S. neared the end of his six-week rotation on the acute-care ward, he realized that his treatment plan for K. would not be followed on that ward once he was no longer there to assume responsibility for it. When it comes to providing continuity of care, an intern, whose patients disappear from his life every six weeks, cannot be a family doctor. Recognizing this, Dr. S. sought to have K. transferred to the psychiatric ward for children, where he would be given nurturant attention and would be less likely to be subjected to invasive testing.

Dr. S. persuaded a sympathetic senior physician (a child-development specialist) to support the transfer by offering this rationale: K., whose primary "medical" problem was susceptibility to infection, ran a high risk of infection on a hospital ward where he was exposed to "big bad bugs." This is a term used by hospital personnel to describe the virulent strains of infectious organisms that develop through natural selection in the hospital environment. Some say that these organisms thrive even on antibiotics as a culture medium. As one house officer put it, "They suck on gentamycin Popsicles for breakfast and eat chloramphenicol pies for lunch." K.'s lack of resistance to infection left him easy prey for these bugs, and his chances of infection were only increased when his skin was broken in drawing blood for tests. Thus, in what Dr. S. and the physician he consulted saw as a destructive cycle, infections led to more testing, and the testing led to more infections.

So K. went over to the psychiatric ward. Urging the psychiatrists to get in touch with him if any problems developed, Dr. S. briefed them on K.'s frequent infections and left instructions for these to be treated empirically. He also visited the child regularly during his off-duty hours. In this unofficial, almost subversive way, hollowing out a place for himself "between the lines" of authority in the hospital, Dr. S. continued to treat K. as his personal responsibility and to act as his physician. He was still serving as K.'s "advocate," though now without the authority to back up his recommendations.

K. thrived nicely on the psychiatric ward for about ten days before he developed his first—and last—fever there. The psychiatrists, feeling that they couldn't take the risk of leaving an organic condition undiagnosed and untreated, transferred him back to acute care for evaluation. Psychiatrists are often sensitive to the accusation of ignoring organic causes of illness. In this case they did not see it as taking a risk to transfer K. back to a ward full of big bad bugs and big bad house officers. They saw it simply as the right thing for them to do—even though K. had had a complete set of lab cultures and had responded consistently to empirical therapy for infection.

Back on the acute-care ward the diagnostic machine, no longer impeded by Dr. S.'s iconoclastic presence, went into full and impressive (albeit misguided) operation, with the house officers showing complete unanimity of purpose. They, too, felt that they couldn't take chances; or as a colleague put it, "If he dies without a diagnosis, then we have failed." By their conception of scientific medicine one had to find a cause before one could treat. Each of K.'s increasingly frequent, increasingly generalized infections brought on a new round of tests to determine its cause. In addition K. was the object of intensive and extended evaluation to determine the basic cause of his immune deficiency and his failure to thrive.

A host of distinguished specialists descended on K. The responsibility for K.'s care, to the extent that it had ever been fixed in Dr. S.'s hands, had by now been diffused among a coterie of specialists, each interested in applying a particular diagnostic technology to a particular part of K.'s anatomy. It had become "medicine by committee." No one doctor could be held accountable. After all, no one doctor could possess all the knowledge thought to be relevant to K.'s problems.

Over the next nine weeks K. underwent the following procedures: CT scan; barium swallow; upper GI; abdominal ultrasound; gastric biopsy; small-bowel biopsy; esophagoscopy; a second bone marrow biopsy; numerous cultures of blood, urine, stool, and throat; six lumbar punctures; serial blood gases; a prednisone stimulation test; screens for adenosine deaminase and nucleoside phosphorylase deficiency; urine assay for vanillylmandelic acid; and repeated b-cell and t-cell function tests. Most readers will not know what each of these tests is. Nor can we know what it must have been like for a two-year-old child (one who could not communicate in words) to be subjected to all these procedures.

What did the tests reveal? Nothing decisive. There were persistent abnormalities of white blood cell function, as before, indicating a compromised immune system. But there were still no grounds for distinguishing between a primary immune deficiency and an immune deficiency secondary to severe malnutrition.

The malnutrition, meanwhile, was becoming more severe, since under the barrage of testing K. stopped eating again. The staff compensated for this by putting in a hyperalimentation line—an intravenous line passed from a vein in the arm to the large vein that empties into the heart—through which K. was given all the nutrients needed to survive. But the hyperalimentation line carried only calories, not love, and by this point K. had been badly weakened by the combined effects of constant infection, starvation, and testing—so much so that he had to have infusions of blood to make up for iatrogenic blood loss from all the tests. (The word *iatrogenic* refers to complications brought on by the medical process itself.)

K.'s next scheduled test was a biopsy of the thymus gland. Whether he sought to avoid this—in the only way now left to him —is not known. In any case he had had enough. Two days before the scheduled test his breathing became very rapid, and he began to lose what little color he had. First his mouth turned blue, then his hands and feet, then his entire body. A vigorous two-and-one-half-hour resuscitation attempt was unsuccessful.

Shortly afterward, the man known as the "feeding team" walked up to Dr. S. in the outpatient clinic, to which he had now rotated, and laid a hand on his shoulder. "Do you know?" he said. "K. died today."

"God damn it!" said Dr. S. "God damn it!"

Other reactions to K.'s death were equally in character. His mother didn't show much response, and the senior resident wondered why. Both parents, saying that they wanted to know whether they should have any more children, asked an intern —and she took the question seriously—whether K.'s disease could be "inherited." The physicians involved, having failed to find a precise cause for K.'s disorder in all their testing, tried again at the autopsy, hoping to find one cause (perhaps an incurable underlying condition such as a cancer) that would explain what had happened to K. They tried again two months later at the clinico-pathological conference on the case. Again no luck.

One of the residents, commiserating with Dr. S., exclaimed that she had never seen such a valiant resuscitation effort. "Why, at one time he had three IV drips going at once! He was spared no test to find out what was really going on. He died in spite of everything we did!"

("In spite—or *to* spite?" thought Dr. S.)

"Nothing could have been done to save him," she went on, "because everything that could have been done *was* done."

("Yes," thought Dr. S., "nothing could have been done— which might have saved him!")

In the pediatric section of the hospital where these events took place numerous well-planned playrooms and multicolored walls hung with engaging designs present a bright, open face to child patients, as do the staff, who are trained to be friendly and reassuring to the children. There is even an "attending" physician assigned to patients like K. who do not have their own private physicians. Yet Dr. S. had seen children who did have private physicians, and whose families were better off financially than K.'s, get the same kind of treatment that K. did.

All this made the case that much more disquieting. No one in the hospital was evil. Everyone was trying to do the right thing, scientifically and morally. In spite of everything they did, or because of it, or for unrelated reasons, the patient died.

The people who "attacked" K. with needles were not sadistic. Nor were they thinking of the income that their procedures would generate for the hospital. They saw and felt the suffering they caused the child, and were distressed by it. They were quite capable of empathy, yet their "scientific" consciences, as distinct from their "personal" consciences, would not allow them to let up on the testing. But what if their "scientific" conceptions turned out actually to be *un*scientific?

No one can say for sure that they were. Yet it is worth noting that while every drug used in K.'s treatment has been thoroughly studied for its side effects, there is one "drug" which has not been subjected to the same scrutiny. It is the most potent, widely used drug in medicine: clinical reasoning. If there is any drug which, when used inappropriately, can kill a patient, it is the reflex reasoning done in the name of diagnosis and treatment. We don't know if it killed this particular patient. But we can look closely at how Dr. S. went about handling K.'s case and how his method differed from that of the physicians who succeeded him on the acute-care ward. When we articulate the assumptions, the thought processes, the clinical strategies that guided the two approaches to this case, we may find ourselves revising our notion of what constitutes scientific practice in medicine.

In general, the two approaches valued different kinds of information and went about getting that information in different ways. These preferences are linked, of course, since a given mode of investigation tends to yield a particular kind of information. Most of the physicians involved in K.'s case were looking for "hard," "scientific," "objective" biological data. They sought these data through precise measurements of organic processes. For example, a genetically based immune deficiency might be discovered by taking a bone marrow biopsy. On the other hand, Dr. S. and his collaborators (such as the child-development specialist and the "feeding team" specialist) took seriously the causal role of subjective psychological factors as well—the child's emotional state, his relationships with the people around him, and his reactions to medical procedures. They realized that their own actions toward K. would be interpreted by him in the context of his family's past actions. These factors do not lend themselves to precise laboratory measurement. Consequently Dr. S.'s diagnostic tools included observation over time and subjective judgment.

These psychological variables are also not easy to isolate from one another, or from other causes. Working on the assumption that K.'s immune deficiency may well have had both genetic and environmental causes, Dr. S. knew that he probably would not be able to tell just how much each was responsible for K.'s condition. But he was comfortable with this uncertainty, because he felt that ongoing treatment and observation would reveal to what extent he could successfully treat K.'s lowered resistance as a complication of malnutrition, and to what extent he would need to investigate its causes further. Dr. S.'s approach assumed that a patient's condition might have many causes, that the relative influence of these causes might change with time, and that the various causes together might act in a way that none would separately. Thus he took into account genetic, nutritional, and psychological factors, even though each of these alone might not be sufficient to account for K.'s illness.

To the other physicians, however, every effect ideally could be traced to a single cause. They seemed to work on the principles that once one cause has been found, it is not necessary to look for other causes, and that the sort of cause worth looking for is one that can account for all that is happening to a patient. For every condition that K. developed, whether acute (a particular fever or ear infection) or chronic (his immune deficiency and failure to thrive), they tried to find one causative factor that would explain how that condition came about. They did so by conducting tests that isolated and measured one hypothesized cause at a time while holding other factors constant or ignoring them entirely. Even when psychological causation *was* considered, the one-cause model was adhered to. K.'s running a fever on the psychiatric ward was taken to "disprove" the psychological hypothesis, and he was immediately sent back for medical examination. The psychiatrists and acute-care physicians did not seriously consider that psychological and physiological causes might both be present, or that causes might come and go with time.

As these other physicians saw it, treatment could not be undertaken scientifically without first having a definite diagnosis, while to Dr. S. the primary purpose of diagnosis was to enable one to treat. He attached less value to the diagnosis of incurable conditions. By the same token, he was quite prepared to treat experimentally without having a very sure diagnosis, on the grounds that treatment could be a form of diagnosis, a way of obtaining information while helping the patient. Dr. S. and the other physicians undoubtedly would have agreed in the abstract that diagnosis is not an end in itself, but a means of discovering the appropriate treatment. In fact, though, the acute-care milieu placed primary emphasis on establishing a diagnosis, while Dr. S., having a more pragmatic disposition, kept treatment foremost in mind.

These divergent biases shaped the course of K.'s treatment under the two medical regimens. Dr. S., by emphasizing the feeding and nurturing of the child, tried to bring about a gradual, day-by-day improvement in his condition. In curtailing diagnostic tests he accepted a small risk of failing to discover a serious condition that might cause a large negative outcome, perhaps a fatal one. This risk was unacceptable to the house officers who took over K.'s care from Dr. S. In their zeal to avoid it by testing for every remotely relevant disease, they undertook stressful procedures which brought about a gradual, day-by-day deterioration in the boy's condition. To the extent that they noticed this downward progress, they considered it an unavoidable consequence of their efforts to achieve a large (though unlikely) positive outcome, i.e., a definitive diagnosis which, if the condition diagnosed was treatable, could lead to an instant cure. However, the progressive weakening of K.'s condition led in the end to the very outcome they were so concerned to prevent.

Several observations can be made about the clinical reasoning of this latter group of physicians:

First, in focusing on extreme outcomes, they disregarded incremental effects. Preoccupied with large gains and large losses, they didn't see that a succession of small losses can add up to a total loss. Dr. S. was sensitively attuned to incremental changes—the small gains from feeding, the small losses from drawing blood. Therefore he tried to put K.'s condition on a gradual upward course. Since his treatment program was interrupted, however, we cannot say whether small gains ultimately would have added up to a large gain for this patient.

Second, they failed to take into account the effects of their own actions. Working from the assumption that K.'s illness had only one cause—the one they were looking for—they naturally saw themselves as observers—*only* as observers. To them *the* cause lay somewhere in K.'s body, so they had no reason to consider whether their own procedures might also influence his condition, perhaps decisively. As human beings they could share the pain they caused him, but as scientists they were committed to ignoring it. Dr. S., working from a more flexible, inclusive conception of causality that allowed for many causes operating at once, was in a better position to assess the possible effects of his own actions, and to see them as part of an overall web of causes, which included K.'s prior experiences with his family.

Third, they failed to weigh the costs of their procedures (the stress to K.'s system brought on by testing) against the benefits. If five lumbar punctures had shown no positive findings, what did they expect to learn from the sixth? What was to be gained from subjecting K. to a small-bowel biopsy which, if it revealed anything, would likely reveal an incurable condition? Many of the tests performed were, in fact, designed to identify diseases for which there was no known treatment. If a primary immune deficiency had been shown to exist, it could not have been treated except by a bone marrow transplant, for which K., in his depleted state, was not a candidate. What, then, was the purpose of the testing? Was it to treat K. more effectively or to give the clinicians the reassurance of certain knowledge?

What was lacking in this clinical approach was any notion of probability. The questions that needed to be asked about each diagnostic or therapeutic procedure were "How likely is this to do good? How likely is it to do harm?" Similarly, there was no assessment of values. "What, in this situation, is good? Whose good are we working for? What is best for the patient? What does the patient want?" All of these questions were implicit in Dr. S.'s approach, where the assessment of probabilities and values formed the basis for estimating the probable costs and benefits of any action under consideration.

Without this framework for clinical decision-making, the diagnosis and treatment in the latter phase of K.'s hospital stay proceeded according to certain unexamined assumptions. The search for more information was seen not as a way of estimating probabilities, but of achieving certainty. All actions not directed toward that end were discouraged as "risky." When the psychiatrists faced the choice of keeping K. on their ward with a fever or sending him back to acute-care for further "observation," they didn't see it as a choice between two gambles. They saw it as a gamble versus a safe and sure alternative. So did the house officer who ordered a septic workup on K. during Dr. S.'s absence from the ward. The physicians who acted out the dominant clinical philosophy felt that it was "taking a chance" to treat K.'s infections empirically. They saw no serious risk, though, in relentless diagnostic testing, which they regarded as having either a good or a neutral outcome. If they discovered something, they were ahead of the game. If not, K. was no worse off than before. The problem was that with every exploratory procedure (though again, not necessarily because of it) he did get worse.

To Dr. S. it made more sense to consider *every* decision a gamble, and to choose what seemed the best gamble among the available options. Each time he ordered antibiotic treatment for K.'s infections (without having the slightest idea what caused the infections), he was playing the odds, since the treatment had worked whenever he had tried it previously. To him that was the scientific method. He reasoned that, as in playing cards, everything you do or don't do is a gamble. In blackjack do you take a hit and risk going over 21? In medicine do you accept the side effects of a diagnostic procedure in order to gain new information? If you believe, as did the other physicians, that diagnostic tests come just about free of charge to the patient's well-being, then you don't have to weigh the costs versus the benefits. If you believe, as did Dr. S., that you pay for each card you take, then you must weigh the price of the card against what you could win by taking it.

When the likely costs of playing out a hand exceed the likely benefits, you throw in your hand and pay for new cards. In medicine when do you give up on an unpromising line of treatment? Apparently never, judging by the physicians who performed six lumbar punctures (i.e., spinal taps) on K. without learning anything. You'd think they might have stopped after two or three. But although they knew how to work up a patient, they didn't know when to stop the workup. Even those who wanted to stop felt that somehow they couldn't. After all, they had to play the game by the rules, and the only rule they knew was to try to obtain a certain diagnosis, even if the diagnosis meant that nothing could be done. In their view, since K. was getting worse all the time, there was all the more reason to do the punctures. They had no criteria by which to stop testing, unless an incurable disease was discovered or the patient died. And so they went by the rule "Stop if nothing more can be done," rather than simply, "Stop if it's just not worth doing any more." With actions that were seen as "risky," however, their rule was to stop immediately when there seemed any possibility of losing the gamble. They accepted a degree of risk by letting K. be transferred to the psychiatric ward, but as soon as he developed a single complication there, they thought it necessary to bring him back to the (ostensibly risk-free) acute-care ward.

These physicians took every opportunity to exercise their considerable skills and were understandably reluctant to leave things to chance. They had to "Do something!"—a commonly felt imperative in medicine. It wasn't only the fear of malpractice claims. It can be frustrating for a highly trained person to have to just watch and wait. Dr. S. dealt with this almost universal anxiety by thinking of watching and waiting, and being with the patient, as "doing something," as skills in the same league as diagnosing and treating. Instead of struggling against the arbitrary power of chance, Dr. S. tried to develop skills for dealing with situations in which chance—probability—plays a major role. Thus in this instance he thought it best to let "tincture of time" make the diagnosis and begin the treatment. His successors on the ward decided otherwise.

This is not to say that if only the case had been handled differently, the patient would have lived. Dr. S. himself recognized that K. might well have had a genetically based immune deficiency or other organic disorder that would likely have killed him before long. Unlike some nurses who told Dr. S. that the cause of death for K. should read "institutional murder," Dr. S. did not claim that the hospital's treatment of K. "caused" his death. Believing as he did that our knowledge of causality is uncertain and that many causes may operate simultaneously, Dr. S. had to concede that if treated differently K. might well have died sooner, or not for another seventy or eighty years, for any number of reasons. But he understood what a philosopher friend of his had in mind when on hearing the story he commented, "In medicine, unlike elsewhere in life, you are considered much less culpable for killing than for failing to save a life."

2

UNCERTAINTY
IN SCIENCE

The story of K. is not simply a case of one doctor being more humane and sensitive than other doctors. All those involved tried to be humane and sensitive. The two different ways of thinking, feeling, and acting that can be found in K.'s story have as their source two different conceptions of medical science. Dr. S. thought about the case differently from the other doctors. He also had a different way of coping with the emotions that anyone would feel when trying to treat a patient such as K. By thinking differently and feeling differently, he was able to act in a way that was as humane, sensitive, and effective as both he and the other doctors wanted to be.

Dr. S.'s way of thinking and that which was "standard practice" in the hospital differed so significantly that they can be said to represent two *paradigms* of thought: an old one, the mechanistic, and a new one, the probabilistic. The term *new paradigm* is today commonly used when what is meant is a new idea. A paradigm, however, is not just one new idea. It is a way of looking at the world, a way of perceiving reality and structuring knowledge. It marks the "burning questions" that people strive to answer in that area of knowledge called science as well as beyond. In particular

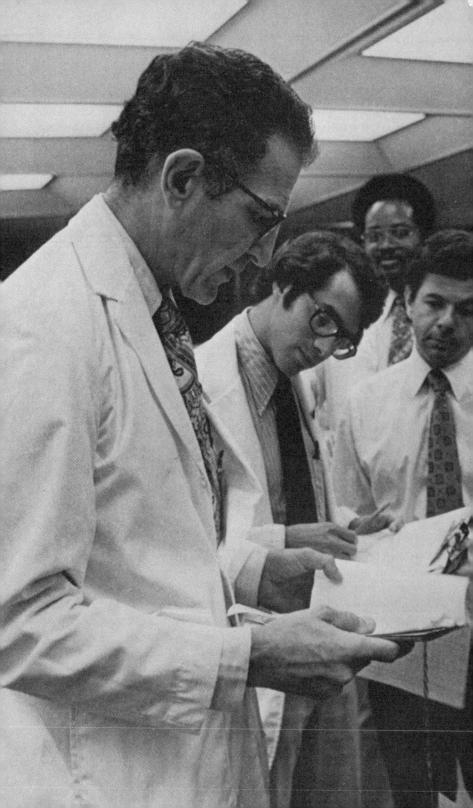

it focuses the energies of science by encouraging the asking of certain questions and discouraging others. It sanctions certain methods for answering these questions and rules out others. It even contains guidelines for what is an acceptable answer and what is not. In these ways a paradigm embodies the standards by which scientists decide what is legitimate and what is important.

We believe that the Probabilistic Paradigm represents not just a new way of doing physics, but a new approach to reality —that is, a new way of thinking, feeling, and acting. We shall explain what the new paradigm means—first in physics, then in medicine, and then as it extends to everyday life.

What we mean by paradigms, paradigm shifts, and the Mechanistic and Probabilistic paradigms in particular can be seen by analogy when we look at this drawing of two faces. Is it

FIGURE 2-1

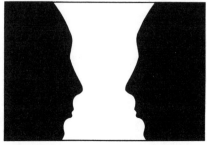

Vase or Faces?

two faces in profile or is it a vase? You may stare at the drawing for a long time and see only the faces. Once you discover (or someone points out) the outline of the vase, you will always be able to see it when you look at the drawing—but you will still be able to see the faces as well. The two images will come in and out of focus in a way that may be disconcerting until you get used to the idea of seeing two alternating images in a single drawing. Then you will have learned what to expect. You will have learned that the drawing will look sometimes like one thing, sometimes like another, and sometimes like both (but not like anything else). The instability of the image will have become stable.

Seeing the two images rather than either one alone opens up new possibilities for what images can be (i.e., stable or unstable). Similarly, a paradigm shift provides not only new knowledge, but new ways of thinking about what knowledge is. The Mechanistic Paradigm sought (and, in its day, found) answers that could be known with certainty, answers that were always the same—like a drawing that always conveys only one image. The discovery in modern physics that such certain, unchanging answers could not be found was at first disconcerting. Once physicists accepted the idea of uncertainty, however, they found that they could work with it and be comfortable with it when it was quantified in terms of probability. Even though they could not be certain, they could still have an idea of what to expect—as when the weather forecast predicts an eighty percent chance of rain for tomorrow. When you learn that a visual image can be unstable, your expectations of what an image is change, so that you are now able to understand an alternation between two images. Similarly, when the paradigm of physics shifted from the mechanistic to the probabilistic, physicists' expectations of what knowledge is changed to allow for probability, or *degrees* of uncertainty.

The Mechanistic Paradigm:
Three Criteria

At least since the time of Sir Isaac Newton, physics has served as a model for other sciences, and science has been taken to be a model of rationality for society. Let us look at an everyday life situation and see how a "commonsense" approach to it reflects the assumptions of mechanistic (Newtonian) physics.

Imagine that an American newspaper sends a reporter to investigate the causes of unrest in a small foreign country. The reporter's mission is to get "the facts," or as they say in the trade, the "who, what, when, where, and why." The possibility that the reporter's presence in the country may affect what the people there say and do is not considered, since, after all, he is only one person in the midst of a population of several million. Besides, he's just an "outsider." As for the reporter's own opinions and reactions, he has been trained to suppress them as completely as he can, and in any case to leave them out of his reports. The editors are confident that they will be getting an "objective" descriptive account, as free from bias as is humanly possible, of what is going on "over there."

In 1686, in Book III of the *Principia Mathematica,* Newton (1953) explicitly set down what we can now understand as the three criteria of the Mechanistic Paradigm. That wasn't how Newton thought of them, of course. He regarded them simply as rules for good scientific practice. To him anything else was not science. But we can use Newton's rules to distinguish Newtonian science from what followed as well as preceded it.

Criterion #1:
Deterministic Causation

For every observed effect the scientist seeks to isolate a specific cause or set of causes, as if it alone can account for the effect. For example, Newton used gravity to account for the motion of the heavenly bodies. Suppose our reporter attributes the demonstrations and disorders he has observed to "economic deprivation." This is a *unicausal* (one-cause) explanation. If, on the other hand, he lists several causes and explains how together they have brought about political unrest, he is using a *multicausal* (many-cause) explanation.

The multicausal explanations (like the unicausal explanations) used in the Mechanistic Paradigm are *deterministic*. A scientist using such an explanation claims that it is complete

—i.e., that the list of causes is exhaustive and that the way they come together to produce the effect in question does not change. "Unfavorable economic conditions always cause unrest" is a unicausal deterministic explanation. An example of a multicausal deterministic explanation is this: "Unfavorable economic conditions, in conjunction with religious fervor, always cause unrest." In either case causal relationships in the Newtonian scheme are taken to be certain and universal. That is, "A causes B" means that we can completely specify the conditions under which A causes B. When we have such a complete list of conditions, then we can count on A causing B whenever those conditions occur. In the Mechanistic Paradigm both unicausal and multicausal explanations are acceptable as long as they are deterministic. Unicausal explanations are somewhat preferred, however, as they seem to give a more deterministic account.

Criterion #2:
The "Experimentum Crucis"

In our journalistic example the reporter is performing an *experimentum crucis,* or "crucial experiment," if he goes into the country with a specific hypothesis that he believes he can test by holding constant all other potential causal factors. For example, he might decide, "Either economic hardship or religious fervor is behind it all. I'll just wait and see what happens when economic conditions improve. If there is still unrest, then I'll know for sure that it's religious fervor."

The Newtonian "crucial experiment" is a test that establishes once and for all a deterministic causal relationship of the sort described by Criterion #1. Newton thought that his theory of light had been conclusively proved by a certain crucial experiment with a prism, since no matter who did the experiment, the result would always be the same. To "prove" that A causes B, the experimenter varies A, while holding everything else constant, and observes how B in turn varies. It is assumed that the experimenter can account for and control all possible causal factors. The experimenter is assumed to be a detached observer in the sense that, aside from his planned manipulations, he does not influence the observed effects. Since cause-and-effect relationships in the Mechanistic Paradigm occur with one hundred percent regularity, and since there is no distortion brought about by the act of observation, the results of an *experimentum crucis* can be reproduced by anyone who does the same experiment.

Criterion #3:
The Objective/Subjective Dichotomy

By any definition of science, scientific knowledge must be useful, and to be useful it must be reliable. If it is to be reliable it must be public, in the sense that scientists must be able to talk about it and agree on what it is they are talking about. In the Mechanistic Paradigm, where scientific knowledge must be *absolutely* reliable, the only knowledge that is thought of as being public (or capable of being made public) is "objective" knowledge—that is, knowledge of a world existing independently of the observer. Newton stated that all his evidence was objective and thus incontrovertible. Just as our foreign correspondent puts his feelings and reactions "out of his mind" when he addresses the reading public, so the Mechanistic Paradigm's experimenter dismisses from the realm of science his or her own beliefs, attitudes, and values. Since these are subjective (that is, not independent of the observer), they are assumed to be private (that is, not capable of being communicated and agreed upon). The strict separation of subjective and objective knowledge is consistent with the first criterion of the Mechanistic Paradigm, which requires that knowledge be certain and universal. The possibility of such a separation is consistent with the second criterion, which holds that what is observed is independent of any attributes of the observer. In this century, however, both of these assumptions have been called into question.

From the Mechanistic
to the Probabilistic

Since the 1960's the notion of objective, bias-free journalism has been looked at with growing skepticism. It has become only too evident that a reporter cannot be without bias, and that this bias cannot help but influence the way the reporter interprets and presents the news. The "New Journalists" of recent years have given a prominent place in their articles to themselves, their feelings, and their experiences, sometimes to the point of telling us more about themselves than what they are reporting on. Even so, the reaction against the mechanistic idea of journalistic objectivity has been useful.

Consider all the things that can happen when our American reporter tries to be objective about the politics of a small foreign country. True, one reporter wouldn't seem to have much impact on a whole country. But suppose he is arrested as a spy. Suppose the government seizes upon his intrusive presence as a pretext for rallying the country to unity. Even if nothing so dramatic happens, it is quite likely that the people he comes in contact with will speak and act differently when they are being observed by a foreigner. They may hide their feelings, or they may "show off," even staging demonstrations inspired by the presence of TV cameras. The reporter, meanwhile, in his effort to be objective may try to minimize the emotional effect on himself of what he sees and hears. He may affect a Hemingwayesque toughness that not only will be felt in the tone of his reports, but also will make the people of the country see him as "another one of those distant, impervious Americans." This stereotype will condition their behavior toward him, which in turn will help shape his view of them, and so forth. Finally, when the dispatches he sends home are published, the people he is writing about may be pleased or offended. These reactions, too, will become an ingredient in the complex relationship between the observer and the observed.

Such effects have been noted in science. In what was regarded as a classic experiment in learning theory, cats were trained to escape from a box by rubbing against a vertical rod in the center of the box, which opened a door at the front of the box. The front of the box was made of glass so that the experimenters could observe the cats. Not taken into account, however, was the fact that the cats could observe the experimenters as well. As later researchers pointed out, rubbing against vertical objects (animate or inanimate) is something that cats typically do when in the presence of people or other cats. Rather than learning how to get out of the box, the cats were simply "greeting" the experimenters in a way that came naturally to them (Moore and Stuttard, 1979).

It isn't just cats who respond to the presence and the interest of experimenters. The famous studies of worker productivity at the Hawthorne Plant of the Western Electric Company in the 1920's and 1930's showed that people do, too (Roethlisberger and Dixon, 1939). Initially the Hawthorne researchers found that small experimental groups of workers, some given better lighting and some not, all showed increased productivity. In fact, their productivity increased even when their work area was *less* well lit than before. Naturally the experimenters were puzzled by this "Hawthorne effect." They eventually found that the workers in all the experimental conditions appreciated the small-group atmosphere as well as the friendliness and leniency of the experimenters who acted as their supervisors. It was a lot better to work under the experimenters than to work under the regular foremen out on the factory floor. Again, what the experimenters unwittingly did just by organizing the scene for observation had more effect on the outcome than their deliberate experimental manipulations.

Characteristically, before one paradigm is replaced by another, scientists working within the old paradigm usually do everything they can to salvage it. First, they try to dismiss as illegitimate or irrelevant the problems that the paradigm can't solve. When the problems refuse to go away, scientists tinker with the paradigm to try to make it accommodate the new data or new issues. In the case of our hapless reporter the editors might try to reduce his bias in regard to the politics of his assigned country by briefing him extensively on the culture and values of its people. This, however, would still not eliminate his bias, which is what editors working within the Mechanistic Paradigm would want to do. So they might decide to send a second reporter to correct the bias of the first, a third to correct the bias of the second, a fourth to correct the third, and so on. By the time enough reporters had been sent, the reporters themselves would become a source of unrest. The country would no longer be what it was before they came.

Physicists went through similar sorts of contortions before they finally gave up on the Mechanistic Paradigm. Around the turn of the century physicists began to be troubled by a range of observations that did not fit into the paradigm. For example, according to mechanistic principles light had to consist of waves or particles, not both, just as the drawing at the beginning of this chapter would have to "be" either a vase or faces. Yet depending on how light was observed, it sometimes looked like waves and sometimes looked like particles. At first physicists discounted such observations as stemming from human and technological limitations. With bigger and better machines for observing, they thought, the problems would resolve themselves.

Einstein's theory of relativity was a last-ditch effort (on the part of a man who to the end of his days expressed the hope that "God does not play dice with the universe") to save the Mechanistic Paradigm by abandoning Newtonian conceptions of space and time. The decisive break with the paradigm came with quantum mechanics, for which Einstein (among others) laid the groundwork, although later he disavowed some of its implications. What Einstein resisted and what quantum physicists such as Niels Bohr and Werner Heisenberg accepted was that chance and cause were not mutually exclusive categories. Rather, to understand that "A causes B" was to see that there was some necessary degree of chance called probability in the relationship between A and B. Quantum mechanics placed probability right at the center of the universe (Bohr, 1969).

Not that probability in itself was a new idea. According to a half-confirmed legend the mathematical theory of probability came into being when two seventeenth-century mathematicians came to the assistance of a gambler. The gambler, Chevalier de Mare, asked his friend Blaise Pascal to advise him on some perplexing questions of strategy that arose in the course of what today would be called "shooting craps." Out of the ensuing correspondence between Pascal and Pierre de Fermat came the theory of probability.

Although Newton in the seventeenth century had little or no awareness of probability (Hacking, 1975), in the following two centuries the concept was easily incorporated into the Mechanistic Paradigm, but only as a "theory of errors," a way of accounting for imperfections of observation and measurement. People were fallible; instruments were inexact. Probability defined acceptable limits within which experimental findings could differ from what the theory predicted. Actual results, actual experiments, and actual scientists were, after all, only approximations of the ideal.

But the ideal was still Newtonian determinism. In theory one could know with certainty the state (position, velocity, direction of movement, etc.) of a given object at a given time. And if one didn't, it was only because the instruments of measurement were imprecise. Perfect the instruments, and certainty would emerge. If one knew the deterministic law governing the behavior of the object, one could then, simply by solving an equation, know with equal certainty the state of the object at any other time. It was a closed system.

As the twentieth-century physics of quantum mechanics emerged, however, the state of the object came to be understood to involve a degree of uncertainty. Even in areas such as planetary motion, where for most practical purposes classical mechanics sufficed, there were cases where the kernel of uncertainty predicted by quantum mechanics was precisely what was of interest to astrophysicists. Nor could there be any hope of eliminating that uncertainty with bigger and better machines that would locate and observe the object more clearly. For the uncertainty now was no longer a matter of perception, but of the very nature of reality. Previously it could be said that the world was certain, although human beings could only know so much about it. Now it was in the world itself that uncertainty resided.

Cause-and-effect relationships, being subject to change and chance, could now be understood only in terms of probabilities.

Probabilistic causality in turn made possible the discovery of the Heisenberg Uncertainty Principle, which holds that an object cannot be observed without having its position and movement affected by the act of observation. Subatomic particles behave in some ways like people whose feelings change on the spur of the moment when they are questioned by a reporter. When light is shone on them, subatomic particles change their position and momentum in such a way that both together cannot be predicted with certainty.

The Heisenberg Uncertainty Principle meant that the object or process being observed could no longer be treated as an isolated system. Now the observing subject (the experimenter) was as much a part of the system of causes and effects as the observed object. Thus Heisenberg's principle undermined the second and third criteria of the Mechanistic Paradigm—that is, the notion that there can be a decisive experimental test and the strict separation of the objective and subjective aspects of knowledge and of reality (Heisenberg, 1958).

The Probabilistic Paradigm: Three Criteria

When we sent our American reporter to investigate the causes of unrest in a foreign country, we learned that the search for causes continually creates as well as uncovers new causes. It is impossible to hold all these contributing factors constant by performing an *experimentum crucis;* they just won't stand still. And despite the best effort to use objective reporting techniques, the subjective bias of the reporter transforms what he observes. In other words, the Mechanistic Paradigm doesn't work.

How can we get around these problems so that we can find out what is going on in that small country? We can do so by accepting a degree of uncertainty in our findings. Instead of trying to eliminate the reporter's bias, we can acknowledge it and work with it. Having tried to understand how the reporter's values will affect his observations, we can see what, given those values, he says about the country. Or else we can choose two or three reporters for their divergent perspectives and interpret their accounts with their biases in mind. In either case a process of active interpretation rather than simply acceptance of revealed truth is required.

Ludwig Wittgenstein (1958), the modern philosopher who understood so well the delicate relationship between knowledge and uncertainty, compared the *experimentum crucis* to the sterile exercise of reading a second copy of the same newspaper in order to verify the content of the first. It is, of course, more informative to read two newspapers—say, a leftist and a rightist one—which is not to say that the reality will be found in between the two, but that, wherever it is found, it can be understood critically through contrast. Even a distortion, if understood critically, can shed light on the truth.

This approach to journalistic investigation is consistent with what we will call the Probabilistic Paradigm in science. Our analysis of the foundations of quantum physics yields three criteria (parallel to those of the Mechanistic Paradigm) which define this new paradigm of scientific investigation.

Criterion #1:
Probabilistic Causation

When we ask how something came about, we usually answer by saying either "This was what caused it" or "It happened by chance." In the commonsense reasoning that Newton made into a science, we don't think that something could have a cause or causes and *also* happen by chance. But this is just what happens in modern physics, where a world that is made up of causes and effects is still an uncertain world. It is not simply that we cannot know all the causes; it is that causes themselves operate to some degree by chance (Bunge, 1979).

In its more sophisticated applications the Mechanistic Paradigm allows that a particular effect may have many causes and that a particular cause may have many effects. Yet uncertainty is not allowed to come into the picture. The mechanistic scheme leaves out the possibility that causes other than the ones we are looking at may be contributing to the effects we observe. One of these causes, of course, is ourselves, since we change what we look at by the very act of observing it. The deterministic model (even in its multicausal form) also does not consider that causes may change with time, and may do so in a way that cannot be predicted. Things that were not causes may become causes, while things that were causes may cease to be causes. What was once a cause may become an effect and vice versa—the "chicken-or-the-egg" question. Causes may also have reciprocal effects on each other. As a result it is not possible to specify what will be or will not be a cause at any given moment.

Causal explanations that not only allow for more than one cause, but also acknowledge the degree of uncertainty inherent in causal relations, are referred to as *multicausal stochastic.* The word *stochastic* refers to influences changing probabilistically with time. Under the Probabilistic Paradigm, causes may act and interact differently at different times, the same effects may not always have the same causes, and the effects of a given cause (and vice versa) cannot be isolated with certainty.

Our reporter is employing a multicausal stochastic explanation if he understands that the political events he observes are subject to an ever-changing pattern of causation, with one cause being the way he interacts with the people he is writing about. The way they act toward him changes his attitude toward them, which in turn changes the way he acts toward them, which in turn changes their attitude toward him, and so forth. Often these changes may be very slight, but sometimes they are noticeable—as, for example, when the people become more intransigently anti-American because they read an article in which the reporter makes what they consider a slur on their religion. Even aside from the reporter's influence on events, the country's destiny is being shaped by a constellation of political and economic forces that is never fully revealed and never quite the same from one moment to the next. When one day's dispatch is filed, it is time to start working on the next.

Criterion #2:
Experimentation as Principled Gambling

In the Mechanistic Paradigm the idea of deterministic causation makes experimentation a simple matter: just manipulate the variables and record what happens. Working from the assumption that one or more causes can be specified with certainty, experimenters can hold some possible causes constant in order to measure the effect that others have (whether singly or as a group). The data dictate the result. In the Probabilistic Paradigm, on the other hand, multicausal stochastic causation negates the very idea of an *experimentum crucis.* If patterns of cause and effect are subject to chance and change, then no one experiment can be "crucial." As with our fast-breaking journalistic updates, no one experimental finding represents the "last word."

What method of experimentation is appropriate for a world in which (1) it follows from the first criterion of the Probabilistic Paradigm that causal relationships cannot be known with certainty and knowledge is subject to change, and (2) according to the Heisenberg Uncertainty Principle, one cannot observe without thereby affecting what is observed? Both of these conditions require that the experimenter interpret the significance of the data. Since the experiment itself does not provide absolute confirmation or refutation of any hypothesis, the experimenter must choose which hypotheses to accept and which to reject, just as we all must choose which newspaper accounts to believe. The experimenter makes this choice on the basis of the consequences of believing and acting upon one hypothesis rather than another.

By "consequences," however, we are not referring to external reward and punishment, as in the case of the scientists who found it useful to believe in the ideologically motivated scientific theories approved by Hitler or Stalin. Rather, what we mean is analogous to winning or losing a gamble. Gambling is, after all, making choices in the face of uncertainty. When we think in terms of the Probabilistic Paradigm, we can see anything we do as a gamble. We gamble on whether an experiment is worth doing, and we gamble (even after the experiment is done) on which hypothesis are worthy of belief. In the Probabilistic Paradigm we can choose a hypothesis to believe and act upon as we would choose a horse to bet on. Similarly, the decision to do an experiment is a gamble, and the results of the experiment present us with further gambles which we can choose to accept or reject. We then have a chain of gambles, any one of which can be called an experiment, or a chain of experiments, any one of which can be called a gamble.

On what basis do we make these choices? What consequences are we concerned with? We want to believe and act upon hypotheses that are true. We also want to achieve good outcomes (to win instead of losing). In the science of gambling that is practiced under the Probabilistic Paradigm, we do both; we seek both the true and the good. Since we cannot be certain of either, however, we must add a third stipulation—that of "justification." We can say that we are acting upon a true and good belief when we can justify our actions and beliefs to another reasonable person by explaining why they are true and why they are good. Thus we choose hypotheses that are "true, good, and justified."

This kind of gambling is both similar to and different from what we usually think of as gambling. Let's say you believe that a certain horse is going to win a race. The consequences of acting or not acting on this hypothesis (i.e., betting or not betting) depend on whether the hypothesis turns out to be true or false. If, for example, you act upon a hypothesis that turns out to be false (i.e., bet on a losing horse) or do not act upon a hypothesis that turns out to be true (i.e., fail to bet on a winning horse), you lose your bet. The same is true when a hypothesis is being tested in the laboratory or the doctor's office rather than at the racetrack.

As with any gamble, the consequences of choosing one hypothesis or another can be understood, up to a point, as a matter of costs and benefits. What do you stand to gain if your horse wins? What do you stand to lose if it doesn't win? How likely is it that the horse will win? Would you rather put your two dollars on an even-money horse (one that will return only two dollars if it wins because it is considered to have as much chance to win as to lose) or on a long shot? Would you still make the same choice if you were betting ten dollars or fifty dollars instead of two dollars? Similar questions are bound to occur to the scientist gambling that it will be useful to act on a given hypothesis.

We often try to understand the costs and benefits of a gamble by referring to probabilities and values. When we gamble we keep in mind the probability of something happening (e.g., our horse winning the race) and the value it would have for us if it did happen. But is that all we think of? Suppose, for example, you get inside information that a race has been "fixed" so that one horse is sure to win. Even though the probability (a "sure thing") and the value of winning are both high, you may decline to bet on principle. That is, you may believe that to win a bet by cheating is not a good outcome, in terms of its effects on others and on your own character.

Despite such examples of individual scruple, the gambling that people do for recreation and for profit can often be characterized as unprincipled. In science, on the other hand, our choice of gambles is guided by a number of principles. These principles grow out of some crucial differences between gambling under the Probabilistic Paradigm and what we usually think of as gambling. Normally gamblers bet against known odds for a definite reward. Most gambling games are structured so that some people win while others lose; there is a fixed pool of winnings that the players simply exchange (with the house, if there is one, taking its cut). In science it is not that simple. The probabilities, the rewards, the potential winnings, and the value of winning are discovered in the course of gambling. Indeed, finding out the odds can be the very purpose of the gamble, rather than merely a means toward gaining a material reward.

In science the idea of "winning" a gamble takes on a different meaning. Since what is to be won is knowledge, not money, there is no limit to what can be won over a period of time, and what is won by one person is not necessarily lost by another. As scientists make use of the knowledge they have won, they produce more knowledge. This knowledge is not only about the subject under study, but about how to gamble and what to gamble for. One experiments to get a better idea of the odds and of how the game works, so as to be able to gamble more consciously and more skillfully.

The principles of gambling under the Probabilistic Paradigm make it possible to gamble consciously and effectively in an uncertain world—the world described by the first criterion of the paradigm and by the Heisenberg Uncertainty Principle. They tell the scientist what to keep in mind while gambling, what rules to follow consistently (and when they may be broken) in order to have a good chance of a good outcome.

One such principle is that one must be aware of the context of uncertainty that surrounds experimentation and be ready to question one's observations, one's assessments of probability and value, and one's hypotheses. Even when the hypothesis under consideration has apparently been confirmed by experimental results, there remains the possibility that some other cause or causes, as yet unknown, have contributed to those results. A degree of doubt, of skepticism in interpretation, is called for.

As one doubts nature, so one must doubt oneself. According to Heisenberg's principle one cannot observe without affecting what one observes. In order to work within the Probabilistic Paradigm, therefore, one must keep in mind the possible consequences of one's actions as an experimenter. One must ask whether the apparent confirmation or disconfirmation of a hypothesis may have resulted from some unforeseen effect of the act of observation. In other words, one must be a self-aware experimenter. Whereas a gambler is primarily concerned with deception by others, a scientist is most concerned with his capacity for self-deception.

Actually, one may not have any problem learning to doubt the order of nature, or to doubt one's hypotheses, or to doubt one's own actions. The uncertainties that appear in one's very

observations and experimental results will give one ample reason to doubt. In a probabilistic world not every trial will work
out; not every piece of data will confirm a hypothesis; and even
when it does, it is not entirely clear what is being confirmed.
Under these conditions it is easy for doubt to become paralyz-
ing and for the experimenter to accept defeat at the hands of
what seems to be total uncertainty. Wherever there is doubt,
therefore, one must be prepared to give the benefit of the doubt
—to nature, to one's hypotheses, and to oneself as an experimenter.

In the first place, when dealing with probabilities one cannot
change one's hypotheses with every new piece of data. Just as
one cannot evaluate a new strategy for playing blackjack on
one trial, so in science one must be willing to pursue a line of
action that is not immediately rewarding in order to learn what
the probabilities are in the long run. Thinking in terms of
probabilities requires some faith that there is order in the
world. Under conditions of complete certainty such faith would
not be necessary; under conditions of complete uncertainty it

"But you can't go through life applying
Heisenberg's Uncertainty Principle to *everything.*"

would not be possible. The idea of probability, on the other hand, implies that an uncertain world is not a chaotic one. Some things merit a higher degree of belief than others. If one trusts that there is an order, a probabilistic one, underlying phenomena, one will be able to stay with a course of action, even without knowing its consequences, long enough to learn its consequences in general and not just in one particular case.

Even when the probabilities have been established through a series of observations, there remains some uncertainty about what exactly has been proved. One must therefore give the hypotheses under consideration the benefit of the doubt before deciding which one to credit. Since there can always be some doubt left as to whether all possible hypotheses have been considered, one must be willing to act upon the one that seems most truthful and useful to act upon while at the same time being ready, if necessary, to reconsider previously discarded hypotheses. The Greek philosopher Heraclitus said, "You never step in the same river twice." For most practical purposes, however, the river remains the same. Just as the river flows downstream, so causes come and go, but very often not enough to make a difference. Where they do make a difference is a matter of judgment, experience, and interest.

Just as one trusts that one has not been out-and-out deceived by nature, so one must trust that one has not completely deceived oneself. While acknowledging that "observer effects" are intertwined with one's results, one must be able to suspend doubt at least long enough to act and then critically assess the results of one's actions. There is, for example, no question but that photographs are taken from the point of view of the photographer and reveal the interests of the photographer, but one can still look at a photograph and learn something about the world beyond the observer.

In summary, then, one must question reality, one's knowledge, and one's methods; and yet sooner or later one must trust sufficiently to choose. One can only interpret one's observations in a probabilistic world—in other words, comprehend the regularities as well as the irregularities of that world—if one extends to oneself as an observer and to what one observes a trust that is not blind, but critical. Being critical means being conscious of one's choices, getting some perspective on them, attempting to assess the consequences of various alternatives, and making choices by criteria that reasonable people can understand. This principle of critical choice, coupled with a degree of trust, sums up the principles we have considered.

Together, these principles give scientists a set of rules that they can agree upon as reasonable guidelines for their efforts and as a basis for communication between one scientist and another. At the same time, they enable the individual scientist to act in accordance with a long-range plan and agreed-upon goals and values amid inconsistent results and shifting fortunes. They help the scientist answer the crucial question, "When does one change one's mind?" For there are costs to giving up a hypothesis and starting over—costs that are referred to as "retooling costs." In a probabilistic world when does new information warrant one's incurring those costs? All one can do is to choose those experiments that seem most likely to yield the kind of information that will let one know whether or not it is worthwhile to change one's mind—and then to interpret the results in accordance with the principle of critical trust.

To understand the second criterion of the Probabilistic Paradigm in its broadest implications, we can start with Niels Bohr's interpretation of the Heisenberg Uncertainty Principle. According to Bohr (1969), Heisenberg's principle links the observer and the observed within a system of mutual influence in which the same laws apply to both. In other words there is not the absolute, unbridgeable difference between a scientist and an electron under the Probabilistic Paradigm that there is under the Mechanistic. The distinction drawn under the Mechanistic Paradigm between the straightforward behavior of physical objects and the complexities and uncertainties of dealing with people disappears under the Probabilistic Paradigm. No longer is the experimental situation set apart, in its precision and controllability, from the multitude of interactions among people as well as objects that occur throughout life. Under the new paradigm the same kinds of judgment apply. What it means to accept a belief about the motion of particles is much the same as what it means to accept a belief about a person. So we can look at the way we understand people as a model for the way we might learn to understand electrons.

When we meet a new person, we have to trust our observations about the person. When we see the person do something we don't understand, we give the person the benefit of the doubt —that is, assume that the person is acting rationally until we are shown otherwise. Similarly, we trust that the seemingly inexplicable behavior of subatomic particles can be explained —if not by a theory that we currently hold, then by another. When we see a person act in a way that isn't entirely consistent, we realize that nobody does the same thing all the time, and we trust that there is an underlying pattern of regularity in the person's actions. In physics, too, we look for relationships of probability, not certainty. We expect patterns to emerge, if not immediately, then in the long run. Finally, when we interact with another person we are self-aware. We realize that we affect and are affected by that person. Thus we ask, "Is part of what I observe in this person a response to my own behavior? Have I made this person act that way?" So it is in physics with the Heisenberg Uncertainty Principle.

It is not only the other person who is affected by the interaction, of course. When we decide whether or not to accept someone as a friend, for instance, we are certainly affected by our decision to look at that person in one way rather than another. To give a stark example, the Nazis, by seeing the Jews as subhuman and treating them as such, changed not only the Jews but themselves. Not only did some Jews act in subhuman ways when forced to live under subhuman conditions, but the characters of some Germans changed so that it became "all in the day's work" for them to treat other people as subhuman.

In science, too, our characters are changed by the decisions we make. Our methods of observing and understanding, the values we uphold, the principles we follow become habits that in part define what we are and how we see ourselves. Whenever we make a choice, we are strengthening or weakening our principles, or choosing new principles. In this respect as in others, the practice of science cannot be disassociated from what is normally thought of as ethics.

What scientific knowledge now requires is the ability to look at oneself as one looks at the objects of one's observation—that is, to see oneself as being made of the same matter and subject to the same laws as they are. What ethical knowledge requires is the ability to look at the objects of one's observation as one looks at oneself—that is, to begin by assuming that they are made of the same matter and subject to the same laws as oneself. Only for good reason should they be treated differently. Thus, although the second criterion of the Probabilistic Paradigm does not ensure that scientists will treat ethics as a part of science (for people can develop compartmentalized awareness), it guides the practice of scientists in such a manner as to encourage them to do so. This is further encouraged by the third criterion of the paradigm.

Criterion #3:
The Continuity of the Objective and the Subjective

In science, as elsewhere, whatever claims to be knowledge must be capable of being publicly discussed. Even if there is disagreement, there must be some basis of agreement so that public debate can take place. As we have seen, scientists working under the Mechanistic Paradigm take the view that such agreement and debate are not possible with subjective knowledge, since whatever is subjective is assumed to be inherently private and irrational. It is no wonder, then, that scientists under the old paradigm seek to experiment in a value-free manner. For such scientists the influence of subjective values upon their objective results is a contamination to be eliminated at all costs, since it threatens the claim that these results constitute knowledge.

We now know, however, as we saw under Criterion #2 of the Probabilistic Paradigm, that it is impossible to eliminate subjective knowledge from scientific inquiry. The effects of the experimenter's values (whether consciously or unconsciously expressed) on experimental methods and results have been noted in contexts ranging from Heisenberg's "observer effect" in physics to Robert Rosenthal's (1969) "experimenter bias" in psychology. As in our example of international news reporting, subjective knowledge is inseparably a part of what is considered objective knowledge. The question is whether or not scientists acknowledge its presence and try to account for its influence. Because scientists under the Mechanistic Paradigm have not dealt consciously with the influence of their values on their scientific practice, that influence has expressed itself through unconscious habit. But it has been there nonetheless.

If objective knowledge is not as fully objective as would appear from the Mechanistic Paradigm's strict dichotomy, what about subjective knowledge? Is it purely subjective? Are values private and irrational—and nothing more? The way values have been understood under the Mechanistic Paradigm is illustrated by the practice of public-opinion polling. Whereas poll-takers attempt to eliminate their own values and beliefs so that their "objective" interviewing techniques will not be qualified by subjectivity, they treat the values and beliefs of the people they interview as if these were unqualified by objectivity. The pollsters contact people individually, in isolation from the family members, fellow workers, and friends with whom they normally discuss public issues. The procedure, by implying that all values are equally private and equally irrational, encourages respondents to express the most selfish and individualistic of values. This is another "experimenter effect" understandable in terms of the second criterion of the Probabilistic Paradigm. What the pollsters look for—and what they get—is a collection of preformed opinions untempered by public discussion and shared experience. Private, irrational preferences become fixed as inert data ("hard figures") through the *experimentum crucis* of polling.

In real life, however, we do not hold our values and beliefs privately. We form and maintain them by living and working with other people. We share our values and beliefs with others and as a result may either change our minds or find our original beliefs confirmed and strengthened. In this way we try to establish what values rational people must agree on and what areas of disagreement and variation are reasonable. The town meeting embodies this kind of interchange. There people develop their values while seeing and hearing others (all of whom, unlike the "neutral" pollster, have an acknowledged stake in the outcome) defend their values and, by doing so, themselves. Through the give and take that occurs at such gatherings, the members of a community decide what rules they all must follow in practice and what differences will be respected. It is ironic that public-opinion polling, which reflects the assumptions of the Mechanistic Paradigm, is (with its trappings of science) a more recent development than the town meeting, which is closer in spirit to the Probabilistic Paradigm.

Just as there is a subjective aspect to objective knowledge (such as knowledge of electrons), as we saw under Criterion #2, so there is an objective aspect to subjective knowledge (such as knowledge of feelings). On the one hand, we find that we need to take values into account when we are being rational, as when we are practicing science. On the other, we find that we *can* be rational when we are dealing with values. Even in the realm of the subjective, reasonable people can find grounds to agree or disagree. It is not a case of "anything goes." For example, although a reasonable person may value his home over his car, or vice versa, it would be more difficult to understand his valuing his car over his life. Only when people reach some degree of agreement about what are reasonable values to hold can they practice science together according to an agreed-upon set of rules. Values that affect people collectively need to be created by people collectively.

Thus science under the Probabilistic Paradigm is more like a town meeting than a public-opinion poll. An experiment becomes an opportunity for the discussion and interpretation of values and beliefs, which are subject to the same kind of critical scrutiny and debate as experimental methods and data. Such values and beliefs, while subjective (in the sense that they are held by individuals and not "proven" by conclusive experiments), can and must be public, in the sense of being justifiable to other reasonable people engaged in the scientific enterprise. Through this process the subjective component of objective knowledge is revealed, and subjective values, by being articulated and explored rationally, become a form of knowledge. Thus the sharp dichotomy between the subjective and the objective under the Mechanistic Paradigm becomes, instead, a continuum, where knowledge may be more or less subjective and more or less objective, but not all one or the other.

It is an uncertain world that scientists study and that we live in. Therefore, as the philosopher Hilary Putnam (1978) reminds us, no one can afford to disregard such knowledge as is possible, be it of values or of electrons, just because there is some element of subjectivity in it.

What Is Probability?

Another area in which subjective judgment comes into play under the Probabilistic Paradigm is in the understanding of probabilities. Although mathematical probability theory has existed since the seventeenth century, we still don't know what probability really means. Everyone agrees on the rules for calculating probabilities. But what lies behind the numbers?

Imagine trying to decide between two interpretations of probability as the basis for science, one of which is identified with the experiment in the laboratory, the other with the gambler placing a bet with a bookmaker. Where one interpretation speaks with the authority of mathematics, while the other has its source in mere "belief," it is clear which one most scientists (or anyone, for that matter) would have more confidence in.

The two interpretations are the "objective," which flourished in the heyday of the Mechanistic Paradigm, and the "subjective," which originated in the eighteenth century but was neglected in the mechanistic era until its reemergence in the 1930's (Lee, 1971). (Since then it has been increasingly used.) The objective interpretation is based on "relative frequencies," the subjective on "degrees of belief." We can illustrate each by the way it arrives at the probability of a coin coming up heads.

Using the objective interpretation, you would flip a great many coins and see how often they come up heads. If you flip one coin, you cannot predict whether it will come up heads or tails. If you flip one hundred coins, you can predict that somewhere around half of them will turn up heads. The greater the number of trials, the closer the result is likely to be half heads and half tails. Thus the "objective" school defines probability as "a limiting value of a relative frequency as the number of cases increases to infinity." With a coin flip, of course, that value is fifty percent.

In the subjective interpretation the probability of a coin turning up heads is thought of in these terms: "How much do you believe that it will turn up heads? How much would you bet on it? At what odds?" The language of gambling expresses subjective judgment in numerical terms. We recall, of course, that the whole idea of probability had its origins in gambling.

It is understandable that the objective interpretation of probability was widely accepted under the Mechanistic Paradigm. It fit in with the mechanistic emphasis on objectivity, and its reliance on laboratory trials was consistent with the notion of an *experimentum crucis.* With its assumption that an infinite number of trials was needed to reproduce the ideal mathematical result, this version of probability gave scientists under the Mechanistic Paradigm a theory of errors which explained deviations from ideal experimental results.

The objective interpretation is not, however, consistent with the three criteria of the Probabilistic Paradigm. The inconsistency became apparent when paradoxes were found not only in quantum physics, but in the most mundane areas of science. These paradoxes can be expressed in everyday language by means of Gedanken ("thinking") experiments like the following (Putnam, 1979):

Gedanken Experiment #1:
"The Life or Death of Schrödinger's Cat"

In this paradox, named after the creator of the Schrödinger wave equation in physics, a cat with the regal name of

Mittendorf Plantagenet is placed in an opaque, soundproof box with a capsule of cyanide that will be released on the occurrence of a random "outside event" such as the detection of a cosmic ray. Mittendorf is left in the box for a time interval during which the probability of the outside event's occurring (by statistical laws) is fifty percent. If this grisly experiment is performed only once, what is the probability that "Mitt" will be found dead when the box is opened?

Part of the paradox here is that the cat's fate, while yoked to an event which has a known probability of occurrence, is itself decided only once. If probability is defined solely in terms of frequency of occurrence of a particular outcome over a series of trials, what probability can we assign to a unique event? According to the relative-frequency interpretation, the probability of a unique event such as Mittendorf's death is either one or zero. But this clashes with our theoretically derived probability of fifty percent for this unique event. We can thus see that the relative-frequency definition of probability is far too restrictive for physics today. This paradox disappears if we instead use a non–frequency-based interpretation of probability.

Many of the events to which physicists assign probabilities, such as some cosmic phenomena, are nonrecurring. Probabilities based on the notion of relative frequency are of little use here. Even in cases where relative frequencies *can* be calculated, some form of subjective judgment is required. In the case of the repeated coin flips the mathematical formulation of a probability that approaches fifty percent as the number of flips approaches infinity is useful, but it is based on the assumption that the coin is as likely to come up heads as tails on any one flip. It also presupposes that one coin flip is just like another. Both of these assumptions represent subjective judgments.

We can see this more clearly where the judgment of similarity is more difficult to make. When we say, "There is a ninety percent chance of rain tomorrow," are we just saying, "There is a ninety percent chance of rain on days like tomorrow"? How can we tell which days to put in that category? What days are just like tomorrow? Whenever we group things into categories for the purpose of calculating relative frequencies, we are making a subjective assessment of similarity based on our prior knowledge and experience.

In no case do the data alone dictate the probability. Always an element of human understanding is present. When we derive probability estimates from a theory, as in quantum physics, we are making a subjective judgment to the effect that the case in question is explained by the theory (and therefore by the probabilities generated from it) and that the theory itself is worthy of being held. When we apply probability estimates to a particular case, as in medicine, we make judgments based on our knowledge of that case. A patient who on the basis of available data is said to have a ten percent chance of having breast cancer is an individual. Our estimate of the probability must take into account our knowledge of the patient as an individual who may somehow differ from other patients in the ten percent category.

Here is a second Gedanken experiment, one that reveals another paradox in the use of "objective" probability estimates (Hempel, 1965):

Gedanken Experiment #2:
"How much would you bet on a raven being black?"

Imagine a law of the form: All ravens are black. You see a bird that you are certain is a raven but can't quite make out its color. But knowing the law you exclaim, "I'd stake my soul, by God, that that bird is black!" All of a sudden, a bolt of lightning strikes, the heavens darken, and a sinister yet familiar figure approaches you and sticks out his hand: "What would you like me to stake against this soul of yours?"

If we really knew with certainty that all ravens were black, it would be entirely rational to bet *anything* against *nothing* that this bird would fit the pattern. And yet no matter how many black ravens (and *only* black ravens) we saw, we would not be likely to make that bet. Moreover, we would not be considered irrational for refusing to do so, since people make an intuitive distinction between observational truths (such as "All ravens are black") and logical truths (such as "If all ravens are black, and if this is a raven, then this is black"). The former are considered risky to bet on; the latter are not. It seems that our subjective gambling decisions do not reflect a belief in a universe where everything is determined.

This is a case where our subjective probability estimate (say, the proverbial "99 and 44/100 percent") differs from the relative-frequency estimate, which, based on all ravens that have ever been seen, would be one hundred percent. Which is the more useful estimate? In the first place, to assign a probability of one hundred percent (certainty) to a statement based on observation rather than logic is legitimate under the Mechanistic, but not the Probabilistic Paradigm, whose first criterion (that the world is an uncertain place) it violates. So we would not make such estimates if we wish to work within the Probabilistic Paradigm. Beyond this, as has been shown by the philosopher Abner Shimony (1970), such estimates are inconsistent with the rules of probability. That is, a person who bets that statements based on observation are *always* or *never* true can be put in the position of having what gamblers call a semi-Dutch Book made against him. A *Dutch Book* is a series of bets set up so that the gambler must lose no matter what the outcome. With a semi-Dutch Book the gambler can only lose or break even, not win.

To illustrate how a Dutch Book works, we can use an example from boxing history. Let's say you and a friend agreed that Muhammad Ali should be a three-to-two favorite over Joe Frazier in a championship fight, and you bet six dollars on Ali against your friend's four dollars. Then another "friend" convinced you that Frazier was going to win, and you agreed to bet six dollars against four dollars on Frazier. If Ali won, you won four dollars on the first bet but lost six dollars on the second. If Frazier won, you won four dollars on the second bet but lost six dollars on the first. Either way, you lost two dollars. With your inconsistent probability estimates, you made a Dutch Book against yourself.

Our gambling phraseology gives us a way of answering the

question, "Does the subjective interpretation of probability mean that 'anything goes'? Is any probability estimate as good as any other?" Not quite. True, with subjective probability estimates there is no one correct answer, as there is when probabilities are calculated from relative frequencies. But when we think of our estimates as odds at which we would be willing to bet on something happening, we are giving ourselves a stake in the outcome and thus disciplining our choice of probabilities. If we stand to lose by making self-contradictory bets like the one on Ali and Frazier, we will avoid making such bets.

Consistency, then, becomes another principle that guides our choice of gambles. We limit ourselves to those gambles that do not allow a Dutch Book (or semi-Dutch Book) to be made against us. A variation of the consistency rule is the requirement of *transitivity,* which means that our choices should be consistent when more than one choice is involved. If we bet on horse A against horse B and also on horse B against horse C, in both cases accepting unfavorable odds, we'd better not be so foolish as to accept the same unfavorable odds on horse C against horse A (a sure loss no matter which horse wins). Finally, the same consistency rules that apply to our probability estimates should apply to our value assessments if we want to avoid a Dutch Book. As applied to values, transitivity, for example, means that if we prefer apples to oranges and oranges to pears, then at the same time we will prefer apples to pears.

Subjective probability assessment fits all three criteria of the Probabilistic Paradigm. It acknowledges that we cannot define categories so strictly as to exclude a degree of uncertainty even in those relationships where observation apparently reveals ironclad regularity (Criterion #1). It requires that people choose their probability estimates rather than have them revealed by an objective experiment (Criterion #2). It implies that probability cannot be clearly separated from other forms of knowledge, including values (Criterion #3). The Probabilistic Paradigm makes it possible to have a subjective understanding of probability and to make use of subjective probability assessments. The subjective interpretation of probability in turn provides an example of how we can use subjective knowledge. It thereby encourages us to look at feeling and value as additional sources of knowledge.

In practical terms the subjective interpretation assumes that people can and do arrive at reasonable probability estimates without necessarily having observed the outcomes of many similar trials. Moreover, it makes those estimates available to science. In medicine, for example, it allows probability estimates to be derived not only from tables of figures, but also from the subjective judgment of the doctor, patient, and family. It means that a doctor's knowledge of a particular patient's history may be more useful than statistical tables in assessing the likelihood that the patient has a particular disease or will respond to a particular treatment. And it means that there may be times when the patient or the patient's family are better judges of these probabilities than the doctor, especially a doctor who does not have prior knowledge of the patient.

Applying the Probabilistic Paradigm

Certainty is an age-old dream. It has taken different forms in different eras. Before the mechanistic age people sought comfort through ritual in the face of uncertainty. There were periods, for example, when people living at the mercy of uncontrollable natural forces gained a measure of psychological control by anthropomorphizing those forces and seeking to dominate them through the use of magic. Under the Mechanistic Paradigm people gained some real control over nature by acknowledging its separateness and learning how it worked. People watched—first with wonder, then with complacency—as diseases were wiped out one after another. It seemed as if the world were moving toward greater certainty.

In the twentieth century new areas of uncertainty have presented themselves: diseases that resist cure, irregularities in the movements of heavenly bodies and subatomic particles, the disruption of environmental balance, the threat of nuclear destruction. There is a renewed focus on things that human beings cannot control. To this we can respond in two ways. One is to recognize the usefulness—indeed, the necessity—of the Probabilistic Paradigm and to apply it as broadly as possible as a way of coming to terms with uncertainty. The other is to retreat into ritual—namely, the rituals of science and technology that so recently gave us the comfort of apparent certainty. Thus the continuing attraction and influence of the Mechanistic Paradigm in our time. There is always need for a little magic.

A paradigm that is dominant for generations puts down strong roots in the unconscious (of which it is a reflection). Despite the commonsensical ring of probabilistic thinking when we hear it in a weather forecast, much of what we call common sense is in fact mechanistic thinking. To overcome the inertial force that the old paradigm exerts unconsciously and implicitly, we need to apply the new paradigm consciously and explicitly. We also need to apply it systematically *as* a paradigm, using all three criteria in an interconnected way. When we try to apply one criterion at a time, the new way of thinking is easily undermined by the familiar habits of the old.

This is where applying the Probabilistic Paradigm differs from casually invoking the language of probability. To speak of using "part" of the new paradigm makes no more sense than to say that seeing only the faces in the drawing after seeing only the vase is a new form of perception. Yet the history of science offers many instances where some aspect of the Probabilistic Paradigm (such as probability) is used, but not the paradigm itself (Hacking, 1975).

However, once we see things in terms of a new paradigm, we can't go back to the old. When we have seen the vase and the faces together, we can't go back to seeing just the one or the other. When the new paradigm becomes familiar, it can exert a force equal to that of the old paradigm in its day. When this new way of thinking becomes so familiar as to be part of the consciousness of a culture, it will not only have revolutionized physics, but will also be a new world view. This vision will have particular impact in an area such as medicine where the concerns of science and the everyday meet.

3

UNCERTAINTY
IN MEDICINE

It is inconceivable, given what we understand a paradigm to be, that during a given era the effects of a paradigm shift would be confined to one discipline such as physics. There may be questions about how the new paradigm translates from one science to another, or beyond science altogether, but it is clear that such translations will occur. A world that understands Newton's laws as special cases of more complex relationships will sooner or later learn to apply the same perspective to the subtleties of social and emotional existence as to the physical.

Indeed, people who work in a wide range of fields have been announcing, predicting, or calling for the adoption of what amounts to the Probabilistic Paradigm in their disciplines. In *The Restructuring of Social and Political Theory* (1978), Richard J. Bernstein reports that the mechanistic "value-free" method of collecting facts and arranging them in the form of deterministic laws is being strongly challenged within the social sciences, which are becoming more hospitable to subjective interpretations and indeterminate causality. Economist Lester C. Thurow, speaking of "The End of Newtonian Economics," notes that "economics, along with much of modern science, is being drawn in a direction where events are perceived to be much more stochastic and much less deterministic

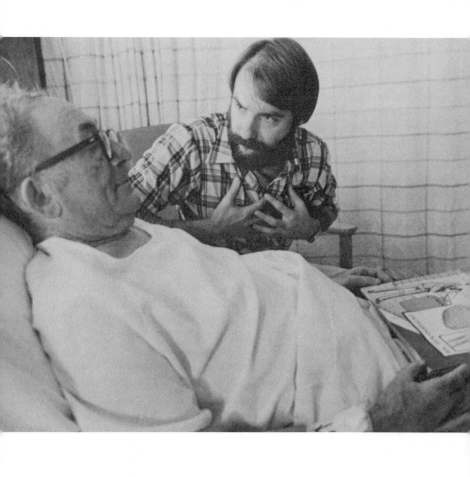

than had previously been thought" (1977, p. 86). The British philosopher Stuart Hampshire contrasts "the two centuries of philosophy dominated by Newton's physics," which "naturally transferred the idea of unalterable laws to human affairs," with the twentieth-century study of biological systems, which "exhibits the sovereignty of chance, luck, and contingency, and provides examples of sudden and substantial changes due to small unpredictable displacements, of little causes producing great effects, and of explanations by probabilities." Hampshire concludes that the human species "is no less exposed to risk than any other species of animal, except that human beings are better equipped to calculate some of the risks and to take out some insurance" (1979, p. 42d).

Where does all this leave medicine? Medicine as an applied science (both biological and social) has not kept up with these changes in scientific thinking. It is not helping people recognize uncertainty, calculate risks, and take out insurance—that is, gamble. In the words of G. Gayle Stephens, M.D., former president of the Society of Teachers of Family Medicine, "Medicine has not noticed that the tides of its intellectual fortune have gone out in the past seventy-five years. Now we are grounded on a shoal. . . . In comparison with physics we are in a pre-Einsteinian phase of existence. We still worship Newton. Physics was forced to deal with the dilemmas of determinism sixty years ago. In medicine it is not discussable even today" (1979, p. 18).

The Mechanistic Paradigm in Medicine and Its Breakdown

The mechanistic philosophy of medical practice which gained ascendancy in the nineteenth century (replacing what we now term the superstition and fancy of prior ages) and still underlies what we call "modern medical science" is expressed most clearly in Claude Bernard's *Principles of Experimental Medicine,* published in 1865. Bernard, one of the founders of modern medicine, made explicit and implicit references to Newton's work in expounding what we can now recognize to be the three criteria of the Mechanistic Paradigm:

Criterion #1:
Deterministic Causation.

I acknowledge my inability to understand why results taken from statistics are called *laws*; for in my opinion scientific law can be based only on certainty, on absolute determinism, not on probability (Bernard, 1957, p. 136).

Criterion #2:
The "Experimentum Crucis."

As a science, medicine necessarily has definite and precise laws which, like those of all the sciences, are derived from the criterion of experiment ... the principles of experimental determinism must be applied to medicine if it is to become an exact science founded on experimental determinism instead of remaining a conjectural science based on statistics. A conjectural science may indeed rest on the indeterminate; but an experimental science accepts only determinate, or determinable phenomena (Bernard, 1957, pp. 139–140).

Criterion #3:
The Objective/Subjective Dichotomy.

Only determinism in an experiment yields absolute law; and he who knows the true law is no longer free to see a phenomenon otherwise (Bernard, 1957, p. 140).

These prescriptions—which express the nineteenth century's growing confidence that calculation and controlled experimental comparison would give man mastery over his environment, be it natural or social—have even today a satisfying ring of assurance and tidy rationality. In fact they guide much contemporary scientific research. Where they can lead, however, is intimated in the story of K., the twenty-one-month-old boy in Chapter 1. Without realizing it, the physicians who were responsible for K.'s care in the hospital practiced according to the three criteria of the Mechanistic Paradigm. They did so by thinking it inappropriate to treat K. until they could find *the* cause of his condition (deterministic causation), by believing that diagnostic testing would reveal this determining cause without itself affecting the state of K.'s health (*experimentum crucis*), and by disregarding K.'s obvious resentment of the testing and their own distress at having to cause him pain (objective/subjective dichotomy).

The case of K. is just one illustration of the medical problems that cannot be solved through the application of these three criteria. Doctors now confront a very different set of diseases from the ones they faced in 1900. Medical technology under the Mechanistic Paradigm has licked diphtheria, tuberculosis, smallpox, and polio, only to find that the people who aren't dying of these diseases are living to contract hypertension, heart disease, and cancer. Treating chronic degenerative conditions that take diverse forms and have no (or many) known causative agents can be as different from treating acute infectious conditions as measuring the velocity of an electron is from measuring that of a toy wagon. Here the diagnosis and treatment are much less clear-cut. The doctor, patient, and family may have serious differences about what is wrong and what to do about it.

Along with these different diseases have come other problems that frustrate the straightforward technological solutions of the Mechanistic Paradigm (which indeed may be helping to create them). There is the problem of cost—higher and higher medical bills, insurance bills, tax bills. Then there is the suspicion, the mistrust, that has come between patient and doctor. Many people, once they realize that a doctor is not the idealized mechanistic scientist who can be trusted blindly to come up with the right answer, seem not to be able to trust doctors at all. Patients sue for malpractice, while doctors gripe about patient "noncompliance" and devise manipulative strategies to make patients comply. Medical care suffers because patients and doctors don't get along with each other, and one reason they don't is that their expectations of each other are grounded in the Mechanistic Paradigm.

The Probabilistic Paradigm in Medicine: Three Criteria

Against Claude Bernard's three criteria of Newtonian medicine, we can set the three criteria of the Probabilistic Paradigm. Again we can take our illustrations from the case of K., but this time from the way Dr. S., the intern, handled the case.

Criterion #1:
Probabilistic Causation

It is recognized that a patient's condition may have more than one cause, that it may not be possible to separate the effects of each cause, and that the same observed condition may have different sets of causes at different times. In the case of K., Dr. S. put much less emphasis on diagnostic testing than did the other physicians because he thought it unlikely that the patient's condition had a single treatable cause that could be revealed by testing. Instead he looked for a number of possible causes (genetic, environmental, psychological) operating in combination with one another in a way that was affected by chance. Among those possible causes were his own diagnostic and therapeutic actions.

Whenever he observed K., Dr. S. realized that he might be contributing to some change in K.'s condition. So he observed, then acted on his observations, then observed the effects of his observations and actions as well as other known and unknown causes. He kept in mind that each effect that he observed could also be a cause, and vice versa. Finally, whenever he observed the operation of causes, he also was observing the operation of chance. Thus, although he was able to form some expectations about K. as he gained more experience with him, he was still open to being surprised.

Criterion #2:
Experimentation as Principled Gambling

Given that the relevant variables cannot be perfectly controlled through detached observation and manipulation, doctors and patients working within the Probabilistic Paradigm treat diagnostic procedures as gambles, to be evaluated according to how fruitful they may be for the patient. Dr. S. understood that extensive diagnostic testing (the *experimentum crucis*) had not revealed and was not about to reveal a determining cause or causes of K.'s illness. Even after all the tests were completed, the data still needed to be interpreted so that choices could be made as to which hypotheses to act upon.

The outcome of each diagnostic or therapeutic gamble did not dictate which gamble to choose next. S., the observer, had to make that choice on the basis of principles which included self-reflection. While trusting himself, he had to be critical of himself at the same time. This was what he did when he acted upon the observation that the testing he himself had ordered was having some deleterious effect on K.'s emotional well-being, eating habits, and ability to withstand infection. Instead of aiming for an illusory diagnostic precision, he undertook exploratory treatments designed to assess over a period of time the relative importance of possible contributing factors such as malnutrition, lack of parental nurturance, and the kinds of germs found in any hospital environment. Recognizing that his own actions would in any case affect the patient, he sought to make that effect a constructive one by whenever possible giving him love and food and protecting him from pain.

In this kind of empirical therapy, diagnosis becomes a form of treatment, and treatment becomes a form of diagnosis. Experimentation is extended outward through time and space as physicians and patients learn from their actions and consciously adjust their subsequent practice. The physician becomes part of the experiment and, along with the patient, changes in the course of the experiment. For example, S. saw the interns and residents around him become more "hard-boiled," losing the capacity to feel love for their patients, the more they did painful diagnostic procedures on children. But that is not the only way in which doctors are transformed. In a more hopeful vein, the experience of a medical practice—the shared experience of doctors and families—can create a growing understanding that is expressed in the form of subjective probability estimates. Medicine, instead of trying to live up to an outmoded model of laboratory science, can then become a science of action, a science of practice.

Criterion #3:
The Continuity of the Subjective and the Objective

Not only the doctor's knowledge, but the patient's knowledge, the patient's feelings, and the doctor's feelings are considered to be of crucial importance in diagnosis and treatment. The goals and methods of treatment, rather than being determined solely by the physician's conception of "scientific" (i.e., technological) efficacy, are evaluated in line with the patient's and the doctor's values. When the patient's values are different from the doctor's, they are still given the benefit of the doubt and considered to be reasonable unless shown to be otherwise. Not that "anything goes," of course. Both the doctor and patient need to apply critical scrutiny to their own and each other's values as these affect the issues at hand. For example, Dr. S. did not simply accept K.'s preference not to eat (even to the point of starving to death) as a reasonable value judgment, although he might have done so in the case of a patient dying of a degenerative disease. And many times S. questioned himself, saying, "Am I fooling myself? Could it be that all the other doctors are right and I am wrong?"

S. found it hard to draw a sharp line between the objective and subjective aspects of K.'s case, since feelings (both the patient's and his own) told him a great deal about the illness and its treatment. Instead of dismissing the feelings of pain that he shared with K. as an irrational concern, S. tried to make sense of them and to see what he could learn from them. The other doctors experienced such emotions too, but they neither paid attention to these feelings nor considered the effects that other feelings they had (e.g., their need for certainty) might have on their actions toward the patient. S., on the other hand, listened closely to his own reactions as well as to those that K. conveyed through his moods, behavior, and eating habits. He assumed that the feelings that the child was showing were basically the same kinds of feelings that he had. Even though it appeared that the way K. was acting wasn't doing him any good, S. conceded that maybe K. did know what was good for him. Maybe he was trying to tell the doctors something. It was clear, at least, that the way K. felt would have a lot to do with how well he responded to treatment.

Subjective Probability Assessment

The three criteria of the Probabilistic Paradigm encourage the use of subjective probability assessment, which K.'s case also exemplifies. Since relative-frequency statistics were not available for a condition like K.'s, the house officers had no way of making use of probability. Instead they did virtually every possible test in their search for certainty. Dr. S., on the other hand, made use of his subjective judgments (based on observation, experience, and empathy) about how much the testing was likely to reveal, what various treatments were likely to accomplish, and what would be good for K. and what would not.

Even where relative frequency statistics are available, they are only a starting point, not an end point, for clinical judgment. They must be translated into subjective probabilities for the individual patient. There is a saying in medicine that every patient is unique. But to what extent a patient is unique and to what extent similar to other patients is a matter of judgment. Anytime one uses relative-frequency statistics for a particular patient, one is making the subjective judgment that this patient falls into the category of patients to which the statistics apply. One is acting on the belief that there is nothing special about this patient, no extraordinary circumstances that one has overlooked that would put the patient in a different category. Such a judgment is another kind of gamble, another guess that is educated by experience and guided by principle.

Benefits of the New Paradigm

Taken together, the criteria of the Probabilistic Paradigm give us a new way to think about and practice medicine. If in some ways they seem to confound common sense, in other ways they reaffirm it, for they restore a respect for the many-sidedness of reality that was lost in the oversimplifications of nineteenth-century science. It is a wonder that medical practitioners ever could have thought that the causes of complicated conditions *could* be known with certainty; that the doctor-patient interaction would *not* influence the course of an illness; that knowledge about microbes and bacilli *could* be separated neatly from knowledge about attitudes, feelings, and values; that *people* could not also be pathogens (as in K.'s case). The

64 A NEW SCIENCE OF MEDICINE

prevalence of these myths in our time is a tribute to the staying power of the Mechanistic Paradigm. Its rigidities, which passed unnoticed through the era of triumphant microbe hunting and superspecialization, now prevent medicine from adapting to the needs of a more complex environment.

Suppose the Probabilistic Paradigm were widely adopted by people who provide medical care and take part in medical decisions. If doctors, patients, and families were to think in terms of probabilities rather than certainty (and observe the other criteria of the Probabilistic Paradigm), would the problems that beset medicine today, such as high cost and doctor-patient conflict, be closer to solution? There are good grounds for believing that they would.

1. Cost. The passion for certainty keeps costs high. It leads physicians to use whatever technology is available to obtain an elusive diagnosis, and it leads patients (who have become "consumers" under the influence of the profession and the media) to demand such diagnostic overkill. Even when physicians themselves do not see a need to perform all the prescribed procedures, they may do so anyway to protect themselves against malpractice suits in which the courts apply medicine's own standards of certainty. By those standards a doctor must do everything necessary to be as certain as possible before acting.

The Probabilistic Paradigm, on the other hand, holds that certainty is unattainable not only in fact but in principle. Therefore we no longer need to use the ideal of certainty to judge how much uncertainty about a patient's condition is tolerable, how much greater certainty can reasonably be attained, and how much effort and resources should be spent in seeking more information.

Probabilistic thinking encourages people to adopt a broader definition of "cost," not only the monetary cost but other kinds of costs as well. Let's turn from the life-or-death situation of K. to the routine "lab work" that we perform or submit to during almost any office visit. If we think for a minute, we can identify several potential costs of laboratory testing:

— financial costs (whoever pays)
— costs to the patient in pain, feelings of violation, and risks of physical harm (such as radiation, allergic reaction, blood loss, and infection)
— costs of extra paperwork for busy personnel and overburdened facilities
— misdiagnosis and/or emotional stress resulting from laboratory errors
— the diversion of time, skill, and energy from other diagnostic modes (e.g., sensitive personal observation) to the reassuring rituals of impersonal diagnosis
— the risk of alienating both the physician and the patient from the diagnosis, which is no longer a product fashioned jointly by the physician and patient in the process of history-taking and physical examination, but a product stamped out by a machine which has access to a part of the patient hidden from both patient and physician

Of course, we can't think about all these things every time we take a throat culture; nor should we. We would never get anything done if we didn't form habits and routines. But while habits are necessary, it is also necessary that they be grounded in principle and on occasion critically reevaluated. Doctors and patients alike need to have an underlying consciousness of the costs and benefits as well as the principles at stake. They need to develop an instinct for asking, "What's it worth, and to whom? And am I fooling myself?" before reaching for the throat swabs. Looked at in this way, some of the lab work that is now routinely performed will turn out to be justified; some of it will not. And, in terms of this broader definition of "cost," the same will be true for other things that are done in the name of good health: office visits, hospitalization, medication, surgery, and so forth.

2. Doctor/Patient Conflict. The Mechanistic Paradigm has no notion of principled conflict. Indeed, it has no provisions for handling conflict at all. Diagnosis and treatment are regarded as a smooth, impersonal process—an *experimentum crucis* controlled by the physician and designed to yield objectively valid results. No allowance is made for any desire the patient may have to share control of the process. No allowance is made for values and feelings (either the doctor's or the patient's) and therefore for differences in values or feelings. Any conflict that occurs is outside the bounds established by the paradigm.

One way in which the Probabilistic Paradigm would help doctors and patients deal with conflict more constructively is simply by substituting more realistic, probability-based expectations for the mechanistic expectation of certainty. When people are led to expect a definite answer, a definite cure, they may quite understandably blame each other when things go wrong. The malpractice suit is the patient's way of blaming the doctor; the charge of "noncompliance" is the doctor's way of blaming the patient. Under the Probabilistic Paradigm the fact that things may go wrong, and that it may or may not be anybody's fault, is acknowledged from the start.

Conflict does not go away under the Probabilistic Paradigm. On the contrary, it is built into the paradigm. Since doctor and patient are both scientific observers whose observations are affected by the point of view from which they observe, their feelings and values are recognized as having a legitimate and necessary role in their decision-making. Where they differ, the conflict between them can be seen (though it may not always be) as a reasoned disagreement between people who, in order to be able to work together at all, have made a prior agreement about what actions are rational and ethical in an uncertain world.

There is then a basis for people in the midst of conflict to appeal to each other by rational means, and there is the hope that they will keep an open mind and be influenced by reason. When one learns to see oneself as one sees another and to see another as one sees oneself, one can have a sense of communality with another even amid disagreement. When doctor and patient work together under the Probabilistic Paradigm, each does not have to see the other as a different kind of person, a natural enemy in the jungle of mechanistic relationships. Each can trust (until shown otherwise) that the other is not out to "get" him or her, whether with a surgeon's knife or a legal judgment.

Six Medical Choices

Does the Probabilistic Paradigm's approach to medicine differ from that of the Mechanistic Paradigm in every case? Will the use of the Probabilistic Paradigm completely alter all the normal everyday procedures followed in physicians' offices and hospitals? Yes and no. Again we can look to physics for an analogy. In physics there is a range of problems for which the results obtained by using the probabilistic methods of quantum physics are the same as those obtained by using Newton's laws. In this category are all those high-school physics problems such as, "What is the speed at which a block sliding down a 3-inch plane inclined at 30 degrees, with a given coefficient of friction, will reach the bottom?" Here the effects of the observer, as well as other factors taken into account in quantum theory, are insignificant. They do not enter into the calculations. In these "limiting cases" of the Probabilistic Paradigm in physics, it is just as accurate—and much easier—to stick with the old methods. The physics of Newton is not valid for the problems that Einstein and Heisenberg addressed, but for practical pruposes it is still valid for the problems that Newton addressed.

A similar distinction can be drawn in medicine. Just as it would not pay to apply the principles of quantum mechanics to every homework problem in high-school (Newtonian) physics, so there are classes of medical problems for which the Probabilistic Paradigm itself would dictate, on grounds of principle and cost, what amounts to the mechanistic approach. In these instances people who have had some experience working within the Probabilistic Paradigm have concluded, after keeping an open mind to the possibility of applying probabilistic methods directly, that it isn't worth the trouble to do so, since they would end up doing essentially the same things as they would under the old paradigm.

"Essentially" is, however, an important word. Even when the same decisions are reached under the Probabilistic Paradigm as under the Mechanistic, they are made in a manner and spirit

governed by the new paradigm, not the old. They are not dictated by the data, but chosen critically, with a consciousness of
the context of uncertainty in which choices are made and a
readiness to make different choices when necessary. A physicist today who makes use of Newton's formulas is not about to
forget that such formulas have only limited application in the
context of modern physics as a whole. Similarly, doctors and
patients who have learned to think in terms of the Probabilistic
Paradigm and to apply it fully—as a paradigm—cannot just put
on blinders and go back to thinking mechanistically. Probabilistic considerations will be implicit in all their decisions, even
those that could also have been reached by the mechanistic
route.

Here are three pairs of cases that illustrate where the two
paradigms lead to similar medical decisions and where they
lead to different ones. For each of the three criteria on which
the two paradigms differ, there is one case where the decisions
reached under the Mechanistic Paradigm are adequate, and
another where the Probabilistic Paradigm appears better able
to handle the many ramifications of the situation. Of course,
while each case primarily illustrates one of the three criteria,
it also illustrates the other two, since the three criteria work
together.

It will be noted that in the three "mechanistic" cases the
doctor alone makes the decisions, while in the three "probabilistic" cases the patient and the patient's family are (or ought
to be) involved. In the Probabilistic Paradigm, where values,
feelings, and subjective judgment play an important role in
decision-making, the doctor, patient, and family are all also
"observers" whose points of view influence the outcome. With
each patient being seen as an individual rather than a statistical unit, patient and family participation are necessary to give
expression to the various causes, some of them unknown to the
doctor, that may affect the patient's illness and its treatment.
Even in our "mechanistic" cases, where standard medical
procedures are clearly required, the Probabilistic Paradigm's
focus on the patient's and family's feelings would still be useful
in dealing with the special psychological circumstances that
surround any "case."

Criterion #1:
Causality

Pneumonia is one of those infectious diseases to which the Mechanistic Paradigm's unicausal deterministic model is usually applicable. Hypertension is one of those noninfectious diseases to which it is usually not applicable.

Case #1.
Pneumonia.

A forty-three-year-old woman enters the hospital emergency room with a two-day history of fever and shaking chills, cough and rusty-colored sputum production, and, most recently, acute shortness of breath. Microscopic examination of a stained smear of the phlegm reveals numerous pus cells and pneumonia-causing germs. A chest X ray shows extensive lung involvement. When bacteria are grown in the laboratory, a diagnosis of pneumococcal pneumonia (pneumonia caused by a particular type of germ, the pneumococcus) is made. The patient is hospitalized and placed initially on intravenous penicillin therapy. With the results of the sputum culture in, this therapy is continued.

The assumptions of the Mechanistic Paradigm help the intern in a busy emergency room function well in the diagnosis and treatment of this case. In particular the intern can act as if pneumococci were the one and only cause determining this patient's illness. This simplifying assumption, though it may lead to ignoring other possible causes (e.g., environmental), is likely to do no harm here (Bursztajn and Hamm, 1979).

Simplifying assumptions of this sort are part of what is meant by *heuristics.* Heuristics are strategies with which people attempt, within the limits of their knowledge and time, to solve problems. Working from the assumption that this woman's illness has only one cause, the intern does not act upon the possibility that she may at the same time have a bronchial neoplasm (cancer of the large airways), which also can cause infection and accumulation of fluid in the lungs. (This possibility is considered only later as part of a differential diagnosis, a long list of possible diagnoses that is often produced in discussion with a senior physician the next day, but which does not affect one's initial choice of action.) Statistically this assumption is justified, but it still represents a judgment. It can be reconsidered if the illness does not respond to treatment in the time it would normally take for pneumonia to show improvement.

Case #2.
Hypertension.

A fifty-five-year-old man comes to his physician's office with a blood pressure of 160/100. History reveals that this is hypertension of over five years' standing. A hypertensive workup, consisting of diagnostic tests which involve taking X rays of the kidney after injection of dye, is undertaken. These tests include an intravenous pyelogram (IVP), in which dye is injected into a small vein in the forearm, and a renal arteriogram, in which dye is injected directly into the artery that supplies the kidneys. The results are negative. Treatment with medications is then initiated. The patient's blood pressure is reduced and becomes well controlled.

It sounds reasonable to test for the physical causes of hypertension, find none, and then begin treatment for "essential hypertension" (the name given to those cases of hypertension that are of undetermined origin)—until you realize that ninety to ninety-five percent of all cases of hypertension, having as yet no detectable cause, fall into the "essential" category. Thus the benefits of testing are questionable, whereas the costs of these tests may be considerable in terms of money, pain, and possible severe side effects. The IVP occasionally touches off an allergic reaction which in rare cases can be life threatening. As for the arteriogram, in one or two out of every thousand cases it causes the artery to thrombose (i.e., to clot at the site).

Why perform the tests, then, except in those special cases where they are clearly called for? To the physician trained in the Mechanistic Paradigm's model of causality, essential hypertension is not a very satisfactory diagnosis. Such a physician works from the heuristic principle: "Find the cause, then treat" (or the surgeon's "You can't cut what you don't see, and a chance to cut is a chance to cure"). Without a known cause there is no clear basis for treatment, and the physician is uneasy with whatever treatment he undertakes. For this physician it is worthwhile to find a definite answer for five or ten percent of the cases at the cost of unnecessary testing for all the others.

Some physicians, however, would not immediately perform an extensive diagnostic workup in this case, but rather would begin treatment with drugs and/or life-style changes (low-salt diet, exercise, stress reduction, etc.). If this regimen were to bring the patient's blood pressure under control, they would proceed no further with the diagnostic workup. Physicians using such a strategy would consider this a problem well solved, even though no "cause," in the Mechanistic Paradigm's deterministic sense, had been revealed. They would feel no particular anxiety in having to deal with a "mysterious" disease like essential hypertension.

By the standards of the Mechanistic Paradigm this strategy is "unscientific." A doctor who takes such an approach is considered—and may consider himself—an empiricist, or one who does "what works" rather than what science dictates. But according to the Probabilistic Paradigm this approach *is* scientific. Where illness is seen as having a range of possible but uncertain causes, it may be reasonable to deviate from the rigid two-step model of diagnosing a cause and then treating it. Therapeutic action may be scientifically based upon the estimated probabilities and values of possible outcomes. As a strategy of investigation it is reasonable to use the patient's response to clinical therapy as evidence for refining one's knowledge and thus one's actions. This was what Dr. S. did when he used K.'s response to being fed and nurtured as a kind of diagnostic test.

The difference between dealing with K. and a patient with hypertension is that the latter can work out the methods of diagnosis and treatment with the doctor before these are begun. Once the diagnostic imperative of the Mechanistic Paradigm is challenged, once it is recognized that there may be more than one right thing to do, once values and principles as well as probabilities are taken into account, then it is no longer only the doctor who can make the necessary choices. The patient's values and principles are every bit as important as the doctor's, especially when you consider who is on the receiving end of the tests and treatments.

Suppose, for example, that the patient thinks it worth the costs of testing to go for the five or ten percent chance of a more specific diagnosis. There are a number of reasonable grounds for such a preference. For one thing, some people value certainty more than others do. Besides, it isn't only the tests for hypertension that have costs, but the treatments as well. With drug treatment these may include money, inconvenience, a daily or even thrice-daily reminder that one is a medical patient (perhaps with a social stigma attached), and side effects. The most common side effect is drowsiness—a high cost indeed for an active person who may have experienced no symptoms and no apparent disability from the disease itself. To avoid these costs, the patient may accept the costs of the workup, which offers at least a slim hope of a surgical cure. Or the patient may choose to try life-style modification alone in an effort to control his blood pressure without drugs. If this is unsuccessful, he may decide that he would rather risk the long-term consequences of hypertension (which include an increased probability of heart or kidney failure, heart attack, and stroke, and therefore a shorter predicted life span) than put up with the medications.

Of course, the doctor will have something to say about these choices, and so will the patient's family. Since both the illness and its treatment are so closely tied in with the patient's daily life, the family needs to be fully informed about the choices and to participate by expressing preferences. For example, if the "diagnostic treatment" involves diet, family members will be buying, preparing, and perhaps eating somewhat different foods. If it involves experimenting with drug dosages, they may for a time have to put up with a "doped-up" breadwinner and assume some of the responsibilities that are normally his. If they are unprepared for these adjustments or unwilling to make them, they may exert pressure on the patient to give up the treatment and become what physicians under the Mechanistic Paradigm call "noncompliant." On the other hand, it is often the family that can persuade the hypertension patient to value his long-term responsibility to stay alive and healthy over the day-to-day inconvenience of taking medication.

Such treatment decisions and the manner in which they are made are part of the diagnosis and thus themselves become causes of the patient's condition. For example, by participating in the decision-making, the patient may become more relaxed and therefore may show a lower blood pressure reading. This, too, is part of the treatment to which the patient is observed to respond. Of course, in talking about diagnosis as a form of treatment and treatment as a form of diagnosis, we are moving from the question of causality to that of the nature of experimentation, which is the second of our three criteria of science.

Criterion #2:
Experimental Method

Here the issue is between the controlled, value-free *experimentum crucis* of the Mechanistic Paradigm and the more flexible, ongoing information-gathering techniques of the Probabilistic Paradigm, which presuppose that the information gained is observer-dependent.

Case #3.
Broken Leg.

A five-year-old boy is brought into the emergency room after a fall. The child's ankle is swollen, tender, and painful. Suspecting that it is broken, the doctor has it X-rayed. Discovering a fracture, he sets it and then puts on a cast.

In this case, the physician appropriately takes actions consistent with the Mechanistic Paradigm. He suspects a single determining cause of the patient's distress, one that can be located in the body: a broken bone. He verifies this with an X ray, which is the crucial experiment: the child is controlled by being immobilized; the doctor takes himself and his subjective hypotheses out of the room. The X ray reveals whether the bone is broken, and the appropriate action (which has been determined through previous experimentation) follows.

Here there seems to be no question of the patient's condition changing when the doctor looks at it. Of course, as the risks of radiation exposure have become better known, it has become clear that repeated X rays can themselves be a cause of future illness. In addition to such long-term effects there are immediate contextual factors that may deserve consideration. For example, a child who has been seen repeatedly for "falls" that result in broken bones, each broken bone having been treated properly but without regard to the context in which it occurred, may one day come in dead, a victim of child abuse. A doctor who suspects child abuse will have to make some sensitive subjective judgments about how far to pursue that hypothesis.

Case #4.
Juvenile Onset of Diabetes Mellitus.

A two-year-old son of a diabetic mother is admitted with coma, labored breathing, and dehydration, all signs of a system thrown out of balance by diabetes. Within a day careful management brings an end to the crisis. It is then decided to bring the patient's blood sugar level under tight control prior to discharge. To this end, morning, afternoon, and evening blood sugars are obtained daily by repeatedly drawing blood from the veins (when they can be found). Over the next two weeks tight control remains elusive in spite of increasing insulin dosages, with the patient continuing to show evidence of sugar and a small amount of ketones (a breakdown product of fat) in the urine. The patient's blood remains free of ketones and is not overly acidic throughout. The patient has become emotionally frazzled while in the hospital, with the three-a-day multiple venipunctures becoming regular battles between staff and patient. Finally the mother takes matters into her own hands and takes her son out of the hospital. His physicians then give up their original goal of tight control of his blood sugar levels. Instead they put him on an insulin regimen which keeps him from having either too low or too high a blood sugar. As the patient is carefully followed at home with minimal invasive testing, his insulin requirements decrease.

In this case the mechanistic approach was tried, only to be abandoned in favor of the probabilistic. Working from the hypothesis that the child's high blood sugar had one determining cause—not enough insulin—the physicians arranged an *experimentum crucis* to test this causal relationship by keeping the child in the controlled environment of the hospital. While every other factor that might affect the blood sugar (such as diet) was held constant, the insulin dose was systematically varied and its effect on the blood sugar level recorded. This is the ideal experimental method under the Mechanistic Paradigm.

Only it did not work. It did not take into account other causative factors—the hospital environment, separation from the mother, etc.—that also may have affected the child's blood sugar. By regarding these factors as constant, the doctors were unable to observe their effects either singly or in combination with one another. In the artificial experimental environment of the hospital the child felt uncomfortable. The factors which in his home made for his comfort and thus could have aided his recovery were controlled out of existence.

For this patient a satisfactory blood sugar level depended on both environment and insulin. As nearly as we can tell, it was lack of sufficient insulin that put him in the hospital, and lack of a proper environment that kept his blood sugar from stabilizing once he was there. In this case it was the patient's mother who decided to gamble. Her "experiment" consisted of taking the child out of the hospital and seeing how he did at home. This empirical treatment, which was not geared toward isolating any one variable, revealed more than did the attempt at an *experimentum crucis* in the hospital setting, which turned out to obscure important causal relationships.

Recognition that the hospital environment in this case was both a causal factor itself and a restriction on other causal factors calls into question another assumption of the *experimentum crucis*—that the act of observation has no effect on what is observed. Drawing blood from the child three times a day made him angry and anxious, which led to a release of adrenaline, which in turn increased the amount of sugar found in the blood that was drawn. The fact that the child fought desperately each time his blood was to be drawn finally led his mother and then the physicians to realize that the experimental conditions were making it impossible to find out what they were designed to find out. It took so long to reach this common-sense observation because the Mechanistic Paradigm, with its insistence on the separation of the observer from the observed, predisposes physicians to ignore the doctor-patient interaction as a possible source of scientifically valid diagnostic information.

The probabilistic approach eventually followed in this case took into account the various causal factors that might be present, including those growing out of the interaction of the observer with the observed. It also asked another sort of question. If this child felt and acted differently in the hospital than at home—i.e., was under increased stress, which in turn affected his blood sugar—what was the use of learning how his blood sugar responded to insulin in the stressful hospital when he was not going to continue to live there? Such knowledge might be of interest to researchers, but it would not do much good for this patient.

The question of what knowledge is worth obtaining cannot be answered without raising a question of value. Under the Mechanistic Paradigm questions of value in treatment are given consideration in the sense that in treating a patient the physician acts for the good. But it is assumed that scientific investigation (including medical diagnosis) is a value-free process of finding out "what is." Under the Probabilistic Paradigm the question of values forms a part of any inquiry. For one thing, the experimenter's values influence his or her choice of which of many possible causes are important enough to look for, and in what way. A doctor who pays attention to the patient's and family's points of view will see a different set of causes than a doctor who does not do so. Moreover it is not only the doctor but the patient and family as well who are observers, and so their values, too, will affect what is observed.

Under the Probabilistic Paradigm diagnosis is approached in the same way as treatment—with a consciousness of the values involved. The probable value of the information to be gained is weighed against the probable costs of obtaining it. In the case of the diabetic boy, practitioners working under the Probabilistic Paradigm could place a high value on such information as (1) the effect of the doctor-patient interaction on the hospital test results, and (2) whether the dose of insulin necessary in the stressful hospital environment might not result in a dangerously low blood sugar when the child is in his normal home environment. As things stand, although these considerations are often noted, children are still placed in the hospital to "determine" their insulin requirements. Under the Mechanistic Paradigm, which has no systematic way of dealing with values in scientific investigation (and in fact explicitly disregards them), the wrong questions are often asked.

Criterion #3:
The Subjective and the Objective

The question of values leads directly into our third scientific criterion—the legitimacy or illegitimacy of subjective knowledge in scientific investigation.

Case #5.
The Comatose Patient.

A thirty-year-old man is brought in, semicomatose, following a fall from a twenty-five-foot scaffolding. Although his blood pressure, pulse, and respiration are initially stable, his neurological status (as measured by level of consciousness, nerve function, reflexes, etc.) progressively deteriorates, with the pupil of the right eye becoming dilated. A neurosurgical procedure is initiated to relieve the pressure from the accumulation of blood between the surface of the brain and the skull.

The physician handled this case according to the diagnosis-treatment model of the Mechanistic Paradigm. Once one knows what *is,* one knows (or figures out) what one *ought to do.* The doctor determined what was wrong with the patient, using his observations of the patient's body as objective data. The diagnosis in some sense dictated the treatment.

Neither value judgments nor subjective information played a major part in this case. Objectivity was made possible by the complete separation of the observer from the observed. The patient alone was the object of scientific observation; the physician alone observed. Since the patient was not fully conscious and his family was not available, he did not participate as observer or decision-maker and did not express subjective knowledge, feelings, or values.

It should be noted that to find a case where subjective information did not play an essential role, we had to choose one where the patient was semiconscious and critically ill, and where the available choices were limited by the need to act quickly. In such a situation one must to some extent depend on habits dictated by custom. The doctor did have to make the subjective judgment that the patient fell into the category of "acute subdural hematoma" even though he did not have all the "classical" findings (which few patients ever show). Even when the doctor acted from habit in this seemingly mechanistic "limiting case" of the Probabilistic Paradigm in medicine, the doctor was making critical choices.

Case #6.
Cancer of the Large Intestine.

An eighty-five-year-old man with widespread cancer of the colon has previously indicated that he does not wish to have any heroic measures taken which would prolong his life. In the five-year course of his disease he has become progressively more confused. Now his bowel becomes obstructed, and he is rushed from the nursing home to the hospital. The surgeon who is called down to the emergency room exchanges greetings with the patient, performs a physical examination, and proceeds quickly to perform a colostomy. The operation involves having the intestine empty directly through a hole made in the skin, thus circumventing the obstructed area.

Clearly this case demanded careful attention from the physician. The patient may have had a number of good reasons not to want this operation. At worst the operation might have left him less comfortable and more dependent on medical aid (e.g., by having to empty his feces into a bag). Anesthesia disrupts an old person's life by leaving him confused, and some people believe that it also hastens the destruction of brain cells, pushing the person toward senility and—again—leaving him more helpless than before. Whatever the costs of the surgery, if it didn't stand a reasonable chance of making the patient *more* comfortable and better able to take care of himself, he may well have felt that at this point there would be little benefit in

prolonging his life by such extreme measures. Given the patient's wishes and his condition, it is not at all clear that he
should have been operated on.

Many people would find this decision worthy of serious ethical consideration.The lack of such consideration by the surgeon in this case may be considered an expression of the Mechanistic Paradigm. It is grounded in the assumption that,
given a particular cause of distress, a particular procedure will
cause its relief. The standard procedure for relieving a colon
obstructed due to cancer is a colostomy. This surgeon did not
think it necessary to consider other aspects of the particular
case.

What he failed to consider were the patient's values, the patient's knowledge (in this case, the patient's prediction concerning whether he would survive the operation and what
change it was likely to make in his condition), the doctor's
feelings (which are important both as a barometer and a stimulus to the patient's feelings), and that part of the doctor's clinical judgment of probabilities that is not derived from objective
fact and statistics. These are forms of subjective knowledge
deemed irrelevant under the Mechanistic Paradigm. The surgeon deprived himself of all of these sources of potentially
useful knowledge, which for him did not exist on the same
plane as "objective" knowledge about the relief of colonic ob-
struction by surgery.

Within the Probabilistic Paradigm subjective and objective
knowledge do exist on the same plane and are used in conjunction with each other. In keeping with the Probabilistic
Paradigm, the surgeon could have used his own subjective
knowledge and personal experience, along with the patient's, to
estimate the probability that the patient would survive surgery
and that the operation would effectively decompress the colon
without debilitating side effects. The patient at some prior time
could have been encouraged to estimate the value (for him) of
continuing to live with cancer, as well as the costs of going
through another operation. When the emergency arose, the
doctor could then have gambled for the patient in keeping with
a shared understanding of what his own and the patient's values were. Where these differed, he would tend to give the pa-

tient's values the benefit of the doubt, assuming them to be reasonable and consistent with general principles unless there was good reason to believe otherwise. Such deliberation might or might not have changed the surgeon's decision to operate. But whatever the decision, it would have been the patient's as well as the physician's, and would have taken into account a much wider range of considerations than did the decision that was in fact made.

Applying the New Paradigm to Medicine

Physicists look at such things as subatomic particles and heavenly bodies; physicians look at biochemical processes inside the human body and at the way human beings live. Is it reasonable to say that physicists and physicians can look at these very different things in much the same way? Although a physician does not do what a physicist does, a physician can appeal to the same standards of rationality that a physicist does. Physicist and physician both study relationships that when looked at superficially appear reassuringly certain, that when looked at somewhat more deeply become hopelessly uncertain, and that finally yield to understanding by means of probabilities. Neither can claim to find universal deterministic laws to explain the causation of a particular event. Both must recognize that they influence what they observe, whether the position and motion of a tiny particle or the well-being of a patient under examination. Indeed, the application of the Heisenberg Uncertainty Principle should be more intuitively obvious in the latter case than the former. (Obvious, that is, were it not for the pervasive influence of the Mechanistic Paradigm.) Of course people change when they interact with others. Of course the way people feel affects whether they are sick or well.

The recognition of these simple and yet complex truths would make medical science and medical practice very different from what they have been for the past hundred years. It would bring what are called the "art" and "ethics" of medicine into the realm of the science of medicine. There has always been a place in medicine for clinical judgment that is based on personal experience and intuition and that takes into account intangible factors such as the physician's knowledge of a particular patient or family. Traditionally this kind of skill has been thought of as "the art of medicine." Under the Probabilistic Paradigm, where it is known as subjective probability assessment, it is taken as seriously and utilized as fully as any other scientific tool. Similarly, although individual doctors may do their best to practice ethically, medical ethics will continue to have only a limited effect on practice as long as doctors are trained and rewarded for practicing a science that does not include ethics. It is as a science that medicine is respected and listened to, and it is within a scientific framework (that of the Probabilistic Paradigm) that the art and ethics of medicine can be practiced with impact.

If anything will bring about the participation of patients and families in medical decision-making, not as a charitable gesture or a response to political pressure but as an unquestioned part of scientific medical procedure, it will be the adoption of the Probabilistic Paradigm. Those who campaign for doctor-patient equality will note that in the Probabilistic Paradigm the patient and the patient's family have equal status with the doctor as scientific "observers" whose observations contribute to the outcome, even though they do not observe in the same way as the doctor. Three of the studies in this chapter show the disadvantages of leaving out patient and family participation, which would have fit naturally and inevitably into the probabilistic procedure.

Case studies later in this book show the advantages of practicing by the Probabilistic Paradigm for all concerned. Patients and their families gain the opportunity and the responsibility to participate in decision-making and influence decisions in accordance with their values. Doctors gain the benefit of the patient's and family's knowledge and the support that comes from sharing the diagnostic and therapeutic dilemmas which previously they have borne alone. More flexible decision-making strategies, together with the consideration of a wider range of possible causes, lead to better decisions and better health care, and the mutuality of the process increases trust between doctor and patient. Costs are reduced in some areas (e.g., by cutting down on unnecessary testing), increased in others (e.g., by having doctors spend more time working with patients and their families). However, even the costs of using the new paradigm—particularly the cost in time and effort—may not be as great as they now appear. Once the use of the paradigm becomes a matter of habit, doctors and patients can carry out the requirements of probabilistic thinking naturally and smoothly as they go about their work, just as they now do in the case of mechanistic thinking.

The problem is that the use of the Probabilistic Paradigm has not yet become a habit. It is the Mechanistic Paradigm that conditions our habits, in medicine and elsewhere. It is easy to feel superior to the physicians who took so long diagnosing K.'s illness that they had no time left to treat him. In retrospect our criticisms of them seem only commonsensical. But at the time it seemed only commonsensical to do what they did; anyone might have done the same. By almost unanimous consensus of the personnel involved, what they did was what a conscientious doctor "should" do; it was the essence of good sense in medicine. It is, in fact, how doctors are trained to do their work. And not only doctors. Almost all our experience in life directs us toward seeking certainty.

Some physicists believe that learning Newtonian physics is a handicap to learning relativistic and quantum physics. The same effect can be seen wherever the two paradigms are applied. To use the Mechanistic Paradigm even where it seems to work satisfactorily (as in the first of each of the three pairs of cases in this chapter) is to gain a short-term benefit at a long-term cost—the "retooling cost" spoken of in the previous chapter. Our minds get used to thinking in terms of whatever tools we use. When we use a crude tool such as the Mechanistic Paradigm, we become less able to take up a more subtle instrument such as the Probabilistic Paradigm when we really need it. Using an outmoded way of thinking even "for convenience" is not without its side effects. The overworked intern in the emergency room may find the Mechanistic Paradigm useful in many instances, but the doctor who is thus trained may find it hard not to treat the whole world as an emergency room.

What is true for doctors in the emergency room is true for all of us throughout our everyday lives. If the Probabilistic Paradigm is such an effective tool for medical decision-making, why don't we use it? As the next chapter will show, we don't use it because the way we live—at home and at work—reinforces the habits of mechanistic thinking, feeling, and acting.

4

UNCERTAINTY IN EVERYDAY LIFE

Dr. S. understood the way his patients thought from the way he himself thought when he wasn't being a scientist. "Damn table!" he would blurt out when he stubbed his toe against a table leg. It was the table's fault. Then as he hopped around in pain, he would shake his head and think, "Boy, am I a klutz!" It was his fault. It was hard for him to think about more than one cause at a time when his foot throbbed with pain. As a doctor S. saw himself as a scientist who practiced consciously by the Probabilistic Paradigm. But when he wasn't giving special attention to the way in which he was thinking, he would fall back into thinking *un*consciously, as others did, in terms of the Mechanistic Paradigm.

In dealing with his patients and colleagues and in critically examining his own practice, S. realized that thinking takes place in contexts—contexts of feeling, contexts of prior experience and learning. People learn to make decisions long before they come to a doctor's office. They learn it at home and in school, at work and in the supermarket. There they learn to make decisions that "feel right" to them. Whether those decisions are right or are being made in a reasonable way is another matter.

Science serves as a standard of rationality for society. When people seek to do what is right in their daily lives, they look to science for guidance. This has been true, at any rate, since science assumed a dominant place in Western society in the era of the Mechanistic Paradigm. The Social Darwinism of the late nineteenth century illustrates the ease with which science (in this case the illegitimate extension of the biological theory of evolution as "the survival of the fittest" to social and economic survival) replaced the fading "Protestant ethic" as a justification for competitive business practices. The era of Social Darwinism was also the era of Claude Bernard in medicine, the period when the influence of the Mechanistic Paradigm began to reach out beyond science to business and industry, the consumer marketplace, and the family. The notion of a scientific paradigm, in its narrowest construction, refers to the conditions under which scientists work. As we shall see in this chapter, the Mechanistic Paradigm has come to represent the conditions under which everyone works and the conditions under which everyone lives.

Why does the Mechanistic Paradigm rule everyday decision-making at a time when it has been fundamentally questioned in the sciences? It survives in part because it has helped to create social institutions that in turn help to perpetuate it—for instance, a profit-oriented economy and a weakened family. Clearly, changes in these institutions would have an impact on the way people think, in medicine and elsewhere. But the reverse is also true—that by learning a different way of thinking, people can begin to create new social institutions and new living conditions for themselves.

As realistic as he was about the odds against people learning to think probabilistically, Dr. S. didn't think that people's actions were determined by their socioeconomic or family backgrounds. If he had thought so, he would have been thinking unicausally. People have the capacity and the responsibility to make choices. Indeed, this book is about the way S. and his patients learned to make choices and how other doctors and patients can do the same. But to learn to make choices effectively, one needs to be aware of the conditions, favorable or unfavorable, under which choices are made. To understand how people think, one needs to consider the mind that thinks, the family that transmits one way of thinking or another, and the society that generates and sustains that way of thinking.

When people get sick and go to a doctor, they don't stop thinking the way they normally do. When people are in pain, they seek explanations for what caused the pain. The explanations that are right at hand are those that people learn throughout their lives—i.e., those supplied by the Mechanistic Paradigm. Moreover, even people who are capable of thinking rationally most of the time tend to fall back on rigid habits of thought when in the presence of the pain and fear that accompany illness or injury (like S. when he stubbed his toe). If S. was going to teach people to think probabilistically, he would have to keep in mind the reasons why people are sometimes afraid to be rational even when they have the capacity to be, as well as the reasons why people often are not capable of being rational even when they are not conscious of fear.

Labor Without Love:
The Workplace

At fifty-four Eleanor Perk had a chronic cough which was not responding to treatment. She had had asthma on and off for eight months. It surely wasn't doing her any good to sit in on those smoke-filled meetings every morning at the prestigious law firm where she worked as an executive secretary. Eleanor had developed a special role in her twenty years with the firm. Every morning she was called in to the meeting, where she took notes which she then organized, summarized, and gave out to the people who attended the meetings—several of whom smoked cigars. S. sought to relieve Eleanor's plight by giving her a note telling her employers that she should not be required to work in a smoke-filled room.

A month later, her cough having subsided, she was back with a new complaint. Her employers had responded to S.'s note by telling her, "You don't have to be in on the meetings. There's other work to do in this office." There was—but it was the work of a junior secretary. "Sure, Doc," Eleanor lamented, "I still get the same pay, but when I go home at night it feels as if something is missing. I mean, all I do is type letters. The way they speak to me now, it's as if they don't know me from one of the 'temporaries'; it's as if I haven't been doing this job for twenty years. They specify how to type everything down to the dotting of the *i*'s. And when I'm finished, someone is always looking over my shoulder. I won't get fired, mind you, but I am made to understand that if I don't do things just the way they want me to, consequences will follow."

"Consequences?" asked S. "Is this anything new?"

"Well, in some respects it's always been this way, I guess. The fellows I was working for before, if they didn't like something I did, they'd let me know about it."

"Then how is this different?"

"It's this way. Now that I'm just one of the girls again, I'm expected to produce just so much by the end of the day. If I don't type my share of this or that report, the girl who's waiting to work on it the next day is going to be stuck. That's part of it. There's also a different feeling now. Before it was as if the rules didn't apply to me. Now it's 'company policy this,' 'company policy that.' For instance, I've been told that it's against the firm's policy for me to change one word of what I type. It used to be that I had some responsibility. Oh, I put down what was said at those meetings, but I also put my two cents in when I wrote those reports. I felt as if I was making something of my own, not just recording what somebody else said.

"Maybe it's okay for a lot of the girls there. After all, they're being promised a career. Stick with the firm, and the firm will take care of you. But there's nothing for me in starting over at the bottom at this point in my life. It's no fun doing what I'm doing. Doc, I need something for my nerves, you know, some of that Valium stuff. Look, we tried it your way, and look where it got me. The firm didn't change. They just put me in a different place."

Eleanor Perk's words illustrate the way the management of a modern labor force discourages critical thinking by exerting control over workers. In his book *Contested Terrain* (1979), Richard Edwards lists three forms of control exerted by management: direction (specifying task requirements—or, in Eleanor's words, "They specify how to type everything down to the dotting of the *i*'s"); evaluation (assessing performance and correcting mistakes—". . . someone is always looking over my shoulder"; and discipline (rewarding and punishing to reinforce compliance—". . . I am made to understand that if I don't do things just the way they want me to, consequences will follow").

Edwards goes on to identify three styles of control (listed in order of their historical appearance). In *simple* control the boss or bosses exercise power personally, through direct contact with workers (". . . if they didn't like something I did, they'd let me know about it."). *Technical* control, epitomized by the assembly line, occurs when work is paced by a mechanical or technological process rather than by immediate human command ("If I don't type my share of this or that report, the girl who's waiting to work on it the next day is going to be stuck."). *Bureaucratic* control is exercised through an impersonal rule of law ("Now it's 'company policy this,' 'company policy that' ") and through the firm's power to bestow or withhold long-range rewards ("After all, they're being promised a career. Stick with the company, and the company will take care of you.").

By employing these three styles of control, management places itself at a progressively increasing distance from the labor force. As this distance increases, managerial authority can take the form of deterministic laws, as it did in Eleanor's case ("company policy"), or else can become so arbitrary in interpreting rules that uncertainty reigns ("who knows what they'll come up with next?"). Either way, workers are unable to challenge authority as they did when the boss was right there giving orders and hearing complaints. As in Eleanor Perk's case, they are taught that it is futile to try to think for themselves in order to influence the process of production. Thus one effect of Eleanor's old job on her health was a cough. Her new job had more serious, long-range effects, such as a dulled capacity for thinking (or at least a habit of not thinking) and a sense of losing control of her life. Here Eleanor learned a way of thinking, feeling, and acting—the mechanistic way—which would affect the way she made choices (or left them to chance) concerning her health as well as other aspects of her life.

Links between a way of thought and a type of economic system have been pointed out before, for instance, by Max Weber in his demonstration (1930) that Protestant religious beliefs were conducive to the development of what we call the free-enterprise system. Similarly, it was no mere coincidence that the Mechanistic Paradigm established itself in science in an era characterized by an expanding, increasingly industrialized market economy, for its three criteria admirably serve the needs of such an economy. This is not to say that the profit system can flourish only under the Mechanistic Paradigm, or that only a profit-oriented economy can tolerate a mechanistic science. Rather, it is to observe that mechanistic science had both tangible benefits in the applied science of industrial production and intangible benefits in the molding of industrial society. With its exaltation of the "objective" (the production and accumulation of material resources) over the "subjective" (feelings that were potentially disruptive to a smooth-running order) and its insistence on single causes, the Mechanistic Paradigm was well suited to a society single-mindedly pursuing the goal of rapid economic development.

How is the paradigm inculcated and critical thinking discouraged in the worker? The classic example of modern industrial production is Henry Ford's assembly line. In *Captains of Consciousness* (1976) Stuart Ewen (quoting a 1939 Federal Trade Commission report) characterizes Ford's "line production system" as using "expensive, single-purpose" machinery run by "quickly-trained, single-purpose" workmen to mass-produce a standardized car. In the juxtaposition of expensive machines with inexpensive workers, we see the worker being fitted to the machine rather than vice versa. When the relationship between worker and machine is modeled on that of machine and machine (or machine and product), the operation of the three criteria of the Mechanistic Paradigm is evident.

In the term *single-purpose* we can discern the deterministic causation of Criterion #1. Or in Henry Ford's own words (from *My Life and Work*):

> The net result of the application of these principles is the reduction of the necessity for thought on the part of the worker and the reduction of his movements to a minimum. He does as nearly as possibly only one thing with only one movement (Chandler, 1964, p. 39).

Each worker's contribution is reduced to a single repetitive act designed to produce a single invariable effect. The worker is not expected to influence the process, but simply to do what is asked, to comply. In this way the worker is not seen as a cause, but as one more variable (along with capital, raw materials, and machines) to be manipulated as if in a scientific experiment (Criterion #2).

This last analogy is not ours. While Ford was pioneering the assembly line, factory owners were introduced to "scientific management" by Frederick W. Taylor, who advocated "taking the control of the machine shop out of the hands of the many workmen, and placing it completely in the hands of management, thus superseding 'rule of thumb' by scientific control" (Hofstede, 1978, p. 453). Taylor divided the workers in a factory into isolated experimental groups. He observed them, timed them, and manipulated their working conditions to determine how they could be motivated to work most efficiently. Years later, ironically enough, the discovery of the "Hawthorne effect" (discussed in Chapter 2) demonstrated that Taylor's application of the *experimentum crucis* to the workplace had been fatally compromised by experimenter effects that could have been anticipated under the Probabilistic Paradigm.

Workers who ran the new machinery were trained and controlled in the same manner as the machinery itself—by the cookbook rules that then constituted "science." No mutual influence between worker and management was allowed for. Moreover, what the scientifically managed worker thought or felt was of no interest to management except insofar as it affected production. The worker was being paid to act in an "objective" manner, not to question the values and goals of production. If a worker was bored, alienated, tired, or ill, performance would be reduced. These subjective states, therefore, like the worker himself, became objects of concern to management, to be dealt with through the evolving science of industrial psychology.

In the myth of "disinterested" observers, devoid of feelings, scientifically manipulating workers "uninterested" in their jobs, brimming with distracting feelings, we have the objective-subjective dichotomy that is Criterion #3 of the Mechanistic Paradigm. By that criterion the objective and subjective aspects of knowledge can be neatly differentiated, "and never the twain shall meet." Scientists and their methods are considered to be objective. Furthermore objective data traditionally were thought to be the only suitable objects of scientific study. By the twentieth century, however, it became possible (or so it was thought) to study subjective, irrational feelings by objective, rational methods. Sociologist Richard Sennett, in *The Fall of Public Man* (1978), traces the historical development by which emotions became "facts" that could be detached from the contexts of living in which they occurred and placed under the microscope of mechanistic science. In such science objectivity is seen as a strength, a resource for gaining knowledge and control, while subjectivity is seen as a weakness by which people can be manipulated. This point of view was enthusiastically taken over by managers who saw themselves in the objective, scientific, controlling role vis-à-vis their workers.

Of course, Ford's assembly line and Taylor's "scientific management" represent the industrial practices of 1910 or 1920 rather than those of today. Taylor's crude manipulations in the name of science have given way to "human relations" management, which is thought to be *more* scientific in that it embodies a subtler understanding of psychology. Today's managers are prepared to take into account a range of subjective factors in job satisfaction (which they still consider irrational) and to allow for considerable interchange between workers and management in establishing company procedures. Still, there is reason to question how much things have really changed. The methods may be flexible, but the goals of production and profit remain fixed and are not open to question. Although workers are encouraged to ask, "How can this be done?" the question, "Is this worth doing?" is not considered a legitimate one. The control exerted over the work force may be subtler than in the past, but it is control nonetheless, and by its very subtlety less accessible to modification. The "enlightened" workplace can still be seen as being run on mechanistic lines, in that workers are denied the opportunity to think and make critical choices about what they produce, as well as the subjective satisfaction that comes from doing so.

It isn't only the factory or clerical worker who is subject to this system of control and its unquestioned goals. Another of S.'s patients, Jerry Matthias, found that being promoted from a stressful assembly-line job didn't do him any more good than being demoted did for Eleanor Perk. Jerry had begun to develop high blood pressure at a time when he was having trouble keeping up with the pace of the assembly line. He wasn't lazy or negligent; on the contrary, his insistence on taking proper care with each piece caused him to linger over it until the next piece was upon him. A competent and intelligent worker, Jerry thought he could put the stress of his job behind him when he moved up to a junior management position. As a manager Jerry was now responsible for making this area a "profit center" for the company. Instead of having to keep up with the pace of the line, he had to set the pace for others according to standards set by higher management.

The new job was no easier on his blood pressure. "I used to think it was the guys on the line who were under pressure," he told S., "but I feel like I'm still on a treadmill. You want to know who's under the most strain? Not the guy who's actually putting the machines together. It's the guy you see standing around with a cup of coffee. Take a good look at that guy. He may not have to be at a particular place at a particular time, and he may not have to produce x number of widgets per minute, but he does have to produce x number of dollars per month. Only he doesn't always know exactly how to do it, and nobody can tell him. That's what he's standing around trying to figure out, and that's where the stress comes in."

Food Without Nourishment:
The Marketplace

S. was looking out the window as his last patient of the day, Jerry Matthias, drove up for his blood pressure check. The car Jerry was driving was a model that had recently made the news as having been recalled to remedy a potentially life-threatening defect in the fuel storage system. S. wondered whether Jerry had taken his car in yet. So when Jerry came into the office S. remarked, "Bet you're not the only one who's been in for an exam lately."

Jerry looked at him.

"You've probably had your car in for a checkup too."

"Oh, that recall. Yeah, I got a notice in the mail about it a few weeks ago. Haven't gotten around to it yet. Don't know if I will."

S. looked—and was—astonished. "What do you mean? From what I read in the paper, that gas tank business is a pretty serious thing. Aren't you concerned? What about your family?"

Jerry was getting angry. "And suppose I miss half a day's work to get the car fixed? That's half a day's pay gone, down the drain. What about my family then? They have to eat, you know."

S. thought that the exchange he was having with Jerry was likely to affect the blood pressure reading he was about to take, but he persisted. "What about doing it when you get home?" S. inquired. As a doctor he was genuinely curious about why someone wouldn't do a "simple little thing" that might beneficially affect his health or safety.

"Yeah, I guess I could do it then," Jerry answered slowly. "But by then I'm too damn tired. When I'm tired, the odds don't feel the same. Look, Doc, you're the one who always talks about costs and benefits. When you weigh the probability that my gas tank is going to blow up against the sure loss of half a day's pay, which would *you* choose?"

"I guess it depends on how much money you have to begin with. If you have enough money, the value of half a day's pay goes down some."

"Besides," Jerry said, "I don't know how seriously to take this recall stuff anyway. Sometimes I think it's just a lot of government red tape. That's a good little car I've got out there. Like they say on TV: 'Build your own car to your every desire.'"

S. had seen the ad. He had seen lots of them. "You" as a consumer could "build your own car" by taking your pick from among the selection of options offered by the company to create the illusion of choice, the illusion that you were producing instead of consuming. Speaking of options, one option Jerry couldn't choose was the option of not driving. "Don't get me wrong," said S. "I know all about the hassles of owning a car when you're too busy working to maintain it properly. Sometimes I wonder if it's all worth it—were it not that I absolutely need it." S. suddenly wondered whether "absolutely" was quite accurate. "How about you, Jerry? Could you do without your car? Would you consider taking a bus to work?"

"A bus? You think I'm crazy? Listen, Doc, I'm so goddam dog-tired when I get out of work that I don't want to get on any bus. I want to get into *my* car and stretch out and hit the road. That car is the only thing I've got that's really mine."

"With all these recalls, though, you've got to admit they don't make them like they used to."

"I know that, but I need a car that looks new. People see me in the parking lot. I'm in management now, and everything about me has to look good, including my car. You know how it is these days, Doc. It's not what you are; it's what you wear."

Whatever this conversation did for (or to) Jerry's blood pressure, it set S. to thinking. Jerry's "noncompliant" response to the auto recall notice told S. something about all the patients who (much to his exasperation) didn't bother with their physical exams and other preventive health-care measures. They were probably just as tired as Jerry. They, too, must be concerned about the half-day's pay they would lose by coming to the doctor. And what better way to rationalize these real concerns than by an appeal to the odds? "It won't happen to me." "My car won't be the one to blow up." "I won't be the one to get breast cancer, so why bother with the monthly self-exam?" Why bother to take care of yourself, or your car, when you didn't have to? It was hard enough to take the time when you were really sick or when the car wouldn't run.

In medical school S. had been taught to expect two things from patients. They would come, and they would pay. But he was beginning to realize that, for many of his patients, coming and paying were not simple things. Paying was not simple because they had other things to spend their money on. Coming was not simple because they had other things to do with their time, such as earning a living. Most of his patients needed to earn a living, especially when "really living" meant having to buy the kinds of things they spent their working hours making.

Jerry's plight illustrated the production-consumption cycle in which so many people were trapped. Jerry had to have a new car so that he could keep up appearances on the job—and keep the job. Once he had the car, he needed the job all the more so that he could pay for the car. People have been willing to "buy" a lot more than cars in order to keep their jobs. On January 5, 1979, *The New York Times* reported that five women employees of a West Virginia chemical plant had had themselves sterilized after a company official told them that they might lose their jobs because of the danger of exposing unborn children to lead poisoning. "He even said he felt sure our health insurance would cover the operation," said one of the women. "We did it because we were afraid," said another. For the sake of their jobs these women "consumed" a medical procedure approved by their insurance companies. If Eleanor Perk had known what was in store for her when she gave up a job that put her health at risk, she might have gone on consuming cigar smoke against medical advice.

In order for goods to be produced at a profit they must be consumed. In an economy of scarcity people are valued for what they produce. In today's economy of artificial abundance, as described in Stuart Ewen's *Captains of Consciousness,* people are valued for what they consume. From the point of view of the corporate producers people should see themselves as having needs that can be met by commercial products. That is, they should see themselves as consumers. Richard Sennett's account of the rise of the department store in the latter half of the nineteenth century shows how people who previously expressed their social identity by haggling with merchants were induced to gain satisfaction from the passive, impersonal "act" of buying standardized, fixed-price merchandise. By various stimulating presentations mass-market retailers persuaded people to think of products for which they had no practical use as representations of their own personal experience and character. That was the beginning of the consumer society.

In motivating people to consume, the economic system organizes consumption, as it does production, according to the three criteria of the Mechanistic Paradigm. Criterion #1, deterministic causation, is reflected in all the advertising that promotes this or that product as a source of certainty. The Mechanistic Paradigm creates the need for (and expectation of) certainty; manufacturers and advertisers purport to answer that need by packaging certainty in brand names: "You can be sure if it's Westinghouse." How easy it was, in K.'s case, for hospital personnel to turn that habitual way of thinking into "You can be sure if you take a blood culture (or do a spinal tap, or whatever)." In the simplistic, mechanistic world of advertising a single cause has a single effect; one stimulus elicits one response. If you have a headache, take Anacin. If you have underarm odor, use Ban. If your life could use a "shot" of power and glamour, get a Mustang. It is hardly a model for learning to think probabilistically.

Advertising does not mention uncertainty or multiple causation. It is not in the interest of General Motors or Ford to encourage consumers to question whether one needs a powerful, flashy car rather than some alternative means of transportation. It is their business to make and sell cars, and the choices among cars that they offer a consumer like Jerry Matthias correspond to the limited choices among tasks and working conditions that the more enlightened factory managers offer their workers. Nor is it in the interest of the drug companies to portray headaches as a multicausal problem so that people might see themselves, their family lives, and their jobs as being among the causes of their headaches. Instead, a magic pill or other product is sold as a "technical fix" for medical, personal, or social problems.

Criterion #2, the *experimentum crucis,* is invoked throughout the system of consumption. First, there are the crisp "scientific" findings that advertisers cite in support of their claim of superiority for their product: "Studies show that Aspirin Plus is better than aspirin." "With Fluropaste you get twenty-seven percent fewer cavities than with Brand X." Second, it is with the detachment of the mechanistic scientist that advertisers manipulate the market by influencing people, creating "new markets," and then "responding" to the needs they have helped to create. To the advertiser the consumer is an object to be experimented upon, and thus the advertiser's relationship to the consumer is the same as the "scientific" manager's relationship to the worker. Finally, advertising instructs the consumer to do his or her own *experimentum crucis* by buying the product and observing its effects. "Try it; you'll like it" is the message, with its neat juxtaposition of experimental manipulation and determined outcome. "Try our product," the advertisement is saying, "and it will have a planned, predictable, demonstrable effect on your life." The message aims to limit the consumer, like the worker, to a series of repetitive, single-purpose acts (in this case buying and using products). It ignores the fact that the effect of using a product depends on how and when one uses it; it is context-dependent. While the product may make one feel good, it may also damage one's health, put one deeper into debt, or give one a false sense of security.

A person who understands both the headache and the headache pill in context (the context of a person's life in society) can see himself or herself as a cause and as acted upon by other causes. This complex awareness, however, will have to come from a source other than consumer advertising, which usually portrays causation in all-or-none terms as being "out there" in the objective world ("take this pill, and your headache will vanish") or within the person in the subjective world ("build your own car to your every desire"). Advertising plays on these extreme emotional reactions by giving people a fantasy of omnipotence in response to a world where what happens to them is too often beyond their control.

According to Sennett, "The celebration of objectivity and hardheaded commitment to fact so prominent a century ago, all in the name of Science, was in reality an unwitting preparation for the present era of radical subjectivity" (1978, p. 22). As psychoanalyst Joel Kovel (1978) points out, the two extremes complement each other in the interest of the economic system, which requires that people be "objective" enough to do what is required of them at work, but "subjective" enough to want the income they get from working and the consumer goods that their paychecks can buy them. The subjective desires of the consumer not only guarantee a market for industry's products, but also ensure a compliant work force, since people must keep their jobs to be able to gratify their desires.

In other words, people must be objective as producers, subjective as consumers. The Mechanistic Paradigm, with its clear-cut separation of the objective and subjective realms (Criterion #3), is the ideal vehicle for maintaining a radical distinction between producer-consumer roles. This radical distinction allows people to be easily controlled in both roles. Indeed, the very word *consumer* puts people in a passive role, so that even when they assert themselves, it is only to seek "consumer power."

When Jerry Matthias decided some months later to approach his employers for a position of greater autonomy, he realized that he would first have to get off this treadmill of worker-consumer dependency. As he told S., "You better sit down. I sold my car last week, the day before I went in to talk to them. I knew that unless I had some money in the bank, I wouldn't have the guts to quit if they turned me down."

S. couldn't believe it. "You're kidding. So what happened?"

"They gave me what I wanted. I could have gambled and kept my car, as it turns out. But who's to know?"

The drastic step Jerry had taken was an attempt to get out of the economic corner in which he had found himself. By facing up to the power of the economic system, he had taken a step toward freeing himself from it. If he wanted to enjoy his work more (i.e., get more subjective gratification out of it), he might have to be a little more objective in restraining his desires as a consumer.

Industry pays close attention to the feelings of consumers, like those of workers, so as to manipulate them. Hunger must be converted into a craving for Cheerios, natural cereals, Mc-

Donald's hamburgers, cookbooks, or diet books. Among the needs that industry capitalizes on (without pausing to consider their origin) are those created by the conditions of life in our society, such as Jerry Matthias's need for a car that would impress his clients and Eleanor Perk's need for a tranquilizer to counteract the frustrations of her job. Advertising also *creates* needs which it then supplies products to satisfy: the need for junk foods, the need for elaborate cosmetics, the need for a slender physique, the need for flashy cars. Those who manufacture and market consumer goods sometimes claim that they are simply responding to needs that are rooted in human nature. People do need food, clothing, and shelter to survive; they need to sleep, eliminate waste, be with other people, and sometimes receive medical attention. It is when the survival not of people but of corporations is at stake that the list of human needs becomes much longer.

Given most people's lack of control and fulfillment in the productive sphere, it is understandable that for many people these consumer needs take the form of an addiction. When people are uncertain of their relationship to the physical and social environment—uncertain about how much (if any) control they have over their destinies—they seek compensatory sensations that *are* certain. If one can't really do anything, if one can't make meaningful choices, one can at least feel good. So Eleanor Perk pops a Valium pill, and Jerry Matthias tears about in his car ("the only thing I've got that's really mine"). But there is no nourishment in this kind of consumption; it is a fleeting satisfaction that does not remove one's basic uncertainties or equip one to make critical choices.

Eleanor Perk asked S. for Valium because she wanted a drug to suppress the critical thinking which she had learned to use in her previous job, but for which there was no place in her new job. The drug would also deaden the pain and anxiety that came with not being able to think critically and be a productive human being. "Look, Doc, can't you just give me the Valium?" she exclaimed. "I'm getting a lot of flak for speaking up to those guys. I can't just shut off. I can't shut off the way I've been working for the past twenty years. Maybe the Valium will calm me down so I can do things their way. Look, I try to shut off, I try to be just a cog in the machine, but then I get panicky. I get panicky when I don't feel alive. Maybe this pill will help me with that feeling, too, huh, Doc?"

What could S. tell her? "You could change jobs," he suggested. "At my age?"

For S., who would have preferred to change the world, there was sadness as he reluctantly gave Eleanor the prescription for Valium. With it he gave her the best explanation he could of why things were the way they were in her life. He suggested that she join Nine to Five, the organization seeking better working conditions for secretarial and clerical workers. With the group's support she just might be able to change things in her own office, and she would in any case gain a sense of purpose in working with people who had similar grievances and similar goals. S. also arranged for Eleanor to come in periodically and speak with him about her job and her habits of consumption, so that he could work with her in preventing her from developing an addiction to Valium. And he didn't doubt that she *would* keep coming back, if only for prescription refills.

Turning the pages of the latest medical journals, S. wondered whether things ever really changed. Nearly a decade before, S. and a group of like-minded physicians had protested the sensationalist advertisements for tranquilizing drugs, such as the one showing a frustrated driver stuck in traffic, that appeared throughout the most prestigious medical journals. These advertisements implied that the way to deal with problems in society was to make people less anxious rather than to seek solutions for the problems. Appealing to the professed standards by which the journals evaluated articles for publication, S. and his colleagues prevailed upon the editors to require more responsible content in the text and illustrations of advertisements. S. was proud of this success; he had helped change the system. But had he? There were still just as many tranquilizer ads, even if they were more subtle. They no longer had such imflammatory pictures, but the names of the drugs were still printed in big, bold letters designed to register in a harried physician's mind. The drug companies still expected doctors to comply with the ads by prescribing their latest products, and doctors still expected patients to comply with the prescriptions. In the marketplace, as in the factory, the message was still the same.

Exchange Without Trust: The Family

The message is the same at home too. A person's capacity to think critically is developed and exercised in the course of being with other people. The workplace and the marketplace are two of the social contexts in which people learn an implicit paradigm of thought, feeling, and action. The doctor-patient relationship is another. But the first and most important of those contexts is the family. The family is where a child learns strategies for dealing with uncertainty, with pain and fear. These strategies can be mechanistic or probabilistic; they can deny uncertainty or make use of probability.

In a world in which both science and industry follow the mechanistic paradigm, it would be surprising if the family did not transmit it as well. Furthermore the operation of the Mechanistic Paradigm has served to weaken the family by isolating its members from one another and reducing their capacity to take effective action together. Thus weakened, the family can still transmit ingrained habits of mechanistic thought, but it cannot (and indeed is not encouraged to) provide the experiences necessary to teach the critical thinking and the trust required under the Probabilistic Paradigm.

A number of social institutions have contributed to bringing the Mechanistic Paradigm into the home and weakening the family as a social unit. The economic system as a whole has colonized the family, made it fair game for profit-seekers, and reduced it to a cluster of individual producers and consumers playing specialized roles (including that of the professionalized homemaker practicing "home economics"). Such a family cannot be a productive community in which family members gain self-respect and strengthen their ties with one another by producing goods together. As Christopher Lasch has noted in *Haven in a Heartless World* (1977), the "helping professions" (medicine, psychology, education) have substituted their own ministrations for traditional family ties and thereby undermined family authority.

Finally, the mass media, particularly television, have taught the family to see itself in mechanistic terms. According to Sennett, over the past two hundred years a society of actors (people creating and playing public roles in relation to one another) has given way to a society of *voyeurs* (strangers passing one another on the street, trying to find out as much as possible about one another while revealing as little as possible about themselves). Television represents the culmination of this historical development. Its version of mechanistic authority (which goes along with the boss, teacher, doctor, and Lasch's emotionally absent parent) is the face on the screen that a child or adult can turn on or off, but not argue with, persuade, or engage in a process of mutual influence. This mechanistic, on-off choice is the only kind of choice possible in the world of passive consumption. Even when family members watch a TV program together and talk about it, they can't change the next episode.

The mechanistic thinking which the family absorbs from science and society centers around the notion of the single determining cause (Criterion #1). This scientific version of the primitive belief in single causes expresses itself in the illusion of total power and the dread of powerlessness. Unconsciously one tends to attribute causality entirely to oneself ("I did it") or to forces outside oneself ("It/they did it to me"). At their extremes these two habits of belief characterize the aspects of personality called *narcissism* and *paranoia* respectively. Although these terms are used in psychiatric diagnosis, where their focus is on abnormal instances, their existence in everyday life illustrates the mechanistic thinking that can manifest itself in anyone. We all have streaks of narcissism and paranoia. Like Dr. S., we all tend to blame ourselves or the table when we stub a toe or bang a knee.

These tendencies within a family are reinforced by the mechanistic vision of experimental manipulation (Criterion #2), where people are left thinking of themselves as either the controlling experimenter (narcissism) or the controlled experimental subject (paranoia). Whichever role is assumed, other family members are seen in the opposite role. Daily existence then becomes a struggle over who is going to be in control. There is no wonder that there is fear of losing, since the stakes are high.

Criterion #3, too (the subjective-objective dichotomy), finds its way into family life. People may identify with their subjective wants and needs and see themselves as alienated, helpless victims at the mercy of powerful objective forces beyond their control. Or they may identify with these objective forces (science, "hard facts," industry, money, disease germs, and technological cures) and thereby distance themselves from their feelings, including their feelings toward family members.

What are the effects of this mechanistic thinking on the family and its members? What follows is an extreme portrait, one that may not apply literally to any particular family, but that applies in greater or lesser degree to all families whose members face the considerable uncertainties of today's world without being able to do so consciously and thus be able to share the risks in a mutually supportive way.

Family relationships governed by the Mechanistic Paradigm resemble the relationships of the workplace and the marketplace. To apply a distinction made by psychologists Margaret Clark and Judson Mills (1979), they tend to be *exchange* rather than *communal* relationships. In an exchange relationship (as represented, for example, by a business contract) people gratify their needs individually in a spirit of pragmatic cooperation. They give one another benefits in order to get comparable benefits in return. Such benefits create reciprocal obligations. They must be paid for, if not in money, then in kind. "What's in it for me?" is the ever-present question. In a communal relationship (for example, the mutuality of a loving relationship) no such obligations are incurred. Benefits are given and received, but not on a quid pro quo basis. It is, in fact, considered inappropriate to "pay off" one benefit with another. Rather, the people involved are understood to care about one another's well-being and to respond to one another's needs as they arise. In a relationship of this sort to satisfy another's needs is also to satisfy one's own.

The love and mutual support that exist in a communal relationship transcend any mathematical distribution of goods. In an exchange relationship, however, people bargain for their share of a supply of goods, or benefits, that is viewed as constant. The concept of exchange fits nicely into the Mechanistic Paradigm, every criterion of which implies a dichotomy. Hypotheses are either true or false (Criterion #1). One is either an experimenter or an experimental object (Criterion #2). Knowledge is either objective or subjective (Criterion #3). Thus mechanistic thinking is "either-or" thinking. Something is either yours or mine, not ours. All that can be done is to divide up the spoils (whether in a civilized or a cutthroat way). Sheila M. Rothman, in an article entitled "Family Life as Zero-Sum Game," speaks of the current tendency of psychologists, feminist leaders, and various organizations to champion the cause of one family member against all the others:

> Since the family is a battleground, every member should have, and now does have, its own Clausewitz . . . Whatever the precise nature of the advice, one assumption is common to all of it: family life is a zero-sum game. Some interests must be sacrificed to others. What is good for wives is not necessarily good for husbands and what is good for mothers is not necessarily good for children. Where our predecessors saw harmony, we see discord. Where they saw mutuality of interest, we see conflict of interest (1978, p. 397).

The Mechanistic Paradigm predisposes people toward exchange rather than communal relationships because, unlike the Probabilistic Paradigm, it does not provide for trust. When nothing between complete certainty and complete uncertainty is acknowledged, there is no use for trust and no way for trust to occur. Without trust people cannot cope with the uncertainty that they do face. And they face a great deal of uncertainty—including uncertainty about the people around them.

In a world where the economic system and its subsidiary institutions tend to split up families into atomized individual units, and where the Mechanistic Paradigm provides a way of thinking by which families split *themselves* up in the same way, family members tend to see one another as competitors. In the mechanistic world view the family's nurturance (the food, love, and care symbolized by the mother's breast) becomes the single cause of one's well-being, an object to be fought over and consumed. The family members do not see themselves as participating in and helping to produce support for one another in health and illness. Instead they see that support as an object to be received, and they fear the loss of what they depend on as an infant fears the loss of the breast. Seeking to control the source of nurturance, one sees others in the family as objects to be dominated lest one be dominated by them.

An extreme example is what is called the "addictogenic" family. People who become drug addicts often have a childhood history of inconsistent treatment, of being kept in perpetual uncertainty by emotionally distant parents. Addiction can be seen as the perpetual search for certainty of experience through the pill, shot, or bottle that eases the pain. In the relationships through which the addict obtains the desired substance, he manipulates as he felt himself to be manipulated, exploits as he felt himself to be exploited, to get the nourishment that he never had (and never has) quite enough of. As with narcissism and paranoia, the pathological example has its everyday counterpart. In the addict's desperate clinging we can see the addictions of everyday life that social psychologist Stanton Peele and Archie Brodsky analyze in *Love and Addiction* (1976). The addict's fear—of his own weakness, of being close to other people, of uncertainty—is everyone's fear.

Alienation within the family and fear of uncertainty set up a vicious circle. The less people can be sure of, the more they fear the unknown. The more uncertainty (lack of trust) people experience in their closest human relationships, the more emotional pressure they feel to deny uncertainty generally. Fear of uncertainty in the outside world can lead people to compensate by being more rigid and blindly trusting in their family relationships. Once this blind trust is shattered, as it must be in an uncertain world, what comes to take its place is blind mistrust and cynicism. With less trust to fall back on, people become less able to face uncertainty. Thus they require even greater certainty in their interpretation of the world and in their conduct of their relationships. They think, feel, and act more rigidly. In the absence of critical thinking people have a difficult time breaking out of this cycle, and it tends to perpetuate itself in ever-worsening degrees.

Faced with fear, faced with pain, faced even with the degree of uncertainty involved in everyday decision-making, people revert to primitive means of warding off the demons. One of these is to retreat into the fantasy of certainty. People tend to be most rational when they are with other people, for it is then that fantasy is continually corrected by reality. In the mechanistic family, with its isolation and emotional distancing, people are not really with one another very much, and fantasies of both the narcissistic and paranoid types are left free to grow.

How do people keep these fantasies from becoming utterly debilitating and destructive? How do they keep the fear within bounds? By applying the simple strategies of the Mechanistic Paradigm for warding off uncertainty. By doing "what's always done," people can achieve a superficial certainty that carries with it the hope of averting an uncertain future.

Forming exchange relationships in the family is one such strategy. That way, at least, the potentially deadly family competition will be civilized, and one will be sure of repayment if not of love. Within these mechanistic relationships family members play rigid roles, i.e., formulas for repetitive action that reduce the individual to a single purpose or a set of disconnected purposes. These roles may be permanent or semipermanent (e.g., breadwinner, homemaker/hostess, child-development expert, specialized teen-age consumer), or they may rotate among family members, as in the case of the stereotyped "sick role" and nurse/doctor roles that people assume in times of illness. Either way, there is no capacity or opportunity for flexible responses. One can only act out the script, follow the rules.

By understanding the impact of the Mechanistic Paradigm on family life, we see the origins of the modern family as described by Christopher Lasch: emotionally distant parents who, having power only in the family, have no power even there; children who, having nothing else around with which to build an identity, cling to phantom parents. This is a family that lacks the authority to give children principles by which to orient themselves in an uncertain world. Without meaningful authority there cannot be the kind of meaningful rebellion that tests the limits of assurance and discovers the consequences of action.

When the family is a community of trust, when its members share the losses as well as the gains, the pain and fear as well as the pleasure and hope, it is safer for the individual to go out in the world and gamble. Even when out in the world alone, one still has one's family to fall back on. And if we assume that people can tolerate uncertainty only up to a point, then the less uncertainty one has about one's family—the less uncertainty that the family will be there when needed—the more uncertainty one can accept and cope with elsewhere. Thus the presence of love and trust in the family makes it more likely that children will learn to think critically and make rational decisions.

The gambling that is practiced under the Probabilistic Paradigm, the leap of faith by which one transcends one's immediate interest and commits oneself to a communal relationship—these require a flexibility of mind and spirit that few people achieve without close trusting relationships. A family that lacks strong mutual trust cannot transmit the habit of active, critical thinking, but only the passive consumption (whether of television programs, ideas, or decision-making strategies) that is its mode of existence. In sum the family that has been formed by the Mechanistic Paradigm can teach its offspring only the Mechanistic Paradigm.

According to social psychologist Herbert Kelman (1963), there are three ways in which children learn from their parents (and people influence each other generally). The first, most primitive way is through *compliance.* Compliance is based on the hope of reward and the fear of punishment. To obtain compliance from a child, the parent must be actively present, ready to impose sanctions. The second, *identification,* occurs when the child follows the parents' teachings not so as to obtain the parents' approval, but to have a satisfying relationship with the parent by being like the parent or being what the parent likes. The child is influenced not by the parent's actual physical presence, but by an inner presence, a favorable image of the parent that the child adopts as a model: "I want to do it the way Daddy (Mommy) does" or "I want to be what my parents think of as a good child." The final, most developed stage is that of *internalization,* in which the child (adult) acts so as to achieve his or her own ends and maintain his or her own values. The parent's teachings are kept in mind, but it is no longer the parent's power or the parent's image that maintains them. Having internalized the parent's description of what actions lead to what consequences, the child is doing not "what Daddy (Mommy) does," but "what I do."

Normally, a child learns by all three processes in turn. The child accepts parental dictates (compliance). The child follows the parents' example (identification). The child shares experiences with other family members and draws conclusions which sometimes confirm and sometimes challenge parental authority (internalization). But in the modern family as described by Lasch, children do not have the experiences that lead to internalization. Children listen to their parents not because the parents have something to teach them that will help them face uncertainty (internalization), but because not to listen calls forth the primitive fear of pain, loss of nourishment, and death (compliance). There is nothing to do but to comply —or not comply. Children who do not learn what it means to apply rules flexibly can only apathetically comply or cynically "get away with" not complying. At best they can identify and "do what Daddy (Mommy) does." Alternately, they can identify with cult heroes outside the family and in so doing devalue the family.

In the mechanistic family, then, learning proceeds by compliance and sometimes identification. But the Probabilistic Paradigm and the decision-making strategies it entails are sufficiently complex that they require internalization. They must be learned by taking action and interpreting the consequences, not by playing roles and following rules. They cannot, therefore, be taught by many families today.

Thinking in the Midst of Pain and Fear: The Doctor's Office

The case of K. points to the close connection between the mechanistic pattern of family life and the way people think, feel, and act when they or others are ill. K.'s family, overwhelmed by the conditions of their lives, denied their child the nourishment he needed to survive. Hospital personnel, seeing a child crying out for a mother, wanted to do right by him. But they could not openly act on their desire to give him loving support in an uncertain situation. Instead they had to act out the professional role of objective experimenters pursuing a diagnosis. Themselves afraid of uncertainty, they took so much care to avoid the loss they feared that they created a situation where little could be gained. And yet in so doing they only acted (as well as thought and felt) as almost anyone else would.

There are a number of parallels between family relationships and the doctor-patient relationship. Both are intimate relationships in which people must together confront uncertainty, pain, and fear. Both involve decisions that require a capacity for critical thinking. In the doctor's office as at home people learn to make these decisions through compliance (with instructions), identification (with the doctor as gambler), and internalization (of strategies of critical thinking). The relationship between patient and doctor, like that between family members, can be an exchange or communal relationship.

The two relationships also intersect in several places, such as the "sick role" and caretaker role that family members take turns playing. The doctor's office can be a place where family relationships are either reproduced or changed, since the doctor's authority as a representative of science and as one who can heal pain can provide a model, whether mechanistic or probabilistic, for authority in the family. Today the dominant pattern is the mechanistic one. The science practiced in the doctor's office is usually mechanistic science, and healing proceeds along the lines of "One shot and it will all be gone." Pain here is not seen as something complex, something that may have many causes, something that one may have to live with. Rather it is seen as an offending particle to be surgically removed. From such experiences with physical pain the child learns to deal with other pains, other losses. If a finger hurting from a splinter has a single cause and a simple remedy, perhaps a broken heart does as well. Or so we think.

Not surprisingly, mechanistic thinking is especially evident in people's explanations of how they come to be ill. Traditional medicine has until recently focused on germs "out there in the air" as the primary if not sole cause of disease, as if people were powerless against such external causation. In the most extreme form of this kind of thinking—a paranoid thought disorder—one may find a person accusing others of poisoning him by injecting or implanting him with germs. Some exponents of holistic health swing equally wide in the opposite direction, claiming that the way a person lives is what brings on or prevents illness. Here the all-powerful "I" of narcissism becomes the sole cause of all that one experiences. Both sides are abstracting half-truths from a context of multiple causation, a context that includes (in addition to germs and personal lifestyle) environmental factors and people's relationships with one another in the workplace, the neighborhood, and the family.

Even when people do think in terms of multicausal explanations and probability, they may still revert to mechanistic thinking in the context of medicine, where life and health are at stake and pain and fear (particularly the fear of death) are ever-present. Even the most intelligent, well-informed, self-possessed people get scared when they are in a doctor's office.

Probably the doctor is a bit scared too. It is difficult for people to think rationally when they are scared. Instead they become rigid in their thinking. They go back to the way they used to think when they were children, a way of thinking that is less than fully conscious.

In speaking of narcissism and paranoia, we have noted an affinity between mechanistic thinking and unconscious processes. The fixation on single causes, the stark "either/or" quality of all three criteria of the Mechanistic Paradigm—in these elegant formulations of Newton's we hear echoes of a primitive response to life. Is it the case that the Mechanistic Paradigm during the past few centuries has shaped unconscious as well as conscious thinking, or that the Mechanistic Paradigm simply formalizes unconscious tendencies that are fixed in the human psyche? For our purposes it does not matter whether the chicken or the egg came first; the effects we observe are reciprocal. What matters is that when the fear of death is touched off, the unconscious reaction that occurs takes the form of mechanistic thinking. This close connection between thought and feeling means that a doctor who is concerned with the way patients think must also be concerned with the way patients feel.

Although it is in medicine that we find mechanistic thinking at its most extreme, it is also in medicine that there may be a hope for change. If people learned from their families how to cope with pain and fear without resorting to mechanistic ways of thinking, they wouldn't need to learn it in the stressful moments of illness. But since most people do not learn this in the family, they need to learn it somewhere else. The doctor's office (or wherever doctors and patients meet) provides a setting where people can confront these issues consciously and gain practice in probabilistic thinking. Both the efforts of probabilistically minded physicians like Dr. S. and the energy coming out of the "active patient" movement suggest that the doctor-patient relationship may be just the place to break old patterns of thought, feeling, and action and try new ones that will then make themselves felt in the family, the workplace, and the marketplace. Medicine has been very effective in teaching the Mechanistic Paradigm; perhaps now it can teach the Probabilistic Paradigm.

PART II

CHANCE
AND CHOICE

5

DECISION ANALYSIS
IN MEDICINE

When Dr. S. began his practice, he thought to himself, "No more K. cases!" In reviewing the case of K., he saw how mechanistic thinking could defeat the best of intentions. From hindsight the outcome had a tragic inevitability. What had been missing in that case was probabilistic thinking. S. would have to learn to think probabilistically and share his understanding with patients. He and they would have to learn to modify uncertain knowledge on the basis of new information (in the hope of making it less uncertain), while acting on the basis of information that would still be uncertain. Since one way of gaining new information was by acting, decision-making would become a matter of acting, understanding the results, and reevaluating; acting, understanding, and reevaluating—always with an awareness that a degree of uncertainty would remain, fluctuating but never disappearing.

This was easier said than done, especially for people who were not already comfortable dealing with uncertainty by means of probabilities. How could the Probabilistic Paradigm be translated into decision-making methods that people could use? What would those strategies look like when set down on paper? What would they sound like in discussions between husband and wife, parent and child, patient and doctor? What

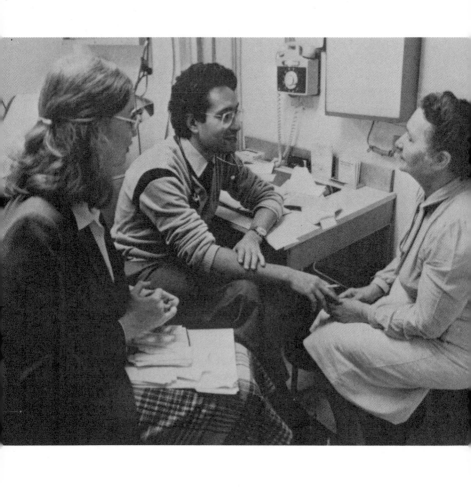

would they feel like to someone who was just learning them?

S. and his patients needed tools for turning the abstractions into concrete plans of action. When one such tool, decision analysis, first presented itself in medical publications (and in some medical-school curricula), S. naturally was receptive. Decision analysis had its origins in World War II when the Americans and British found that mathematicians could solve certain strategic and tactical problems better than the generals could. Out of this experience came a series of attempts, in which the mathematician John Von Neumann and the economist Oskar Morgenstern (1944) were pioneers, to apply systematic mathematical methods to decision-making. Decision analysis has been one outgrowth of these efforts. First used in economics, public-policy planning, and business investment and marketing, decision analysis is now being applied to other fields, including medicine. It is used in situations where one faces a sequence of choices, each having more or less uncertain consequences—a sequence so complex that people doubt their capacity to make the best decision intuitively (Raiffa, 1968).

In a medical situation, for example, one might test for one disease, get a negative result, try a treatment for another disease with no noticeable improvement, try another treatment, gain a partial alleviation of symptoms, and so forth. How can one keep all the relevant variables in mind simultaneously? How can one tell at the beginning of the sequence which choice is likely to lead to better outcomes several steps down the road? Decision analysis provides a way of laying out on paper the sequence of choices and their possible outcomes. By estimating the probability of each outcome at every step of the way and the desirability of the possible outcomes at the end of the sequence (e.g., death, complete recovery, partial disability, daily medications for life), one can mathematically calculate what, consistent with one's values, is the best action to take.

Some doctors look upon decision analysis as a promising tool because it seems to offer a way around all the factors that confuse people when they make decisions in medicine: economic pressures, family conflicts, and the pain and fear that accompany anyone to the doctor's office. With decision analysis it seems that, just by sitting down and working it all out on paper, a doctor and patient can coolly detach themselves from the hurly-burly of these pressures and just abstract the elements necessary for making a rational decision. Now that decision analysis (and its products, e.g., recommended approaches to particular diseases) is being made available to doctors and patients as the vanguard of probabilistic thinking, it is possible that each of us will meet up with it sooner or later in the doctor's office. Even if we don't use decision analysis ourselves, people around us will be using it, and their use of it will have consequences for our lives.

By learning about decision analysis, as S. did, we can decide intelligently whether, when, and how to use it. We can do so by seeing to what extent it is an aid and to what extent a barrier to thinking critically. In this and the following chapter we will be looking at S.'s experiences with decision analysis in order to see whether it can be of much day-to-day use to doctors and patients and whether (both in itself and as it is commonly applied) it is compatible with the three criteria of the Probabilistic Paradigm.

Whether or not we decide to make much use of decision analysis, it can still be a good learning tool (like the training wheels on a bicycle) for probabilistic thinking. Its formality can be helpful for the beginner (Dreyfus and Dreyfus, unpublished). Chance, choice, probability, value—all these are laid out in black and white. By going through the steps of decision analysis at least once we will know better what to keep in mind when we make decisions probabilistically in the more informal way that we refer to as gambling.

A Test Case

As the brief case example in Chapter 3 suggested, it doesn't make much sense to say, "Find the cause, then treat," when it comes to hypertension. As of now ninety to ninety-five percent of all cases of hypertension have no known cause, and in the remaining cases a cause may be discovered only with great difficulty. Nonetheless, in almost all cases elevated blood pressure can be reduced to acceptable levels, with a consequent reduction in complications and deaths. Still, treatment remains problematic. In a given case there may be reasons to consider drugs, life-style modifications, surgery, or no treatment at all. Moreover the effectiveness of treatment for a particular patient may vary greatly over time. For example, if an irregularity in the artery leading to one kidney *(renal artery stenosis, stenosis* means "narrowing") is corrected by surgery, the condition may recur a few years later in the artery leading to the other kidney. A drug regimen may keep a person's blood pressure controlled under some circumstances but not others. Indeed, it may take considerable experimentation before a combination of drugs is found that will stabilize the condition for a time. Even when an effective treatment is found, the patient, preferring the illness to the side effects of the drugs, often will stop taking the medication. Paradoxically, with hypertension it tends to be the treatment rather than the disease that initially brings unpleasant symptoms. Without treatment (except in severe cases) the patient may feel fine for many years. With treatment the patient may suffer side effects, such as drowsiness.

Hypertension is a very common chronic condition that people can live with for years without knowing they have it. A severe case may be brought to a doctor's attention when a person complains of headache, chest pain, dizziness, or shortness of breath, but the illness is most often discovered when a person's blood pressure is taken during a routine physical examination. It can have dramatic, sometimes fatal consequences, such as heart attack or stroke, but these typically do not occur until middle age or later. The doctor may be primarily concerned with preventing these harmful consequences of the illness in the future, whereas the patient may be primarily concerned with minimizing the inconvenience of the medication in the present. The very complexities involved in the diagnosis and treatment of hypertension together with its prevalence and potential consequences make it an important testing ground for decision analysis.

In his early years as a family doctor, at the time when he was investigating decision analysis, S. came up against an unusually challenging case of hypertension, that of Mrs. Pinelli, a thirty-five-year-old bookkeeper and divorced mother of three school-age children. When Mrs. Pinelli began to have severe headaches and chest pains, she went to S.'s nearby office, where a nurse took her blood pressure. "Just wait here a minute," said the nurse as she back-pedaled out of the examination room. "You can tell me!" Mrs. Pinelli called after her. "I know all about it! I've had it before!" Indeed, her blood pressure was 240/120, a dangerously high reading. (Although "normal" blood pressure depends on such factors as a person's sex, weight, and history, readings below 140/90 can roughly be considered normal.) She told Dr. S. that a few years earlier she had had another outbreak of severe hypertension, which had been "cured," according to the surgeon who operated on her, by a renal artery bypass operation. In taking her history it became apparent to S. that Mrs. Pinelli had been working at a furious pace. To make sure that she would rest, he hospitalized her. He was mainly concerned that she might have a heart attack or stroke at any time, and in the back of his mind he was also aware that he did not want to be held responsible for what might happen to her at home.

This was not the typical sort of hypertension (the kind that cannot be treated surgically) that S. was accustomed to dealing with. There was, therefore, some uncertainty, but there was also the fear that, should anything dreadful happen to this woman, he would be blamed. S. felt vulnerable, which was no surprise in the current climate of unreason, where controversy brings fears of malpractice claims.

In the hospital Mrs. Pinelli's blood pressure was quickly brought down with medications taken by mouth. Once back home with her children, Mrs. Pinelli began seeing Dr. S. at his office to work out a plan for controlling her blood pressure. He wanted to stabilize her condition with medications and then consult a specialist to see if this unusual case warranted further investigation.

After some delay he was able to obtain the records of Mrs. Pinelli's previous hospitalization. As is so often the case, he had to make decisions before the patient's records even arrived. The records told him much (though not all) of what he wanted to know about her medical history. Three years earlier Mrs. Pinelli had been found to have hypertension and had been placed on medications. But, as she put it, she "didn't have such a hot time with the pills," which made her drowsy. Because of her young age and severe hypertension, an X-ray study (arteriogram) of the arteries supplying her kidneys was performed. It revealed that a surgically correctable condition was present in both arteries, but was more severe in one than the other.

At that time surgery was looked upon as the preferred method of treatment for renal artery stenosis. "The way it was told to me," Mrs. Pinelli reported, "it could be cured by surgery. So why stay on pills the rest of my life?" She was referred to a surgeon at a leading teaching hospital, who successfully performed the renal artery bypass, and her blood pressure came down to normal. A few months later she had a falling-out with her doctor and stopped going back for follow-up visits. It was thus impossible to tell just when in the three intervening years she had relapsed.

S. had mixed feelings about being Mrs. Pinelli's doctor. He wanted to support her every step of the way, as long as she needed him, but he realized that to do so would require a good deal of work on his part. He knew that Mrs. Pinelli couldn't afford to pay for a fraction of the time he would spend making referrals, obtaining information, and so forth. Still, he wanted to give her complete care. If he gave her anything less, he would feel as if he were abandoning his patient.

His forebodings increased when Mrs. Pinelli began to express the same discontent with the medical regimen that had led her to have surgery the first time. The pills were making her dopey, she said. She couldn't do a good day's work, and she couldn't take proper care of her children. Besides, she insisted, it made no sense to try to treat her condition without looking at her kidneys, where the cause of her hypertension had previously been found.

Dr. S. agreed that she had a point, but did not want to rush into expensive and painful tests that might well not show anything. Instead he suggested that Mrs. Pinelli use decision analysis as an aid in making an informed decision. He delegated the task of conducting the lengthy briefing in this method to Jeanne Aaron, medical student then in training at his practice, who did some preliminary research to clarify the choices and the probabilities. She would then sit down with Mrs. Pinelli and lay out the options, so that Mrs. Pinelli could reach a decision on the basis of her own values and principles.

When Mrs. Pinelli returned for her next visit, Jeanne was ready. She explained to the patient the principles of decision analysis and the main courses of action open to her. "We all agree, don't we," Jeanne said, "that it doesn't pay just to do nothing about this." She looked up at Mrs. Pinelli for confirmation. Mrs. Pinelli gave the expected nod, but did she agree? From her earlier episode to the present she had shown a clear preference for doing nothing except when she developed symptoms that she couldn't ignore. Then, when she had to do something, she looked for a quick and total solution through surgery. S. and Jeanne, notwithstanding their own belief that drug therapy probably was the best choice for Mrs. Pinelli, would need to be aware of her tendency to oscillate between avoidance and the search for a magical cure.

Jeanne, however, tried to deal with Mrs. Pinelli on a rational level without first working with her to establish a shared sense of what it meant to be rational. She reviewed with her the problems connected with surgery. The fact that one renal artery had been bypassed was no guarantee that the artery to the other kidney (which was also, but less severely affected) would not become narrower in the future. Progression of such lesions (pathological distortions) commonly occurred only up to about the age of forty. Until then the picture could always change, and not for the better. If Mrs. Pinelli stayed on drugs for another five years before having surgery, she stood a much better chance of avoiding having to go through the operation yet again. Furthermore there was now a clear preference to turn to surgery at any age only as a last resort. The issue of recurrence after surgery did indeed concern Mrs. Pinelli. "I was never even told that there was any chance of its recurring," she said bitterly. But she had something else on her mind as well. "Someone" *had* told her that "no one knows anything unless the arteriogram is done."

A tension developed between the two women as they staked out their positions:

J.A.: Tell me how you feel about taking medications.

MRS. P.: I don't like it.

J.A.: How much don't you like it?

MRS. P.: A lot. It just seems like every time I turn around I'm popping pills.

J.A.: Would you feel better with just one pill?

MRS. P.: Better than with what I'm taking now.

J.A.: So it's the number of pills that's bothering you.

MRS. P.: Yes, and the idea that I have to depend on them for the rest of my life. But I'll take them for the rest of my life if the arteriogram says I have to.

J.A.: What if you only have to depend on them for five years, and then have surgery when it's more likely to cure your hypertension for a longer time? How much would it bother you to have surgery now and then have your blood pressure go up again, the way it did this time?

MRS. P.: Couldn't it be that this thing just flared up again? I mean, do I have to keep taking all these pills, or can we cut down on them once my blood pressure is down?

Throughout the session Mrs. Pinelli's hopes for a quick and simple answer were heard (and who could blame her?). She and Jeanne discussed the possibility that she was not having a relapse of renal artery stenosis at all, but rather a completely unrelated episode of essential hypertension (i.e., hypertension with no known anatomical cause or surgical cure). Both of them jumped at this explanation—Jeanne because it would mean that an arteriogram would be useless, Mrs. Pinelli because she mistakenly thought that a form of hypertension that didn't require surgery might be cured, not just controlled, by medication. She clung to the hope of someday being able to stop the medications.

When Dr. S. returned, Jeanne summed up the discussion for

him. "Mrs. Pinelli's main concern about the pills is the number she has to take," said Jeanne. "It really bothers her to take all these different pills every time she sits down to eat." Indeed it did, for as Mrs. Pinelli put it, "Sometimes you don't eat at all when you're taking all those pills." But her *main* concern, as she had made clear, was with having to be dependent on pills for the rest of her life. Jeanne also told S. that "Mrs. Pinelli is frustrated by the way her first operation turned out. She went into it thinking it was a permanent cure. So she's not sure she wants to go through surgery a second time until there's a better chance that this won't happen again." This was all very logical to Jeanne, but it was not Mrs. Pinelli's logic.

Mrs. Pinelli was indeed frustrated and bitter. Although her surgeon years earlier might have told her that her hypertension could recur, all she had heard was that she was "cured." That was all she had wanted to know while she was enjoying the luxury of not having to worry about doctors and pills. Now she felt betrayed. She paid no attention to the fact that her chances for a surgical cure would get better in years to come. Rather, she demanded all the more insistently the surgical cure that she still believed in, but felt she had been cheated out of. She had in fact raised several objections to Jeanne's idea of waiting until she was forty to have surgery, but it was as if Jeanne had not heard her. People have their own ways of talking and their own ways of listening.

With Dr. S. in the room an uneasy truce took hold as both the student (who had been doing most of the talking) and the patient deferred to the doctor. Mrs. Pinelli, who was not as anxious to confront S. as she had been with Jeanne, appeared more open to considering all the options. Taking his cue from Jeanne, S. indicated that newly developed medications might make it possible in the coming years for Mrs. Pinelli to get by on one or two pills a day. Mrs. Pinelli tried to bargain with him, saying, "If we can just get it down *close* to normal, can't we stop the pills for a while and see what happens?" S. told her, "With the kind of hypertension that you have it would be very unlikely that that would work." But he assured her that she had a right to have surgery if she so decided, and that whatever decision she made need not be considered permanent. "It's not as if it's signed, sealed, and delivered once and for all," he told her. "There are new drugs, new operations, and there is new information coming out all the time. The idea is to make a good decision now and then review it from time to time. And there's never any one right thing to do. For the time being you're safe, because your blood pressure is controlled. As long as that's the case, you can take your time and be sure you know what you want to do before you do it. You don't have to rush your decision."

Jeanne added, "Just wait till we do the decision analysis! That'll clear everything up." The three of them closed ranks around that sentiment and went through the decision analysis that Jeanne had prepared.

The Procedure

When Jeanne Aaron did the decision analysis with Mrs. Pinelli, she went through a standard procedure, parts of which involved the patient's participation. We will not draw full detailed diagrams or work out all the calculations here. Rather, we will outline the procedure and suggest what each step entailed for Mrs. Pinelli, Dr. S., and Jeanne.

Drawing the Tree

Jeanne's first step in preparing the decision analysis was to construct a *decision tree*. A decision tree is a diagram that shows a set of possible actions to take, the possible results of each, another set of choices stemming from these results, their possible results, and so forth. The tree consists of a series of "choice points," where the decision-maker decides what to do, alternating with "chance points," where the world (or reality, or fate, or nature) responds to the decision-maker's action in one of a number of ways. In the treatment of hypertension at least four initial courses of action might be considered: (1) drug therapy; (2) life-style modifications such as diet (e.g., low salt), exercise, or stress-reduction techniques such as meditation; (3) testing for surgically correctable causes; (4) doing nothing now and living with the subsequent consequences of the illness.

Jeanne wanted to present Mrs. Pinelli with a decision tree that would be easy to understand, yet would do the job. She and S. went over the four main options and decided, without consulting Mrs. Pinelli, that doing nothing would be unacceptable and life-style changes alone would be insufficient. Jeanne accordingly began her tree with two basic choices, as shown in Figure 5–1. She then filled out the branches with possible results and subsequent choices. "It will be simpler for her this way," she told S. "We'll make it easy for her."

This diagram is simplified for demonstration purposes, since the actual tree might involve taking more than one action at a time. For example, S. undoubtedly would give Mrs. Pinelli drugs to control her blood pressure while she was undergoing tests. Moreover, "drug treatment" represents many possible choices, not just one. However, S. and Jeanne began the "drug" branch of the tree with what seemed from their experience to be the best choice of drugs; they drew later branches on the tree to represent other combinations of drugs in case the first did not keep Mrs. Pinelli's blood pressure controlled. Most doctors, for example, begin the treatment of hypertension with diuretics— drugs which, among their several effects, promote salt loss from the body. Once S. and Jeanne had mapped out the possible diagnosis and treatment on the decision tree, they had to ask themselves and Mrs. Pinelli some questions about probability and value and perform a few calculations to come up with a strategy for action.

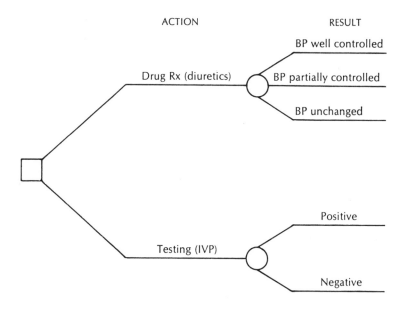

Partial Decision Tree
for Hypertension—Mrs. Pinelli

ACTION   RESULT

                                               BP well controlled

        Drug Rx (diuretics)   BP partially controlled

                                               BP unchanged

                                               Positive

        Testing (IVP)

                                               Negative

FIGURE 5-1

Prior Probability Estimate

S. and Jeanne first asked: "What is the prior probability that the patient has the disease in question?" In order to figure out which tests have the best chance of revealing useful information and which treatments have the best chance of success, it is necessary to estimate how likely it is that the patient has one disease or another. In some cases the doctor and patient must estimate probabilities for several possible underlying conditions so that they can direct their diagnostic and therapeutic efforts toward those that are most likely to be present.

Probabilities may be estimated with the help of statistical

tables on the frequency of occurrence of the disease in question for patients in certain categories of age, sex, symptoms, and so forth. They may also be estimated subjectively, on the basis of the patient's understanding of his or her past history and the doctor's experience with other patients and intuitions about this patient. Even when tables of data *are* consulted, the doctor and patient must make critical judgments about how reliable the tables are, whether the information in the tables is up to date, and how the statistics apply to the unique case of this particular patient. Even when one looks up numbers, one is still at best making educated guesses.

Mrs. Pinelli knew that she had hypertension. What she wanted to know was whether she had one of several rare types of hypertension that could sometimes be corrected by surgery. In particular she wanted to know if she still had the condition that was diagnosed at the time of her previous episode: *renal artery stenosis* (RAS). When one or both of the renal arteries is partially pinched off, high blood pressure can occur.

Given that at least ninety to ninety-five percent of all cases of hypertension are of the "essential" variety, it follows that renal artery stenosis is not very common. Its statistical frequency among both men and women with hypertension is only four percent. Since Mrs. Pinelli had a prior history of this condition, S. and Jeanne judged the probability of its being the cause of her hypertension now as seventy-five percent.

Revised Probability Estimate

The second type of assessment that S. and Jeanne had to make was: "Given additional information, what is the revised probability that the patient has the disease in question?" In an uncertain world we are always adjusting our probability estimates on the basis of new information. Today's newly revised probability estimate becomes a prior probability estimate for tomorrow's information-gathering. For example, before Mrs. Pinelli had her blood pressure taken or showed any symptoms of hypertension, the probability of her having RAS was practically nil. Once she was found to have high blood pressure, the probability jumped to four percent. That figure could in turn be revised by looking at her history as well as by undertaking further tests and treatments. The "risk factor" charts that appear on doctors' waiting-room walls testify to the fact that many different kinds of "signs"—age, sex, weight, family medical history, personal medical history, occupational stress, exposure to disease carriers or disease-causing agents, diet, exercise, alcohol and tobacco use, appearance of symptoms—can raise or lower by a few percentage points the probability of a person's having a particular disease.

By the time a medical decision analysis is begun, many of these factors (vital statistics, life-style, symptoms, prior history, family history, preliminary tests) are already known. These are incorporated into the estimate of the probability that the person has the disease. Further refinements tend to come from test results and from the observation of how the disease responds to treatment (or what "natural course" it takes without treatment). S. knew how Mrs. Pinelli felt, how old she was, how much she weighed, how she spent her work and leisure time, whether she had previously had RAS, and what her blood pressure reading was. What remained was to prescribe medication or administer more sensitive tests and then see what happened. S. still wouldn't be *certain* whether or not she had RAS, but (at the cost of time, money, and possible side effects of testing or treatment) he would have more to go on.

The ways in which choice and chance combine to bring about good or bad outcomes are shown in general terms by this simplified decision tree (Fig. 5–2). This tree presupposes, just as doctors and patients usually do, that test results are always accurate. It shows that the decision to treat or not to treat (without testing) may be right or wrong, but it makes it appear that the decision to test is never wrong. Indeed, if test results were always accurate, testing would always be the best choice (provided that there existed some real doubt to be resolved by testing, that the condition the test might reveal had some known means of treatment, and that the costs of testing—time, money, pain, risk of complications—were not excessively high). Under the Probabilistic Paradigm, however, it is recognized that no

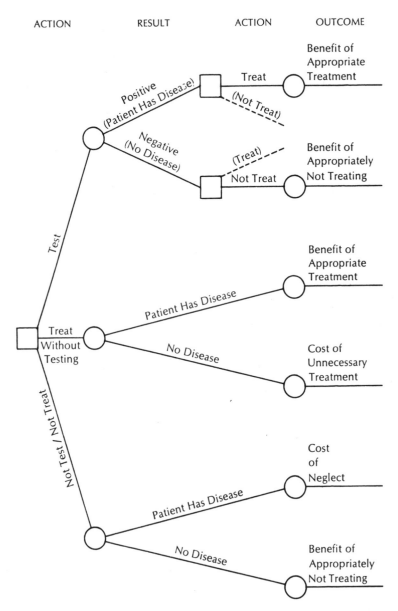

Outcomes of Testing and Treatment Options
(when accuracy of test is assumed)

ACTION   RESULT   ACTION   OUTCOME

Positive (Patient Has Disease)
Treat — Benefit of Appropriate Treatment
(Not Treat)

Negative (No Disease)
(Treat)
Not Treat — Benefit of Appropriately Not Treating

Test

Treat Without Testing

Patient Has Disease — Benefit of Appropriate Treatment

No Disease — Cost of Unnecessary Treatment

Not Test / Not Treat

Patient Has Disease — Cost of Neglect

No Disease — Benefit of Appropriately Not Treating

FIGURE 5-2

one test constitutes an *experimentum crucis* that resolves the diagnosis once and for all. A lab result is just another piece of information, and does not guarantee certainty. Most diagnostic tests are marketed with reminders of how often a test result will be in error. However, in practice many physicians do not pay sufficient attention to this information.

This state of affairs can be represented on the decision tree by substituting the branch shown in Figure 5–3 for the "test" branch in Figure 5–2. Along with the costs of unnecessary or inappropriately withheld treatment, the tree now shows the costs of inaccurate or misleading test results—those which identify a disease that isn't there (false positive) or fail to identify one that is there (false negative).

Even a small percentage of false positive results can make a test almost meaningless in cases where the prior probability of the patient's having the disease is low. Here is a case that S. remembered from his decision analysis course. Suppose that a certain type of cancer occurs in five out of every thousand people. Now assume that ninety-five percent of the people *with* this cancer will have a positive test result for the disease, while ninety-five percent of those *without* cancer will have a negative test result. On a National Cancer Day testing program at work you get a positive result. What do you estimate is the probability that you have the disease?

Most people's estimates are way off. Out of a large group of practicing physicians, more than half thought the probability was greater than fifty percent. Actually it is just under nine percent. Among all the people taking the test, most of those who get positive results do not have cancer. Common sense doesn't seem to work very well in interpreting test results of this sort. We can, however, make use of a mathematical formula that the Reverend Thomas Bayes proposed for just such purposes in 1763. We will not spell out Bayes's Theorem here; it can be found in any textbook of probability theory. What is important for understanding Mrs. Pinelli's case, and decision analysis in general, is the fact that test results must be interpreted in conjunction with other probabilistic information. When we make use of a diagnostic test, we are going from one probability esti-

Outcomes of Testing
(when accuracy of test is uncertain)

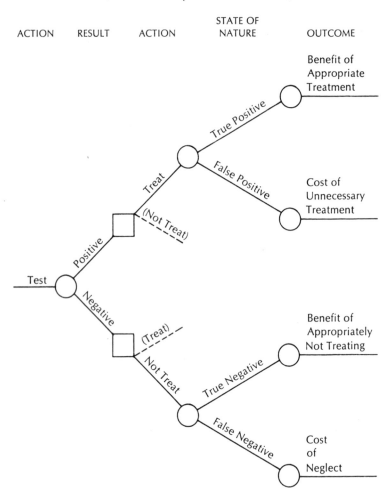

Definitions:

State of Nature: underlying reality
True Positive: disease is present; test result is positive
False Positive: disease is not present; test result is positive
True Negative: disease is not present; test result is negative
False Negative: disease is present; test result is negative

FIGURE 5-3

mate (the prior probability) to another (the revised probability) via a third (the information yielded by the test).

For renovascular hypertension the tests in question are the *intravenous pyelogram* (IVP) and *arteriogram,* two X-ray procedures (using injected dye) described in Chapter 3. Usually a doctor who suspects RAS or a related disorder will first do an IVP, which can reveal kidney malfunctioning. If the IVP suggests that there may be an insufficient blood supply to the kidney from the renal artery, the doctor may proceed to do an arteriogram, an uncomfortable and slightly risky procedure that gives an X-ray picture of the artery itself. The two tests are part of what is called a "hypertensive workup." In some cases they can provide grounds for going ahead with renal artery bypass surgery.

On the other hand, the accuracy rate for these procedures must be taken into account. With the IVP, for example, we can estimate from past experience that only seventy-eight percent of hypertensive patients *with* RAS will have a positive IVP (which means that there will be twenty-two percent false negatives), while ninety percent of those *without* RAS will have a negative IVP (which means that there will be ten percent false positives). Using Bayes's Theorem, we can calculate that a positive IVP would increase the probability of Mrs. Pinelli's having RAS from seventy-five to ninety-six percent, while a negative IVP would reduce the probability to forty-two percent. For Mrs. Pinelli a positive IVP would suggest that an arteriogram might be useful diagnostically. It would not, however, dictate the decision to do an arteriogram—especially since the arteriogram has its own error rate and since even a positive arteriogram is no guarantee of a successful surgical cure. Most doctors, in fact, now would advise against surgery for people whose hypertension can be controlled with medication. Because the primary purpose of the IVP and the arteriogram is to identify a surgically correctable condition, and because at Mrs. Pinelli's age the probabilities do not favor surgery, she and S. would choose the workup only if her values strongly favored either having the diagnosis for its own sake or seeking a surgical solution (which, as before, might only be temporary) (Pauker, 1976).

Probabilities of Outcomes

Having made the best estimates they could (using all the available information) of the probability that their patient had each of the diseases in question (in this case, renovascular versus essential hypertension), S. and Jeanne then made a third kind of assessment: "Assuming that the patient has a given disease (or no disease), what is the probability of each of the outcomes that may occur if a given test or treatment (or none at all) is administered?" In other words, on the decision tree each "state of nature" (e.g., the presence or absence of a disease) leads to a "choice point" (e.g., taking or not taking a particular action). That choice will have further "chance" outcomes—i.e., outcomes for which probabilities can be estimated. The estimating is done in the same way as with diagnostic probabilities, that is, by subjective, critical judgment, sometimes with the assistance of statistical data obtained from experimental studies or compilations of clinical experience. Subjective judgment, based on the doctor's own clinical experience and the patient's personal experience, is needed to decide which statistical categories are relevant to the case at hand.

These probability assessments, together with the patient's eventual value assessments, constitute a way of measuring the costs and benefits of each action under consideration. Costs and benefits include not only the true or false information gained from a test and the success or failure of a treatment, but also such factors as lost time, physical strain, and the risk of infection. Some of these side effects (e.g., whether a patient will have an allergic reaction to a medication) must be assessed probabilistically. Others, such as the monetary cost of the test or treatment, occur so dependably that they can be entered on the decision tree as "tolls" along with whatever other outcomes the test or treatment may have. A bottle of pills, for example, might or might not bring down Mrs. Pinelli's blood pressure, but she would have to pay the pharmacist to find out.

On Mrs. Pinelli's decision tree the two initial branches split off into many smaller branches as choices led to outcomes that necessitated further choices that led to new outcomes, etc. If one drug or combination of drugs didn't work, another would be tried. If the IVP or the arteriogram did not reveal an operable condition, then a nonsurgical option would have to be pursued. At those points the "test" branch of the tree, which had one branch leading all the way to surgery, split off into other branches that looked like the initial "drug treatment" branch. On all the branches "choice points" alternated with "chance points" until a set of final outcomes was reached, these being the estimated levels at which Mrs. Pinelli's blood pressure would eventually be stabilized given various combinations of actions and consequences.

Finally, since S. and Jeanne could not reasonably expect Mrs. Pinelli to assign values to blood pressure readings like 180/120 or 130/90, they had to translate these figures into descriptions of probable consequences for her life. Included in the overall picture were such factors as life expectancy, degree of disability, discomfort, and cost. Mrs. Pinelli could attach a value to a scenario such as "normal life span without stroke or heart disease" or "$——— a year in medical expenses, ——— side effects of drugs, and ——— probability of stroke or heart disease."

Value Assessment

The fourth kind of assessment required by decision analysis, one that Mrs. Pinelli had to make for herself, was "What value does the patient place on each possible outcome?" (In some cases the values of the patient's family or the doctor may also be relevant.) Mrs. Pinelli had to give numerical value assessments. One way to obtain them would have been to ask her to rate each possible outcome, for example, on a 0 to 100 scale. A score of 0 could be given to the worst possible outcome (immediate death, which is a four percent probability with renal artery bypass surgery and a one-tenth percent probability with the arteriogram), while a score of 100 could be given to the best possible outcome (living out her life without serious complications from hypertension). She then would assign numbers between 0 and 100 to descriptions of the other possible life scenarios.

It was not so easy, however, for Mrs. Pinelli to evaluate on a one-dimensional scale such diverse scenarios as "one month of urinary frequency, then stably controlled hypertension," "$180 per year, drowsiness, plus controlled hypertension," "develop nonfatal coronary artery disease in two years," and "develop fatal coronary artery disease in twelve years." How could she compare all these things on one scale? And how could S. and Jeanne be sure that she really thought that an outcome she called a "60" was as much better than a "40" as an "80" was better than a "60"?

A procedure called the "lottery method" (Raiffa, 1968) has been devised to help people assign numbers to outcomes in a meaningful way, as well as to take account of people's attitudes toward risk. The procedure involves setting up a hypothetical lottery between the best and worst possible outcomes and asking the patient to choose between playing the lottery and having the outcome that is being evaluated. The probabilities of the two extreme outcomes in the lottery are adjusted until the patient is indifferent to the choice between taking the outcome under consideration and taking his or her chance on the lottery.

The lottery method can be presented as a game, "The Devil and Mrs. Pinelli." A mysterious stranger with an uncanny resemblance to Dr. S. appears before Mrs. Pinelli and says, "Would you like to play a game?" He then produces a big jar full of black and white marbles. From the jar he takes out various combinations of them, always totaling one hundred marbles, but in different proportions of black to white. He then mentions one of the possible outcomes that Mrs. Pinelli faces. "If I give you a choice," he tells her, "between developing nonfatal coronary artery disease in two years and playing a lottery in which you have as many chances of the best possible outcome (living the rest of your natural life without serious complications) as the number of white marbles I hold out, and as many chances of the worst possible outcome (immediate death) as the number of black marbles I hold out, which do you choose?"

Clearly if the Devil holds out a hundred black marbles and no white ones, Mrs. Pinelli will choose the certainty of developing nonfatal coronary artery disease in two years. If he holds out a hundred white marbles and no black ones, she will choose the lottery. But as he tries various proportions of white to black between these two extremes, she becomes less sure of her preference. Finally he hits upon a combination—say, sixty white marbles and forty black—where she just doesn't care whether she gets to play the lottery or the certainty of the intermediate outcome. The two are of equal value to her. Getting coronary artery disease in two years is worth as much to her as a sixty percent chance of living out her life without complications due to hypertension and a forty percent chance of immediate death. In doing this procedure she will have assigned a value of 60 to the outcome, "developing nonfatal coronary artery disease in two years." Continuing in this way, she estimates the values of all the listed outcomes.

Calculating Expected Values

Once the four kinds of probability and value assessments have been made, probabilities can be entered on the decision tree for all possible outcomes along the various branches, along with values for those that represent "final," real-life consequences for the patient. The next step is to calculate the *expected value* (or expected utility) of each possible outcome. In commonsense terms, the question, "How much is this outcome worth to me?" boils down to "How much would I like or dislike this if it happened?" *and* "How likely is it to happen?" The expected value, then, is the value of a possible outcome multiplied by the probability that it will happen. If, under a given set of conditions, "developing nonfatal coronary artery disease in two years," to which Mrs. Pinelli has given a value of 60, has a ten percent probability of occurrence, then its expected value is 6. If it has a probability of twenty percent, then its expected value is 12. If we could repeat the same choice many times, the average result in the long run would be close to the expected value.

Making the Decision

At each of the final "chance points" on the decision tree the expected values of all the branches coming out of that chance point are added up to get an overall expected value for the choice that leads to that chance point. (For example, if at one of the final chance points of Mrs. Pinelli's decision tree there are three branches with expected values of 72, 18, and 3, the expected value of the choice leading to that chance point is 93.) There will be more than one such choice at that point on the decision tree. The choice with the highest expected value is kept, and its expected value is passed on to the branch that leads to that "choice point" from the previous chance point. Thus at any chance point we choose the action with the highest expected value. Occasionally there may be reasons for doing other than maximizing the expected value, as when we want to go for the best possible outcome or avoid at all costs the worst. Normally, though, we would choose to maximize the expected value, especially since to do otherwise would leave us open to having a Dutch Book (a sure losing bet) made against us, as explained in Chapter 2.

Working back along the branches of the tree in this manner, we chart a strategy for action that tells us the best choice to make at each choice point in response to whatever has happened at the previous chance point. With this strategy we are anticipating all eventualities that have been incorporated into the decision tree. The strategy indicates which of the initial options leads to the highest expected value. In Mrs. Pinelli's case, not surprisingly, it favored taking medications for blood pressure control, as opposed to testing for renal artery stenosis.

Algorithms

When S. had met Mrs. Pinelli, his first thought had been "If only there were an algorithm!" When decision analysis has been done for a number of similar cases, it is sometimes possible to "package" the resulting strategies in the form of an *algorithm,* a sequence of instructions for solving a problem. Algorithms are based on prior explorations of the probabilities and values involved in a given set of situations. An algorithm may take the form of a general decision tree (like the one for hypertension) which can be adapted to the needs of particular patients, thus saving doctor and patient the prohibitive effort of structuring a new tree for each case. Or it may simply be a table of therapeutic recommendations for patients classified according to age, sex, symptoms, diagnosis, and so forth.

Successful examples of the use of decision analysis in medicine have led some doctors to hope that medical practice in the future will be conducted increasingly with the aid of algorithms. Ideally, they speculate, a patient like Mrs. Pinelli should be able to "plug in" her values to a preexisting algorithm for hypertension and, whether by consulting tables or by feeding the data into a computer, come up with recommendations for action at each choice point. As yet, though, there was no algorithm for Mrs. Pinelli, and there might not ever be one. So Jeanne Aaron had to work out the decision tree from scratch and go through it with Mrs. Pinelli from beginning to end.

Decision Analysis Spurned

Mrs. Pinelli wasn't too happy with the "answer" (predictable though it was) that came out of the decision analysis. She agreed, however, to think things over for a week, during which Jeanne would find out whatever additional facts might help answer her questions. "This is quite a disease," said Mrs. Pinelli.

The next week, however, when Mrs. Pinelli came in, she immediately said, "Look, I want to see a specialist." S. sent her to Dr. Alan Berg, a prominent internist who specialized in hypertension and related conditions. He and S. were old friends and fellow students who had remained on the best of terms.

Dr. Berg chatted amiably with his new patient and then got down to business. He agreed to do some preliminary tests, including an IVP, but said that in all likelihood he would be treating her high blood pressure with medications. The interview proceeded smoothly until Dr. Berg concluded, "Unless I am satisfied that I have exhausted every possible avenue of medical treatment, I will not be comfortable sending you back to surgery. I think we can treat this thing well enough medically to prevent you from needing surgery again." Mrs. Pinelli shot back, "How are you going to prevent me from feeling like a zombie all the time?"

This was the first indication Dr. Berg had of Mrs. Pinelli's anger at doctors and medicine. Questioning her further, he soon realized that what she wanted was to exhaust every possible avenue of *surgical* treatment before going back to medications. Acting as the "good" doctor who was responsive to his patient's wishes, he went against his own judgment and put Mrs. Pinelli in the hospital for ten days. There he put her through a complete workup (including an arteriogram after a negative IVP) which he could have predicted would be inconclusive and wasteful—to the tune of thousands of dollars taken from the pockets of insurance subscribers. He did it to satisfy Mrs. Pinelli's desire to "know for sure" so that she might then become more amenable to taking medications.

S., meanwhile, wondered what was happening. When he found out that Mrs. Pinelli was in the hospital being tested, he was irked. His instructions, it seemed, had been ignored. The investment he had made in engaging Mrs. Pinelli in critical thinking was going down the drain. So he telephoned Dr. Berg and said, "Hey, Alan, I want my patient back! I only referred her to you for consultation."

It turned out that S., instead of writing Dr. Berg a note, had simply checked off on the referral form a box marked, "Please see and follow with us." Dr. Berg, who later said that he was too busy to read check marks on forms, had assumed that S. was giving him full discretion to handle the case. Although he often had patients referred to him by family doctors from upstate, he did not think of patients in the city as having family doctors. When local patients came to him, he usually ended up becoming "their doctor."

Dr. Berg apologized for the misunderstanding, sent S. the test results, and told Mrs. Pinelli that from now on she would be going back to her family doctor. This development was as big a surprise to her as it had been to Dr. Berg. She, too, had thought that Dr. Berg was now her doctor, her case being of the sort that required a specialist's attention. But she went where she was told to go.

The arteriogram showed that (as would have been expected after a normal IVP) Mrs. Pinelli's previous arterial bypass was still working properly and that there was no clear indication of any progression of stenosis in the other renal artery. There would be no surgery. Back in S.'s office, Mrs. Pinelli reported that, with the catheters and the hot dye going through her body, the arteriogram had been like "a torture rack." She didn't ever want to have one again. But at least it had reconciled her to taking pills for the rest of her life. Still, she made wistful allusions to new pills and new diagnostic tests that would be coming out in the next few years. (There was hope for surgery yet!) In the meantime, on Dr. Berg's suggestion S. was trying out some pills that didn't make her feel so sleepy as before. His strategy was to increase the dosage gradually so as to bring down her blood pressure without knocking her out. Her pressure was still only partially controlled (about 155/100), but he thought it better to achieve a partial success than to bring on disagreeable side effects that would lead the patient to stop taking the medication.

Mrs. Pinelli felt the same way. She was more comfortable with S. and Dr. Berg than with her previous doctor, who had threatened her with heart attacks and strokes if she missed taking one pill. "Dr. S. knows that I skip a pill once in a while," she confided to a nurse in his office. "He knows that it's my choice and that I know what I'm doing. Can you imagine what it feels like to have to walk around the room to keep from falling asleep—and then to hold a pill in your hand that you know will make you feel even *more* that way?"

Mrs. Pinelli indicated what her deepest concerns were when she said, "I'll be satisfied to keep my blood pressure not too far above normal. I'll chance what happens later. If I die when I'm fifty because of this, by then my kids will be able to take care of themselves. My youngest is six years old. Now is when I have to take care of her. If the pills make me so groggy that I can't work, or if my blood pressure goes so high that it kills me, what will she do?"

Mrs. Pinelli could have expressed these values through the decision analysis procedure. Her concern for her children would have had as much weight in her decisions as she chose to give it. Yet she didn't care to find this out. She was willing to lie still for the arteriogram, but she wouldn't sit still for the decision analysis. She viewed the procedure as biased (as Jeanne presented it), abstract, and irrelevant. When Jeanne had told her the four basic options, she had said, "Oh, I know all that stuff already." Somehow the procedure didn't give her the room she needed to express her own concerns in her own language.

Decision analysis assumes that a series of decisions extending into the future, although admittedly influenced by intervening events, can be anticipated and structured in advance. It is not easy to adjust a decision tree when people come to conceive of later decisions differently after having experienced the consequences of prior decisions. For example, in Mrs. Pinelli's case each decision introduced new psychological factors which predisposed the patient and doctors to make subsequent choices that were not anticipated by the decision analysis. In retrospect it is hard to see how they could have been anticipated.

Take, for example, Dr. S.'s decision to hospitalize Mrs. Pinelli immediately. Her blood pressure had to be brought down quickly, and S. wanted her to be in a place where she could be monitored. Nothing, however, was actually done in the hospital that couldn't have been done in her home or in his office. Even if she had confirmed his worst fears by having a stroke, it is not clear that she would have been much better off having it in the hospital. Yet S.'s reflex reaction was (as almost any doctor's would have been) to hospitalize her, not only because she somehow felt that she would be safer in the hospital, but also so as to protect himself against possible professional criticism. Since his decision *was* a reflex reaction, it is unlikely that he could have made his motivations accessible to decision analysis ahead of time.

That initial decision set in motion a chain of unintended events that led to the unnecessary arteriogram. When S. put Mrs. Pinelli in the hospital, he reduced his own contact with and influence over her and exposed her to the influence of house officers, nurses, and technicians who expressed their own version of an aggressive surgeon's mentality: "When you test, you can see, and to see is to know. Once you know, you can cut, and to cut is to cure." This visual, tangible imagery made a powerful impression on Mrs. Pinelli. Ironically, this woman who was so angry at doctors and hospitals accepted (as a result of her present and previous hospitalizations as well as her whole life experience in this society) much of their picture of reality.

By the time Mrs. Pinelli saw Dr. Berg, she had been given so much contradictory information (as when she heard Dr. S. arguing with another doctor in the hospital) that she felt all the more justified in her impatience and in her demand for a precise diagnosis, which Dr. Berg felt powerless to resist. When he implicitly reinforced her "visual" image of diagnosis by authorizing an IVP, he may have unwittingly made the next diagnostic operation, the arteriogram, almost a *fait accompli.* Although both he and Dr. S. had told Mrs. Pinelli that an arteriogram was not likely to be a useful procedure for her, the message she kept in mind was one that she got from a house officer: "You can see some things on the IVP, but you can see everything on the arteriogram. If you have gone this far, you might as well go all the way."

Going to the hospital, insisting on seeing a specialist, having an IVP and then an arteriogram—each decision almost automatically touched off the next rather than being viewed in isolation and made on its own merits, as in decision analysis. All concerned made decisions by and large unconsciously and sometimes irrationally. Their reasons for making the choices they did (e.g., S.'s concern that his actions be professionally and legally defensible, Dr. Berg's respect for "patient's rights," Mrs. Pinelli's sense of responsibility toward her family) generally made sense at some level. Decision analysis ideally would have reflected such concerns. It would have been difficult if not impossible, however, for these three people to include in the decision analysis all the various and sundry considerations that ultimately guided their actions, some of which they were not conscious of, some of which they would not have been comfortable dealing with explicitly and publicly, and some of which they never could have predicted would come up.

Throughout the case, decisions were influenced by unexpected events and situational factors. The patient and her two doctors were operating in the context of disagreement, inadequate communication, and territorial conflicts among doctors; a clash of assumptions and perceptions between patient and doctor; a changing understanding of the treatment of the disease in question; and a health-insurance system that provides no incentive for patients and doctors to consider the cost of unnecessary procedures and no reimbursement for the time a doctor spends speaking with a patient. These contextual issues were not extraneous to the decisions at hand: they were essential elements in those decisions.

Mrs. Pinelli's "decision analysis bypass operation" left Jeanne Aaron disappointed and frustrated. Jeanne was still "high" on decision analysis. "It would have worked if she had only listened!" she exclaimed to S. "After all, it gave her what turned out to be the right answer!"

S. wasn't so sure. He realized that he and Jeanne, inexperienced as they were at the new technique, might not have presented it as clearly as possible. Maybe they hadn't given it a fair trial. On the other hand, what experience he had was beginning to teach him that one cannot say much about any tool or instrument without considering the contexts in which people use it. It had required an expensive, futile technical procedure (the diagnostic workup) to satisfy Mrs. Pinelli that she didn't need surgery. S. had tried to satisfy her instead with another technical procedure—decision analysis. It would have been better, he realized, if he could have gotten through to her in her own language. "People often say that a picture is worth a thousand words," he might have told her, "and you may think that a picture of your renal artery is worth a thousand dollars. But you know, sometimes you can see something and still not be sure what it is. There may be many ways of interpreting it. Even looking at a picture involves a gamble."

In the future S. would not take for granted, as he had with Mrs. Pinelli, that his patients' understanding of the decision-making process was—or should be—the same as his. Even in cases where he did use decision analysis, he would ask questions like, "What does this mean to you? What do you want to do with it?" Involving a patient like Mrs. Pinelli in decision-making might mean challenging her, as by saying, "So you think an IVP is worth doing? Well, what would you bet me, and what odds would you give, that it will reveal anything useful?" It would mean showing her and all his patients that they could work with him to create their own gambles.

6

DECISION ANALYSIS: USE WITH CAUTION

As time went on, S. found himself thinking of decision analysis more and more in the past tense. His patients' reactions led the way. Some, like Mrs. Pinelli, turned away from decision analysis altogether (and sometimes turned away from S. along with it). Others thought they had to follow it slavishly. Whenever S. would ask them, "What do you say about this?" they would throw the question right back at him: "What does the decision analysis say?" Although patients tended to be all too receptive to the "answers" that came out of decision analysis, it was often hard to engage them in the process of arriving at an answer.

For S., working with decision analysis had been a way of learning how to make decisions probabilistically over time. Somewhere at the back of his mind the formal decision-making framework still structured his thoughts (cf. Raiffa, 1968). Occasionally, when he wanted to clarify his thinking about an unfamiliar problem, he would "rough out" a decision tree, usually one that involved just one or two decisions rather than a long string of them. The procedure as a whole, however, turned out not to be flexible or efficient enough to handle the diverse situations he faced in his practice, where it sometimes seemed as if little remained the same from one day to the next, and

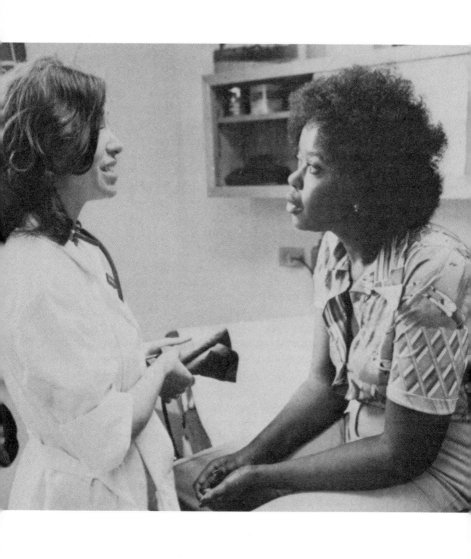

there wasn't much time to pause for reflection. To judge decision analysis by its own criterion: it usually didn't do S. and his patients enough good to justify all the effort it required.

S. had come to see that there are two major difficulties in using decision analysis. One is that the procedure is only as reliable as the various kinds of data that go into it, and those data all contain some degree of uncertainty. The other is that decision analysis involves some presuppositions that have their origins in the Mechanistic Paradigm. Not only do people tend to use decision analysis (like everything else) mechanistically, but it doesn't easily lend itself to being used any other way.

Garbage In, Garbage Out

Decision analysis ends with a set of exact-sounding numbers. By the time the calculations are finished, one can easily forget that those numbers began as more or less imprecise observations in an uncertain, changing world. Before a decision tree can be drawn and numbers written along its branches, people have to make judgments about possible causal relationships, about probabilities, and about values. The degree of confidence one can place in the results of decision analysis depends on the degree of confidence one can place in these human judgments, which are not made any more certain or permanently valid by being expressed in numbers and operated upon mathematically.

Causal Relationships

The very structure of a decision tree is based upon some assumptions about the world. Before one can estimate how probable it is that a given set of symptoms or test results has been caused by one disease or another, one must draw branches on the tree for whatever diseases have a *possible* causal connection with those visible signs. Similarly, one draws branches for those tests or treatments that have some relevance to the diseases in question, and for those outcomes (improvement, no improvement, side effects, etc.) that can reasonably be expected to follow from the actions taken. These choices, although they may be well supported by experience and knowledge, are still choices and need not be irrevocable, for one's knowledge of what causes can have what effects may change. If one examines standard decision trees (e.g., for hypertension), one can see where they might be redrawn on the basis of recently acquired knowledge. One must continually ask whether there is enough new information to warrant redrawing the tree.

Probability Estimates

"Four percent, seventy-five percent—what do those numbers have to do with me?" asked Mrs. Pinelli during a subsequent conversation with S. "Oh, I know that you changed them 'just for me' because I had had kidney artery trouble before. But how could you tell that the numbers you finally came up with out of your head were any more tailor-made for me than the numbers out of the tables?"

S. saw what she was getting at. It wasn't that there was anything illegitimate about either statistics or subjective judgment as a basis for probability estimates; after all, these were all that one had to go on. Rather, Mrs. Pinelli was pointing out the incompatibility between the exact numerical expression of probability estimates and their inexact origins. She saw through the precision of the form to the imprecision of the substance. What she said held for both objective probability estimates (those based on frequency data) and subjective ones (those based on individual or collective judgment). And indeed, S. realized that there were problems (not disabling, but sobering) with both kinds of probability estimation.

In the case of objective, frequency-based estimates, not only the numbers themselves but the methods used to obtain them have a reassuring aura of precision. For example, the data on which probability estimates are based may come from experimental studies comparing the efficacy of different treatments. In one type of study subjects are randomly assigned to experimental groups receiving one or another treatment (or a *placebo,* a physiologically inactive substance administered as if it were an active medication). Such *randomized* studies represent what we commonly think of as "exact science." Yet according to Criterion #2 of the Probabilistic Paradigm, the results of randomized clinical studies (like any other experiments) are affected by the process of experimentation. What the experimenters do and how the experimental subjects react are influenced by their knowledge that they are administering or receiving one treatment rather than another.

Such effects may be minimized through the use of the double-blind technique, in which neither the patients receiving an experimental treatment nor the doctors administering it are told which treatment it is. The double-blind procedure works well with drugs, which are easily disguised. It does not work in more complex situations that require conscious participation by patients and doctors (e.g., home versus hospital birth). Especially when the double-blind precaution is taken, randomized studies tend to be elaborate and costly. There is also the problem of how the results for both groups are affected by the knowledge that this is, after all, an experiment. Randomized studies also entail a potential ethical dilemma, in that half of the experimental patients do not get what may turn out to be the better of the two treatments being tested.

Given these shortcomings of the randomized method, even with double-blind controls, many investigators have searched for a better approach. There is, in fact, an experimental technique that is more probabilistic in spirit, more sensitive to the changing nature of the world, and fairer to subjects. This method assigns subjects to experimental groups on a *sequential* rather than randomized basis (Weinstein, 1974). In this "two-armed bandit" approach to clinical research the experimenters try out the treatments under consideration in the way a gambler might find out which of two slot machines pays off more often. Here patients are treated one at a time instead of all at once as in randomized comparison studies. The first patient is given Drug A. If this patient recovers within the number of days established as the criterion for "cure," then the second patient is also given Drug A. If the second patient does not show the requisite improvement, then the third patient is given Drug B. This drug likewise is used as long as it "works." If it doesn't work for one patient, the experimenters switch back to Drug A for the next.

The sequential method has the ethical advantage that the number of patients given each treatment is roughly proportional to the effectiveness of the treatment. The better a treatment turns out to be, relative to the other treatment(s) tested, the more patients will have received that treatment during the experiment. Moreover, this type of experiment embodies the principle of stochastic causality within the experiment itself. In contrast with the static time frame of a randomized study, sequential trials stretch over a period of time during which changes in probabilities can be picked up if they occur. Although changes in probabilities may not often occur in the length of time it takes to do a study, they can occur, say, if bacteria mutate so as to become resistant to a previously effective drug. In psychiatry, for example, new treatments (both drug and otherwise) tend to be very effective at first and then to become less so, whether because the doctors and patients using the treatments become less enthusiastic or less careful, or simply because the treatments are given to other patients besides the selected group of initially responsive patients (Tourney, 1967). An ongoing sequential study would be a good way to measure this psychiatric Hawthorne effect.

Notwithstanding the advantages of sequential trials, no experimental method can do away with the uncertainties of experimentation or the complexities of the world. Tables of data, whether obtained from research studies or recorded clinical experience, contain built-in layers of uncertainty. As psychologist Ward Edwards has observed:

... My friends who are expert about medical records tell me that to attempt to dig out from even the most sophisticated hospital's records the frequency of association between any particular symptom and any particular diagnosis is next to impossible—and when I raise the question of complexes of symptoms, they stop speaking to me. For another thing, doctors keep telling me that diseases change, that this year's flu is different from last year's flu, so that symptom-disease records extending far back in time are of very limited usefulness. Moreover, the observation of symptoms is well-supplied with error, and the diagnosis of diseases is even more so; both kinds of errors will ordinarily be frozen permanently into symptom-disease statistics. Finally, even if diseases didn't change, doctors would. The usefulness of disease categories is so much a function of available treatments that these categories themselves change as treatments change—a fact hard to incorporate into symptom-disease statistics (Edwards, 1972, pp. 139–140).

When it comes to applying the data to the individual case in practice, yet another layer of uncertainty is added. With both diagnostic and treatment probabilities, subjective judgment is required. For example, S. had a diagnostic probability table which gave the likelihood that a middle-aged male smoker who coughed had lung cancer. A patient of S.'s fit into this category, but he also had worked in a coal mine and had a family history of tuberculosis. There was no information in the table pertaining to such a patient; indeed the table could not possibly account for every variation and refinement of its basic categories that an individual patient might present. Yet S. had to account for these additional facts in estimating the probability that his patient had lung cancer rather than tuberculosis or black-lung disease.

He had to do the same when it came to treatment. Although hypertension, for example, is often associated with stress and anxiety, most of S.'s colleagues believed that elevated blood pressure could not be lowered by minor tranquilizers. In an algorithm for hypertension the probability that the condition could be successfully treated through the use of such medications would be listed as 0. S. disagreed. He regarded some of his patients with mild hypertension as anxious people whose blood pressure varied with their state of mind. Departing from the data, he explained to patients the costs and benefits of various treatment options, including minor tranquilizer use. Where this unorthodox treatment was chosen by the patient, it was successful about fifty percent of the time. In this way S., like any doctor, was able to build up a set of informal, mostly unwritten probability tables of his own which sometimes departed from the statistical norms so as to be consistent with his experience.

Whether or not objective probability data exist (all the more so when they do not), subjective judgment must play a part in estimating probabilities. Subjective judgment is no less fallible than tables of figures. An advantage, perhaps, is that it is less likely to appear infallible and to be thought of as such, especially in a world where people are not comfortable dealing with probabilities.

Mrs. Pinelli was not alone in finding the concept of probability not entirely compelling, and indeed a bit foreign. Most people, having been brought up under the Mechanistic Paradigm, have some difficulty even thinking in terms of probabilities, let alone training their senses to make good subjective probability estimates. And the estimates they do make can't help but be affected by the mechanistic assumptions that in varying degrees underlie everyone's thinking today. For example, by not taking into account the first criterion of the Probabilistic Paradigm (which holds that causes can come and go over time), people tend to estimate the probability of a future event based on their best guess as to the probability of its happening in the present. Moreover, people tend to be as confident in predicting events in the distant future as they are about events in the near future. This can lead to overconfidence. As patients and doctors gain practice in estimating probabilities, they will do better at it. But the numbers they come up with will still be no more than estimates.

Values

Values, too, can be estimated by objective and subjective methods. So-called objective techniques involve finding a numerical scale that exists independent of the observer and can be applied to any medical situation. The scale most commonly used is that of dollars and cents. On this scale the consequences of illness and treatment are measured in terms of how much future income the patient will lose. Such a monetary measure of values is rather obviously incomplete, for it does not include consequences other than lost work time, such as pain. It also values human lives in an unequal and unfair manner. On this scale a secretary's life might be worth only one fifth as much as that of her boss.

Since values have an inherently subjective quality (although by Criterion #3 of the Probabilistic Paradigm they are not *wholly* subjective), various measures have been proposed to take subjectivity into account. The "lottery method" described in the previous chapter is one such technique that takes into account subjective attitudes toward risk. Mrs. Pinelli, however, had some choice words to say about this "game."

"How can you talk about money and years of life in the same breath? Lottery, indeed! I don't play games where my life is involved. That was a big reason why I said enough to the whole decision analysis business. What I wanted instead was some solid information to sink my teeth into, like the information the arteriogram can give you: a picture that shows you what's wrong and how to fix it."

As S. understood, Mrs. Pinelli had her reasons for placing value on things, but Jeanne in her enthusiasm found it difficult to listen. Also, a measuring procedure that aligns all values along one dimension obscures the fact that many decisions call forth values that cannot be easily compared. These may involve principles that constrain choice, "thresholds" below which some values cannot be compromised. To use an example given by legal scholar Laurence Tribe (1972) in his critique of formal decision-making methods, social planners cannot bargain away one person's arms and legs because another person would gain more "satisfaction" in numerical terms by having them cut off than the first person would lose. The citizen's right to breathe clean air can be measured against the industrialist's right to pollute the air for a productive purpose—but not to the point where the citizen cannot breathe at all without suffering a severe health hazard. The value of the preservation of human life cannot be reduced to numbers.

Such discontinuities in values tend to occur where individual satisfaction clashes with the common good. They also can occur, however, within the value scheme of a single individual. How can numbers, arrayed on a one-dimensional scale, adequately convey a paradoxical attitude such as this: "It is unacceptable to me to lose my eyesight—I can't see how I could go on living; but then I guess I wouldn't just kill myself if I were blinded—not right away, at least"? This seeming contradiction is a common human sentiment, one to which we cannot do justice by saying that the person values death at "0" and blindness at "5" or "10." Mrs. Pinelli exhibited a similar complexity of response as she oscillated between trying to do something about the symptoms of severe hypertension and resisting the side effects of the medication. Yet she had an underlying concern that made sense of the apparent contradiction—namely, her fear of being disabled as a parent, whether by the illness or by the treatment. She had her reasons for valuing the things she did, but these became less clear when her values were reduced to numbers.

The lottery method is designed to enable people to express their attitudes toward risk. These attitudes, however, may not be consistent over the range of situations people face. Someone may be much more averse to risk in Russian roulette than with a roulette wheel. Someone may like to gamble at the racetrack, but not in the doctor's office. Another context that influences evaluation is that of the progression of items as they occur in thought or speech. In reflection or conversation there is a natural order in which various possibilities come up for evaluation. Presented in a different order, the possibilities might be evaluated differently. The lottery method, by setting up its own necessarily arbitrary order of presentation, may thereby affect the expression of basic personal values about life and death, health and illness (Bursztajn and Hamm, unpublished).

The lottery method is grounded in the belief that people can make better assessments of their values by making "choices" than when they try to state their values directly. While this may well be true, the kinds of choices people make in an imaginary lottery may not have much to do with the choices they would make in the context of their lives. "I don't care what the numbers say," Mrs. Pinelli said. "There are just some things I can't tolerate. Like walking around being drowsy all the time. I've got to work to support my family. I'm not going to take the slightest chance of leaving them without a home." Mrs. Pinelli's image of her children blocked out all other considerations. A decision analyst would be quick to point out that she could have used the procedure to express the overriding value she placed on her family's well-being. She could have, yet she didn't, because she didn't see the lottery method as a compelling representation of the choices she faced in "real life." It is when choices occur naturally, in the context of living, that people are best able to think about and act on their values.

Refining the Use of Decision Analysis

There are a few technical precautions that can serve to remind doctors and patients of the uncertainties of the data in decision analysis and help those who use decision analysis keep their minds open to new information. One is the practice (as yet not generally followed) of dating all decision trees and algorithms that are disseminated for general use. People who make use of such tools should have the opportunity to judge how likely it is that the information on which a decision tree or algorithm is based has been superseded by more recent findings. Ideally dates should be given both for the structuring of the options and their outcomes and for the data used in estimating probabilities, since both kinds of information can change. Although value assessments will not often appear on a general decision tree, some trees may contain hypothetical value assessments for "typical" patients in certain categories. These, too, should be dated, since the values assigned to outcomes can change on the basis of, for instance, the development of new pain relievers.

Irrespective of how recently the expected value was calculated, one need not and perhaps should not invariably choose the course of action leading to the higher expected value. In a world where perfect information is not available, it makes sense once in a while to check where the "road not taken" would have led one. As opposed to a *deterministic* decision rule, which keeps one on the "best" road, a *stochastic* decision rule recognizes that there is some value to exploring alternate routes occasionally to see whether in some cases one of them might be better than the "best" road. With a stochastic decision rule the greater the difference in expected value between the "best" road and an alternate route, the less often one would chance the latter.

A doctor might, for example, use a stochastic decision rule in treating patients with some kinds of coronary artery disease. For some such patients medical treatment has a higher expected value. For others the expected value of coronary artery bypass surgery is higher. Since these expected values represent "best guesses," it may be worthwhile to explore whether the one treatment really is better than the other for groups of patients for whom the expected value difference is small. How, though, would one allot patients to the treatment that is believed to have the lower expected value? The only ethical way to do so, it would seem, would be by sharing the decision with the patient, so that the patient could knowingly choose whether or not to accept the treatment with the lower expected value.

Tables giving the treatments with the highest expected value for various categories of patients with coronary artery disease have been developed by cardiologist Stephen Pauker (1976), who has pioneered in the use of decision-analytic methods in medicine. The tables indicate probability "thresholds" at which the expected value for one treatment becomes higher than that for the other. A stochastic decision principle can be applied to these tables in the following manner. Suppose, for example, that a particular man with an extremely devastating form of coronary artery disease has an eighty-eight percent chance of having his chest pain relieved by coronary bypass surgery. If this patient is in such great pain that he places a very high value on relief of pain, then Pauker's table of thresholds would recommend surgery as better for this patient than medical treatment. But the table also provides a threshold for changing that decision. It stipulates that surgery is better as long as the probability of a successful operation is above four percent. That is, this person finds his pain so unbearable that he would be willing to have surgery even if the chances of success were only four percent. Given this information, a deterministic decision-maker would choose surgery on the basis of its higher expected value. A stochastic decision-maker would probably choose surgery, on the grounds that the difference between eighty-eight percent and four percent is a decisive one, but might think twice about doing surgery in every such case if its probability of success fell closer to the threshold—say, below ten percent—because of the possibility of error in the probability estimates, as well as of patient-by-patient variation in expected values.

Whether or not one ever uses stochastic decision rules in a mathematical form, one needs to keep in mind the principle that underlies them. If decision analysis is to be used within the Probabilistic Paradigm, it cannot be used as an *experimentum crucis* that purports to make choice unnecessary. Decision analysis does not tell doctors and patients how to act; rather it contributes evidence to be considered in making choices critically. This is true whether one is using standard decision trees and algorithms or a decision tree constructed especially for a particular patient. Even after the structure of the tree and the data have been adapted to the circumstances, needs, and values of the patient, one cannot suspend critical thought. One must still say to oneself, "Okay, I've come up with a nice numerical 'answer,' but does it make sense? How does it match my understanding of the world? Does it jibe with my intuitions?"

Mechanistic Presuppositions
of the Method—and Its Users

Although to use decision analysis as an *experimentum crucis* is to defeat its purpose, that's just what people tend to do. Since people are trained to think in terms of the Mechanistic Paradigm, they are not likely to use decision analysis in a manner consistent with the Probabilistic Paradigm. Furthermore decision analysis itself is based on some mechanistic assumptions.

The Assumption of Fixed Structure

Decision analysis seeks to anticipate all questions. In reality, though, some questions arise only after other questions are answered. In Mrs. Pinelli's case it seemed that everything was turned upside down once the process got under way. The issue was decided by questions that never were anticipated when the decision tree was structured (such as whether it was Dr. Berg's job to take over Mrs. Pinelli's care or simply consult with Dr. S.) and questions whose meaning changed in the course of events (such as what having an arteriogram meant to Mrs. Pinelli). The strength of decision analysis as usually used is its commitment to answering a predefined question; its weakness is that it does not encourage one to redefine the question. Jeanne Aaron, for example, did not concern herself sufficiently with finding out what questions were important to Mrs. Pinelli.

Throughout his work with families S. saw how important time and experience were in changing both the questions and answers of decision-making. He observed that, in the process of making choices and acting on them, people explored what they were and defined what they wanted to be. As they chose one way of acting rather than another, they learned about and indeed changed their values. When a man and woman decided to have a child, they were choosing to become a father and a mother. They were changing themselves as individuals and creating themselves as a family. As the family changed in the course of the pregnancy, not only the decisions they faced but the way they thought about those decisions changed. Not only the values and probabilities but the mind-set within which these were perceived was being subtly altered by new experience. Decision analysis, with the mind-set neatly laid out in a tree, could not automatically accommodate these changes, nor those that subsequently took place when the man and woman decided, by making choices over time, what kind of father and mother they were going to be. When Mrs. Pinelli voiced her concern for her children's welfare as a crucial factor in her own decisions, she was defining the kind of person she aspired to become—and was becoming. This process occurred in the context of everyday life and everyday choices.

When S. began attending births, he tried to structure his own and the family's assessment of alternatives (hospital versus home, anesthetized versus nonanesthetized, etc.) as an ongoing decision analysis. He would draw flow diagrams with decision points throughout the pregnancy, labor, delivery, and postpartum period. But how could he talk about the "expected values" of "outcomes" when a large part of the value of the birth experience for the family came out of a nine-month process of making choices, facing uncertainty together, and accepting personal responsibility for these choices in a manner that would set the tone for their future decision-making? How could he measure the survival and health of the baby "against" the satisfaction the family derived from the experience when the meaning of the "outcome" was so greatly influenced, even created by the manner in which the family felt themselves to have brought about the outcome?

With Mrs. Pinelli, too, decision analysis assumed a stable set of values. Yet her way of dealing with her hypertension did not support this assumption. When she felt the symptoms to be unpleasant and disabling, she did something about the illness. When she felt the side effects of the medication to be unpleasant and disabling, she stopped doing anything about the illness. If her actual decision tree (as opposed to the one Jeanne laid out for her) could be visualized as having two main branches labeled "do something" and "do nothing," then each branch could be seen as leading her back to the beginning, whereupon she would take the other branch. Instead of a series of branches going in the same direction, her tree would look like a pair of linked loops. In this respect Mrs. Pinelli was not so unusual. Decision trees do not adequately represent the circuitous paths along which people may be led by their unstable values.

Ironically one of the experiences that contributed to changing Mrs. Pinelli's values and her actions was the experience of using decision analysis. "It's funny," she said in retrospect, "they told me that decision analysis would be a way to think about what to do. But by the time I was finished, the last thing I wanted to do was to think at all. All those boring questions, and those numbers—what did they have to do with anything? You might say I couldn't see the forest for the 'tree.' So when Dr. Berg talked about doing things that you could *see,* I jumped right up and told him that that was what I *wanted.* I was so tired of thinking, I just wanted to have something I could see, like when you've been working so hard that all you can stand to do is look at a movie for two hours." In other words, just as decision analysis is changed by the person who uses it, so in this case Mrs. Pinelli was changed by decision analysis.

As S. learned to observe and experience decision-making more consciously, he realized how well the process illustrates the first and second criteria of the Probabilistic Paradigm. In a world where information is shaped by the act of eliciting it, where the tool changes the user and the user changes the tool, where answers prompt new questions and decisions create further choices, people need decision-making procedures that are sensitive to change as it occurs. Decision analysis locks people into preexisting categories for decision-making. Of course, one can always redraw the tree, but that takes work. It is easier to deny the new perceptions, the thoughts and feelings that don't fit. With all its good intentions decision analysis can sometimes lead to what psychologists Buzzy Chanowitz and Ellen Langer (unpublished) call "premature cognitive commitment," or what S. would call a closed mind.

The Fact-Value Dichotomy

According to the third criterion of the Probabilistic Paradigm facts are perceived in terms of people's values, and values are facts about people that can be rationally understood and discussed as other facts can. Decision analysis, however, by its very structure separates facts—which are dealt with rationally through probabilities—from values—which are not considered to be rationally discussable. Mrs. Pinelli's outburst against "that silly game" (the lottery method) was a reaction to her feeling that S. and Jeanne were patronizing her by treating her values as completely irrational and therefore somehow childish. In her view her values were rationally justifiable, since they were grounded in her sense of the responsibilities of an adult.

S. could hardly fault Mrs. Pinelli, or any of his patients, for having trouble making the separate judgments of probability and value that went into calculating the expected value. In Mrs. Pinelli's words, "Jeanne multiplied the value by the probability to get the answer. But I think I was doing a little of that just to get the 'value' in the first place. So weren't we doing the same thing twice?" Of course, Mrs. Pinelli wasn't supposed to figure the probability into the value. The procedure called for her to evaluate first how good or bad something would be if it happened to her, and then how likely it was to happen. These two estimates together would make up the expected value. It is unrealistic, however, to expect people to be able to draw such a sharp line between probability and value. People evaluate a possible event in terms of its meaning for their lives. If she were asked, "What if the sky fell in?" Mrs. Pinelli would find it hard to focus on the seriousness of the consequences. Such a question would strike her as an abstract exercise, a "game." If, on the other hand, she were asked, "What if you lost your job?" she would feel the hypothetical consequences more intensely—not because they would actually be more dire than those of the sky falling in, but because they would be more likely to happen.

Bias Toward Quantifiable Data

There is a fable about a drunk who was seen groping around on the ground in the light cast through a doorway. A passerby asked him what he was doing. "I'm looking for my key," the drunk replied. "Where did you lose it?" "In the alley over there." "So why are you looking here?" the passerby asked with surprise. "Because it's light here." Similarly, decision analysts may tend, without even realizing it, to look where their method sheds light rather than where light needs to be shed. Where decision analysis sheds light is on "hard facts"—those that can be expressed in its own language of numbers and mathematical calculation.

As Laurence Tribe puts it, "Even the most sophisticated user is subject to an overwhelming temptation to feed his pet the food it can most comfortably digest" (1971, pp. 1361–1362). Taking an example from criminal law, he tells of two analysts ("one a legal scholar and the other a teacher of statistical theory") who, in estimating the probability that a palm print resembling the defendant's would be found on a knife used as a murder weapon if the defendant was or was not the murderer, simply equated the probability that the print was actually the defendant's with the probability that the defendant committed the murder. They disregarded the obvious possibility that the defendant committed the murder without leaving a print, or that someone else incriminated the defendant by using a knife which already bore the defendant's print. These possibilities did not easily fit into the analysts' formula, and therefore (apparently) were not considered.

If two highly trained observers could make such an error under the seductive appeal of "mathematical machinery," what about juries—and the rest of us? S. and Jeanne Aaron, two trained medical observers, may well have committed a similar oversight when they did not include a "life-style modification" branch on Mrs. Pinelli's decision tree. The effects of life-style modification on high blood pressure are no less real than those of medications and surgery. They are, however, less well documented statistically.

In a decision-making economy whose currency is numbers, measurable entities (e.g., "facts" with known probabilities, "values" based on financial costs and benefits) drive out unmeasurable entities (e.g., "facts" with unknown probabilities, "values" based on moral principles and sensibilities). Tribe suggests that if questions of guilt and innocence are rephrased as questions of mathematical probabilities, the scope of legal reasoning will be severely narrowed, and jurors may lose the capacity to draw upon a broad context of moral and social values in reaching their verdicts. The issue he poses is equally relevant to medicine, where patients, families, and physicians must make decisions as sensitive and as urgent as those made by juries. The child K.'s need for love could not be quantified as easily as could his diagnostic test results. Mrs. Pinelli's desire to remain alert and lucid while her children were growing up could not be quantified as easily as could her blood pressure readings. Were these concerns therefore not worthy of consideration? A society that implicitly answers in the negative by practicing a narrowly mathematical approach to decision-making or by holding up that approach as a norm is choosing to see itself in a technological light. The people who live in such a society will have difficulty seeing those parts of themselves on which the light does not shine.

Assumption That Reality Can Be Broken Down into Analytical Units

Things take on meaning from their contexts (Dreyfus and Dreyfus, unpublished). If you unscrew a ball-point pen and say, "This part is worth two dollars, and that part is worth one dollar, so I'll sell either part individually or sell the whole pen for three dollars," you are assuming that the whole is the same as the sum of its parts. But if you were on an island where there were no other pens with interchangeable parts, what would either part of the pen be worth individually? If you had nothing to write on, what would the whole pen be worth? What good is a brain without a heart? What would Mrs. Pinelli's life mean to her outside the context of her family?

When Mrs. Pinelli complained that it was not so easy for her to separate value from probability, she was pointing out that the context in which an object exists is part of what the object is, just as the object is part of the context. When decision analysis separates facts from values, one cause from others operating along with it, an individual's welfare from that of the family or community, an illness from a person's life history, one decision from the context of other decisions that define its significance, it turns decision-making into something rather artificial and academic. Of course, some such simplifying assumptions do have to be made if decision-making is to proceed at all, whether or not decision analysis is used. But those who do use decision analysis need to be aware of the special kinds of simplifying assumptions that it entails and the questions these raise when decision analysis is translated into actual decisions. For example, decision analysis will have a better chance to be used critically if the people to be affected by the decisions can create the categories of the analysis rather than simply assuming preformed categories.

Assumption That the Structure of the Tree Is "Given" Rather Than Chosen

Mrs. Pinelli was dissatisfied with some judgments that S. and Jeanne made both at the beginning and the end of the decision analysis. "Why didn't the tree have a branch for doing nothing and then seeing what would happen?" she asked. "Decision analysis is supposed to show *all* the options, but Jeanne only showed me the options that *she* thought were good." For their part S. and Jeanne had given Mrs. Pinelli the "standard" tree for her blood pressure level in order to make the work of decision analysis manageable for her. Since "all" the options would represent too long a list, some judgments had to be made. Still, S. and Jeanne didn't take into account the possibility that what was "standard" to them might not be acceptable to the patient.

When it came to interpreting the probable consequences of each of the "final" outcomes for Mrs. Pinelli's health, she again had questions. "I can't see the point of just saying, 'probability of a stroke in sixteen years.' What's a stroke? Why, they say my mother had three strokes before she finally died of a heart attack at the age of eighty. None of them slowed her down one bit. On the other hand, Uncle Joe had one stroke, and 'puff'—a vegetable. What I want to know is how likely I am to get the kind of stroke that Uncle Joe had. I don't care about any old stroke." Again, the categories that S. and Jeanne set up didn't meet the patient's needs.

Mrs. Pinelli's two complaints show that judgment is required in knowing how much to include in a decision tree. In the first place the decision to draw more or fewer branches is a matter of judgment (Raiffa, 1968). One must evaluate what is to be gained from further subdividing reality as well as from pruning options that may be irrelevant (such as, in Mrs. Pinelli's case, "doing nothing" and "life-style modification"). Second, there is nothing in decision analysis itself that dictates where to stop the chain of actions and results and declare a set of outcomes to be "final." It is not the causal structure of the world, but one's own sense of what causal relations are important, that brings about that choice. To S. and Jeanne "probability of stroke" was a reasonable stopping point. To Mrs. Pinelli it was not.

Again, the need for judgment does not invalidate decision analysis, since anything one does in a probabilistic world requires judgment. Nonetheless, the fact that Mrs. Pinelli threw up her hands at all the details in a procedure that she called a crude oversimplification suggests that the procedure may be at once too complex and too simple. It generates more distinctions than most people can comfortably work with, and yet it doesn't necessarily get to the distinctions that matter to people.

Mathematical Reasoning on Trial

In an article on the use of mathematical decision-making methods in legal proceedings, entitled "Trial by Mathematics," Tribe shows, on the basis of some of the theoretical considerations presented here, that these methods are not the unbiased, "value-neutral" tools that decision scientists would like them to be. Rather, they are full of unacknowledged biases. Mathematical evidence and mathematical arguments can be and have been manipulated so as to distort the legal process and subvert justice. Most people are familiar with the story of the French Captain Alfred Dreyfus, who in 1899 was accused of betraying state secrets to the Germans. The prosecution established its case by using "expert" witnesses who testified to the extremely low probability that certain resemblances between Dreyfus's handwriting and the writing on the incriminating letter could have occurred by chance. Subsequent review showed that the mathematical "proofs" contained in this testimony were worthless. Yet according to a historian quoted by Tribe, the defense counsel and the government commissioner, who admitted they had understood nothing of these arguments, "allowed themselves to be impressed by the scientific phraseology of the system" (Tribe, 1971, pp. 1333–1334).

In another case Tribe cites, this one dating from 1968, witnesses to a California robbery described the perpetrators as a woman with a blond ponytail and a black man with a mustache and a beard who drove a yellow car. A couple who matched this description were convicted after the prosecutor argued that there was only a one in twelve million chance that a randomly chosen couple would have all the characteristics listed. The California Supreme Court reversed the conviction on four separate grounds. First, the prosecutor's estimates of the frequency of occurrence of each characteristic individually were not supported by any evidence. Second, the prosecutor multiplied the probabilities for the separate occurrence of each characteristic to get the probability of the joint occurrence of the combination of characteristics. This would be valid only if the various characteristics occurred entirely independently of one another rather than in relation to one another, which in this case they clearly did not. For example, men with beards often also have mustaches. Therefore, if one out of every ten men has a beard and one out of four has a mustache, the probability that a man has both a beard and a mustache cannot be said to be one in forty, but is actually closer to one in ten. Third, the quantification of these probabilities diverted the jury from considering the more difficult to quantify but equally crucial question of whether the prosecution's witnesses were mistaken or lying. Fourth, the probability that a randomly chosen couple would have the same salient characteristics as the defendants did not (as the prosecutor claimed it did) reflect the probability of the defendant's innocence. For in a sufficiently large universe of suspect couples—say, twenty-four million, or thirty-six million—there might likely be several couples with these same characteristics, each of whom would have an equal probability of guilt. In this case the prosecutor made opportunistic use of mathematical probabilities, the defense attorney (at least until the appellate hearing) was too bewildered to make effective rebuttal, and the jury was swayed from its better judgment by the spell of the numbers.

Tribe's concern is that the explicit use of mathematical probability in legal trials, as well as in establishing standards of legal proof, may undermine legal reasoning. Mathematical proofs are subject to exploitive misuse because their valid use involves complexities not easily grasped by lawyers and jurors. They also are likely to distract judges and juries from deciding the simple questions of fact and the complex questions of moral intention that traditionally have been the province of law. We may assume that jurors make implicit probability estimates in arriving at their verdicts, just as all of us do in daily life. To quantify such estimates explicitly using Bayesian computations would, however, fundamentally change the character of legal decision-making. It would put into jeopardy, Tribe believes, two fundamental principles of law: the presumption of innocence and the "reasonable doubt" criterion for conviction. Thus if we choose to "try by mathematics," we as a society will be changing what we value and what we are.

From Decision Analysis to Gambling

In his discussion of the symbolic, expressive function of the rules of trial procedure Tribe makes an important distinction between dead ritual and what we might call rules to live by:

> Some of those rules, to be sure, reflect only "an arid ritual of meaningless form," but others express profoundly significant moral relationships and principles—principles too subtle to be translated into anything less complex than the intricate symbolism of the trial process (Tribe, 1971, p. 1391).

Rituals that are arid involve activities done mindlessly, repetitively, uncritically; i.e., mechanistically. Rules to live by, on the other hand, can ultimately enhance the possibility of critical choice rather than suppress it. They are similar to rituals insofar as they take some things for granted, but they do so in such a way as to allow one to keep an open mind. Even in the Probabilistic Paradigm, one begins with assumptions. One cannot keep an open mind if everything is open to question, for then chaos ensues. Where everything is taken for granted, or where nothing is taken for granted, the result is the same—the negation of critical choice.

Rules to live by embody principles used consciously and explicitly, so that they can serve as standards to be held up, lived up to, argued with, dissented from, and occasionally broken. The principles of the law are richer and more useful for having been derived from ethics rather than from the mechanistic science of the nineteenth century. They acknowledge the moral consequences and practical implications of uncertainty without lapsing into utter relativism, since in law something must finally be decided. "Reasonable doubt" is such a principle. For there to be reasonable doubt, there must first be doubt; then there must be reason.

It is thus apparent that similar principles can be arrived at from several different directions: from ethics, from the rules of law, or from the Probabilistic Paradigm of twentieth-century science. It is not surprising that there is often a convergence among the principles drawn from such different areas. For all of them represent human wisdom as derived from experience, wisdom that encompasses the good as well as the true.

Medicine has both rituals and rules to live by. There are, on the one hand, the savage rituals of contemporary medicine, like the unnecessary tests that K. was subjected to and that Mrs. Pinelli was taught to request. Doing things over and over again makes us less fearful, because then we know what to expect. It is a way to assert control in the face of uncertainty. But the assertion is strained, the control illusory, because the reality and the terror remain, though they may be inaccessible. And so, again and again, doctors and patients act out the ritual of "looking at the picture," so as to be sure not beyond *reasonable* doubt, but beyond all doubt.

There are, on the other hand, principles and rules to live by in medicine—the manners and mutual respect between doctor and patient along with consideration for their different areas of authority. It is these principles and rules—ancient in their ethics, modern in their acknowledgment of the unknown—and not the "arid rituals" of the present that need to be revived and strengthened.

Decision analysis, designed to help people free themselves from the dead rituals of medicine, came in S.'s eyes to look like a dead ritual itself. It was at once unconvincingly abstract and forbiddingly detailed. It aspired to a formal precision that broke down when one looked closely at its component parts. Decision analysis, it seemed, would be of little day-to-day use to doctors and less to patients. There might even be times when it would come between doctors and patients, if Mrs. Pinelli's reaction was any indication. "I just didn't trust myself after that whole business," she recalled. "The more Jeanne talked, the less I knew what to do. That's why I just nodded 'yes' to whatever she said and then asked to see a specialist. I just didn't know what to think, so I wanted to talk to someone who did."

For doctors and patients to face uncertainty together, S. realized, there had to be trust between them. If people became too uncertain about themselves and each other, they would flee from the additional uncertainties that medical decision-making presented. They would flee, presumably, back to the comforting rituals of mechanistic practice, the "seeing" and the "doing."

Rejecting the "elusive ideal of wholly objective, impersonal, and detached instrumental analysis" as "not only unattainable but destructive," Tribe has called for "a subtler . . . and more complex style of problem solving" (1972, pp. 107–108). Principles for decision-making are needed that can be used in the contexts in which people actually make decisions. What is needed is a way of thinking that doctors and patients can use together, one that seems natural to people because they already use it in their daily lives, one that encourages people to reason instead of diverting them with calculations, one that engages people in examining their own lives in order to create their own probabilities, values, and categories for making choices.

S. developed such a method through trying to explain to patients in their own language what it meant to make decisions probabilistically. He would say, for example, "It's like betting on the horses, or on a poker game. You're given the odds, but then you have to decide what you think the odds of winning really are. If you can get betting odds that you think are favorable, and if you can afford to bet, then you bet. How much you bet depends on how much you can stand to lose, how much you want to win, and what it's all worth to you. When you come here from now on, just imagine that you're going to the racetrack or the casinos in Las Vegas; but, of course, science will be there to guide you, and so will I."

Already in his mind's eye S. saw the big neon sign flashing in front of his office: YOU PAYS YOUR MONEY AND YOU TAKES YOUR CHANCES.

7

UNCONSCIOUS AND CONSCIOUS GAMBLING

To most people the word *gambling* suggests abdicating control of one's fate in the face of total uncertainty. The idea of "taking chances" with one's own or a loved one's life and health sounds foolhardy and irresponsible; the idea of a doctor's gambling with the lives of patients seems repugnant. Yet we recall that under the Probabilistic Paradigm everything a scientist does in order to gain knowledge is a kind of gamble. Acknowledging a degree of uncertainty in the world, the scientist gambles not as an abdication of control, but as a way of exerting a degree of control. The gambling that Dr. S. and some of his patients adopted as a model for medical decision-making wasn't the Las Vegas-style recreational or profit-seeking gambling, but rather this scientific gambling under the Probabilistic Paradigm. Although (as we shall see) the card game and the casino are models that are sometimes followed in medicine as it is currently practiced, our intuitions are correct when they tell us that these are not good models for gambling in medicine.

Making decisions under conditions of uncertainty is a form of gambling. Like the gambler the decision-maker (whether or not with the help of formal decision analysis) seeks informa-

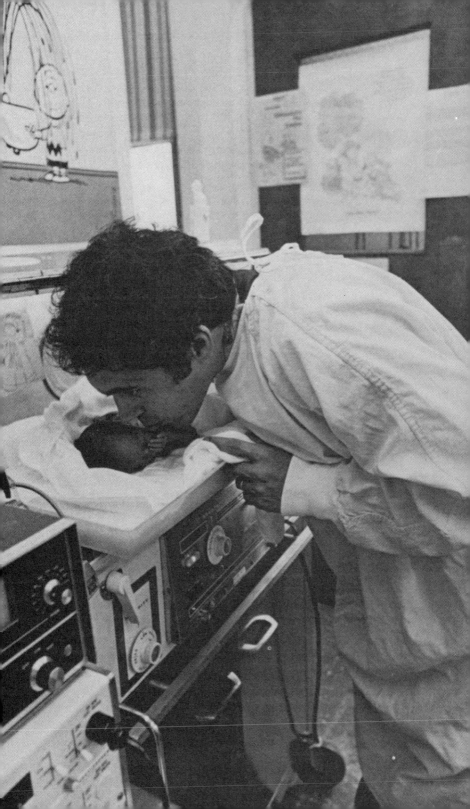

tion about possible gains and losses and then weighs the gains against the losses in terms of their probability and value. Nonetheless, there are some important differences between what we usually think of as gambling and the kind of gambling that is done in science, including the science of medical practice.

Clinic or Casino?

In casino gambling or in betting among friends, we can choose whether to play and how much to bet. We can set limits on the stakes, and we can quit while we're ahead or throw in our cards when the game gets rough. In medicine, on the other hand, the decision to gamble is not a voluntary one. In most cases we don't decide when to get sick. We can walk out of the doctor's office or hospital, but that choice is itself a gamble. Even if we stop going to the doctor, there is still uncertainty.

All choices in life are gambles. That is, we act with hope, but there are no guarantees. All choices that are worth thinking about (including many that we make without thinking) are worth thinking about as gambles—whether they are choices to act, to seek more information, or to believe something, or choices *not* to act, seek information, or believe. It is a gamble to go to the doctor or not to go to the doctor, to diagnose or not to diagnose, to treat or not to treat.

Moreover, in such real-life gambles the stakes may be higher than in recreational gambles—sometimes as high as life and death. Gambling in life is more than just a game. The consequences of our choices are not limited to an artificial sphere of activity, but are felt throughout our lives. We never know quite how much we are risking on each throw. We have all the more reason, therefore, to make those choices consciously, with some critical understanding of how we are gambling and what may be at stake.

Paradoxically, though, it is more difficult to gamble consciously in life than in a game that is set apart from life. In a game we at least know that we are gambling. In real life, where we are not deliberately doing something that is called "gambling," we may tend to gamble unawares. It is easier to gamble with eyes open when the stakes are limited and well defined than in the kind of real-life gamble where we don't know whether we've won or lost (or how long it will take before we will know), and where we rarely win or lose irrevocably. No wonder we don't always know, or want to know, that we're gambling. Gambling consciously would mean looking uncertainty in the face and acknowledging that we don't have as much control over our lives as we like to think.

Then, too, at the back of our minds lurk the distasteful images of the compulsive gambler, who is driven to seek the sensations of gambling regardless of the results, and the professional gambler, who lives by winning at others' expense. These are not images of how we want to live. No wonder Mrs. Pinelli didn't go along with the "lottery game" when she was facing life-and-death issues.

There is no simple antidote to our emotional discomfort with gambling, but we can describe what it means to gamble in science under the Probabilistic Paradigm and note how different this gambling is from both the compulsive and exploitive styles of gambling. In medicine, for example, one wins a diagnostic gamble by believing and acting on a correct diagnosis or by rejecting an incorrect diagnosis. One loses by believing and acting on an incorrect diagnosis or by rejecting a correct diagnosis. One wins a treatment gamble by trying a treatment that works or by not trying a treatment that would not have worked. One loses by trying a treatment that does not work or by not trying a treatment that would have worked. A correct diagnosis is one that can do the patient some good and that is true; this also holds for what can be considered a correct treatment. In scientific gambling, then, we seek not only the good outcome that the horseplayer or casino patron seeks; we also seek truth. Nor are the two easily separated. In the experimentation practiced under the Probabilistic Paradigm, one way of finding out is by taking action, which in turn can affect what is learned.

Treatment can lead to diagnosis, while diagnosis affects the course of treatment.

A type of gambling in which the true and the good are sought differs from the competitive gambling in which one person must lose for another to win. In competitive gambling a group of friends may arrange a card game or football pool in which there is a "pot"—a fixed pool of goods—that changes hands in the course of the game. Some players win, others lose, but the total amount won equals the total amount lost. This is called a "zero-sum game" (a term used in Chapter 4 to describe family relationships based on the principle of exchange). A casino or racetrack operates in the same way, although here the "house" sets the odds so as to skim off a small percentage of the total amount exchanged by the players. In a zero-sum game the doctor and the patient would be gambling against each other— hardly an attractive model for the doctor-patient relationship. However, the scientific gambling that we are applying to medicine more closely resembles another kind of gamble, one in which all the players can win or lose together.

Such cooperative gambling can be illustrated by a party game. Several cone-shaped objects are placed in a large, narrow-necked bottle. Each player holds a string attached to one of the cones. Only one cone at a time can be drawn out of the neck of the bottle. When the players are rewarded individually for the speed with which they get their cones out, they all tend to pull on their strings at the same time. The cones bunch up inside the neck of the bottle, and a traffic jam ensues. When the players are rewarded for teamwork, they cooperate by pulling out their cones one at a time.

Gambling in science takes this cooperative form because there is no fixed pool of winnings. Goods are not simply exchanged, but produced, in the form of knowledge that can be shared. This gambling differs from recreational gambling in that it not only draws upon all our knowledge and experience, but also contributes to it. The stakes are indefinite not only on the losing side, but on the winning side as well. For example, a physician and family who gamble well in their handling of a death can create a positive, nourishing experience even in the face of a large loss. A physician and family who are insensitive in their handling of a birth can rob it of some joy and so suffer loss even when the birth has a "successful" outcome.

Cooperative gambling proceeds according to the principles that govern scientific investigation under the Probabilistic Paradigm. Guided by these principles, one does not gamble in the unprincipled manner of the recreational or acquisitive gambler. Rather, one gambles with an attitude of critical trust toward the operation of cause and chance in the world, toward the gambling strategies with which one seeks to understand cause and chance, toward oneself as a gambler, and toward those with whom one is gambling. In each instance one has some doubt, but one also extends the benefit of the doubt. These principles make it possible for people gambling together (such as a patient, family, and doctor) to make the best of uncertain situations. They make it advantageous, therefore, to face uncertainty and gamble consciously rather than unconsciously.

Unfortunately, this model of cooperative, principled gambling is not always followed in medical practice. This is not surprising, since people are still guided more by the Mechanistic Paradigm than by the Probabilistic. The following case, which S. observed when he was an intern, shows how people sometimes gamble against rather than with each other in difficult medical situations. S., although he had not yet made a habit of thinking of medical decisions as gambles, sensed that there might have been another way to go in this case, a way that might have lessened the family's and the physicians' suffering. The case is a study of unconscious and conscious gambling.

A Double-Edged Gamble

A three-day-old baby looked as if she might have two severe medical problems. For one thing, she "looked funny." Her features were distorted in a way that suggested Down's syndrome, a genetic disease characterized by chromosomal abnormality.

Down's syndrome is commonly known in America as mongolism. Having Down's syndrome would mean being physically and mentally retarded for life. As if this weren't bad enough, the baby looked blue and had difficulty breathing—signs which pointed to heart trouble. In addition to doing a chromosome typing test for Down's syndrome, the family and the hospital staff considered the choice of whether or not to diagnose the heart trouble by catheterization. If a surgically remediable heart condition were found, they would then face the choice of whether to operate.

Both parents were in their mid-thirties. They had two other children. The father found it natural to do most of the talking, and the doctors found it natural to talk mostly with the father. The mother participated in the decision-making by speaking privately with her husband. This role was most comfortable for her because it was her customary role within the family, as well as because she was still exhausted from giving birth. Since it was the father who articulated the family's concerns, the doctors could not tell to what extent his wife agreed with his decisions. This would not have concerned them if he had agreed with *their* decisions. As it turned out, however, serious differences arose.

The father, whose primary concern was with whether the child had any prospect of a normal life, chose to test for Down's syndrome. He did not want to do anything about the heart condition until he had the result of the chromosome analysis, which would take a minimum of three days. Under pressure from the hospital staff he did agree to have the baby catheterized. However, he refused to sign an operative permit, which would have authorized the doctors to operate immediately if they found something they could operate on.

Catheterization revealed "critical aortic stenosis," a marked narrowing of the main artery through which blood is pumped from the heart to the rest of the body. The effects of this condition can be minimized for a few days by carefully administering cardiac drugs and regulating fluid intake. However it is best operated on quickly. Since the father refused permission to operate until the Down's test result was known, the baby was placed on medication to keep up her blood pressure. The catheterization had been a useful procedure, since it established the probabilities on which further action (or nonaction) could be based. And yet the doctors had almost refused to do this procedure without having an operative consent form signed in advance, since for them the only reason for catheterizing was to be able to operate. For them, that is, diagnostic information was meant to be used not only to inform the choice, but to dictate the choice. They wanted the decision to operate to be predetermined. It did not occur to them that it might be better to wait and then evaluate that particular gamble in the context in which it arose—the context of the baby's condition and the parents' feelings at the time.

"It's all so clear and simple," said the senior resident. "You just do the operation." But it was not so clear and simple. The operation promised only to relieve, not cure, the condition. By a senior clinician's rough estimate it might increase the odds from two out of ten to three out of ten that the child would survive and have a chance at normal development. Nobody told the parents this, however. They told them only that the baby would surely die without the operation, but that with it she might have a chance to live. Nonetheless, the father had a pretty realistic understanding of the situation. He sensed that this was not, and would not be, a normal child. He was aware that (1) she might have Down's syndrome; (2) the operation, even if successfully performed, might leave her with a serious heart condition; and (3) even if the operation could give her a normal heart, she might already have suffered brain damage.

The next couple of days were a very difficult time for the baby's parents. Now that an operable condition had been discovered, the doctors stepped up the pressure on the father to operate. With the nurses, like a chorus in the background, chanting, "Don't just stand there; *do* something," the doctors confronted the father: "You mean you're not willing to do anything to save the baby's life?" Driving a wedge of shame through the distressed family, they asked him whether he thought his wife incapable of raising a disabled child. They threatened to take him to court and get an injunction forcing him to let them operate. Warning that the baby would likely die while the father was waiting for the Down's test result, they threatened not to revive her if her heart stopped. In this way, they insinuated, the father would be responsible for his child's death.

It is easy to imagine a reasonable way in which the last threat might have been worded. The doctors might have said, "Well, if that's the way you feel, then we don't see any reason to take extraordinary measures to save the baby if she arrests." And it is easy to see how the doctors would not have wanted to fight a battle with one hand tied behind their backs. Still, by being unwilling to give the father the benefit of the doubt (i.e., to assume until shown otherwise that he was a reasonable person to gamble with), they made it almost impossible for him to gamble reasonably with them. Indeed they made it a matter of reproach that he was gambling at all! Apparently they were unaware that they, in doing what they thought was the "safe" thing, were gambling, too.

As is often the case, the reproach served to bring the father into line. He could not easily bear so many accusations, insinuations, and threatened complications of his family life from respected authority figures. While he may have felt that it was best for the baby to die, he could not accept that prospect in such concrete and immediate form. At that point, however, S., who was one of several interns assigned to the case, promised to resuscitate the child if necessary, so that the father could get the information he wanted before deciding to act. By sharing the gamble with the father, S. sought to make it possible for him to gamble consciously.

The father was trying to find out the odds that the child would have Down's syndrome. But none of the doctors knew. "We don't know what the statistics are," they all said. Some of them offered optimistic predictions on the basis that Down's syndrome occurs more commonly in conjunction with heart lesions other than critical aortic stenosis. These considerations, in fact, had little bearing on the case, since the question at hand was not "What is the likelihood that a newborn child with Down's syndrome will have critical aortic stenosis?" but "What is the likelihood that a newborn child with critical aortic stenosis will have Down's syndrome?" Finally the father decided that since three out of four doctors thought the child would turn out to have Down's syndrome, the probability was therefore seventy-five percent. About the only conclusions that can be drawn from this exchange of misinformation are these:

1. Most doctors are not comfortable making subjective probability estimates in the absence of "objective" relative-frequency data.
2. The idea of probability is sufficiently complex and ill-understood that it can easily be distorted into an instrument of confusion, manipulation, and control.
3. When denied access to reasonable probability estimates or a reliable basis for making them, people will make their own estimates, however ill-founded.

After two days the father, who previously had said only that if the Down's test came back positive he would refuse to operate, announced his intention not to act to save the baby's life even if she did *not* have Down's syndrome, since she clearly had a very limited life ahead of her. The sudden revelation angered the only doctor besides S. who had supported the father all along. This doctor, a young cardiologist, *had* given the father the benefit of the doubt. Now he felt that the father had shown himself to be unworthy of his trust. He didn't take into account the conditions that made it difficult for the father to act reasonably and consistently. Concluding that he could no longer give him the benefit of the doubt, this doctor joined the others who were trying to shame the father into accepting surgery.

The father, capitulating to the pressure, then consented to the operation, which was performed immediately. The next day the test result came back negative for Down's syndrome, but by then the baby had died. "If only your husband had agreed to operate earlier . . ." wailed the nurses to the mother. (Again, the delay probably only slightly diminished the child's already unfavorable prospects for survival.) The father was left with feelings of shame; the mother was left questioning her husband's judgment at a deeply serious moment in their life together. It was, in a sense, a broken family.

Afterward, as a way of quantifying the biases of the physi-

cians (including his own), S. made up a quick version of decision analysis for the young cardiologist, to see how sensitive the
decision would have been to different probabilities: "Taking
the probability that this child would be capable of normal development as ninety, seventy, fifty, thirty, or ten percent, which
of the following options would you choose?"

1. Obtain a court injunction authorizing surgery.
2. Manipulate feelings of shame to induce the father to
   operate.
3. Adopt a neutral position.
4. Support the father if he decides not to operate.
5. Manipulate feelings of shame to induce the father not to
   operate.

The heart specialist chose options 1 and 2 at fifty percent and
above, 3 at thirty percent, and 4 at ten percent. S. chose options
1 and 2 at ninety percent, 3 at seventy percent, and 4 at fifty
percent and below. Although no "official" estimate of this
baby's chance for survival and normal development had been
made, in retrospect the senior cardiologist's best guess was that
it was not better than thirty percent. The younger heart specialist was left feeling that he should have adopted a neutral position, while S. felt that he ought to have supported the father's
decision more publicly.

As this case was actually handled, it seems fair to say that
human feelings, family prerogatives, and medical realities
were violated by those whose responsibility it was to respect
them. Shame is a dangerous drug, with severe side effects and
high costs attendant upon its use. This does not mean that it
should never be used (there are such things as child neglect
and wife beating), but that, like other dangerous drugs, it
should not be used indiscriminately.

How might S. have used a gambling model to define the alternatives more clearly for this family, and to make the physicians more sensitive to the family's needs and priorities? First,
he might have laid out the decisions that were required in the
form of a bet or a series of bets. When one bets on a coin flip,
the outcomes look like this:

OUTCOME

BET		Heads	Tails
	Heads	**Win**	**Lose**
	Tails	**Lose**	**Win**

Here the value of the available choices was similarly affected by the contingencies of the outcome:

CONDITION

ACTION		Down's	Not Down's
	Operate	**Worse**	**Best** (if operation works)
	Not Operate	**Better**	**Worst**

There were two possible bets here. The surgeons, by choosing to operate, were betting that the child did not have Down's syndrome. The father, by choosing not to have the operation done, was betting that the child did have Down's. This is an oversimplification, since the doctors stood to gain by operating (by their values) whether or not Down's syndrome turned out to be present. The father, on the other hand, had reasons not to operate even if Down's was not present, since he was also concerned with the possibility that the heart operation might not prevent a cardiac-related disability comparable in severity to the retardation produced by Down's syndrome.

The father and the doctors chose different bets for one or both of the following reasons: (1) they evaluated the probabilities differently, or else just paid attention to different possibilities, the father being more concerned with the Down's contingency, the doctors with the Not Down's contingency (cf. Kahneman and Tversky, 1973); (2) they had different values. The doctors were most concerned to save a life (and exercise their skills) while the question of the quality of the life saved did not stand out in their minds. The father was most concerned about the costs of raising a child with a serious disability (of whatever origin). The doctors also felt that failing to save a life by not operating was far more reprehensible than taking a life by having the child die right after the operation, as in fact she did. Or as one senior surgeon put it, "Sometimes we have to be executioners" (that being, at least, a skill). The father, on the other hand, did not see letting a baby with severe defects die as a reprehensible act.

The feelings of the doctors and the father might be paraphrased as follows (although it is highly unlikely that either side articulated what is written here, even to themselves): One of the surgeons might have thought, "If I let this child die, then in the future I am committed to letting other children die. This would be a precedent. I find it all very painful. Though I could stand the pain of letting this one child die, I could not do the same thing again and again and again. That's just too painful for me. So I'll draw the line right here. I'll commit myself to operating to try to save this child, because that's the only policy I can imagine following consistently." The father might have said to himself, "This is the only time I'll ever have to decide whether or not to let a child die. Though I can stand the pain once, I couldn't stand having over and over again the pain of letting her live, which I would have to if it's going to be matter of repeated operations. Therefore I'll accept the pain I can more easily endure—that of letting the child die once."

Conceiving of the choice as a gamble would not have provided an "answer" to this dilemma. What it *would* have done was to reveal plainly that there *were* value differences involved, and that these needed to be addressed by all concerned. Once these differences had been brought into the open, the family's values would likely have been honored, provided that these did not violate societal values protecting infants from indifferent or malevolent parents. In this instance society's values would have left considerable leeway for responsible people to make different decisions.

The use of the gambling model also would have made clear

that probability estimates were required for making those decisions, and that the family needed to be better informed about the probabilities than they were in the actual case, where they were left in near-complete uncertainty about the likely outcomes of actions that were presented to them as moral imperatives. On the basis of the probabilities and values, the father's gamble could have been seen in a clearer light. The doctors and nurses who thought him callous and inhuman might have understood that three days and a small reduction (from thirty percent to twenty percent) of the baby's chances for a healthy existence were a painful price that he was willing to pay for more information and some time to make up his mind.

Once the gamble had been analyzed, S. might have sat down with the husband and wife and said, "We all have mixed feelings about what to do. Can we come up with a course of action that will incorporate all those feelings? If not, can we set some priorities and agree to leave some differences unresolved? Whatever happens, it won't be that one of us was right and the others wrong. Some gambles are reasonable; others are not. In many situations it would not be reasonable not to try to save a baby's life. In this case, although there are differences among us, we all have good reasons for making certain choices. It may be right to operate immediately and have a child with Down's syndrome. It may be right to wait, even if we find out only after the child has died that she did not have Down's. The main thing is to know what we are gambling for and why."

Gambling and the Unconscious

The doctors in the Down's syndrome case gambled unconsciously, in the sense that they did not admit to themselves that they were gambling. They also gambled badly, both in that they did not work together in a trusting way with the family with whom they shared the gamble, and in that their choice of gambles (whether right or wrong) was not justified by their stated reasons for choosing it.

We can also imagine other ways of gambling badly. Suppose the baby's father had said (as he did not) that he and his wife preferred not to have the baby operated on because, having already reconciled themselves to the baby's death, they did not want to open themselves up again to the possibility of disappointment. They would rather just accept their "fate." Hope brings anxiety in its wake, and disappointed hope makes a bad outcome worse, so why not just accept the worst? This choice, absurd on the face of it, makes a kind of sense if one cannot bear anxiety and possible disappointment as costs of trying to better one's condition.

People differ in the degree of anxiety that uncertainty arouses in them. They also differ in their ability to bear the anxiety they experience. If, for example, you give children a basketball and watch them take their shots, you will find that some stand so close to the basket that they almost always get the ball in, while others stand so far back that they almost never get it in. Still others stand at an intermediate distance, where they have a reasonable, but by no means certain chance to score (McClelland, 1958). Presumably, as they practice and improve, they step back farther from the basket, where they can continue to face a challenge. These individuals either feel less anxiety or are better able to bear it. Those who choose either the safe situation or the impossibly difficult one are trying to get away from anxiety by moving to a situation of very low or very high risk.

When people are made anxious by uncertainty and also do not tolerate anxiety well, they will be more likely to gamble unconsciously and, in so doing, to choose certain kinds of gambles (Fuller, 1975). Moreover, anxiety about uncertainty is characteristic of the unconscious, so that anyone, regardless of personality, who is gambling unconsciously is likely to be in full flight from uncertainty. Unconscious thinking (in particular, what in the psychoanalytic literature is called "primary process" or "id" thinking) tends to take the form of mechanistic thinking. The unconscious polarizes the world into yes or no, all or none, good or bad, rather than seeing it in more subtle degrees of probability or value. It assumes one's own values to be universal. Its causal explanations (as noted in Chapter 4) are unicausal and primitive: "I am the cause" (narcissistic) or "the Other is the cause" (paranoid). Either "I cause everything," or "I cause nothing."

The narcissism of the unconscious is expressed in the belief that the outcome hinges solely on the application of skill, as by a physician: "I can be the cause of all. If I take over, it will turn out right." It also is expressed in the gambling error of paying attention only to one's own wins or losses instead of to the actual probabilities (e.g., the number of "tens" remaining in the blackjack deck). This error can take the form of what is called the postmortem fallacy ("if I have been losing, I must be doing something wrong") or the gambler's fallacy ("if I have been losing, perhaps now I'll win"). Either way it reflects the egocentric assumption that all that matters in the world is what happens to oneself; there lies the cause of it all. This kind of mechanistic thinking, which assumes that the future will be like the past, can result in actions that make this a self-fulfilling prophecy. In contrast, probabilistic gambling also relies on past experience, but only if understood critically, i.e., in terms of the variables that actually influence the probabilities, including (but not confined to) those that engage the emotions of the gambler. The critical gambler is one whose hopes and fears are tempered by realistic expectations.

Just as unconscious thinking considers only one cause at a time, so it considers only one outcome at a time. The outcome it tends to focus on is the most extreme, so in the unconscious all consequences resolve themselves into either life or death. Every choice is one of "to be or not to be." The unconscious does not weigh costs and benefits or hold various outcomes in some kind of emotional balance. Instead it responds to the stimulus most immediately at hand, to whatever possible outcome is most salient emotionally. Thus instead of an expected-value strategy for gambling (which entails weighing costs and benefits, probabilities and values), the unconscious follows what in game theory is called a *minimax* decision strategy, which seeks to minimize the maximum possible loss. A minimax strategy ignores probability and is concerned with only one outcome, the worst, which it seeks to avoid. (In medicine, as in the unconscious, the worst outcome is death.) As such it is appropriate not for a probabilistic universe, but for a completely uncertain universe (where probability is useless) or a completely certain universe (where probability is unnecessary). The world of the unconscious is the world of the primitive, oscillating between these extreme states of total understanding and control (self as omnipotent cause) and no understanding and control (other as cause, self as impotent).

This fear of maximum loss, together with the anxiety about uncertainty that is strongly felt under the Mechanistic Paradigm, leads to the avoidance of risk, since risk involves both uncertainty and the possibility of maximum loss. The risk that is most to be avoided, according to this logic of the unconscious, is that of death, for death in the savage universe of the unconscious is maximum loss and maximum uncertainty (no one knows what it really is). Death is the ultimate fear that lies behind the minimax strategy. It is also what some doctors and hospitals, in the K. and Down's syndrome cases and throughout contemporary practice, have shown themselves to be quite literally preoccupied with, sometimes to the exclusion of other values. Doctors often speak of what they do as "saving lives," although few medical situations involve life-or-death issues. Behind the choices of gambles that doctors make (such as the choice in the case of K. to avoid the worst outcome at all costs) there lurks the fear of death.

In the cautious, insecure world of minimax strategy a sharp line is drawn to separate the permissible from the unthinkable. Beyond this line gradations of value cannot be entertained, since all possibilities are regarded as intolerable. For example, given these choices:

   a) to kill a patient
   b) not to do anything for a patient, who then dies
   c) not to try very hard for a patient, who then dies
   d) not to do everything for a patient, who then dies
   e) to lose a patient while doing one's best

the last is the only acceptable outcome for many doctors. All five of these outcomes involve cost for the patient (death), but the first four also involve cost for the doctor—the cost of believing and having it believed that one did not do everything to prevent the patient's death. The problem with this bias is that, while (e) is best for the doctor, (d) may in some instances be best for the patient.

This, then, is how the Mechanistic Paradigm and the use of unconscious processes reinforce each other. When one's thinking is guided by the Mechanistic Paradigm, with its unattainable standard of certainty, one becomes anxious when one sees that one is taking chances. Since one cannot avoid taking chances, one seeks to avoid the anxiety by closing one's eyes to the fact that one is taking chances. What one sees with one's eyes closed is the possibility of death. With this fearsome prospect in view one understandably seeks the assurances that the Mechanistic Paradigm offers: certainty (Criterion #1), control (Criterion #2), and objective knowledge (Criterion #3). The more one shuts one's eyes, the more difficult it is to open them again.

The Probabilistic Paradigm offers a way to break this vicious circle by reducing some of the emotional costs of gambling. Since certainty is not set up as the standard for knowledge under the Probabilistic Paradigm, people do not feel (on top of the anxiety inherent in uncertain situations) the added anxiety of trying to make these situations certain. The Probabilistic Paradigm enables people to acknowledge their values, including the value of reducing anxiety, and to act consciously to reduce anxiety if that is a desired end. It enables people to cope with the anxiety associated with risk by seeing the feared outcome not as certain to occur (as the unconscious would have it), but as having a probability of occurrence that can be estimated and lived with. Even death can be contemplated in a more realistic, less overwhelmingly frightening way. Because gambling under the Probabilistic Paradigm is not as scary as under the Mechanistic, it can more easily be done consciously. And consciousness in turn makes it possible to gamble according to scientific principles.

How do we break out of the mechanistic cycle and initiate the probabilistic one? We can't gain control of our gambling without understanding the factors, internal and external, that customarily exert control over the gambles we take. When we gamble unconsciously, we aren't really making our own choices. In part it is the unconscious that exerts control. But there are other controlling factors as well, and these lie outside ourselves.

Who Controls the Game?

Just as people individually feel more or less anxious about uncertainty, people together find themselves in—and create—situations where such anxiety is felt and heeded to a greater or lesser degree. It has been observed, for example, that surgeons, in the aftermath of an unexpected death on the operating table, prefer to operate on hopeless cases. The reason they usually give for doing this is that they wish to practice their technique. What they are also doing is choosing a low-anxiety task in a situation where their anxiety level has been temporarily raised. Just as anxious people avoid middle-range risks (high uncertainty) in favor of high risks (almost certain failure) and low risks (almost certain success), nearly anyone may do so in anxiety-provoking situations. Just as people who seek the approval of others tailor their gambling strategies to gain that approval, nearly anyone may do so in situations where the approval of others is crucial.

People are sensitized to how others take risks. If someone does so in an unusual manner, he is identified as a gambler, and his risk-taking is thereby considered excessive. Since anxiety can be caused just by seeing others take what appear to be unacceptable risks, people often seek to limit the amount of risk-taking that others do. In situations that bring out such concerns, people are put under considerable pressure to avoid dreaded consequences by gambling as everyone else does. For example, the father in the Down's syndrome case, who on his own was able to respond reasonably to uncertainty and risk, was reduced to confusion and inconsistency in the stressful situation created by the hospital staff.

Unfortunately most of us spend much of our lives in similarly stressful situations. The world described in Chapter 4—a world of "exchange" relationships and zero-sum games in the family, the workplace, and the marketplace—is guided by the workings of the unconscious and by the Mechanistic Paradigm. In the absence of trusting relationships in which the emotional burdens of uncertainty can be shared (indeed, in the presence of relationships that generate suspicion and self-seeking behavior), we find ourselves much of the time on guard. After all, someone else's gain is likely to be our loss. We react to uncertainty with fear, and we react to fear with self-protective strategies. For example, when we have to do our jobs under the threat (explicit or implicit) of being fired for departing from ritual, or for thinking critically, we will tend to make a habit of thinking mechanistically. Our gambling will be furtive, our strategies automatic. Such gambling resembles the gambling that is done at the casino and the racetrack, not in the scientist's laboratory.

All this does not magically change when we walk into a doctor's office. On the contrary, the threats are more severe, the risks even less acceptable in a setting where life as well as livelihood is at stake. Here even people who elsewhere in life gamble consciously and cooperatively may slip back into fear and ritual.

Medicine is not only a science; it is also a social institution. To be a science today medicine needs to follow the Probabilistic Paradigm. To be a social institution today, it can only follow the Mechanistic Paradigm. As in other workplaces and marketplaces, people who gamble unconsciously have their choices of gambles controlled by corporations intent on profit. A Las Vegas hospital created an unwitting parody of the kind of gambling that goes on in medicine today when it established a lottery to pull in the customers on weekends (when people usually don't go into the hospital unless they have to). Anyone who checks in on a Friday or Saturday (usually for nonemergency surgery) automatically is entered in the sweepstakes. The winner gets a four-thousand-dollar vacation trip, or (for those too ill to travel) the equivalent in cash. And if you die while you're in the hospital, your winnings go to your estate. Of course, the "house" gets its cut too.

Medicine, like many activities that people engage in together, is a mixture of cooperative and competitive (zero-sum) gambling. The patient and the doctor (and the hospital if one is involved) are gambling together for the patient's health. The doctor also is gambling for experience, the satisfaction of exercising skill, and a professional reputation. The doctor and the hospital are gambling to make money, and the patient (when not completely covered by insurance) is gambling not to lose money. Finally, all three parties are gambling for control. To the extent that they can control the gamble, they are all better able to win the stakes they are gambling for. But control is itself part of the stakes, since people—and institutions—get satisfaction from exercising control. Control would not be an issue if medicine were a cooperative gamble guided by scientific principles. The fact that it is an issue points to the zero-sum aspect of gambling in medicine.

In commercial gambling establishments the "house" controls important elements of the game. In medicine the doctor's office or hospital is the house. Here the house does not control the odds as a casino does, but it does control information about the odds. Whereas in gambling under the Probabilistic Paradigm information is produced in order to be shared, in the zero-sum gambling of the casino (and the hospital when it acts like a casino) information is hoarded so that it can be selectively shared and withheld. For example, in Mrs. Pinelli's case the hospital personnel freely shared information with the patient about how much an arteriogram might reveal, but failed to mention that the data thus revealed were not likely to be useful.

By knowingly or unknowingly giving the gambler a false impression of the odds, the house can influence the gambler's choice, as when the house staff exaggerates the dangers of a condition to ensure a patient's cooperation. The most extreme bias in the presentation of odds is the claim that one course of action is a gamble (a matter of probability) while another is not a gamble (a matter of certainty). When a doctor tells a patient, "You're taking a chance by taking care of this condition at home rather than in the hospital," without adding that it is also taking a chance to go into the hospital, the doctor, though not intentionally deceiving the patient, is simply thinking in the way that comes naturally—i.e., in terms of the Mechanistic Paradigm. The doctor, too, is gambling unconsciously, but in such a way as to control the patient's gamble on behalf of the hospital.

Along with information the house controls contingencies that affect the outcome for the gambler. In the Down's syndrome case, for example, the doctors pressured the father to sign an operative consent form by threatening to withhold life-saving efforts that might later be required. In everyday medical situations the threat is neither so explicit nor so drastic; it can simply take the form of the selective withdrawal of the acceptance, approval, and affection that many people seek from a doctor. Through these means of control, doctors and hospitals (often out of a sincere desire to do what is good for the patient) induce patients not only to stay in the "game" longer than they need to, but to raise the ante by betting on what are probably unnecessary technical procedures. Patients, like tourists in Las Vegas, can get swept up into the game, staking more than they initially intended.

It isn't only patients, though, whose gambling is controlled by the corporate interests that constitute the "house." Doctors who gamble unconsciously are also susceptible to such control. A doctor's effectiveness is always on public trial, with judgment being rendered by patients, peers, and the courts. Doctors are afraid to be called gamblers. They are afraid of being singled out as unorthodox for failing to participate in the rituals of defensive medicine, rituals that grow out of a fear of failure and a preoccupation with the approval of others. The day-to-day reliance on "safe" procedures alternates with the daring emergency operation where the doctor becomes a hero by succeeding but has nothing to lose by failing.

S. found that the setting mattered too. He gambled differently with his patients in the office, the home, and the hospital. In his office, where he was the "house," he tried to share the control with patients as much as he could (though he didn't flatter himself that he was completely successful). In a patient's home the family was in a sense the house, although S.'s medical knowledge and authority gave him some control as well; there, too, a cooperative spirit prevailed. When the hospital was the house, however, S. sometimes felt as if he and the patient were gambling together *against* the house. The physicians in training known as house officers (as S. well knew from having been one, as well as from his later dealings with them) were like casino employees, running the tables by the rules of the house. S., on the other hand, as a private "attending" physician, felt more like a tipster, picking up inside information that might help the patient and family turn the odds in their favor, but unable to influence the outcome as much as he would like.

S. concluded that he and his patients would be able to take control of their gambling decisions only by learning to gamble consciously—by taking the gamble, as it were, of thinking of themselves as gamblers and learning the skills needed to be scientific gamblers. As S. was to learn, gambling skills are equally useful whether one is gambling with the house in a spirit of cooperation or against the house in a tense adversarial atmosphere. Perhaps most important, they can provide a way of getting from the latter state to the former.

Skill and Chance

To gamble is to acknowledge the part that chance plays in all events. And yet gambling is itself a skill, the skill of dealing with chance. In order to gamble consciously and effectively we need to distinguish between situations that are largely governed by chance and situations in which skill can be decisive (Langer, 1975). We can then turn what we might call "chance situations" into "skill situations" by applying the skills of gambling.

By "chance" situations we mean those where nature must take its course; by "skill" situations we mean those where human action can influence the outcome. Thus when we speak here of "skill" versus "chance," we are talking not about the degree of predictability that a situation exhibits, but about the degree of control that one may exert over it through the exercise of skill. One can almost always predict the course of a common cold, but one cannot change it. We therefore consider a case of the common cold to be a predominantly chance situation, different in degree, not in kind, from a roll of the dice. The probabilities of the outcomes are different, but the two situations are equally uncontrollable.

Skill situations satisfy our natural urge to *do* something, to be in control. On the other hand, there are times when we would just as soon put down the burden of responsibility and leave things to chance. Thus two common errors in gambling (including medical gambling) are to interpret chance situations as skill situations and to interpret skill situations as chance situations. A gambler who tries to "psych out" the roll of the dice is trying to apply skill to a chance situation. A gambler who sits at the blackjack table and plays without keeping track of the cards that come up is leaving a skill situation to chance. In medicine to disregard chance and use skill inappropriately is a form of defensive medicine. To neglect necessary skills and rely inappropriately on chance is a form of malpractice. Ironically, the wish to control, like the wish to relinquish control, leaves us open to having our choices controlled by the unconscious or by others who are gambling against us.

A third error is to treat the "skill versus chance" distinction as an all-or-none thing. In situations where skill is found, so is chance, and vice versa. Skill and chance situations can be thought of as existing on a continuum, both in actuality and in people's perceptions of them, as illustrated in Figure 7-1. At all points on the diagonal running through the box, the degree of skill, as opposed to chance, that people choose to apply matches exactly the degree of skill, as opposed to chance, that is required by the situation. Appropriate responses to situations are those that fall on this line. The dots appearing elsewhere in the box represent instances in which people's perceptions of a situ-

The Skill-Chance Continuum

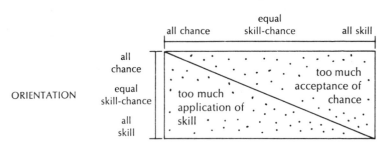

FIGURE 7-1

ation do not match the actuality. The greater the distance between a dot and the line, the less appropriate the response.

For the sake of simplicity it is useful to think of situations as involving *predominantly* either chance or skill. In a predominantly chance situation a chance orientation is appropriate, a skill orientation inappropriate. The reverse is true in a predominantly skill situation.

The trick is to identify the skill and chance aspects of the situation. Suppose, for example, that a woman in her late sixties is dying of bowel cancer. Nothing can be done to save her life. If we are looking at the life-or-death outcome, then by our definition this is a chance situation. (The cards have already been dealt.) If, on the other hand, we are looking at the possibility of making the woman more comfortable with loving care and supportive treatment (caring and supporting being skills), then this is a skill situation. (There is still an opportunity to bid on the cards that have been dealt.) To try to alter the course of the patient's condition by performing investigative procedures would be to treat a chance situation as if it were a skill situation. To say that nothing can be done to make the patient feel better as she is dying would be to treat a skill situation as if it were a chance situation.

Figure 7-2 shows that this one case can illustrate an appropriate acceptance of chance (1); an inappropriate acceptance of chance (2); an inappropriate application of skill (3); and an appropriate application of skill (4). (In this and subsequent diagrams, the inappropriate choices will be shaded.)

Leaving aside the issue of nurturant care (important as it can be, not only for a dying patient but for any patient), we can use two other cases to illustrate the skill-chance distinction with regard to "purely medical" outcomes, as shown in Figure 7-3. A child has a runny nose and sore throat. A common cold is diagnosed and left to run its course, although medication may be given to ease symptomatic discomfort. That is a predominantly chance situation. Another child comes in with severe ankle pain. X rays are taken so that a possible fracture can be identified and, if present, treated. That is a skill situation. But if viral cultures are taken to isolate the specific organism causing the common cold (even though there are no antibiotics to kill such a virus), or if the child with ankle pain is simply sent home without being examined and told, "It will get better in a few days," then we have again confused chance with skill, or skill with chance.

It is unlikely that any reputable doctor would make either of these elementary mistakes when dealing with a common cold or a possible broken ankle. But in the case of K. (Chapter 1), physicians with the best training and the best intentions made *both* mistakes. They inappropriately exercised the skill of diagnostic testing, when the precise identity of K.'s condition

Skill and Chance: Terminal Cancer

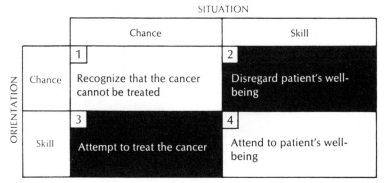

		SITUATION	
		Chance	Skill
ORIENTATION	Chance	**1** Recognize that the cancer cannot be treated	**2** Disregard patient's well-being
	Skill	**3** Attempt to treat the cancer	**4** Attend to patient's well-being

FIGURE 7-2

Skill and Chance: Common Cold and Ankle Pain

SITUATION

		Common cold (Chance)	Ankle pain (Skill)
ORIENTATION	Chance	**1** Do not investigate cause	**2** Do not investigate cause
	Skill	**3** Investigate with viral cultures	**4** Investigate by examining

FIGURE 7-3

could, after a while, have been left in the realm of chance, and they failed to exercise fully the skills of feeding and nurturing, which might have benefited K. Dr. S., who held different views about which skills would influence the outcome, did not make these mistakes here (which is not to say that he never made them). Note that this case, as represented in Figure 7-4, differs from that of the dying cancer patient, where neither kind of skill could have affected the medical outcome. In K.'s case the use of inappropriate skills may have hastened the patient's death, while the use of appropriate skills might have saved the patient's life.

Skill and Chance: The Case of K.

SITUATION

		Chance	Skill
ORIENTATION	Chance	**1** Dr. S: do not investigate cause beyond a certain point	**2** Hospital physicians: do not concentrate on feeding and nurturing
	Skill	**3** Hospital physicians: investigate cause without limit	**4** Dr. S: feed and nurture

FIGURE 7-4

Overdiagnosing and undernourishing are errors made commonly under the Mechanistic Paradigm, which does not acknowledge (as the Probabilistic Paradigm does) that even the exercise of skill is always a gamble. The Mechanistic Paradigm places emphasis on skills that can be exercised with an appearance of precision, such as diagnostic testing and technically oriented treatment. More subtle skills, such as diagnostic "watching and waiting" and nurturant treatment (food, love, comfort), it abandons to chance. "That's not science," it says. But the Probabilistic Paradigm makes possible a science of chance, which in turn changes the nature of skill as well as the relationship between skill and chance. The fact that the effects of nourishing a child are difficult to measure, and obviously involve a large element of chance, no longer justifies disregarding them or the skills they entail.

The inappropriate use of skill in chance situations is one of the rituals by which people, including doctors, cope with the anxiety aroused by uncertainty. A better way of coping, one that answers the same emotional needs without denying reality, is by using the skills of gambling. These include assessing causes and effects probabilistically, estimating probabilities and values, understanding the effects of time and social context on gambling decisions, dealing with the emotions that arise in the course of gambling, and recognizing and avoiding the common errors of gambling. Most of all, gambling under the Probabilistic Paradigm means being able to do all of these things with other people in a relationship where uncertainty is shared. In this kind of gambling the doctor, patient, and family ideally can work together with the openness and mutual respect of fellow scientists.

S. encouraged patients to be his partners in gambling, as we see in the following case:

A seventy-year-old man had a feeling of tightness and discomfort in his legs whenever he climbed stairs or walked a short distance. On examination Dr. S. found weak pulses in the thighs and below. S. diagnosed a reduced blood flow to the legs—insufficient for exercising—caused by clogged blood vessels. He said to the patient, "I have no way of treating your condition medically. If you want to do something about it, you will need to go to a specialist to see if it can be treated surgically. Surgery helps some people, but it also involves risks. At your age you may prefer to accept the restrictions this condition places on your life. Or you may accept the risks of surgery in an effort to improve it. If it gets worse, and the circulation is blocked off completely, you may eventually be forced to do something about it. In any case you should get more information from a specialist to help you decide whether you want to have surgery now. If you don't have surgery, that's a decision, just as it is if you do. You know how the racetrack works. If you bet on a race, you want to know the odds on each horse before you bet, and you may want to hedge your bet. It wouldn't make sense to bet on one of the horses, or not to bet on any of them, without knowing the odds."

Here S. was sharing his perspective on reality so that he and the patient could engage in common action. Working with patients in this way made S. feel as if some of the load had been lifted from his shoulders. It's not that he was "punting," or passing the buck of responsibility to ill patients who may just have wanted to be taken care of. Rather, instead of taking full responsibility to impose order on an uncertain world, he was sharing responsibility with patients and with chance.

What patients gain from such an exchange is a chance to learn some of the doctor's detachment. A doctor has less to win or lose on each gamble than a patient does. Doctors also get more practice in gambling, more experience in winning and losing. The doctors who gamble best for their patients are those who can, when needed, take a certain emotional distance from their gambling, though not to the point of losing empathy and gambling recklessly "for the fun of it." Patients who gamble with a doctor like S. not only can learn to achieve better outcomes, but also can gain some perspective on the wins and the losses. They can take responsibility for choosing reasonable gambles, but still be able to live with themselves—and with uncertainty—if they lose. Thus when doctors and patients gamble together, both can learn not only to see each gamble from up close, as a patient feels it, or from a distance, as a doctor approaches it, but to move back and forth between the two points of view (Havens, 1976).

Since gambling, with its characteristic skills and attitudes, acts as an analgesic for anxiety in cases of uncertainty, it is not surprising that it, like other analgesics, can be overused. A harried doctor may try to shed too much responsibility by habitually turning skill situations into chance situations, i.e., "punting." It is nice to be able to blame one's failures on chance. Given human nature and the conditions under which doctors must work, some doctors will use the notion of gambling to let them off the hook in difficult situations, just as few doctors today, in comparable situations, go to the narcotic cabinet. If doctors, who are gambling only for their reputation, time, and the feelings they share with patients, feel a need to escape, then it is not surprising that patients, who are gambling for life and health, will also seek relief. There will be some who will say, "It's all up to chance," and continue smoking or, like Mrs. Pinelli, stop taking their medications.

Although gambling is open to abuse, the primary effect is to enable patients as well as doctors to use skill to live with their anxiety rather than to allow anxiety to reduce their skill. Through the experience of gambling, patients will gain a better sense of the probabilities, that is, of which contingencies are controllable and which are not. They will then be able to make better choices in the future. Beyond this, the very act of making an informed choice can give a patient a sense of being in control, which in itself may reduce the stress of illness and with it the physical as well as emotional damage suffered by the patient. In keeping with the second criterion of the Probabilistic Paradigm, both the consequences of particular choices and the habit of making choices have an impact on one's experience, capacities, and character. A habit of making choices consciously, and recognizing a degree of uncertainty in one's choices, can produce a stronger, wiser self.

8

GAMBLING SKILLS FOR MEDICINE

Once he realized that one could not avoid gambling, S. set out to learn to gamble well. If he were going to have to gamble anyway, he ought to be able to tell the difference between a good gamble and a bad gamble and act on the good one. This skill, he reflected, was the same as the scientist's skill of choosing the hypotheses most likely to yield true and good outcomes. It was as important for his patients as it was for him. Patients sought the good, in that they wanted to get well. They sought the true, in that they wanted to understand why they were sick and how they might get well. Understanding was what gave patients a sense of control—and some real control—over their fate. As S. came to see, though, it would have to be an understanding of gambling as well as of medicine.

Gambling strategies are heuristics, or rules of thumb for solving problems. As we saw in Chapter 7, people generally gamble according to unconscious heuristics. By gambling unconsciously, they don't have a chance to learn from experience, correct gambling errors, and exercise gambling skills.

As S. became a more conscious gambler, he began to look critically at two types of heuristics: (1) preferences for one type of gamble over another; and (2) patterns of gambling decisions

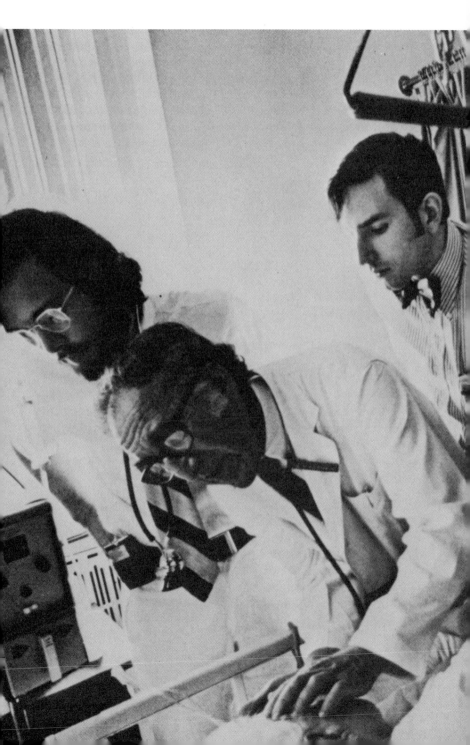

over time. In the course of his clinical practice S. asked himself what kinds of gambles he favored and under what conditions he changed his gambling choices. In both areas he found himself making what he later judged to be mistakes. In gambling, however, unlike decision analysis, learning from one's mistakes is part of the method. Whereas in decision analysis the "irrational" human factor tends to undermine the method, the gambling approach involves a human rationality incorporating common sense, perception, experience, and feelings. It recognizes that human beings are capable both of acting and of evaluating actions in many different ways, and that what is a mistake in one context may not be in another.

Gambling Preferences

People tend to prefer some type of gambles to others. Sometimes it is reasonable to act on a particular gambling preference; sometimes it is not. One must make a judgment about whether an act is reasonable in a given situation. Like the judgments that scientists make, this is a judgment about whether acting on a given preference is consistent with what we know to be true and what we know to be good. Thus the purpose of gambling consciously is not to learn to gamble in some ideal way, but to understand how we do gamble so that we can decide whether or not we are gambling reasonably.

A few gambling preferences are logically inconsistent, as we have seen in the so-called Dutch Book situation. These preferences can be called mistakes. Other preferences are specious, in that they do not serve the gambler's interest in the way the gambler imagines they do. A gambler may, for example, habitually seek what seem to be skill situations in the belief that his skill can almost always overcome chance. Another gambler, believing that he is "lucky" or lacking confidence in his skills, may habitually seek what seem to be chance situations. These preferences are specious if they are maintained without regard to the contexts in which the gambles are chosen. As we have seen, the preference for either skill or chance situations can be a reasonable one, but only when applied in an appropriate context.

As S. began to watch how he and others gambled, these were some of the common gambling preferences that he observed:

1. Preference to avoid gambling.   In a society that understands itself and its environment in terms of the Mechanistic Paradigm, the uncertainty of gambling makes people anxious. People who don't want to gamble choose gambles that don't look like gambles at all. For example, they may go into the hospital (or, as doctors, bring patients into the hospital) in the belief that the hospital is a "safe" environment whereas taking care of the condition at home would be "taking a chance."

When people who don't want to gamble *are* aware that they are gambling, they prefer to have a "sure thing"—a gamble they can't lose. Suppose someone is given the choice of these two gambles:

Gamble A:	90% chance of winning $10
	10% chance of losing $1
Gamble B:	50% chance of winning $2
	50% chance of winning $1

Gamble A has the higher expected value, by far. One would almost surely win more by choosing it over a series of trials, and would probably win more by choosing it once. Yet some people would choose Gamble B, simply because they wouldn't want to risk losing anything. And this would be the right choice for a person who wandered into the casino without having any money to pay off a loss. In the never-never casino that offered such bets, this gambler could build up a small bankroll by betting Gamble B the first few times, and then switch to Gamble A.

Gamble B likewise may have been the right choice for Dr. S.

in the case of K. Faced with a starving child who had no resources of physical or emotional strength, he could not risk depleting the child's strength further by testing (losing one dollar) to try to gain a definite diagnosis (winning ten dollars). Actually the odds on his winning that bet were more like ninety percent against than ninety percent for. So instead he chose the conservative option of feeding and emotionally supporting K., which might more or less benefit him (winning two dollars or one dollar), but would be unlikely to hurt him. Once K. had built up some reserve strength for surviving traumatic investigations, Dr. S. could reevaluate the option of going for the jackpot (the ten-dollar diagnosis).

Of course, the odds were not quite so favorable for Dr. S. as Gamble B indicates, since K. stood some chance of dying of an undiagnosed infection while he was being nurtured back to health. Real life seldom offers us gambles that we can't lose. When we think we have found such a gamble, it is usually because we deny the possibility of losing and imagine that a loss would be really just the same as maintaining the status quo. In choosing Gamble A, the doctors who treated K. didn't take into account the possibility that the tests were contributing to the deterioration of K.'s condition. To the extent that they even saw themselves as taking a gamble, they thought they were betting to win ten dollars (by finding the diagnosis) or *lose nothing*. For them (though not for K.) the gamble came free of charge.

When the possibility of losing cannot be avoided, those who prefer not to gamble choose gambles in which there is little difference between winning and losing (i.e., where there isn't much to lose). When given a chance to remain at status quo or risk an equal chance of gaining or losing an equal amount, people tend to prefer to stay where they are. In a "double or nothing" game, where the choice is between a sure five dollars and an equal chance of having ten dollars or nothing, "gamblers" will take the bet, but our culture encourages the conservative choice of keeping what one already has. For example, a disease is controlled at a tolerable, though moderately disabling level by medication. Radical surgery offers the chance for a dramatic improvement or complete health, though at some risk of greater disability or death. A person who prefers gambles with less variance of outcome will stick to the medication. On the other hand, a surgeon trained to regard any condition of less than perfect health as unacceptable, or a patient whose self-esteem is tied to the notion of perfect health, may well choose the gamble with greater variance.

This and other preferences can be illustrated with a probability distribution curve, where the possible outcomes are laid out from left to right in order of ascending value, and the probability of each outcome is represented by the height of the curve at that point. For the sake of simplicity the expected value (probability multiplied by value) of the gambles represented in the graphs equals zero. (In other words, if one took any of these gambles many, many times, one would expect to come out with neither a gain nor a loss.) As shown in Figure 8–1, a gamble with little variance of outcomes is the next "best" thing to no gamble at all.

Probability Distribution Curve:
Gambles with Lesser and Greater Variance

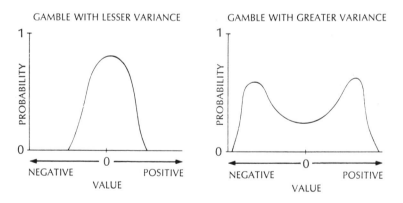

FIGURE 8-1

2. Preference for gambles with positive skew. The term *skew* describes an uneven distribution of probabilities along the value continuum. As shown in Figure 8-2, a positive skew involves a small chance of a large gain, and a large chance of a small loss. A negative skew involves a small chance of a large loss, and a large chance of a small gain.

With a positively skewed gamble there may be a greater overall chance of a negative than a positive outcome, while there may be a greater chance of a positive outcome with a negatively skewed gamble. What attracts people to the positively skewed gamble is the hope of a big payoff. What scares people away from the negatively skewed gamble is the dread of a big loss. In both cases considerations of probability take second place to the hope or dread in question.

The case of K. illustrates positive and negative skew. The physicians who ordered all the tests accepted the small, highly probable incremental losses from testing in order to play for the long-shot win of a definite diagnosis. Their gamble was a positively skewed one. They saw it as a highly responsible gam-

Probability Distribution Curve:
Gambles with Positive and Negative Skew

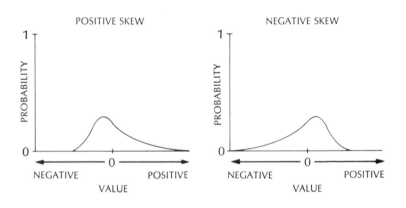

FIGURE 8-2

ble—not a gamble at all, really—because it avoided the risk of a major defeat (failure to diagnose a treatable condition). A negatively skewed gamble was unacceptable to them because it involved that risk (as well as the risk of being sued). Dr. S., on the other hand, accepted that low-probability risk in return for the small, highly probable incremental gains to be derived from good care and nutrition. He reasoned that, rather than leading to either a breakthrough or catastrophe, a sustained investment in one treatment strategy or the other would result in an accumulation of minor gains or losses. These, he thought, would ultimately decide the issue. As S. saw, by repeatedly using negatively skewed gambles one can build up a bankroll that eventually will support positively skewed gambles.

A preference for positive skew reflects a focusing of attention on the most extreme possible outcomes. A big gain surely is better than a big loss. But this strategy, pushed to its extreme, ignores all the outcomes in between and their likelihood of occurrence. It is, in effect, a concentration on values, together with an indifference to probabilities. In the context of complete certainty or complete uncertainty it would make sense, but our world is generally somewhere in between.

3. Inconsistent preferences: the Preference Reversal Phenomenon.
In evaluating a gamble, one may attend primarily to the values at stake, as in the preference for positive skew, or to the probabilities of the outcomes, as in the preference for negative skew. When there are two gambles, one of which offers a higher payoff, the other a higher probability of winning, a person who is asked to choose between them will often choose the one with the more favorable odds. But when the same person is asked how high a price he or she is willing to pay for a "ticket" to make the bet, his or her attention is focused on the payoffs, and he or she will often name a higher price for the gamble with the higher payoff. Thus when the gamble is presented in one or another way, inconsistent responses can occur. This is called the Preference Reversal Phenomenon (Lichtenstein and Slovic, 1971). Although it is something that people commonly do, it represents a logically inconsistent set

of preferences, for which a Dutch Book can be made against the gambler.

In the case of the infant with the heart disorder who was suspected of having Down's syndrome, the father at first paid more attention to probability (the probability that the child would not have a normal life). Later he reversed himself and went along with the doctors, who paid more attention to value (the value of saving a life, and particularly that of saving the life of a normal child, even if there was a very low probability of the latter). The father's change of heart can be understood in terms of the different ways in which he was led to see the gamble. He initially believed that the decision was his to make. What he heard the doctors telling him was "It's your choice." Under those conditions he focused (as most people would) on the probabilities. The doctors, displeased by the choice he made, then let him know that he would suffer the consequences of having made it. "You'll pay for it" was the message he now got from them. Looking at the gamble in this new way, he chose (again as most people would) on the basis of the values.

4. Preference for gambles about which there is information.   People usually prefer gambles where they know something about the odds, whether or not the odds are actually better. This preference is illustrated by the Ellsberg paradox, which was devised by Daniel Ellsberg (1961), later to be known for his prodigious feats of photocopying. To take a hypothetical example from medicine, suppose someone in your family has leukemia, which leaves patients particularly susceptible to infections that tend to be fatal if not treated. Two drugs have been developed for treating these infections, but their effects are different for each of the three major types of leukemia: t-cell, b-cell, and null-cell. Drug X cures infections in patients with t-cell leukemia, but not b-cell. Drug Y does just the opposite. Neither drug is effective in cases of null-cell leukemia. The two drugs cannot be used together; a choice must be made.

Suppose further that at this stage of the disease tests can show only that this patient has a 33.3 percent probability of having t-cell leukemia. The tests cannot distinguish between the b-cell and null-cell variants, and thus the probabilities of these remain unspecified. Given the following possible outcomes (where + stands for survival and 0 stands for death), which drug would you choose?

Case I

OUTCOME

		T-cell (33.3% chance)	B-cell (0–66.7% chance)	Null-cell (0–66.7% chance)
CHOICE	Drug X	+	0	0
	Drug Y	0	+	0

Now consider a different case in which drugs X and Y are both *effective* against null-cell leukemia (all other conditions remaining the same). Now your choices look like this:

Case II

OUTCOME

		T-cell (33.3% chance)	B-cell (0–66.7% chance)	Null-cell (0–66.7% chance)
CHOICE	Drug X	+	0	+
	Drug Y	0	+	+

In the first case most people choose drug X. They are more comfortable with a known probability of one third than with a probability that may be anywhere from zero to two thirds. In the second case many of the very same people choose Drug Y. They prefer a known two-thirds probability to a probability that may be anywhere from one third to one. The paradox, as a quick look at the diagram makes clear, is that the two cases offer the same choice. (Drug X helps patients with t-cell, while

Drug Y helps patients with b-cell.) Why, then, do people change their preference so as to get the known odds in each case? One reason is that they prefer certainty to ambiguity—to know for sure what the odds are. Another reason may be that most people, when dealing with life and death, expect the worst. So, although there is no reason to believe that the odds in the indefinite condition are closer to, say, 0 than 66.7 percent, one's instinct is to believe that this is the case.

People prefer to have information about the odds even when the information is known to be unreliable. Take, for example, the standard medical practice of taking six blood cultures to compensate for false negative results (i.e., where the test fails to record something that is there). A blood culture is a test performed to determine whether or not bacteria are present in the blood. If they are (i.e., if there is a true positive culture), it means that they are being carried throughout the body, posing the threat of infection wherever they might lodge. K. had over forty blood cultures, with the consequences we have seen. To take six, on the other hand, is normal practice in many instances. In fact, the accuracy of the test does improve (say, from seventy percent to eighty-five percent) by taking three cultures rather than one. From then on not only are there diminishing returns (in true positive results) from taking additional cultures, but there is an increase in false positive results (where the test records something that is not there) from contamination, to say nothing of the trauma and blood loss.

Most people would argue that the costs of a false positive blood culture are less than those of a false negative. The latter might mean a patient's death. Sooner or later, though, the costs of false positive blood cultures add up: the financial and social costs of treating patients who should not be treated, the side effects of such treatment, the occasional failure to diagnose a treatable condition in a patient for whom initiating antibiotic treatment on the basis of a false positive blood culture shuts off further investigation. Pushed to its extreme, the standard medical preference for avoiding false negative cultures exemplifies the preference for information, however inaccurate. One prefers to have something to believe which isn't true than to have nothing to believe at all.

5. Preference for gambles with a higher expected value. In saying that other gambling preferences lead people to make choices that are against their own interests, our standard of comparison has been the preference for gambles which have a higher expected value. This is a reasonable standard. Other things being equal, the gamble with the higher expected value is the better gamble. But when are "other things" (e.g., the values of all the people affected by a decision, the consequences that a decision will have at different times) equal? As we saw in our discussion of decision analysis (Chapter 6), there isn't any single numerical scale on which the satisfactions of different individuals—or of the same individual at different times, in different situations, or in different moods—can be measured.

In the case of decisions in which, say, immediate human wants are weighed against the welfare of future generations, the health and safety of individuals against productive activity benefiting large numbers of people, the calculation of expected values cannot possibly encompass the many values, interests, and points of view that are involved. The same is true for what are thought of as purely individual decisions. As Mrs. Pinelli's case illustrates, people experience mixed feelings, unconscious motives, changes of mind. People gamble differently, depending on whether they are alone or with other people, whether they are taking the same gamble many times or just once, and whether they are focusing on long-range or short-range consequences.

A person will assign one expected value to the gamble of eating a hamburger when in the presence of a freshly cooked hamburger, another when in the presence of a bathroom scale. Which expected value is the correct one? Each is correct in its own context. True, in the presence of the hamburger one may try to calculate its expected value as if one were in the presence of the scale, so as to resist temptation. But that is a choice, made on the principle that the consideration of long-range consequences provides a better context for decision-making than the consideration of short-range consequences. Expected values take on meaning from the principles by which one gambles.

Such principles are in turn established in the process of making choices—of gambling. Simply in the course of living, people develop their own repertoires of intuitive decision-making methods that take into account the various contexts in which the consequences of decisions are experienced. One way of making decisions is to calculate expected values mathematically. But when one lets the number that represents expected value dictate the decision, rather than keeping it in mind as information that may be further qualified by thoughts, feelings, and experiences, one may be avoiding the responsibility of considering the contexts in which one gambles. By making one's gambles one's own through exercising one's capacity to reason, one strengthens that capacity by establishing principles and strategies for future gambles. Being able to say why one chooses something involves both self-definition and insight. In the long run, being able to say "this is who I am" may be more important than making the choice with the highest expected value.

Gambling Over Time

When he laid out medical decisions as gambles—and as choices between gambles—S. focused on some of the same issues as he did when he was doing decision analysis. Here, too, he was concerned with probability and value. Here, too, he was making choices on the basis of at least an informal estimate of the expected values of possible outcomes. "How likely is this to happen? How good or bad would it be if it did happen?" These questions, he found, were as central to the gambling method as to decision analysis.

But he learned that there were differences as well. He discovered that one of the strengths of the gambling model is its sensitivity to time. When he thought of his decisions as gambles, he found it natural to think in terms of the Probabilistic Paradigm. As a scientific gambler he acknowledged that the world changes (Criterion #1) and that the relationship between the world and the decision-maker changes (Criterion #2). Time, together with the feelings of the people involved in the decision (Criterion #3), creates a fluid context in which decision-making occurs. As time passes, probabilities change; values change; information changes; feelings change. The results of one gamble affect the next. Time also gives people who have an interest in the outcome a chance to influence the gambler's decision. The gambling framework, by incorporating the context of time, enables people to make decisions that are suitably sensitive to a complex and changing environment.

Even in what we ordinarily think of as gambling, the effects of time can be observed as people place their bets and wait for the outcome to be decided. At the racetrack a collective anxiety can be sensed as the odds fluctuate during the half hour prior to each race. As the clock runs down to post time, spectators agonize over whether to bolt from their seats and place a last-minute bet, perhaps "hedging" a bet they have previously made on a different horse. In medicine a treatment plan is decided upon, and the doctor and patient wait to see how well it is working. They, too, may have to decide whether to change horses in midstream.

Once the bet is won or lost, the gambler must interpret the results. Future gambles will be based not simply on the results of previous gambles, but on the gambler's interpretation of the results. In this sense gambling closely resembles scientific experimentation under the Probabilistic Paradigm, where the data, rather than dictating the conclusions, must be interpreted by the experimenter. When a doctor prescribes a treatment for strep throat, inflammation of the intestine, athlete's foot, or hypertension, the doctor must evaluate the results when deciding whether to follow the same treatment strategy, either in continuing to treat the same patient or in treating future cases of the same disease. Perhaps the strategy was wrong in the first place; perhaps it has been made obsolete by changing conditions; perhaps it is appropriate for some cases but not for others. Perhaps it was the right strategy but simply hasn't been given enough time to work.

There is, unfortunately, no simple way of interpreting the results of past actions for the benefit of future decisions. In fact, people often misunderstand and misapply such information, either because they don't perceive the situation correctly or because they don't think clearly about it. Like preferences for individual gambles, patterns of gambling over time may be based on specious assumptions. People may habitually react in ways that do not in fact lead to better gambling decisions and better results. Two of the most common misinterpretations are referred to as "postmortem hindsight" and "the gambler's fallacy." S. knew them both well from his own experience. He knew that he had to be as conscious of his long-range gambling strategies as he was of his individual gambles.

Postmortem Hindsight

It seems natural to assume that a gamble won was a good gamble, and that a gamble lost was a bad gamble. People almost inevitably change their probability estimates from hindsight (Fischhoff, 1975). They underestimate the degree of uncertainty that existed before the outcome became known, and revise their probability estimates upward or downward depending on whether the event in question did or did not occur. The fallacy in this is that a gamble would not be a gamble if chance did not intervene. A gamble would not be a gamble if the best decision always led to the best outcome. Sometimes a wise strategy does not win. Sometimes a foolish strategy does win. One win or one loss in and of itself says little about the probability of winning or losing, or about one's skill in choosing a gamble. Yet people commonly take pride in a win or blame themselves for a loss, as if the outcome really had been a matter of only skill rather than of skill plus chance. People sometimes give up a good gambling strategy, just because of one bad outcome, and switch to one that has less chance of winning.

In order to avoid this error, it helps to remember that past decisions were based on estimates of an uncertain situation, and that these estimates must be evaluated not only on the basis of what is known after the fact, but on the basis of what was known—and not known—before the fact. A technique that

S. found useful was to record his probability estimates before the outcome became known. Such written information, he found, can correct the bias of memory and act as a check against later overreactions.

A *series* of wins or losses, on the other hand, may provide real information about probable outcomes, and one may appropriately revise one's probability estimates—and subsequent actions—on the basis of this information. In this way one may profit from one's mistakes. To do so, however, one needs to have the attitude of critical trust that the scientist employs when testing hypotheses and accumulating data. A gambler who does not doubt himself will be unable to question what appears, on the basis of one lucky shot, to be a winning strategy. A gambler who does not give himself the benefit of the doubt will be unable after an initial setback to pursue what might ultimately be a winning strategy.

Translated into gambling terms, the scientific principle of critical trust tells the gambler that it doesn't pay to take the outcome of most individual moves in a game too seriously. But it does pay to try to understand how the game works and to develop a strategy for making one's moves accordingly. The sense that one is following a sound strategy can bolster the gambler against the disappointment that arises from individual losses—and the temptation to react with rash shifts in strategy. When it becomes clear, however, that a strategy isn't paying off—that the outcomes are going against the probability estimates on which the strategy is based—then it is time for a new strategy. And even if a run of losses is due only to bad luck, one may have to revise a sound strategy and bet more cautiously in order to avoid losing all of one's resources.

The "Gambler's Fallacy"

If a fair coin comes up heads three times in a row, what are the odds that it will come up tails the next time? The correct answer is one out of two, but many people will say the odds heavily favor tails. This is called the "gambler's fallacy." Coins do not have memories, and their behavior when thrown up in the air is not affected by their past history. Yet many people assume that there is some pressure on the coin—or dice—to even out the odds on the next throw. This assumption is based on a misinterpretation of probability. Chance outcomes do tend to even out according to probability, but only over the long haul. It is true that the odds that a coin will come up heads four times in a row are only one out of sixteen. So are the odds on any specified sequence of four coin flips, such as heads-tails-heads-tails. But these low odds are for the *combined* outcome of four coin flips, not for the fourth alone. Once the coin has come up heads the first three times (an event with a probability of one out of eight), the odds on the next throw are just the usual one out of two. A person who walked into the room without knowing about the first three flips would correctly assume these odds, and such a person would, after all, be observing the same outcome as the people who have been in the room all along. On the other hand, if a coin keeps coming up heads, maybe it is a trick coin. In that case it is appropriate to revise one's probability estimate on the basis of this new information. The revised estimate, however, would be in the opposite direction from that predicted by the gambler's fallacy.

If, in the case of the child K., the doctors who did all the tests were to justify their actions by saying, "We've had such a long run of negative test results, we're bound to get a positive one soon," they would be committing the gambler's fallacy. As in this instance, the gambler's fallacy can encourage the gambler to stick to a losing strategy in the belief that his luck is about to change, while the fallacy of postmortem hindsight (which says that a lost gamble was an unwise gamble) can lead the gambler to give up too quickly on a strategy that appears to be losing. Let's say a medication is prescribed which may or may not alleviate a given condition. If the medication did not work immediately, a doctor working from postmortem hindsight might give up on it, ascribing the result to insufficient skill ("I prescribed the wrong thing"). A doctor who believed in the gambler's fallacy might keep trying the medication long after its inadequacy was demonstrated, in the hope that luck would change.

The gambler's fallacy combines with postmortem hindsight in a way that makes gambling-house owners happy—and rich. People have a tendency to attribute their wins to skill and their losses to chance. It is in the interest of the house to encourage this way of thinking, because it leads the customers to stay in the game whether they are winning or losing. The gambler on a winning streak wants to "keep doing what works" (assumption of skill). The gambler on a losing streak invokes the gambler's fallacy, with its promise of a reversal of fortune (assumption of chance). Both believe that future prospects will be favorable. Partly on account of these inconsistent interpretations, people tend to take more risks when they are winning big or losing big. Another reason is that as the game goes on and the winnings or losses mount, each dollar (proportionately and psychologically) means less than the one before.

Unconscious, emotionally driven gambling can be costly enough in the casino. It can be even more costly when it is applied to real-life gambling, as in medicine. Suppose a husband and wife are concerned that a hereditary condition that one of them has, such as club feet, may be passed on to their children. If they have a child who does not have the condition, they may think it that much less likely that the next child will inherit it (postpartum hindsight). If they have a child who does have the condition, they may think that the odds will be that much better for having a normal child the next time (gambler's fallacy). The probabilities do not justify either of these inferences.

Commitment Strategies

Readers of the Sunday newspaper in a large metropolitan area learned of the "million-dollar baby," a two-and-one-half-year-old boy in a local hospital who had been resuscitated fifty times in his short lifetime. These recurrent life-or-death sieges had left him with permanent brain damage. His body riddled with needles and tubes, he led a miserable life. The newspaper article, which commemorated the first million dollars spent by the child's family and by society to keep the child alive, praised the hospital's heroic effort. But someone with different values (someone who valued the common good or the quality of life as well as the survival of an individual) might have regarded this heroism as a perverse commitment to a lost cause.

How does one decide when to stick to a gambling strategy and when to abandon it? Would the doctors of the "certainty" school who treated K. ever have reached a point where they would have stopped testing? And if Dr. S. had remained in charge of the case, might he have had to rethink his own strategy if K.'s course had turned downhill despite all the food and love he was getting? How does one maintain a valid strategy when there is pressure (from oneself and others) to change it? How does one discover that one's commitment to a given course of action is irrational or unnecessary and that reevaluation is in order?

Changes in strategy can, of course, be built into a plan of action, as demonstrated by Dr. S. in the following case. A two-year-old boy had had a birth defect which had caused food to pass from his stomach into his lungs, sometimes causing pneumonia. Even after the problem was corrected, the boy continued to struggle when he was fed, because he associated food with pain and illness. Since he was seriously undernourished and underweight, S. decided to feed him only through a gastric tube going directly into his stomach, thus removing a major source of irritation and conflict while he nurtured him in other ways. The treatment plan called for feeding the boy by mouth again when he reached a certain weight, for at that point feeding would no longer be a life-or-death issue. This is an example of a planned change in strategy. In devising a plan of action, it makes sense to allow for anticipated change. But in an uncertain world one cannot allow for every possible change.

In the face of setbacks and unexpected developments people feel a need to maintain a commitment to a course of action—a commitment that is sometimes justified and sometimes not. It is a question of when it is worthwhile to pay the "retooling costs" that a change in policy entails—a question (to cite again the scientist's principle of critical trust) of when to doubt one's gambling strategy and when to give it the benefit of the doubt. Sometimes a commitment to a strategy is a commitment of principle; sometimes it is a commitment of fear and rigidity. To the extent that K.'s doctors felt "If we stop testing now, then all the tests we've done will go to waste," or "We've invested so much in testing that we can't switch now," they were showing a rigid commitment to their strategy and a reluctance to abandon "sunk costs" and incur "retooling costs." Sometimes, by a psychological process called "cognitive dissonance," people show a greater commitment to a strategy that doesn't appear to be working than to one that does, as if the lack of apparent benefit from pursuing the strategy necessitated a greater resolve in defending it, perhaps to prevent embarrassment. In the case of K., doctors invested their honor in sticking to a strategy in the hope that it would eventually work, as if the acceptance of new information constituted a damaging admission of error.

People have strategies for maintaining consistent behavior, as well as for maintaining the flexibility needed to change, when faced with doubts raised by themselves or by others. The same commitment strategies that bolster a "bullheaded" stubbornness can also defend commitments to principle or to sound policy. Whether the strategies are being used constructively in a given instance depends on the value of the commitment itself.

Psychiatrist George Ainslie (1975) has analyzed the ways in which people question their commitments and the strategies they use to reaffirm them. People reconsider their strategies for a number of reasons, such as internal conflict about the rightness of a decision (conflict which may have existed before the decision was made), fluctuations of mood, and conflict with other people. A major threat to consistency comes from what Ainslie calls specious preferences. A person embarked upon a course of action aimed at achieving a highly valued long-range outcome may be tempted off course by a more immediately attractive alternative. This dilemma is expressed by the Greek myth of the Sirens, who lured sailors to death by overriding with the beauty of their singing the sailors' long-range preference for living. Odysseus wanted to hear the Sirens, yet be able to resist them. He accomplished this by having himself tied to the deck while stuffing the ears of his crew with wax and instructing them to continue past the Sirens regardless of how he struggled and pleaded. In other words, he suppressed the crew's capacity for perception and his own capacity for action.

People's capacities for perception and action are routinely suppressed when they are sedated before surgery. This is done in part because many people who decide weeks in advance that an operation is in their best interest become anxious about the pain and risks as the hour of the operation draws near. The same sort of anxiety is known to affect couples who are about to get married. Many more people would call off their weddings during the final days before the ceremony were it not for the fact that by then society has taken the matter out of the couple's hands by interposing elaborate arrangements that would be embarrassing, inconvenient, and costly for the couple to cancel.

Ainslie calls these additional contingencies "side bets," in that they do not affect the probabilities on which the original gamble hinges, but simply change the value of the overall outcome by adding new outcomes to the equation. A person can make these additional rewards contingent on doing what will be rewarding in the long run (or punishments contingent on not doing so), so as to compensate for the specious reward that comes from deviating from that strategy. Since the appeal of the specious reward is usually that it is immediately gratifying, the same should be true of the payoff from the side bet. Giving a patient a tranquilizer before an operation changes the immediate value of having the operation (by making it more comfortable). Side bets can also involve financial costs and benefits. For example, a dentist or a psychiatrist may stipulate that patients will still have to pay for appointments that are canceled within twenty-four hours of the scheduled time. That will make a person think twice about canceling an appointment out of last-minute fear. Or a side bet may be based on psychic costs and benefits. One can strengthen one's commitment to a course of action by affirming the commitment publicly. If you tell enough people, including your family, that you're going to get married, then you'll look like a fool if you don't.

Side bets are one method by which people make themselves act in a manner consistent with long-range goals and policies. Another is simply to give more attention to the anticipated outcomes whose value reinforces the original decision. For example, one can deliberately think about the benefits of surgery and not think about the discomfort and risk. That most people find this mental discipline difficult to achieve is illustrated by the modern medical versions of the Sirens' song—smoking and overeating. One may "know" that one will benefit in the long run by not smoking or overeating, but that distant reward is hard to keep vividly in view when the immediate pleasure or emotional relief of the cigarette or the dessert is at hand. The longer projected life span that the nonsmoker enjoys is not a very tangible value at any given moment; likewise, the increased personal attractiveness that comes from losing weight is not yet evident when a person is just beginning to eat less. Some people can substitute for those delayed rewards a sense of increased self-respect from doing the right thing. This subjective self-rewarding is a kind of private side bet: a person who fails to do the right thing loses self-respect. If a person needs more tangible rewards and punishments to make the consequences of smoking or overeating sufficiently salient, the person can create them through side bets as in behavior-modification techniques.

Commitment in the Face of Opposition

Not only do people themselves have mixed feelings about carrying out the decisions they have made, but others may disagree with those decisions. They may estimate the probabilities differently, or they may value the outcomes differently. Even when those others are not betting directly against the person making the decision, as in a competitive game, their interests may conflict with those of the decision-maker. For example, what is good for the patient may not be good for the doctor or for other members of the patient's family. All are affected by whatever action is taken, and yet only one action can be chosen.

The opposition of other interested parties is thus another

important source of conflict for the decision-maker. There are several ways in which other people can try to reverse a person's decision. They can make it physically impossible for the person to carry out the decision, as by putting him under anesthesia or declaring him mentally incompetent and institutionalizing him. They can call attention to implications of the decision, and of other possible decisions, that the person had not considered seriously enough (such as other outcomes, other probabilities, other values). Finally they can set up side bets, just as the decision-maker can. They can raise the ante by adding unpleasant contingencies which make it more costly for the decision-maker to stick to a bet, or they can tempt the decision-maker with positive rewards for switching.

All of these avenues of influence are illustrated by the case of the baby whose father refused permission to operate on her heart condition until he learned whether or not she had Down's syndrome. The doctors who disagreed with this decision threatened the father with a court injunction which would have taken decision-making power away from him. They called attention to the negative consequences that they thought his decision would have on the infant's chances for survival. Mainly, though, they put him under various kinds of pressure which increased the costs of maintaining his position. They insinuated that, as an added outcome of his choice, he would be regarded—and would have to regard himself—as a bad father and a bad husband. As yet another outcome, they implied that they would not resuscitate the child if an emergency occurred. The man's wife (perhaps influenced by the doctors) added a contingency of her own—that if his decision proved wrong she would not forgive him. The doctors and the wife were serving notice that they would blame the man for losing a gamble they disapproved of, but would not blame him if he lost a gamble that was acceptable to them. No wonder the man broke down after two days!

It is appropriate that people sometimes can change each other's minds, since decisions can be wrong, and the interests of others may legitimately overrule the decision-maker's own. On the other hand, since this is not always the case, it is also useful that people have commitment strategies by which to stay firm in their decisions when pressured by others. These strategies are the same as those used when the questioning of one's purpose comes from within oneself: side bets, selective attention, and even, as in the case of Odysseus, the relinquishing of one's physical capacity to change one's decision.

When people use such commitment strategies, when people make choices about where, when, and how long to apply such strategies, they are doing more than simply influencing a single decision or set of decisions. To establish a policy and stick with it in the face of initial failure or disappointment is to build character. Indeed, to do so inflexibly is to build a character armor which in the process of protecting the self can also serve as its prison. But to do so consciously, on principle, with an awareness of the risks and a readiness to change when change becomes advisable is to educate oneself about probability and strengthen one's capacity to cope with uncertainty. By the second criterion of the Probabilistic Paradigm, the making of a decision changes the decision-maker. The effect of making one choice may not be noticeable, but as making choices consciously becomes a habit, its impact on character is cumulative. By taking responsibility for one's choices and their consequences, one trains oneself to make further choices—to be a full participant in a difficult but not entirely unknowable or uncontrollable world.

Gambling in Practice

The following four cases from S.'s practice demonstrate ways in which the gambling approach to probabilistic thinking can be used beneficially by doctors and patients. The first case, incidentally, is one in which the hospital setting, instead of frustrating gambling with institutional conservatism, made it easier to gamble:

A baby born two weeks after his expected birth date had some initial difficulties in maintaining a constant body temperature and was taken to the intensive-care unit for observation. Dr. S. encouraged the baby's father to feed him two hours after birth; immediately thereafter, the baby stopped breathing and had to be resuscitated. Initial tests, including a complete blood count, did not suggest a possible infection. To explore whether there might nonetheless be an infection, more invasive procedures such as a lumbar puncture (spinal tap) and blood culture would be required. S. decided to forgo the tests for the time being. Other doctors questioned his decision, saying, "Why do we have the baby in the intensive-care unit, if not to perform tests?" He replied, "That's just it. If the baby were not under such constant observation, we might play it safe, do the tests, and wait for the results before treating. But here, where we can test immediately if something goes wrong, we don't need to test unless something goes wrong. Meanwhile, we can begin treatment and see how that works." Under this regime the child thrived and was spared not only the tests, but the three days of penicillin and kanamycin that are routinely given after the tests. In this case S. made two gambles on the patient's behalf. He gambled on an early feeding, and lost. But since he had gambled consciously, he could interpret the results realistically, instead of imagining more drastic reasons for the baby's breathing failure. He gambled on not testing, and won. Both, however, were good gambles, since they were made under conditions where the consequences of losing could be limited and where there was a good probability of recouping a loss.

A young woman's transplanted kidney began to fail while she was pregnant with twins. Since the pregnancy contributed to the strain on the kidney, S. considered it necessary to deliver the twins early. But as the woman's family doctor, taking into account such issues as her desire to have children and his own commitment to saving the babies if possible, he did not want to deliver them so early that they would have little chance to survive. A minimax strategy would dictate delivering the twins at the earliest possible time so as to avoid the death of the mother. The expected value strategy which S. and the woman actually adopted, however, entailed weighing the probabilities of survival for the mother and babies given the time chosen for delivery, along with the value of the mother's and babies' lives. The twins were delivered after thirty-two weeks of pregnancy, when both they and the mother would have a good chance to live.

A twenty-year-old woman had a sore throat which gave the appearance of strep throat, along with headache and swollen lymph nodes. S. had the choice of waiting one to two days for the results of a throat culture, which would confirm or disconfirm the diagnosis of strep throat, or treating with penicillin immediately, either with one injection or a ten-day supply of pills. If the woman did have strep throat, immediate treatment would relieve her symptoms without the need for a return visit, and would almost surely prevent complications (as would, in all likelihood, delayed treatment). On the other hand, the costs of using penicillin included the possibility of an allergic reaction to the drug, resulting in the patient's being denied a useful treatment when she might really need it on some later occasion. If she did not now have strep throat, this cost would be incurred without benefit. S. estimated the probability that the woman had strep throat at fifty percent. Given the estimate, he felt that the decision should hinge on the patient's values. Explaining the costs and benefits to the patient, he asked her to take her own gamble. She chose the penicillin shot, which he administered. He also took a throat culture for the purpose of educating his clinical judgment.

An elderly woman presented symptoms suggesting a diagnosis of arthritis of the neck. S. told her, "I'm ninety to ninety-five percent sure that that's what you have, and I'm willing to treat you now on the basis of that estimate. If treatment works, fine. If it's still bothering you in a couple of weeks, we can look at it again. On the other hand, if you want to spend a hundred dollars on tests, we can narrow down the area of doubt and come close to a hundred percent assurance. But I should warn you that the conditions that make up the other five or ten percent are not easily treatable anyway. It's your choice. I'll go either way with you on it." The patient asked, "What do we have to lose by treating for arthritis if that's not what I have?" S. replied that there was not a great deal to lose in terms of side effects or lost time and expense, and the patient agreed to begin treatment.

The gambling approach illustrated in these four cases presents options, probabilities, and values so that people can see them all together as part of a larger picture. When S. and his patients made decisions in this manner, they had a sense of greater control; they also felt the personal responsibility that went with that control. The language of gambling is not a panacea, a flight from responsibility. It is, rather, a constant reminder that there is no panacea. It is a language of responsibility in an uncertain world.

When S. and his patients gambled consciously together, they created their own categories for decision-making as they went along. Working in the contexts of everyday living, they could change their categories as the contexts changed. Among the most important contexts were the relationships patients had with their families, with the people they worked with (or worked for), and with S. as their doctor. People didn't make decisions as an abstract exercise; rather, they were influenced by the feelings they shared with others. If S. was going to help people make better decisions, he would have to understand those feelings. His own relationships with patients and families would have to be the kind of relationships that would foster wiser gambling.

PART III

RELATIONSHIPS

9

A FAMILY

If any one case taught S. that scientific gambling was more than an intellectual exercise, it was that of Rose Heifetz. Confronted with breast cancer that was well advanced before it was diagnosed, Rose had to gamble on a choice of treatments, as well as on how to face the possibility of death. Rose did not face these gambles alone. Her family and even S. himself shared the gambles with her. Yet this family still had much to learn about what it meant to share a gamble, and as a result Rose was not able to gamble as effectively as she might otherwise have done. As for S., he was learning even as he was teaching.

The irony was that the Heifetzes wanted to gamble consciously and, on the strength of their medical backgrounds, were well equipped to do so. Rose, a psychiatric social worker in her early fifties, knew about all the latest "holistic" therapies in psychology and medicine. Her husband, Herb, a statistician on the editorial staff of a medical journal, was conversant with the language of the physicians with whom he was in contact. Together they were prepared to consider carefully a wide range of options in cancer treatment. But they were less prepared to

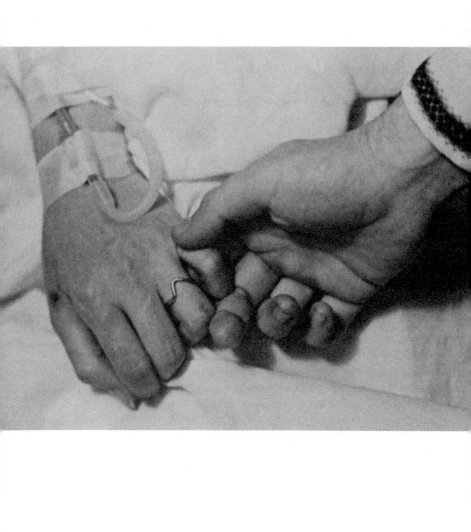

share the feelings that would arise in a situation of great uncertainty, where life itself was at stake.

Rose and Herb had been living apart for almost a year; that had something to do with it. However, they still saw each other frequently, in the company of their two grown children and three grandchildren, and continued to support each other in their respective careers. With all the estrangement that has come to exist among families who live under one roof, the Heifetzes' situation was in some ways a common variation of normal family life. Illness strikes families in good times and bad; it struck the Heifetzes at an awkward, unsettled moment in their life as a family. Still, it was as a family—with all the complications thereof—that they responded.

By the time Rose went to a doctor to confirm that she had breast cancer, it had already grown to be a massive tumor that had spread to the lymph nodes in her armpits. The odds on her ultimate recovery could scarcely have been worse. But if anyone could beat the odds, Rose thought, it was she. She believed that she formed a special category of patient to whom the statistical probabilities did not apply. After all, they were just "averages," and she was not average.

In many ways Rose *was* special. In addition to being very knowledgeable in medical matters, she had the strength of will to undergo a year-long "detoxification" program (a diet aimed at removing the "poisons" that had accumulated after a lifetime of bad eating habits) under the supervision of a nutritional consultant. This regime had left her clear-skinned and thirty pounds lighter. No longer troubled by frequent colds, she was more attractive and energetic than she had been in years.

On the other hand, in spite of her professional experience with breast cancer and her observations of the way women whom she had counseled had reacted with denial (such as by refusing to believe that they had cancer or were at risk of death), her own initial reaction was similar. In fact, even when the lump had become too noticeable to ignore, it had taken her a few weeks to pick up the phone and call a doctor. In part, this was because she needed some time to get used to the prospect of dying. In addition, her holistic approach to her health, much as it strengthened her in other ways, may have contributed to her reluctance to acknowledge that she was seriously ill.

One might wonder—as S. did, for instance—why this medically sophisticated woman had not had annual breast examinations or done monthly self-examinations, which might have revealed the presence of the tumor at an earlier stage. Perhaps she would have if breast examinations had been associated with the alternative health movement rather than with the medical profession. As it was, she seemed to feel that if she just ate right, lived right, and felt right, she wouldn't get sick; so why bother with examinations? By the same logic, however, if she did get sick, she might well wonder whether she had lived right after all. Hard as it was for Rose to face the fact that she might have cancer, it was even harder when she feared that she was the cause of it. When there was hope of a good outcome, the belief in oneself as the cause of one's health and illness could lead a person to gain knowledge and thereby gain control. The same belief, when there was fear of a bad outcome, could lead a person to avoid knowledge and thereby give up control.

Rose might have taken even longer to look into her condition had she not been able to call upon Herb for support. When she told him of her condition, Herb offered to accompany her to the doctor's office and to help her gather and interpret medical information and make the necessary decisions. Rose cried and accepted the offer. Herb was, as he put it, "able to be helpful in the way I had always been helpful. An intellectual role was the most comfortable one for me to play." He knew that Rose had wanted more from him emotionally than he had given during their years of marriage. If he could not or would not be her husband, he could at least be an involved, responsible friend and researcher.

What Rose was later to call her "odyssey through medicineland" did not begin, as it would have for many people, with a visit to a family doctor. Although she had met S. at a professional meeting and formed a favorable impression of him, she did not think first of him when she became ill. Thus S. was not involved in the early stages of her care, and he only knew about her initial decisions and experiences from what she and Herb told him later.

The doctor Rose called was an oncologist (cancer specialist), who did a biopsy (i.e., excised a piece of the breast mass for analysis) to verify the diagnosis of cancer that his examination of the lymph nodes indicated. Given Herb's connections, Rose found it natural to go first to a specialist. She chose this one in particular because he had a reputation for not sugar-coating the truth. Indeed, when she returned with Herb to see the oncologist along with a radiotherapist, she found them positively grim. "Look," she finally told them, "when you're with me, it's okay to smile."

In these physicians' opinion the treatment of choice was radiation plus drug therapy. Although no treatment could guarantee that a cancer which had already spread would not remain in her system and subsequently recur, nonsurgical treatment seemed a better bet than mastectomy (surgical removal of part or all of the breast) to arrest the tumor's growth and reduce its size. The particular type of drug therapy chosen was based on the knowledge that a lack of estrogen (female hormone) inhibits the growth of some forms of breast cancer. In order to see whether Rose's tumor was sensitive to the drug Tomaxifen, which neutralizes estrogen, the oncologist ordered additional tests performed on a tissue sample that had been preserved from the biopsy.

At the end of the session the oncologist and the radiotherapist answered Rose and Herb's questions and told them to feel free to call if anything further needed to be clarified. Some questions did arise when the couple discussed the visit that weekend, and Herb called the hospital on Monday to relay them to the doctors. But it happened that this was the first week in August, and he was told that both doctors had gone off on two-week vacations that day. Was anybody covering? Yes, but these doctors would need to familiarize themselves with the case. Frustrated as they were by what they experienced as abandonment, the Heifetzes nevertheless decided to wait for the oncologist to return rather than involve another doctor. Besides, under the circumstances it was easier to wait a little longer for the bad news.

When he got back from vacation, the oncologist reassured Herb that "a week or two doesn't matter anyway." This reassurance was immediately undermined when he couldn't locate the Tomaxifen test results. With a sinking feeling Herb wondered whether the lab work had been done at all and whether (as a result of tissue spoilage) Rose might have to go through another biopsy. Several days later the results were located: Tomaxifen could be expected to retard the growth of Rose's cancer. Rose and Herb were relieved, but the delays and mixups had shaken their trust in physicians.

Herb began to accumulate a thick file folder full of information about various treatment programs. He made it his task to evaluate the claims of numerous variations of conventional and holistic therapy (some of which invoked widely differing criteria of evaluation). He reviewed published research and consulted with people he trusted, and still there were no sure answers.

The first question to be resolved was whether to go along with Rose's wishes and the oncologist's recommendation and refrain from surgery. Rose and Herb decided against surgery for the following reasons: (1) The statistics on outcomes of surgery for Rose's sort of advanced breast cancer were not as encouraging as those for the combined radiation-drug therapy treatment. (2) Even the surgeon they consulted did not recommend surgery for cancer this advanced, since he felt it might interfere with the body's capacity to resist the spread of the disease. "When the *surgeons* say don't do surgery," said Herb, "when they're telling you not to come to them and do their thing, it's hard not to listen." (3) Rose had a general philosophical bias favoring "natural" remedies, those that interfered as little as possible with bodily functioning. Though drugs and radiation were objectionable to her, surgery was even less acceptable to this woman who didn't smoke and would not take aspirin for headaches. Besides, she was confident that she was in such good overall health that she could lick this illness without surgery. (4) Surgery would involve a difficult convalescence and would have residual effects on Rose's chest and arm areas. (5) Rose would not choose to be disfigured unless she absolutely had to. "It might be different if I had a loving husband who'd be there whatever I looked like," she explained, "but now that I'm on the market again my breasts are important to me." Later she added, referring to the breakup of her marriage as well as to her mother's having committed suicide while she was still a young child, "I've lost enough in my life. I'm not about to lose my breasts too."

Rose made these remarks some weeks later when she brought S. up to date on how she had dealt with her illness before he was involved. They were part of her interpretation of cancer as "a disease of separation and loss" and of herself as a "cancer-prone personality." With her mother's suicide she suffered emotional deprivation at an early age. Then she led an isolated life until she married Herb and began to raise a family. When she lost that bond too, she became, by her account, psychologically vulnerable to cancer.

Rose's life history and emotional state may well have been contributing causes of her illness. In proposing them as the only causes, however, she appeared to S. to be falling back on mechanistic thinking, as surely as if she had been giving an account more compatible with the standard medical model's search for a causative agent such as a virus. S. could see how, both despite and because of the Heifetzes' familiarity with scientific methods, their thinking was so strongly influenced by the Mechanistic Paradigm. Here was a couple who felt a lot of mistrust toward each other in the aftermath of their recent separation. They had lost some vital parts of their family relationship, the parts that went with living together. Without the support that they might have given each other in better times, they didn't have the emotional freedom to think critically about life-and-death matters. What they did have was a way of thinking and feeling urged on them by their upbringing, education, and unconscious promptings, a way that enabled (or compelled) them to blame themselves and each other for a misfortune that had many causes, some of them unknown.

Rose was in no position to think critically when she felt alone and abandoned. Living on her own, uncomfortable about calling on her family for support, and unsure about how much support there was to call upon, she had little choice but to deny the terrifying prospect of disabling illness and death. When she decided early on that the statistics on mortality from breast cancer were insufficiently refined to fit her special case, she was, on the one hand, quite reasonably making a subjective probability estimate that took into account her special capacity to respond to the illness knowledgeably and effectively. On the other hand, by refusing even to incorporate the available statistics into her subjective estimate, she was seeing herself as entirely special, or unique, i.e., not subject to the same uncertainties that other people were. "Think of all the anxiety I'd have if I believed the statistics!" she explained. She couldn't bear the anxiety because she felt she had no one with whom to share it.

So she imagined herself the all-powerful cause of her condition, and when she wasn't feeling so powerful, she imagined her family to be the cause. In citing the breakup of her marriage as the final "separation" or "loss" that left her susceptible to cancer, she seemed by implication to be pointing the finger at Herb. And when she suggested that she had decided against surgery in part because she no longer had "a loving husband," she was assigning to Herb a lion's share of responsibility for that choice (a choice that might have life-or-death consequences).

After he got to know the family, S. wondered whether Rose was blaming Herb as a way of holding on to what was left of their relationship. The relationship, at least as she saw it, no longer existed as a full communal bond, by which Herb would feel an unconditional commitment to help care for Rose. Perhaps, though, she could still keep it going as an exchange relationship by saying to him, in effect, "Since you caused this pain, I have a right to ask you for help." In fact, Rose may not have needed to remind Herb what he "owed" her. He may well have felt committed to supporting her, as he said he did, simply because she was the person with whom he had shared so much of his life. In fact he invited her to move back in with the family, but she declined to do so. She may not have been quite sure of his devotion. Now that they were living apart, she may not have trusted him to be at her side when she needed him. And in a world of isolation and loneliness, a relationship held together by guilt or blame would be better than no relationship at all.

For whatever complex reasons, Herb committed himself to sharing the gamble with Rose. He was involved, not only with his mind and his expertise, but with his feelings. He had loved Rose for too long to accept easily the prospect of her dying. He may indeed have felt guilty about having put her "out on the market" where the loss of her breasts would be a disadvantage to her. And he may not have completely given up on the possibility of a reconciliation with her.

Herb and Rose did not, however, acknowledge all the different feelings they had toward each other. Instead they settled back into their old, comfortable roles. Rose expressed some of her feelings by ascribing magical causative or curative powers to them, while Herb played what he described as a "detached" scientist gathering "hard data" and hoping that the data would make his decisions for him. He became the professional patient advocate—a role originally modeled after that of a concerned family member—in a family where concern could be expressed only in the language of mechanistic science. The Heifetzes tended to speak of "data" on the one hand and "feelings" on the other. Yet feelings, along with data, entered into every decision they made.

The big decision, they felt, was to go with a combination of nonsurgical treatments. As Rose later told S., "I put together my own package—a piece here, a piece there—out of the best of both traditional and alternative medicine." The "traditional" part of the package was the relatively noninvasive form of medical intervention represented by the radiation and drug therapy. The main issue here was that of sequence. Tomaxifen originally had been used to shrink tumors before applying radiation, so that less radiation would be necessary. Recent studies, however, had shown that Tomaxifen interferes with the effects of radiation (but not vice versa). Rose's doctors therefore decided to go ahead with radiation first. Herb objected that since radiation only works at the site of the tumor at which it is directed, while Tomaxifen affects cancer cells throughout the body, it might be of more urgent importance to retard the spread of the cancer with the drug than to attack the tumor with radiation. It was a choice between gambles.

After weighing the priorities, Herb and Rose went along with the doctors' choice. Rose began a four-month course of escalating doses of radiation for which she had to go to the hospital daily—an exhausting, dispiriting procedure. Tracing the extent of the tumor with a dye, the radiotherapist precisely mapped out the area to be irradiated on a grid. At one point Rose was hospitalized for radiation implants. Filaments were placed directly into the tumor and then removed several days later.

Meanwhile she continued to see the nutritionist who had prescribed her "detoxification" program, a person in whom she placed a good deal of trust. Her anticancer diet consisted of dietary restrictions together with vitamin supplements and enzymes that the nutritionist believed would break down cancer cells by making them more permeable to outside agents. (The vitamins and enzymes sometimes numbered a dozen in a single meal.) The diet was based on a little that is known and much that is guessed about the relationship between cancer and nutrition. Among the nutritionist's recommendations were the following: Cancer patients suffer an extreme deficit of Vitamin A, so add Vitamin A. A fatty diet is associated with breast cancer, so cut out fat. The liver, which must eliminate the toxins produced by cancer and cancer treatment, can be strained by having large amounts of carbohydrates to convert into sugar, so limit carbohydrate intake. Cultivation of cancer cells in the laboratory requires a saline solution, so no salt. Actually, *all* living cells are cultured in saline solution, which as a culture medium has a different function from salt in one's diet. A person would die without body salt. Other aspects of this diet were equally debatable. Much indeed is known about variations in the incidence of various cancers in regions with different diets, but the curative value of dietary modification has not been established. Still, Herb went along with Rose's view that any treatment should be tried in the absence of evidence that it was incompatible with another treatment or otherwise harmful. If it might do some good, why not?

On this principle Rose went to a number of different practitioners simultaneously. Along with regular visits to the oncologist, radiotherapist, and her nutritionist, she undertook a program of "visual healing imagery" (Simonton *et al,* 1978; Fiore, 1979), which sought to mobilize her body's defenses against malignancy by having her visualize them in action, and saw a conventional psychotherapist to deal with her anxiety about death. If nothing else, drawing upon varied specialists gave her a feeling of having a support system and being actively engaged in her own care. A firm believer in "mind as healer, mind as slayer" (Pelletier, 1977), she was determined to work up some positive emotional energy to combat the illness that emotional stress had, she felt, in part caused.

For Herb, though, this meant more far-out approaches and extravagant claims to investigate. The file folder grew thicker and thicker. Finally he threw up his hands and cried, "No more!" He was having his troubles with "establishment" medicine as well. The oncologist and radiotherapist were only infrequently in touch with each other, let alone with the nutritionist. The resulting duplication of effort was sometimes harmful to Rose, as when she took the same blood tests two weeks in a row because each doctor didn't know what the other was doing.

Herb, along with Rose, experienced considerable stress in dealing with doctors and medical facilities. When Rose was hospitalized to have the radiation implants removed, Herb thought it would be nice to celebrate by picking her up afterward and taking her out to dinner. (She had been told that she would be able to leave the hospital a few hours after the procedure.) Upon arrival Herb was greeted by a security officer, who told him that he had five minutes to bring Rose down before his car would be towed. As Herb remembered it, up on the ward he found Rose walking around in a stupor. She was pale, lethargic, and irritable. "Are you sure you're okay?" he asked. "Maybe we'd better ask the nurse." While Rose stood by mumbling, the nurse reassured Herb that a doctor had said that his wife was able to go home. The next day Rose couldn't remember anything that had happened. Herb hypothesized that she had had to be anesthetized more heavily than expected for the implant removal, but that the staff, once assured that she had survived the procedure, had not checked up on her afterward. As in the case of the child K., the hospital personnel appeared not to be concerned with smaller, subtler gains and losses. Later Herb regretted that he had not questioned the judgment of the absent doctors when his own eyes had made another judgment.

When the radiation treatments were over, Rose did her own

version of the *experimentum crucis* by temporarily discontinuing her vitamin and enzyme supplements. "Within two days I was miserably sick," she reported. "That experiment was one hundred percent evidence of the value of my diet. I didn't need any more evidence." In her confidence that the only cause of her symptoms was the cause that she manipulated (her diet), Rose ignored evidence of other possible causes—in this case, the fact that people who have radiation treatment almost always feel as she did forty-eight hours after the treatment is stopped.

Herb, meanwhile, was finding it increasingly difficult to apply the *experimentum crucis* model to the situation at hand. He was beginning to realize that he was facing decisions he couldn't make by using what he had been taught was the scientific method. How was he to apply research data from mice to human beings? How much credence could he give to the words of a true believer? He was an old hand at collecting "hard data," but was much less confident when the need for subjective judgment in decision-making became inescapable.

He also was learning that he wasn't able to be as objective as he had hoped in conveying information to Rose. In trying to provide the "facts" she needed while also giving her reason to hope, he was treading a thin line—especially since he was not comfortable thinking about facts and hope together. In his concern over Rose's reaction to potentially devastating information he found himself unable to be a detached observer. "My mind played tricks with me," he later recalled to S. "I wouldn't hear things, or I would unconsciously distort them. The facts would get transformed in my head." He was coming face to face with the second criterion of the Probabilistic Paradigm. He had been trying to live up to the idealized conception of a mechanistic scientist that he had formed in the course of working for a scientific journal. Every time he rationalized, made unwarranted inferences, and evaded the worst possibilities, he learned how an observer creates the data as he interprets it. But what he considered a failure on his part was really a kind of growth. Herb was beginning to realize that even in science one could not deny feelings.

In any case, he wanted help. He felt out of his depth in a sea of data and conflicting claims. It was then that Rose mentioned the family doctor whose name she had been keeping in the back of her mind in case she ever needed him. "You need him now," Herb told her.

S., too, remembered his earlier meeting with Rose Heifetz. It felt odd to have as a patient someone whom he had met as a fellow professional. Seeing Rose as someone like himself, he felt closer to her and to her illness than he would have liked. Even more than usual he wanted to be of help.

At first, though, with Rose's treatments well under way, he wondered how he could be of help. It wasn't (as he originally hoped) by working directly with the various practitioners who were treating Rose. Some of these practitioners, being outside the medical system he represented, had no reason to honor his position or his authority. And the ones who *were* part of the system seemed too intent on protecting their turf to yield any of it to him. Or else they were too busy, and so was he. He never once met the oncologist or radiotherapist.

Not that it mattered to Rose. She was glad enough just to have someone to go to when she didn't feel well and wanted to know whether her symptoms were related to the cancer and its treatment. For example, when she had mucus and a metallic taste in her mouth, was this from the radiation? But perhaps the most important thing she and Herb got from S. was a sense that here was a doctor who cared. He arranged to speak with them at least once a week, and if they didn't call him, he called them. "I've got a doctor who calls *me!*" announced Rose to her friends.

S.'s contribution was to support the Heifetzes both intellectually and emotionally in the decision-making process. Much of what they wanted him to look into was completely new to him. He couldn't do the legwork himself; he didn't have the time, and no insurance plan would pay for it. So he simply read the materials Herb collected and reacted to them on the basis of his clinical experience. As he did so, he saw that Herb had a point of view, however much he claimed otherwise. Herb's bias was to give too much credence, to take too seriously the claims of various therapies. In the delicate balance between doubt and trust that every scientist (or scientific gambler) must strike for

himself, Herb erred on the side of giving too many approaches
the benefit of the doubt. He did this not only with the materials
he researched, but also in interpreting what S. said to him.
When S. tried to level with Herb about the odds against survival
for a woman whose breast cancer was as far advanced as Rose's
was, Herb understood the message as something less grim. S.,
however, did not yet feel comfortable about pressing the point.

Among the various treatments that Rose and Herb presented
for his consideration, some struck S. as potentially helpful,
some as useless or even harmful. When he spoke on the phone
with the nutritionist, for example, S. was angered by her claim
(with no evidence to substantiate it) that her diet could serve
as a primary treatment for cancer, as well as by her marketing
with great fanfare what he thought of as standard principles of
good nutrition. Still, a good diet (along with medical treatment)
might well contribute to a favorable outcome.

S. granted that, although some of the measures that they tried
were of dubious rationale, the Heifetzes' energetic efforts may
have helped Rose avoid the depression that can accompany a
grim diagnosis. By being active in her own care, by busying
herself with many small decisions, Rose gained a sense of accomplishment and hope which made her feel better and may
have helped keep up her physical strength. Still, there was a
substantial likelihood that the eventual outcome would not be
favorable. Even if the unlikely came to pass and things turned
out well, many of the choices Rose and Herb made would
nonetheless be far from having been scientific gambles. S. wondered whether Rose and Herb were maintaining a frenetic
pace of activity so as not to have to acknowledge the large role
that chance, rather than their own skill, would play in the
outcome. He could hardly blame them if they were.

It occurred to him that he might be patronizing this family
by encouraging the hope they placed in long-shot cures. But on
the whole he felt that he was building trust so that they could
learn to estimate the probabilities more realistically. By his
willingness to entertain new approaches, by his implicit and
explicit assurances that he didn't consider the Heifetzes crack-
pots for looking into remedies that he could not endorse, he
extended to them a trust that they could then reciprocate. He

let them know that he trusted their judgment, and they in turn came to trust his. To Rose it meant a great deal that she had a doctor who kept in touch with her, who was considerate of her feelings, and who respected her thinking. The more certainty she felt about her relationship with her doctor, the more uncertainty she could accept about her illness and its treatment. Now she could keep a more open mind, acknowledging that orthodox medical approaches had some benefits and unorthodox ones some disadvantages.

Not that she hadn't thought critically before meeting S. She had accepted radiation treatment (which some of her colleagues were as much opposed to as Herb's were opposed to megavitamins and psychic healing) and rejected such all-or-none schemes as residential care in a Mexican natural-healing retreat. But it was S. who supported her growing willingness to look critically at the "natural" remedies that she was predisposed to favor, such as Laetrile, the controversial apricot-pit extract that is illegal as a cancer treatment in the United States. S. said, "I do not find any evidence that Laetrile works, and therefore I see no rational basis for using it. But I can understand your reasons for wanting to try anything, and it certainly won't get in the way of my being your doctor if you do want to use it." This advice gave Rose and Herb the emotional space they needed to make a rational decision. Herb had accumulated a vast file of sometimes contradictory findings on Laetrile, some of the positive results having seemed sufficiently credible to warrant further investigation. But in the end he and Rose passed up the Laetrile program.

In making it possible for the Heifetzes to be more rational in their choice of options, S. became perhaps a little less rational both in what he said and what he thought about the overall prognosis. In the relationship of trust which he established with the family, he was coming to feel like "one of the family" himself. He liked Rose, and he didn't want to see her suffer. It wasn't any easier for S. than it was for the Heifetzes to admit that skill might be powerless to overcome all the effects of chance. He shared this feeling with the Heifetzes so that they might understand why other doctors sometimes came across as grim, especially when confronted with cancer. They responded by telling him that they were comfortable with his saying, "I don't know." Indeed, his willingness to say "I don't know" was what enabled them to trust him as much as they did.

The problem was that he did know more than he felt able to say. In their readiness to accept "I don't know" as an answer, the Heifetzes were treating the unspeakable as merely uncertain. It would be necessary at some point to turn uncertainty into probability, but this they were not yet ready to do. S. somehow felt that he did not have their permission to speak about death, that Rose would regard the mention of death as an intrusion, or perhaps even as a cause of the very possibility of death that S. wished they could all look at together. On S.'s side, if one of his principles was to honor the truth, another was not to impose it. In order for him to be able to present the gamble to the Heifetzes as it really was, they would have to participate in creating the categories of the gamble. They, and not S. alone, would have to be able to acknowledge the possibility of death. It would take more time and more trust before they would be ready to hear the unwelcome message.

Under the circumstances, then, S. let himself be carried along, half consciously and half unconsciously, by the Heifetzes' energy and by their hope. It wasn't that he told them anything that wasn't true. But when they would make a remark that might have struck him as a denial of the probability of death, he would let it pass. He stretched to the limit to give the benefit of the doubt to the things they said. In the presence of such a compelling, strong-willed woman as Rose, S. almost became a believer. On some level he shared her feeling that, yes, she *had* lost enough; why should she lose her life too? With any patient he would hope for the best; with this patient he was persuaded to expect the best. He did not want to dampen Rose's fighting spirit. He wanted to support her determination not to give in to the illness, and yet he felt that sooner or later she would want to face the truth of her prognosis.

After six months of radiation and Tomaxifen, Rose went to the oncologist for a routine checkup. She looked so healthy that the doctor almost didn't recognize her when she walked into the office. To his surprise (since he had hoped to shrink the tumor in a year) there was no tumor left, either in the breast or in the lymph nodes to which it had spread. Finding on examination no evidence for even identifying Rose as a cancer patient, he told her that he had no basis for estimating the probability of recurrence. Actually such remissions are common after the first course of treatment for breast cancer. Even a complete remission did not alter the fact that Rose had had advanced breast cancer. But the oncologist found it all too natural to join in Rose's relief and delight. "Just keep on doing whatever you've been doing," he told her—which meant continuing the Tomaxifen for a few months as a precautionary measure and staying indefinitely on a moderate, "maintenance" version of her diet.

When these results were relayed to the radiotherapist, he jumped up with excitement. Previously so pessimistic, he, like the oncologist, reacted with unguarded joy. It was as if Rose's unexpected reprieve was a reprieve for all concerned. Indeed, the Heifetzes became the toast of the medical community, in which they already were well regarded. Each of the practitioners Rose had consulted, "establishment" and otherwise, regarded her apparent success as a personal vindication. She soon received a number of invitations to do taped and filmed interviews and speak before self-care and holistic health groups as model patient.

S., too, joined in the general optimism. While Rose had been fighting her desperate battle with cancer, he had accepted her treating the situation as one of complete uncertainty ("I don't know"). Now that she was in remission, he accepted her treating it as one of complete certainty. When she spoke of her illness, it was in the past tense. "For a while I wanted to die," she told S., "but when my body called my bluff I realized I didn't want to. I made myself better. I did it, and it makes me feel so powerful, as if I can do anything and don't need anybody to help me. I have every intention of not getting this cancer again." Her fear that she had been the cause of the cancer had been translated into a belief that she had been its cure. Behind her bravado there lay a concern about who really would help take care of her if she became ill again. But S. couldn't quite get down to that level with her. "Okay," he would say to himself, "we'll talk about it the next time she comes in." But each time there were so many other things to talk about that they just didn't get around to it.

What they talked about instead (besides issues that came up in the course of the medical checkups) was a recapitulation of the successful experience they had had together. Rose included S. prominently among the practitioners to whom she liberally gave credit for her recovery, and S. showed an understandable disinclination to interrupt such praise by bringing up disturbing complexities. Rose also was more than happy to honor S.'s way of thinking. "When people ask me to what I attribute my recovery," she said, "I tell them I really can't say that any one ingredient 'did it.' But I know from the reactions of all those doctors that by doing all those things together I came out a lot better than chance." S. assented to this multicausal stochastic explanation. "Your approach didn't focus on a single cause, or even one cause at a time, but on many different causes working together in ways that you and your doctors couldn't understand and that might have changed over time. It wasn't as if you could say, 'We'll add the diet to the radiation treatment and increase our chances of success by twenty percent.' Who knows how the diet may have interacted, for better or worse, with the radiation or the drug therapy? It was more a case of 'Here we've done all these things, and together they've worked so far.' "

Talking about the Probabilistic Paradigm is not the same thing as practicing it. Sometimes talking about it can be a way to avoid practicing it. Yet in Rose and S.'s case the very act of talking in terms of the Probabilistic Paradigm, even in a defensive way, seemed to remind them of its implications. Perhaps by reviewing a successful experience in dealing with one kind of uncertainty, they became comfortable enough to look at other uncertainties. Perhaps they were building up an additional fund of trust with all the praise and encouragement they gave each other. In any case, Rose finally began to raise, or give S. permission to raise, some issues that were of vital importance to her.

As she spoke of the support Herb had given her during her illness, Rose began to voice other concerns. Yes, Herb had been a big help, and she was grateful for that. But what about the time he disappeared for two weeks on a research project while she was home convalescing? Herb was accessible by phone, like a doctor, but he was not accessible in the heart. He was a man of honorable words, sensitive words, but where were the feelings? Herb had never been a man of feeling.

S. asked Rose how much support she had had from her children. "They were too busy to be bothered," she said. "Living alone like I do, there have been times when I've really needed bodies around to help me, like when I've been too tired to prepare a meal. It would have been marvelous to have someone come around to my apartment and help with the housework or simply visit me when I didn't have the energy to go out and socialize. My daughter thought she was being supportive by helping Herb with all the reading, which was really supporting *him;* I'd rather have had her come over and watch TV with me. And did my family take me out for a big celebration at the end?"

S. felt uneasy when she said "the end." Again she was talking as if the ordeal was over and she was cured.

Rose answered her own question. "Not on your life. You should have seen how blasé they all were about it. The only one who showed any emotion was my four-year-old grandson, for God's sake! And if I bring any of this up, they tell me I'm laying a guilt trip on them. My daughter says to me, 'You act as if you were always hungry. Whatever we gave you would never be enough!' And now they tell me I didn't let them have enough candy when they were kids!"

S. reflected that this was indeed a family of the mechanistic era, fighting over food and other forms of nurturance. It was a case of people starving one another, perhaps beginning with Rose's mother, who hadn't cared to live long enough to give Rose a good start in life.

"Well," Rose concluded, "I've never been celebrated in my family, so what else is new? I survived this time by my own strength, and I'll go on surviving alone."

"I get the feeling," S. ventured, "that deep down you feel uncertain about who's going to take care of you if you ever relapse."

"Uncertain is right!" Rose exclaimed, becoming suddenly

agitated. "That's why I'm so determined that I won't get sick again. I can't afford to be sick. What would I do? Where would I go? Who could I count on? Why, I have friends who are more like family to me than my family."

"They may have to become your family," said S.

After a brief silence Rose mused, "The only way this cancer will ever come back is if I again let myself sink into despair."

S. could understand how he and Herb had both kept silent about some of the grimmer possibilities. Neither of them wanted to be the bearer of bad tidings who would lead Rose into despair. If that was what Rose thought could bring back the cancer, who, after all, would want to be the guilty party? S. was relieved, therefore, when Rose told him that she and Herb wanted to have a series of family-counseling sessions with him. Having been forced together by illness after they had decided to live apart, they saw how their feelings toward each other were both keeping them together and keeping them apart. Perhaps S. could help them better understand these feelings.

Their view of the family, like much else in their lives, was colored by professional jargon. "The family doctor," pronounced Rose, "is in a perfect position system-wise to help structure the management of the family. He also is there to help family members with their feelings about what it's like to have Mama as a patient." Her first sentence might be said to represent the chaff, her second the wheat, of contemporary therapeutic approaches to the family—and of S.'s family practice. What S. found encouraging, however, was the Heifetzes' realization that they would need to understand themselves as a family so that they could understand Rose's illness and the way they thought, felt, and acted with regard to it.

By now S. had a clear sense that he had been colluding with Rose and Herb in excluding one of the possible outcomes—death—from the gamble that they were consciously making together. Now that Rose was in remission, now that the three of them had some trust and some experience in working together, he felt both compelled and permitted to share with Rose and Herb his concern that this outcome was a real (perhaps even a large) possibility. In making the choice to do so, he realized that he was taking a chance. For he was acting against one of the messages he had been getting from the couple: "Don't rock the boat when things are going so well." But there was clearly another side of the Heifetzes that wanted to gamble consciously even where death was concerned. After all, these were people who placed considerable stock in learning, knowledge, and truth. So was he. It thus would have been out of character for all three of them just to sit back, let nature take its course, and enjoy what would probably be only the temporary success of the treatment. Rose's taking the initiative concerning family counseling strengthened S.'s belief that she and Herb held it as a principle, as he did, to gamble as honestly, as scientifically as they could. The side of them that wanted to know the truth had come to the fore.

The family-counseling sessions began where Rose's previous conversation with S. left off—with the stalemate she had reached with her children. "I don't complain anymore." She shrugged. "They don't want to hear it. I got the message, and I comply with it." To say that one complies with a one-way message, rather than that one interprets and thereby helps create it, is mechanistic in the sense that one does not acknowledge one's own part in the interchange that produces the message. Rose had, after all, helped produce the family that was giving her this message. But it was less painful to think of herself as complying—to think of her family as an external force acting upon her.

Still, in a family where no one wanted to hear anyone complaining, things were difficult enough in times of health and good fortune. When serious illness presented itself, the simplest way to make life bearable was to deny the possibility of death. Everyone participated in the denial—Rose by imagining that she alone among women with advanced breast cancer could give herself a favorable prognosis, Herb by being a data-gatherer, and the children by assuming an even greater distance than usual from their mother. For Rose the unpalatable choice was to deny her feelings and the reality behind them or to use guilt ("You caused it") to make her family listen.

One night, after a difficult evening with Herb at his house, their daughter had come back with Rose to her apartment be-

cause Rose appeared to be so upset. In an attempt to be reassuring her daughter had said, "Look, I'd do this for anyone." Rose
was not reassured. The remark touched off her fear that even
to her family she was no different from "anyone." Rose hastened to add that her upset on that occasion had been "purely
emotional, nothing to do with my daughter or my illness"—as
if "subjective" emotions could be separated from their "objective" context. Again, fear was driving Rose back to mechanistic
thinking. She was living in too cramped an emotional space to
think freely.

The same was true for Herb, who during the initial counseling sessions was silent much of the time. In an effort to break
through the wall of guardedness and mutual suspicion and get
Rose and Herb talking to each other, S. began making provoca-
tive paraphrases and interpretations of what they were saying.
("So Herb is not to be trusted? How does it feel not to be trusted,
Herb?") He hoped that, in reacting to these statements, they
would start responding to each other's feelings.

What emerged was that Rose and Herb, like Rose and the
children, were at a standoff. Rose could trust Herb, as she put
it, "not to let me starve in the gutter," to support her in professional and medical matters, and to be, by his lights, fair and
dutiful. But she could not trust him to be available to her in a
fuller sense. For his part Herb saw no reason why he couldn't
be "very close friends" with Rose. She, on the other hand, still
hadn't given up on him as a husband. She wanted him "to be
a companion, a playmate, a lover, a comforter; to be honest and
not run away when I'm upset." Those were the things she had
wanted all along, although she had been the one to move out
once the situation had come to seem hopeless. "For God's sake,
Herb!" she exclaimed, turning to face him for the first time.
"You think I feel welcome in your home when I know that I'll
hardly be cold in the ground before you'll find a replacement?"

S. was beginning to see how little choice Rose had. A person
who felt herself to be interchangeable to her husband and "just
anyone" to her children might well seek whatever immortality
was to be gained from the approbation of a retinue of health
professionals. Through them, if not through her family, she
could keep alive a record of the good she had done in the world.

Without the consolation of being able to leave behind such a record death could only mean (as it does when it is experienced in the unconscious) total separation, the annihilation of the self.

What makes death a gentler prospect is the conscious awareness that one's memory will be carried on in the lives of others. As the dying Socrates in *Phaedo* was internalized by Plato, all of us hope to be internalized by our families. But in the atomized, dog-eat-dog world of today, that hope cannot always be convincingly maintained. Rose Heifetz was an assimilated Jew who did not see her memory surviving in a community and a tradition. She feared death as much as she did because the structure of her family (and of the society of which her family was a part) did not allow her to glimpse a connection between herself and those who would come after her. Once she died, the connection would be broken (Lifton, 1979).

S. found it so hard to confront her about her evasive strategies because he saw that there was little else she could do. She was living her life under the conditions that her life had established for her. By now he could understand what Mrs. Pinelli, the thirty-five-year-old woman with hypertension, had meant when she said that she didn't care if she lived beyond fifty as long as she lived to see her children grown. What was it to be fifty and unconnected? But if up to that point you had lived for your children, perhaps your memory could continue to live in and through them after your death.

"So now you two have split up for good," S. said to Rose and Herb, wondering what kind of response he would get. Rose answered by saying that she didn't think she could trust Herb. S. wondered how easily she could trust anyone after her mother had died while she was still a child. "Could you learn to trust him short of being husband and wife—say, just at the level of his taking care of you when you're ill?" Could she assume a flexible distance toward her husband and trust him about one thing if not another—trust him, that is, critically instead of blindly? Rose didn't think she could. "I guess that's my *schtick,*" she said. "That's just how I feel." She was declaring her feelings, but in a way that defined for herself an area of subjectivity where she could not be challenged. It was as if to say, "I am the only cause of 'my *schtick,'* which I know you won't accept, but which you can't take away from me, either."

Herb, meanwhile, had "issues of my own" that he was exploring through the separation and that kept him from making the commitment Rose wanted from him. Both of them were working on an individual level, clinging to "issues" that they saw as subjective, private, and not subject to reason. S. did not think that any movement would be possible that way. Not that he was trying to bring about their reconciliation as a couple. It was just that, simply from their past relationship, their "issues" concerned each other. They needed to work them out with each other rather than with the fantasy images of each other that arose when they tried to work them out alone.

At this time, though, there did not seem to be enough trust between them. Whenever the counseling sessions became too tense or reached a standstill, S. let the couple withdraw from their intense emotional currents and remind themselves how well they had cooperated with each other during Rose's illness. S. hoped that they might learn to gamble with each other in everyday life as they had gambled with each other—and with him—in an emergency. Having learned to trust a doctor who sometimes said "I don't know," perhaps they could learn to trust each other when they said "I don't know" about their feelings toward each other.

Where Rose's prognosis was concerned, however, it was time to go beyond "I don't know." By this point, S. thought, the Heifetzes would not be able to deal realistically with their family relationships unless they faced the reality of Rose's illness. If he let them go on talking complacently about Rose's "self-cure," he would not be doing what deep down they wanted him to do.

To get to the probabilities, he began by pointing gently to the uncertainty. "It would be nice to be out of the woods with this cancer."

Rose looked at him. She appeared both hurt and angry. "Why talk about that now? For now I am out of the woods—what else is there to say?"

"I know you've heard this said before," said S.

Rose swallowed hard. "Not lately, it seems. I guess the idea of an uncertain future looked a lot better when things were going badly. But when you talk about it now, it's almost as if you don't want me to stay well." She paused. "But of course you do. I know that."

"We all want that very much," Herb added.

"So much so," S. went on, "that we find it hard to talk about the possibility that you may not stay well. We have to remember that the odds aren't what we'd like them to be."

Rose shook her head sadly. "As hard as we've all worked . . ."

". . . some things can't be changed." Herb had finished the sentence for her.

S. sensed that he was not the only one who felt relieved.

Once Rose and Herb found that they could accept the possibility (and perhaps the probability) of a recurrence of Rose's cancer, they were able to talk more openly about its real and imagined causes. In subsequent sessions they began to be relaxed enough to talk to each other about themselves as a family. They could open up and express greater honesty, greater humor, and less simple meanings.

Here S. gambled again in order to show the Heifetzes a mirror of the mechanistic thinking that they were outgrowing. Again he made their implicit beliefs and feelings explicit, thereby exposing them to critical rationality, as when he said to Rose, "You wouldn't blame Herb for your cancer," or to Herb, "How does it feel to be a cause of your wife's cancer? How would you feel if she died of it?" Of course, he did not intend these remarks and questions literally. Rather he was bringing to the surface long-held irrational attitudes in the hope that these could then be acknowledged and repudiated. This process was especially valuable for Rose, who in her irritation with S. ended up defending Herb as *not* having been the cause of the illness.

S. now explored Rose's fantasy that she had called the cancer into being to show that she needed Herb and then vanquished it to show that she didn't need him. It was with considerable satisfaction that S. heard her enunciate a multicausal stochastic explanation of the cancer: there were many causes, and Herb was in a sense a cause and in a sense not a cause. Perhaps now she could give up the all-or-none attitude toward Herb by which she insisted on trusting him blindly and then was disappointed. Perhaps she could consider whether she wanted to have him as a friend. She admitted, at least, that she did not know him as well as she thought she had.

As Rose inched away from her blind trust in Herb, he showed signs of giving up his blind acceptance of himself. Perhaps he did not have to be the emotionally evasive intellectual he had always been. As he put it, he was, at any rate, learning:

> I've always played the rescuer without realizing how I wasn't responding to Rose's emotional needs. My way has been to solve problems; if there wasn't a problem to solve here and now, I felt I couldn't be of use. This recent experience has enabled me to hear better when Rose is upset. My eyes were opened when I learned that I could just listen to her, hear her, support her, and that that would be helpful, even if I didn't solve any specific problem.

If Herb had been more in the habit of giving himself due credit, he would have realized that, in alleviating Rose's loneliness, he was "solving a specific problem."

Perhaps it was not as easy as he thought to be "just very good friends" with someone with whom he had been intimate for twenty-five years. In one of the last sessions with S., Herb spoke in probabilistic terms about the past, present, and future:

> Being alone has given me the time and the freedom to explore the issues that are important to me. I had blamed Rose for a lot of what had gone wrong between us, but as I saw myself re-create the same patterns in other relationships, I realized that some of these barriers were of my own making. I saw that I, too, was a cause. And I saw that I couldn't erase all the years of our relationship and all the good things about it, even if I was not ready to get back into it. Then Rose's cancer took me away from my own preoccupations and showed me that I don't have forever to deal with them. Time is a thief; it won't stand still while I explore other sides of myself. Right now I am still very unset-

tled. I still want very much to be good friends with Rose, but I don't know how easy that will be. I know that we will be better friends if I can respond to her more spontaneously and sensitively and can let her know when I need her.

S. more than once acknowledged the courage Rose and Herb showed in coming in for family counseling. They would not have taken that gamble, he said, if there had not been a great deal between them. Nor would their relationship have lasted as long as it had if it had been all bad. Wherever there were strong feelings, there were always mixed feelings. In their efforts to resolve their relationship with a clear hello or a clear good-bye, Rose and Herb had lost touch with their mixed feelings and thereby further confused matters. They could achieve some degree of clarity if they accepted their mixed feelings, either by getting back together and accepting that there would be conflict or by separating and accepting that there would be grief.

S. hoped that they would be able to make this choice, either on their own or through further counseling. Again, however, time proved a thief. S.'s counseling sessions with the Heifetzes ended when Rose was hospitalized after complaining of swelling in her abdomen. Although Rose and Herb would not believe it at first, S. gently made clear to them that the cancer had reappeared, only now in a part of the body that was inaccessible to the treatments that had eliminated the tumor in her breast. Once the effects of the illness began to make themselves felt in her daily life, Rose gave up her apartment and accepted Herb's invitation to move back into her old home with him and their daughter. Her spirit and determination not to give in to the illness, not to "go gentle into that good night," had had a chance to steel itself through a shared understanding of the prospect of death. When death came, as it did before long, it came to a troubled family, but a family nonetheless.

10

TRUST

If Dr. S.'s patients found it hard to reconcile his concern with gambling with his interest in being a scientific practitioner, they were even more puzzled about what either of these ideas had to do with trust, which he spoke of in the same breath. Trust seemed too "soft" a notion for the precise language of science. And where was there less trust than in gambling? At least in the image of gambling that most people carried away from film Westerns, where the card sharks would sit around the table, each with one hand poised at his waist, ready to come up shooting at the first hint that one of the others (always it was one of the others) was cheating.

On S.'s side, he was as concerned as any of his colleagues were with what was now commonly referred to as the "doctor-patient relationship," but he felt that to talk about that relationship chiefly in terms of "rights" and "powers," as most of the books currently written either for patients and doctors were doing, missed the point. As he practiced, and as he shared his thoughts and feelings with his patients, he and they came to see that trust was at the center of probabilistic medical practice. Only when trust was established did it make sense to start thinking about "rights" and "powers," and when trust was es-

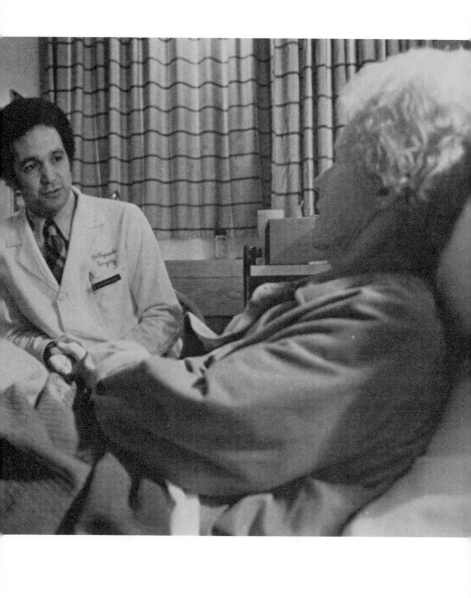

tablished, it was often no longer so necessary to think in those terms at all.

From sad experience he knew what trust was like under the Mechanistic Paradigm. For the patient, at one extreme, it came down to "You're the doctor. I'm putting myself in your hands. Whatever you say goes." But how easily blind trust turned to its opposite, blind mistrust, when things did not work out, or when he had to tell the patient something that the patient did not want to hear. Then, too, some of the very people whose fathers and mothers had blindly trusted their family doctors would approach S. full of suspicion: "Watch out, he's in it for himself. Either he'll say I need more time with him so he can charge me more money, or he'll rush me out the door so he can make money on other patients." This fluctuation between blind trust and wariness was not confined to patients. S. would assume that patients automatically took prescribed medications and, when they didn't, would feel rejected by this "noncompliance." "How can I go on being your doctor?" he would think. It was also easy to be cynical from the start. "What's he here for?" he would catch himself thinking. "What's his hidden agenda? I'll bet he's here just to get a drug prescription out of me."

Both absolute trust and absolute mistrust are intertwined with the Mechanistic Paradigm's denial of uncertainty. To accept a person at face value and not look any further is to deny the possible existence of other, unseen causes that may sometimes influence the person's actions. However, to disregard completely what is on the surface and only to look beneath it for a "hidden agenda" that represents "the" cause of a person's actions is equally mechanistic. Either you see the cause of something, in which case you trust it completely and have absolute trust that a good outcome will follow; or you don't see it, in which case there is no sense of understanding and control, and you have no trust at all. This is the "show me" attitude of the *experimentum crucis,* where the "facts," bereft of understanding, reveal the determining cause with certainty. With blind mistrust, on the other hand, no facts are sufficient to shake the fixed belief in a patient's or a doctor's ulterior motives.

Under the Probabilistic Paradigm scientists do not draw conclusions directly from the evidence; nor, of course, do they disregard the evidence. Scientists (including physicians) who work within this paradigm recognize that evidence takes time to appear, that it requires interpretation, that it is never complete, and that it can never ensure complete control over the outcome. Instead of performing an *experimentum crucis* to settle the issue once and for all, the scientist may take provisional action that leaves room for further evidence to reveal itself. Under the Probabilistic Paradigm trust (like other "soft," subjective factors) becomes a part of science itself. This is not blind trust, however, but a kind of reasoned faith that must be critically reevaluated as new evidence emerges.

When we recognize that even in science the evidence is not immediately apparent, that even science requires a degree of trust in uncertain findings, it becomes easier for us to be trusting in our relationships with people, including the doctor-patient relationship. Doctors and patients who are mindful of the Probabilistic Paradigm do not decide all at once whether they find each other trustworthy. Rather they begin by accepting each other, make an initial estimate of how far to extend their trust, and then keep an open mind.

At any point along the way deciding to what extent to trust someone is a gamble. It is a decision like any other, one made on the basis of probabilities, values, and principles. Without a willingness to gamble, without the recognition that in an uncertain world one must always gamble, there can be no trust.

Without trust, on the other hand, the encounter between doctor and patient can take the form of a competitive, zero-sum gamble. When doctor and patient see each other as adversaries, and thereby as untrustworthy, they may tend to be short-sighted and to engage in the kind of actions whereby one cuts off one's own nose to spite one's opponent's face (e.g., by withholding cooperation so that one can later say, "I told you so!"). It is then that the patient and doctor are gambling against rather than with each other.

Trust allows for a different type of gamble, a cooperative gamble, in which doctor and patient share a time perspective that allows them to keep playing instead of folding up their game (and maybe drawing their guns) after a single loss. Trust allows time for both parties to evaluate critically whether a given diagnosis is a reasonable basis on which to proceed, whether a given treatment has had a chance to work, or whether a given doctor can work well with a given patient. Trust allows doctor and patient to stick with a decision long enough to assess its long-range as well as immediate outcomes; it also gives them time to change their minds and recoup their losses. Conversely, time is what builds trust—especially when it is time spent gambling consciously together.

Engendering Trust

S. often wished that he could trust his patients more. Having been "burned," however, by missed appointments and broken agreements (especially when it came to taking medications), he found this difficult to do. He could simply have gone on reflecting, with some sadness and anger, on how untrustworthy his patients were. But his growing understanding of the Probabilistic Paradigm, together with his willingness to listen to what his patients were telling him, led him to realize that his patients weren't the only ones who might not be able to be trusted. Before he could think about trusting them, he would have to consider his own causal role. He would have to become trustworthy.

There were several ways in which S. learned to gain the trust of his patients. One of the most effective was just by being with them for a long time. When people get to know each other over a period of time, they reveal themselves to each other as trustworthy or untrustworthy in large and small ways. Sometimes, of course, what is revealed makes people turn away from each other. In most cases, however, increased familiarity builds increased trust. It was important to S. that what he communicated about himself should make his patients more comfortable with him and more willing to gamble with him.

S. worked for trust between his patients and himself by acknowledging uncertainty, by not trying to make things seem more certain than they were, by making clear that he and his patients were gambling and that he was willing to learn whatever he could to gamble with them more effectively. To avoid the disillusionment so often brought about by doctors who seek to gain absolute trust by encouraging in the patient a sense of absolute certainty about what outcome follows what course of action, he spoke in terms of probabilities and admitted when he reached a point where he did not know or where no one could know. Uncertainty did not mean, however, that any one course of action was as good as any other. Acknowledging his own causal role as an active observer, S. articulated his values so that his patients would know where he stood.

It wasn't enough that they know that he knew the "facts" and that he would tell them when he didn't know. They also needed to know how he selected and interpreted the facts so that they could work with him in thinking critically about the decisions they needed to make together. He found that while people often started out trusting him on the basis of external indicators of his expertise (his various degrees), they ended up trusting him by seeing what his biases were and how he obtained working knowledge on a day-to-day basis.

S. also inspired trust by being available to his patients (within reasonable limits) where and when they needed him. For instance, he went to people's homes to attend births and to visit those who were bedridden or who could not easily get around. Much to his surprise, he had to emphasize to patients his nighttime and weekend availability (in rotation with his partners). He found this out when someone would call him in the morning after having been ill during the night, in the belief that he could not be reached except during his normal office hours. Sometimes family members would even take the sick person to a hospital emergency room, thinking that this was the only alternative to going without medical attention until morning. "We didn't know we could call you," they would say. To S. it was a sad thing that people could no longer trust doctors to be available when they needed them. He had to tell people that if he was to be their doctor, he would be their doctor even at 2 A.M.

S.'s on-call availability was an important ingredient in establishing trust. Though he was quick to acknowledge his resentment at being awakened, he appreciated the opportunity that the after-hours calls represented. For one thing there were occasions when those phone calls allowed him to follow up observations made during a prior contact. Moreover, it was by being close to people at moments of crisis that he really became their family doctor. It was a rare chance to get to know a family. "I think it's important that you would get up at this hour to take care of your sick child (or parent)," he would tell them. "If you can be awake, I can be awake." By putting himself on the line for people at such moments, he built up a reservoir of trust that carried over to the times when he was not physically with them. Once they knew that he would come when they needed him, they could believe him when he reassured them that they didn't need him. Even when he answered a late-night call by saying, "You can stick this one out yourselves and call me in the morning," the family could feel that he was, in a real sense, there with them as their doctor.

S. found that people who might at the drop of a hat call upon the hospital emergency room or the night shift of alert strangers at a prepaid health-care facility did not presume upon his availability. They knew that he had human needs that were not to be lightly overridden. This was a good thing, for there was a danger that his willingness to serve might become a tool to make people dependent on him. S. and his patients fashioned guidelines to help them decide when they needed him (a crucial gamble that everyone faced once in a while). "Knowing when to call a doctor isn't always easy," he would tell them, "but I know you wouldn't call unless you felt it was important. You wouldn't call in the middle of the night just for a cold, but severe pain that you can't relieve on your own is another matter." In this way he let people know that it was as important for him to be able to trust them as for them to be able to trust him. Dependency there was, as there always is in relationships between people. But in a trusting relationship the dependency is mutual.

S. learned from his patients that small gestures could make a big difference when it came to establishing trust. A patient of his who was concerned with women's perspectives on medical care suggested that he should do more than just set up a screen for women to use when changing their clothes in the gynecological exam room. Since then he made a point of leaving the examination room so that the woman could have the room entirely to herself while she undressed. Instead of dividing the territory with her, he tried to say by his actions, "Just as you're important enough for me to answer your calls at night and come to your home, so you're important enough for me to inconvenience myself by leaving the room so that you can have some privacy."

Patients told him the same thing in their own ways. When a couple planning a home birth asked S., "Is there something *you* like to eat that you'd like us to have in the house?" they were telling him that they wanted to break bread with him, to establish a relationship of mutual respect and trust. A week after he had made a home visit to a sixty-seven-year-old woman who was nearly incapacitated with a pulled muscle in her upper back, the woman's daughter called to tell him that the anti-inflammatory drug, local heat, and massage he had prescribed had worked very well. When she told him, "I had my doubts about it," it was as if she were also telling him, ". . . and I trust you enough to tell you about them." To S. the call would have been useful whether or not the treatment had worked. These follow-up reports, which made it possible for him to learn from his successes and failures and from his patients' beliefs and doubts, were a way in which his patients took steps toward building mutual trust.

It wasn't always easy for S. to acknowledge uncertainty and share it with his patients. Some people were surprised and unsettled when he admitted that there were things he did not know. In retrospect many of them appreciated his extending them this trust, but at first they felt, in the words of one expectant father, that he had "thrown us a curve." Patients who were used to doctors handing out orders with crisp authority tended to react to S. in one of two ways. Some thought him wishy-washy and ill-informed. Even though he was as sure of his facts as he could reasonably be, a doctor who spoke of gambles could not inspire confidence in these patients. Others were so used to an authoritarian approach that they didn't even hear that S. was saying anything different. They simply assimilated what he said into their own framework. For example, he might tell the parents of a child with a fever, "Right now it looks like just a virus cold—annoying, not dangerous, and, frustrating as it is, not curable by any means now available. If he develops any complications such as labored breathing, drowsiness, or crying as though in pain, call me back so that we can take another look." In the few cases where the child took a turn for the worse, some parents judged S. to be a poor doctor, as if he had not qualified his initial assessment. Yes, it was risky to practice probabilistic medicine.

On the other hand, the patients who came to S.'s practice asking to be actively involved in the decision-making process were the ones who were most enthusiastic about learning scientific gambling. They were the ones who most readily adopted the principles of critical doubt and critical trust from the Probabilistic Paradigm. When it came to initiating a trusting relationship, these patients were S.'s teachers.

Initiating the Gamble

Both the doctor and the patient can take the risks and initiate the gambles that make for a trusting relationship. In the most trusting, most satisfying relationships both sides do some of the initiating. Initiating such a gamble feels different from reciprocating it, and there is something to be learned from both. Given the way doctor and patient roles have been defined in our society, S. as the doctor often found himself doing most of the initiating. But there were some patients who came prepared to take the lead.

Charlotte Martin, a thirty-nine-year-old divorcee who had had her first child a dozen years before, was an unusual prenatal patient for S. to be seeing, in that she was not now married and was of advanced age for childbearing. She knew that she faced a difficult decision about whether to continue with the pregnancy, and she wanted a doctor who would not pressure her to make the decision and who would be supportive whichever path she chose. She began by letting S. know that she was willing to trust him enough to share the preconceptions she had formed about him. "A friend of mine recommended you as being 'dry'—that's how she put it. She said that while you're slow to warm up, you're a very warm person. I guess that's what I'm comfortable with, what with my WASP upbringing. I may come across as cold at first too."

S. stiffened. In his mind he had a commitment to openness of communication, but in his heart he was embarrassed to find himself out on the table for review. At first trying to evade the issue, he replied woodenly about the importance of feeling comfortable with a person one chose to work with. Somewhere in his upbringing and professional education he had decided that being himself—acknowledging his feelings—was unbecoming to him as a person and a physician.

After speaking for a while in generalities about trust, he felt safe enough to answer Ms. Martin directly. "I guess I am a bit dry," he remarked, "and I hope you will find me warm deep down. I've heard enough people have that reaction to me to believe that it must be true. And I've actually changed so as to reveal such warmth as I do have. But seeing myself as others see me is not easy. It has been a blind spot for me, as it is for most of us. Had I not been practicing medicine in this context where I couldn't ignore or deny the way I was coming across to people, I might never have had the chance to change."

This relationship got off to a good start in part because Ms. Martin gambled on sharing with S. the feelings she had about him, and in part because S. gambled on revealing to her his feelings about himself. Both learned something by playing out of character instead of automatically assuming the attitudes that have become hardened into so-called doctor-patient roles. Not only did the patient initiate, but it was the doctor who was being "examined." Patients show trust each time they stand still while being examined by the doctor. That trust is enhanced when the patient sees that the doctor, too, is willing to stand still for examination. On the doctor's side it helps to feel what it's like to be a patient once in a while. A taste of the vulnerability that patients feel all the time can help close the emotional gap that inhibits trust.

It is easy to talk about gambling; it is not so easy to gamble when you have a lot at stake. Some patients are initially hesitant to accept the gambling approach, and with good reason. The kinds of gambles that one takes with one's health are different from those in a "game." When gambling is presented with glib confidence by a doctor who can afford to feel detached from the outcomes of the "game," the patient is quick to realize that it is not the doctor's body, the doctor's pain, the doctor's life, that are at stake. The doctor takes risks, too, but these risks are much smaller, and thus the doctor stands at a greater psychological distance from the gamble.

Because he did not want to fall into glib detachment about the feelings of the people he was treating, S. was willing to be, like his patients, sometimes even an object of observation—to be "objective" about himself and to have others be objective about him. If his relationship with a patient could not be equal in terms of magnitude of risk, it would be equal in that the patient's feelings about him would be as important as his feelings about the patient. Recognizing his own reluctance to gamble with his self-esteem (as when he asked his patients for comments, positive and negative, on the care he was providing), he came to understand how courageous it was for patients to initiate the sort of trusting relationship that made principled gambling possible. His appreciation grew for patients such as Charlotte Martin who took the initiative in getting involved in the decision-making under conditions where there was some uncertainty.

When a patient initiated, S. was ready to reciprocate. After two months of prenatal visits a couple who were planning a home birth told him that they were now confident that he could handle their delivery. S. replied that he now had confidence in them too. At first they were slightly taken aback; this was not something they would expect to hear from a doctor. But they were intrigued as well, and they pursued the subject until S.'s meaning became clear. He was telling them that not only did they depend on him, but he depended on them. This was not the supermarket, where "home delivery" was a service performed for the consumer. It was, rather, a relationship of mutual reliance.

Another couple, after extensive consultation with S., decided that they could not have a child at the present time and reluctantly chose to have an abortion. In the course of the discussions they asked S. whether the procedure was a difficult thing for him to do. He replied that he had doubts and sadness whenever he performed an abortion, even though, on balance, it could be an important contribution to a family. A week later the woman sent him a letter that said:

> I appreciated your honesty in expressing the difficulty you felt in carrying out what we had agreed upon. You walked well the delicate line between being open and passing judgment. In sharing your feelings you made it so much easier for us to acknowledge our own mixed feelings, which below the surface are very much there. Thank you.

What S. in effect had said was, "I'm strong enough to do this without denying the sadness and doubt that come with it. You don't have to pretend to me that you are happy about this in order to go through with it." He trusted this couple enough to share with them his sadness and doubt, and they in turn trusted him enough to let him share theirs.

Sharing the Gamble

For S. trust began with his getting clear on the difference between sharing and shirking the gamble. As he shared responsibility—which he did as much as possible for each patient—he felt himself becoming more rather than less responsible. He also saw that patients who wanted to be actively involved in the decision-making process were increasing rather than detracting from his responsibility. By trusting him, yet doing so critically, these patients were seeing him as he was, rather than as some paternalistic fantasy figure that a doctor so easily evoked. They trusted him and themselves enough so that they did not have to hide behind an illusion that he could never live up to.

Soon he felt it his responsibility to act in such a manner that, even when he was dealing with a frightened child, there could be some sharing of the choices and uncertainties of the gamble. Even a routine procedure like taking a child's throat culture was transformed when it was seen as an opportunity to involve the patient in the decision. A throat culture is useful for distinguishing a bacterial (streptococcal) infection, which can be treated with penicillin, from a viral infection, for which only symptomatic treatment and "watchful waiting" are available. Even for an adult it is uncomfortable to have the cotton tip of the culture stick touch the back of the throat. For a child the discomfort is compounded by fantasy. Thus when six-year-old Lena had to have a throat culture taken, S. carefully explained the procedure and its purpose to Lena as well as to her mother. His next step normally was to tell the mother to hold the child on her lap, securing her arms, legs, and head so that she couldn't jump when the stick was inserted.

Then Lena's mother stopped him. "Look," she said, "I remember that when I had to have a throat culture done, you asked me to hold still. At least you can ask Lena whether she wants to give it a try to hold still by herself."

Of course, S. had already involved Lena in the gamble of taking the culture; why not involve her in the gamble of restraining her from hurting herself? The procedure would be more acceptable to her and would mean more to her if he didn't simply talk over her head to her mother. So he turned to Lena and said, "Even though this test is only painful for a second, it's scary when it's happening. When the cotton touches someone's throat, the person often jumps back without thinking, like this." Lena laughed as S. jerked his head and shoulders back and his arms up and out. "When someone with a stick in her mouth jumps like that—and it's hard not to—she can really get hurt. So that you don't hurt yourself that way, I can ask your mother to hold you tight. Or you can give it a try by yourself." Lena answered, "I want my mother to hold me." "Okay," said S., "but after it's over I want you to tell me how it felt and whether what I'm telling you turned out to be right."

After the procedure S. congratulated Lena for being brave and for helping him find out whether she needed medicine for her sore throat. "And your mom had the chance to show how much she cares about you by not letting you get hurt," he added. Then he showed her the office laboratory where the germs would be grown in a culture medium. She watched the technician plant her culture and put it in the incubator. Later that week her mother told S., "Lena really got a kick out of that throat culture. She didn't stop talking about it all evening."

S. learned that he could gamble directly with a child of Lena's age as well as with her family. In the case of eleven-month-old Toby he could not gamble with the patient. Instead he gambled with the family as a means of establishing the conditions that made trust possible.

Toby had been running a high fever. S. checked him over, saving for last the examination of the ears, which would be most upsetting to the child. But wax filled both canals, blocking the view.

There were many reasons why ear wax was called the bane of a pediatrician's life. S. had memories of being drained physically (he had to stoop down over the table to align himself with the tiny ear canals); of falling behind on his schedule (it often took an extra ten minutes to do the job properly); of the sight of bleeding from the canal that sometimes was induced by the metal curette used for wax removal; of parents upset over a crying, bleeding child ("What a butcher!" their faces, if not their words, seemed to say); of screaming, frightened babies with God knows what perception. It was with such experiences, perhaps, that bad feelings toward doctors began.

Heretofore S. had assumed that there was no alternative to cleaning out the ears—unless one wanted to do nothing about a possible ear infection. But when the wax was particularly resistant and there was a high probability of an ear infection, his experience in structuring decisions as gambles led him to see another option—that of beginning antibiotics along with ear drops to dissolve the wax. In a day, with the wax gone, the antibiotics could be discontinued if an infection was not found. This gamble, which would involve another visit, entailed all the usual costs of using antibiotics without what was called a "definite diagnosis," together with the benefits of avoiding the horror show of wax removal while still treating the infection (if one was actually present). With this alternative in mind the standard procedure of ear cleaning could become a choice instead of a necessity.

S. shared the gamble with Toby's parents. "Even though I've been removing wax from children's ears for years and am good at it, I sometimes nick the ear canal with my instrument. Then there is bleeding, and no one likes to see blood. You get upset, I get upset, the baby gets upset. Not that it's dangerous. It's like a nosebleed, and it will heal in a few days. I'd say it happens to me about once in twenty tries. But you ought to know about it so that you can decide whether or not to go ahead."

Toby's parents decided to go ahead. By having an explanation of the choices, they were prepared to participate not only in making the decision, but in doing the procedure and living with the risks it entailed. They continued to be involved as the three of them huddled over Toby on the table, father holding his legs, mother his arms, and S. at his head. "The procedure, so far as I can tell, shouldn't be painful unless the canal is nicked. He'll be screaming mainly out of fear and resistance to being immobilized," S. told the parents as they took up their battle positions. First S. used the otoscope to see the wax. He formed a mental image of it, removed the otoscope, and then went after it with a curette.

Throughout the procedure the distraught baby was soothed by his mother. "Good Toby. The doctor is just trying to help you. You'll be okay." Although Toby was too young to understand the words, S. thought that he was likely picking up their tone and intent.

When enough wax had come out for S. to say with reasonable assurance that the left ear was normal, he suggested that all four of them "come up for air" before getting down to the right ear. After taking a few deep breaths, they resumed their positions around the table. Once exposed to view, the bulging drum of the right ear offered convincing evidence of infection. The procedure had been accomplished without any bleeding. Had this not been the case, S. felt that Toby's parents would have understood and felt themselves to be part of what had happened. They all could share in the responsibility.

"One small child and three grown-ups to handle him!" the father exclaimed. They all smiled.

Mistrust in the Family

Sometimes the trust S. showed in patients came as a surprise to them because they were not used to being trusted in their families. In such cases S. worked to establish trust between himself and the family. This would sometimes reawaken trust in those families where it was dormant.

Fourteen-year-old Rodrigo Santos sat in sullen silence while his mother told S. about the earache that had kept him awake the previous night. "It seems," said S., "that you don't want to be here at all."

"I feel better now," Rodrigo finally said, "so why bother coming?"

"You and your mother don't seem to be in agreement about this," S. persisted. Instead of minimizing the disagreement and getting down to treating the earache, S. articulated the mother's and son's conflicting positions so that both could be honored in making a decision—a necessary prelude to trust.

"Listen, Doctor, when I was a child in the Islands," said Mrs. Santos, referring to the Portuguese Azores, "I once had a terrible earache. There was no doctor, and I suffered for three days. That's why I want to have my children's ears checked."

"So ear pain has a special meaning for you," S. commented.

"I never heard that story," said Rodrigo.

"If you listen long enough," thought S., "there is always a 'story' that helps explain the other person's feelings and actions." S. went on to explain that, in the case of an earache, the possibility of ear infection made it prudent to check with a doctor even if the pain went away. He encouraged Rodrigo and his mother to make such important decisions together and reminded them that they could include him even in their emergency health decisions by calling him at night, if necessary, instead of waiting until the next day.

There were more extreme, troubling instances of mistrust in the family. Dolores Clayton was a woman in her thirties who complained of pain in her ribs. Recently she had been hospitalized because a small bone near her eye had been fractured. How had this happened? Actually her husband had beaten her, but in the hospital emergency room where her ribs had been X-rayed (revealing no fracture), she had said that she had "fallen." In the emergency room, where there isn't enough time to build trust, patients give expedient answers which an overworked staff is all too happy to accept. Dolores had also lied to her employer about why she had had to stay home from work. It was clear that she had mixed feelings. She was ashamed of the truth, and she was ashamed of lying. She didn't want her husband to be put in jail, but she was about ready to leave him.

She had to have some initial trust in S. even to admit that she had been beaten, and he did not want to presume upon that trust. "So this is the first time he's ever beaten you," he said. No, she replied, he had done it several times. S. did not want to make her feel cornered by bombarding her with questions. He listened, and she was able to volunteer that her husband was beating her because she couldn't stop gambling her money away.

They proceeded in the same conversational mode, which gave the patient room to express her viewpoint without having to align herself on the "yes" or "no" side of a question. Dolores was able to fill in the background of her story. Brutally beaten by her father, sometimes for no reason at all, she had as a child found an escape in gambling, where at least she had some notion of what the rules were. Once married, she had not gambled again until her husband had left her, briefly, a couple of years earlier. When asked whether she was winning much money, she said she always lost; the game was probably rigged.

S. tried to express his own values without passing judgment on either her or her husband. Her husband's beating her, he suggested, wasn't doing either her or her husband any good. Dolores stated that her husband was now ashamed of his act and concerned about her. He had offered to drive her to S.'s office.

After listening to her breathing to check that her lungs were normal (a broken rib might puncture a lung), S. presented the "gamble" of doing another X ray versus prescribing pain medication. Dolores smiled when he mentioned gambling. "This isn't like the gambling you've been doing," S. told her. "It's not a game, and so far as I know, it's not rigged. But you should keep a sharp eye out anyway." S. didn't see much payoff from another X ray, so the choice came down to a weak pain medication versus a strong one such as codeine, along with a binder to restrict chest movements. "I can give you some medication that won't take all the pain away, but it will take away some of the pain, and the chances of your getting hooked on it are less." Drug addiction, he felt, was something to watch out for in a person addicted to gambling.

He concluded by stressing that this was a serious and a sad thing that had happened. He gave her the name and address of a shelter for battered women, and she took the responsibility of deciding whether and when to report the beatings. When he suggested contacting a therapy group, she replied that she would probably leave her husband instead. "Then he doesn't care for you?" S. asked. No, she told him, her husband did care for her and was in most respects a good husband and father. He did not beat their children. "Well, maybe you should leave him, but keep an open mind," said S. in parting.

The next week she called and said that the pain was worse and that she needed stronger medication. Now the odds had changed. A new X ray, which she and S. agreed was called for, revealed a fractured rib. The fracture, too small to show up on the original X ray, probably had been made worse by strain. This meant revising the gamble on the pain medication as well. "I think I can avoid getting hooked on the codeine," Dolores told S. "What do you think?" S., too, thought that she was ready to use the drug responsibly. He prescribed codeine along with the weaker medication so that she could choose which to take depending on the severity of the pain at any given moment.

"Maybe the pain is all in my head," said Dolores. "Well, there is a broken rib there," S. reminded her. "On the other hand, the way you perceive the pain depends on whatever else is going on with you. And drugs alone won't help you with that. Speaking of which, now that we know that your rib has been broken, maybe it's time for me to see your husband." He gave her a note informing her employer (and her husband) that she needed to stay home from work with a rib fracture.

Upon reading the note, her husband agreed to come in with her to see S. the following week. At that time she reported that she had needed the codeine only twice during the week. S. and Dolores's gamble that she could bear the responsibility of making that choice had paid off. In a mistrustful world in which she had had no control over her life (as when her father had beaten her), she had sought the illusion of control over uncertainty in pathological gambling—where, however, she always lost, so that she still had no control. S. was showing her that she might gain some control even by choosing between two bottles of pills. Here she could gamble and sometimes win.

In order to remove some of the strain of her family situation S. was establishing a mild therapeutic dependency in Dolores. They discussed it and agreed that (again remembering her potential for addiction) they did not want to let it go too far. Before meeting with her and her husband, he told her that as a physician he would not be doing family counseling with them on a continuing basis. They would have to learn to talk to each other directly, not just through him. Not surprisingly, though, he found himself doing a considerable amount of relaying and transmitting as their joint session began. He began by telling Charles Clayton that he knew that he had broken his wife's rib. "She beats me verbally," Charles countered. "Maybe that's so," said S., "but that's still a broken rib."

The broken rib was real, and so was the verbal abuse. S. noticed that whenever Charles started to speak, his wife cut in and caused him to stop talking. S. unobtrusively encouraged Charles to continue by keeping his eyes focused on him while he was talking, even after Dolores interrupted. After that the husband and wife started talking to each other. S. supported them in doing so by emphasizing the courage it took for them to come in together and talk things over. "Maybe I'm wrong," he told them, "but the two of you wouldn't be here if it were all bad between you."

Charles's side of the story was that, having had to keep several younger brothers in a fatherless family away from the temptations of the street, he lost his head whenever he saw his wife gambling. "You sound as if you don't trust gambling very much," S. remarked. "Maybe you're not that comfortable being here, which is certainly a gamble." Indeed he was not. "And the only way you can stop your wife from gambling is by beating her." S. was articulating Charles's thought processes so that he could examine these critically and make his unconscious choices conscious. After all, S. reminded him, Dolores had been gambling a lot more since he had started beating her.

With all his distaste for gambling, Charles was taking a big gamble. He was showing considerable courage and involvement in his marriage by speaking openly to a doctor, an authority figure who might be taking evidence against him. S. returned his trust, and his wife's, by assuring them that everything they said would be held in confidence. He showed them the chart where he had written only the words, "Family seen for family counseling." "I'm gambling too," he added. "If things get worse between you and the law is called in, I could be charged with not reporting a crime." Since they were taking the risk of meeting with him, he would take this risk, given Charles's agreement not to beat Dolores again. Although he urged the couple not to discount the healthy commitment they had to each other, further commitment on Dolores's part would not be healthy if the beatings continued.

S. agreed to see the couple one more time. After exploring their mixed feelings about making contact with a social-service agency to begin family therapy, both Dolores and Charles felt that it would be easier for them to do so if they knew that they could share with S. their initial experience with the agency. It would still take courage to go to the agency. S. suggested that Dolores make the call to set up the appointment with her husband listening in—a precaution that was needed at this early stage to nurture the small amount of trust remaining between them. In letting his own availability be tied to their taking this step to further their own well-being, S. was willing to have his own presence be at stake in a side bet. The Claytons did see him for a final visit after contacting the family therapist.

S. made it possible for this couple to gain some control over uncertainty in their relationship with him, in the hope that this control would carry over to their relationship with each other. He had shown them how to create ground rules for a trusting relationship, and he believed that by taking the additional gamble of family therapy, they would be able to go on from there.

Gambling Against the Odds

It was particularly difficult to overcome the odds against critical trust when a patient wasn't sure if anyone, including herself, could be trusted. This was the case with Barbara Reilly, who came to S. for the first time with a complaint of back pain. Her first baby had been a "crib death" casualty five years earlier. At that time her husband had shown the first signs of the muscular dystrophy that had since confined him to a wheelchair. Two weeks before her visit to S. she had had a second child, whom she brought with her to the doctor's office. "You might say," she joked bitterly, "that my husband is my first child."

During her pregnancy Barbara had strained her back while helping her husband out of bed. A doctor had prescribed Percodan (a mild opiate), which she had continued to use after her back problem had cleared up. Now she told S. that she had reinjured her back and needed more Percodan.

S. wasn't so sure. He did not like to prescribe a drug with the addictive potential of Percodan before he knew the patient well enough to trust her when she said she needed it. "That's quite some baby you've got there. Look how she looks up into your eyes. You must have your hands full, what with your husband and this little one as well. No wonder you are in pain."

Barbara Reilly began to cry. "I'm sorry," she said.

S. didn't think she had to apologize. "Maybe there is a better way to express the sadness you feel, but crying is certainly one good way to do it, and it sounds like you have lots to feel sad about. What a beautiful baby—bundles of joy, people call them. People must think you're the happiest woman in the world. They forget that even beautiful babies can make you angry! Everyone is cooing over the baby, but you're the one who has to change her diapers."

"Sometimes it can drive me crazy," she said. She soon made clear to S. that her need for Percodan was caused as much by the strain of being alone in taking care of the baby and her husband as by her back pain. She felt burdened by both her husband and baby and may have blamed herself for the death of her first child. With so little going for her she may have seen doctors as opponents whom she needed to outwit in order to win the one thing that eased her pain.

This was one of those situations of mutual mistrust where each party was trying to get an "angle" on the other. "What's she after?" S. found himself thinking. "Is she just giving me a story so she can get a prescription?" And on her side, "How can I 'reach' this guy? What story do I have to tell him to make him give me the pills?" Each of them had a hidden agenda. The question was how to bring it out into the open.

How could S. gain this patient's trust without prescribing the Percodan? He thought that here it would have to be him who took the initiative. Should he hedge his bet by giving her what she wanted in the hope that she would stick with him long enough to learn to gamble with rather than against him? Or would giving in to her demands only inspire a superficial, cynical form of trust? There was just one gamble that he felt right about taking, a gamble that he chose on principle even though it meant he would risk losing her at the outset.

"Listen to that!" he said, calling attention to the baby's cries for food. "When this baby wants something, she really wants something. She won't give you a chance! It's good to know that ten years from now she won't need you quite so much. But she'll still need you, and you'll have to think about how you can best take care of yourself so that you can give her what she needs through the coming years."

It wasn't only the baby who wanted something right away. S. dramatized the baby's demands in order to mirror what the mother herself was doing. At the same time, he held up an image of the mother as different from the baby—as an adult who, being responsible for others, could not give way to immediate impulse. The image also had in it a time perspective, a reminder that decisions could change with time and that decisions made now would influence decisions made later. S. wanted to help Barbara Reilly be aware and unashamed of her mixed feelings toward the baby and her husband so that she could accept and live with these feelings. If she was going to be making the important decision about using a highly addictive drug, then it ought to reflect both the joys and anger in her life —both, rather than whichever one was uppermost at the moment.

Regarding that decision, S. gently reminded Barbara that there was more than one cause of her pain. Percodan would remove one of those causes, but it would reinforce others. For a person who did not have much control over her life, giving up responsibility for her life to an addictive drug would in the long run only make things worse. S. felt uncomfortable telling someone what to do, but he would not practice "consumer medicine" in the sense of giving the patient whatever she wanted. The more they talked, the more apparent it became that her craving for Percodan was not a free, informed, adult choice.

Having acknowledged the feelings and experiences that had led to this craving, he offered her oxazepam, a less potent drug, an anxiety-reducing agent, that would help her bear the pain without having quite the same addictive potential as Percodan. This drug, he thought, was less likely to affect her capacity to make choices as she learned to live with those things in her life that caused her pain or began to take steps to change them. "We're both taking a chance that this drug won't work very well," he admitted, "but in the long run Percodan won't work either, and you and your husband and baby will be playing a risky game if you go on using it."

When it came to drugs, though, Barbara Reilly was not nearly so ready to gamble with S. as Dolores Clayton had been. "Why don't you just give me the Percodan," she demanded. There followed a tense exchange during which Barbara became visibly angry. "Who wouldn't be angry?" said S. "There's lots to be angry about." He wanted her to feel safe in expressing her anger, so that she could live with it instead of letting it dictate her decision. Living with anger, however, was not the same as making it or the situation that caused it go away.

In the end she agreed to a trial of oxazepam, though she wasn't very happy about it. She had not gotten what she wanted. S. asked her to make another appointment. "To get the most out of it," he added, "it would be good to have your husband come in with you. I'd like to see how his illness may be affecting yours, whether your load can be lightened in caring for him, and whether he can start helping you care for the baby." He hoped that she would keep the appointment.

In extending his trust to Barbara Reilly, S. spoke to what was best in her, the responsible wife and mother rather than the demanding child. People drift into blind trust or mistrust when they do not feel strong enough to trust themselves to make choices. By learning to make rational choices through principled gambling with a doctor, Barbara Reilly might learn to trust her own capacity for decision-making along with someone else's. As her trust and strength grew, she could see herself more as a person making choices under conditions of uncertainty. She could also begin to see those choices as having effects on others as well as herself.

As S. was learning in his practice, people look for certainty because it is easier to deal with than uncertainty, especially when one is alone. Uncertainty takes more effort, more mental and emotional energy. There is, therefore, only so much uncertainty that one person alone can stand. As a patient and doctor (or husband and wife, or parent and child) acknowledge uncertainty together and trust each other to recognize and deal with it, they become more certain of each other's support. This leaves them more energy to deal with their uncertainty about themselves. As they learn to trust others as well as be more comfortable with themselves, they can be more open to facing, rather than denying, what uncertainty there is out in the world and making it more manageable by turning some of it into probability. Uncertainty is decreased when it can be expressed in probable expectations, expectations that can be critically trusted: about oneself, about others, about reality.

Reestablishing Trust

Admitting his uncertainty was a gamble for S. But it was a gamble that he generally preferred to take. He might as well let people know that things might turn sour, since this was bound to happen sometimes whether he said so or not.

He was particularly sensitive to the issue of trust in the case of home birth. Because there were almost no other doctors in the area who attended home births, he did not have clearly agreed-upon professional norms to fall back on if his actions were questioned. Here, where he had less control over uncertainty than usual, he knew that he needed some help in putting the Probabilistic Paradigm into practice. He needed to be able to rely on the family's desire to assume responsibility, not only by participating in the delivery but by consciously taking on the risks. But he had his blind spots, as when his fear of reprisal from a disappointed family (which could have more serious consequences for him in an area where he did not have the support of his peers) led him to trust the family less. His wariness, in turn, led them to trust *him* less. Beneath the idyllic surface a home birth was a place where trust could be strained to the limit. On the other hand, the home birth situation provided a certain measure of safety for S. He could generally count on the kind of families who chose home birth to take up the slack in maintaining or repairing a trusting relationship when his courage and critical thinking failed him.

Margaret and Bill Benson were among the many couples who came to S. for a home birth without having known him previously. Unlike most families, however, the Bensons were disappointed by the way their birth went.

As with most of the families whose births he attended, the Bensons preferred that Margaret not have an episiotomy (an incision that widens the opening of the birth canal). This gamble, which the three of them had discussed in advance, had a high probability of success, since S. and the laboring mother could almost always prevent significant tearing of the perineum by various "natural" techniques. In Margaret's case, however, he neglected to perform one of these techniques—that of keeping his hand on the perineum while the baby's head was coming out so as to allow the perineum to stretch in a controlled manner. A severe laceration occurred, with S.'s lapse being a probable contributing factor. To compound his blunder, S. tried for an hour to sew up the tear at home, only to have to give up and admit Margaret (with her baby) to the hospital for treatment by an obstetrician-gynecologist. "Some home birth," thought Margaret.

Several weeks later Margaret came in to tell S. how disappointed and angry she and her husband were. After telling everyone how "great" her birth had been, she realized that it hadn't been so great. The pictures the family had taken of the birth showed clearly that S. had not kept his hand on the perineum. Naturally the Bensons blamed S. for their not having had a good birth experience.

S. accepted complete responsibility for his error. Margaret pointed out that the laceration might have occurred regardless of what S. had done (lacerations sometimes occur even after episiotomy). Still, S. made clear, his oversight probably had been a cause. He told her that he felt that he had let her down and thanked her for initiating the discussion of a subject that both of them found difficult to talk about.

Margaret mentioned that the family had noticed S. kneeling in an uncomfortable position during the delivery, but had not thought it their place to say anything about it. S. assured her that, were he ever to be her doctor again, he would want her to trust his willingness to listen and be corrected. As it turned out, it was not only the family that had noticed something amiss. Paula, the birth attendant, had seen S.'s error but had not called attention to it at the time for fear of causing the Bensons to lose faith in him. She hadn't trusted either S. or the family enough to let them see her take issue with S. "What happened might have been avoided," Margaret concluded, "if we had all trusted one another enough to risk taking the initiative."

S. told Margaret that he and Paula had agreed to keep an eye on each other in the future and correct each other when necessary. Nothing could change the outcome in Margaret's case, but she would at least know that other women might benefit from her experience. In stressing the need for a full and free interchange among the family, the birth attendant, and himself, S. was talking about a kind of trust that transcended hierarchical distinctions. It was not a matter of doctor versus nurse, doctor versus family. All had a stake in trust.

S. wondered whether Margaret would have liked him to have taken the initiative in exploring this problem with her, instead of leaving it to her to contact him about it. He took a chance and asked her. "Yes, I would have appreciated it," she replied. His failure to contact her had been an unconsciously chosen losing gamble, just as Paula and the Bensons had lost by not speaking up in time to correct S.'s error during the delivery. Building trust requires taking risks, and on this occasion S. and Margaret regained trust by speaking frankly with each other.

The photographs the Bensons took of the delivery would have been damning evidence in a malpractice suit. The Bensons, however, had built up enough trust during their brief prenatal relationship with S. to bring their grievance to him rather than take it to court. "We took this gamble together," Margaret explained. "You can trust us to know the difference between a mistake and bad faith." As she left, she shook hands with S. and said, "I hope we'll see each other again." The Bensons, who were already members of a prepaid health plan, were not to be among the families who adopted S. as their family doctor after going through a birth with him. But they were ready to consider him for their next home delivery.

From this encounter Margaret felt reinforced in her conviction that you could tell someone (even a doctor) that you were angry at him without having either one of you drop dead from the explosion. To confront someone with your anger, you had to trust that person and know that he trusted you. Her belief was strengthened that there is a middle ground between blind trust and vindictive retaliation. When you have come to trust someone over a period of nine months, it doesn't make sense to throw it all away because of one careless moment. Better to check out whether the person you thought was so good could really be so bad. You might confirm your initial trust or your subsequent disillusionment—or, again, something in between.

Betting on Oneself

What S. learned from this and other encounters was that trust breeds trust. What he did or did not do was only one cause of his patients trusting or not trusting him. He realized as well that his own observations and expectations of his patients' untrustworthiness influenced them to live up—or down—to his expectations. He also realized that, if he wanted to be trusted, he could not blindly trust himself. At times he would need to ask his patients or coworkers for help, as in checking that he manually supported the perineum during a delivery. When he felt himself to be under time pressure while making hospital rounds, he would ask the nurses accompanying him to watch him carefully and inform him of any omissions in his clinical procedure. In doing so, he was making a side bet that created an added immediate reward (approval or lack of criticism) for doing what was consistent with a larger, long-range goal (attending to his patients' well-being). Asking family members, birth attendants, or nurses to monitor his performance at crucial moments was a side bet that S. often made when he felt himself slipping into gambling in his own rather than his patients' interest.

In gambling on whether he needed help and whether he needed to make a side bet on his being trustworthy, S. was able to go beyond the mechanistic impulse to look to the patient or the situation for *the* clue, *the* piece of evidence that would decide the issue. Just as he made probabilistic estimates of the trustworthiness of his patients and coworkers, so he decided on a probabilistic basis whether he could trust himself. He would look at the context, including the patient, his own past experience with that particular type of problem, and how he himself felt at that moment. The "experiment" now took into account not only the patient, but the doctor as well. It included the feelings the patient evoked in him and whatever he could apprehend of the feelings he evoked in the patient. Whether he could handle a particular problem was a gamble, a gamble that he shared with patients so that he and they could approach it as carefully as they did other gambles.

What he learned from people such as the Bensons was to regard both himself and his patients as causes. Along with them he was taking a step away from the primitive thinking that saw causation as occurring either entirely inside or entirely outside himself. If everything were to be caused by the actions of others, then he would be powerless, and he would not be able to trust those who had power over him. If he himself were the cause of everything, then he would not need to trust anyone else, and he would soon become untrustworthy. ("Absolute power corrupts absolutely.") The primitive feelings of doctors tended toward the latter extreme—that of megalomania. But what about the primitive feelings of patients? These often took the form of frustration at the patient's lack of control over uncertainty. The very mistakes a doctor made (however unfortunate the consequences) served to demonstrate the doctor's power to influence events. What, then, was left for the patient to do but to demonstrate control in an equally negative way by the nose-thumbing gesture of noncompliance? If the doctor could be a cause of an unsuccessful outcome, so could the patient. So ran the perverse logic of primitive emotion.

It did not take long for S. to agree with the Bensons that the structure of the doctor-patient relationship was itself not conducive to trust. A relationship where the doctor, as "experimenter," held all the cards left the patient nothing to do but to trust blindly in "doctor knows best." When this trust was shattered either by errors on the doctor's part or by an element of chance that no amount of skill or goodwill could eliminate, blind trust turned to blind resentment. It was essential, then, for S. to involve patients in facing uncertainty by gambling with him. But it was equally essential for the patients' well-being. By becoming S.'s gambling partner (an active partner, not a silent partner who invested the resources of life and health without taking part in gambling decisions), a patient could learn where S.'s blind spots were and thus could *critically* trust this well-intentioned partner.

Even more important, by making choices, patients could test their own authority and power in an uncertain world. Like S. himself, they would now have the burden and the privilege of learning to trust themselves—the privilege outweighing the burden, since only a person who has some control over events needs to be trusted to use that power responsibly. Thus when misfortune occurred, doctor and patient both would know themselves to be strong enough to accept a fair share of the responsibility of the sadness and the fear. Both would know themselves to be a cause (so that they would not feel powerless), but not the only cause (so that they would not feel completely to blame). In a probabilistic world they would be able to share the sadness and the fear with that set of other causes called nature. Through the experience of gambling, on the other hand, they would feel that they had enough power and enough skill (the skill of gambling) to bear the burden of some of the responsibility and the sadness themselves.

There is a big difference between sadness and helplessness. It is easier to feel sad when one believes that there is a chance to do something about the sadness. When one has had some success in gambling in the past, the odds are that one will not be without hope or without resources in the future.

Living with Anxiety—
and with Regret

S. learned that patients grew stronger through making choices, however much courage they needed at first to do so. He wanted the same thing to happen to him. He, too, did not always feel secure in the presence of uncertainty. He, too, was learning to make better choices.

He had gone through a considerable evolution, for example, in the way he treated those patients who chronically presented a variety of aches and pains that had no apparent organic cause and for which the likely diagnosis was "anxiety." He would explain to these patients, as he had to Dolores Clayton and Barbara Reilly, that feelings are manifested in bodily stresses and that it usually did not make sense to treat the mind and body separately. But what was the next step?

There was a time when he simply recommended family counseling as more honest and more effective than drug therapy. "That's the way you deal with these things," he would say. Then he would worry about whether the patient would come back, let alone bring the family in. As often as not the patient didn't come back, and S. was left to blame the patient or himself. Denying uncertainty in his presentation to patients, he was left with the anxiety of "Will they or won't they?" which he dismissed by looking for a certain determining cause—a flaw in their character, a diagnostic label such as "borderline personality"—when they "didn't."

Later S. became less mechanistic both about assigning responsibility for failure and about the values involved in making treatment decisions. While he still believed that the odds usually favored family counseling, he had come to realize that the world was such that some people could not change their lives. For these patients, sad as it was, drugs were better than nothing at all. Since no treatment was certain to work, S. presented patients with a series of options which he counted off on his fingers. One, do nothing and go on living with the symptoms. Two, get a second opinion about possible organic causes.

Three, take an antidepressant drug or a tranquilizer. Four, talk things over with S. or with someone else, with or without the participation of family members.

When S. left the choice in the hands of the patient or family, he felt "clean." No longer was he biased in favor of one choice or another. Whatever the patient wanted to do was fine—including not coming back at all. For a while S. thought of himself as "the transformed doctor." He certainly was less anxious, and he thought that he truly was practicing probabilistically.

After a while, though, he became dissatisfied with this approach as well. Previously patients didn't come back because he was too directive; now they didn't come back because he didn't seem to care. If he was too involved before, he was too detached now. He had made himself less anxious by turning away from uncertainty altogether, perhaps to avoid the anxiety he would feel if he faced it directly. The patients also could not get sufficiently involved in their own treatment, as a result of the packaged, take-it-or-leave-it way in which he presented the options. When it was a matter of choosing among "one, two, three, or four," patients were just choosing which option to consume instead of producing their own options.

So S. gradually learned to accept each case as having some unique possibilities. He now tried to help people see how they could create choices for themselves, choices to which his principles as well as theirs would speak. Without overlooking the fact that situations constrained people's choices, he helped people see their part of the responsibility for arranging those situations. All the while he helped them bear the responsibility by assuming responsibility himself in his interactions with them.

He recognized that if there could be said to be a "germ" that caused anxiety, this germ was uncertainty. He was willing to work with patients so that he and they could build up an immunity through measured inoculations of uncertainty in an active decision-making process. He, the doctor, was inescapably a part of that process. He took into account that anxiety was contagious, that anxious doctors made for anxious patients as well as vice versa. Of course, too little anxiety could be as bad as too much; he and the patient had to be careful to avoid quarantining themselves from uncertainty altogether.

How many transformations would he have to go through, S. wondered, how many layers of mechanistic skin would he have to shed before he could finally feel that he was doing it "right"? By now, though, having made some choices for himself, he felt strong enough to live with regret over the mistakes he had made, to know that he would someday live with regret over the mistakes he was still to make, and to trust himself enough to go on. His patients were growing to expect no less.

11

COMPLIANCE VERSUS CARING

S. found that probabilistic medicine often was easier to think about than to practice. It was hard enough to practice in a world where there was little critical trust; it was doubly hard in the world of medicine, a world full of pain and fear.

When people came to S., they often were in pain. Even when they were not, they might well fear that they would suffer pain, either right there at the doctor's hands or in the coming months and years. Sometimes it was first the pain and then the fear, S. reflected, as in the case of an elderly woman with breast cancer. At other times it was first the fear and then the pain, as in the case of a man who had had a heart attack. Whenever this man would think about what intimate terms he was on with death, the pain in his chest would soon follow. Most often the two came together and were so intertwined that only when they became memory would they finally separate. Where there was sickness, there was always a heart broken with the pain of sadness for one's lost health (and sometimes youth). There was also the fear that it could mean facing death alone, or (where death was not yet an issue) that life would never again be the same.

Many of the people who came to S., therefore, were in no mood for probabilistic thinking. They wanted the consolations

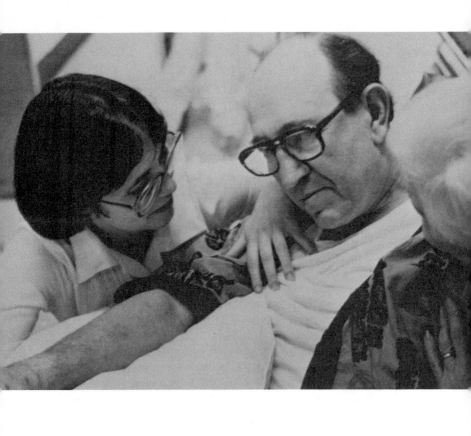

of certainty, the security of being told what to do. They wanted to be taken care of, and S. wanted to take care of them. When the pain and the fear got to be too great (as they could with any patient), it was understandable that S. would slip into the traditional doctor role and that his patients would slip into the traditional patient role. He would take care of them by telling them what to do, and they would comply with his edicts. Then there was little probabilistic reasoning, little of the spirit of doctor and patient gambling together. But S. consoled himself that at least the pain and fear could be held at arm's length.

S. would have gone on in this belief had it not been that his patients did not always comply. For example, they did not always take their medications as they had agreed to do. When he would ask them, "How can I take care of you if you don't listen to what I say?" he would feel anger and sadness. It was when he realized that the anger and sadness he felt were partly his and partly his patients' (for they, too, were angry and sad) that he stopped asking the question rhetorically as a reproach to his patients and began asking it seriously. How *could* he take care of patients who didn't comply? It was a question that he and they needed to answer together.

As they explored this question, S. learned that patients looked at the compliance issue from a perspective very different from his own. Taking medications often complicated people's lives. There was no saying how the medication would work—that it would work at all, or that it wouldn't make them sick—until they tried it. He couldn't tell them, as the advertisers did, "Try it; you'll like it." What he could do was to invite them to call him about any problems they had with the medication. But he could understand that they might throw up their hands if it didn't work right away. They might even blame him.

Remembering Mrs. Pinelli and her hypertension, S. realized that many patients weren't interested primarily in building a relationship with him. They came to him often as a last resort after finding that their pain didn't simply go away or respond to home remedies and over-the-counter drugs. They were looking for immediate relief, not a long-range commitment to deal with a problem. Little in their experience gave them reason to hope for anything more.

Compliance was a new term in the medical lexicon. *Caring* was an old one. Doctors had long spoken about caring for patients; only recently had patients' compliance with doctors been spoken of in the same breath. Reflecting on the current medical preoccupation with compliance, S. wondered whether caring could be separated from compliance in the doctor's office—or, for that matter, in the family. He wondered whether people knew how to care without exacting compliance in return. After all, they were living in a world where caring between husband and wife, brother and sister, parent and child—or anyone, for that matter—was often seen as part of an exchange.

In the course of his practice S. began to learn that he could take care of patients without insisting that they comply by treating his wishes as cookbook recipes. He no longer felt that he was engaged in an exchange or an implicit contract whereby a patient "owed" him compliance in return for care. Once he was able to untangle the question of caring from that of compliance, he could look afresh at the question that concerned him most: how one could care for people in pain and fear through the practice of probabilistic medicine.

What his patients helped him see was that he could best care for them when he neither demanded compliance nor adopted an indifferent, "anything goes" attitude. People sensed when he didn't care. To be involved with his patients, S. needed to stand by his own values while respecting theirs, and to support them in doing what he and they thought was right. Sometimes the outcome would not be what he desired, as often from the patient's choice as from what are called "natural" causes, and about some of these times there was nothing left to do but to be sad.

The "Hateful Patient"

An experience that taught S. to separate caring from compliance involved a patient who became so distasteful to him that his usual eagerness to care turned to a plea of "Oh, God, why won't she find herself another doctor?" It was only when his plea was answered and she found herself another doctor that he realized it hadn't been all her doing. She had become, in the words of a *New England Journal of Medicine* article (Groves, 1978), a "hateful patient." This had happened in the context of her relationship with S., a relationship that had been the sort of zero-sum game one would find in the mechanistic family. It had taken this doctor-patient relationship to make the woman, Mrs. Nagel, a hateful patient.

Mrs. Nagel was a woman of seventy whose cultivated speech and fund of medical knowledge seemed out of place in the cluttered studio apartment that S. would come to know as her home. Mrs. Nagel had hyperparathyroidism, a difficult to diagnose condition. Since hyperparathyroidism mimics the symptoms of other common conditions such as the flu, every instance of fatigue or loss of appetite became an opportunity for Mrs. Nagel to pit the family doctor's opinion against that of a specialist.

During her first few visits with S., Mrs. Nagel rambled on with complaints about other doctors until he finally felt he had to tell her to stop. She left his office in a huff, accusing him of not paying attention to her. He brooded about his "failure." Mechanistically, he considered himself to be the sole cause of her departure. Now it was "his" fault; before long it would be "hers."

Several months later she called him again and asked him to make a home visit. When he arrived, she began by apologizing for dismissing him so abruptly, but then proceeded to ramble just as before. Finally S. risked confronting her. "You know," he said, "if you keep talking about other things, I'm eventually going to tell you to get back to the subject at hand, and you'll just get so angry that you'll cut things off again, right? Well, then, I'll be glad to be your doctor if you'd like me to, but for us to get on with finding out what's wrong, you'll need to stop talking when I ask you to."

It worked. She complied with his wish. S. had shown Mrs. Nagel a picture of herself that she would acknowledge was accurate. In risking an uncertain reaction from her, in challenging his own mechanistic assumption that she would take off angrily, all because of him, he felt that he was also undermining *her* assumption that she could control *his* reactions (as she did everyone else's) by making him so angry that he would do something he would come to regret, and she would get to be the victim again. What he might also have done was to offer her the responsibility of asking him to stop talking when she saw fit. He might have said, "If you think I'm being unreasonable, tell me so." Although Mrs. Nagel was not responsible enough to handle much power in her relationship with S., this bit of equality might have given her some insight into what it was like to have a doctor's responsibilities. It might also have shown S. what it felt like to be on the other end of the judgments he made about the way patients took up his time. This reciprocity might have been the basis for empathy and trust between them.

S. was enthusiastic about his "breakthrough" with Mrs. Nagel, but in a probabilistic world the course of a relationship is not determined by the first encounter. S. had given little power to Mrs. Nagel within their relationship, but in a sense he had given her complete power. If he made all the rules, she could break them all, which she did by calling him several times a week with the same complaints. She let him know in the teasing manner of an unfaithful lover that she was seeing other doctors on the sly. S. felt that as her family doctor he would be able to sort out her maze of symptoms only if he were given access to the findings of the other physicians. Whatever his intentions, she interpreted his concern as a demand that she trust him blindly. She delighted in playing doctors off against one another, showing each of them how unimportant he was to her.

Such treatment wore S. down until he jumped at the provocation. He told her that he could not be her doctor if she called him all the time with insubstantial complaints and didn't tell him when she saw other doctors. He saw in her concealment of information a lack of trust in him, but in making an issue of this when there wasn't enough trust between them to begin with, he was unconsciously playing the jealous lover to her unfaithful one. His blowup gave her a pretext for walking away from him again.

The next week he called her—a first for him—and told her he had had "second thoughts." "Look," he said, "however you want to use me is fine. You're free to call me as often as you want and talk to me about anything you like. Tell me about the other doctors; don't tell me about the other doctors. You have your idea of what a family doctor is, and I have mine. For one thing, I need to be paid for my time. Medicaid doesn't pay for phone calls. If you won't come in and see me so that I can bill Medicaid, I'll bill you for the time we spend on the phone. There, my cards are on the table. I'll send you a letter which summarizes this conversation. If you want to sign it and return it to me, we can use it as a contract specifying the terms under which I'll take care of you." Mrs. Nagel thought this was a fine idea.

No sooner had he sent the contract than it was signed and returned by Mrs. Nagel. And no sooner did he allow himself an expression of relief than Mrs. Nagel called. She had found a loophole in the contract and was about to make use of it. "I need a home visit right now," she demanded. "I won't tell you over the phone why I think I need it. It costs too much to talk to you on the phone. I would much rather just follow the contract."

S. felt outwitted. She was complying with the letter, but not the spirit, of the "contract." The way he had written it, however, it was pretty clear that to follow it to the letter he would have to comply with her wishes. Now that the shoe was on the other foot, would he comply? He went to see her.

Again he had risen to the occasion; again it didn't last. A day after he had seen her at home, she called again with the same request. He responded that he would not go to her home again so soon for the same problems, but that she could see him in the office if she liked.

She became furious with him. "I pay you good money, so you've got to come and see me. Read that contract of yours; it specifies our deal. You're not holding up your part of the bargain. I am doing what the contract says I should, and you're not." Chagrined, S. nonetheless stuck to his resolve and asked her to renegotiate the contract. She refused, and he never heard from her again. He knew that she would continue to find other doctors. For his part he felt so drained that he would not call her back.

The burden of this encounter hung over him. A few months later he tried to examine whether anything he might have done could have made a difference. He did not want to fall back into the mechanistic pattern of blaming either himself or Mrs. Nagel, as if either were the sole cause. He no longer thought of Mrs. Nagel as intrinsically a hateful patient. As he got more deeply into probabilistic practice, however, it occurred to him that he would have had much to gain and little to lose in his last encounter with Mrs. Nagel by telling her explicitly (as he was telling her implicitly) that he didn't trust her: "Right now I don't trust you to be able to decide when you need a home visit and when you don't." He had since learned that even when you don't trust a person, you can still convey a degree of trust by saying so. Some people respond to being taken seriously in this way by taking on more responsibility for their choices; Mrs. Nagel might or might not have been one of them. Her life was predicated on the conviction that she didn't need to be responsible, since no one acted responsibly toward her. In the end S. failed to shake that belief. But one could hardly blame him if he, too, came out of that encounter feeling that life was a bit unfair.

As he continued to examine the case, he began to understand some of the reasons for Mrs. Nagel's anger and how he had contributed to it by his insistence on compliance as a condition for caring. Here was a lonely, elderly woman, scared to death of being made dependent by her progressively more debilitating and painful disease. No wonder she made so many calls and so many requests. Since she did not trust anyone, let alone herself, her solution to her pain and fear was to find as many doctors as possible so that she would not be completely dependent on any one of them. She felt that she could not trust anyone to stick by her in the midst of her intense pain and fear. She expected that she would lose Dr. S., and, sure enough, through her constant testing of S. she was not disappointed. Once again she would find herself all alone in the world.

As she saw the world, every relationship was a zero-sum game with one party or the other being to blame and thus somehow deserving the pain and the fear. She would "comply" with S.'s wishes so that she could later point the finger at him. She was eager to accept the contract, for it gave justification for her anger at Dr. S. when, as she had expected, he would not comply—to the letter—with the exchange it specified. In this way she could blame him for failing to protect her from pain and fear, and maybe even for having caused them in the first place. Blaming him let her forget for a moment how sad and precarious her situation was. It let her proceed with the illusion that, in an eccentric version of the *experimentum crucis,* removing S. as one would remove a splinter would produce the desired outcome of removing the pain and fear.

For his part it occurred to S. that his insistence on compliance might not have been entirely motivated by his wish to take care of her. An example was his initial demand that she tell him whenever she was seen by another doctor. By letting her know that he didn't feel able to care for her otherwise, was he making a self-fulfilling prophecy? By quickly jumping to spell out for her the consequences of her failure to comply, was he telling her that he was expecting, maybe even wanting her to fail to comply? In her "failure to comply," was she complying with the hidden message, implicit in the compliance model, that patients such as she are expected not to comply? He saw that her consulting other physicians had served some unacknowledged desires of his own. It meant that some of her demands for care as well as some of her anger would be directed at the other doctors instead of at him. It had also given him justification for the anger that he felt toward her. Thus he was able to win the power struggle and to rid himself not only of the anger engendered by this patient, but of the patient herself. Mrs. Nagel was being "compliant" with his hidden wishes when she was being "noncompliant" with his stated wishes.

Reflecting on his encounter with Mrs. Nagel, S. wondered whether by basing his caring relationships with patients on compliance he was treating grown people like small children. Was it any wonder, then, that some patients would respond like children and even attribute to him the magical powers of the mechanistic scientist, who by changing this or that variable could make their pain and fear disappear? When such expecta-

tions were disappointed, as sometimes they must be, anger
would follow. By now, even when S. *could* make the pain and
fear disappear, patients would be using the most primitive version of the Mechanistic Paradigm, whereby he was the only
cause. They would need only the slightest provocation to consider him not only the sole cause of cure for their pain and fear,
but of the pain and fear themselves. When treated as children,
patients would fall back on a mechanistic notion of causality
and would think of S. as they long ago thought of their mothers
and fathers.

S. realized that, though he was using the criteria of the
Probabilistic Paradigm, he was following them like cookbook
rules rather than internalizing them as an interdependent system. Thus he could be drawn into Mrs. Nagel's zero-sum compliance game, an exchange relationship where he would make
concessions to her as the price of getting his way. The two of
them so arranged it that theirs was a competitive relationship,
with the loser being "stuck" with the sadness that, together,
they could not find a way to share. By being angry with each
other, they attributed the sadness to the "fact" that the other
was "making me sad," and thus named the other person as
somehow the cause of the sadness.

Although both of them were thinking mechanistically, S., as
a "scientist" in the Mechanistic Paradigm (not to mention his
being healthy and having family and friends) ultimately had
the upper hand. His initial reaction had been to steer clear of
patients such as Mrs. Nagel. They took up too much of his time
and energy and, he felt, took away from the care he could be
giving other patients. He could feel sufficiently justified in his
anger to label Mrs. Nagel "hateful," as if that were a classifica-
tion to be applied to an individual rather than a result of interactions between people. On reflection, however, S. saw that
he had swung over from the narcissism of total self-reproach
to the paranoia of seeing this patient as the sole cause of her
hatefulness. This enabled him to hold Mrs. Nagel's anger and
sadness at arm's length, just as she had sought to hold her pain
and fear at arm's length by being angry at him.

S.'s reconsideration of his interactions with Mrs. Nagel allowed him to accept his share of the responsibility for what had happened. He recognized that as long as he was operating on the compliance model, he could arrange matters so that with almost any patient the need to struggle against rather than work with him could come to the surface. He could get away from Mrs. Nagel, but not from himself.

S. resolved to become more conscious in forming relationships with patients that were based on shared rather than competing needs. Sharing between doctor and patient could not, of course, be total. It was the patient's life, the patient's health, that were on the line. Still, a caring person could share pain and fear that he could not directly feel. Instead of squaring off in a game that pitted the needs of one against the needs of the other, doctor and patient could gamble together to meet needs that were shared as well as needs that were not shared. With this hope S. stopped struggling to achieve compliance and tried to offer caring without strings attached.

Complying with Oneself

S. remembered Mrs. Nagel when he met Henry Kane, a twenty-year-old epileptic whose seizures were not well controlled. The kind of seizures that Henry Kane had could not be completely prevented under the best of circumstances, but matters were made worse by the fact that for periods of time he refused to take medicine. Henry had little experience in self-reliance; his family seemed accustomed to his being dependent and perhaps unwittingly encouraged it. While Henry was in the hospital after having fallen and cut his scalp during a seizure, he and S. arranged that he would be discharged to a halfway house, where his medications could be further adjusted and he could gain some distance from his family entanglements. Without telling anyone, Henry went straight home instead of to the halfway house. He also did not pick up his prescription and failed to keep an appointment with S. for a follow-up visit as was previously agreed upon.

At first S. stood in awe of the powerful forces that kept Henry as he was. How chaotic, how distrustful Henry's world must be. S. didn't see how he could continue to be his doctor. Then, remembering Mrs. Nagel, he called Henry. They set up an appointment. When the time came, Henry was there.

S. addressed Henry in a way that he had never quite brought himself to use with Mrs. Nagel. He was about to say, "Henry . . ." when he caught himself. Though he often called patients by their first names, it seemed to have the wrong implications in the case of this grown man whose family still treated him as a child. "Mr. Kane," S. said, "it is very hard for me to believe anything you say after you behave as you do over and over again. I sense that your life is full of mistrust, and it hurts me that I, too, cannot trust you. I'll still be your doctor if you want to be my patient, so long as you know that right now I don't trust you."

Going by Henry's unresponsive face, S. couldn't tell if his words had even registered. But although he had lost his initial gamble of trusting Mr. Kane, he would still gamble on trusting him with the knowledge of his suspicions. After his experience with Mrs. Nagel he knew better than to assume that one brave gesture would create a higher level of trust. But perhaps it was a beginning.

What S. was doing was a far cry from what the drug companies implied he should be doing, i.e., manipulating the patient to achieve compliance. In their advertisements, such as the one entitled, "Patient Compliance: The Missing Link in Successful Control," the drug companies were marketing the second criterion of the Mechanistic Paradigm. They were claiming that, even if many causes were present, manipulating one cause, one variable (the "missing link"), would change the outcome decisively. The object to be manipulated was the patient. In the drug companies' mechanistic science patients were put into the role of compliant subjects who did everything they were told to do.

In Henry Kane's case, however, this was the role he already

had in his family, where he was, in effect, told to be sick. No wonder he couldn't do what S. told him to do. He couldn't comply with S. in being well because he was already complying with his family in being sick. If S. had tried to make Henry Kane comply, he would have put him into an untenable situation, as well as entering into a zero-sum game with the family over who was going to tell Henry what to do.

In his family Henry Kane had learned that he would be cared for only if he complied with his role as the cause of the family's troubles. When someone else got a cold, it was clear to everyone that Henry, "the sick one" who had always been prone to colds, had been the cause. When one or another family member met with a setback in the outside world, all would agree that the need to "take care of Henry" was the cause of it all. The more pain and fear was laid on Henry, the more he assumed the sick role, the more his brothers and sisters wanted to get away from him. And yet they were bound to take care of him by the same unspoken contract with which he was complying in being sick.

As Henry became more helpless, his brothers and sisters were all the more determined to show that they were different from him. But in the back of their minds lurked the fear that they, being of the same flesh and blood and the same genes as he, might not be so different after all. So they went to great lengths to show how different they really were. The way they showed it, however, was by taking care of Henry's every need while he was "sick," but having nothing to do with him while he was "well." Although their wish was to be as far away from him as possible, their behavior ensured that the ties of dependency that bound Henry to the family, and the family to Henry, would be far stronger than the genetic ties they feared.

S.'s task, then, was not to show Henry Kane how to comply; he could do that all too well. Mr. Kane was now in a weak, dependent position, and S. could not honestly treat him as he would most patients. But there were ways of caring for a person that did not involve manipulating him into compliance. Clearly Mr. Kane was not now able to internalize the principles of the Probabilistic Paradigm and practice them independently. Perhaps, though, he could begin by identifying with S. as someone who could do these things. In S., Henry Kane would have a model of a conscious gambler. If he liked what he saw in S.'s way of thinking, feeling, and acting, he might make it in some measure his own.

It would do no good to try to make Mr. Kane comply with anyone else's ideas about what he should do. What mattered was what he thought was right for himself. The real issue for S. was to see if Mr. Kane wanted to make a choice—to choose to be an independent, self-respecting human being—and then help him get beyond his fears and uncertainties so that he could live out that choice, i.e.: comply with his chosen self.

Henry Kane needed to learn in the most basic ways how to take care of himself—to get around the city, to achieve some financial independence, to manage his epilepsy without having it manage him, and even to articulate some of his thoughts and feelings. He was afraid to learn these things, since he feared that he would lose his family's support if he did. For the same reason he was afraid to stop having frequent epileptic seizures, which were a comforting sign of his dependency on the family. And yet he also was scared to death of the seizures and found them unpleasant and humiliating. This was the place where S. decided to try to break into the closed system of Mr. Kane's dependency. "Shall we take a chance on working together?" he asked him, hoping that at some level Mr. Kane would want to gamble on himself.

"Nothing ventured, nothing gained, I guess," replied Mr. Kane.

"What makes it so hard to take the medication?" S. asked.

"Well, what usually happens is that there is no way I can remember to take it three times a day. I need someone to remind me, but my family gets tired of it after a while. And once I stop taking it and have a seizure, it's a pain to start again."

The first gamble S. proposed was to switch to a medication that Mr. Kane would have to take only once rather than three times a day. "I'll bet that if we do that," said S., "you won't forget to take the medication so much. And the less you forget, the fewer seizures you'll have."

"Let's give it a try," said Mr. Kane. Instead of a "game" where he took his medication as the price of keeping S. in his corner, patient and doctor were now on the same side.

Even though their talks were still one-sided (for Henry Kane didn't yet trust himself enough to say what he thought and felt), S. carefully brought him around to a different attitude toward his illness and treatment. Since it was as yet impossible to stop the seizures completely, there was no reason for Mr. Kane to think that he had "failed," lost the gamble, if he happened to have a seizure. He and S. were going for a reduction of the probability, not an all-or-none result. Nor did Mr. Kane have to think, if he forgot one dose of his medication, that the bet was lost and he might just as well forget his medication altogether. True, he increased the probability of a seizure every time he forgot to take the medicine—and that was what they were trying to avoid—but he would raise the odds much more by forgetting repeatedly than by forgetting once. So there was still every reason not to forget the next time. There was a thin line between "it's okay to forget it" and "it's not okay to forget it," just as there was with patients who were gambling on themselves when they tried to stop smoking or overeating.

As in those cases, S. helped Mr. Kane understand that the consequences of a single lapse, in terms of the habits he was trying to learn, went beyond the physical consequences alone, which often were negligible. In the language of gambling, S. was setting up a side bet whereby Henry Kane could enhance his own self-respect every time he took the medication. As Mr. Kane put it, "You know, it's funny—the more I bother about myself, the more I think I'm worth bothering about."

On the other hand, S. thought it important that both of them understand that the consequences of forgetting a dose were not so dire as to mean that Mr. Kane would lose the whole of his self-esteem. "Who doesn't forget sometimes?" S. would say on those occasions when Mr. Kane would come in and tell him that he had forgotten a dose here and there. Though Mr. Kane would continue to forget once in a while, he did so less and less frequently. Moreover, when he did forget, he would resume the medication with the next dose instead of stopping completely and refusing to take it.

Controlling Henry Kane's seizures was an important first step in his treatment not only because he would be able to get around more confidently by himself if he were not subject to such frequent attacks, but also because his fear of being "out of control" during a seizure stood for his sense of not being in control of his life and in his family relationships. S. helped him achieve some control over the frequency of his seizures by familiarizing him with some of the known causes of epileptic attacks. Failing to take the medication was a cause. Drinking, which Mr. Kane had been doing with the tacit encouragement of his family, was a cause. Emotional agitation was a cause, and a person who kept his feelings pent up as Henry Kane did was often agitated.

As their relationship evolved, S. and Henry Kane were able to set up a regular visit schedule so that he could continue to count on seeing S. even without there being a crisis. He needed to see that, in contrast to his family situation, getting well did not mean that he would lose his ties to S. He could still count on S.'s care even after he stopped being completely dependent on S.'s presence. In time—and it would take time—Henry Kane would no longer have a stake in being sick. Now that he was beginning to identify with S. and internalize the principles S. followed, he could begin to deal with the uncertainty that he would always face, while knowing that others would work with him even if he was able to help himself. S., at least, would do so; perhaps those who lived with him would too.

In the months that followed, Henry Kane became more articulate. With S.'s encouragement he took an adult-education course in emergency medicine, a subject he chose out of his increasing awareness of and responsibility for his illness. Since the purpose of the course was to teach people to respond to just that sort of occurrence, it gave Mr. Kane a natural format for practicing the steps he and S. had worked out for him to take when he felt a fit coming on. First he would lie down. Then he would tell the people around him what was going to happen. "Don't worry," he would say. "It'll be okay as long as I can breathe. Keep the airway clear if it gets blocked. It'll just take five minutes, and then I'll be dazed for a while." This procedure had worked quite well at home with his family.

It happened that Mr. Kane did have a seizure in class. As he described it later to S., "It came out okay, and the people did the right things, but they were really scared, and afterward a lot of them didn't seem to want to look at me or talk to me all evening. And this was the kind of thing they're all supposed to be there for!" People have different ways of distancing themselves from what they fear, and just at that moment Henry Kane's family's way of smothering him with sympathetic attention was looking a little better to him. It did not surprise S. that Mr. Kane suffered a setback as his family drew him back into its protective folds. But while he had been changing, his family had been changing too. As the others in the family saw Henry take the gamble of stepping out of his sick role, and survive, they found the courage to do the same. S. was now able to begin working with the family as well as the patient to try to understand what had happened. Slowly the rigid roles that had characterized this family became more flexible, and the family began to break out of its mechanistic mold.

Over the next few years, as the family members learned to share the risks of gambling rather than load all the fear and pain of an uncertain world onto Henry's illness, their capacity to bear fear and pain grew. At the same time, the amount of fear and pain Henry's illness caused them became less as they began to understand the illness probabilistically. They were learning that epilepsy is an illness with many causes, some of which they as well as Henry could control. For example, as Henry learned to express his feelings, the frequency of his seizures decreased. His brothers and sisters learned to see that having one possible cause of epilepsy (some of the same genes) in common with Henry no longer meant being predestined to the same fate.

When they no longer had to differentiate themselves from Henry on the basis of who was caring for whom and who was complying with whom, the other members of his family could tolerate far more initiative on his part. They could be with Henry as a family, sharing experience and risk, rather than manipulating a passive, compliant, sick subject in order to hide from the uncertainty they could not tolerate.

Acknowledging Strengths and Admitting Differences

The difficulties that S. encountered in caring for Henry Kane and his family and for Mrs. Nagel were exceptional. Even so, he learned something about caring from each of these cases. Caring sometimes meant supporting people in their efforts to comply with their own choices, as S. had done with Henry Kane. Sometimes it even meant supporting people when their choices did not comply with his own wishes, as he would like to have done with Mrs. Nagel. Having learned these lessons, S. could apply them when caring for less troubled families such as the Fowlers and the Neills.

When the Fowlers brought in their two-month-old, whose birth at home S. had attended, for a well baby checkup, they reported that the baby was fussing for several hours each evening despite all their ministrations. S. assured the couple that this behavior was normal. He explained it as a kind of developmental stage through which infants pass. "After all, he's still largely a reflex person," said S., pointing to the baby's easily elicited startle response. "There isn't that much he can do, and crying is one of those things. As soon as he begins to relate more discriminately to the world around him, you can count on this kind of crying coming to an end.

"Remember, we don't know what the experience he is having is like. We can't even assume that it's unpleasant. We just can't get inside his head. But you feel responsible to make him feel better, anyone would. And what you find out is that you can't do everything about it. Then you feel helpless, and maybe the baby does too."

S. knew how insecure many new parents felt. He believed that they were doing well, only they were the last to know it. His faith wasn't blind. Sure, there were things he encouraged them to do differently, but he did so in the spirit of refining an already amazing piece of craftsmanship, the family. All too often people simply are unacknowledged for being themselves. They are always being put down. Even the efforts of experts to assist can have the effect of undermining self-confidence. So he made a point of letting people know what a good job *they* were doing, and of offering them understanding and support. He also wanted to show them that he cared for them even though they were doing well. There did not have to be something wrong for him to care. He believed that the parents' feeling good about themselves was as important to a child's well-being as any of the traditional things he did, such as giving polio vaccine.

The more pain and fear there was, the harder it was for people to gamble with a doctor. S. began to realize that some of the pain and fear entered into his practice not from the patient's home, as with Henry Kane, but from the very fact of a person's becoming a patient.

It isn't easy to be a patient. People feel bad and find it difficult to express themselves (it is often hard even to describe a pain). They may feel stupid for being inarticulate, for having delayed seeking attention, or for having come for a trivial purpose. They may be ashamed to disrobe, particularly when they do not know the doctor. S. thought it essential to acknowledge this discomfort and to put people at ease so that they could provide better information and collaborate in their treatment.

When S. encountered patients who readily, even insistently collaborated in their treatment, he admired their courage in choosing to do so in spite of all the barriers. However, they often presented a different kind of challenge. There were some who insisted that the compliance shoe be on the other foot, that the doctor give them what they wanted, such as this or that tranquilizer, or they would take their business elsewhere. They presented S. with a difficult dilemma. He did not want to impose his values, yet he did not think that "anything goes" was a responsible position to take. So, depending on the patient and the request, he would try to work out some agreement. When an agreement simply could not be reached, he had to say, "Would you like me to refer you to another doctor for this?" More often he could continue to care for a patient or family while agreeing to disagree with a particular choice that they made.

It happened that way with the Neills, a professional couple in their late twenties. Elizabeth Neill had had three abortions in the past four years. The last of these had been performed by

S. Afterward he invited the couple to discuss contraceptive methods with him. As they spoke, it became apparent that the couple had previously spent a good deal of time examining the subject. "We've had this same discussion before with other doctors," said Elizabeth, "and the best we could come up with was the rhythm method. We've done everything. We keep track of the temperature, and we even use the mucus test." The couple's reasons for deciding against an IUD and the pill were based on an evaluation of the side effects of both. They rejected a diaphragm or condoms on the grounds that these would detract from the sensuality of their sex life. And they were both clear that they did not want to have children just yet.

After getting to know the couple better in the course of several visits, S. could not help but wonder whether their choice was not being constrained by an excessively rigid definition of sensuality made necessary by the otherwise fragile bonds between husband and wife. But the couple did not see that as a problem that they wanted to deal with just then. S. let them know that he disagreed with their choice, but that he could live with the disagreement and continue to offer them support and care. He and the Neills agreed to disagree for the time being.

Caring in the Midst
of Pain and Fear

S. had come far in internalizing the Probabilistic Paradigm and applying it to caring for the frightened or pained patient. One such situation was blood drawing. It was especially difficult for S. when he encountered a person with a morbid fear of needles and of blood taking: Some people would faint right in the office. At first S. tried to tell these patients that this fear was not in their best interest. For example, to pregnant patients he pointed out that their inability to give blood not only interfered with prenatal care, but could become a significant hazard should a sample of blood or an intravenous treatment be needed in an emergency. He soon realized, however, that such statements, left by themselves, smacked too much of "compliance" and too little of "care."

Again his patients became his teachers. There was eighteen-year-old Ginny Meher, tears in her eyes, ready to walk out of his office: "No one is going to draw any blood from me. You're not going to stick me with a needle." Ginny had always been "scared to death" of needles, and now it was just too much. She had come to S. because her menstrual period, which had always been "like clockwork," was now, two weeks after its due date, yet to appear. She was worried when she walked into S.'s office. She was afraid that she might be pregnant and had no one, not her mother or her boyfriend, with whom to share that fear. Ginny's father was long dead, and she felt that her mother, a "very religious woman," would be "shocked." Tommy, her boyfriend, was away in the service, and this was something that she did not want to tell in a letter or over the telephone.

The urine test for pregnancy gave an ambiguous result. The results of S.'s pelvic exam were less ambiguous. He told her, "There is a good chance that you are in the very early stages of pregnancy." The thoughts that just then rushed through Ginny's mind were accompanied by a numbing, a deadening of her body, and by tears which came to her eyes but did not roll down her cheeks. After she had talked with S. for a while about the choices she faced, the thoughts were now of a different sort, but the feeling of deadness through her body and the tears poised on the edge of her eyelids still remained. It was when S. mentioned that blood would need to be drawn to confirm that she was pregnant that her outburst came.

She was surprised by her anger at him. "I am sorry, Doctor. I know that you want to help me, but I just can't stand needles." By now S. had realized that despite his best efforts to be helpful (and in part because of them), the fear and sadness that Ginny was feeling would have to be shared between them.

She had entered the office scared, thinking that she would hear "the worst": that she was pregnant. She was feeling sad ("robbed," she would later say) that something which under other circumstances would be joyful would now only be an occasion for pain. S. took great care to make the pelvic exam as comfortable as possible. He explained what he was going to do and how it was likely to feel at each step, referring to the illustrations and diagrams that lined the walls. He was so successful that during the exam she felt far calmer and safer than she did when she stepped through the door. She felt somehow reassured; she felt that as long as he took care of her, he would be able to keep the fear, pain, and sadness at arm's length.

So when Dr. S. reentered his office after the pelvic examination and told her that he thought she was pregnant, she was outraged. Although she fought hard not to show it, she felt somehow betrayed. The fear and sadness returned, and the gratitude she had felt toward S. during the pelvic exam, when she saw him as the cause of her calmness and confidence, turned into resentment. She couldn't help but see him now as the cause of her pain. This person who could ease her pain the way her mother had long ago when as a child she would bang her knee, this person who could ease her fear and make her feel safe the way her father had when he walked with her through a tough neighborhood, aroused in her both sadness and anger when the pain and fear came back. He had brought her the "bad news," and now she was more scared and panicked than before at the prospect that she would soon have to make a choice under conditions of uncertainty—to go through with the pregnancy or abort. She felt somehow "robbed" of her youth by the prospect of making that choice. It was one that did not make any sense in terms of the ambitions and ideals she had had while growing up.

"I know I am a coward, and I am ashamed of that, but I'm upset enough today," she told S. He felt that if she walked out of his office right then and there, feeling deeply ashamed, with the question of whether or not she was pregnant still a bit up in the air, she would not feel strong enough to make the critical choice that needed to be made. He decided to gamble rather than just watch her walk out. He did not tell her that she had to comply with his wishes and just *had* to have the blood drawn. He didn't doubt that she would have gone along with the blood drawing if he had phrased his request as an edict. But that would have resulted in her leaving his office completely dependent on him and as ill-equipped to deal with the uncertainty she would soon face as if she had left without the blood test, feeling independent but ashamed.

S. took a different approach, saying, "I wish I could tell you that this blood drawing is going to be painless, but it won't be. God knows, you're in enough pain already, but you've been in tough spots before." For the first time since she had entered his office, a smile crossed Ginny's face. "I guess you've had to deal with patients who've had a far tougher lot than mine," she said, "but they couldn't have been as scared as I am right now." He shook his head. "You're not the only one. Just now there's more than one scared person in this room." "You, scared?" Her voice had in it now both sadness and a certain relief.

They talked a while longer. At first it was in general terms about how much courage it took to allow oneself to be scared, to feel the pain, to face uncertainty. Ginny soon was sharing with S. her experiences with needles and doctors as far back as she could remember, and the thoughts and feelings she would have whenever she had to have blood drawn. Finally she said, "Okay, which arm?" "Your choice," he answered. She stuck out her left arm, explaining, "I am going to need my right one to write a letter to my boyfriend tonight."

S. went ahead and drew the blood, telling Ginny exactly what he was doing at each step: "Now I am rubbing your skin with the alcohol swab." "Now I am putting on the tourniquet." At each step she watched what he was doing and told him what she was thinking and feeling. She felt as if she was drawing the blood herself. At the end, when she felt faint, she heard him say, "If you feel like fainting, it's okay. It's safe—both you and I will be here to take care of you."

PART IV

FAMILY DECISIONS

12

DEATH
IN THE HOME

By now it was a familiar story. "Do you make house calls, Doctor?" asked the woman on the phone. He guessed that she was middle-aged. "My mother is riddled with cancer—breast cancer. The surgeons at the General Hospital said that there was nothing more they could do and that we should find her a local medical doctor. Now my mother is very, very weak and in pain. She doesn't get out of bed anymore, and she has a sore on her back. Since she had a stroke a few weeks ago, she has trouble talking and swallowing. She wants to stay at home, and we want that too. When could you come over, Doctor, and tell us what you think we should do?"

"Does she know that she's dying?"

"Yes, she's known it for a while now."

After S. had seen his last patient of the day, he checked the map, picked up his black doctor's bag, and headed into a neighboring town about ten minutes away from his office. "Nothing more to do," he thought. "Here I go again." He now felt the anxiety of being exposed to death and that of entering into a family's intimate life during a crisis. And it was always different in the home. The family would need support in whatever course they chose, support which he could give.

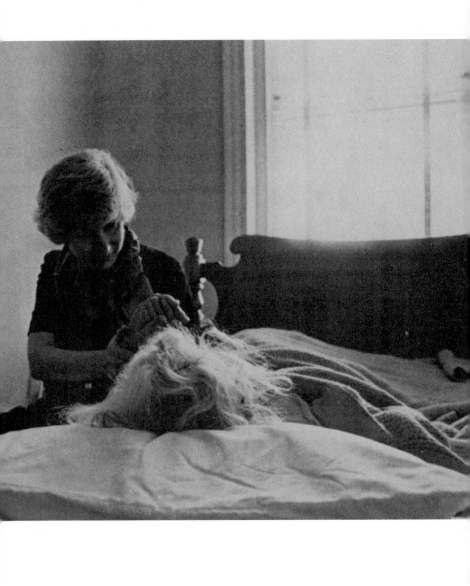

Eighty-year-old Mabel Gormley lived on the second floor of a two-family house on a quiet side street. Her daughter and son-in-law, Jessie and Norman Cavanaugh, lived on the first floor. It was not a fancy house or a fancy neighborhood, but the Cavanaughs, like their neighbors, were proud of the way they kept up the home in which they had been living for many years.

Another daughter, Jenny O'Farrell, lived nearby with her husband and two unmarried daughters. Both the Cavanaughs and the O'Farrells also had married children who lived in the neighborhood where they had grown up. This family did not fit the stereotype of the mobile nuclear family in contemporary American society.

Dr. S. introduced himself and was ushered in to see the old woman, who was lying in bed in her own bedroom. As he examined her, he saw how weak she was. There wasn't much skin on those bones. She couldn't sit up, and her chest didn't move much when she breathed. She was very deaf and very scared and very tired. What he said to her had to be relayed to her by her daughter, who leaned over the bed as she spoke. Mrs. Gormley was afraid, her daughter told S., that he would say that she had to go to the hospital. It was hard to tell, but while he was examining her she took his hand and squeezed it. After discussing the situation with the family in Mrs. Gormley's presence, he said, "Well, you asked me to tell you what I think you should do, but I'd say you have a choice to make."

Jessie Cavanaugh leaned over the bed again. "Mama, it's okay," she said. "The doctor says it's okay. You can stay." A look of relief appeared on Mabel Gormley's face.

S. went into the living room to speak with the family. He felt that although it might make him comfortable to speak to his patient in an extended fashion, it might not do her much good. So he tried to get a better idea of how she felt by finding out how her family felt. From his impressions of this family he decided that their statements probably did reflect her wishes. But he would be open to changing his mind.

Various questions concerned him. When Mrs. Cavanaugh had asked him on the phone to "tell us what you think we should do," was she asking whether they could responsibly care for their mother at home and how they might best go about doing so? Or was she asking him to be the one to tell the old woman that she had to go to the hospital? Was she becoming too much trouble for them? Did they feel themselves unable to undertake day-and-night nursing care? It would be very understandable if they felt that way. But if such were their decision, he did not want the responsibility "dumped" on him, as he had experienced with other families. He wanted to help this family shoulder the decision themselves.

Perhaps, though, he was being too wary. He didn't really have that feeling about Mrs. Gormley's family, anyway. Undoubtedly they had mixed feelings about what they were doing, and he thought it best that they be aware that they did.

"What made you decide that you wanted to keep your mother at home?" he asked.

"It's not our decision," replied Mrs. Cavanaugh, gesturing toward the bedroom where the patient lay. "It's my mother's decision entirely. She wants it that way. Give her the credit, Doctor. She's not the kind of person who'd let them keep her drugged in a nursing home."

The credit and the blame, thought S. "It's your decision too—all of you," he said. "After all, you'll be the ones who will be doing the work."

Mrs. Cavanaugh, who by now was doing most of the talking for the family, reminded S. that "it's my mother we're concerned about. The last thing we would want is for her to suffer because we decided to keep her at home."

"In some ways she may suffer less here than in the hospital," he reassured them. "You can do a lot to keep her comfortable, and she will feel better being among the people and things she has cared about all her life."

"And how about all the suffering she'd go through in a nursing home?" Mrs. O'Farrell broke in. "A few years ago, when she broke her hip, they put her in a nursing home for therapy after the operation. I went to visit her the first day, and it was as if she didn't know me. Whether she was heavily medicated, or whether she was scared out of her wits at seeing all those other people, I don't know. But I couldn't even make out what she was saying. Her speech was thick. This wasn't my mother. As soon as I saw her I knew she wasn't in her right mind."

S. commented, "The staff may not have been aware of how much she had changed. They may have assumed she was always that way. You could tell the difference because you knew what she was really like."

"I just couldn't take it," continued Mrs. O'Farrell. "I went right home and told my sister, 'We have to get her out of there.' " As she spoke, she glanced toward her twenty-two-year-old daughter, Audrey. "That night I told my husband and all my children, 'If I ever get to be that way, don't ever put me in that nursing home.' "

"It sounds like *you* have some very definite feelings about putting your mother in a nursing home again," said S.

"That same night my husband and I brought her home in an ambulance," Mrs. Cavanaugh related. "In just the few minutes I spent in that nursing home, I saw all kinds of drugs being mashed into ice cream for the patients. I turned to my husband and said, 'Those poor people. Whoever gets that concoction won't see the light of day for a year.' "

Her sister added, "In just one day she was stuffed so full of drugs that it took her until the next morning to regain control of herself. In a day or two, when the drugs had worn off, she was herself again."

"She felt at home," S. said gently.

"We think it was the drugs," reiterated Mrs. Cavanaugh.

S. doubted that it was only the drugs. "So you've all had experience with the way they treat old people in some nursing homes, and *one* of the things they do is to substitute drugs for people, for love." He was concerned that if they blamed drugs for everything, they wouldn't be able to choose freely to give their mother pain medication when she really needed it. Blaming everything on drugs was like relying totally on drugs. They needed to see *people* as a cause. "Who made the decision to put her in the nursing home?" he asked.

Jessie Cavanaugh was the first to answer. "It wasn't the doctor. It was the social worker who said she had to be in a nursing home. The social worker thought she was helping by doing that. The doctor didn't agree with her, but we didn't even know that. We thought, 'That's what the social worker says, that's what the doctor says, so that's what we have to do.' We didn't think we had a choice."

"You don't have a choice if you don't have anyone to take care of you," her sister went on. "But when there are people like us who want to help, the doctor should listen to them."

"The family makes these choices possible," S. explained. "I have had patients like your mother whose families were unable to care for them at home, or who didn't have families at all. In those cases the only choice I could live with was to put them in the hospital." As he spoke, he reflected sadly on the story of the doctor and the social worker. Everybody passes the buck, and nobody makes the decision. Either it's "*I'm* the doctor, and *I'll* decide," or "Don't look at *me.*" Things just "happen," and nobody takes responsibility. Responsibility isn't a matter of ownership; it's a matter of sharing. He wanted to share responsibility with this family.

Just then Norman Cavanaugh spoke for the first time. "Jessie's father died in a hospital. He was thrown in a room with five other men; apparently they were all considered 'goners.' The nurses did what they could, but they all knew they were waiting to die, one after another. Is that any way for a guy to leave this world, with a bunch of guys in a room and nobody caring about them?"

"In this nursing home they have six or seven nurses taking care of one hundred people," said Mrs. O'Farrell. "They hardly have time to feed or bathe them, let along show them some concern. Most of these poor people die of a broken heart. They don't have anybody coming to see them and kiss them and hug them."

"As if those things didn't matter," said S.

"You can't buy love. Look at what people pay to go into hospitals and nursing homes, just to be drugged to sleep. Whether they give all those drugs to ease the pain or to keep them quiet I don't know."

"Sometimes it's hard to tell the two apart. Think what a better position you're in as a family. You have six or seven people to help care for one person."

Since S. couldn't get to know Mrs. Gormley by speaking with her, he asked the family what she was like. Since her radiation treatments at the General Hospital Mrs. Gormley had been going downhill fast. At first she just sat in her chair, afraid to get up. She said it was because of her fear of breaking a bone, but her wish to stay still seemed just as much a way for her to dig in her heels. Then she took to her bed. According to her daughters she was a shy person who wanted to be with people she knew best. Her biggest fear was that of being taken away from her loved ones.

S. wondered to what extent the fear of death is entangled with the fear of separation from the familiar. People are afraid of childbirth because they don't see it, don't know anything about it. It is the same with death. When people saw death and lived with death from their earliest years, perhaps it was not so overwhelmingly frightening, especially if they could see that the dead did not lose all contact with the living, that they were remembered. Death is an unknown. It is made even more fearsome and mysterious when it is put out of the way in sterile institutional settings, when the dying person is left alone in a strange place with all connection to the familiar stripped away beneath the hospital "johnny."

"My mother has a lot of courage," said Jenny O'Farrell, "but she also has a lot of fears. She's never wanted to take vacations or go out with groups of people. She's more comfortable staying at home."

"It takes a strong person to die away from home, but it also takes a strong person to die away from the hospital," S. commented. He was glad to see Mrs. O'Farrell take such a balanced view of her mother. Yes, her mother was a wonderful person, but she wasn't perfect. Dying at home was an expression of courage and also an expression of fear. It was a way for the dying person to say "no" to death. With that perspective the family would be better able to get through the tasks that lay ahead.

They had wanted to know whether they were "doing the right thing." He told them that he thought they were. He was willing to support them at home if they were willing to put in the necessary nursing care. There were no double-blind controlled studies to demonstrate that one choice was clearly better than the other. He doubted that there ever would be such studies. How could you isolate and measure all the variables contributing to the effects of treating patients with different medical needs and family situations at home versus in the hospital? Even if there were some data, he and the family would still have to make subjective estimates of what the probabilities meant in their situation, and of what their values were. They would have to gamble.

Either way, home or hospital, was a gamble. Most doctors thought only of the home as a gamble. In so doing they were simply showing a preference for the gamble with the more certain outcome. In the hospital you knew more or less what was going to happen. But the hospital, too, had its risks. As Dr. S. told Mrs. Gormley's family, either choice had its advantages and disadvantages. There was no sure thing. They had a choice between two gambles—going to the hospital or staying at home. (A third gamble, not yet available in their community, would have been a hospice, an institution that allowed the terminally ill to be cared for in homelike surroundings.)

S. made clear that he was not wedded to the choice of staying at home. The important thing was for the family to make the choice and to reevaluate the choice critically on a continuing basis. To do this they had to feel free to change their minds. "It won't always be easy," he told them. "There may be times when you'll want to change your minds. You should talk about these concerns when they come up. You don't have to keep your mother at home. The hospital is always there as a backup. My experience has been, however, that most families are able to get over the hurdles they face. Not all, but most. And it's okay with me if you change your minds."

It was not that he didn't have feelings of his own about the issue. His feelings were becoming clear enough to the family. At first he felt a bit ashamed of not being a bit more "disinterested" in the family's choice. He realized, however, that his role was perhaps to balance other social pressures. It wasn't easy to keep a dying relative at home these days with almost everyone doing the opposite.

"There are some things you'll need to do. For one thing it will be very helpful to rent a hospital bed from a medical-supply house. A hospital bed is higher, which makes it easier when you're turning or changing her. It goes up and down, and it has side rails to keep her from falling out. You can raise her head for feeding and adjust the angle for her comfort." He wondered, though, if the hospital bed was also a touch of "home" for a physician who found himself on strange turf. He had fantasies of yelling out for his order book and dressing the family up in white uniforms. He would have to be careful to avoid being carried away with these fantasies.

"Then you'll have to get to work on the pressure sore at the base of her spine. It comes from lying in bed too long in one position. Pick up a soft cushion filled with lamb's wool—that will take the pressure off that spot. Turn her from side to side every hour and apply ointment to the sore. This may cause her pain, but in the long run you'll be saving her pain. That's about all you'll need to know for the time being. I'll arrange for a visiting nurse to be with you during the day, and I'll come back in a few days to see what else you can do to keep your mother comfortable. We'll talk then about the things you may have to deal with in the later stages. Meanwhile, call whenever you need to, day or night."

Yes, S. thought as he was leaving, these were strong people. Sure, they were concerned about whether this was "the right thing to do." Who wouldn't be? In these times it was an unusual thing to do. How easy it was for him to fall into the professional trap of assuming that he was indispensable. Yes, they needed him, but not so much as he might like to think. They knew a great deal already. They only needed to be assured of how much they knew and how much they could do.

They did need some reassurance, of course. They weren't used to making such large decisions for themselves. In a way, they weren't used to thinking critically. Take Audrey, who had a dead-end job as a secretary in the very hospital where her grandmother had been given radiation treatments and sleeping pills. She had been taught to spell and define medical terms, but not to use them creatively. She was being paid to do her job, not to exercise the capacity for thought that her family had given her.

Her mother and aunt remembered more about what it was for a family to make its own choices. They had learned it from *their* mother, who—even more than they—had lived by her own labor. Her reward was that she would die at home, surrounded and comforted by her family rather than by machines and attendants. Of course, she had suffered in her life, but she had been able to teach her children something about critical thinking. They were showing the benefits of her teaching when they took her out of a nursing home and chose not to put her in a nursing home again.

In recent years this family had not had so many opportunities to make decisions that affected their lives. They were glad to have this opportunity, even if exercising it felt a bit like exercising long-unused muscles. They saw themselves in the mirror Dr. S. had held up for them: uncertain, afraid, yet strong underneath it all. They did have mixed feelings about doing all that work. But now that the choice was presented to them, they saw why it was important for them to do it. Perhaps they didn't want to think of themselves as abandoning their mother. But it was much more that they simply would not abandon her. What they felt was not guilt or shame so much as love. They just had to get used to the very new—and very old—idea that love didn't have to mean putting someone in a hospital.

Dealing with death aroused complex and contradictory emotions in S. It forced him to acknowledge his vulnerability as a doctor and as a human being. For one thing he could not help but share the pain, anger, and fear of the dying person and the family. The routine of the hospital, the orders and details, were no longer available to preoccupy him and deflect these emotions. Nor was the glamour of the intensive-care unit, the occasional life saved "just last week in the same bed," available to console him. For a doctor trained to treat and to cure, it was very difficult just to wait and let die.

Then, too, in the mortality of the dying person he treated, S. could not help but glimpse his own mortality. There were times when he looked away from that mirror, when what he saw there brought more pain and fear than could easily be borne. There were other times when he looked directly at it, when he sought out the opportunity to have a hint of what death was like. He tried to remember each death for the sake of the dying patient and for his own sake. There were times when he could see another side to death, when he could see it as the last gift of the dying person to the living. He was grateful, for that hint could enable him as well as the family gathered at the bedside to confront more consciously their own deaths to come. His thoughts turned to an essay of E. B. White's. He would return that night to underline a passage:

> I do not experience grief when I am down there, nor do I pay tribute to the dead. I feel a sort of overall sadness that has nothing to do with the grave or its occupant. Often I feel extremely well in that rough cemetery, and sometimes flush a partridge. But I feel sadness at All Last Things, too, which is probably a purely selfish, or turned in, emotion— sorrow not at my dog's death but at my own, which hasn't even occurred yet but which saddens me just to think about in such pleasant surroundings (White, 1977, p.89).

He had mixed feelings as well about his own undeniably important role in supporting the family of the dying person. There was a tinge of guilt, maybe even shame, at the voyeuristic, intrusive, busybody aspect of his going into people's homes when they were most vulnerable, most exposed. Did his calm, helpful demeanor mask a self-centered thirst for experience? Was that what he did it for? Did he just enjoy the kudos bestowed upon him? Did he do it so that he could glory in having lived with his own mixed feelings while trying to help the family make the best of the situation? Well, he thought, better to do the right thing for the wrong reasons than not to do it at all. He was hoping that it *was* the right thing, that it *did* help families. That was a better gamble, he decided, than to see himself as totally corrupted, a mere victim of these times, and let nature (no, not nature but "the system") take its course.

When S. returned a few days later, Mabel Gormley was resting as comfortably as her condition permitted in the hospital bed that her family had obtained. The family and the visiting nurses had begun the nursing-care routines that he had out-lined. Mrs. Gormley looked better, and everyone was pleased.

"Tell me, Doctor," Mr. Cavanaugh asked, "is there any hope? If we do all the things you tell us, is there a chance that she might rally?"

"No," replied the doctor. "She may have her good days and bad days, but at this late stage there's nothing you or I can do to stop the spread of the cancer, any more than the doctors at the General could. You are caring for her, not curing her. Your job and mine is to help her die in comfort, dignity, and love." S. was careful to see that the family would keep sight of the truth. And that meant telling the truth in a kind way, so that the family would understand it without being driven to crippling fear or denial. When this family brought up the possibility of a miraculous remission, he gave them a straight answer. He would not use uncertainty as an excuse to justify vagueness about the odds. Vagueness was a means by which doctors—including S. himself at times—could keep control over their patients' and their own feelings. S. did his best to give his patients reliable probability information, along with some idea of the margins of precision, so that they themselves could exercise some control.

As far as the family was concerned, there was no reason to put Mrs. Gormley in the hospital unless there was some hope of recovery. As Mrs. Cavanaugh put it, "People think that if you don't go to the world's best hospital and spend all the money you have, you're not doing the right thing. That makes no sense."

S. agreed. "You would have paid anything to save her if you could have. But that's not what's at stake now."

The family did, however, have one major concern about providing home care. "What if something happens?" they wanted to know. "What if there is an emergency and we don't know what to do?"

"Things *will* happen," S. answered. "She is going to get worse. She will have more pain. You will have to do more and more for her." He explained the progressive deterioration of a dying patient by drawing an analogy with pregnancy and birth. "When we're taking care of a pregnant woman we watch for possible complications that may cause us, along with the woman and her family, to reconsider our decisions about the birth—for example, whether we will have the birth at home. The odds are very low, however, that any particular complication will occur, and there is a good chance that none of them will. With death we can be more certain—though not completely certain—that more and more complications will occur along the way: difficulty in eating, difficulty in breathing, loss of contact and communication. Perhaps *complications* is the wrong word, since these things are just part of dying. But whatever you call them, as time goes on, they raise the ante for taking care of someone who's dying at home. You recall my telling you that you could always change your minds."

"But, Doctor," Mrs. Cavanaugh objected, "you see these things all the time. For us they're all new."

"That's right. She is the only mother you have, and this is the only time she will die. I have to gamble a lot, and I win some and lose some. From that experience I get a pretty good idea of the odds. That's what I'm trying to share with you. I wish I had a crystal ball, but the best a doctor can do is to speak of probabilities rather than certainties." Still, he couldn't expect them to be as capable of detachment as he was, nor would he be capable of detachment if the dying person were a member of his own family. For she was their mother, and he knew how much more he had cared about his mother than any doctor had.

"Let's look at some of the choices you are likely to face in the coming days and weeks. By anticipating them, you may be able to make better, more conscious decisions. What if your mother develops pneumonia, as old people often do when they're ill? Will you want to treat it or not? Pneumonia used to be called 'the old man's best friend.' Now, though, we have drugs and machines that can bring people through it. It may not be easy to withhold those treatments from your mother even if that's the kindest thing to do."

The word *machines* brought up the respirators that could keep Mrs. Gormley going for days or weeks. Being away from those reassuring backup resources was one of the things S. found scary about treating people at home. Yet how often he had anguished over the plight of some old people, for whom the miracles of modern medicine—the machines that could keep them alive—had become a form of unwitting torture. "Please let me die!" they would say to the nurses behind the doctor's back.

It turned out that Mrs. Gormley's family had a pretty clear idea of how they felt about life-prolonging technology. "If it gets to the point where her life depends on a machine," they explained, "then we know that she wouldn't want any part of it."

Despite the family's statements on the matter, they still needed Dr. S. to explain what the machines would and wouldn't do. He told them that Mrs. Gormley would almost surely die within a few weeks. If a respirator were to be used to keep her alive beyond that point, it would not reverse the course of her illness; nor would it keep her conscious and able to communicate with her family. It would just keep her breathing. "Even so," he said, "I know how hard it is for a family to say, 'No, that's enough.'" This acknowledgment of the inevitable mixed feelings surrounding such a decision made it easier for them to make an informed choice not to use a respirator. As Mr. Cavanaugh put it, "A few days, a few weeks—at least we have some idea. Instead of it all being new to us, we have some facts to go on." In other words, S. was turning pure uncertainty into probabilities.

Another highly charged issue for this family was that of pain medications. "When she needs it," S. explained, "use this acetaminophen and codeine mixture for pain."

"But how will we know when she needs it?"

"Sometimes you will find yourself giving her the pain medication because she tells you she needs it. At other times you will be left on your own. Those are the times that are tough. It won't be easy to tell whether you are giving her the medication for her comfort or for your own—because she can't stand the pain or because you can't stand to hear her moan. Moaning is sometimes a signal that the person can't stand the pain, and sometimes a way for her to bear the pain. If her moaning means that she wants the medication, and if you don't give it to her, you will feel as if you're causing her suffering. On the other hand, if you give her the medication automatically every time she moans, you will be making yourselves more comfortable, but you also might be taking away from her what self-control and pride she has left, which is making her death bearable to her and you. Each time this choice comes up, you will be gambling that you understand whether she would prefer to have relief from pain or consciousness and clarity of mind. The more she is drugged, the less she will be able to share her last days with you. You will also be putting your own preferences into the equation. It might be worthwhile to sit down with her now, while she can still speak to you, and ask her on which side she would want you to err when in doubt."

"We don't have to ask her," Jenny O'Farrell stated emphatically. "As sick as she's been, there have been nights when she's told us, 'I've already had two aspirins today; don't give me any more.' She even said it the night she fell on the floor and couldn't get up. I know my mother. I'm the same way. Even in the hospital I wouldn't take sleeping pills." Mrs. O'Farrell could easily put herself in her mother's place. Someday she *would* be in her mother's place, and her daughter would be in hers. Audrey was getting some clear instructions.

"That's where a nurse in the hospital might have just given her an injection," said S. "But you listened to her because you are her daughter. This is one of the most helpful things you're doing for her—just listening and accepting and trying to understand her feelings, even the most painful ones, without falsely reassuring her. Since you do know your mother, you can trust your own feelings about her in a way that a nurse can't. Not only can you afford to spend more time with your mother than the nurse can, but you've had years already to get to know her. Since you know how she has lived, you can help her die the same way.

"You will have to find the answers to the problems that come up in your knowledge of yourselves as a family. All I can do is tell you about the situations I have seen families face. You will have to keep an open mind and choose what to do each time. And sometimes you will have to change your minds, and live with having made a mistake, and live with regret."

In a home visit there was always the feeling of being a guest on someone else's turf. In the office, even when one consciously tried, it was hard to shake the ingrained inequality of the doctor's and patient's roles. In the office it was so easy to see the patient, stripped of his or her life context, merely as a carrier of disease. So easy, then, to focus on the disease—to see treatment in terms of a magic bullet, of pills. Being in a patient's home left no doubt that the patient's autonomy, his or her capacity for deciding how much or little of modern medicine to take, was real, real in a family context, where the patient was connected to family members by long-forgotten yet still strong ties of nature and nurture.

This "case" had been going on long before S. ever got involved in it, as the patient had been sick a long time. But then the family had been living together and developing their own unique ways of getting along with each other and coping with the world for a long time also. Doctors had been involved with the illness only intermittently; the family had been involved continuously, minute by minute. Their decision to call S. had come near the end of a long chain of events. Though it would be a "cop-out," he thought, to say that his actions were of no consequence, it would be a fantasy to believe that he controlled the entire flow of events and decisions.

For S. questions like these made his participation in a birth or death at home more than a good human-interest story. It was a challenge not only to the heart, but to the mind as well. S. saw himself right on the frontier of scientific medicine, with all of the excitement and risk that he could ever hope to have.

He thought back to his first visit to the Cavanaugh home, when the family had shown some surprise that he so readily supported their choice. "Look at the facts," he had begun to tell them, then stopped himself. Another cop-out, he thought. As if all a doctor had to do was find the facts. Well-prepared house officers on rounds rattled off "the facts" on patients' charts as if any observer would see the same facts and then proceed to act on them. That wasn't the way it was, either on the hospital floors or out here in "real life." Those house officers changed the facts they looked at, and so did S. He was a cause of the decision to care for Mrs. Gormley at home, as were her children and grandchildren. If the family had been less willing and able to take care of her, the decision probably would have been different. If S. had not encouraged them to think that they and he would be "doing the right thing," the decision might well have been different. People, not facts, had made this decision.

S. also rejected the mechanistic interpretation that cancer was *the* cause of Mrs. Gormley's condition. While in the hospital she had been treated as though her problem was solely one of cancer. Once the hospital had done all it could about the cancer, it had "nothing more to do." For S. there was much more to Mabel Gormley than her cancer. She was a person with a history, a value system, and needs: needs for food, shelter, clothing, disposal of body wastes, relief from discomfort, and love. It was no accident that she wanted to be at home. She had always been at home. Home was where her supports were. It was where she had worked to support others: first as a mother who loved, taught, made food, and did so many other things that often are not recognized and appreciated. Then, as a grandmother, she did these things, somehow the same things and yet somehow so different.

This patient's condition was not determined unicausally by her cancer. It was the result of the interaction of a number of causes which would come and go as they had come and gone in her life, all depending on the context; for example, the pollutants in the air she breathed, the carcinogens in the food she ate, the feelings of anguish she had here and there felt while continually exposed to various stresses that could be felt even in her family's home. To respond to the special needs that cancer presented did not mean that all the other causes operating on and off in her life had to be ignored.

In medical school S. had learned to find the one correct solution, as one found the "facts," by experimenting. One could do an experiment, for example (or look up statistics obtained from such experiments), to see whether the home or the hospital provided a better environment for a person in Mrs. Gormley's condition. Actually, there had been and could be no such experiment, in part because Mrs. Gormley's condition could not be reduced to a set of controllable variables, and in part because the very act of experimenting would change what was being experimented upon. Now, practicing in real life under conditions of uncertainty, S. experimented by making a series of choices (gambles) and seeing what further choices they led to, all the while bearing in mind that all his actions, including his observations, were influencing the always tentative results of his experiments. Having made the initial decision to treat Mrs. Gormley at home, he and the family (as fellow experimenters) could see how she was doing and whether they were able to continue that form of treatment. Their choices, along with the illness and other causative factors, created new sets of circumstances requiring new choices.

Finally S. rejected the exaltation of objective data in favor of close attention to both objective and subjective (feeling) data. He took into account how the patient and family felt about where she wanted to die just as much as he did the report from the pathologist at that large hospital from which Mrs. Gormley had found her way back home.

S. was beginning to understand not only the kinds of gambles that the home and hospital represented for Mrs. Gormley, but also why many people did not see them both as the gambles they were. People thought you couldn't lose by going to the hospital, but only by staying at home. At home you could either win or lose. In the hospital, while you could lose as far as life and death were concerned, you somehow felt that you wouldn't lose because at the very least you would be doing the "right thing."

S. well understood that feeling. He knew what it was like to have someone close die in the hospital. He had been there many times. For the family it was always the same story: the visiting hours; the quick word with the private doctor; more frequent words with the nurses and house physicians; the trips back and forth. It all seemed so regular, like clockwork. The only hint of doubt, of the gamble, would come when you were home again, waiting for the call in the night that you knew would come but never knew when. Whereas when the person you loved was at home, dying where he or she had lived, you lived with the doubts and the risks day and night. Instead of settling comfortably into the thought that you had "done everything you could," you had much more left to do.

In reality, though, the hospital was as much a gamble as the home, as S. had learned in the case of K., the young child for whom he had unsuccessfully tried to make a "home" within the hospital. With K. the house officers had lost their "hospital" gamble. Whether S. would have won or lost his "home" gamble he did not know. But he had won enough such gambles since then to choose a similar gamble when he supported Mrs. Gormley in her desire to stay at home to die. Most doctors, like the ones who treated K., would have done otherwise. When he had begun taking care of patients at home, S. had felt uncomfortable about choosing a gamble that many of his colleagues would have regarded as unusual. But now it seemed like the least he could do.

Later that week S. received a phone call from one of the visiting nurses, who reported that Mrs. Gormley complained of considerable pain when she was moved. Because of this the family was not putting her on her bedpan, and she was urinating in bed, which in turn aggravated the bedsore. The nurse asked S. whether she should put a catheter into the patient's bladder, thus solving all these technical problems at one stroke.

S. did not order catheterization just yet. Instead he asked the nurse to work out a solution with the family. They might try to locate more precisely where Mrs. Gormley was feeling pain when she was turned. They might be more firm in reminding her that having to be moved was part of what it meant to stay at home. At the same time, they might explore any feelings they had that they were being cruel in causing their mother pain. Another approach was to increase the pain medication at the times when she needed to be moved. Then again, they could just have the catheter put in, at some risk of infection. But would it be such a bad thing for the old woman to die of an infection when she was about to die of cancer? In any case, S. wanted the choice to be made by the patient and her family rather than by the doctor and the nurse.

Again it was Mrs. Cavanaugh who articulated the family's decision: "No tubes if there's no chance of cure." She reminded her mother—and herself—why it was necessary to undertake the disagreeable task of moving her. After a while she sensed that her mother, even while continuing to object to being moved, still seemed more comfortable after being moved. She felt good at having been able to overcome her own reluctance to cause pain in the interest of sparing her mother what she felt was an unnecessary violation of her natural functions.

As soon as she got up each morning, Mrs. Cavanaugh would go to her mother's room, turn her, and clean the bedsore. After letting her dry off for an hour she changed her clothes. At eight thirty, when a home health aide arrived, Mrs. Cavanaugh went to work. She spent her lunch hour at home assisting the aide, then returned home for good at five when the aide went off duty. At that point it was up to the family. Mrs. Cavanaugh did what she could to get her mother to eat, but if she didn't, well, S. had told them that that might happen. Then the others trooped in for the evening. Mrs. O'Farrell (who, like Mr. and Mrs. Cavanaugh, had a full-time job) was there almost every night. Audrey and some of the other grandchildren came often, while others stayed away, saying it was "spooky." They, along with the ones who did come, were afraid.

The night was left to the Cavanaughs. Mrs. Gormley usually slept well, but if she was restless, her daughter would stay with her. Sometimes Mrs. Cavanaugh would wake up and hear her mother talking incessantly. If she sensed that she was not going to quiet down and become comfortable after a reasonable time, she would give her the pain medication. Mrs. Cavanaugh could go by her instincts about whether her mother needed the medication. It would be harder for a nurse to do that. She could adjust the medication to her mother's needs rather than the need to keep the ward quiet or get things done on schedule or keep harried personnel available for other tasks. As a result Mrs. Gormley needed little medication on the whole. Sometimes she didn't need any from one night to the next. It seemed that just being at home was half the medication.

Her last days contained many conscious moments. Although no one ever knew how much she was aware of as she passed back and forth from wakefulness to sleep to somewhere in between, her eyes always opened to the sight of the bureau, the mirror, the pictures on the wall—the things that had accompanied her through healthier and happier times. Her senses opened to sights, smells, and sounds of many years' familiarity. And into her fragile consciousness came her daughter Jessie, her daughter Jenny, her sons-in-law and grandchildren and even great-grandchildren, kissing her good night and good morning, kissing her hello and good-bye. They all had felt that they could do nothing for her, and yet they did a lot.

While Mrs. Cavanaugh did most of the physical chores, the others in their own ways worked too. It takes energy to move your mother onto a bedpan, and it takes energy to feel sad that she is dying and to extend to her some last kindnesses. People lose time from their own jobs when they take care of sick and dying relatives. This family gave up their leisure time to do something that was emotionally draining, that took as much energy as any job. The Cavanaughs and O'Farrells each, in effect, held down two full-time jobs.

No one would want to be reimbursed for loving someone. But the family could at least have been paid for doing the work of nurses, work for which taxpayers and insurance subscribers otherwise would have been billed. The economic system is not, however, set up to reward such work. People are encouraged to buy a gadget or a pill to help them do something they could just as well have done for themselves. Our economic system takes people's skills, processes them, and sells them back at a premium—just like food.

This family had to rediscover their capacity to do a traditional job. Their neighbors told them that they must be very brave to do what they were doing. Doctors, hospitals, even friends were saying that they couldn't or shouldn't be doing it. They themselves couldn't be sure. No wonder they needed a little encouragement from Dr. S! But they had something else besides his help; they were able to draw on memories of what it had been like to see someone die a generation or two before. Just forty or fifty years ago it had been a normal, routine thing to die or be born at home. Back then they didn't even take the body right out of the house as they did now (as if it would contaminate people), but held the wake at home too. Jessie Cavanaugh remembered how as a child of seven or eight she had seen her grandmother laid out on her bed. Maybe she hadn't fully understood, but she hadn't been scared out of her mind. So now when a friend told her, "If it was my mother, I just couldn't deal with it," she said, "You will when you have to." She began to have the feeling that she and her family weren't just doing it for themselves, but for others as well.

In the beginning what was particularly difficult for everyone was the strange feelings that came up when they were preparing to bathe the old woman, change her clothes, or clean up the mess that she could no longer keep from making. There is no getting around it; urine and feces smell bad. When a baby does it, somehow it's a sweet smell. Incontinence in an old person, on the other hand, turns a lifelong relationship on its head. Now the children and grandchildren were nursing someone who had given them life, taught them strength and competence. From this person they had learned how to live and work. Could they stand to see her fade away? Would they be able to see this once idealized person as flesh and blood and yet also as spirit still; reduced to childlike messing and yet still something more; powerless and yet still powerful? Would reality crowd out memory, or would memory crowd out reality? These unpleasant, scary things are what the sanitized medical apparatus (an unholy alliance of vested interests and people's own fears) shields people from. If the Cavanaughs and O'Farrells were heroes to take on a heavy burden of unpaid work, even more were they heroes to face these fearful things that taught them more than they had known about what a human being is. S. could see his task as supporting such extraordinary, yet everyday heroism.

Norman Cavanaugh had never imagined that he would get so uncomfortably close to his mother-in-law. "How can I do this?" he would think before entering her room. But then he said to himself, "Somebody's got to do it. I'll do it, that's all." Each day things got a little easier. It was amazing, he reflected, what people could do when they had to.

His wife was deeply troubled about violating her mother's privacy. She knew her mother as a modest, shy person "from a different era" who "wouldn't even tell us about the birds and the bees." Now she had to touch her mother in places where she never had before. She had to separate the physical functions of those parts of the body from the myths and fantasies that surrounded them. In touching her mother, she discovered something of what it must have meant to have her mother touch her in the same places a long, long time ago. In her mother's dying she had a glimpse, darkened and transformed, of her own beginnings.

The family also faced their fear of death. At first Jenny O'-Farrell could not get used to the idea that her mother was dying, that she was going to lose her and never see her again. All of the child's fears of being left unfed and unprotected were reawakened. Yet day by day, as Jenny watched her mother suffer, the fear somehow dissipated. It came to seem right, or at least necessary, that her mother should leave her at this time.

Audrey, who in previous months and previous illnesses had tried to talk her grandmother out of being afraid to die, now just sat by her bedside and talked. It scared her to see her grandmother become less and less able to tell who she was, or who anybody was. So Audrey talked, not so much for her grandmother, who couldn't understand what she was saying, but for herself, because it made her feel better to pretend that her grandmother did understand. And as her grandmother got worse, she felt herself—felt everyone—getting better.

Audrey surprised herself. They all surprised themselves. Mabel Gormley's children and grandchildren "couldn't do anything for her"; but if all they could do was change her diapers, they still were doing something for her. And she still was doing something for them, even as she had long ago when she changed their diapers. She was giving them the courage to find out about themselves. It is said that a sudden death is more merciful than a "lingering" death. But Mrs. Gormley was not lingering. No longer physically or mentally active, she was actively a part of an exchange of strong feelings. As her own strength ebbed away, she was helping to produce strength in her family.

A sudden death may in some respects be more merciful for the person dying. Had she been offered the choice, perhaps Mrs. Gormley would have chosen a quicker death, like the one her son-in-law's mother had. The elder Mrs. Cavanaugh had been ill, but had not been considered near death when she suddenly collapsed one day while she was sitting in the living room talking with the family. The youngest granddaughter, a girl in her teens who only with great reluctance could bring herself to visit Mrs. Gormley as she lay dying, had been very close to her other grandmother. It was as if there hadn't been time to say good-bye.

The first snow of the season was falling on the night when, a few weeks after his first two visits, S. received an urgent call from the family. The patient was agitated, "out of her head," and her daughters felt that things were getting out of control. S. always found it disagreeable to leave his warm apartment once he was settled in for the night. When possible he made his house calls on the way home from the office. He especially dreaded being awakened during the night when he felt least confident about going out into the world to apply his incomplete knowledge. At two in the morning he had to make decisions without aid. Sometimes, though, it could not be helped.

As he drove through the night to the Cavanaugh home, he reminded himself that as a doctor he couldn't just leave the family with a parting word of advice and think his job was done. He remembered when he had prepared this family for the way a dying person might refuse to eat after a certain point. Family members needed to be told that this refusal was part of dying and not a sign of their own inadequacy. But there is no getting away from the frustration that people feel in being unable to do anything in the face of a refusal of food—in the face, that is, of death. S. saw it as part of his job (even if it wasn't taught in medical school or paid for by Blue Shield) simply to *be* with them to help them deal with that frustration. When he first spoke with Mrs. Gormley's family, S. knew that they would call him again and that he would come, even if his knowledge was not always what they needed.

Mrs. Gormley now looked very, very old. "It's okay," S. said to the worried family. "She is on her way out. I don't know exactly when, but it looks like we're getting near the end. This is the way people often are at that stage. Who can say what she's feeling now? It would be nice to be closer to her, but we can't be. She must be very frightened of dying. Who wouldn't be? The delirium is a normal response to that. You can look at it as a way of withdrawing, of blocking out the fright. It's nature's way of keeping people comfortable. Just accept it. Don't fight it. You're doing fine."

At this time he brought out into the open an anxiety that many of them (especially the younger ones) must be feeling. "One of you will discover her in bed dead—cold, blue, lifeless. How will you feel about that? Who would want to be the first to find her?" Along with the near-certainty of Mrs. Gormley's death was the large, looming uncertainty of who would have the responsibility of finding her dead. It was like a wheel of fortune, a game of chance with no skill attached to the gamble. In speaking about this with the family as a whole, S. sought to reduce their anxiety in advance, as well as to encourage a common sense of responsibility by making it clear that this was a gamble that they all shared. Whoever found her dead would not be at fault.

Two days later Mrs. Cavanaugh went to her mother's room and found her blue and breathing very slowly. She was crossing the threshold of death. She was clear-browed and calm, like someone looking forward to the long, long rest that she had earned by all her suffering. To her daughter she looked beautiful. Mrs. Cavanaugh, who had long resisted the idea of her mother dying, felt at ease now. This was the way her mother had wanted it. Somehow this was so much easier to accept than to have had a call from the hospital telling her that her mother had died.

The family members assembled around the old woman's bed. No one of them alone would bear the responsibility of finding her dead; they were assuming that responsibility collectively, as a family. The gathering was like one of the deathbed scenes on which the literature of past generations turned, but are rarely found in our own. Although Mrs. Gormley had no opportunity for final instructions and explicit farewells, each person in turn was able to step up to the bed and kiss her good-bye. Soon her breathing stopped.

After she died, the family called S.'s office as he had instructed them to do. Since S. was not on call that night, it was one of his partners who went out to the home. This was another way in which home care required cooperation. The same doctor couldn't be on call every night—not if he wanted to have a family of his own.

The doctor pronounced Mrs. Gormley dead, filled out the death certificate, and stayed with the family until the undertaker came to take the body. "How many doctors would do that nowadays?" said Mrs. Cavanaugh to her husband and sister. His presence gave the family a lift, a bit of encouragement when they needed it.

A few days later S. spoke with the family by telephone. They all agreed that Mrs. Gormley had "died well." As Mrs. Cavanaugh phrased it, "The whole thing was like a puzzle that fell into place as she was dying." Still, S. added, she *had* died. They would all have to live with that.

For S. the last piece in the puzzle was never quite in place. Even though the patient was dead, the family was still alive. A doctor who was not concerned with the family would have considered the job done when the death certificate was signed. S., whose reaction to Mrs. Cavanaugh's first call had been to wonder whether her family really even needed him, had to remind himself that his job was not done. Although Mrs. Gormley was dead, she continued to live in the thoughts and feelings of her family and continued to influence their lives.

So S. would stay in touch with the family (who by now expected no less). After all, not only Mrs. Gormley, but the whole family had been his "patients." He had tempered the savage fantasies that the young children (and their elders) brought to great-grandma's death with the sad, but far gentler reality. He had figured out a lot of little ways for everyone, himself included, to say good-bye. Everything he said and did in that house had an effect (he hoped therapeutic) on the family; but when he submitted his bill to Medicare, he would not be able to name the family as the patient.

S. was touched when, a year later, on the anniversary of Mrs. Gormley's death, he was invited back to the Cavanaugh home to review the experience with the family. Norman Cavanaugh spoke for the whole family when he said, "For me this has been a new part of life that I'm learning about. As I get older I'm trying to adjust to death myself. It seems it's not as terrible as

I thought it was. It's just another thing that we go through. We're born, we live, and we die." For his wife this new acceptance of death, an acceptance that came from having "seen" it, was only a small consolation for the seeming unfairness of her mother's having had to suffer as she did. Jessie Cavanaugh, it seemed, still had mixed feelings. "Who wouldn't?" said S.

Audrey certainly did. "It was the most important experience of my life," she exclaimed. "Not that I'd want to go through it again with my own mother. This was hard enough to accept as it was."

"It will take a lot of courage," Dr. S. cautioned her, "but you'd be surprised how much courage you have, just as your mother was surprised this time." Later, in the course of a discussion of medical treatment in institutions, Audrey said, "When I watched my mother take care of my grandmother, I pictured myself doing the same for my mother in thirty or forty years. You'd never put *her* in any nursing home!"

Along with everyone else, S. shared his reactions to the experience. "It was very special for me as well. In order to come here I had to open myself up to all my own fears about dying. I also learned something from it as a doctor. You handled things beautifully. What we all learned I can share with other families."

The family expressed concern that it was so hard to find a family doctor. They had a family doctor from years back, but he was too old now to make house calls. "It's a sad situation when you can't get a doctor to come to your house," said Mrs. Cavanaugh. "You can't get an old, sick person to the office, so the only alternative is to put her in the hospital."

S. managed a wry smile. "So doctors, who should be keeping people out of hospitals, sometimes are a cause of people being put *into* hospitals."

"And once they're in," Mrs. O'Farrell volunteered, "it isn't the doctor who takes care of them, but the nurses and aides. So what's the difference if a person stays home? You can have nurses at home too."

S. was made uncomfortable by all the praise that was being directed at him for his extraordinary involvement with this family. He enjoyed basking in their appreciation, of course, but at the same time he felt angry and sad. What a commentary on modern medicine and modern society that the experience of making decisions and exerting control even in the midst of death should be so novel for people. "Why does this have to be something special?" he asked. "This should be the way it always is."

"Absolutely," said Mr. Cavanaugh. "Why should this be such a 'brave' thing to do? It's perfectly normal. I think everybody ought to face something like this. It would be a good experience for anyone."

"Nobody encourages people to do this," S. interjected. "Doctors don't encourage it because they're scared too. They're afraid other doctors will criticize them for doing something risky. Doctors are a little afraid of something they aren't used to doing, just as families are."

He spoke to them again about uncertainty, about which Norman Cavanaugh commented, "The only certain things are death and taxes, and we've made the best deal we could with both." S. reviewed with them the principles that had guided them and the gambles they had chosen together—how they had turned out, and how else (being gambles, after all) they might have turned out. He mentioned also some gambles that they had not chosen—*could* not have chosen, things being as they were. They were not wealthy people who could arrange their schedules to suit their convenience and hire servants to do the "dirty work." They did not live in a community (who did?) where they could choose to have their neighbors come and help care for an elderly person. These things, in all probability, they could not change. But it was good to be reminded every once in a while that the world did not have to be as it was.

There came a moment when deep emotional currents could be felt beneath the surface of the discussion. When they spoke of the decision not to prolong Mrs. Gormley's life by artificial means, Mrs. Cavanaugh was quick to give S. all the credit. "I'll tell you who made that decision, folks," she stated, pointing a finger at the physician. But S. reminded her of their discussions. He wanted it to be remembered as a decision for which they all bore some responsibility.

Other things were said that day that were very satisfying for

S. to hear. When he asked the family how they felt about not being reimbursed by Blue Cross for nursing services, someone said, "That's okay. We got something out of it." Someone else added, "When we remember our mother, we will remember the way she went out of the world and the things we did to help her."

But there were mixed feelings too—probably more than they could easily admit to a doctor. Mrs. O'Farrell gave an inkling of these with this enigmatic utterance: "Sometimes it's harder when you're close to someone. There's more to cope with when you're close."

S. glanced at Audrey and thought of the concluding paragraph of Kafka's *Metamorphosis,* which describes a family that has been released by death:

Then they all three left the apartment together, which was more than they had done for months, and went by tram into the open country outside the town. The tram, in which they were the only passengers, was filled with warm sunshine. Leaning comfortably back in their seats they canvassed their prospects for the future, and it appeared on closer inspection that these were not at all bad, for the jobs they had got, which so far they had never really discussed with each other, were all three admirable and likely to lead to better things later on. The greatest immediate improvement in their condition would of course arise from moving to another house; they wanted to take a smaller and cheaper but also better situated and more easily run apartment than the one they had, which Gregor (the dead son) had selected. While they were thus conversing, it struck both Mr. and Mrs. Samsa, almost at the same moment, as they became aware of their daughter's increasing vivacity, that in spite of all the sorrow of recent times, which had made her cheeks pale, she had bloomed into a pretty girl with a good figure. They grew quieter and half unconsciously exchanged glances of complete agreement, having come to the conclusion that it would soon be time to find a good husband for her. And it was like a confirmation of their new dreams and excellent intentions that at the end of their journey their daughter sprang to her feet first and stretched her young body. (Kafka, 1948, p. 132).

Together with grief there is relief at no longer having the dying person in the house to attend to. Energy that was drained by dying can go back into living. The family can acknowledge this (without being overwhelmed by the shame that such a feeling can bring) when they have had the dying person in the house and have known what it took to care for her.

13

BIRTH
IN THE HOME

One of the greatest satisfactions S. had as a family doctor came from being able to experience all stages of life, and with them an extraordinary range of human feelings. Within a single night, for example, he might witness a death and then a birth. Having just left a family stricken with sadness, he might ring another doorbell to find a family at a moment of hope and confidence.

One of the best times for families to learn to gamble consciously and take their destinies in hand was during the months of pregnancy and the intense hours of labor. The positive energy and hope that a family invested in a birth (a momentous event, yet one that the family could prepare for) made it an ideal time to learn a way of thinking that could be applied to other situations in medicine and in life. Birth combined the predictable with the unpredictable, skill with chance. It was a series of gambles over a nine-month period in which changes in strategy, anticipated and unanticipated, might occur at any time. Moreover, the sort of gambling a couple would engage in, especially if this was the birth of their first child, would be the basis upon which the couple could begin to define itself as a family, the husband and wife growing to become also a father

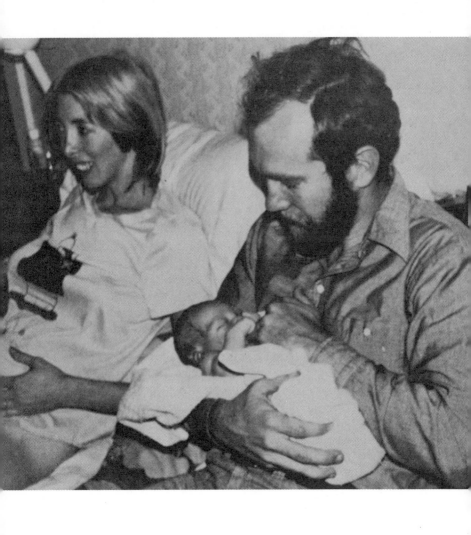

and mother. This was true for any birth, but it seemed most true for a home birth, in which the gamble had an extra dimension. Here none of the participants, least of all S., were likely to forget that they were gambling together.

Initial Visit

S. breezed into his "prenatal" office to meet a couple interested in using his practice for maternity care.

"Hello, I'm Dr. S. Welcome."

"I'm Roberta Johnson and this is my husband, Bob Williams."

"I understand you're pregnant."

"That's right," Roberta replied. "I'm three weeks late with my period, and the pregnancy test I just had here was positive."

"Were you planning a pregnancy at this time?"

Roberta and Bob exchanged glances. Finally Roberta said, "I guess it was a bit of a surprise. "We're getting used to the idea by now, though we've had our ups and downs about it."

Before S. had a chance to explore these feelings further, Roberta quickly added, "We came here because we'd like to talk to you about a home birth. We understand that your practice is one of the few that do home births."

"Yes, we're open to the idea of home birth. What makes you want to have one?"

"Several things. First of all I just don't like hospitals. I find them very unpleasant places. I've had some really bad experiences with sick relatives in hospitals. To be perfectly truthful with you, doctors are not my favorite people. Also, hospitals are for sick people, and I don't consider pregnancy to be a sickness. Sure, I know that things can go wrong and a hospital might be necessary, but I'd like to cross that bridge when I come to it. The other thing that scares me about hospitals is that they do things to you—like using a monitor, IV, and episiotomy. I think that when you're at home you can avoid those kinds of things. Also, you can have all your familiar things around. You can have your friends and family there. It's your own place—you know what I mean?"

"Are you familiar with the changes that hospitals have made in their maternity services to make them less 'hospitallike'?"

"The birthing rooms? I've heard about them, and I guess they're a step in the right direction, but still I'd like to try a home birth if it's possible. Even though this is our first child, I've done some talking and reading, and at this point I think that I want to be at home. We'd like to hear your views."

"Okay. A home birth is fine if your medical history, physical examination, and pregnancy course don't show significant risk of any problem that would be hard to handle at home. Also, you have to be willing to accept the risk that is there. You need to know that even though everything looks okay going into labor, you could die and your baby could die—that's the ultimate kind of risk that I mean. Now, let me soften that a little. Having a baby anywhere carries a risk of death—a small risk in these times, to be sure, but there nonetheless. The hospital has its kind of risk and the home its kind. I'm not saying the home is less safe than the hospital for the low-risk mother. There's no evidence I know of to support that claim. But you must understand that a situation could conceivably arise in the home where your having been in the hospital instead would have made the difference between life and death. It may be only one in a thousand or more, but if you're the one, it's a hundred percent for you."

"I know there is risk, but I don't think I'll be the one," Roberta interjected.

"It would be nice if the things we don't want to happen to us wouldn't happen to us, but we can't count on it. No matter how skillful I am or how well prepared you are—that is, assuming neither of us makes a human error—there is a tiny but real chance beyond our control that there will be a tragedy. You've got to face that just as I've got to. I put it to you straight because I'm not here selling home births or, for that matter, hospital births. I appreciate the benefits of home births—I've learned to appreciate them because they've been important to quite a few families I've worked with—but I'm not ideologically committed to them. We have wonderful home-like births in the hospital, too. My concern is that you have a good birth experience, wherever you have it." He paused, and they all shifted a little in their seats.

It was S.'s practice to bring up the subject of death early on with couples choosing home birth, but not with those choosing hospital birth, even though the risk of a tragedy, as far as he could tell, was no greater in the one setting than in the other. While the home might not be more likely to be a cause of death than the hospital, it was a different cause. Having a baby die at home would heighten a couple's sense of personal responsibility for the tragedy and could make it harder to live with. It was easier to be angry at the hospital than at oneself.

Bob broke the pause. "One of the reasons we've come to you is that we'd like to have maximum control over the pregnancy and delivery. We understand, correct me if I'm wrong, that you involve patients actively in decisions affecting them."

"That's quite correct—with, however, one 'but,' which is that sometimes in labor things can happen so quickly and so unexpectedly that there simply isn't time to talk. You've got to move and move quickly. That's where trust—in both directions—comes in. So during labor I'll have to take a more active role."

"I can understand that," Bob responded.

"Let me get back to home birth for a moment," said S. "The determination of risk is ongoing. We look at the choice of home versus hospital all the way along during the pregnancy—right into labor and beyond. If the odds change for the worse and technical maneuvers available only in the hospital can lower the overall risk, then we'll have to shift to the hospital. Just as we have to accept some risk in the hospital, so we have to accept some risk at home. The question is, when does the risk at home become unacceptable? We have a printed policy—you'll get a copy—which spells out what we think are unacceptable risks. For example, aside from risk factors such as age and complications of prior pregnancies (which wouldn't apply to you), an unacceptable risk could come from an illness such as diabetes or high blood pressure, or from a complication such as prematurity or lack of progress in labor. Our policy also states that you have to be within twenty minutes of one of our backup hospitals, and that you have to have certain supplies ready in your home for the birth. You'll need to take childbirth education classes as well, so that you'll know what you're doing by the time you go into labor. We won't deviate from our policy unless you come up with some good reasons why we should. And after you go into labor, I don't find it so easy to accept 'good' reasons."

"You make it sound so technical; it sounds like you have as many rules as the hospital," Roberta replied.

"It may sound that way at first, but what we're interested in is coming to an agreement, rather than your obeying a rule. Read the policy over and let me know any special conditions in your case that might justify our having a different understanding from what is spelled out here. The more we can anticipate what may be special about your labor, the more we can come to an agreement ahead of time about when to move to the hospital if that becomes necessary. That way I won't have to make the decision myself during labor." He paused. "Basically you have the freedom to have the kind of birth you want. It is your birth, after all."

Roberta's expression changed. "If anything happened to my baby, I'd never forgive myself."

"Never is a long time. Anyway, responsibility is a tricky thing. You are responsible for your choices, but things still happen which are beyond your control. Even when you *can* blame yourself, that doesn't mean you don't ever forgive yourself." For a moment they were all silent. "Well, this has been a hard discussion, but a necessary one; the odds are that you'll do fine with a home birth. By the way, I never did get around to asking you what kind of work you do."

"I'm an urban designer," Roberta replied.

"And I'm a computer programmer."

S. noted their occupations in the record. "Any questions?"

"We'll save them for the next visit." They looked at each other. "We're pretty well agreed that we want to come to this practice."

"Let's set up a visit soon so we can do a physical exam and go into your medical history. Let me walk out to the front desk with you and make sure you get all the literature, our policies and fees, and the phone number of the birth attendant, Paula. Be sure to get in touch with her. She'll be working with us right along."

Physical Examination

S.'s prenatal room was more like a classroom than a doctor's office. There were diagrams on the wall showing the anatomical structure of the female pelvis and changes in the uterus over the course of pregnancy. S. referred to them as he did the physical examination. On the ceiling over the brown wooden examination table was a humorous poster showing how to build a rainbow. Women found that it took the edge off a sometimes awkward situation and, rather than being distracting, allowed them to focus on what they and the doctor were doing. S.'s office was in many ways nonstandard. It reflected the suggestions of his women patients and colleagues. Stirrups were "optional," and there had never been any takers.

"I've always disliked this part of the examination," Roberta muttered as she placed her feet at the corners of the table and shimmied her buttocks down to the edge.

"What's it been like for you?" queried S.

"I don't know. I feel so exposed. I'm a little embarrassed, I guess."

"Who wouldn't be?" S. replied. "When I started doing pelvic examinations, I was embarrassed too. Let's talk a little about the exam before we begin. I need you to participate in this pelvic examination. It's not something I can do alone. Before we get to the rectal exam, I'll feel your uterus and ovaries. Now, these organs can't be touched directly. All an examiner can do is get a sense of what's between his or her hands, the one pressing up from below in the vagina, the other pushing down from above on the lower abdomen." S. brought his hands together by way of illustration. "By your relaxing, you allow the examining fingers to come closer together to feel what's in between."

Roberta nodded.

After checking the tone of Roberta's perineal muscles and commenting on the importance of toning exercises, S. visualized her cervix with a lighted speculum. With a mirror Roberta could see it too. She propped herself on one elbow and with her other hand brought the mirror down to her buttocks. "Well, what do you know," she said with a look of surprise on her face. "It's so small. How will the baby ever get out? Bob, come on over here and take a look."

After they had finished looking, S. withdrew the speculum. "Now let's check the measurements of the birth canal. I'll feel for the landmarks I pointed out to you on the wall charts. As I do, I'll tell you what I'm doing." Following this part of the exam, S. was able to say, "Feels like a roomy pelvis. Good."

Next S. positioned his hands for the bimanual examination. He could feel Roberta tense up.

"Now what I want you to do is to 'let go' of the tension in your muscles, and I'll let you know if I can tell the difference. Now let go. Good. Now, let go some more. Great. I can feel most of your uterus except on the right. Yes, that's the muscle to relax. Fine. Feels almost six to eight weeks size. Now your right ovary —good. And the left—good. Now the rectal exam." "Ugh." Roberta winced.

"All done." The bimanual and rectal exam had taken sixty seconds. S. withdrew his hands. "Why don't you get dressed; I'll be right back," S. said as he left the room. When S. returned, Roberta was dressed and seated. It was easier now for them to speak as equals.

"You were very helpful," S. said.

"So were you," she replied.

"How did you feel about the exam? Was it comfortable for you?"

"Okay, I guess. Better than usual. As I mentioned, it was a little embarrassing, though after I spoke up, I felt more at ease. Pelvic exams have always been uncomfortable for me since I first had them. I guess I still tense up, even now."

"You didn't say anything about pain today. Does that mean that there wasn't any?"

"Well, for the most part."

"You mean there were parts that were painful that you didn't tell me about?"

"Well, yes."

"What stopped you from speaking up?"

"Oh, I don't know. I guess it's awkward for me to tell a doctor what to do."

"I see. Look, if you don't tell me, how can I know? The easiest way for me to know what you're feeling is for you to tell me."

"I'll keep that in mind. Okay, tell me, did I relax enough for you to do a thorough exam?"

"Yes, it was a good exam. You should have no problem with a vaginal birth. Of course, you can't be sure till you're in labor, but for now everything looks okay. Speaking of labor, the pelvic exam reminds me of labor in this sense: as the baby moves down the birth canal and begins to stretch out the perineum, one of the ways to help ease the baby out is to let yourself open up, as you did during the pelvic exam. Also, when the head emerges or, as we say, 'crowns,' we let the perineum stretch out ever so gradually—to prevent tears and minimize the need for an episiotomy. We'll tell you to 'push,' or to 'pant' so you won't push. In other words, we'll let you know how your perineum is responding. Just like today when I let you know when you were relaxed, or weren't."

S. turned to Bob. "What do you think of all this?" he asked him.

"Sounds good to me. It was interesting to see Roberta's cervix and hear about toning up the pelvic muscles." He grinned. "Of course, I can't tell you how the exam felt. I've always thought that Roberta was some kind of sissy with her fear of going to the dentist or gynecologist. I guess her antsiness today is part of the same thing."

"You've not been exactly sympathetic?"

"No, not exactly," Bob replied. Roberta nodded her agreement.

S. noticed that Bob was still grinning. He guessed that Bob, too, had been embarrassed. A form of sympathy, he mused. "Well," he said, "it might be good to review with each other what went on here today. One thing among many that you can learn about during a pregnancy is how you respond to each other's feelings."

Roberta changed the subject. "We'll be seeing Paula, the birth attendant, today right after we're through. I've kept a three-day record of my diet, and I want to go over it with her."

"As far as general precautions are concerned," said S., "nutrition you've already taken care of. Smoking is a risk to the baby —smaller size and greater chance of respiratory infections after birth. Alcohol can harm the fetus. I'd stay away from alcohol and other drugs, including over-the-counter medicines, especially during the first trimester (the first three months of pregnancy). Also, be sure to use a seat belt when you're in a car. As your uterus grows bigger, use just the lap belt under your uterus and around your hips down low. Everyone else in the car should buckle up, too, because if you're in a crash nonrestrained passengers can fly into you. All of these things will help you exert some control over the outcome of the pregnancy. You can't completely prevent problems in pregnancy, but you can avoid some risks. Even though, together, these measures might make only a few percentage points' difference in rates of complication, each point counts."

After Bob and Roberta left, S. reflected on his parting words. Here was a place, he realized, where he advised families to gamble so as to avoid an extreme outcome. A pregnant woman who was used to smoking or drinking would be more or less uncomfortable if she stopped. S. thought it "right" for her to accept the high probability of such moderate discomfort in order to avoid even a low probability of serious harm to the baby. This was the same argument that other doctors gave for accepting the moderate discomfort of giving birth in the hospital instead of at home, and yet he did not agree with them. Some families placed a high value on the comfort and integrity of their home life; some families placed a high value on the pleasures of smoking and drinking. He was inclined to honor the one set of values, but not the other. At the same time, he would not attend home births in cases where he thought it unsafe to give birth at home, and yet he would attend births where the mother-to-be had disregarded his warnings against smoking or drinking heavily.

Although he was not entirely comfortable with these inconsistencies, he realized that different gambles were appropriate in different contexts. Besides, he was not about to pretend (to families or to himself) that he did not have values.

In asserting his values, however, he did not want people to conceal from him the way they lived or to avoid coming back to him out of a fear of "failing" and disappointing him. Though he worked out agreements with patients by which they would stop smoking or lose weight or take pills for hypertension, he wasn't about to stop being someone's doctor because he or she failed to live up to such an agreement. His commitment to the patient as a person went beyond his commitment to a way of treating a particular disease. Nonetheless, S. felt his open-mindedness strained to the limit when someone was careless with the life and health of an unborn child. That, to him, was an unprincipled gamble.

S. also sought to have the father share in the increased concern for safety and health that made itself felt during pregnancy. It was another way in which a family learned to share the gamble rather than gamble against each other. What might start as an agreement by the father to share the inconvenience of wearing seat belts or giving up smoking out of fairness to his wife might become a real commitment to better living habits on his part, which would benefit the entire family. These were the kinds of choices that changed individuals into family members.

A Principled Gamble

If a concern for his professional reputation was only a thought that crossed S.'s mind when he cared for a dying patient at home, it was an ever-present preoccupation when he attended a home birth. Here he was clearly flying in the face of accepted obstetrical practice. Talk about gambles, he might even be risking his livelihood. S. hadn't entered this professional lion's den without very careful thought and evaluation of the evidence. It was barely a generation since birth, seemingly once and for all, had moved from what was considered the unsafe setting of the home to the scientific security of the hospital. In the 1930's and 1940's there were good reasons for preferring the hospital. But conditions change, causal relationships change, the odds change. Now it was possible for the low-risk mother to have sanitary conditions, adequate monitoring of fetal health, and prompt initial care of emergencies outside the hospital. S. believed it to be a gamble worth taking, but he was willing to change his choice of gambles, just as he had done once before when he started doing home births. He had chosen that gamble on the basis of new information, and he would need further information to reevaluate it. So he was documenting each home birth and subjecting his overall experience with home birth to both internal and external critical review. Even as the home birth service that he and his partners provided was becoming better established, he did not let himself forget that it was still a pilot project. Although he did not think it likely that on the basis of the evidence they would decide to discontinue the project, he was not about to close his eyes or his mind.

He had carefully examined the evidence drawn from studies done in many countries on the safety of out-of-hospital births. The findings pointed to the same conclusion—either no differences or the home had better outcomes for low-risk patients. This was true in Holland with its fifty percent of births in the home compared with Sweden with its one hundred percent in hospital, in England before births shifted sharply from home to hospital in the 1960's, or in the United States in the 1970's where in one study more than one thousand births at home were compared with a matched comparison group in the hospital (Kitzinger and Davis, 1978). It was true in a 1979 report by the Maternity Center Association of New York City of its three-year experience working in an Upper East Side town house birthing center staffed by midwives (Faison *et al.*, 1979). Not only were the center's births safe, they were only one third as expensive as hospital births during a time when soaring health-care costs became an object of national concern. (Despite these data the center, which housed all of two birthing suites, was bitterly opposed by the obstetrical community in New York.) Although the existing studies left something to be desired, S. thought it a good bet that no strong link between site of birth and safety would be found.

To be sure, the standard of safety set in the best of today's hospitals was impressive. In university hospitals such as the ones S. worked in, the neonatal death rate for babies born after at least a thirty-seven-week gestation and without congenital abnormalities was calculated to be 4 per 1000 (Neutra *et al.,* 1978). Whether that figure could be equaled or improved in the home was hard to tell, especially when the data could not be viewed out of its social context. It was one thing to do home births in Holland where the entire health-care system (including the emergency transfer apparatus) was supportive; it was another thing to develop a service in an American city where the congested traffic could not always make way for ambulances, and where most obstetricians could barely restrain their hostility toward home delivery. For the comparison between home and hospital to be fair, resources comparable to those lavished on the hospital setting would have to be invested in perfecting the home birth support system, including transfer to hospital.

S. could envision, for example, a modern version of the famous flying squads of England, where mobile vans were equipped with the trained personnel and equipment necessary to give anesthesia and perform emergency surgery. Expensive? In itself, yes, but it would very likely cost less to provide mobile backup for home births than to have everyone give birth in the hospital. As long as society did not appreciate the potential savings, however, home birth would not be fully supported. S. was left having to be more tentative than he otherwise would have been in his advocacy of home birth for his place and time. His own work as a home birth practitioner—with its close attention to safety, its excellent outcome record, and the appreciation it brought from families—was the best advocacy he could offer.

It was not only his own work, he reflected. He would not have been able to attend home births at all had it not been for the open-mindedness of some established obstetricians who made their hospital services available to him even though they had reservations about home birth. And couples like Bob and Roberta, by choosing home birth at a time when it was not yet fully accepted, were taking a gamble on principle, one that would benefit other families in the future as well as themselves.

Families like Bob and Roberta typically took an interest in the social, economic, and political implications of the controversy over site of birth. As their relationship with S. progressed and they became more comfortable with one another, and as the uncertainty that surrounded their own upcoming birth gave way to a shared understanding of probabilities, they could discuss the broader picture. There were, for example, the implications for hospitals and obstetricians if out-of-hospital birth were to become a widespread movement. In one sense there were significant cost reductions to be realized. But at whose expense? So long as the profit motive lurked unacknowledged in the background, rational debate—let alone critical choice—would be difficult.

Electronic fetal monitoring was a case in point. Monitors produced a continuous tracing of uterine contractions and fetal heart rate, allowing for early detection of signs of distress in the fetus. In just a few years the use of monitors had become almost standard obstetrical practice. Although fetal monitors were being used almost as routinely as anesthetics or infant bottled formulas had been in the past (it was the "lunatic fringe" of the preceding generation of women who had begun the now well-established return to breast-feeding), they had not been demonstrated to make a significant difference in the care of the low-risk labor (Neutra *et al.,* 1978). (About high-risk labors there was little question.)

This evidence notwithstanding, an unacknowledged, profitable, and (in our society) almost inevitable alliance between well-motivated, dedicated academic obstetricians and manufacturers of fetal monitors had, it seemed to S., almost prejudiced the outcome of the debate before it could get off the ground. Many obstetricians claimed that there was no such thing as a low-risk labor and feared not to use monitors lest a malpractice suit for a misadventure be based on this omission. Of course, monitors were not available in homes, further casting doubt (for those who saw things that way) on the wisdom of out-of-hospital births.

S. and his partners were the first family doctors in the city to be interested in maternity care in recent years. At the same time, midwifery had again been legalized in the state (although not for home births). The family doctors and midwives, together with the families they served, were reclaiming an area of medicine that had long been exclusively controlled by obstetricians. In calling upon the obstetrician for consultation and support rather than for direct care of the low-risk pregnancy, the new practitioners were, to be sure, carving out for themselves a slice of the economic pie. But they and the families also were creating a new philosophy of birth, one which held that birth was not a medical problem, although medical problems could occur along the way. This critique of established practices had already helped bring about changes in hospital birth procedures, such as the use of birthing rooms.

The out-of-hospital birth movement was one expression of a revolt against professional dominance. By working with families like Bob and Roberta, S. was aligning himself with an important shift in public values. In so doing he was more than willing to give up some measure of control and play by mutually produced rules. Whose birth was it, anyway—the family's or the doctor's? S. had to catch himself whenever he lapsed into the jargon of his medical-school days when he, the doctor, "delivered" babies. To be accurate, he now said that he "attended" births. He was quite clear that mothers were the ones who delivered babies. The difference in words was not incidental. It reflected a different understanding of birth and a different way of arriving at decisions.

Some of the new experience S. was acquiring was painful, as much because of peer disapproval as because of his own failures and the accidents of nature. If things fell apart in the hospital, the doctor was largely cushioned against criticism by the safe institutional setting. But if a serious problem occurred at home, everyone would say, "I told you so." He remembered how awkward he had felt when he had to bring in Margaret

Benson (Chapter 10) for suturing an extensive perineal laceration (something that at times is unavoidable in home or hospital). He could read the disapproval on the faces of the doctors
and nurses he called upon to help him. So far he had had only
one death—a stillborn who had died during a very short labor
before he and the birth attendant had arrived. This death undoubtedly would have occurred even if the mother had planned
a hospital delivery. That may have been the "one in a thousand." Although stillbirths occur in hospitals too, in the home
he had to call in the medical examiner to investigate. It was not
only a sad but also an anxious moment. S. felt as if he were on
trial and feared that a complaint might be raised. But the examiner found that it had been an unavoidable death.

S. had to guard against the extremes of disabling fear and
complacency. He rehearsed emergency procedures while keeping the rarity of emergencies in perspective. Yet he knew that
he could not stand apart from his environment in the manner
of a detached scientist coolly manipulating experimental variables. Like it or not, he lived in a climate of opposition which
affected his emotions and in turn his actions. What others
thought of his choice of gambles affected his self-esteem; it
might also affect his ability to think clearly. He was concerned,
for example, that, to avoid disrupting a rich family experience
and exposing himself to criticism in the hospital, he might
deny to himself that there was a real need to transfer someone
for whom it was no longer safe to be at home. Because he was
aware of these potential "experimenter effects," he established
principles to guide the choices he had to make under pressure.
For example, he and the birth attendants agreed to observe
each other closely and voice disagreements openly. By trusting
each other enough to subject their uncertain perceptions to
each other's scrutiny, they sought to be worthy of the trust
families placed in them.

For S. the risk of failure and the excitement of achievement
that characterized medical practice were two sides of the same
coin. He enjoyed the emotions of birth, wherever it took place:
the pain, fear, laughter, joy, relaxation, closeness—the sense of
drama and triumph. Still, there was something special about a
home birth. Even though the home did not contain all the life-

saving technology of the modern hospital, there was nonetheless a kind of security there, along with a warmth that the
hospital could not match. (The traditional image of distant
flickering lights across a field from an isolated farmhouse on
a cold winter night came to mind. Maybe that's how it felt as
he arrived.) Perhaps the relaxed atmosphere—the friends and
relatives (including children), the familiar surroundings and
food, the quiet lights, the sense of celebration, played an important part in supporting the laboring mother. She didn't have to
go anywhere; she just stayed put. Where was she more at home
than in her own home? The trappings of the home were collectively a cause, one among many, in a successful outcome. They
were not the only cause, though, as those who left things to
chance in an unattended home birth appeared to think. These
families, in S.'s view, were engaging in the same kind of unicausal thinking as those who regarded the hospital as the sole
cause of a good outcome.

S.'s role as a doctor, too, was only one factor among many. He
was a cause, but the kind of cause he was varied from one home
to the next. Sometimes the most important thing he did was to
contribute to the family's peace of mind. He sometimes transformed a tense scene into a confident one simply by reassuring
a couple that all was well with baby and mother, even though
it might not feel that way at the moment. The reality of it was
often changed merely by his observing and being there, which
enabled all concerned to feel that if the crunch came (and at
rare times it would), he would be there to do what needed to,
and could, be done.

Pregnancy and birth provided an exciting opportunity for S.
and a family to work together probabilistically. Every case
represented a unique and ever-changing combination of causal
factors. No two labors were exactly alike, physically or emotionally, and no two families responded to the stresses and
strains in exactly the same way. Every family had its own values, its own way of supporting the laboring woman through her
pain, its own way of expressing and discharging tension. For
some the home would be a source of anxiety, for others a source
of comfort. When did a woman really need hospitalization?
When did a labor become "prolonged"? At what point in the

vast range of variation did the "normal" become "abnormal"? These questions called for highly sensitive, individualized judgments. They were questions of value and questions of probability. S. could estimate the probabilities only by drawing upon his and others' past experience in attending births, his experience with a particular family, and the family members' experience with one another.

Life would be a lot simpler if he could ignore the changing pattern of causation over the course of pregnancy and birth, ignore the effects of his procedures on what he observed, ignore the effects of the woman's and the family's feelings (not to mention his own) on the outcome. Wouldn't it be nice if he could have one answer for everybody! Given that he was concerned with value (avoiding serious complications), he originally had found it hard to be concerned as well with probability (how likely such complications were to occur). He was trained to be oriented toward extreme outcomes—the tragic death, the dramatic rescue. And indeed, the hospital was a good place to be if an extreme outcome was at all likely. On the other hand, it was good to be at home if all was expected to go well.

Whenever he became too preoccupied with avoiding maximum loss, he thought back to the well-meaning physicians who had scheduled exhaustive diagnostic tests day in and day out for the starving child K.—or for elderly patients, some with incurable illnesses, who needed rest more than anything. Beneath this dueling with the specter of maximum loss lay the fear of death. Though it was the patient's death that was in the forefront of a doctor's mind, lurking in the background was a concern with his own.

Just as he could not give everyone the same answer, so he could not tell anyone that the same answer was right from beginning to end, even over a nine-month pregnancy. For S. the beauty and the difficulty of childbirth lay in its being a developing, unfolding event. A woman's body was undergoing progressive physiological modifications. A child in the womb was growing, ever more noticeably, to the point where it came to dominate the feelings, thoughts, and actions of everyone in the family. To this new presence the family's life was continually adjusting itself. How could one be sure that the answer that seemed right at the beginning of this process would still seem right at the end?

Roberta and Bob came to Dr. S. in October. The due date for their baby was estimated to be June 15. In the eight months that intervened any number of complications could occur, along with the normal, but never quite predictable evolution of parental feelings in the mother- and father-to-be. The gamble would be constantly changing, right from the initial meeting, history-taking, and physical examination. S. would be on the lookout, as Roberta and Bob would be, for any changes that might tip the balance in favor of the hospital gamble as against the home gamble. There were some cases where the initial gamble was to choose a hospital birth, but that gamble was changed to a home birth as the pregnancy progressed. Still, he was much more on the lookout for events that would change a planned home birth to a hospital birth than vice versa. He hoped that, as experience with home birth grew, this would not have to be the case.

Nausea

The leaves had stopped falling when Roberta, ten weeks pregnant, came to Dr. S. in despair. "I'll tell you, this morning sickness has just about done me in. I spend about four hours each day absolutely miserable—retching and sick to my stomach. Paula said to take some pilot crackers while I'm still in bed in the morning and then to eat frequent small meals, but nothing helps. I have never felt so awful in my life. When will it end? It makes me wonder whether it's all worth it."

"Well, I'm sure you already know that nausea is a common, possibly even normal part of early pregnancy. It doesn't harm the baby; nor does your temporarily eating less affect the baby's growth. It's related to hormonal changes and rarely lasts more than three months, usually less. I know that three months or

even one day is too much, feeling the way you feel. The point
is that it does end. When the things you've tried don't work,
some women choose medication. According to the best evidence we now have, the medicine we prescribe has not been
found to be harmful to babies, and often provides relief. Nevertheless, lots of women stay away from it unless forced to the
wall, because they fear harming the baby."

S. thought it extremely important to be attentive to what were
called the "routine" or "common" problems of pregnancy. Engaging with Roberta on the common, everyday issues was a
way of developing trust for the big issues that lay ahead. There
was nothing routine about this nausea to Roberta, just as there
was nothing routine about Mrs. Gormley's death to her family.
S. had to guard against automatic responses. If he was really
listening to Roberta, he would know it by feeling closer to her
by the end of the interview. On the other hand, the fact that
dealing with morning sickness *was* routine to him enabled him
to give her some perspective on her suffering.

"It must be hard to be so uncomfortable physically when
you've had mixed feelings about this pregnancy in the first
place. Do you want to talk about those feelings?" he asked her.

"Yes," she replied. "They have been on my mind." Roberta
then confided to S. her worries about holding onto her job after
the baby's birth, her concerns about the changes in her relationship with Bob, and her fears about the pain and discomfort
of childbirth.

"Just now you're really feeling the costs of having a child. I
don't blame you for wondering whether it's all worth it. Your
nausea has brought these normal worries to the surface. I
wouldn't blame you if you changed your mind altogether. But
you should ask yourself whether morning sickness is a good
reason for changing your mind. I mean, to take an extreme
example, you could get rid of the pain from a tooth extraction
by killing yourself. Or—and this is something you'll be facing
soon—you could yell for pain medication (which we don't give
at home) at the first twinge of discomfort in labor. If you can
get through this morning sickness, you'll be better prepared to
face that crisis when it comes. You want to be careful not to

relinquish your power to make important long-range decisions with and for your family (including this unborn child) by trying to make those decisions when you're in pain."

"You mean it won't be peaches and cream from here on in?" she replied with a sad smile. "I guess I will be giving up some things to have this child."

As often happened in S.'s experience as a family doctor, a medical symptom had revealed a deeper problem, in this case an unresolved issue in the family. Why did it have to take a symptom—physical discomfort—to get people to talk about something so natural, so understandable, so *permissible* (if permission were his to give) as mixed feelings about an event that would irrevocably alter their lives? He marveled that so many couples had to be with a doctor to air their mixed feelings, even to each other.

Being a family had gotten so complicated. It used to be that people just had children automatically, whatever anxiety they felt about it—and wasn't there always some anxiety? Now there was often doubt as well. These days it was accepted that a man and woman might question whether they wanted to have a child, but often they weren't equipped by experience to ask each other that question and answer it together. Often they acted not as a family but as competing individuals, with the child as a new competitor that the mother had to "cut in" to the game by depleting her own reserves. Some birth techniques seemed to emphasize the baby's comfort at the expense of the mother's, while some feminists contended that the mother's well-being was of primary concern.

How could a family get beyond such an either-or situation, a zero-sum game where one player lost when another won, and the doctor (or lawyer) was always there to take his cut? S. remembered the "cones in the bottle" game, where if the players competed with one another, no one ended up ahead; instead, the cones all got stuck at the neck of the bottle. He resolved to stress the principles of cooperation and fairness as issues for families. The sharing of risk was a principle which needed to be observed within a family if the family was to gamble wisely.

The Rubicon Crossed

For eight weeks during the winter Bob and Roberta attended childbirth education classes, where they supported and were supported by couples at different stages of pregnancy. At the same time they continued their regular prenatal visits to Dr. S.'s office. S. kept an eye out for anything that might indicate possible complications, such as protein in the urine or high blood pressure or blood sugar. He also was attentive to the couple's changing attitudes. He knew from experience that a couple that came in one week expressing doubts and fears about a home delivery might come in the next week saying, "This home birth idea is the greatest thing!" S. cautioned them against such denial of doubt. "Keep an open mind," he would tell them. He wanted them always to remember that they were a little afraid, so that they might not ever be too afraid.

Similarly, they needed to be aware of their responsibility without being awed by it. More than one agitated parent-to-be had alternated between wanting to lock the doctor out of the house and passing the whole thing off with false assurance: "Don't worry, honey. Dr. S. will take care of it all." Whenever S. heard the words (or the sentiment), "You take care of it, Doc," he was quick to disclaim such sweeping responsibility and power. Both he and the family needed to be aware that the responsibility was shared.

These mixed and shifting feelings often were tied up with doubts about the pregnancy and about the couple's future as a family. When Roberta and Bob came in for a prenatal visit on the Ides of March, which marked the end of the sixth month of pregnancy, it appeared as if all doubts had been resolved. Roberta looked relaxed, pleased, and perfectly healthy.

"How do you feel?" S. asked her.

"Great. It's funny now to think about the time I was almost ready to give up on this pregnancy."

"Well, I guess by now you've crossed the Rubicon," said S. He wanted to give the couple a chance to articulate whatever mixed feelings might remain.

Roberta laughed. "Oh, yes. We haven't been thinking along

those lines for a while now. At this point I guess we're as clear as we'll ever be that we want this child. Pregnancy, childbirth, and beginning a family have brought to the surface all kinds of feelings for me. All of a sudden I'm going from being my mother's daughter to being a mother myself. I've learned a great deal about myself and my own family too. Not all the things are pretty. But I am learning to live with these mixed feelings."

Bob smiled. "And I'm learning to live with Roberta living with mixed feelings. Until this pregnancy I always expected her to be Ms. Joy and Comfort. But when we found out that she was pregnant, other feelings came up for her, feelings of anger and sadness. She trusted me to bear with her while she expressed those feelings. That gave me courage to express some of my own. All this has been tough, but it has drawn us closer."

The Hospital Visited

Roberta waddled and Bob walked into the room. By now she was thirty-two weeks along. S. reviewed her record. Her blood pressure and weight gain were normal and there was no protein or sugar in her urine. The measured size of the uterus was "right on target."

"Well, your exam looks good; how was your visit to the hospital?"

Bob replied, "The birthing room was quite nice, much nicer than I had expected."

"But it's still a hospital; there's no getting away from it," added Roberta.

"When you need the hospital," said S., "there's nothing like it. In fact, I wouldn't be willing to attend births at home (since there are alternatives available) without a well-equipped hospital twenty minutes away to back me up. The hospital obstetricians bend over backwards to involve me and the family in decisions requiring our participation, like whether or not to do a cesarean section. There is far less of this 'play by the rules or else' than at some other hospitals I could tell you about. Given the fact that the hospital staff—both nurses and doctors—are strangers to the families we work with, I am impressed with how accommodating they are."

"I'm glad to hear that," Bob replied. "I think you're right. It is comforting to know they're there. It almost feels as though we're getting something for nothing. After all, we won't actually be paying the hospital to serve as a backup unless something goes wrong and we wind up there. So we get our peace of mind for free."

"On the other hand, by choosing a home birth, you are cutting the costs of care, yet have no incentive to do so."

"You mean, for example, our insurance won't pay for the birth attendant."

"Right, even though you will be saving your insurance company and its subscribers well over a thousand dollars."

"It's a crazy system, isn't it?" Roberta reflected.

"Unless you're in it for the money," quipped S.

To which Bob reacted, "I guess gambles that are best for profit are not always best for people."

"Anyway," said Roberta, "we're willing to consider the hospital if things go wrong. You know, if the odds change. It's easier to think about the uncertainty now that we're sure that we want the baby after all."

S. smiled. "I'm feeling increasingly comfortable working with you. See you in two weeks."

Coming to an Agreement

Through the spring, as new green leaves replaced those that had fallen during the difficult early months of Roberta's pregnancy, the prenatal visits focused increasingly on the delivery. Whereas S. usually preferred to wait until patients brought up difficult topics, the time was now growing short. Since one of the tasks that remained was to prepare the couple further for getting through labor without anesthesia or pain medication, at the thirty-four-week visit S. said, "You know labor is going to be painful."

Roberta responded, "Yes, we've gone over that in our childbirth classes. I've talked with a number of women about labor pains, and it's the kind of thing that's hard to imagine until you're actually having it. I know that I can use the breathing that we've learned, the massage, and all that."

"It would be nice if study would make it painless," S. sighed.

"But suppose I need something too. Do you bring pain medicine with you, just in case?"

"No, we don't use pain medicine at home. I know you've been over this in your classes, but let's go over it again. First of all, many of the reasons drugs would be necessary would also require care in the hospital anyway. But more important is the fact that drugs, even when they are carefully and critically used, as they are now in most hospitals, can depress the vital functions in you and your baby. So, even though the additional risk is slight, we don't feel it is a risk that we want to take at home. In the hospital it may be a different gamble, since the kinds of problems that drugs can create can generally be handled by the equipment and expertise available there."

"You mean that if I want to keep my options open I have to go to the hospital?"

"Yes. It's like with many other choices: take one turn on the road, and you can't take the other. You will have some choices at home that you wouldn't have in the hospital, but pain medication isn't one of them."

"But can't we just play it by ear and see how bad the pain is going to be?"

"Well, you know how I feel about keeping an open mind. But there are times when you have to commit yourself to a gamble ahead of time and stick to it on principle. I think that you have to decide about analgesics *before* labor. I say that because it's almost too hard a decision to make while you're *in* labor. Many women, particularly in first labors, reach a point where they feel that they can't make it. They've practiced all their skills—breathing, massage, knowing what's happening to their bodies

—all that. And they reach a point where they feel like they're falling apart. 'Do something! I can't go on!' " S. said, raising his voice and flailing his arms, eliciting a smile from the couple. "And then we say, 'You're okay and the baby is okay.' It's hard to reconcile the way you feel—which might be awful—with reassuring words like these. Now, if you ask a woman who feels like that whether or not she wants pain medication, what do you think the answer will be?"

"I can imagine what it will be."

"Right. It's almost not fair to expect someone whose feelings are so intense to think rationally."

"In other words, we ought to decide ahead of time, when we can still think clearly," said Bob.

"There are several things to consider," S. continued. "First, when you feel that things are at their worst, when you're 'falling apart,' you're usually in transition—the time when the cervix is dilating most rapidly. In other words, you're almost to the top of the mountain. If you can hold out a bit longer, then you'll be in a position to push, which many women feel gives them a new kind of control over their pain. Second, what you're talking about is several hours of pain out of a lifetime. I've not yet known a woman who in retrospect would have wanted to have the pain medicine she didn't get. Third, this is an opportunity to learn about pain and sort out what part of it comes from fear. There are few other situations in which pain is normal—that is, doesn't mean that there is something wrong—and comes and goes so that you can observe it and yourself. Here's your chance to experience it for what it is."

"Sounds like she'll have more control over it than I will," Bob said animatedly. "I don't know if I'll be able to stand it."

"That's a good point. I'm glad you brought it up. The people around a laboring woman often have difficulty tolerating her pain. They have the urge to do something; they feel responsible. Also, the woman might yell and scream and accuse those around her of not caring, of sitting on their hands. Husbands we've known have had the impulse to throw us out of the house and move right to the hospital. It's hard to be with someone who's so uncomfortable and not do something. It's hard to say no to a request for pain medicine unless you're honoring a prior agreement to do so. It's almost asking too much of anyone to be with someone who is in pain, and yet not feel responsible for it. If you don't do something for her this time, you might wonder whether you can ever look her in the face again. Under these circumstances just being with someone isn't easy, and it's not the same as doing nothing."

"Like when I'm in a funk, it's hard for Bob to take. He tries to humor me—he'll do anything but just leave me alone." She turned to Bob. "And when I tell you to leave me alone, you get upset. Sometimes you go and take a walk, but that's not what I meant."

"Well, I must own up to it," replied Bob, "that I can get pretty upset with Roberta when she's in one of her moods—like around her periods."

"Well," continued S., "here's your chance to talk through what a person can do that's most helpful to another in distress. We've got to remember, Roberta, that the pain will be yours, all yours, not ours. But that doesn't mean we are turning our backs on you. We're going to support you in your decision to handle the pain without medicine. Our job is to keep cool if and when you feel you're falling apart."

"But what if the pain gets to be too much?"

"I'll be keeping an open mind and listening closely to the messages I get from both of you. Even though we're now committed to no pain medication and home birth, you'll need to trust that I know you well enough by now to recognize when the pain gets to be too much. Also, all this discussion presumes a normal labor. If there is a problem with the labor, then we'll be dealing with a different set of issues."

"Well," she said, "you have certainly seen me in some pain already, like during the pelvic exam and when I had the morning sickness. Bob can be of some help to you too."

"I'm counting on that," said S. "And remember, I'm committed to being your doctor all the way, whether the birth is at home or in the hospital."

"That makes me feel much more comfortable about going ahead with a home birth without pain medication," said Bob.

"I guess that up till now being in pain and being alone always meant the same thing to me," Roberta remarked.

Bob looked at her. "You've never said that to me."
"I guess I've never quite said it to myself."

A Crisis of Confidence

It was an unusual request over the phone to "talk things over in the next day or two." Roberta's office was on S.'s route between hospitals, and she and Bob agreed to meet him there. S. was glad to be able to see them at her workplace.

"I'm glad that you could see us on such short notice," began Roberta, now thirty-six weeks pregnant, "and that you could come to my office." She paused and then continued, "It's hard for us to say this, but now that we're coming down to the wire with this birth, we're having some second thoughts about you as our birth attendant. Let me say that basically we like you a lot and think you're a good doctor. But a few things have happened which alone might not mean anything, but taken together have shaken our confidence in you somewhat.

"First, there was the time when I sprained my ankle early in the pregnancy and you told your assistant to wrap the wrong foot. Second, when we did that screening test for blood pressure complications during labor and it was abnormal, you didn't react to the report; your nurse practitioner overheard your assistant in the hall and told me to increase protein and fluids and to rest on my left side for an hour twice a day. Finally, when you noticed the yeast infection in my vagina two weeks ago, you disregarded it; yet when I mentioned it yesterday to you you started me on medication. I guess what we're worried about is that you'll overlook something during the labor. We felt we had to discuss these concerns with you now."

S. swallowed hard. "Do you feel the same way, Bob?"

"Who doesn't make mistakes? I'm not as concerned about each item as is Roberta, but the fact that she's concerned is what concerns me too."

S. then spoke to each of the points, admitting error in part and also legitimate differences of approach. "In some cases I change my own mind as to what's the best gamble. But I can understand your doubts. What can I say? I'm the one who keeps stressing the importance of trust. I certainly have more trust in you for sharing these doubts about me. I'm unhappy about the mistakes. I also erred in not working out the options with you about that yeast infection. That is our agreement when the treatment for a problem is uncertain, and I broke the agreement. I wouldn't blame you one bit for asking me to bow out."

Roberta shook her head. "Well, I'm glad we can agree that you've broken the agreement. As I said before, we really want you to be there, but we wanted to reassure ourselves that we have a common understanding."

"I feel better too," said Bob. "At least we know that if differences arise, we can see them for what they are."

"And I appreciate your talking with me about this," S. replied. "I'd like to attend your birth. I'm looking forward to it."

"Good, we're looking forward to it too. Come, let me give you a tour of the office."

For S. to say that he looked forward to the birth was an understatement. He still found it hard to acknowledge to his patients the degree to which they inspired and educated him. As long as he could hear them, they would help him become the kind of doctor he wanted to be. On the other hand, recognizing that he was a cause wasn't always easy on his ego. Moreover, he had to guard against the pitfall of becoming "just one of the family" and slackening his professional alertness. Notwithstanding the egalitarian doctor-patient relationship he fostered, with its active family participation and negotiation, there were still decisions that he alone would have to make. That was what people expected him to do—especially when it came down to labor. If a move to the hospital was called for, he could not allow himself to be swayed by the family's disappointment or by his own. If the family was ready to run to the hospital for pain medication when in fact labor was progressing normally, then, too, he would have to speak with authority, though in such a way as not to compromise the family's participation in the decision.

On the Alert

At the thirty-seven-week office visit Roberta's urine showed a moderate amount of sugar. S. then drew a blood sample for sugar (glucose) determination. The report came to his desk first thing the next morning. The blood glucose was mildly elevated.

That was the thing about "normal" pregnancy. You never knew for sure whether or when it would turn into something else. The presence of sugar in the urine late in pregnancy was very common and most often normal. Usually it resulted from a temporary and harmless change in the capacity of the kidneys to recover filtered glucose. But it could also signify diabetes, an impaired capacity to process sugar in the body. A glucose tolerance test could help make the distinction.

S. was on the alert for diabetes because, without producing any symptoms at all, it could increase the chances of a stillbirth as well as result in an extra large baby that would have trouble passing through the birth canal. Furthermore, a baby born of a diabetic mother was prone to complications at birth such as breathing problems and low blood sugar, sometimes accompanied by seizures. The diagnosis of gestational diabetes was one that S. much preferred to make—when he had to make it at all—before rather than at birth. He well remembered one nine-pound-plus baby, one of his first home births, who stopped breathing and turned blue for seconds at a time. S., who had already left the scene, had to return to the home. The baby's breathing was shallow. S. packed everyone into his station wagon and drove to the hospital. It was scary. The baby did well while tests done on the mother showed a diabetic pattern.

This was not a good way to discover minimal diabetes, and S. never forgot the lesson. In fact, there was a danger that he might be overshooting in the other direction: finding the borderline cases of diabetes where there were no good data on outcome and treating them like high-risk pregnancies. It was understandable that he was sometimes overcautious, since he practiced in a milieu where many of his peers believed that there was no such thing as a low-risk pregnancy.

"Hello, Bob," S. said on the phone. "This is Dr. S. calling. I want to let you know about the report on Roberta's blood sugar. It was on the high side—not much—and I'd like to recheck it."

"Funny that you should call. We were just about to call you. Roberta's waters broke about ten minutes ago."

"Really!"

"We've already called Paula. Here's Roberta now. I'll put her on."

"Hi. It's hard to tell how much came out, maybe a cup of clear stuff. I was in bed, and I just felt it coming out, so I sat up. It soaked the floor. It's still coming out."

"Are you having any contractions?"

"No, not yet."

"Well, sounds like you're about to go into labor. You're just at thirty-seven weeks, which is our cutoff point for home birth in terms of prematurity. Paula will call me after she sees you. If you go into labor, we'll make a decision about home or hospital."

"Okay. Hey, what was that you were telling Bob about my blood sugar?"

"It was a little elevated, and we'll have to deal with that. But we may not have time to deal with it in the way we would like. Right now we'll have to see whether you're indeed going into labor."

The Birth

S. slowly put down the phone. It was still May, and Roberta's due date was June 15. "Uh, oh," he said to himself. "Could be trouble." He caught himself. "Well, a gamble different than expected, anyway." Whether Roberta had diabetes was still an open question. Moreover, premature babies were at greater risk of complications at birth. It was a risk he was reluctant to take. And if Roberta didn't go into labor following the breaking of her bag of waters there would be another problem: the danger of infection. Once the protective membranes had broken, bacteria from the vagina could enter the uterine cavity, infecting it and the baby. Infection could break out with lightning speed, and the monitoring techniques to detect its earliest signs —temperature rise, elevation of the white blood cell count, and the appearance of pus cells in the leaking fluid—were good but not that good.

So there was some danger in waiting. Traditionally, if Roberta's cervix was "ripe" for labor, labor would be induced, but that would mean no home birth. "Watching and waiting" also had its advocates, though. But it was one thing to watch and wait in the hospital and another, in the eyes of those opposed to home birth, to do so at home. In the home, too, a traditional obstetrical view was that the couple couldn't be trusted to take the temperatures and to refrain from activities like sexual intercourse and tub baths which might flush bacteria up the birth canal.

If you had a woman in the hospital, you could at least control what she was doing. You could place her in an *experimentum crucis* where you didn't need to trust her and her husband to follow the rules themselves. Many of these "rules" had arisen in impersonal clinic settings where trust was minimal. They might make sense as a response to this lack of trust. Once established, however, the rules took on a life of their own.

So here he was, here they were, faced with another decision with a number of elements: borderline maturity, borderline blood sugar, and ruptured membranes without (as yet) signs of labor. He caught himself momentarily wishing he had a pocket computer with a programmed decision analysis. But what good would that ever do? There was no way he could place this unique patient into a preexisting statistical category, and even if he could, placing her there would still be a judgment, a gamble. Talk about gambling—twice in one morning new gambles had arisen.

When Paula called, she reported that mild contractions had begun. Paula had a "sense" that this baby was of good size and that the labor would proceed normally. She felt that the couple's wish to stay at home was reasonable even though there was a question of prematurity.

S. felt a load on his shoulders over the question raised by prematurity and possible diabetes. The answer he came up with was: "Share the dilemma with them. Let them know that there may be a slightly increased risk for the baby and that the hospital on a technical level might offer some advantages. Review with them, in these changed circumstances, some of the things that make the home gamble different from the hospital gamble: the greater variance of possible outcomes, the slightly greater chance of a very negative outcome, and so forth. Remind them that they had agreed to go to the hospital in circumstances like these, and that if we're going to change the principles by which we're gambling, we should do so consciously."

Thirty minutes later Paula called again. She had just checked Roberta and found her cervix to be dilated to four centimeters, a sign of labor. That issue, at least, seemed resolved. S. asked to speak with Roberta and Bob. He presented the choice and the risks to them, and they strongly indicated their preference to stay put even if it meant slightly modifying agreed-upon principles. "Well, as long as you've given it some thought," said S. "It's a decision we all have to take responsibility for."

Paula felt surer than ever about the home birth. S. respected her judgment. From experience she had learned what the probabilities were, and she had a good understanding of the situation. "Okay, Paula, call me when things heat up."

S. went back to seeing patients in his office with Liz, a medical student. There were a few progress reports through the day. By late afternoon a milestone was reached when the baby's body rotated from a "posterior" position (with the face pointing to Roberta's front) to an "anterior" one, optimal for labor. Paula, who had worried about the slow progress until that time, had found useful and reassuring Roberta's mother's observation that her three labors had been just that way—starting slowly from posterior and speeding up following rotation, which had occurred, as it now had in Roberta's case, relatively high in the birth canal. Maybe Roberta, too, would follow this "family" pattern. This was the kind of data that the probabilistic approach, sweeping wide in its search for relevant information, was more likely to take advantage of than the mechanistic. In its own way it was as useful as any statistically constructed labor curve.

About eight that evening, with the day's last patient waiting to be seen in the office, Paula called back: "She's at eight centimeters. You'd better come. Her contractions were so mild I didn't check her until now. I'm amazed that she's moved so fast."

"I'm on my way. Would you check with Roberta to see whether it's still all right to bring that medical student we talked about a few weeks ago, Liz, to watch the birth. She's welcome to come? Fine." S. put down the phone and poked his head into the office of one of his partners. "I've got to go. Come, let me introduce you to Mrs. B., whom I was just about to see. I'll tell her I've got a delivery."

S. grabbed the oxygen tank and home birth bag, a big black kit designed for veterinarians and chock full of equipment including emergency drugs, plasma, IV tubing, needles, syringes, specula, laryngoscope, and infant resuscitation breathing bag. He asked Liz to take Roberta's medical record and the "ultrasound" instrument from the OB examining room. The ultrasound was useful in recording the baby's heartbeat during the final contractions when the heart might no longer be in easy range of the stethoscope. They packed S.'s car and drove off.

Even though it was after rush hour, traffic was still heavy as he crossed the bridge connecting two parts of the city. Heavy spring rain had delayed many in getting home. He was getting frustrated as the traffic backed up. "Talk about uncertainty," he thought. "When you deliver in the home, you don't control the conditions under which you get there." He was getting angrier at the traffic until he remembered the time in the hospital when he couldn't find a free nurse to assist at a delivery because so much was going on at the same time, as well as all the times when obstetric nurses delivered babies because the doctor didn't get there on time. He realized that he was getting angry because he was comparing what was happening now with an ideal standard of hospital perfection—the perfectly oiled machine. The machine didn't always work perfectly either.

Fifteen minutes later they turned off the major artery. "Right at Williams' Market to the third house on the left," said the directions. Shabby three-decker wooden homes. Past two men working on a car at the corner under the streetlight. A truck trailer was parked on a side street. The neighborhood was just as Paula had described it after her preparatory home visit two weeks earlier.

They quickly unpacked the car. The birth kit and oxygen tank were heavy; the sidewalk slippery. Up the stairs to the porch. The door was unlocked. A young man greeted them and directed them to the bedroom in the rear. A quick glance told S. that things were not under control.

That was an understatement. Roberta was, simply stated, panicking. "Do anything—take me to the hospital, give me an anesthetic, anything—but end this pain." Bob was even more unnerved. He looked like he could barely contain his anxiety and anger.

It was time for firm action. S. quickly put on a sterile glove and persuaded Roberta to hold still long enough for him to check her cervix and the position of the baby. Paula simultaneously applied the ultrasound to Roberta's abdomen, and the reassuring hoofbeatlike sound of the baby's heart was broadcast through the room for all to hear.

"Roberta, you're fully dilated!" S. exclaimed. "You can begin pushing now. You're over the hump. No wonder you felt like you were losing control. You're fine and the baby's fine. Relax! I know it hurts, and you're okay—do you understand? Now let's all get to work to get this baby out. There is more work to do, you know. Now, Bob, you come around to her side. I want you to keep eye contact with each other during contractions."

If ever S. had to give an example of how he couldn't observe the "facts" without changing them, it was now. He was prepared to go even further if necessary. There were times when he had to remind a couple of the agreement they had made to have a home birth. They had wanted this kind of birth, and he had been willing to support them. He didn't think they should let the passion of the moment overturn a well-worked-out plan. If it came to that, he would remind them that if they wanted an anesthetic, they would have to move the whole show to the hospital. There were times when a firm hand was called for.

"First, let's position you better," he told Roberta. "Lying on your back isn't such a good idea. Let's prop you up with these pillows behind your back and get gravity working for you. You'll be in a better position to 'push' if this makes you comfortable, and the baby will get more blood from the placenta."

For the first time he could pay attention to the people present. There was Jim, who had come to the door; his wife Sarah; and Alice, Roberta's mother. A whining dog was locked up in an adjacent room.

"Now you don't have to push now, Roberta. Try and see if it helps you feel better. The baby will be born whether or not you push." He had to speed up his probably too lengthy instructions because another contraction was starting up and competing for Roberta's attention.

Half an hour later Roberta's face was flushed and moist. She was no longer available for verbal interchange, although between contractions she could nod her understanding of the observations and guidance of her coaches. S. noticed, almost in passing, that she was no longer breathing in any special pattern when she wasn't bearing down. Breathing techniques were a central part of natural childbirth instruction. The couples whose births S. attended (at home or in hospital) learned the techniques, but learned to use them selectively, as needed.

S. didn't insist upon any particular set of rules for breathing. Here, too, there was choice, just as there was in the matter of "pushing the baby out," which women traditionally were told to do. With S. they pushed only when they were comfortable doing so. Unless, of course, delivering the baby quickly was important. Then the mother would be told to push and to push hard. Speedy delivery was in order, for example, in the case of abnormal and noncorrectable slowing of the fetal heartbeat, signifying possible fetal distress. In general, though, what babies needed to be born was time and patience. Much of the interventionist mentality of obstetrical practices, especially in the past, it seemed to S., had to do with the pressures, economic and otherwise, to hurry things along.

By now Paula had stopped applying warm wet towels to Roberta's perineum. The lore of midwives was that this moist heat increased blood flow and stretchability of the tissues. She continued circular movements around the vulva, stretching the by now pursed-out lips with her gloved and oiled fingertips between the lip and the emerging head.

Sarah held a mirror near Roberta's buttocks so that she could see the baby's head emerge. "Here's your baby. Put your hand down here and feel the baby."

S. checked the baby's heart after each contraction. Paula predicted that several more contractions would do it. S. positioned himself on his knees next to Roberta in order to assist Paula with an extra pair of hands for the baby. With the contractions Paula told Roberta, "Pant, don't push," so as to decrease the expulsive force. Just after the last contraction eased, Paula asked Roberta to push "just a little; easy, easy." As Roberta bore down, the head slid through the stretched vulva. S. felt around the neck and reported that it was free of umbilical cord, which sometimes becomes twisted around the neck and needs to be disentangled or cut so that the baby can be born. He then suctioned the mouth with a nozzled rubber bulb.

At this point S. asked Roberta to bring her hands down to grasp the baby as it emerged. This freed his hands to support the perineum and ease it over the shoulder as the baby slid out. "It's a girl!" Roberta had delivered her own baby!

The baby cried lustily and pinked up. Roberta and Bob cried too. "Apgar eleven," said S., turning to Liz. The Apgar score, the standard rating scale of newborn function (named after anesthetist Virginia Apgar, who first proposed it), takes into account color, heart rate, quality of respiration, muscle tone, and responsiveness to stimuli. A perfect score, often seen in unmedicated births, is ten points. "Apgar eleven" is a way of saying "better than perfect."

S. wrapped the newcomer in a warm receiving blanket and asked Roberta to put her to breast. She sucked immediately, and her mother's uterus contracted in response. Within minutes the placenta, assisted by gentle tension on the cord by Paula, emerged. S. breathed a sigh of relief. One of his major concerns was the possibility of hemorrhage that revolved around delivery of the placenta. Paula inspected Roberta's vagina and reported that there were only a few "skid marks," i.e., small, superficial tears which required no stitches. No episiotomy had been done, and these small tears would heal on their own.

Amidst all the celebrating, though, S. had to keep an eye out for any signs of bleeding. In situations when the uterus was lax and there was bleeding, the husband would be asked to suck his wife's breasts (if the baby did not) to stimulate the reflex clamping down of the uterus. This was unnecessary for Roberta. Of course, there were always the drugs (Pitocin and Ergotrate) as a backup if these maneuvers, coupled with massage of the uterus, failed.

S. caught Roberta's eye. Her face was relaxed. She was beaming and overwhelmed. He felt he would never forget that expression.

While Paula was cleaning Roberta up and repositioning her, S. checked the baby and recorded his examination findings in the record. He gave the baby vitamin K and treated her eyes. Paula filled a rubber examining glove with ice cubes, tied it at the wrist, and applied it to Roberta's perineum to reduce swelling.

In the relaxed afterglow, while the new parents enjoyed the privacy of the bedroom with the baby, the other participants reviewed the birth over tea, a birthday cake with the newborn's name already iced on it, and Sarah's guitar music. "I'm glad you stood by the family's wish for a home birth," S. told Paula. He turned to Roberta's mother, with whom he had had only passing words in the heat of the delivery, and asked her how she had found the birth.

"Well, I was dead set against the home part of it. It's not easy to overcome what you've been led to believe is the right way. But let me tell you, I was so out of it when Roberta was born that I barely remember what happened. You've got to hand it to these young people and to people like yourselves for being so sensible about what you're doing. I think it's great. I'll never forget it. I wish my husband had lived to be here too."

"I have to thank you as well," S. replied. "You made an important contribution. Do you know that your telling Paula about your labors—turning from posterior to anterior—was the piece of information that tipped the balance in favor of staying at home instead of deciding that labor had stopped progressing?

And just your being here—what a source of support that was for all of us."

Just then Bob came in with a tray of wineglasses filled with champagne. "Well, we almost, it felt, came to blows," S. remarked to him. "And here we are. We can say that we lived through some pretty strong emotions. I'll never forget it. When I see you again to check the baby, I'll know that we sweated it out together and that we handled our emotions just long enough to get through—but emotions there were!"

They embraced. S. knew that he was doing all the talking. He also knew Bob well enough to know that he was speaking for both of them. It was the trust that Roberta, Paula, and the two men had developed that had enabled them to contain the frustration they felt with one another and to produce the result they had all worked for. S. and the family could build upon this trust in the future. For a family doctor birth was just one episode (though a uniquely important one) in working with a family.

All agreed that this had not just been the birth of a baby, but the birth of what in this family was a new idea—the idea that a family could consciously make decisions *as* a family. All of the questions they had faced together, all of the decisions they had made—whether to have the baby; the choice of a doctor; the planned home birth; what to do about the morning sickness, the elevated blood sugar, the borderline prematurity; the difficult yet unmedicated labor—had built toward something larger: a way of gambling consciously at the important moments in their lives. "You could have made the same sorts of decisions in a hospital or birth center," said S., "but since you wanted to do it at home, I'm glad that you were able to."

Just as each successful experience of gambling during the pregnancy (whether the gamble itself was won or lost) gave Bob and Roberta added confidence for approaching the next, so the overall experience would lead them to believe in themselves a bit more, even amid all the pressures (and these weren't going to go away) that could undermine any family's belief in itself. It wasn't blind confidence; they had lived through things that easily could have gone wrong, and they knew it. They would always have to face uncertainty, but with a growing capacity to turn it into probabilities. As they learned what they could accomplish, they would rightly set higher probability estimates for success in the things they attempted. And with a growing backlog of consciously held experience, successful and unsuccessful, they would not interpret each new success— or failure—as meaning that the world had only a friendly—or demonic—face to show them. Together, they were becoming rational instead of reactive human beings.

PART V

CONTEXTS

14

MEDICAL MILIEUX

While Dr. S. visited patients in their homes several times a week, few of these visits were to help someone die or be born. But the births and the deaths, with the special character they took on in the home, served to remind him of some important, yet often unasked questions about the visits with patients that constituted the major share of his daily experience. Where did they take place? Who was visiting whom? How did the site affect the nature and quality of care? Did people (himself included) make decisions differently in different sites? If the questions were not asked, the choices could not be made consciously.

S. saw patients in a number of different places: his office, their homes, hospitals, nursing homes, and just about anywhere in an emergency. He sought to learn and teach critical thinking in all of those sites. But to do so he had to learn and teach critical thinking *about* the sites. He and his patients had to think critically about the probable consequences of choosing one site rather than another. For he knew from experience that things do not remain the same when taken out of one context and put in another. Even something as concrete sounding as a symptom has little meaning outside the

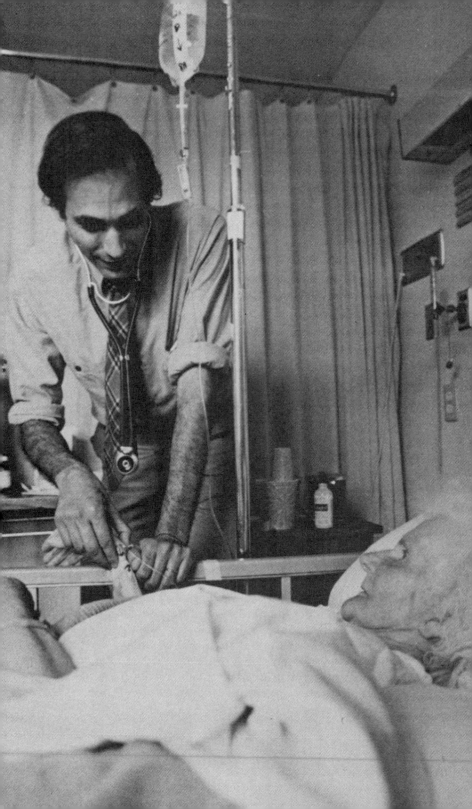

contexts in which it appears. S. sometimes "cured" patients who suffered chest pain (what doctors call *angina pectoris*) on exerting themselves in a stressful job situation when he told them to "take it easy" and move around less. S. removed the symptom by changing the context; in a different context it might reappear.

As with the disease, so with the treatment. Although it cannot be said that the site completely determines the type of care that is given, it does have an effect. It has the largest effect when people take it for granted, when they do not realize that they are making a choice. Going to the hospital or staying at home is a choice people make that in turn makes other choices more likely, though not inevitable. In the hospital people can become passive before the operation of technology; in the home people can become passive before the operation of nature. By being aware of the implications of their choices, families and their doctors (as S. well knew) can make better choices of site and better choices within whatever site they choose.

These days the hospital (or, in chronic cases, the nursing home) has become a habit—i.e., still a choice, but one made by default. At one time the sick were cared for in the home. Illness was something that happened—and was dealt with—within the family. In those days no medical technology could do any better than home treatment. Today many people who otherwise would have died are alive because of hospitals and hospital technology. Still, patients and their families need to consider in any given case whether they are entering a hospital or nursing home because it is the right choice in that situation or because they have drifted into it, swept along by the currents of habit formed under the Mechanistic Paradigm.

What is profitable for a few tends to become the habit of many. S. aimed to break the institutional habit and reopen the home-versus-hospital question as a conscious choice for families. They hardly needed to hear a case made for the hospital when so many social and economic pressures combined to push them in that direction. On the other hand, some families now were making a case for the home because they wanted to retain the power of choice through the course of the illness, rather than surrender it to institutional personnel.

There are some visits that one doesn't like to make, like the last social call on an old friend who is moving out of town. And there were some house calls that Dr. S. didn't like to make: the ones where he and the family faced the painful, at times agonizing decision of whether an ill person—especially an elderly person—should stay at home or go to the hospital. The patient, if he or she was alert enough to know, rarely equivocated: Stay at home! "Don't put me in a nursing home. Whatever else you do, don't do that!" On the other side was the view of an involved relative such as a son or a daughter (if the patient was fortunate enough to have one): "My father simply can't take care of her anymore; he's old and sick too. And we haven't any room at our house. Besides, we're working people; who would stay with her?"

S.'s role in all this was an equivocal one. A family that wanted to keep a sick relative at home would look to him for support. His involvement made home care a viable alternative. A family that didn't want to take care of the patient at home might find it easier to attribute the decision to him: "The doctor says you've got to go to the hospital." In such cases S. would say, "I don't want to be the bad guy to your mother, who is my patient, after all. The fact is that she could stay at home if you could take care of her there. Tell her that, though you love her, you can't do it anymore. If you had unlimited money and if there were more supports for families, then you could do it and would want to. But that's not the way it is."

The hospital, one anguished daughter had pointed out, was a place where her mother could get used to being cared for away from home; this would make it easier to place her in a nursing home. That was the idea—to make the transition in palatable stages: from home to hospital, then from hospital to nursing home. On such visits S. felt more like the sheriff evicting an old friend than a family doctor sending a patient to the hospital to get better. If the patient got better, she would probably go to a nursing home. If she got worse, she would go to her eternal resting place. Either way the hospital would be a way station.

That was how the hospital made things easier for the family. It also made things easier for the patient—and for S., the doctor.

He remembered a woman in her eighties whom he had treated at home for a blood and joint disorder. She spoke only Portuguese, and S. could communicate with her only through her niece. He had left the two women with written instructions and what he had thought was a clear mutual understanding about the medications the patient was to take, only to find on his next visit that nothing had been taken as he had ordered. The patient had run out of some medications without telling her niece; her niece had changed S.'s instructions without telling him; and the old woman had ended up taking some things he had told her *not* to take. S. was left puzzled and confused about what medications the woman had actually taken. No one—not the patient, not her niece, not S. himself—had assumed the responsibility of seeing that what they had all agreed to was carried out.

At that moment the controlled environment of the hospital looked very attractive to S. There he and the patient and family did not *have* to take responsibility. On the other hand, even if they wanted to take responsibility, they still could not. Insofar as taking responsibility itself was a cause of a successful outcome, there would be costs, for each act of taking responsibility increases one's capacity to take responsibility, and each failure to take responsibility diminishes that capacity. In fact, S. considered fostering that capacity to be one goal of treatment.

In the hospital responsibility was diffused among different "services." If the patient had a fracture of the hip, which was often the final straw, she would wind up on the orthopedic service. Chances are that the orthopedist wouldn't know her and would defer to a social worker, who wouldn't know her either. The family doctor, who had no clearly defined role on the orthopedic service, could easily hide in the fuzziness of responsibility made possible by specialization. In fact, it took a lot of conscious effort on S.'s part to remain involved at all—asserting himself on the ward, with the social worker, with the house physicians who welcomed excitement and challenge, but who weren't always as interested (nor were they expected to be) in the "routine" cases where the job was to make an ailing elderly person more comfortable and to extend her conscious life.

S. was aware that he brought a mind-set to the care of his patients that was different from the one that he had learned in the hospital and that was still current there. His mind-set, like that of the hospital physicians, could imprison as well as liberate. Each setting had its own bias. To remind himself of the strength of those biases and of the need for critical thinking in any setting, he would recall three cases: one that showed the hospital in all its glory and all its excess, one that revealed the mixed blessings of the home, and one in which critical judgment (together with an appreciation of the family context) enabled him to use hospital technology to advantage.

S. was asked to see Evelyn Dewey by her longtime friend and former neighbor, Florence Peterson, who had been given his name by the Visiting Nurse Association. He arrived late one winter afternoon at her first-story, one-bedroom flat after having gotten lost in a neighborhood unfamiliar to him. A quick look around the apartment told a lot: an obese, elderly, white-haired, pleasant (even charming) woman who looked less than her ninety-one years, sitting in a chair, huffing and puffing; red, oozing, swollen legs. Dishes and garbage in the sink; unmade bed; clumps of dust on the floor. How long had she been this way? She must have slipped gradually, over many months, into what at a glance looked like congestive heart failure.

"She hasn't seen a doctor in twenty years," said Florence, a woman of about sixty. He didn't need to be told that it had been a long time. Could this have been prevented? He doubted that congestive heart failure could have been prevented, but its effects could have been tempered. He was often called in late when the disease was advanced. It wasn't ignorance; frightened old people wished so hard for it not to be true that their better judgment was impaired. The slow, insidious process by which the heart slipped into failure made it easy to deny that it was happening at all.

At first Evelyn Dewey seemed to have her wits about her, but the longer S. stayed with her, the more her mental deficiencies —what doctors usually called "senile dementia"—became apparent. The questions by which he tested her reasoning and memory (such as "How much is 7 from 100?" and "Who is the president of the United States?") were always painful to ask, no matter how gentle he tried to make them. Her answers confirmed his impression that she was mildly intellectually impaired, but still could reason and feel.

He checked her over: blood pressure in the normal range; rapid pulse; clear lungs (a surprise—he had expected to hear the sounds of fluid in the lungs); swollen abdomen probably full of fluid so that the liver, which he had expected to find enlarged with backed-up blood, couldn't be felt; legs very swollen.

"Looks like it's your heart. It's not pumping as strongly as it needs to," he concluded as he returned his examining equipment to the black doctor's bag.

"I think it's my arthritis. That's why I can't walk. My heart's just beating fast from all the excitement. I'll be okay. Don't know why you're all making such a fuss," she said.

Florence thought otherwise. "Since Christmas, about six weeks ago, I've come in once or twice a week to do the shopping and pay the bills. But I can't take care of her, and there is no one else. I think she needs to go to hospital."

"I agree," replied S. "Some time in the hospital to get things under control, and you could be in shape to come home again."

"No, that's out of the question. I'm staying right here, period. I'm an old woman, and my family is all gone—except Florence here, who's like family to me. All I have left is here."

S. could sense that Evelyn valued living longer less than she did maintaining her pride and autonomy. He knew there was little point in arguing with her. Who was he, after all, to tell her what to do? "Okay, let's give it a try. If treating you at home works, great! If not, then you may have to go to hospital." He knew that by meeting her halfway and allowing her to participate in the decision, he, a stranger, would be building up trust which could be tapped for the more difficult decision that lay ahead. Later he made sure to explain to Florence that they were taking a gamble, so that she would share in the responsibility.

After drawing several tubes of Evelyn's blood for chemical analysis, S. gave her two prescriptions. "One is for digitalis, which is a heart tonic," he explained. "The other is for a fluid pill to help get rid of the excess water and salt your body has stored. I'll call the VNA nurse to see you tomorrow; she'll give you an electrocardiogram. I'll be back the day after." He left his phone number on a piece of paper in case she needed to call him before then.

He doubted that it would be all that simple. He questioned whether she could or would take the medications as directed. In this first visit he hadn't checked her medicine cabinet, which he often liked to do. Was she like so many other older people he had met who maintained a veritable "drugstore" of medications collected over the years, some of them out of date or no longer in use, trying a little bit of this and a little bit of that?

The next day the visiting nurse called S. back to say that she hadn't been able to get into the apartment with her portable EKG machine. Evelyn hadn't been able to get out of her chair, where she had sat since S. had left the night before. All that time she had held in her urine and hadn't been able to get to the pills that Florence had left for her. The nurse had had to call Florence, who hurried over from work with the key and helped her get Evelyn to the toilet.

While driving for a second time to her apartment, S. pictured Evelyn Dewey sitting immobile in her chair. How much like Mabel Gormley, he marveled, who in her dying days had sat as if glued to her chair, afraid to move for fear of disrupting the tenuous equilibrium that kept her frail body functioning. He wondered whether it was just a coincidence that Evelyn had declined so precipitously right after his visit. Was she frozen in her chair by her illness or from the fright of having been seen by a doctor, what with the looming threats of nursing home and death that his presence must have brought menacingly close? Had the gentle questions he had asked her not been as gentle as they might have been?

When S. arrived, he articulated as a conscious decision what everyone must have felt was a forgone conclusion. It was time to go to the hospital. Florence persuaded Evelyn to go by reminding her of the days when she had been a volunteer driver for the Red Cross. "Think back, Evvie. For twenty-five years you took people to the doctor or the hospital and back home again. Well, now it's your turn."

S. phoned ahead to the emergency room at City Hospital to

tell the house officers about Mrs. Dewey. He didn't know the doctor at the other end, and the exchange felt impersonal, although proper. "After you get a look at her, give me a call. I want to see her before we take the next step."

Evelyn and Florence left in an ambulance. Evelyn thought she would be back soon. S. told himself later that he ought to have discussed with her the probability of her ever returning home, which—not for "medical" reasons, but on other grounds —was not very good. This was to be her farewell to independent, private living. S. was being the sheriff again.

S. came down to the emergency room after the doctors there had called him back. They agreed with his diagnosis of heart failure. They, too, noted the absence of fluid in the patient's lungs or distension of the veins in her neck—findings that, if present, would have completed the picture of garden-variety heart failure.

"The team from the ward will be down soon. No need for you to wait. We'll take care of everything." It seemed so natural, so polite, for them to make this gesture. And so easy for him to leave. He had many other things to do, among them getting home to dinner on time for a change.

He caught himself. A real "family doctor" would not leave his patient here among strangers without personally making the transfer to the ward and letting the staff know that he was her doctor. He, like everyone involved in the case, was concerned with the patient's well-being. Yet he had let himself become preoccupied with getting home for dinner, just as the house officers and nurses, with their greater emotional distance from the patient, were attuned to their own convenience as well as to the pressing needs of other patients. That was the whole point of having a family doctor—someone who stood at varying distances from the case, so as to be able to see it from the patient's and family's "personal" viewpoint as well as the "professional" one of the trained physician. If S. didn't look out for his patients, who would? Yet it was not always such an easy thing to do.

In this case it was to be harder than he yet knew. He stayed with Evelyn in the emergency room, so that all the procedures done there were undertaken in consultation with him. In any event, the initial tests, such as the EKG and chest X ray, were not much of a strain on the patient. Their benefits were clear, and their costs were relatively low. But what would happen when Evelyn was on the ward and the prospect of further tests arose? S. would no longer be with her. He later realized that he ought to have instructed the ward personnel to inform him immediately of any significant changes in his patient's condition, even during the night. He might have told them, "She's an old woman; she's frightened; she's been sick a long time. Let's do only what we need to do and look for small changes over time." He might have said these things. . . .

In the emergency room Evelyn was given additional digitalis intravenously along with oxygen administered through nose prongs. The chest X ray showed a massively enlarged heart, an accumulation of fluid in the left chest cavity outside the lungs, and an increased amount of fluid in the lungs themselves.

The ward team, too, was struck by the massive swelling of Evelyn's legs and the absence of distension of her neck veins. The latter could be explained, consistent with the likely diagnosis of congestive heart failure, by her dehydrated state. This explanation would make further testing unnecessary. But the ward team thought of another possibility, especially in view of her labored breathing: pulmonary embolus. According to this hypothesis blood clots had formed in the veins of her legs. Some had broken loose and, having been carried by the venous system through the right side of the heart into the vessels of the lung, had lodged in the branches of these vessels. So, following their commitment to thoroughness, they phoned Dr. S. and urged him to authorize a lung scan, a procedure that involved injecting radioactive dye intravenously and then counting the radioactivity over the lung fields.

It seemed like a reasonable step to S. as well. It was hard to argue with the house staff when they were right there on top of the situation, while he was at the other end of a telephone line. He couldn't take a look at Evelyn and see how she was doing. And if he disagreed with the house officers' recommendation, they might ask him to come in and look for himself. Besides, S., too, was afraid of "missing something." In this instance it didn't take much for him to be drawn into the prevailing mentality. "Maybe they do know something that I don't," he put it to himself. And he was quick to acknowledge that they did know a lot about acute care, since they saw acute illnesses every day that he only ran across occasionally.

The lung scan was negative—no signs of embolus. Struck by the bulk of Evelyn's abdomen, the house doctor had also requested an ultrasound examination. This test bounced sound waves off her intraabdominal contents and gave a scan picture of her abdominal structure: it revealed a lot of fluid in the abdominal cavity, a finding consistent with heart failure. No new information.

Once in her room on the hospital floor Evelyn was thoroughly questioned and examined by an intern and again by a resident and a nurse. They all wrote detailed notes in her record listing her various problems and the plans to attack them. Among the problems were heart failure, heart murmur, confusion, and weakness of her left arm and leg, this last suggesting that she had had a stroke on the right side of her brain sometime in the past. That part of the brain is known as the "quiet side," since in most people it does not control such functions as speech or memory. Often no one, including the patient, notices a mild stroke when it occurs on this side.

Evelyn was finally settled in late that night in a room with three other seriously ill patients. Her vital signs—temperature, pulse, respiratory rate, and blood pressure—were taken every four hours, day and night. The nurses and aides were always running in and out; if it wasn't Evelyn's vital signs being taken, it was someone else's. The treatment begun at home and in the emergency room was continued. But an important component of that treatment—rest—was being neglected.

By the next day Evelyn, who had hardly slept now for several days (a fact which everyone had overlooked), was more confused. The treatment for heart failure continued, and plans were made to do the studies that would shed light on the list of identified problems, all of which represented stable, "underlying" causes rather than variable causes such as stress, fatigue, and disorientation.

The next morning Evelyn went to the X-ray department for plain films of her skull and a repeat chest X ray. While she was

there a phonocardiogram (sound analysis) and an echocardio-
gram (sound picture) of her heart were performed. She then
went to the nuclear-medicine department for a brain scan. The
brain scan gives a picture of the distribution in the brain of an
intravenously injected radioactive solution. Following this was
an electroencephalogram. S. missed her on his rounds because
she was getting these studies. Sadly, but predictably, none of
the studies added much to what was already known. They had
been motivated by the hope of an unexpected breakthrough
and the need to avoid future regret.

By evening Evelyn looked much worse: increasing shortness
of breath, confusion, irritability. In her lucid moments she
complained of pain in her back. The original intern being off
that night, the house officers on call, fearful that she would die,
asked and received S.'s permission by phone to do three things.
They wanted to tap her chest with a needle to draw off the fluid
in the pleural cavity which was compressing her lung, and
then to give her morphine, an old remedy for pulmonary
edema. Morphine was a two-edged sword. It could relieve the
sense of suffocation; it also depressed the drive to breathe. So
while it helped with one problem, it left another in its wake.
Hence the third request—if necessary, to pass a tube, which
would then be attached to a mechanical respirator, through her
mouth into her airway.

In addition to the symptoms observed by the house officers,
there were ominous changes in the electrocardiogram. These
signaled a malfunction in the rhythm of the heart, likely due
in large part to a toxic reaction to the digitalis, although so
many things were now happening that it was hard to quantify
the contribution of each. If not dealt with, this dysfunction
could lead to heart standstill or to ventricular fibrillation—a
rapid quivering action of the heart which renders it ineffectual
in pumping blood and unable to sustain life. This dysrhythmia
had to be treated, so the drug lidocaine was administered intravenously. It quieted down the heart, but also irritated Evelyn's brain, so that she became more confused. Because she
looked so bad, her vital signs were now ordered hourly—
whether or not she was sleeping at the time. She was also
moved to a small single room near the nurses' station so she

could be watched more closely. The room had no windows or plants. The contrast between her new "home" and her old apartment couldn't have been more striking. The change would have been disorienting even to a younger person with intact senses and mind, yet none of the tests that the house officers relied on could measure its impact. An *experimentum crucis* cannot measure the fluctuation of feelings, including those caused by the experiment.

While the hospital functioned efficiently and smoothly, S. couldn't help being struck by the succession of new faces, every eight hours, who tended to his patient. He barely knew them himself. How must it have been for someone in Evelyn's condition? When did visits become visitations?

Evelyn's deteriorating condition made it necessary to increase the frequency of blood sampling from her veins to monitor her changing chemistries. Since respiration was becoming an issue, blood had to be taken from the artery in her wrist to measure oxygen levels. Each puncture made Evelyn wince. Sometimes she had to be stuck several times to draw blood. Her bruised arms told the story.

By now Evelyn was moaning and restless. It appeared likely that she was having a reaction to the morphine. So she was given a morphine antagonist, which, while it could reverse the effects of morphine on her consciousness, could also depress the respiratory drive in its own right and therefore make mechanical respiration more likely.

That night S. spoke to Florence Peterson on the phone. She expressed confusion, anger, and concern. "She looks much worse. I can't for the life of me understand why a woman that age has to be subjected to all those tests. She's exhausted. Why can't they just leave her alone to rest?" Florence's words echoed S.'s concerns and spurred him to honor his own inclinations. Things had gotten out of hand.

The next morning S. found Evelyn wildly thrashing. She had knocked away the oxygen mask. She only half knew where she was.

Finally S. acted. Turning off the oxygen and the room lights, he told the technician who came to draw blood that he had changed his mind. He sat down next to the old woman and asked her where her back hurt. Then he rubbed her back, talking softly to her all the while. He told her what a good person she was and how much he enjoyed being her doctor. He told her that her heart was doing better (which it was) and that she just needed a chance to rest. Unlike some of the young nurses who, winking to each other at what seemed her childish complaints, tried to assure Evelyn that this or that wouldn't really hurt, he let her know he understood that she was suffering. Evelyn seemed to enjoy the back rub until finally she fell asleep.

S. had never done anything like this before. He, the doctor, was doing something that was normally left to nurses and aides, assuming they weren't too busy with vital signs and IV's. After all the technical work was done, he saw that a simple act was needed just to make the patient feel good. He took the responsibility of giving the back rub himself instead of delegating it to the staff. An hour of his time—the *doctor's* time—just being with a patient! The staff could take their cue from that.

While he was rubbing Evelyn's back, S. reflected on his feelings toward her, toward the house officers, toward himself. He realized that he had been ambivalent all along—on the one hand reluctant to tax Evelyn's meager strength, on the other hand afraid to "miss something." It really was a case of the left hand not knowing what the right was doing. Busy with other patients in other places, he had let fear and inertia gain the upper hand. Talking to Florence and actually seeing the state Evelyn was in had made him conscious of his mixed feelings. Had he still been ambivalent, he would have come down hard on the other side and thundered at the house officers for being callous and destructive. But it was hard to be angry at them when he recalled that he had gone along with their decisions. A system of thought and action that was bigger than all of them together had led people of goodwill—himself as well as the house officers—to do the wrong thing. Still, it wasn't enough to blame the system. The only way to counter its influence was to take responsibility. He would set the example.

Leaving Evelyn sleeping peacefully in her room, he ordered the digitalis temporarily stopped and reduced the frequency of vital signs to once every four hours. He gently reprimanded the house officers for their overzealousness, including himself prominently in the critique. He had been angry with these less experienced physicians, but he felt that he should deal with them as thoughtfully as he dealt with patients, and he knew that putting them on the defensive was not the way to help them learn. "We've done a good job so far with her heart failure," he explained. "She developed it over many months, and it will take a while to reverse it. Let's not rush things. She's an old woman who has been through a lot. She's tough. Look what she's survived. Now let's give her the day off. None of these neurological conditions you've been looking for are ones that we could or would treat anyway. There's a high cost to finding out about them, so why bother? Let's just let her have some ice chips, plenty of good nursing care, and visits from her friend Mrs. Peterson. Yes, she could die; whatever we do, we'll have to take that chance."

He was telling them frankly that this was a gamble, whatever course they chose. The gambling skill that the house officers best understood was that of avoiding the maximum loss (death). They would have to learn other skills in order to gamble well. House officers also had a limited time perspective, since they usually only saw patients during a brief crisis of acute illness. As Evelyn Dewey's family doctor S. was in a position to remind them that patients generally have a long life span before and after hospitalization.

It was only natural that the house officers exaggerated the importance of the tests and treatments they performed, as if these constituted an *experimentum crucis,* and were not fully aware of the duplication of procedures that often occurred. In the case of K., for example, to each month's new rotation of interns every fever K. ran called for a spinal tap. A family physician would have observed a succession of six spinal taps, each one further straining K.'s system without revealing anything new. Such a physician would have seen the cumulative effect of medical investigation on K.'s health, instead of assuming (as one who observed only one test could reasonably assume) that each test simply documented the child's condition without changing it. Yes, S. thought, it was tough to be just one person trying to temper the effects of a hospital machine that could continually throw fresh personnel into the breach. But being just one person had its advantages too. It gave one the perspective of continuity, which in turn made it possible to practice probabilistically.

After S. spoke to the house staff, an embarrassed intern apologized. "I had no idea she was ninety-one," she said. "She looked much younger, and I thought we had to go all out to pull her through." S. later wished that he had clarified the issue further, both to the intern and to himself. The intern was saying, in effect, "I didn't know you were just letting her die peacefully." The issue was not whether or not to try to save this patient. The issue was what course of action had the best chance of saving both her body and her soul. K. had been as young as Evelyn was old, and no one could say that the house officers had not "gone all out to pull him through."

S. had not then had the authority to turn off the hospital machine. Now he did. The machine was turned off.

In a way it seemed that the machine had come close to killing Evelyn. In a way it seemed that it had saved her life. For her condition improved, and after about ten days she was out of danger. The signs of heart failure were almost gone. Her weight had come down due to the loss of both retained water and accumulated fat. S. had observed that obesity was often a factor in the problems of the elderly. At her new weight Evelyn's heart, assisted by the digitalis and diuretics, had less work to do. He knew from experience that to have gotten her to lose weight preventively would have been next to impossible. In this respect, ironically, the trauma she had gone through had reinforced the beneficial effect of her medications.

S. made it a point to phone Florence daily during the critical period. It was the beginning of a working relationship that would result in her becoming a patient of his too. At first Florence felt embarrassed to have spoken up as she did. S. praised her for having done so. "You know her best. We value and need your opinion. People seem to think that doctors always know what to do. Well, as you see, we don't. We know how to use our machines, but don't always know whether to use them. We need help from the family. So keep on speaking up."

Florence made clear that what had sustained her in her advocacy was Evelyn's strong "will to go on." In the darkest moments she had cheered Evelyn on by telling her, "You're fighting for both of us."

S.'s relationship with Evelyn Dewey herself was a different matter. He regretted that he hadn't better prepared her for the hospital. In retrospect he knew just what he might have said: "I wish there were some way I could continue treating you at home. But none comes to mind. We gambled, and we lost. Now we'll have to gamble again by going to the hospital. I wish I could say that I'd be there all the time to look after you, but I can't. I'll be just one of many doctors there, and you'll be just one of many patients. We'll continue to gamble together, though we'll now be playing less and less according to rules of our own making. It will be easy for us to lose touch, to get lost in the shuffle of the machine, with its rules and its tempo, that is the hospital. Well-meaning people may perform test after test on you without explaining why. Sometimes you have to use your own good sense and say no to them, or at least ask questions when something they do doesn't make sense."

What could he say to her now, though? She might well have reason to doubt whether she still wanted to gamble with him as her doctor. He had to admit that he had made mistakes. Her judgment about what might happen to her in the hospital had been better than his. Now, however, given what he and she had learned together, he was in as good a position as anyone to help keep the hospital apparatus off her back.

S. felt a bit foolish rehearsing monologues for situations that had already happened or that would never happen. For now he would have no need to speak in serious terms with Evelyn Dewey. She was very easy to please these days, remembering as she did only what had happened the moment before (or, perhaps, a long, long time ago).

As Evelyn's physical condition improved, her mental deficit became more apparent. Her memory was much more impaired than at home, as were her attention and reasoning capacity. Heart failure, drugs, lack of sleep and nourishment, and the hospital environment all could have contributed to her disorientation. S. could not sort out the relative impact of each causal factor. But he knew from experience that to take a person with failing eyesight and reasoning out of her environment with its familiar cues—where she could see and understand things half from memory—would likely break down whatever it was in her that resisted final deterioration. In the hospital she would learn that she was going to be taken care of by others, like it or not. If she had any yearnings to make a meal for herself or put on her street clothes, she was judged to be "going crazy." If being denied these things made her cry, that, too, was "going crazy." What was there to do but go crazy?

Through her illness and hospitalization, Evelyn had suffered an irrevocable loss of independence. She had recovered physically; but, then again, all she ever did was get out of bed and sit in a chair by the window. Who could know whether her heart failure might reappear if she tried to do more? The very idea of "symptoms," he was reminded, was context dependent—the context here being one of very limited functioning. Asking whether Evelyn still had a heart problem was like asking whether a tree falling in an uninhabited forest made a sound.

In the months that followed, for a combination of medical, financial, and geographical reasons—and some plain old red tape—Evelyn Dewey was moved several times from one nursing home to another. She didn't seem to mind, though the moves were a strain on Florence, who had to make all the arrangements. At least Evelyn was able to get into a nursing home reasonably quickly, unlike many other elderly, chronically ill people for whom a nursing-home bed could not be found because it was not profitable for nursing homes to accept people on state assistance. The majority of these patients stayed in acute-care hospitals at enormous expense to the taxpayer, sometimes even forcing hospitals to turn away people who were in immediate need of acute medical care. At least Evelyn, as a widow without assets, was not in the position of elderly couples who were compelled to divorce so as to preserve what savings they had (or perhaps their home) and at the same time qualify for government aid for the ill partner. The irrationality and cost (in human and financial terms) of the system saddened S.

Ordinarily, as old people move around, they have to change doctors. S., however, remained with Evelyn throughout. At each new home he let the staff know that he was her doctor. In him and in Florence, he was telling them, their new charge had friends at court. S. was grateful for the opportunity to get to know Evvie (as he, like Florence, was now calling her), thereby "getting in on the tail end of a long life." The feelings he had for her, though, were mixed: "We've done it again. The miracles of modern medicine have saved another old person. But for what? What will her life be like now? A succession of nursing homes? What kind of life is that?"

In the heat of the struggle for life many an old patient had told him, "Let me die." How could he tell whether or not someone meant it? Though many survivors remained indifferent to the gift of renewed life, some were reinvigorated. What about the ninety-year-old woman who, after all but giving up on herself during a stormy six-week hospitalization, told S. during a home visit two months later that she was "on top of the world"?

S.'s first reaction was to doubt whether feelings and values could ever be interpreted as accurately as, say, lab tests. But a blood pressure reading taken under duress can be as misleading as a feeling insensitively registered. Both require care and attention; both require interpretation. A blood pressure out of context has as little meaning as a woman in labor screaming for pain medication or an elderly patient saying, "Doc, please let me die." Does that statement mean "Please take the pain away" or "I really want to die"? Does it express a stable preference or a momentary delirium? Given that people change their minds, is this patient changing her mind? A doctor who has known the patient in good times and bad, or who is consulting with members of the family, can often make a good judgment, just as a doctor with a good sense of pathophysiology can detect mechanical and procedural artifacts in lab results.

"Without a sense of context," S. reflected, "critical thinking is lost."

No wonder S. thought twice about hospitalization when he was called by the superintendent of a low-income housing project to see eighty-one-year-old Frank McMillan. What he found in the third-floor, walk-up apartment was a short, obese, disheveled, elderly man with massive swelling and redness of his legs from toes to hips. Serum oozed from sores on his inflamed shins. Mr. McMillan could not walk because of the pain in his legs, which he attributed to "joint trouble." Like Evelyn Dewey, he may have found the idea of arthritis a lot less scary than that of a heart condition. Unable to breathe when flat in bed, he had been sleeping upright in a chair for three weeks. One look told S. that Mr. McMillan was probably in advanced heart failure. One look was about all S. got, since he couldn't do an adequate examination without the patient's being able to lie down.

S.'s reflex reaction, even after all that had recently transpired, was to send this man immediately to the hospital. Mr. McMillan pleaded with S. to try to treat him at home. "It's Joe, my brother. He's mentally retarded," he said, gesturing toward a man standing in the doorway, who looked to be in his sixties. "There's no one to take care of him."

"Well," said S., "we agree that something has to be done. I think it's risky for you to stay at home. I can't get the information here in the house that I need in order to treat you effectively. I'd be taking a real chance myself to treat you without knowing more. You could get worse, you know. You could even get worse from any treatment I might prescribe, and I'd be to blame."

Those objections didn't impress Mr. McMillan, who again pleaded for care at home. "I'd just as soon die in my chair," he said.

S. thought back to Evelyn Dewey. "On the other hand," he said, "it's true there's a risk in going to the hospital too. And then there's your brother to consider."

For a moment S. seemed lost in thought. Mrs. Dewey's case was teaching him how the risks of staying home had to be balanced against the risks of going to the hospital. Elderly patients risked being harmed by procedures or drugs intended to help them—risks that became greater in the hospital setting. There the elderly were met with a great enthusiasm for diagnostic procedures which, while they might help in their care, could also drain their strength. They were exposed to microorganisms that often had become resistant to the usual antibiotics and therefore set up infections that were difficult to treat. In a strange environment they were vulnerable to disorientation and depression, especially at night. Their confusion itself then needed to be evaluated, resulting in more tests and procedures to determine its causes: whether a drug effect, a change in the salt concentration of the blood, and so forth—until the only explanation left was the change of environment itself.

S. continued, "You know, Mr. McMillan, it *is* a gamble either way. Thank you for reminding me. Seeing your swollen legs almost made me forget. Why, it's like betting the horses—that's what we're doing. I'll tell you what. I'll gamble with you at home for a week. I'll draw some blood, give you medicine to drain some of that fluid that's causing the swelling, and have the visiting nurse come tomorrow to take an EKG and begin to make other plans for your brother just in case you have to leave here. Is it a deal?"

When S. was satisfied that Mr. McMillan would do his best to get better at home, he shook hands with him and called it a deal. He then called someone from the Visiting Nurse Association and discussed with her how Mr. McMillan might be made more comfortable in his home.

S. could understand Mr. McMillan's feeling about his home. He himself felt comfortable there. Seeing patients in their homes made it easier for him to remember that he was (as the office and hospital settings sometimes led him to forget) a human being. Physicianship somehow had become hard to reconcile with humanity, as represented graphically by his own creature needs. When people offered him a cup of coffee, his professional upbringing cautioned him not to accept it. What an upbringing it had been! Years earlier, during his internship, while working in an intensive-care unit for newborn infants, he and other interns had been shamed into not eating and not going to the toilet, let alone sleeping, during their thirty-six-hour rotation stints. As if taking five minutes to attend to one's human needs was going to harm a baby. Everyone knew that it wouldn't, of course. But there was the tiniest hint of doubt, and in the world of the Mechanistic Paradigm that was enough.

In the home S. found it easier to be himself while also being a doctor. During the hours he spent at a home birth, for example, he ate, drank, used the toilet, took his shoes off, and sometimes even took a nap right there with his "patients." It was a relief for him to experience this kind of wholeness. All the same he had to concentrate on doing the things for which doctors are needed. He couldn't allow the informality to lull his judgment.

In the weeks that followed, Mr. McMillan (S. never felt comfortable calling him anything else) slowly improved. He did well enough to stay at home, thus saving Medicare $300 a day (the average daily cost of hospitalization for heart failure in that community in 1980) minus the modest reimbursements given to S. and the visiting nurse. Joe was able to go on living in the shelter of his brother's household, where he did the shopping and helped with the cleaning and dressing changes.

As S. gradually stepped up the medications, the swelling in Mr. McMillan's legs was reduced, and he felt better. He lost weight, though not as much weight as Mrs. Dewey had lost in a much shorter time. "How am I doing?" he kept asking Dr. S. He was delighted to hear that he was making satisfactory progress. "Let's keep going and keep an open mind on this," S. told him. "Call me if anything seems wrong to you."

The trouble was that S. never fully got him out of heart failure, as he had done with Evelyn Dewey. In the hospital Mr. McMillan would have been put on bed rest and oxygen, but at home, where he had more control, he refused to lie down on account of his breathing difficulty. Spared the acute crisis Evelyn had gone through, he remained more comfortable than she had been and for that very reason was less receptive to heroic measures. The home setting introduced its own bias—that of allowing the patient to live much as he always had. Influenced by that bias, S. did not wish to intensify the treatment very rapidly.

That autumn Mr. McMillan died in his sleep. He died peacefully in his home, in his chair, as had been his wish. It had not been his wish that his brother Joe be left alone to take care of himself. Contrary to his expectation, however, Joe at last report was still living in the apartment and was doing well on his own. Joe didn't want to have much to do with Dr. S., but from time to time S. asked the visiting nurse how he was coming along. He wished Frank McMillan could see his brother now.

* * *

People went to the hospital to be cured and stayed home to die. The hospital was set up primarily to save lives. Everything about the hospital made it possible for patients to believe that they were there to be cured, and that there was no other place where they could be cured. Outside the hospital it was difficult —psychologically as well as economically and culturally—to mobilize the resources needed to have the best chance of saving a life.

Evelyn Dewey and Frank McMillan were in some ways similar; neither of them wanted to die in a place where they wouldn't want to live. But Mr. McMillan unquestionably was more fatalistic about death than Mrs. Dewey. He expected to die, and there were some compromises he would not make to live. She "fought like hell" even in a situation that had its degrading aspects. It was likely that their expectations had affected not only their own internal resistance but the performance of the people who were caring for them. S. wondered if it would be stretching things too far to say that they both got what they were looking for.

Evelyn left the hospital with her life saved and her life at home ended. While it would be impossible to separate the effects of all the causal factors that operated on her in that setting, S. considered it probable that her heart had been strengthened by digitalis (which improved its contractions), diuretics (which drained her excess fluid), oxygen, and a salt-restricted diet. With the exception of an opportune weight loss, all of these factors would have been—in fact were—part of S.'s treatment plan on the basis of the physical examination, chest X ray, and EKG. Further testing failed to modify his original impression of Evelyn's condition. (He wished more doctors would follow the old medical-school adage, "If you hear hoof-beats, don't look for zebras.") In all likelihood the tests had created at least some of the abnormalities revealed by subsequent tests, and the remedies then applied had created further abnormalities to be remedied.

It is conceivable that the treatments that appeared to have worked for Evelyn could have been given her at home if proper support had been available there. But it was not available, as is often the case in our society. Evelyn was put in the hospital so that she could get the nursing care she couldn't get at home. One reason doctors put patients in the hospital is simply to have them rest and be taken care of. Often, though, it doesn't work out that way.

In the hospital it is easy for physicians (unless they stop and think about it) to perform unnecessary procedures simply because the means for doing so are readily available. In medicine as elsewhere, technology is used *because it is there.* Actually, diagnostic testing should be considered *less* necessary in the hospital than at home, because, with the patient under more or less constant observation and all necessary personnel and equipment at hand, the staff can respond much more quickly and effectively in the event of a complication. Less necessary —but still the machines are sitting there waiting to be used. And who would want to live with the regret of not having done an easily available test that had even the tiniest chance of providing lifesaving information?

In Evelyn's case S. had fallen into that way of thinking along with everyone else. In Mr. McMillan's case, too, he had reason to be self-critical. Perhaps he could have done more of the things for Mr. McMillan at home that apparently had been beneficial for Evelyn in the hospital. Why had he not increased the medications more rapidly? Why had he not worked harder to have Mr. McMillan agree to lie down for part of each day, with oxygen being administered during those hours to assist his breathing? Why had he not insisted that Mr. McMillan follow his diet and get more rest? Perhaps because with Mr. McMillan, in his own home, he hadn't had the power to insist —and hadn't had the time and the will to persuade the patient to act in his own best interest. Perhaps, too, it was because he himself had not been thinking critically.

There was no way to tell why one patient lived and the other died, or what judgments one might make about the way the one lived or the other died. They were two different people. Still, S. thought in retrospect that he had probably given too much treatment to the patient in the hospital and not enough to the patient at home. His decisions in each case had been influenced by reflex responses to the site, with all its customary associations. As a result, although both patients did a lot better than they might have elsewhere, it could be argued that neither received optimal care.

In the hospital S. had responded mainly to the acute aspects of the case; in the home he had responded mainly to the chronic. The home was not seen, by families or by doctors, as a comfortable setting for acute care. Like the hospital, it had its own tempo and its own rituals. In accepting both the hospital and the home on their own terms, had S. unwittingly accepted the assumption that scientific medicine could be practiced only in the hospital? Was there a way to practice scientific medicine at home without bringing the hospital into the home and making a family feel like strangers in their own house?

S. could envision alternatives, such as a kind of infirmary or halfway house that would offer hospitallike nursing care while being equipped to provide acute care when necessary. (Nursing homes often did not do this.) Given the choices available in the present, however, he would need to be aware—and to make others aware—of the large influence of site on medical decision-making. This awareness would help him make decisions that would be better both in context and in spite of the context. He now knew what a struggle it could be to maintain one's critical consciousness in a context that drew people in until they were simply overwhelmed.

This could happen both in the home and in the hospital. It was possible—and necessary—to think critically in either setting, and yet each setting contained special barriers to critical thinking. Nonetheless the two were not equivalent—not when all the forces of society and the dominant contemporary habits of thought and feeling drew people to the hospital and, once there, to mechanistic choices and procedures. S. would, of course, recommend home or hospital care to his patients in keeping with their wishes and with his own sense of what was medically appropriate. But to enable families to choose rationally between the home and the hospital, S. would often need to emphasize, as a balance against the force of the hospital habit, the values to be found in home care. To take a value-neutral position, when judgments are skewed by habit, is just to let habit run its course.

* * *

Critical thinking (and the welfare of his patients) also required that S. keep an open mind about medical technology and use it to advantage when its use was called for. A case in which he did so, while working in a hospital outpatient clinic, was that of fifty-six-year-old Albert Riccola, whose daughter brought him to the clinic for treatment of a severe headache that had lasted for four days. S. was not the first doctor to see Mr. Riccola on this occasion. One doctor had diagnosed migraine and prescribed pills. Another, going by the patient's unshaven appearance and history of heavy drinking, had concluded that his headache was caused by alcoholic withdrawal. (He had in fact stopped drinking just when the headaches began.) Still, his daughter was not satisfied. Speaking on her father's behalf (since he spoke only Italian), she shared her concern with S. "He isn't himself," she said. "He used to drink every day, but he also used to shave every day."

S. wasn't satisfied, either. Noticing the visual contrast between the unkempt father and the well-groomed daughter, he questioned why this man would suddenly depart from his habitual way of life. Why had he stopped drinking, let alone shaving? Then there was the additional information that Mr. Riccola had suffered a minor head injury in an auto accident a month before. Conscious of being tired and wanting to go home (this was the day's last patient), S. determined that, in spite of his mixed feelings, he would do a thorough neurological examination. To keep himself honest when he might otherwise have been sloppy with fatigue, he took the precaution of getting the patient's permission (through his daughter) to call in a medical student and demonstrate to her the "standard" neurological exam. Through this side bet he consciously proceeded to increase the odds that he would do a most thorough examination.

The first part of this procedure, the mental-status examination, involved speaking with the patient. With this patient S. had to have the daughter translate the questions and answers. Finding Mr. Riccola partially disoriented and exhibiting some inappropriate judgment, he noticed as well that the daughter seemed uncomfortable with her father's responses. Upon questioning her he was told that "he's making too many puns." This S. would not have known, of course, since the puns were in

Italian. S. thought it worth noting that the patient was behaving contrary to the expectations of his daughter, who, after all, knew him well.

Continuing with the neurological exam, S. discovered very slight divergences in the orientation of the right and left eyes and the right and left toes. He could easily have overlooked these findings had he not committed himself to a meticulous exam by calling in the student. By now he was convinced that there was a good probability of a blood clot pressing on the brain (subdural hematoma), which had likely resulted from the auto accident injury but had only reached a critical stage in the past four days. This diagnosis was confirmed by an emergency X-ray test called a CT scan, which showed the pressure on the brain to be increasing to the point where death from massive brain damage was imminent. Mr. Riccola was immediately transferred to the operating room, where surgeons performed a simple procedure to relieve the pressure. A few days later he was his old self and was able to go home.

In this case S. gambled well by recognizing that the results of one gamble, carefully interpreted, could help him choose another gamble. Taking note of the fact that the patient's daughter was betting her time and effort that her father's strange behavior was worth bringing to a doctor's attention, S. gambled that it would be worth his time and effort to look to her as a source of useful information. This gamble produced information that he used in estimating the probable value of doing a careful neurological exam and making the side bet of calling in a medical student, which, since he prided himself on being not only a good doctor but also a good teacher, motivated him that much more. That gamble in turn produced information that led to his doing a CT scan. In this series of successful gambles each gamble changed the odds for the next. Such a series of principled gambles, under the Probabilistic Paradigm, is what scientific experimentation is all about.

Ironically, a CT scan was one of the tests unnecessarily performed on K. This time, however, there were good reasons for choosing to perform the test. In the case of K., where technology was used mindlessly, a life was lost. In the case of Albert Riccola, where technology was used critically, a life was saved. In the one case critical thinking enabled S. to make use of "soft" data (parental neglect) where other doctors looked only for "hard" data (organically based immune deficiency). In the other case critical thinking enabled S. to discover "hard" data (blood clot) where other doctors saw only "soft" data (alcoholism). In the one case S. focused on a kind of causation that could best be observed in the home; in the other he focused on a kind of causation that could best be observed in the hospital. In K.'s case, the hospital setting extinguished critical thinking; in Albert Riccola's case critical thinking put the hospital resources to appropriate use.

15

CAN IT WORK?

S.'s experience in practicing under the two paradigms of medicine had led him to believe that if medicine were to speak the truth in the twentieth century, it would need to speak in probabilistic terms. By facing uncertainty and thinking critically together, patients and doctors could build trust and thereby gamble cooperatively. Out of uncertainty they could create probabilities. S. had seen it happen in his practice; he had felt the excitement of people gaining some control over their lives—some of the time.

He had seen it happen both at the extremes of human experience, as with Mrs. Gormley's death and Roberta and Bob's home birth, and when dealing with mundane and everyday situations. He had seen it happen under difficult circumstances (and with only partial success) in the care that Joe McMillan gave his brother and that Florence Peterson gave her friend Evelyn Dewey. In all of these cases what the patients and families did made a real difference for all concerned, including S. Yet most of the time this wasn't what doctors and patients did. Even S. and his patients weren't applying the new paradigm as much as he would have wished.

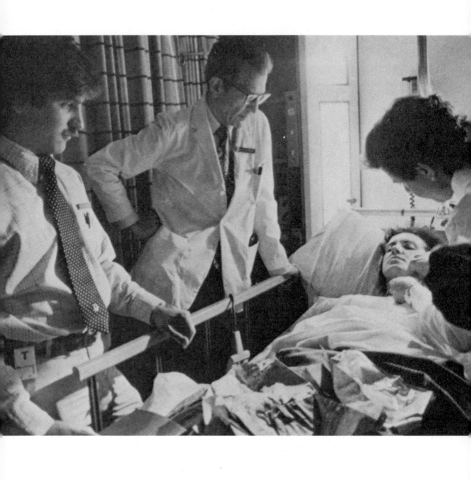

S. realized that his practice was a very imperfect approximation of what he wanted it to be. The same was true of the physicians he recommended when patients asked, "Are there any other doctors who do this?" Why weren't there more physicians and patients who acknowledged uncertainty and made use of probabilities?

It came down to the fact that he, like other doctors, did not practice in a vacuum. He practiced within certain established contexts—the context of widely held beliefs and attitudes, the context of a particular medical system, a particular legal system, the context of limited resources, the context of a way of organizing the production and consumption of goods. In any society a way of thinking supports and is supported by a way of feeling and a way of acting. In our society, as S. was well aware, a way of thinking (the Mechanistic Paradigm), a way of feeling (unconscious fear and denial), and a way of acting (the quest for profit and power) reinforce one another. The barriers to probabilistic thinking that are set up in the workplace and the marketplace make for considerable resistance to the kind of practice S. and his patients were engaged in.

The Limits of Choice

The Probabilistic Paradigm both requires and enables people to make informed choices under conditions of uncertainty. When S. practiced probabilistically, he and his patients made choices together. He viewed much of his work as a process of learning and teaching others how to make informed choices. Yet it seemed that certain choices were almost always closed off. Could people choose to move out of a tenement where their children were subjected to lead-paint poisoning? They might have a choice about whether or not to use the electronic fetal monitor, but they had no choice about whether the monitor was developed, whether their local hospital purchased it, and whether it was overused—all of which decisions would affect their medical bills and insurance rates. Did they have any choice about the stress-related morbidity and mortality fostered by workplaces designed mainly to maximize profits regardless of potential human cost? (Eyer and Sterling, 1977)

S. remembered Mrs. Pinelli, the woman who went through a painful, expensive hypertensive workup that proved to be (and could have been predicted to be) useless. It is not surprising that Mrs. Pinelli failed to make an informed choice. Nothing in her experience as a compliant worker and consumer had prepared her to think critically about the choices she faced concerning her health. She grew up in a society that is not committed to educating people to think critically. At the very most she received "consumer education" in school and from magazines which taught her how to shop intelligently and get the most for her dollar. But this education did not keep her from "buying" the heavily advertised claim that the complete workup was "the best medical care money can buy."

Since probabilistic thinking was strange and foreign to Mrs. Pinelli, Dr. S.'s attempt to introduce her to it was made possible only through a medical student's availability and willingness to donate her time. The exploration of options begun by the student might have led Mrs. Pinelli to forgo the complete workup, thus saving her much pain and her insurance company the cost of both the tests themselves and the days of hospitalization they entailed. But no insurance company was yet willing to invest in the educational process necessary to bring Mrs. Pinelli to the point of making an informed choice. Indeed, in a fee-for-service system the doctor, the hospital, and all their supporting cast stood to profit more by doing *more*, not by doing less. While it is hard to assess the precise impact of this unstated fact on Mrs. Pinelli's decision, it is equally hard to deny that it existed.

It wasn't only Mrs. Pinelli whose choices were limited. S. would have been able to make different choices in treating her if society (through its various reimbursement plans) had placed a higher value on patient education and shared decision-making. As it was, S. was not reimbursed at all for teaching people to think critically and was inadequately reimbursed for many of the things he did in support of people who tried to think critically. He was handsomely remunerated for giving an anesthetic to a woman in labor, but not for working with the woman so that she could handle her uterine contractions without requiring an anesthetic. He could spend an unremunerated hour dissuading a family from transferring an elderly, terminally ill relative from a nursing home to a costly acute-care hospital, while at that same hospital a doctor could make hundreds of dollars in much less time by performing a life-prolonging maneuver such as placing the patient on a respirator. Although the system would pay for Mabel Gormley to be kept breathing by technology, it would not provide as well for her to be given a little "tender loving care" so that she could die in peace and comfort.

Doctors were well aware of the financial advantage to be gained from hospitalizing patients or by performing reimbursable technical procedures in the office. The bias of the legal system also lay in the direction of encouraging the use of expensive, highly profitable technology. A doctor was far more likely to be sued for doing too little than for doing too much. By the same token, practicing "defensive medicine" often meant doing the very things that were profitable to do anyway. So when patients asked S., "Why can't I find other doctors who practice the way you do?" he could have given them more than one reason.

The limitations placed on the choices made by doctors also affected the choices available to patients and families. People could not choose a type of care that no doctors were willing to give. Moreover, people would have to think twice about choosing a type of care for which their doctor would not be reimbursed, since they would have to pay for such care out of pocket. Roberta and Bob's health insurance paid S.'s fee, since S. in "delivering" the baby was thought to be "doing" something. But this insurance policy (which would have paid for a fetal monitor and a team of nurses in the hospital) did not pay for Roberta to be monitored by a birth attendant at home. She and Bob had to make a significant financial sacrifice for a choice that saved their insurance company and its subscribers all the usual costs of a hospital birth (costs that in 1980 averaged $500 per day). Not every family could afford that choice. Mrs. Gormley's family saved their insurance company thousands of dollars by giving the dying woman family care instead of professional and machine care. But not every family could afford to give so much time without compensation.

Finally the hospital itself was not reimbursed for maintaining the backup facilities which patients in Mabel Gormley's or Roberta Johnson's position would occasionally need. If the patient did not *actually use* the facilities, the hospital did not get a cent. It was only natural, then, that hospitals and their personnel were geared toward bringing people into the hospital to be put through the technical procedures for which the reimbursement system was primed to pay.

S. wanted his patients to understand the contexts—economic, political, ethical—in which he and they made decisions, for by understanding, they could perhaps make better decisions. He wanted to tell them about the conditions that constrained their choices—if there was time to tell them, and if it would do any good. Whenever Mrs. Pinelli sat in the office with him during one of her monthly blood pressure checks, he wondered how he could explain it all to her. He wished he could tell her, "You wanted the arteriogram in part because your experience in your bookkeeping job and elsewhere in life has led you to believe that the way to solve problems is by one simple technical operation. On top of that the residents and nurses in the hospital were all telling you that you ought to have the arteriogram 'so you'll be sure.' You see, they face the same kinds of pressures on the job that you do, and they learn the same things. They're afraid *not* to do a procedure that promises to give them certainty. And indeed, the arteriogram does have one outcome that is certain: someone will profit from it; for there is profit in the search for certainty by technical means. And the quest for profit itself reflects a way of thinking in which some single, measurable goal can be exalted over all else. It all fits together in an often jumbled, yet interlocking system, and it's up to us to find a way out of it."

He wanted to tell her these things, but it would have taken his time and her time. They both had other things to do in that time —things that they were being paid to do. Besides, it was all he could do to explain the medication dosages to her so that she wouldn't come in hypotensive (i.e., with her blood pressure abnormally lowered) from taking too much. As S. was learning, there were formidable problems in expecting a patient to use a paradigm in medicine that she wasn't trained or encouraged to use anywhere else.

Sometimes S. did give patients the kind of explanation that he did not attempt with Mrs. Pinelli. For example, when he was treating a so-called hyperactive child, he thought it only responsible to tell the parents, "If you were wealthy, we could do more for your child. We could put him in a school with smaller classes where he would get more personal attention—which certainly won't happen in your public school. But few of us can be wealthy, and so the most we can now do is to give a drug like Ritalin, or experiment with diet or with teaching the child out of school. But these measures do not substitute for the changes in the child's environment that we all too often don't have the power to make. It's the best we can do under the circumstances, but you ought to be aware that under other circumstances we could do something better."

This was what he said when he wasn't too busy or too tired or too overwhelmed, and when he thought that the patient could understand and respond to the information. As a family doctor S. saw patients who differed greatly in their knowledge, intelligence, income, family structure, ethnic background, and ability to speak English. He saw elderly people who had trouble getting to the office, dressing and undressing for examinations, and remembering instructions for taking medication. Some of his patients had no idea what a family doctor was. Some felt a much greater need for certainty than did others. Some were aggressive "consumers" of health care or self-care zealots who acted as if they didn't need a doctor at all, while others were enlightened skeptics who didn't need S. to teach them to think critically. These factors, too, affected people's capacity and willingness to gamble.

The Workplace and the
Marketplace of Medicine

The habits people acquired in the workplace and the market-place did not magically disappear at the door of S.'s office or the hospital admitting room, for these were also workplaces and marketplaces. Medicine is business—big business. S. had been a hospital corporation employee and was now in business for himself. His patients assumed themselves to be consumers, although S. tried to work with them in such a way that they would come to see themselves as more than that.

Yet S. was part of the system too. He was earning a living, and he was also a consumer. Everything from the clothes he wore to work to the prescription pad given him by the drug salesman were tools of his trade which he consumed as he worked. Practicing one of the most profitable occupations in a profit-seeking society, he could not help but be concerned with the economics of his practice. His work, too, was being done for profit as well as principle. Under the circumstances he sometimes found himself shaking his head and saying to himself, "How can it work when it doesn't pay?"

When S. went into practice, he took on all the responsibilities and details of running a small business that was open twenty-four hours a day. He saw, for example, that although he was paid (either by the patient or a third party) for time spent face to face with patients, much of what he did for patients was done behind the scenes. Driving to and from patients' homes and hospitals, reviewing laboratory results, updating medical records, speaking with patients and their families on the telephone, conferring with specialist consultants, doing the paperwork required to support the visiting nurses in their care of homebound patients—these he considered essential services, but from a business point of view they constituted red tape. He estimated that only about sixty percent of the time he spent on the job was billable. In order to cover his expenses (office space and personnel, answering service, etc.), he had to charge a fee for each of those billable hours that made it difficult for the poor to use his practice. He could not survive in business, for example, if any more than a small proportion of his patients were covered only by Medicaid, the federal-state health insurance for low-income people. For a doctor who went into practice to serve the community, this was a sobering realization.

What made it all worthwhile was that he was his own boss, at least to the extent that such freedom was still possible. Within the constraints of professional standards, relationships with colleagues, and economic necessities, he was free to serve his patients as he and they saw fit. The autonomy and control he gained by being in private practice translated into more choices for patients and families. If there were to be only one type of medical care that a doctor could practice, someone like Mrs. Gormley might not be able to die at home, and couples like Bob and Roberta might not be able to have their baby at home. If there were only one type of medical care available, and if everyone worked for the same corporate bureaucracy, S. could easily envision the existence of "company rules" that would constrain medical choices even further.

When he thought back to the case of K., S. remembered the residents and interns, all of them good, compassionate people, as compliant assembly-line workers tending their single-purpose diagnostic machines. K. was passed down the assembly line, with each machine recording its one result. And if the need for certainty on the part of the institution and the individuals involved weren't enough to ensure that K. would get this mechanistic treatment, the corporation's earnings were directly proportional to the length of time K. remained in the hospital and the number of procedures performed on him.

If the case of K. is any indication, the hospital is much like a factory, where work done by machines (i.e., requiring a large investment of capital) is currently more profitable than work done by people (i.e., requiring a large investment of labor). The hospital worker finds his job to be a routine, attending to machines rather than critically using machines to care for people. Whether in using expensive computer axial tomography in place of a thorough neurological exam to rule out possible life-threatening causes of a prolonged headache, or in treating a patient with a bone infection by giving intravenous antibiotics for six weeks in the hospital instead of giving the medication as a pill at home with comparable effectiveness at a fraction of the cost, the bias generally favors expensive, profitable technology. Thus K. Thus Mrs. Pinelli. Thus Evelyn Dewey.

Even though the profit motive is not always in the foreground, this is not to say that it is not always there. It *was* clearly in the foreground, S. found, in some private community hospitals set up as profit-making businesses. There the staff actually made diagnostic and treatment decisions with an eye toward performing the more profitable procedures. This was not how decisions were made in the academic teaching hospitals where S. worked (the ones where K., Mrs. Pinelli, and Mrs. Dewey were treated). These hospitals, while themselves nonprofit organizations, were connected with other institutions (such as drug companies and equipment manufacturers), which profited by their activities. Here the profit motive was served indirectly, through the mechanistic standard of certainty to which the staff was trained to aspire. Engaged in what they saw as the pursuit of truth for humanitarian ends, physicians in the teaching hospitals often ended up performing the same unnecessary procedures which in the private hospitals were motivated by outright greed. Still, "often" is not "always," and misguided idealism is not synonymous with unprincipled self-seeking—which was why S. felt more comfortable in the academic hospital complex (when the services of a hospital were needed at all).

In the medical industry that coexisted with the Mechanistic Paradigm the "need" for certainty insured a "need" for specialized technology, which in turn created a "need" for specialized settings and personnel. (In places where people still got along without these things, an "unmet need" was considered to exist.) If something had to be done with specialized equipment in the hospital, then S. was not the doctor who could do it; somebody else would get the "business." The view that birth, for example, always needed such specialized attention was one with which S., along with couples like Bob and Roberta, disagreed.

S. liked to think of his practice as an alternative to assembly-line medicine—that is, to the anonymity and fragmentation of care that demoralized patients. Yet his practice was tied into the system in a relationship that was in part cooperative, in part antagonistic. S. couldn't do everything himself. He needed the hospital in cases where he did have to call in specialized equipment and highly trained personnel. When he did his neurological examination on the man with the blood clot in the brain, he was thankful that there was such a thing as a CT scan and that surgeons were on call to operate on a few minutes' notice. When a woman about to give birth needed to rest after hours of unproductive labor, he saw how much it meant to be able to bring her to the hospital, sedate her, and keep her under observation while she slept (with the personnel and equipment needed for a possible cesarean section right at hand) in the hope that when she awoke, she would be able to complete a normal vaginal birth. Part of what S. offered his patients, in fact, was the availability of these backup resources and his ability to use them critically and effectively.

Typically, though, patients were pulled into the system as if on a conveyor belt, with neither the patient nor S. having a chance to think critically about the procedures and consultations the patient needed. Mrs. Pinelli was drawn in like a helpless swimmer in an undertow. In her case a specialist physician (S.'s friend, to boot) thought it perfectly natural to assume control of the case from S. and then to relinquish control to the anonymous hospital personnel who ended up having the greatest influence on the patient's decision. Rose Heifetz would be thought of as more sophisticated than Mrs. Pinelli, but sophistication for her meant being acquainted with specialists whom she could see without going through a "middleman" like S. It was hard to win a tug of war with an assembly line.

When Does a Heart Beat Too Slowly?

Patients and their families gave up some control when they went from their homes to the doctor's office; they gave up more control when they went to the hospital. It was with considerable misgivings, therefore, that S. observed yet another level of centralization of medical-care facilities: the regional specialty center, where several institutions joined forces to create a facility or group of facilities gathering together the most prestigious personnel and the most up-to-date equipment for treating a particular condition. This was done with the laudable aim of sharing experience and making the best use of scarce resources for the benefit of patients. However, it also had the effect of limiting the diversity of options and thereby limiting choice for patients, families, and physicians. There was talk, for example, of setting up a regional birth center that would handle all births for people living within a radius of fifty miles. How would Bob and Roberta (let alone S. himself) fit into those plans?

It was in dealing with such medical "conglomerates," sometimes operating unobtrusively within the walls of familiar hospitals, that S. felt most strongly the impotence of the outsider. A case in point was that of a baby born with bradycardia (slow heartbeat) after a normal pregnancy, labor, and delivery (with mild analgesia). S., who was covering for another physician, did not know the family. Called to the hospital to evaluate the baby's condition in the light of the irregularity, S. found nothing abnormal. The baby's heart rate was indeed slow, but it was the same as that of ten percent of all normal babies, and the baby on examination was otherwise healthy and acted normally. Nonetheless unwritten hospital rules (recall Eleanor Perk's "company policy" from Chapter 4) required that the baby be placed on a heart monitor in a special-care nursery, and the nurses indicated that they would not be comfortable deviating from the rules.

S. could read the confusion and anxiety on the faces of the baby's parents. Here he was telling them that nothing was wrong with the baby, yet how could they trust him when they did not know him and the nurses were telling them just the opposite? Whom were they to believe? Just seeing their baby hooked up to a monitor was enough to make the parents worry, and if they worried long enough, they would "want" the baby on the monitor.

In the days that followed, S. tried to have the baby taken off the monitor. By this time the baby's grandmother had mentioned that each of the baby's uncles had been born with the same slow heart rate and none was the worse for it. Meanwhile, though, on the instructions of the chief nurse, the ward nurses had bolstered their position by consulting with a pediatric cardiologist at a nearby hospital. They did this without notifying S., who was at the time the responsible physician. Finally S. contacted the cardiologist directly and, mentioning the baby's normal X ray and electrocardiogram, asked him to look at the baby himself. After being examined and found normal by the cardiologist, the baby was discharged. Through an appeal to machines and institutional authority S. was able to turn off the machine that institutional authority had turned on. "We're glad he called in the cardiologist," said one nurse to another. "We wouldn't have wanted that baby to suddenly die on us."

Who had turned on the machine in the first place? It was not easy to assign responsibility. Several hospitals in the area had merged their neonatal departments with the announced intention of achieving "shared knowledge and coordinated high-level decision-making." What it also achieved, intentionally or not, was absentee authority, remote from and unaccountable to patients, families, and physicians. The lines of communication connecting the various poles of invisible authority ran mainly through the nurses, who were encouraged to "play a greater role in decision-making by consulting with their superiors and freely contacting appropriate personnel at the partner institutions."

It is true that nurses in hospitals generally are not given the chance to think critically and make decisions to the extent that they are capable. Rectifying this discrimination may have been one of the aims of the administrators of the merged program. Whatever their intentions, their actions had the effect of limiting the authority of physicians by implementing policy through highly specialized nurses, who as hospital employees with fewer outside job opportunities were more amenable than physicians to the dictates of the institution. These nurses were a new breed, a breed whose skills were so closely matched to the machines with which they worked that they could not survive outside the temples of high technology. One found many different species of specialists in these temples, all of whom depended for their living on their ability to function smoothly, to follow the rules rather than assume individual responsibility.

A patient or family member or private physician can argue with a staff physician. But how can one argue with a nurse, who, like the minor bureaucrats who appear in Kafka's *The Trial,* has no authority but merely fronts for authority? As in *The Trial* the authority set up by regional medical centers was so diffuse, with no clear chain of command or stated procedures, as to be invulnerable to appeals to reason, principle, or the legitimate authority of experienced and knowledgeable people. Unless, that is, someone put himself out and "made a stink" as S. did. The hospitals were willing to yield in such cases, which were few and far between. After all, they didn't want people to think them authoritarian.

Formula for Consumption

Hospitals and megahospitals were not the only corporate institutions that influenced doctors' and patients' decisions behind the scenes. S. was well aware of the far-reaching power of the drug companies, who subsidized medical journals with their advertisements and who were reaching out with educational programs for doctors on "gaining patient compliance." The drug companies' success in gaining compliance from patients and doctors alike was not lost on other commercial suppliers, for instance the manufacturers of infant feeding formulas.

In 1978 the American Academy of Pediatrics' authoritative Committee on Nutrition issued a set of recommendations concerning infant feeding. Among them were the following: (1) breast-feeding is superior to bottle-feeding both for the mother (in terms of minimizing postpartum bleeding and getting the uterus to contract) and for the baby (in terms of reducing infection and supplying appropriate nutrients); (2) babies should be kept on bottled formula (or, of course, breast milk if it is still being given) up to the age of one year instead of six months as previously recommended, since the formula (which is designed to resemble breast milk) is better for babies than whole (cow's) milk. This recommendation was based on reports that whole milk, with its higher concentration of salt and certain kinds of proteins, may cause allergies and gastrointestinal bleeding in some infants.

For S. the committee's statement was remarkable for what it did not say. Its findings were presented as "scientific data," with no mention of the political or economic context. Actually the committee's first recommendation had already taken place in practice, and the committee was in effect ratifying a shift in society's values. Thirty years earlier breast-feeding had been opposed by most physicians and nurses, who did everything they could to discourage the practice. The La Leche League, a society of breast-feeding mothers, was founded at that time to promote breast-feeding in the face of opposition. For a generation "the data" had dictated bottle-feeding; now suddenly "the data" dictated breast-feeding.

As for the second recommendation, in S.'s view the findings cited did not justify it. The studies of formula versus whole milk between the ages of six months and a year were isolated case histories with no probability factor. S. granted that some babies would show increased sensitivity to some of the ingredients of whole milk. But how many? What were the risks for an otherwise healthy six-month-old? If adverse effects occurred, were they irreversible, or could they be eliminated simply by switching to formula once the baby's inability to tolerate whole milk became evident? It was not even made clear whether the infants studied were over six months old.

The economic implications of the new policy were considerable for both the consumers and producers of commercially prepared formula. Families would be spending more for formula than for whole milk. And their money would be going into different pockets. Formula manufacturers had been suffering a steady loss of their market as a result of the return to breast-feeding. What a fortunate coincidence for them that just when the relevant branch of the medical profession (with whom, it must be added, they had close ties in research and development) officially sanctioned breast-feeding, it also advised

women who did not breast-feed for a full year to continue buying formula for another six months. Now the market that was
being lost in one place could be regained in another.

Because the committee's policy represented a departure
from past recommendations, it embarked upon an educational
program for pediatricians, family-practice physicians, nurse
practitioners, and others in a position to influence people's
decisions concerning infant feeding. The program included direct mailings, announcements in journals, courses for which
physicians received continuing education credit, speaking
tours by prominent physicians and nutritionists, and national
closed-circuit television presentations with telephone hookup
for questions—all underwritten by the formula manufacturers.
A major theme of the presentations was "Problems of Management and Compliance." What, for example, should a doctor do
with a mother who, having started her first two children on
whole milk at six months with no apparent adverse effects,
didn't see why she should treat her third child any differently?
The speakers and brochures advised the doctor to be "supportive," to build an alliance, to use communication skills, to present the new information in a nonthreatening way, to avoid
arousing guilt, and so forth. The goal, however, was to achieve
compliance, not to interpret the data (including the family history of successful feeding with whole milk) with the mother so
that she could make her own choice.

The latter course was the one S. tried to take. Except in cases
where abnormalities in the baby's condition or family history
suggested a greater-than-usual risk of complications from
using whole milk, he told parents, "The advice that's being
officially given now is not to start whole milk until the baby is
a year old. To my mind the evidence on this point is not clear.
I don't know of any harm that would result if you gave the baby
whole milk after six months and then switched back to prepared formula if problems developed. And I ought to tell you
that the companies that make the formulas have a vested interest in pushing the official line. The choice is yours to make."
Although he did not see much likelihood in his being able to
counter such a well-organized, well-financed campaign, he
began writing letters to the American Academy of Pediatrics as

well as to independent research organizations in an effort to clarify the scientific basis for the new recommendations.

The necessity for making the choice, S. reflected, had been created by the omnipresent partnership between big business and institutionalized medicine.

Amending the Mechanistic Constitution

The Mechanistic Paradigm, together with the form that people's relationships tend to take in conjunction with it (power-oriented, profit-oriented, exchange rather than communal), can be thought of as a kind of "constitution" under which doctors and patients practice. Under this constitution doctors and patients avoid feeling uncertain about each other by setting up relationships that have a hierarchical, authoritarian quality, with the doctor and patient playing rigidly defined roles. This kind of relationship fits in well with the rest of mechanistic practice—the assumption that the diagnosis should determine the treatment, the belief that there is one "objectively" right thing to do, and so forth.

It does not fit in well with the needs of our time. Since World War II people have been less and less willing to defer to their doctors. Malpractice suits, outrage over the high cost of medical care, rejection of orthodox medicine in favor of holistic medicine and self-care, and the demand for patients' rights are signs that the mechanistic medical constitution is breaking down. For their part concerned physicians and other health professionals have come up with various "amendments" which introduce some flexibility and responsiveness into the mechanistic constitution. These amendments have made it less likely (though not impossible, as we have seen) for what happened to K. to happen to others. From the perspective of the history of science, however, they represent the same kind of tinkering that physicists did in the late nineteenth and early twentieth centuries in an attempt to save the Mechanistic Paradigm. Such amendments stretch the paradigm so as to enable it to solve particular problems, but they are cumbersome. Although in medicine they have sometimes made it possible for patients' needs to be met and for doctors to practice in a more humane, value-sensitive way, these patchwork devices are themselves undermined by the assumptions of the paradigm onto which they have been grafted. Their significance lies chiefly in that they portend a shift to the Probabilistic Paradigm.

Even the notion of *compliance* (discussed in Chapter 11), chilling as it is, amends the Mechanistic Paradigm by challenging the deterministic assumption that if medicine has been prescribed, it has therefore been taken. It recognizes (albeit grudgingly) that human beings, having a range of feelings, values, and attitudes, are capable of making choices. Nonetheless the compliance model, by failing to recognize that there are sometimes good reasons for disregarding instructions, places a pejorative connotation on the human capacity to choose different courses of action. It has mobilized doctors, backed by drug companies, to work harder at achieving the kind of control allotted to them under the mechanistic constitution.

Other amendments, while not always very effectual, have had the more constructive purpose of legitimizing the exercise of decision-making power by patients and families. The term *informed consent* is used to describe the requirement that a doctor inform the patient (within reason) of the available options and the risks of each. The weakness of this concept lies in the word *consent,* which implies a passive consumer accepting options that the doctor (like a car dealer) presents, rather than participating in creating the options. The words *informed choice* better describe the scientific gambling that patients and doctors under the Probabilistic Paradigm must do together. The *patient advocate* is a new breed of hospital employee who handles complaints and mediates between the patient and the hospital staff. The patient advocate role was created in recognition of the fact that many patients no longer have family doctors or even families to look out for their interests—and in recognition of the fact that medicine has become, like the law, all too often an adversary system. In practice, even with the best of intentions on the part of the hospital, a hospital employee cannot feel fully free to raise issues that may challenge the economic base on which his or her livelihood depends. The *patient's bill of rights,* which is sometimes written into hospital policy or even state law, includes such guarantees as privacy, informed consent, and itemized billing. It is undoubtedly a useful protection as well as a comfort for many people. It might be more useful (and would better reflect a relationship of equality between doctor and patient) if it were accompanied by a bill of responsibilities for patients and a bill of rights for doctors and hospitals. These additions would make clear that patients are participants rather than consumers, and that doctors and hospitals do not retain (as might be assumed under the Mechanistic Paradigm) all rights and powers not specifically given to patients in the patient's bill of rights. The *living will* enables people to specify in writing how they wish to be treated (especially with regard to the use of life-sustaining technology) in the event that they should become terminally ill and unable to communicate. Given the misinterpretations (unintentional and otherwise) that occur routinely with written documents, a living will is most likely to be effective in the context of shared experience, shared expectations, and a shared approach to decision-making among patient, family, and physician. In such a context the written instructions clarify and are clarified by the understanding that exists among the parties (Bursztajn, 1977). What is true of the living will applies as well to all of the "amendments" we have considered. In the context of interpretation supplied by the Mechanistic Paradigm (the context that exists at present) their effectiveness is compromised, their purpose distorted. In a different context—that of the Probabilistic Paradigm—they would be both more useful and less necessary.

S. wanted to help establish that context. Instead of more amendments to the mechanistic constitution, he wanted there to be a new constitution, a new paradigm. His goal, the purpose that gave direction to his work, was the wise use of the Probabilistic Paradigm as a basis for decision-making—first in medicine, and then throughout life. He realized, however, that even the most thoroughgoing attempts to reshape medical relationships and procedures in accordance with the Probabilistic Paradigm might simply produce more amendments to the existing structure of thought, feeling, and action. As long as the Mechanistic Paradigm both governed and was supported by the political and economic relationships by which society functioned, medicine could not stand alone as a place in which people dealt with one another with trust, openness, equality, and a willingness to face the unknown. And though he would have liked to think that there was some prospect of the kind of general social and economic change that would be motivated by the use of the Probabilistic Paradigm, he was pessimistic about the chances of its happening in his lifetime.

Still, it was worth a try, beginning in medicine. He started by sketching out the implications of the paradigm for broader social issues in medicine, such as malpractice judgments and health care funding. What would it be like, he wondered, if the law and the economics of medicine reflected the same principles that guided him and his patients in their daily practice?

Malpractice

Sometimes people misunderstood what S. meant by words like *uncertainty, probability,* and especially *gambling.* They thought that these concepts would give doctors an "out," a way of disclaiming responsibility by attributing bad outcomes to chance. Indeed, in the mistrustful world of the Mechanistic Paradigm, there were some doctors who would try to do this. Some patients wondered whether even S. might not have had that in mind.

Actually nothing could have been further from his mind. Even though S. made it clear that he could not know with certainty, he also made it clear that it was possible to know with some degree of certainty. For example, he could not know precisely what caused Rose Heifetz's cancer or brought about its remission, but he stated with some degree of certainty that Laetrile would not work. In a less than certain world he, like his patients, was responsible for acting on probable knowledge.

Under the Probabilistic Paradigm a doctor would still be responsible for knowing what a doctor should know and doing what it is a doctor's job to do. Malpractice law ought to be able to distinguish between reasonable gambles that just lose and gambles that are unreasonable, whether from incompetence, negligence, or bad faith. When a doctor is held responsible for choice, not chance, malpractice becomes a matter of unprincipled gambling, intentional or unintentional.

This definition, S. realized, would not be so different from the one currently in use. The law as it stands seeks to penalize doctors not for chance outcomes, but for avoidable errors. Deriving the malpractice concept from the Probabilistic Paradigm would have the benefit of clarifying the chance-choice distinction, both in the law itself and, perhaps more important, in people's expectations. Patients who gamble consciously would be less likely to evaluate gambles from hindsight, i.e., to confuse a good outcome with a good gamble, a bad outcome with a bad gamble. Rather they would evaluate gambles as they might have appeared before the fact to a knowledgeable person acting in good faith. Moreover, patients who participated in decision-making would feel less alienated both from the doctor and from the various outcomes. By being able to share the burden of uncertainty from the beginning, they would be less likely to react to disappointment with recriminations. Although malpractice judgments would still be awarded, there probably would be fewer unjustified claims. Without the expectation of certainty doctors would not have such an excessive burden of responsibility.

Under the Probabilistic Paradigm both the doctor and the patient are causes, and as such cannot be completely known or controlled, even by themselves. Acknowledging themselves to be among the causes, patients and families can share responsibility for making and acting upon informed decisions whose consequences they can live with. In this concept of shared (as opposed to diffused) responsibility, in which the patient and family become more responsible without the doctor's becoming any less so, lies the real significance of the Probabilistic Paradigm for medical ethics and malpractice.

Health-Care Funding

If S. had wanted to "sell" the Probabilistic Paradigm, he might have been tempted to claim that its adoption would reduce the costs of medical care. He could not, however, in all honesty make such a broad claim. Quite likely the widespread application of probabilistic thinking in medicine would reduce costs in some areas (e.g., exhaustive, high-technology diagnostic testing) and increase costs in others (e.g., the time doctors spent working out decisions with patients). Less would be spent on machines, more on people.

The costs of medical care depend in part on the kinds of choices people make, individually and collectively. In the present system, however, high costs often result from an absence of choice. The real difference between the present system and the one S. envisioned would be in the way in which the costs would be incurred: who would make the decisions, how consciously and explicitly they would be made, what values they would reflect, how the needs of the individual would be reconciled with the needs of society. An economic solution consistent with the Probabilistic Paradigm would put decisions about the kinds of medical care bought by patients and insurance subscribers (as well as taxpayers) less in the hands of corporate interests and more in those of patients, families, and physicians. People would be choosing what they thought was worth paying for. Even if costs remained as high as they are today, they would not seem so arbitrary and uncontrollable. They would be seen as resulting from considered principles and values.

When the Cavanaugh and O'Farrell families took care of Mrs. Gormley at home, they were made intimately aware of the costs of dying—the costs for the dying person and the costs for the family, the money costs and the costs in time, work, and emotional energy. Without articulating the issue in these terms, they could weigh the costs against the benefits of having

Mrs. Gormley live beyond the point of being able to live a useful or even sentient life. They would have done anything to keep her from becoming terminally ill, but at a certain point they could see that it was time to allow her to die and to go on with their own lives. If Mrs. Gormley had been in the hospital, life-prolonging technology would have been temptingly at hand. In almost any hospital setting today not only she but her family would have been anesthetized from the experience of death and from the costs of caring for a dying person. At home, even if they had been reimbursed for the extra expenses of home care, they still would have experienced the work involved.

S. did not challenge the fairness of the basic insurance principle of averaging out the costs of illness to avoid financial hardship for those who were ill at any given time. As in the case of malpractice claims, he thought it entirely consistent with the Probabilistic Paradigm to say that people should not be penalized for chance events. At the same time, he could not help but observe (as with the Cavanaughs and O'Farrells) that people who participated in making and carrying out decisions concerning their own and their families' health care were in a better position to assume responsibility for the consequences of their choices, both for themselves and for society. Of course, it was not always possible or desirable for patients and families to be so involved in physically carrying out their decisions as Mrs. Gormley's family was. Expensive and remote-seeming technical procedures sometimes were necessary. Still, S. thought, there ought to be some way to bring the consciousness of choice—and along with it the principles of fairness and social responsibility—into everyday medical decision-making.

A system of health-care funding consistent with the Probabilistic Paradigm would give patients and doctors incentives for making principled decisions. By keeping probabilities and values in sight, people could more easily come to principled decisions in a society where limited resources prevent everyone from being reimbursed for everything they might want to do. By how much would a given test reduce the uncertainty of a diagnosis? By how much would a given treatment increase the probability of a good outcome for the patient? These considerations of probability would be weighed against considerations of value and principle. The nature of the illness, for example, would have to be taken into account. A ten percent reduction of uncertainty might be considered worthy of reimbursement in the case of cancer, but not in the case of strep throat. In considering such a reimbursement scheme, however, we also would have to ask whether it is fair for people of greater means to be able to buy the extra ten percent of certainty.

The judgments involved in establishing a health-care reimbursement system cognizant of probabilities and values would be complex and sensitive ones. Who would make them? When he considered this question, S. saw how what he envisioned as an application of the Probabilistic Paradigm could become merely an amendment to the Mechanistic. In a society structured as ours is, guidelines for reimbursement would inevitably be established by a bureaucratic process heavily influenced by profit-seeking interests. Out of such a process would come judgments such as that infants between six months and one year of age should be fed commercial formula rather than whole milk. For a system consistent with the Probabilistic Paradigm such as S. was proposing to work, people would have to be involved not only in their own health-care decisions, but in the political process by which society set up principles for allocating resources. Without such participation patients, families, and doctors would be alienated both from the process and the result.

In attempting to practice the Probabilistic Paradigm in medicine, S. was working to establish trust, both in other people and in the order of a changing universe, so that people could deal effectively with the vicissitudes of reality instead of reacting reflexively out of fear and anxiety. If people could learn trust and critical thinking in the sensitive area of medicine, they would gain, individually and collectively, both the feeling and the actuality of greater control of their lives. They would be less amenable to control by individuals, corporations, or bureaucratic institutions and better able to bring about new ways of thinking, feeling, and acting throughout society. Yet how could people learn to trust in a world that was not now set up to allow for trust? How could people use critical thinking to develop their own rules to live by when the rules they *had* to live by encouraged mindlessness? How could they distinguish between critical thinking and cynicism?

Still, it was a gamble worth taking. They would have to give it a try.

REFERENCES

AINSLIE, G. "A Behavioral Theory of Impulse Control." *Psychological Bulletin,* 82(1975), pp. 463–96.

BERNARD, C. *An Introduction to the Study of Experimental Medicine.* New York: Dover, 1957.

BERNSTEIN, R.J. *The Restructuring of Social and Political Theory.* Philadelphia: University of Pennsylvania Press, 1978.

BOHR, N. "Discussions with Einstein on Epistemological Problems in Atomic Physics," in *Albert Einstein, Philosopher-Scientist,* Third Edition, P. A. Schilpp, ed. LaSalle, Ill.: Open Court (1969), pp. 199–241.

BUNGE, M. *Causality and Modern Science.* New York: Dover, 1979.

BURSZTAJN, H. "The Role of a Training Protocol in Formulating Patient Instructions as to Terminal Care Choices." *Journal of Medical Education,* 52(1977), pp. 347–48.

BURSZTAJN, H., and HAMM, R.M. "Medical Maxims: Two Views of Science." *Yale Journal of Biology and Medicine,* 52 (1979), pp. 483–86.

BURSZTAJN, H., and HAMM, R.M. "On Knowing What Is Good for the Patient: The Uses of Utility Assessment and the Clinician's Intuition of Patient Values." Paper presented at the First Annual Meeting of the Society for Medical Decision Making, Cincinnati, Ohio, September 12, 1979. Unpublished.

CARLSON, R.J., ed. *The Frontiers of Science and Medicine.* Chicago: Henry Regnery, 1976.

CHANDLER, A.D., ed. *Giant Enterprise: Ford, General Motors and the Automobile Industry.* New York: Harcourt, Brace & World, 1964.

CHANOWITZ, B.Z., and LANGER, E. "Premature Cognitive Commitment." Cambridge, Mass.: Harvard University. Unpublished.

CLARK, M., and MILLS, J. "Interpersonal Attraction in Exchange and Communal Relationships." *Journal of Personality and Social Psychology,* 37 (1979), pp. 12–24.

COUSINS, N. "The Holistic Health Explosion." *Saturday Review,* 6 (No. 7, 1979), pp. 17–20.

DREYFUS, H., and DREYFUS, S. "Uses and Abuses of Multi-attribute and Multi-aspect Models of Decision Making." Berkeley: University of California, Department of Philosophy and Department of Industrial Engineering and Operations Research. Unpublished.

EDWARDS, R. *Contested Terrain.* New York: Basic Books, 1979.

EDWARDS, W. "N = 1: Diagnosis in Unique Cases," in *Computer Diagnosis and Diagnostic Methods,* J.A. Jacquez, ed. Springfield, Ill.: Charles C Thomas (1972), pp. 139–51.

ELLSBERG, D. "Risk, Ambiguity, and the Savage Axioms." *Quarterly Journal of Economics,* 75 (1961), pp. 643–49.

EWEN, S. *Captains of Consciousness.* New York: McGraw-Hill, 1976.

EYER, J., and STERLING, P. "Stress Related Mortality and Social Organization." *Review of Radical Political Economics,* 9 (No. 1, 1977), pp. 1–45.

FAISON, J.B.; PISANI, B.J.; DOUGLAS, R.G.; CRANCH, G.S.; and LUBIC, R.W. "The Childbearing Center: An Alternative Birth Setting." *Obstetrics and Gynecology,* 54 (1979), pp. 527–32.

FIORE, N. "Fighting Cancer—One Patient's Perspective." *New England Journal of Medicine,* 300 (1979), pp. 284–89.

FISCHHOFF, B. "Hindsight ≠ Foresight: The Effect of Outcome

Knowledge on Judgment Under Uncertainty." *Journal of Experimental Psychology: Human Perception and Performance,* 1 (1975), pp. 288–99.

FULLER, P. "Introduction," in *The Psychology of Gambling,* J. Halliday and P. Fuller, eds. New York: Harper & Row (1975), pp. 1–114.

GLENN, M.L. *On Diagnosis: A Systemic Approach.* New York: Brunner/Mazel, 1984.

GLENN, M.L. *Collaborative Health Care: A Family-Oriented Model.* New York: Praeger, 1987.

GROVES, J. "Taking Care of the Hateful Patient." *New England Journal of Medicine,* 298 (1978), pp. 883–87.

HACKING, I. *The Emergence of Probability.* London: Cambridge University Press, 1975.

HAMPSHIRE, S. "Human Nature." *The New York Review of Books,* 26 (No. 19, 1979), pp. 42c–42d.

HAVENS, L.L. *Participant Observation.* New York: Jason Aronson, 1976.

HEISENBERG, W. *Physics and Philosophy.* New York: Harper & Row, 1958.

HEMPEL, C. "Studies in the Logic of Confirmation," in *Aspects of Scientific Explanation.* New York: Free Press (1965), pp. 3–51.

HOFSTEDE, G. "The Poverty of Management Control Philosophy." *Academy of Management Review,* 3 (1978), pp. 450–61.

ILLINGWORTH, P.M.L. *AIDS and the Good Society: From Philosophy to Public Policy.* New York: Routledge, 1989.

KAFKA, F. "The Metamorphosis," in *The Penal Colony,* translated by W. Muir and E. Muir. New York: Schocken Books (1948), pp. 65–132.

KATZ, J. *The Silent World of Doctor and Patient.* New York: Free Press, 1984.

KAHNEMAN, D. and TVERSKY, A. "On the Psychology of Prediction." *Psychological Review,* 80 (1973), pp. 237–51.

KELMAN, H.C. "The Role of the Group in the Induction of Therapeutic Change." *International Journal of Group Psychotherapy,* 13 (1963), pp. 399–432.

KITZINGER, S., and DAVIS, J.A., eds. *The Place of Birth.* Oxford: Oxford University Press, 1978.

KOVEL, J. "Rationalization and the Family." *Telos,* 37 (1978), pp. 5–21.

KUHN, T.S. *The Structure of Scientific Revolutions.* Chicago: University of Chicago Press, 1962.

LANGER, E. "The Illusion of Control." *Journal of Personality and Social Psychology,* 32 (1975), pp. 311–28.

LASCH, C. *Haven in a Heartless World.* New York: Basic Books, 1977.

LEE, W. *Decision Theory and Human Behavior.* New York: Wiley, 1971.

LICHTENSTEIN, S., and SLOVIC, P. "Reversals of Preference Between Bids and Choices in Gambling Decisions." *Journal of Experimental Psychology,* 89 (1971), pp. 46–55.

LIFTON, R.J. *The Broken Connection.* New York: Simon & Schuster, 1979.

McCLELLAND, D.C. "Risk-taking in Children with High and Low Need for Achievement," in *Motives in Fantasy, Action, and Society,* J.W. Atkinson, ed. Princeton: Van Nostrand (1958), pp. 306–21.

MOORE, B.R., and STUTTARD, S. "Dr. Guthrie and *Felis domesticus,* Or: Tripping over the Cat." *Science,* 205 (1979), pp. 1031–33.

NEUTRA, R.R.; FIENBERG, S.E.; GREENLAND, S.; and FRIEDMAN, E.A. "Effect of Fetal Monitoring on Neonatal Death Rates." *New England Journal of Medicine,* 299 (1978), pp. 324–26.

NEWTON, I. "Philosophiae Naturalis Principia Mathematica," Book III (1686), in *Newton's Philosophy of Nature,* H.S. Thayer, ed. New York: Hafner (1953), pp. 3–5.

PAUKER, S.G. "Coronary Artery Surgery: The Use of Decision Analysis." *Annals of Internal Medicine,* 85 (1976), pp. 8–18.

PEELE, S., with BRODSKY, A. *Love and Addiction.* New York: New American Library, 1976.

PELLETIER, K.R. *Mind as Healer, Mind as Slayer.* New York: Delacorte Press/Seymour Lawrence, 1977.

PUTNAM, H. *Meaning and the Moral Sciences.* London: Routledge and Kegan Paul, 1978.

———. "A Philosopher Looks at Quantum Physics," in *Mathematics, Matter, and Method,* H. Putnam, ed. Cambridge: Cambridge University Press (1979), pp. 130–58.

RAIFFA, H. *Decision Analysis*. Reading, Mass.: Addison-Wesley, 1968.

ROETHLISBERGER, F.J., and DIXON, W.J. *Management and the Worker*. Cambridge, Mass.: Harvard University Press, 1939.

ROSENTHAL, R. "Interpersonal Expectations: Effects of the Experimenter's Hypothesis," in *Artifact in Behavioral Research*, R. Rosenthal and R. Roshow, eds. New York: Academic Press (1969), pp. 181–277.

ROTHMAN, S.M. "Family Life as Zero-Sum Game." *Dissent*, 25 (1978), pp. 392–97.

SCHRECKER, PAUL. *Work and History*. Princeton: Princeton University Press, 1948.

SENNETT, R. *The Fall of Public Man*. New York: Vintage, 1978.

SHIMONY, A. "Scientific Inference," in *The Nature and Function of Scientific Theories*, R. Colodny, ed. Pittsburgh: University of Pittsburgh Press (1970), pp. 79–172.

SIMONTON, O.C.; MATTHEWS-SIMONTON, S.; and CREIGHTON, J. *Getting Well Again*. Los Angeles: J.P. Tarcher, 1978.

STEPHENS, G.G. "Family Medicine as Counter-Culture." *Family Medicine Teacher*, 11 (No. 5, 1979), pp. 14–18.

THUROW, L.C. "Economics 1977." *Daedalus*, 106 (No. 4, 1977), pp. 79–94.

TOURNEY, G. "A History of Therapeutic Fashions in Psychiatry." *American Journal of Psychiatry*, 124 (1967), pp. 784–96.

TRIBE, L.H. "Trial by Mathematics: Precision and Ritual in the Legal Process." *Harvard Law Review*, 84 (1971), pp. 1329–93.

———. "Policy Science: Analysis or Ideology." *Philosophy and Public Affairs*, 2 (1972), pp. 66–110.

VON NEUMANN, J., and MORGENSTERN, O. *Theory of Games and Economic Behavior*. Princeton: Princeton University Press, 1944.

WEBER, M. *The Protestant Ethic and the Spirit of Capitalism*, translated by T. Parsons. London: G. Allen and Unwin, 1930.

WEINSTEIN, M.C. "Allocation of Subjects in Medical Experiments." *New England Journal of Medicine*, 291 (1974), pp. 1278–85.

WHITE, E. B. "Bedfellows," in *Essays of E. B. White*. New York: Harper & Row, 1977, pp. 80–89.

WITTGENSTEIN, L. *Philosophical Investigations*. New York: Macmillan, 1958.

INDEX

THE AUTHORS

HAROLD J. BURSZTAJN, M.D., is an Assistant Clinical Professor of Psychiatry and Co-director of the Program in Psychiatry and the Law at Harvard Medical School. In addition, he teaches undergraduates at Harvard College and consults to patients and colleagues in medicine, ethics, and the law from his home office in Cambridge, Massachusetts. He is co-author of *Divided Staffs, Divided Selves: A Case Approach to Mental Health Ethics.*

In his published work Dr. Bursztajn has made clinical, theoretical, and empirical contributions to understanding decision-making under conditions of uncertainty in a variety of contexts, ranging from the mundane to the tragic. His work has focused on integrating a psychoanalytic understanding of human choices with behavioral decision theory in the clinical contexts of medicine, ethics, and the law. He is a practicing psychoanalyst and is called upon as an expert in psychiatry and the law in medicolegal cases and legislation. He is married to Professor Patricia M.L. Illingworth.

RICHARD I. FEINBLOOM, M.D., is on the faculty of the Department of Family Medicine, State University of New York

Medical School at Stony Brook. He was formerly Director of the Family Health Care Program of the Harvard Medical School and Chief of Child & Family Health Division, Childrens Hospital Medical Center, Boston. Dr. Feinbloom, a graduate of the University of Pennsylvania, is a founding member and past president of Physicians for Social Responsibility. He is co-author of the original *Child Health Encyclopedia* and *Pregnancy, Birth, and the Early Months*.

ROBERT M. HAMM, Ph.D., is an experienced psychologist at the University of Colorado and author of many studies of decision-making behavior. He has taught at the University of Iowa Business School and conducted research at Harvard Medical School as well as at the Army Research Institute in Fort Leavenworth, Kansas. A classmate of Dr. Bursztajn's at Princeton, he subsequently worked with him in formulating the theoretical framework and empirical studies from which *Medical Choices, Medical Chances* originated.

ARCHIE BRODSKY, a professional writer and social critic, is co-author of numerous books in psychology and health care, including *Love and Addiction, Sexual Dilemmas for the Helping Professional, Home Birth: A Practitioner's Guide to Birth Outside the Hospital,* and *Diabetes: Caring For Your Emotions As Well As Your Health*. He is Senior Research Associate at the Program in Psychiatry and the Law, Massachusetts Mental Health Center, Harvard Medical School. As an activist and commentator he works to enhance autonomy and choice in areas such as childbirth and addictive behavior.